ROGER MACBRIDE ALLEN

ALLIES & ALIENS

This is a work of fiction. All the characters and events portrayed in this book are fictional, and any resemblance to real people or incidents is purely coincidental.

A Baen Books Original

Baen Publishing Enterprises
P.O. Box 1403
Riverdale, NY 10471

ISBN: 0-671-87658-9

Cover art by Paul Alexander

First printing, June 1995

Distributed by Simon & Schuster
1230 Avenue of the Americas
New York, NY 10020

Printed in the United States of America

INTRODUCTION TO THE REVISED EDITIONS

The Torch of Honor and *Rogue Powers* are my first two books. The first deals with the outbreak of the first interstellar war, and the second continues the story, as the war is prosecuted in the midst of humanity's first contact with an alien species.

Jim Baen published the two books, and by doing so launched my career as a science fiction novelist. Jim has now done me the further kindness of offering to publish these two books anew, in a combined volume.

I have taken advantage of this opportunity and revisited the two books with pencil in hand. I have re-edited the two volumes and, I think, improved them both substantially. I have learned a lot about writing since the far-off day when *The Torch of Honor* first slid over the transom at Baen Books, and I have put that experience to work in this edition. They are now better-written books.

Nearly all of the changes I have made fall into three broad categories.

First and foremost, I have simply undone a number of mistakes of style and usage. I managed to catch my foot in a number of literary potholes way back when. I have now taken the chance to fill in many of these same craterlets that obstructed the path of the story. I have tried not to tamper needlessly, and I believe I have retained the original tone and spirit of the works. Indeed, by disentangling a number of muddled passages, I think I have made the intended tone far clearer. I knew what I meant to say back then—now I know how to say it.

Here and there, I have resisted the urge to tinker too much, for fear of overdoing. I tried to improve the quality of the prose while preserving the books' essential personalities. I think and hope I have succeeded. Readers of the original editions might not even notice most of the fairly substantial revision work I have done. That is as it should be. When potholes are filled in properly, they disappear.

Secondly, I have deleted one or two passages in *Rogue Powers* that served no other purpose than to remind the reader of the plot of *The Torch of Honor*. As such material was utterly redundant in a combined edition, I have removed it.

Thirdly, I have corrected a number of technical and scientific errors. By far the most significant of these concerns the geometry of the Nova Sol star system as discussed in *Rogue Powers*. In the book as originally published, I made a huge mistake as regards the conservation of angular momentum. This error has now been corrected. Fortunately, the impact of this error on the story itself was minimal. However, both Guardians and Z'ensam can rest easy, secure in the knowledge that they now inhabit a binary star system that is physically possible.

Although *The Torch of Honor* is the first book of the two, certain events in *Rogue Powers* take place before the action opens in *The Torch of Honor*. Chronologically, virtually all of *The Torch of Honor* takes place between chapters three and four of *Rogue Powers*. Mac and Joslyn Larson battle the Guardians in the New Finnish system even as Lucille Calder makes her first contact with the Outposters.

It was a pleasure for me to return to these two books, these old friends with whom I have not visited in far too long. I am pleased to offer them to new readers, and to readers of the original editions. Both, I think, will take pleasure in reading the volume you now hold in your hands.

Roger MacBride Allen
December, 1993
Washington, D.C.

Volume I
The Torch of Honor

To Dad:
my mentor, colleague—
and friend

In Flanders Fields

In Flanders Fields the poppies blow
  Between the crosses, row on row,
    That mark our place; and in the sky
    The larks, still bravely singing, fly
Scarce heard amid the guns below.

We are the Dead. Short days ago
We lived, felt dawn, saw sunset glow,
    Loved and were loved, and now we lie
    In Flanders fields.

Take up our quarrel with the foe:
To you from failing hands we throw
    The torch; be yours to hold it high
    If ye break faith with those who die
We shall not sleep, though poppies grow
    In Flanders fields.

John McCrae

Prelude

April, 2115

The Finns knew the Guardians had won. It was over. The Guardians had taken the planet's surface, and now the surrender of the great satellite Vapaus would go into effect in a few hours. The Guardians themselves had caused a delay of the surrender by insisting it be negotiated strictly in English. The Finns, desperately playing for time, stalled for as long as possible, taking hours to search for the English-speaking officer they could have produced in moments.

The time was put to urgent use. The last, the only hope, thin though it might be, was the League. Word had to be sent.

Six of the last torpedoes were stripped of armament. Light-speed-squared generators and radio beacons were installed. Recordings that held the vital knowledge of the anti-ship missile system, and what little information the Finns had on the Guardians, were placed aboard.

Word had to get through.

The Guardians had not yet closed the ring around Vapaus. Three tiny one-man ships were launched from the Forward airlock complex, each with two torps strapped to jury-rigged harnesses amidships. The little ships launched at six gees, to fly straight through the Guardian fleet. The enemy's radar was too good to be fooled by any feinting maneuver; speed was the only protection.

It was not protection enough. The lead ship was destroyed in seconds by laser fire from a troop transport. The Finnish pilot's last act was to blow the fusion engines; the resultant explosion created a plasma that jammed every radar screen and radio within a thousand kilometers. That gave the two remaining ships their chance as they flashed into and beyond the gathering fleet.

They dove down to lower orbits, rushing to get the sheltering bulk of the planet between themselves and the enemy's radar before it could recover from the explosion the Finns' lead ship had died in.

They fell toward the planet, gathering speed for a gravity-assist maneuver. One hundred eighty degrees around the planet from the satellite Vapaus, they both changed course, maneuvering violently, one coming about to fly a forced orbit straight over the planet's North Pole, the second heading over the South Pole.

As soon as the ships had reached their new headings, they cut their engines for a moment, and each released a torp. Then the two ships and the two released torpedoes ignited their engines and flashed on into the sky, the torps holding course, the ships again changing their headings.

The southern ship was caught and destroyed by a Nova fighter scrambled from the planet's surface. The northern ship released its second torp and came about one final time, to act as a decoy for the torps.

Soon, all too soon, another fusion explosion lit the sky, marking the point where a Guardian missile had found the last Finnish ship.

The Guardians tracked only the last torpedo launched, and they were able to destroy it.

Of the six torpedoes, two now survived, undetected. Engines still burning, they curved around the world in exactly opposite directions, one over the South Pole, one over the North, their courses bent by the planet's gravity until they came about to identical bearings.

The torps cut their engines precisely over the Poles, just as they reached escape velocity.

Each now rose on a straight-line course starting from a point directly over a pole and parallel to the equator, the paths of the torps also parallel to each other.

Engines stopped, they rushed through space, coasting, trusting to the cold and dark of the void to hide them.

Hours after launch, when they were hundreds of thousands of kilometers beyond the orbit of the moon Kuu, celestial trackers on each torp examined the star field. The maneuvering thrusters fired fussily and touched up the torps's headings. The two torps were now on precise headings for the Epsilon Eridani star system, where the English had their colony world, Britannica. The torpedoes were still far too close to New Finland's sun to go into light-speed-squared. For long weeks they coasted on into the darkness, while, behind them, the Guardians worked their horrors on the Finns.

On one torp, the power system failed and the torp became another of the useless derelicts in the depths of space.

But the other torp, the last one, held on to life. And at the proper moment, the light-speed-squared generator absorbed nearly all the torp's carefully husbanded power and grabbed at the fabric of space around the torpedo.

The last torp leapt across the dark between the suns.

Soon after, with weak batteries, the radio beacon barely detectable, the torpedo drifted into the Epsilon Eridani system.

Just barely, the last torp made it.

Part One
An Empty Grave, A Hollow World

Chapter One

January, 2115

A cold drizzly rain spattered on the faceplate of my pressure suit as the chaplain droned through the funeral service, there at the edge of the empty grave.

The metal and rubber arm of my helmet's windshield wiper slithered back and forth across my field of vision, clearing the rain away. This was probably the only world humanity had bothered to settle where a pressure suit needed a wiper. We all had them, the wiper blades endlessly waving, side to side, like the mouthparts of giant locusts.

They were gone, dead, missing in the depths of space. Sixty of our classmates. Their ship simply vanished en route back from one final training cruise. There had been exactly one hundred of us when we had started out. Of course there had been other losses to our ranks—other accidents, candidates who had been dropped—but now there was this. There were only 34 of us left to stand on the miserable plain.

"Vanity, vanity, saith the preacher," intoned our chaplain. "We bring nothing into this world, and we take nothing out." The words might as well have been a recording. The chaplain's voice made me think of dried-out toast. He talked on in gravelly, portentous tones, plucking old morsels from half the books of scripture, a shopworn service to be dragged out for all funerals and sad occasions. "What is man, that thou are mindful of him?" he asked, his voice raising for a moment, and then sliding back down to a low grumble.

A light blinked on the tell-tale board inside my helmet, and I kicked my radio over to a private channel.

"Mac, this man is awful. Can't we make him be quiet, so we could at least stand here and *think*?" Joslyn asked.

She and I had been married by the same chaplain three months ago. He had taken two minutes over our vows and 45 minutes on a rambling sermon that put half the congregation to sleep.

"Just keep your suit radio cut off," I suggested.

"But then I could still see his great jaw flapping. And now he's glaring at us. Best we listen. Oh, Mac, they deserve a better send-off." She slipped her gauntleted hand into mine and we switched back to the general circuit.

"Dear Lord, we commit to your care and keeping the immortal souls of these the departed. We pray you to welcome and cherish the souls of Lieutenant Daniel Ackerman, Lieutenant Dwight Amoto, Lieutenant Lucille Calder, Lieutenant Commander Joseph Danvers . . ."

Nice touch, I thought. *He's got them memorized in alphabetical order*.

The empty grave was a regulation hole, one meter wide, two meters long, two meters deep. I looked up into the sky through the gloomy overcast at the blue and white globe that hung here. It was there, on that planet, Kennedy, that the tradition of the empty grave had arisen. There, during the Fast Plague, it had been rare to have a body to put in the ground. The corpses had been viciously infectious. The only sure way of sterilizing the remains was to destroy them in the fusion flame of a grounded spacecraft. That was what happened to my parents' bodies—I remember the patches of dim incandescence in the cleansing flame. There was an empty grave there, on Kennedy, a meter by a meter by two meters; on top of it a granite cover slab that bore all the names.

There have always been a lot of funerals without bodies at the edges of civilization, I suppose. There still were. A ship doesn't come back. Somebody pushes the wrong button and a ship explodes. People get eaten. There are lots of ways.

Finally, the cover slab with sixty names on it was carefully set down over the grey concrete shell that defined the grave. A few centimeters of dirty water were trapped in a puddle in the bottom.

We trooped back to the pressurized quarters and the wardroom. There was to be a reception there—a wake, really, even if no one called it by its proper name.

Joslyn and I hung back. We stood on the surface of Kennedy's moon, Columbia, a while longer.

When humanity had first come to this system, Columbia had had a wispy methane atmosphere and a lot of water ice locked up in polar ice caps. Now the engineers were hard at work on a dozen projects to remake it into a better place. Some day their work would be done and this world would live. Already, the air pressure was up to a third of what Earth's was. But it was still a dank, miserable bog of a world, cold and moody, the air poisonous. It rained too much.

Silently, I bid our comrades a last farewell, and we went inside.

Once in our quarters, it took us a while to get out of our pressure suits and into our dress uniforms, with the grim addition of an issue black armband.

I struggled into the midnight black, high collared, rather severe uniform of the Republic of Kennedy Navy. Joslyn, a native of the Planetary Commonwealth of Britannica, was thereby a loyal subject of the King-Emperor of Great Britain. Her uniform was a deep navy blue, with a lower collar, far fewer buttons, and a better cut. Both of us wore the insignia of the League of Planets Survey Service, a starfield superimposed on a rectangular grid. Both of us were lieutenants, assigned to special training classes at the League of Planets Survey Service Training Center on Columbia.

Joslyn checked her appearance in the mirror. *She* said she was five-foot-seven and I was six-four. *I* said she was 170 centimeters and I was 193. She was slender, well-muscled and strong. Her face was oval, her lips full, and she had a full set of dimples when she smiled. Her hair was a shade between brunette and blonde. She wore it in a braid long enough to reach the small of her back. At the moment she had the braid coiled on top of her head, as per regulations. She pulled her tunic straight and checked her profile, giving me a smile and a wink in the mirror.

She satisfied herself as to her own appearance and turned to me. She patted my tunic smooth and brushed some lint from my sleeve. "You'll do," she said, "but if they ever put padded shoulders in those uniforms, you'll never fit through the doorway." Suddenly, she threw her arms around my neck, pulled my head down and gave me a most unmilitary kiss. She looked me in the eye and sighed. "Mac, I do love you so."

I tickled her under the ear and smiled back. "Never mind that stuff," I said "You sure I look okay?"

"Oh, you'll do. That is, if one likes Greek gods."

I looked in the mirror and shrugged. I've always felt I looked like a refugee from a comic book. Broad shoulders, a bit overmuscled, kind of narrow-waisted, my face is long and lantern-jawed. I've got light blonde hair and the blue eyes to go with it. My smile is a little uneven, but it's friendly enough. My arms and legs are long, my hands and feet big. I take the largest size they issue in practically everything.

Growing up I was the kid who tripped over his own two feet and tended to smack into walls. My body got bigger than my coordination could handle for a while there. Nowadays, Joslyn can escort me to the dance floor in perfect safety; I can even waltz. I looked at myself in the mirror and concluded that regulation formal dress made me look about the size and shape of the angel of death—not a propitious image to be running through my mind, given the circumstances.

We headed to the wardroom.

We, the survivors, should have been able to gather quietly together, drawn to each other by the bonds of camaraderie that linked us one to the other, and to the dead. But this was not to be a private occasion. The representatives of a half-dozen governments were here and they had to be treated diplomatically. Some were from nations and planets that opposed the Survey, others from places that were footing the bill.

Joslyn went off in search of drinks. I stood there and

scanned the crowd for a friendly face. Pete Gesseti caught my eye and came over.

Pete worked for the Republic of Kennedy State Department, and was one of those rare people who could actually make you believe that the bureaucracy knew what it was doing. Pete was of medium height, his brown hair retreating toward baldness, his intelligent-looking face permanently calm. A friendly warning from Pete has kept plenty of people out of trouble. Pete had known my father—and Pete had done a lot to keep *me* out of trouble after my father was dead. If not for Pete, I'd probably be just another of the orphan punks that cause Hyannisport police to travel in pairs.

He came over and shook my hand. "This isn't the right sort of occasion, but I haven't seen you since. Congratulations on your commission, Second Lieutenant Terrance MacKenzie Larson, sir."

"Thanks, Pete."

He raised his glass to me and took a sip. Joslyn returned and handed me my drink. "Two more congratulations. Or three. On *your* commission, Lieutenant Joslyn Marie Cooper Larson. On your marrying him. And on his marrying you. Cheers."

We clinked our glasses and smiled. Pete went on, "Sorry I missed the wedding. I understand the Reverend Buxley was spellbinding. Couldn't get leave."

"We understand, Peter. It was pretty short notice." Joslyn said. "Once we decided to marry, we didn't see much point in waiting."

"The wedding aside, at least you didn't miss a trip to some place worth going," I said. "Columbia's not much of a tourist spot."

"True, I suppose. The League should have picked someplace a lot better than this to train you kids. And I have a sneaky idea that putting you in this hole was the deliberate policy of certain people who want the Survey to fail—if you're interested in a little paranoia."

"What?" I asked.

"Mac—tell me this: How does Columbia rate as a training

base for a space-going operation?" Pete had a tendency to snap from one subject to another quickly. He took some keeping up with.

"Well, okay—not so great."

"Make that terrible. You guys should be in free orbit. That way, you want to train in your ships, you just hop out the hatch and go it. Here, since your ships aren't designed to land on a surface, you lose a lot of time taking shuttle craft back and forth. Makes schedules impossible. Even having to fly through this atmosphere is worthless as training. It's a freak, since the terraforming engineers started tinkering with it. It hasn't stopped raining here for years, which must be great for morale. The air would kill you, so you have to wear suits. The methane leaks in anyway, and stinks to high heaven. The whole atmosphere is in transition: all kinds of crud precipitates and ruins equipment. . . ."

"Okay, you've made your point," Joslyn said. "It's not much use as a base. So who is it that put us here?"

"You kids are lucky this is my third drink or I'd still be a fairly discreet diplomat," Pete said. "People who wanted the Survey to fail. People who had friends who arranged for some misguided members of the Kennedy Chamber of Commerce to lobby for you to be based here—if you followed that. People who would like the Survey to fail because the British donated the ten long-range frigates you'll be flying, because your commander graduated from Annapolis, and because the reports are to be published in English. People who think the Brits and the Yanks are plotting to lay claim to all the best real estate out there. Note that Britannica, Kennedy, and Newer Jersey are the prime planets so far—Europa, for example, isn't all *that* habitable. There are some grounds for being suspicious. Anyone you met at this reception speaking French, or German, or Japanese, for example, would probably be just as happy if you had all been on the *Venera* when she went poof."

"You're not suggesting the *Venera* . . ." I began.

"Was nuked on purpose? No. But, on another subject, it has crossed my mind that your friends aren't dead."

"Pete, you're going too fast," I protested. "We're at their funeral, or didn't you notice?"

"Hmmmm." Pete looked around, a bit nervously, and spoke again, in lower tones. "Me and my big mouth. Look, I shouldn't have said anything to start with, but I'll finish the thought and then forget I said anything. All right?"

"All right," Joslyn said, and I nodded my agreement.

"Okay then. The *Venera* fits a pattern. In the last ten years or so, there have been at least 30 cases in which something like this happens: Proven, reliable ship takes off, on a well-known route, the trip announced in advance, and a number of highly skilled people on board. Occasionally there is some evidence—in the manifest, say—to suggest that someone bribed their way on board, or stowed away, or whatever. Ship vanishes. No wreckage, no explanation. The ship ends up listed Lost With All Hands, and they put the files away."

Pete was silent for a moment before he spoke again, gesturing vaguely with his drink. "I get a funny feeling sometimes that someone is setting up shop on some backwater planet. Needs more skilled people than he's got. So he kidnaps the talent he needs."

"Are you kidding?" I asked. "That's crazy."

"Probably," Pete agreed. "Now *forget* I ever said that, because I'd hate to fib and deny any such idea ever went through my head." He sipped his drink.

I stood there, too surprised by the idea to react. Joslyn wasn't going to let the subject drop, though. "Peter—If you believe that, why aren't you out organizing a search party?"

"Joslyn, please don't—" Pete caught the expression on Joslyn's face and sighed. "Okay, I know that look. I give up. I guess I've gone far enough that it doesn't matter. I have several reasons. One: I have no proof. Two: I could not face giving all but certainly false hope to thousands of people who are relatives and friends of people lost on unaccounted-for ships. Lots of ships have been well and truly lost. Can you imagine anything crueler than letting someone imagine their loved ones were still alive? Three: As the saying goes: it's a big galaxy. We've been in star travel for something like a hundred years, and we haven't visited a tenth of the star systems within a hundred light-years of Earth. Four: sooner or later, we *will* stumble across anyone who has been grabbing ships. Next year, next millennium. We'll find them—*if* we keep looking for habitable planets. *If* something like the Survey gets off the ground and is out there doing the looking. I spend a lot of government time on the Survey. My superiors complain about it at times. So let's leave it alone and talk about the weather. It stopped raining yet?"

"Not for another fifty years or so," I said. "We get the message." We murmured something in the direction of a goodbye and circulated among the guests. I went through the motions, mostly on automatic.

My head was whirling with confusion. I had never paid much attention to politics. It had never occurred to me that someone would think ill of the Survey, let alone try and throw monkey wrenches at it. And past that, way past that, the wild thought that all those people might still be *alive* . . . I understood why Pete wasn't wholesaling his theory. I had known him all my life, and it had taken a funeral that might have been mine and a few drinks too many for him to mention it to me. How could he ever bring himself to suggest it to strangers?

And then there were the rumblings that the Survey Service was to be stillborn. We had yet to send a single ship out on a survey mission. Ours, the first class of the Service, had been about a month from graduation when the *Venera* was lost. I had figured the loss would slow us down to a crawl, but could it really stop us?

With all that to worry about, it was a lousy party, even for a funeral.

Some hours after, I was alone in the view room. An overhanging roof shielded the oversize view window from the worst of the rain, making it possible to see something of the dismal surface of Columbia, and of her sullen sky. Now it was night, and Kennedy gleamed boldly down through the high cloud deck. Where was the time to mourn?

I looked up again at the leaden heavens, and thought of the stars behind the dirty clouds.

So many stars . . .

In the vicinity of Earth's sun the star systems were about five light-years apart, on the average. That worked out to about 34,000 stars within a hundred light-years of Earth. Our home Solar System was a good sample of what to expect in an average star system—nine or ten good-sized planets, forty or fifty noticeable satellites, and a few trillion pieces of sky junk running the gamut from rogue moons down to individual atoms and elementary particles.

But there was plenty of variety that went past the average to the incredible. If every human being alive were put to work as a scientist or an explorer, and they all passed their jobs along to all of their descendants, it would still take a thousand years to get together a basic catalog of what we know is out there to learn within that hundred light-years.

Consider the infinite variety of Earth—the geology, the hydrology, the atmosphere, the biology, the physical reality of our ancestral home. Multiply it by the number of worlds waiting to be found, and the dimensions of the problem start to come clear.

Exploration was not something to do out of idle curiosity. Knowing what is out there was an urgent need, and getting more so every year.

Around the beginning of the third millennium, the experiments were performed that took faster-than-light travel from an impossibility to a laboratory trick to a way to haul the freight. Humanity, barely staggering into the third thousand years alive, found that the stars had been dropped in its lap. Some say the breakthrough came too soon, too fast. We could reach the stars before we could truly grasp what that meant.

But there was no turning back. The explorers were already heading out.

Some of them came back, telling of the worlds they had found. The settlers followed in their paths. More than once, settlers went out blazing their own trails. Colonists went out, poorly organized, often toward nothing more definite than the hope that they might find a place to settle and live. Very few of that number were ever heard from again.

Yet, by the year 2025, the United States Census Bureau estimated the off-Earth population as over 1 million for the first time. Ten years later, the figure was twice that, and the pace accelerating. By 2050, rapid emigration and high birth rates had pushed the minimum estimate to 10 million, and the growth rate shows no sign of slowing.

One job of the Survey was to find the missing colonies—or their surviving remnants—and to establish a reliable catalog of habitable planets, so the next generation of colony ships might go out with a better chance of survival.

Our second mission was to catalog the bounty of the starlanes, the incredible riches that literally hang in the sky. What new mineral, born in exotic heat and pressure, waited for uses to be found and markets established? Where were mountain sized lumps of pure nickel-iron orbiting in darkness, waiting for a factory ship to take possession? Where were the lovely green worlds waiting for people to come and live on them? What new plants, new animals, would be worth exporting?

It should have been obvious to everyone there was a need to explore, and just as obvious, it was a job for the governments of humanity to take on. Obvious to everyone except the governments, that is. Governments are supposed to lead the people, but the governments have been way behind the people ever since our race entered space in a big way.

The first crunch came in the 2030's or so. By that time, there were a good half dozen colony planets—and a bad dozen. Nations and consortia that certainly could not afford to do so established colonies anyway. The founding of colonies did great good for the nations that could afford the massive capital expense. But the poor nations that tried it went bankrupt long before their colonies started to pay any returns. The pattern was repeated many times. The nation, or the colony, or both, would collapse and people would start to die. To the richness of space we brought war, riot, pestilence and starvation. It happened in a dozen different ways on a dozen different worlds.

The big nations, and the healthy colonies got tired of bailing out the failures after a while. The United States, the Asian and European powers, the strong colony world—Kennedy, Britannica, Europa, New Alberta, Newer Jersey, and the others—came to the conference table. By every means possible they coerced the little and the weak to join them—The Estonian Republic, The People's Federal Protectorate of Chad, Uruguay, colonies like New Antarctica and High Albania, the supposedly self-contained, but half-bankrupt, habitats in orbit around Earth.

Some big countries were part of the problem: China pulled off some truly remarkable failures in space. Many of the smaller nations and colonies were among the most responsible members of the conference: Sweden, Singapore and her 'daughter' habitat High Singapore; Portugal, Finland, and New Finland were strong backers of the enterprise.

The delegates bickered. They threatened each other. They indulged in backroom deals that are still causing scandals today. But they managed to come up with a treaty.

So, on January 1, 2038, at 0000 hours GMT and Zero hours Accumulated Stellar Time (AST) the League of Planets came into being and its founding document, the Treaty of Planets, came into effect.

By 0000 hours GMT on January 2, or 24 hours AST, the League was evacuating the hapless residents of New Antarctica and treating them for frostbite.

The delegates came up with a system that works. Its basic tenet sets the right of a human being to live over the right of an idiot to run a government as if it was a family business.

When the League came into being, ground rules were set up for the founding of colonies. Colonists could still bug out and vanish if they wanted to, but fewer people did so by accident. Fewer people starved. When the Fast Plague came to Kennedy, the Interworld Health Organizations came in and their aid saved us. There is no possible question on that point. That's why the Republic of Kennedy is very pro-League.

There are other good things. There are fewer tinhorn dictators taking over small colonies with still-weak governments. Trade is reliable, not for gamblers anymore.

I stood there and looked out at the gloomy night. It occurred to me that I must have been pretty naive to think that politics wasn't going to affect the Survey—not with a history like the League's.

I must have been there for nearly an hour, nursing a drink, before an orderly came for me.

"Lieutenant Larson?"

"Mmmmm?"

"Excuse me, sir, but Captain Driscoll's compliments, and could you come to her office right away?"

"Certainly," I said. I followed the young man along the well-known route to Driscoll's office.

The orderly led me into the office and vanished. Joslyn was there already—and so was Pete Gesseti. As I came in, Driscoll was just handing him back a sheaf a papers. He slipped them back into a folder marked REPUBLIC OF KENNEDY STATE DEPARTMENT CLASS A CLEARANCE ONLY *** TOP SECRET.

I exchanged glances with Joslyn but she just shook her head. They hadn't told her anything yet. Pete's expression was one of pure bemusement, a bad job at a poker face.

Driscoll ignored me for a moment and simply sat there, staring into space. Gillian Driscoll didn't do that sort of thing much. A good loud voice that expected to be obeyed was more her style.

She was a small, rather compactly built woman, the sort of person who punched out walls when she felt frustrated. Her face was round, and a bit plain. Her skin had a rough, windblown look to it. She kept her hair cut short to the point of severity, for the sake of convenience. She was capable of using make-up artfully, though, and had presented a better-than-presentable appearance in her full dress uniform earlier in the evening, but had changed back to her usual standard-issue sneakers and coveralls. She fought a tendency to plumpness when she got stuck behind a desk for any amount of time. That wasn't one of her current problems: she led the courses in hand-to-hand combat and survival training. She was of Irish descent, more or less, and her blue eyes and red hair came with a button nose to prove it.

At last, she seemed to come to herself, and saw I was there. "Mac. Good. Sit down. We've got to do some talking here."

I sat down.

Captain Driscoll drummed her fingers on the desk and muttered darkly to herself for a moment. Then she spoke up. "Pete, you tell it. Let me hear it again. Maybe I can think a bit."

"Right," Pete said to her, then turned to Joslyn and myself. "First off, do you know how the Survey Service got hold of the ships you are supposed to fly?"

"Donated by the British, right?" I asked.

"Not exactly. You've got ten ships designated as Survey Ships. They used to be long duration patrol frigates, the plan being to have enough of them to be able to send one or two into a trouble spot and have the ship's firepower hold things together until the political types came in and tidied things up. His Majesty's government contracted for one hundred such ships with Imperial Shipyards, with a clause calling for an additional ten to be built.

"H.M.G. thought the extension clause was *activated* by notification, Imperial thought it was *cancelable* by notification. The contractor was a dozen light-years from the purchasing office. The upshot is that the Brits got ten more ships than they wanted, and the bill for same. Turns out they didn't even need the hundred original ships. So the Brits had the ships with no budget for operating them, and no use for them anyway. So they leased them to the League for a pound a year. Think of it as their taking a tax loss. Now. In the five years since they got stuck, the British have lost a few ships through accident, and on top of which, they now have more real estate to cover. They decided maybe they could use ten more ships after all. The current lease expires in about 45 days—Earth days, whatever the hell that is in hours."

"To conclude the story," Captain Driscoll said, "your friend Mr. Gesseti has just broken a number of laws, regulations and treaties to show me a diplomatic message intercept. Sent from London to the British Embassy on Kennedy."

"Some of the backroom boys cracked their diplomatic code a while ago," Pete said. "We pulled it off the relay satellite, picked it up and read it before the British did—fortunately for you people," Pete explained without a hint of shame. "London was telling the embassy to sort of turn cool on the Survey people. They're pulling their liaison officer soon. And they are thinking of taking the ships back, if politically feasible."

"The cable predates the loss of the *Venera*," Driscoll pointed out. "With the British supporting us at the League, we could weather the loss of personnel. With our establishment intact, it wouldn't be 'politically feasible' for the Brits to grab their ships back this close to graduating the first group."

"But, as things stand now—you're screwed," Pete said blandly.

"So what do we *do*?" Joslyn asked.

"Do. What do we do?" Driscoll pulled open a drawer, extracted a bottle and a glass and poured herself one. "We take our thirty-four surviving crew members, put them on the ten ships which are supposed to have crews of nine each, and send them out before the League bureaucracy has time to cut our head off."

It took a moment before I could react. "Ma'am, Captain, with all due respect, that can't work," I said.

"Mac, you may be right. But unless the survey ships launch *now*, they never will. We have to get them out of orbit of Columbia and at their proper work."

"But can't you rush the next class through? Or use the instructors?" Joslyn asked.

"The very first thing I thought of. The second class—hell, those kids haven't even been *inside* one of the survey ships yet. They aren't anywhere near trained. Most of them haven't done the survival course yet, none of them are checked out on astrogation to the point where I'd even trust them completely on the Kennedy-Britannica run, let alone on a trip between poorly-charted stars. And the instructors, strangely enough, are even worse. Scanlan is the best fusion-reactor and power system expert in thirty light-years—but she's never even been in a pressure suit. Jamie Sheppard is turning you all into experts on your pressure suits, but he doesn't know a damned thing about piloting. No. It's you. Your class. Or we don't go."

Driscoll downed a stiff gulp and sighed. "One more little problem: ten doesn't go into thirty-four. Also, some of the kids aren't quite good enough for three to be a safe crew. But you two." She paused. "You two. Our hottest pilot and a young man who's been at the head of every class and every team he was ever in—what they call a 'born leader.' You two were tops in the class, and you're married—so you're supposed to be compatible. I'm sending out two crews of four. Three crews of three. And one crew of two. You two. I flipped a coin before you came in. Joslyn, you're now a First Lieutenant. Mac, you have the rank—brevet—of Commander, and as soon as I sign this piece of paper, you are the skipper of League of Planets Survey Ship 41. You launch in no more than two hundred hours—before the damn pols can react to the loss of the *Venera*."

Shock was scarcely the word. Me? Skipper? Launch in two hundred hours? The Brits pulling the rug out from under us? Things were happening too fast. I looked around the room in a daze, until my eye met Pete's.

He just grinned. "Congratulations, again."

"Peter, this was your idea," Joslyn said accusingly.

"Wrong that time, Joslyn," Driscoll said. "I worked it out myself. But let's just say his handing me that cable made my conclusions inevitable." For a moment there was a smile on her face. Then, suddenly, she seemed smaller and more tired than I had ever seen her.

"You won't even ask us to volunteer?" Joslyn asked her.

"Would you have?"

Joslyn looked to me, I to her. Her face betrayed an attempt to look only to the rational, to look carefully at what was best, whatever her feelings. I could see the decision she reached, and I nodded my agreement, imperceptibly to anyone but her. "Yes," she said, simply.

Captain Driscoll rose. "Then let the record show such. Lieutenant Larson. Commander Larson. I ask you freely to volunteer for the hazardous duty in question. Answer upon your honor." Her voice took a hard, formal tone.

Self consciously, I stood as well. "I so volunteer," I said hoarsely.

Joslyn remained seated and looked carefully at each of us. "I, too, so volunteer."

There was a long pause. I felt then, and felt for a long time afterward, that things had come too fast. Now our lives were staked to the Survey. LPSS 41 *could* be handled by two people, but it would be very close indeed . . . The silence held for a long time.

"Well, thank God for that," Pete declared, snapping the tension. "Now maybe you can serve *all* of us a drink, Captain."

"An excellent suggestion, Mr. Gesseti." Driscoll pulled out three more glasses and poured.

Pete took his glass and raised it. With a twinkle in his eye, he offered a toast. "To secrets. And to knowing when to have them, and knowing why to keep them."

"To secrets," the rest of us repeated and then we all drank. We were conspirators now; for whatever reasons, we had just agreed to hijack our own fleet.

"One more point," Pete said. "Mac, I don't want to see you piloting a nameless number through space. You have to name it."

"Her," Joslyn and Driscoll corrected in unison.

"So I do," I said. I had to think for only the briefest of moments. "My friends—I ask you to drink to the League of Planets Survey Ship *Joslyn Marie*."

"Mac!" Joslyn cried, very much taken aback. "Don't you dare!"

"Quiet there, Lieutenant," Driscoll said. "Never argue with a man when he's putting your name in lights."

And so, we drank to the new-christened ship.

Joslyn got her revenge on me, though. I've mentioned that people from the planet Kennedy are edgy about being called "American." Objectively, of course, if we aren't American, we're doing a damn fine imitation. Anyway, a week and a half later I discovered that "someone" had christened the *Joslyn Marie*'s three auxiliary craft *Stars*, *Stripes*, and *Uncle Sam*. Worse, *Stars* had gotten a paint job consisting of huge white stars on a blue background, *Stripes* had been covered with red and white stripes, and *Uncle Sam* had both. The first time I brought the newly emblazoned *Stars* down to the surface of Columbia, it seemed to me as if a stunned silence hung over the ground crew. I ignored it as best I could and went to look for my crew, wondering if I could clap her in irons for artistic insubordination.

It promised to be an interesting trip.

Chapter Two

The next morning a notice was posted. It was titled "Revised Crew Lists."

The first lines read:

LPSS 41 *Joslyn Marie*
Larson, T.M., Cmdr. (commanding)
Larson, J.M., 1st Lt.
Volunteer Crew—Billet Complete.

The rest of the ships were listed as well, initially with no crew other than commanders. In twelve hours LPSS 42, 43, 44, 45, 46, and 48 were listed as Billet Complete. In thirty hours, all ten ships were so listed. As nearly as I could figure, every single person volunteered—and volunteered for the ship that Driscoll intended him or her for. Certainly, the ships with crews of four each had one of the lowest-ranking members of the surviving class aboard, with some of the higher-ups there to back them up. The three-crew ships were staffed by the middle-ranking class members. All the scuttlebutt I could pick up indicated Driscoll hadn't coerced anyone else into volunteering. I guess she knew her command.

Survey Base was soon filled with the roar of launching auxiliary craft ferrying supplies, instruments, luggage and incidentals up to the orbiting ships. The parts depot was stripped bare in 50 hours, until the base XO ordered all spares returned to the depot for proper distribution. While I can say that the loyal crew of the *J.M.* returned nearly everything we hadn't installed yet, I can't speak for the other ships. A few aux craft made the run to Kennedy for long-store food that didn't taste like cardboard. We all chipped in on that one.

Every comm channel was jammed with carefully censored goodbye messages to every planet in the League—and none of the messages explained why we were launching so suddenly.

Driscoll was trying to keep the loss of the *Venera* private, even if it could not be made secret. She wanted it under as tight a wrap as possible for as long as possible. She knew perfectly well that there would be a leak sooner or later. Regret-to-inform 'grams had already gone out to the next of kin, of course. These said nothing more than that a son or a daughter, a niece or a nephew, a grandchild, a spouse, had died in the honorable performance of his or her duties. No mention of how, or when, or where, simply a statement that, owing to circumstances beyond human control, the body could not be returned for burial.

If word leaked, and someone higher-up bothered to see what was going on at Survey Training Base, you could bet the launching of the Survey Ships would have been stopped cold. For good. But space was vast, and communications were slow. There was every chance of keeping certain people in authority from discovering the situation for a while.

There was hope, there was a reasonable chance, that the risks Driscoll was running could pay off. The Survey Ships could, in theory, be operated by one person—if everything worked perfectly—and two or three could handle the job under a great many circumstances. A crew of nine was a safety measure, a morale improver, a redundancy system. The mission rules for a crew of nine required that at least three people remain aboard and retain at least one auxiliary ship while the others were on an exploratory job. Now that rule was out the window—or else no one could have ever left the ships. So were a lot of similar regs. All was now up to the commander's discretion.

Driscoll called all the commanders to a meeting to cover such points. Her basic orders were quite simple: gather and return to base as much information as possible without risking your command. Bring the ship back in one piece.

Find some nice real estate, poke around a little, learn what you can out there—*but bring that ship back*!!

The first explorations of the League of Planets Survey Service were going to be *good* publicity. That was a direct order.

Then there was the physical checkout of the ships themselves. That was what kept me awake nights. Had I or had I not gotten a proper reading on the fuel pump pressure in the number three oxy tank? Did that overvoltage mean anything? What about the air plant? One bright point was that we ended up spending most nights on the *J.M.*, which meant working and sleeping in zero-gee. That helped a lot.

The ship was soon in fine fettle, but would it stay that way until we got back? The astrogation team had given us a course that would have the *J.M.* light-years from the nearest shipyard for the next 13,000 hours—about a year and a half, Earthside. Joz and I checked out every primary, secondary, and tertiary backup system every step of the way. then put the diagnostic computer programs through their paces just as thoroughly. *Then* we used the diagnostics to check all our hand-work. Slowly, we squeezed the bugs out.

By the time Joslyn closed down the last access panel and wiped the grease off her nose with an even greasier hand, we had a taut ship. We were proud of her. "Mac," Joslyn said. "I think I can forgive your naming this old girl after me. She is a love."

"I agree. But I'm sure you're a lot more fun on a date." I was mighty happy with both Joslyn Maries. The one with the nice smile cuddled into my arms and gave me a happy kiss, then settled herself over my lap. It would have been *in*to my lap, but we were in zero-gee at the time. Nice thing about zero-gee: laps don't get tired. I stretched out on my command couch and peeked around Joslyn to see a green board. The ship behind that board was a beaut.

The *J.M.* was about 90 meters from stem to stern. At the stern were the three great fusion rocket engines and the support gear for them. Directly forward of the engines was a central core hydrogen tank surrounded by six strap-on fuel tanks. The strap-ons were not to be jettisoned; the *J.M.* could, at least in theory, sidle up to a space-going hunk of ice, a comet or whatever, and tank up by extracting hydrogen from it. It would take an emergency before I would want to try that maneuver. Above the tankage section was a exercise deck. Like the rest of the ship, it was a cylinder fifteen meters in diameter. Its hatchways were set in its centerline, about which it spun to provide simulated gravity. Above this were two decks of staterooms, plumbing, a galley, a library nook, an entertainment screen, and so forth. The topmost deck was the command center, where Joz and I were now. Here were control centers for the planned nine crew members, most of them redundant in one way or another to the primary command chair—where I sat. Joz was to have the pilot's hotseat when we were maneuvering.

Above our heads were the main docking and extra-vehicular-activity airlock sections. Docked nose-to-nose with the *Joslyn Marie*, and thus flying stern-first when docked to the main ship, was the large, blunt-cone shape of the large ballistic lander, *Uncle Sam*. Access tunnels led from here back down the length of the ship to the docking ports of *Stars* and *Stripes*, which sat atop the number one and number four outboard fuel tanks. Unlike *Uncle Sam*, they rode the *J.M.* right-side-up, sitting, inside additional bracing, on their own landing gear.

The *J.M.*, *Uncle Sam*, *Stars*, and *Stripes* were all armed with torpedo tubes and powerful laser cannon. We carried sensitive telescopes, radio gear, and detection devices of all sorts. There were dozens of internal and external inspection cameras all over the ship, wired into the command center video screens. Pressure suits, maneuvering units, a washer and drier, climbing ropes, a biological lab, workshop space, what seemed like an extra ship in spare parts, and a great deal more were tucked inside the hull here and there.

She was a good ship.

We sat there, admiring her, for a long time. For me, at

least, that was the moment she stopped being a piece of metal for holding the vacuum out, and became my home. And she was ready to fly.

Driscoll called us into her office for a brief set of final words before we launched. Driscoll was tired, very tired, and certainly more frightened than we were. It was very quick. She welcomed us to her office, sat us down, politely offered us a drink, and we politely refused. She didn't seem to know where to begin for a long time. She hemmed and hawed about little things, the details of what would come next, all the time toying with the pencils and papers on her desk.

Finally, she plunged in. "Damn it. Do you kids know how proud I am of you?" she asked. "You've truly taken on the world, the galaxy. And you're going to go out there and break your backs trying to wrestle with the unknown. You might die out there, struggling and fighting with the cold and the heat and the vacuum and the loneliness, and yet die well, with your spirit and your heart intact, without fully knowing what it is you are dying for. You can't possibly know. You're too young, too brave, too sure."

She paused, and sighed deeply. She threw back her head and stared at the ceiling for a time before she continued.

"The best clue to what it is all about that I can give you is this: only if you *do* die with your spirit and your heart intact will you have died well—and dying well simply means that you have *lived* well. But I don't truly believe you will die—you are both survivors. If there comes a time when you feel you can't go on, remember that; you are survivors, and use that fact to find the tiny shred of endurance, of courage, of strength you forgot you still had." She paused, and smiled, and we saw that her eyes were shining. "And that's all I have left to tell you." She led us to the door, embraced us both for a moment, and then we took our leave.

A few hours later we were at our command chairs, and a powerful tug was thundering along behind us, providing us the velocity we'd need for our first jump without having to touch the fuel in the *J.M.* tanks. This freed up our fuel for later use and thereby increased our range.

The faster-than-light drive moves a ship at the square of the speed of light. It's usually referred to as C^2, pronounced "cee-squared," even though it isn't *really* the speed of light squared—that's a meaningless expression. The speed of light is 186,000 miles per second, or 300,000 kilometers per second—or one light-year per year.

The C^2 drive is called that because it gives an effective velocity of about 89,000,000,000 kilometers a second, which is close enough to the square of the metric expression of the speed of light. C^2 gets you from the Solar System to Proxima Centauri in about 450 seconds. That is, it would, if anyone had any reason to go to Proxima Centauri. Of course one has to use the C^2 drive well outside the gravity well of a solar system, or end up far, far, far away from the intended destination.

There are other catches, as well—the jump between "normal" space and C^2 takes a big jolt of power. If, God forbid, anything went wrong with your power supply and you got stuck in C^2, well, the edge of the universe is over that way, and no one knows exactly what happens once you get there. Certainly, ships have been lost that way. Less catastrophic, but still very dangerous, is inaccurate astrogation. An error of .09 seconds in coming out of C^2 would put you roughly as far from your target as the asteroid belt is from the Sun.

Navigation computers are good enough these days that pilots can feel safe with about a half billion kilometer miss-factor. The *J.M.* would shoot for about three times that, as we were headed into territory not as well charted as that on the regular space lines. Also, if we came out over the pole of the target star, as we hoped to do, we would have the best vantage point for us to look for planets.

Most star systems (including Earth's) have the plane of rotation of their planets in the same plane as the equator of the star in question. So, if you looked at, say, the Solar

System from the plane of the Sun's equator, the planets, asteroids, and what have you would be moving in orbits that would be seen edge-on from where you stood. If you watched the Earth for a year, that is, one orbit, it would simply appear to move in a straight line from one side of the sun to the other, and then back again, moving once in front of the Sun's disk, and once behind it. From a point far enough away to observe the entire orbit, the change in size of the Earth's disk as it moves toward and away from you, inscribing a circle seen edge on, would be difficult to measure accurately. Seen from the north or south polar regions, however, the orbits of the planets would be laid out before the observer face on and so would be easy to observe. This in turn makes it easy to measure motions of planets and other bodies and put together reasonably accurate charts and ephemerides of their orbits.

What all this boils down to is that it is best to come in over a star system and look down on it, rather than come in at the side and see it edge-on.

Fine. It has been found that planets usually rotate in the plane of a star's equator. So how do we determine where the equator is? One star seen from another is a featureless dot of light.

The standard technique is to use the Doppler effect. Light of a given frequency has a higher *apparent* frequency when it is moving toward you, and a lower apparent frequency when it is moving away from you. The light doesn't change, the way you perceive it does. Obviously, one side of a rotating object will be moving toward you and the other side will be moving away. The difference is measurable over stellar distances. Very careful measurements can usually yield the plane of rotation, and thus the equator and poles, within about ten degrees or so.

Ten degrees is a lot. Stack on top of that the fact that the actual distance to a target star is rarely known to any degree of accuracy, and you'll see that there is a certain degree of luck in Survey work. Get bad data, use it to put your ship in the wrong place, and you'll have to waste fuel getting the ship to where it was supposed to be. Waste too much fuel and you come back early, or not at all. It was possible to "mine" hydrogen fuel from an ice moon. But finding suitable ice was rare, and the process was a long and tedious one.

You came out of C^2 with precisely the heading and velocity you started out with. The stars orbit the center of the Galaxy, just as planets move about a star. Thus, they move relative to each other. A typical velocity difference would be on the order of about seventy kilometers a second. A ship traveling from one star to the other would have to match that velocity shift.

The tug was boosting us up to our required velocity, so that we could match speeds with the star we were shooting for first. Once there, we would make any adjustments needed to our speed and heading, and begin the search for planets.

We cast off from the tug and were on our way. Five minutes later the *J.M.*'s computers decided we were in the right place at the right time and booted us into C^2, and we were off into untraveled regions.

For 4,000 hours or so, say 6 months, the *J.M.* did her job. We visited a half dozen star systems, each magnificently different from the others, each a sore temptation to stay and explore and wonder at for a lifetime at least. The only thing that kept us from staying was the promise of fresh wonders in another part of the sky.

Not only a universe of wonders, but the woman I loved to share them with me. Those were the days of my greatest happiness. Each day I woke to challenging, satisfying work that was not only exciting but useful, vital. Each day was spent with someone I not only loved, but liked. Each day was a new adventure.

Each day, every day, was *fun*.

Imagine yourself standing on a tiny worldlet of tremendous mineral wealth left there by some quirk of the way worlds are born. Imagine standing on that world, staring up at the sky at a world a hundred times the size of Jupiter, knowing that the violent storms you see in its roiling sea of clouds are the birthpangs of a star, its thermonuclear furnaces just flickering into life. Joslyn and I stood in such a place, and knew others would follow, rushing to extract the treasure beneath our feet before the fireball in the sky came to full life and expanded out into space, leaving nothing but cinders where we stood. The end for that world will come in a human lifetime, or perhaps twice that.

Imagine two worlds the size of Earth's moon that revolve around each other, separated from each other by less than 3,000 kilometers. Tidal forces have spawned endless earthquakes and utterly shattered the surfaces of the twin worlds. We named them Romulus and Remus. One day they will smash into each other and leave only rocks careering through the void.

Imagine a world where the air is fresh and sweet, and life very like that on Earth fills the seas and skies and land. There I found—something. I say it is a piece of worked metal. Joslyn thinks it is a chance piece of nature's work, a glob of alloy spat out of a volcano and shaped by the caprice of water and weather. Humanity will settle there soon, and I hope some child born there will dig one place, dig another, and one day prove that ours are not the only minds to have touched that place.

Joslyn and I lived to wander the sky and do as we pleased. It was the happiest time of our life together.

And then they found us.

We were in the vicinity of our sixth target when they did. We had been there for about ten days. We were just about finished with the location-and-orbit survey search for major planets, and were ready to start down from our perch far above the star's north pole to take a close-up look at some of the better real estate we had spotted.

We were in bed, asleep, when the alarm sounded. It was the general alert buzzer, which meant the emergency was rare enough that it didn't rate its own alarm code.

Joslyn and I scrambled out of bed, bounced off a few

bulkheads, and made our way to the command deck. I fumbled a hand to a switch and killed the alert buzzer.

Joslyn, who usually wakes up faster than I do, got the computer to decode the alert before I was even in my flight chair. "It's a courier drone!" she said.

"*What*?"

"You heard me."

"Yeah, but it doesn't make any sense." Courier drones were *expensive*, and the odds of one finding us all the way out here were remote at best.

"Tell the drone that. Get on your board and pull a print-out of the drone ops manual, will you?" Joslyn was studying her screen, trying to squeeze more information out of the words on it.

I typed in a few commands and a book-length manual buzzed its way into the line printer's hopper. I instructed the computer to decode the courier's beacon signal and report the data in it.

"So when is it going to transmit its message to us?" Joslyn asked.

I looked at my screen and whistled. "Never. Don't ask me why, but there's a security block on all the information aboard except the beacon."

"Can we get it to home in on us?" Joslyn was thinking like a pilot—if the drone did the maneuvering, that would save on our fuel.

"The decode of the beacon signal shows tanks nearly dry."

"Oh, wacko. It can't get to us?"

"Not unless you want our grandkids to pick it up. That 'nearly' dry is close to being 'completely.' "

"They shouldn't be, with a direct boost from base."

"I'll bet you who fixes dinner it isn't a direct boost. I think it tried our last survey system first, then headed here."

"Mac! Do you have any idea how difficult it would be to program a drone to do that? The search gear it would need? The instruments? The power? It would have to be *huge*."

"I know, I know, I know. That's why this is a manned ship we're flying. But we left the last system a week ahead of schedule. We're still supposed to be there. And the heading that thing's on is almost exactly the heading *we* used to come from there—and about 120 degrees away from where it would be on a direct boost from Columbia."

"Bloody. You're right. The velocity is all wrong for Columbia, too."

I stared at the screen full of numbers. "Get some rendezvous data. Give us a set of three trajectories—reasonable economy, midrange, and minimum time. I'll make coffee."

"We'll need it," Joslyn said, and started plotting courses.

Fifteen minutes later she had some rough figures to show me. "One percent of our fuel gets us there in a month. Five percent gets us there in a five and a half days." She paused.

"And what's the minimum time trajectory?"

She bit her lip. "Thirty-six hours. Fifteen percent of our remaining fuel."

"Is that assuming we fly the *Joslyn Marie*?"

"Oh, goodness no! All of these are assuming we fly *Stars*. She seems to fly a trifle more efficiently than *Stripes*."

"Fifteen percent . . . damn. Okay, feed the minimum time course to *Stars'* computer. I'll start a systems check on her." I started for the airlock level.

"Mac!" Joslyn called. "We—we can't lose that much fuel! We do that and we might as well pack up the rest of the mission!"

I sighed. "Joz—I know you're the pilot. You're in charge of flying the ship without wasting fuel and keeping our options open. Thanks to Driscoll's coin toss I'm in charge of choosing which option we take. Now, whatever base sent that drone after us, they judged it more important than our mission, or else they wouldn't have sent it."

"But what could they have to say that would be important enough to send a drone after the ship?"

"I don't know. But if it's so important that it was worth

tracking us across two star systems, it's certainly urgent. The party's over, Joz. The real world just caught up." I went below to start on powering up the lander.

What *could* be important enough? I simply couldn't think of a single possibility. I did a rough guess in my head on what the drone would cost, juggling the figures as I worked. The answer was impressive. For a robot ship smart enough to scan one system, search it and then reject it, plus the computers to hack a course to another system, plus the engines, the fusion plant, the C^2 plant, the communications gear—probably more than the *Joslyn Marie*, since it would be a custom job, not mass-produced like the *J.M.*

Getting the *J.M.* for this job was a miracle. What was big enough to *spend* that kind of money?

Three hours later we cast off from the *Joslyn Marie*, leaving her powered down to wait for our return. *Stars* was a trim little ship, and Joslyn even let me do the flying, for once. I lined us up with the gyros to save fuel on the attitude jets, just to keep on Joslyn's good side.

The course was a hair-raising one. We had to blip into C^2 for a few milliseconds, pop out and change our heading, then into C^2 again. All this to avoid falling into the local sun, which was dangerously close to what would be a direct course to the drone. Then a long cruise while we gunned our fusion engine in earnest and lined up for the final jump to the drone's position and velocity.

It was a dull thirty-six hours, beside the few minutes required now and again to monitor the ship and guide the computer through the course. It was not made any more pleasant by the fact that Joslyn was mad at me. While she understood the need to get to the drone fast, she didn't have to like it, and she couldn't yell at the base personnel who had sent it out after us.

Well, she didn't exactly yell at *me*, either, but the effect was the same: what she did was barely speak to me at all.

I was left without much to do besides trying to figure out what the drone was. And I still didn't get anywhere with that.

By the time we were within visual range of the drone, I was more than glad of the change of pace—to say nothing of going out of my mind with purest monkey curiosity.

Stars didn't have all the fancy optical gadgets we had on board the *J.M.*, but she carried a pretty fair long-range camera. As soon as there was the slightest hope of picking up the drone with it, I brought it to bear. And got one of the great shocks of my life. A drone was about the size of a torpedo—maybe 5 meters long, most of that fuel tanks. This thing was the size of the *Joslyn Marie*. Most of it fuel tanks. The only cargo seemed to be in a blister on the apex of the drone. Huge arrows, painted on the hull, pointed to it.

"It must have five times the fuel capacity of the *J.M.*" Joslyn said, her voice betraying as much shock as I felt. Surprise had evaporated all her annoyance with me.

"If they burned all that fuel getting here, they must have tracked us through *three* star systems . . ."

"If not more. And at high acceleration, too. See all the structural bracing?"

"Yes. The aft end is pointed through the direction of flight, too. It must have burned almost all its fuel slowing to a velocity we could match. One thing on the bright side—if the drone has scavenger pumps, we could take the last of its fuel for *Stars'* tanks."

"Even if that monster's tanks are down to one percent, that'd be enough to top us off. Here's hoping. Mac, what could it *be*?"

"We'll know soon."

We approached the giant ship slowly. As we closed to within a hundred meters or so, Joslyn pointed to one side of the screen. "There! A fuel hose waiting for us. They did think to set up a scavenger."

"Good. Maybe we'll have some fuel when this is over. Whatever it is."

I switched on our fueling system and forgot about it. It was an automatic that was supposed to call to a fuel system at a commercial port and request fueling. The port's robots were supposed to come and tend to the ship without bothering the crew. The home office had been kind enough to arrange that kind of service out here.

We came in over the docking port and swung our topside around to meet it, so that the two ships came together nose to nose. I made the docking run in the first pass and activated the capture latches to hold us solidly to the other ship.

We got out of our crash couches and climbed over each other getting to the nose airlock door, both of us burning with curiosity. I cracked open a bleeder valve to match our ship's air pressure with the drone's cabin pressure. There was a brief *whooshing* of air, and I swallowed to make my eardrums pop. At a nod from me, Joslyn undogged *Stars'* hatch, and then opened the drone's hatchway, a meter or so beyond it.

The drone's hatch swung open, revealing the drone's interior. Since the ships were docked nose to nose, we were looking straight down from the top of the drone's cabin. The only thing in it was a great black cylinder, exactly the size to fit through the airlock passage. It was pointed right for the hatchway joining the ships; all it needed was a good push from below to send it through the lock into *Stars*.

We kicked off from the hatchway and drifted into the drone's cabin staring at the cylinder. It was big, and its base was heavily braced against acceleration.

Joslyn hung in midair, fascinated. "My God, it's like a totem pole ready for—"

But a giant, booming voice suddenly shouted out from a speaker by the overhead hatch. "THIS IS A WAR EMERGENCY SITUATION," it roared. "TRANSFER THE CYLINDER TO YOUR SHIP WITH ALL POSSIBLE SPEED. DO NOT DELAY FOR ANY REASON. THE MOMENT AUTOMATIC REFUELING IS COMPLETED, CAST OFF AND RETURN TO THE *JOSLYN MARIE* AT MAXIMUM SPEED. DELAY FOR NOTHING. YOU MAY EXAMINE THE CYLINDER EN ROUTE. HURRY. HURRY. THIS IS A WAR EMERGENCY SITUATION. THAT IS ALL."

I clapped my hands over my ears and heard the great

voice that way. The moment it was over, Joslyn and I looked at each other in something close to shock, and instantly got to work on the cylinder. That wasn't the sort of voice you argued with.

There was a very simple, straightforward quick-release device holding the cylinder to its bracing, and a diagram painted on it in bright red paint, showing how to use it. I pulled at one lever, Joslyn at the other, and the cylinder popped off its moorings with a deep *sprung*. A spring-loaded pusher had been cocked underneath it, and gave it a gentle shove through the overhead hatch, moving it at about a half meter a second. I kicked over to one side of the cabin, scrambled up a set of handholds, and beat the cylinder through the hatch by only a few seconds. I cleared the hatchway and got to one side. The cylinder came through *Stars'* nose hatch, through the access hatch to the lower deck. I peeked down through the access hatch to see the forward end of the great black shape sprouting a set of legs, a tripod, that swung into place and locked, forming a solid support for the thing. The legs touched *Stars'* inner hull and I heard a *thunk, thunk, thunk*—electromagnets coming on to further brace our new cargo.

Joslyn came into *Stars'* forward cabin right behind the cylinder, squeezing past it as she sealed the hatches. The cylinder was a good eight meters long. The part of it poking up through the access hatch took up the entire height of *Stars'* upper cabin. Someone had done some very careful planning—apparently down to figuring out which ship type we'd use.

Just as Joslyn dogged the inside hatch, a speaker hooked into the cylinder came on, cued by radio from the drone. It wasn't quite as loud, but that voice still had authority. "REFUELING IS COMPLETED. CAST OFF. GET UNDER WAY. GET UNDER WAY. THAT IS ALL."

But Joslyn was already at the command seat, working the joystick. She snapped *Stars* through a tight head-over-tail loop and gunned the engine, bathing the drone's cabin in fusion flame, vaporizing part of it. The robot ship was a derelict now, and she wasn't going to waste time being careful of it.

I held on as best I could through the loop and made it to my own couch as she started the main engine and we set out for home. I looked at the base of the cylinder that sat in the centerline of our lander.

What had we gotten ourselves into? War emergency situation?

What war?

Ours, as it turned out.

Joslyn got us under way as quickly as possible, and we did the post-maneuver check-outs in record time. Twenty minutes after casting off from the giant drone ship, we started to take a good look at the cylinder.

The first thing I realized was that it was not quite as awesome an object as I had first thought. Underneath an outer sheath, much of its bulk was padding and bracing against acceleration. We set to work taking it apart.

Inside the packing material were a few odd looking pieces of equipment and a set of very standard playback disks, each marked with a large red numeral. Joslyn pulled the one marked "1" out of its jacket and set it into *Stars'* playback unit.

"Mac—I'm almost afraid to play this thing."

"It's too late to chicken out, Joz—run it."

She pressed the play button. The main screen came to life, first displaying the flag of the League of Planets, and then dissolving to Pete Gesseti's face. Pete? What was he doing in a communication from base? Why not Driscoll? I looked hard at his image on the screen. He was tired, his clothes looked slept in. For the first time in my life, I looked at Pete and thought of him as . . . old. Something more than six month's time had aged him.

But it was his eyes that drew me. They spoke of anger, determination, and some odd hint of faith.

Pete began to speak. "Mac, Joslyn. Hello. They asked me to do this because you both know me. Maybe it'll sound a little better from me. Though it can't sound very good.

"We—the League, all the members, everybody, are at war. Not with each other. With someone from outside. Human, descended from Earth, speaking English. A heavy military force has attacked . . . no, they haven't attacked. They've *conquered* the planet of New Finland.

"The Treaty of Planets requires that the members of the League come to the aid of New Finland. Period. No ifs, ands or buts. The other members of the League have an absolutely binding legal and moral duty to come to the assistance of our sworn allies. We have to help them. And we want to. We need to.

"Maybe this isn't official policy, but it's fact: if the League doesn't fulfill its commitment, it will fall apart. At best, it will become a useless debating club. No one could rely on it. It isn't healthy now. Worse since you've been gone. There are too many bad little signs—infighting, petty squabbles, minor, pointless, defiances of the League. Ugly, mean, little things.

"The League has *got* to hold together, because we don't have anything else. If it goes down, it'll go down the way the League of Nations went down. Straight down into war.

"None of that is pretty, but you need to know how much is riding on this. How much is riding on you."

Pete, or rather the recording of Pete, paused and frowned. He sighed. "It's this way. The New Finns are settlers from a group of people who were leaned on a lot by a big, dangerous neighbor. The old Soviet Union. So they settled far out from everyone else, where no one would be near enough to bother them. They are right at the limits of the physical area of space humanity is known to have colonized.

"The only thing we knew for a while was that we had lost contact with the New Finns. Then a small message drone popped into normal space in the New Britannica system. In it was a message from a group of New Finns who lived on the planet's large artificial satellite, Vapaus.

"They reported that the invaders called themselves 'Guardians,' and that these Guardians were in the process of setting up an anti-ship missile system around the New Finnish system. The Guardians had developed a rather simple gadget which detected the very specific burst of ultraviolet and X-ray radiation a ship coming in from C^2 gives off, and hooked it up to a missile with a C^2 generator of its own.

"The effect is that if a ship appears inside the Guardian-held New Finnish system, it will be detected, and destroyed within seconds of being so detected.

"There are already a number of civilian ships gone missing that were due to call on New Finland. We assume the missile system got them.

"The one ray of hope from the New Finns' message was that the missile array was not completely deployed. At the cost of the lives of several of their men, they came up with the deployment schedule for the missiles.

"If a ship entered the N.F. system from a certain direction by a certain time—670,716 hours Stellar Time, or noon GMT on July 8, 2115, Earthside, it should be able to enter the N.F. system without being destroyed."

Pete swallowed hard. "The only ship, the only people we've got with the slightest hope of getting there on time—well, the ship is the League of Planets Survey Ship 41 *Joslyn Marie*. Your ship is fast. New Finland happens to be out the way of your survey. You're it.

"You have got to go in there."

Pete suddenly looked, not worried or afraid, but embarrassed. "Okay, that's *that* part of it. What you've got to do once you're there is *really* crazy.

"Bell Labs, on the mining satellite Lucifer. They came up with something about the time the *Joslyn Marie* was launched.

"A matter transmitter."

"Oh, boy," I said. A *matter* transmitter?

"They say—well, they say it works on the same principle as the C^2 generator, except with the force, or the field, or the power, or something, rotated through 90 degrees. I'm a paper pusher; I don't understand it. Now this next is the nutty part."

He paused. "They have a lot of faith in it. In the same package where you found this recording, is the receiver, or at least the core of it, for the matter transmitter. You're supposed to get to the planet's surface with it, assemble the receiver on a precisely predetermined spot—and they'll transmit 5,000 troops to you from a light month away."

"Good Lord!" Joslyn cried, drowning out Pete for a moment.

". . . means they'll have to transmit the troops—or the signal carrying the troops, a standard month—30 Earth days, 720 hours—*before* you receive it. Which boils down to mean the troops will be transmitted to you before you could possibly build the device to receive them."

"Joslyn," I said, "this is insane. How could it work?"

"Mac, I don't . . ." Joslyn trailed off to listen to Pete.

"There are more recordings that give you the technical grounding for all this. Some other gadgetry. Learning sets for the Finnish language." Pete's image fumbled with some papers.

"Mac, Joslyn. I dunno. It seems crazy from this end—but not as crazy as it must seem to you. We are very frightened. These Guardians simply *took* New Finland. Maybe they could just *take* us. The message from the Finns say that's the way they're talking. We have to stop them. The guys in the lab came up with the transmitter, and the brass came up with this plan. We're going to put it all in the fastest drone ever made—actually the fastest ship ever made. We're going to try and find you in three different star systems. The drone will launch and cruise at accelerations that would kill a man in minutes.

"There isn't any way for you to send a message saying 'Yes, we got the drone's signal and the cargo and we'll do it.' There isn't enough time. So they'll send the troops no matter what, just hoping you've picked up the ball.

"In other words, if you do it, 5,000 troops are taking a tremendous risk. If you don't, and the signal isn't received; they're dead.

"It is all on you. You are the only chance those troops

have to live, and maybe the only chance the Finns have to regain their liberty." He paused and lowered his voice. "*And I have a very strong, gut feeling that this has something to do with what I said after the third drink at the funeral.*"

My stomach did a flip-flop. The Guardians? They hijacked the *Venera*?

"I have no logical reason, no evidence. But I have a very strong hunch I'm right. If I am, and it is true, our friends won't be on New Finland. They, and others caught the same way, will be back in the Guardians' system. I warned the people who asked me to do this I'd have some cryptic ways of convincing you." There was a bare, brief hint of a smile on his face for a moment.

"Listen, you two. There's a very old poem. From long ago and far away. It's the last way I have to ask you to do this thing, to fight this war for us. Part of it said

> Take up our quarrel with the foe.
> To you, from failing hands we throw
> The torch, be yours to hold it high.
> If ye break faith with those who die,
> We shall not sleep . . .

The torch be yours," Pete repeated. His voice came close to cracking. I was as close as he had to a son, and he was called upon to send me out to war, to die, perhaps.

No, the odds were too bad.

To die, probably.

"Gesseti out."

And we were on our own.

Chapter Three

The spanner nearly jumped out of my hands again, but this time I kept it under control at the cost of a set of rescraped knuckles.

"Damn!" I yelled, sucking at the re-opened cuts. "This is not my idea of a good time."

We were working on one of the torpedoes in the airlock and workshop deck of the *J.M.* Two things made it tougher. The first was that most of the handtools aboard the *J.M.* were intended for use in zero-gee. This meant a tool had to exert equal pressure in two perfectly opposite directions. Otherwise, work would have been impossible. A normal hammer is a good example of why special tools are needed. Hit something with a hammer in a reasonable gravity field and you'll stay in place, pasted down by your own weight. Do the same thing in zero-gee and you'll go flying. Without gravity to hold you, the force of your swing not only will drive a nail down, but you up: an equal and opposite reaction.

So zero-gee tools have counter-action balance weights, counter-rotating collars driven by gears, and so on. The power tools especially look like the results of drunken binges at an inventors' convention.

The second flaw was that the *J.M.* was boosting at two gees toward the calculated transition point for the jump to the New Finnish system. When used in two gravities, a zero-gee spanner is more a weapon for use against one's self than a tool.

There was a third flaw, of course. We were boosting toward the New Finnish system—and neither of us wanted to go.

"Mac, easy with that thing! You've got it tight now, don't strip the bolt."

"Sorry."

"Let's take a break. We're ahead of schedule anyway."

"Sounds good." I tossed the spanner aside and it clattered to the deck with a satisfactorily loud noise. Without further discussion, I followed Joz down to the wardroom for a cup of tea. She puttered about with the makings while I sat and brooded.

"I cannot believe this," I suddenly announced.

"What?" Joslyn asked, her mind more on the tea than me.

"The mission. The whole hare-brained thing. And the way we got into it."

"The way we got into it. You're right. That's the worst part of it," Joslyn said as she brought the kettle to the table and sat down. There were advantages to constant boost: you had homey things like kettles instead of squeeze bulbs. "If I had a chance to do it," she continued as she poured, "I honestly believe I would have volunteered to help the good people of New Finland. I truly do. But I feel so *compelled* by the way it happened, as if I was a piece on a chess board that had no choice but to go where it was sent."

"I don't think Pete liked doing it that way, either. But I don't see what choices he had, either. No one did, since the Finns were attacked. Once that happened we were the only thing the League had. Good old Pete," I said ruefully.

"He certainly pushed every one of your buttons, from the debt you feel to him as your substitute father, to duty . . ."

". . . To the chance that we *might* get a lead on our missing classmates." That was the first time I had called those lost on the *Venera* "missing," not "dead." I realized I was convinced they were alive.

"Don't forget the fate of the League is in our hands." Joslyn said, with just a hint of a smile.

"I haven't, but I'll keep trying." I sipped at my tea and we sat quietly for a minute. "What gets me is there's nothing to stop us from saying the hell with it and pointing the *J.M.* away from the trouble. If we turned and ran, or just destroyed the drone and showed up a year or two from now and claimed we had never found it—if we chickened out, no one could do anything about it.

"Against that, the only thing making us go in and risk our lives for strangers is the feeling that we have to do it." I paused. "And it's enough, I guess. Thanks to the sense of duty they've bred and beaten into us. And I know what you mean about having no choice."

"And now that it's all out of your system, let's go finish the go-cart," Joslyn said, rumpling my hair.

The 'go-cart' was what was left of the torpedo we had started with. Joslyn and I had pulled down the entire nose section. I had been working on installing a crash-couch on to the front end of the torp's motor housing while Joslyn pulled the guidance system out of the nose section and hooked it back up to the decapitated torpedo. She left off the frills: it would pick up a downloaded trajectory from *Stripes'* guidance system and run with those numbers: that was it. The control panel was one button marked "ON."

The crash-couch looked more like a lawn chair, and folded up like one, but it was extremely strong. The *J.M.* carried about ten of them, in case she ever had to carry passengers.

The go-cart was the key to our grand plan for getting me down to talk with the locals and arrange for the little matter of the transmission of 5,000 combat troops. I was to be the only cargo—we did not want to bring in the receiver hardware itself until we had managed to contact the locals.

Along with Pete's message to us had come other recordings, full of such information as our side had.

Most importantly, the League had some information on the enemy. When the alert came in from the New Finns, every intelligence outfit in the League had gone to work, digging into old files, cross checking, trying to figure out the "Guardians." It didn't take long to find out who they were—or at least who they had started out being.

About 60 years ago, at the turn of the 21st century, a collection of fascist and right wing groups in Britain and the United States combined their forces and called themselves the Atlantic Freedom Front, or just the Front—apparently deriving the name from something in 20th century England called the National Front. They staged demonstrations and caused a riot or two, and during the slump at the beginning of the 21st century began to get some attention. They were willing to sign up just about anybody—people like the Ku Klux Klan, The New John Birchers, the remnants of Afrikaners in Exile. They got to the point where they thought they were a lot bigger than they really were.

On March 15, 2008, they attempted to overthrow the British and American governments. Never, at any moment, was either government in the slightest danger—the Front did not number more than a few thousand members on either side of the Atlantic. What was supposed to be a brilliant double coup ended up as little more than a pair of bloody scuffles in Washington and London. Their street thugs were called Guardians of the Front, and they managed to kill a few police and soldiers, and a few innocent bystanders. Mostly, the Guardians just got themselves killed. The leaders, and such of the others as could be caught and convicted were thrown in jail. That was the end of the story, or should have been.

Colonization laws were pretty loose back then—and I guess they still are. Pretty much anyone who could hire a ship and get the needed gear together was allowed to launch and go pick a planet.

The Guardians, or what was left of them, set out to do just that. Not secretly, either—the intelligence kit we got included reproductions of old ads calling for volunteers to start "a New Order in the Skies." They were ready to launch their ship—the *Mosley*—by June 2010.

To no one's great surprise, the Guardians tried to bust their leaders out of jail before leaving Earth. The authorities had been expecting an attempt, but not such a well organized or executed one: the Guardians had been learning. Simultaneous raids on prisons in England and the United

States got the chief hoods out and left a lot of good men dead.

Two hours after the raids, the Guardians and their head men were launching ballistic shuttle craft toward the *Mosley*, and an hour later, the *Mosley* boosted from orbit, entered C^2, and was never heard from again. No one was sad to see them go.

The planet the Guardians had claimed to be headed for was searched some time later. No sign of past or present human habitation was found. The *Mosley* was listed as missing and presumed lost with all hands, and good riddance. Last of the Guardians.

Until New Finland. Unquestionably the same people. They called themselves Guardians. The insignia matched. So did the brutality.

Against them, the League had provided us with only a sketch of a plan: get the receiver down to the planet's surface at the right place and switch it on at the right time.

The League did provide sets of maps, and diagrams of the New Finnish system, drawn up at the time the planet was settled. There didn't seem to be much current information.

There also were language lab gadgets and a complete set of tapes and recordings on Finnish.

But no program of hypnotic teaching, sleep teaching, audio-visual gimcrackery, or anything else is going to change the fact that learning languages is tough for some people, and I am one of them. I came very close to rebelling against sentences like "The cat is on the roof of my grey-haired maternal grandmother's house of flats." That once came out "Grandmother's mother is on the roof with the grey cat on her head."

But Joslyn is one of those people who pick up languages the way my dress uniform picks up lint. She would be. In any event, she was there to see me through it all and help me get Great-gramma and the cat off the roof.

Joslyn tried to use my language problem to say she should be the one to contact the New Finns. But that was clearly impossible. The reports the League had passed along were very definite on the point that the Guardians were barely allowing the Finnish women out of the house. No women were allowed in positions of even minor authority. The only Guardians any Finn had seen were men, though there were rumors of a "comfort corps." Whoever went down there would have to play spy, pretend to be one thing or another at one time or another. That would be merely tough for a man—it would be impossible for a woman. I had to go.

Alone. Up to that moment alone had meant alone together for us. Now I might die, or Joslyn might, and the other would be truly alone, surrounded by nothing but strangers, or perhaps marooned in space.

That was the thing we worked hardest at not thinking about.

We came to the transition point and skittered through the skies for a long minute or so of C^2 flight, the longest jump either of us had ever taken. C^2 doesn't feel any different than normal space, since what the C^2 generator does is drag a bubble of normal space, big enough to contain the ship, into C^2 conditions. The only disconcerting thing was that the outside cameras didn't work. A camera looking at the ship showed it normally, but any lens or port pointed outward showed . . . nothing. At least that was the theory. It didn't look like nothing. Empty space, *that's* nothing. What you saw in C^2 wasn't that. It had no color, no detail, no substance, no evidence of any energies human instruments could pick up. But it wasn't nothing. I feel sure of that, but I couldn't say why. How could eyes evolved to see light make anything of what theory said C^2 required—light that, well, moved faster than light, so to speak . . .

That doesn't make any sense, which is another attribute of C^2.

But then we popped back into normal space and we were in the outer reaches of the New Finnish system. Working as fast as she could, it took Joslyn half an hour to check our position, while I watched every passive detector we had. If the New Finns were wrong, and they had gotten the antiship missiles deployed out this way, we were already dead. The missiles supposedly came in so fast there wouldn't be any point in firing our laser cannon without radar guidance—but we couldn't use the radar without being spotted ourselves. Even so, I had the laser primed and ready to go.

But the hours passed, and we were still in one piece long past the time it would have taken a missile to find us if there were one looking. We were inside, and, for the moment, safe.

Joslyn finally spotted enough of the system's planets to triangulate our position. We were on course: we were on the orbital plane of the planetary system, on the far side of the local sun from New Finland, and headed straight for a fall into the aforementioned sun. We'd brake our fall and roll out into a safe orbit first, of course, but keeping the sun between us and New Finland was the most obvious way to avoid being spotted: a sun makes a pretty fair shield. The easiest maneuver to keep us hidden was a direct fall. By the time we had to fire our main engines, we'd be completely screened by the sun.

Joslyn intended to put us in a solar orbit exactly opposite New Finland's, moving at exactly the same velocity, so that we'd remain hidden by the sun, always 180 degrees away from the planet, but in the same orbit.

But we had about a week of falling toward the sun before we needed to maneuver. That time was private. I won't speak of it, except to say that we were as happy as we could have been, with things the way they were.

At last, it was nearly time for Joslyn to drop the *J.M.* into the proper orbit. We had to get me ready to jump ship before that. I would ride one of the two smaller ballistic landers, *Stripes*, on in the *J.M.*'s current trajectory for a while yet. We wrestled the go-cart onto one of *Stripes'* exterior cargo clamps, swathed it in reflective material and heat-proofing, and stowed my gear aboard the auxiliary ship.

And there was no more time. I had to hurry. If I lost the

race, 5,000 troopers would be trapped for all time inside a timeless bubble of rotated C^2 space, with no receiver to find the bubble and pull them back. If C^2 was un-nothingness, then being lost in rotated C^2 space was undeath. If I lost the race, this solar system had no hope, and others might follow it.

And there was no more time.

We said our last in-person goodbyes in *Stripes'* airlock. We were at war. The odds were that we would never see each other again.

We held each other tight and said things that wouldn't interest anyone else anyway, until the last possible moment, until another moment more would mean Joslyn missing her burn window and losing fuel we couldn't waste.

Hatches clanged shut, I slid into my command couch, took the controls and jogged *Stripes'* thrusters, moving her to a safe distance. I aligned my little ship and edged away from the *J.M.* The bigger ship's engines jumped to life, and the fusion jet took my wife away from me.

I slipped a set of tiny plastic headphones on, and squeezed them tight against my ears, as if that would keep Joslyn a little closer. "Goodbye, kid," I said softly.

"Good hunting, Mac. But save a few of those bastards for me."

"Why bastards?" I asked, smiling in spite of myself. "What have they done to you so far?"

"Well, you're not here any more, are you?"

The great power of the *J.M.*'s engines created a strong plasma, a super hot gas-cloud formed of fusion exhaust particles. It caused static in radio frequencies. As the big ship slowed and I fell onward, the plasma served to jam radio signals perfectly. We were cut off from one another.

The *Joslyn Marie* slowed her fall and eased into orbit behind me, to wait there in the loneliness of space for word from me. If I survived to send it.

I too had to perform a pair of rocket burns, the first one speeding my fall into the sun, the second shifting my path into a tight loop *around* the sun, a gravity-assist maneuver that would flash me across the diameter of New Finland's orbit in less than a month.

It was a tricky maneuver, and might even cook poor old *Stripes* a bit—and me with her—if the cooling system had any problems, but I had to move as fast as possible. There was no hope of using C^2 this close to a sun. I'd be more likely to end up in the center of the star than where I wanted to go. I had to stay in normal space for another reason: the Guardians were looking for ships entering from C^2, and I'd be hard to miss.

Still, it was a long wait, and an unpleasant one, more so as I came nearer the star. I was only 40 million kilometers from New Finland's sun at closest approach. That violated the warranty on *Stripes*, but she kept me safe through it all. Good ship.

The worst of it all was the boredom of space travel. There is very little to do on a ship by yourself. Added to that was the tension of all the unknowns ahead of me; it was not a pleasant time. Mostly I studied my Finnish.

Finally, it was over. One hundred eighty degrees around the sun from the *J.M.*, I arrived at the vicinity of New Finland, albeit travelling at a great relative speed. I couldn't use *Stripes'* engines to slow down: Joslyn and I didn't want the aux ship to get within two million klicks of the planet. Closer, and there was a chance someone might spot her. I had to abandon ship.

That was what the torp, the go-cart, was for. I was to jump ship, climb into the fold-out crash couch, and ride the torp's motor in. *Stripes* would continue on her present course for a long while yet, until she was far enough from New Finland to use her fusion engine without risk of detection. Then she would turn back toward the sun, going into a solar polar orbit that would keep her in line of sight of both New Finland and the *Joslyn Marie* for many months, if she was left undisturbed by the Guardians. While in line of sight, *Stripes* could serve as a relay station for laser messages between Joslyn and myself.

It might have been a dangerous trip up until that point, but it had been far from exciting—or even interesting. That was about to change. I collected all my gear and checked my suit over a half dozen times. I would be counting on it for a long while. Then I gave the guidance pod on the go-cart a download from *Stripes'* astrogation computer. In theory at least, the torp's computer would know where it was and where I wanted it to go.

Before I abandoned *Stripes*, I wrote Joslyn a brief note. Nothing meaningful. But if I got myself killed, as was very likely, and Joslyn recovered the aux ship, I wanted her to have something, some words, that had passed from my hand to hers.

And then I was out the hatch. It took some huffing and puffing to get my oversized, pressure-suited self, my maneuvering backpack, and my equipment bag onto the go-cart in such a way that it would be properly balanced in flight. When I had, I stretched a finger toward the cargo-clamp release button, and a rattling vibration told me I was free of the ship. I reached a little further and shoved hard against the ship's hull. The go-cart and I drifted slowly away. I checked the chronometer in my suit's helmet. An hour until I had to push that single button marked "ON" and get this show on the road. Plenty of time for *Stripes* to get safely distant. I hadn't shoved with great precision: the go-cart was tumbling gently. It didn't matter. I spent the hour watching the gently receding *Stripes* drift around my field of view, to be replaced by a splendid view of New Finland and her single large natural moon, Kuu. I was too far away for any hope of spotting Vapaus, which was my eventual target. I was lucky in that the sun remained pretty much at my back as I tumbled.

And then it was time. I pushed the "ON" button, and the torp's gyros began to whir busily. I felt the vibration through my suit. The guidance pod spotted New Finland and set itself up to home in on the planet.

Without any warning, the engine lit up ten gees at my back and that go-cart *moved*! It was a short life but a merry one, and the torp engine died as suddenly as it had opened up. Without the burn, I would be following *Stripes* as she slowly drifted away from the planet. Now I was moving straight for New Finland, and at a pretty good clip. The torp began to rotate itself along its long axis for the retro-burn about thirty hours later. If the retro-burn didn't work, I was going to drop right into the atmosphere and burn up. I had enough confidence in the torp that I wasn't worried, but I had something else that annoyed me enough to avoid boredom: I was now pointed straight at the sun, almost forced to stare at it. My visor compensated automatically for the glare, but its constant self-adjustment was irritating.

I slapped my sunshield down and set it to OPAQUE. I felt my suit warming up just a trifle in the full sunlight. Nothing the cooling system couldn't handle, but it didn't make the ride more pleasant.

I had a good bit of waiting to do. I spent part of it chewing over the plan Joz and I had cooked up for my getting inside the hollowed-out asteroid world Vapaus.

I had read up on the place. Vapaus had started out in life as a rather routine lump of stone and rock floating through space on an orbit that brought it within easy range of New Finland. The Finns had dragged it into the orbit of the planet and set to work making an orbiting industrial base and shipping port out of it.

The first step was to hollow it out, and trim the oblong lump of rock into a cylinder.

The New Finnish system had several gas giant planets in its outer reaches. The closest-in giant had a small ice moon far outside its gravity well. This moon was mined for ice and the ice was towed to the asteroid's orbit.

The interior of the asteroid was by then a cylindrical hollow which the Finnish engineers proceeded to pack with ice, The mine shafts were sealed with pressure locks. The asteroid was then set spinning.

Giant solar mirrors were brought into position around the asteroid, and tremendous amounts of light and heat were focused on it.

The stone melted like butter.

The heat-pulse hit the ice-filled interior. The ice boiled off into super-heated steam and inflated the asteroid the way a child's breath inflated a balloon.

The engineers having done their math properly, the pressure locks blew off at the right moment. Ninety percent of the water escaped to space, and then the pressure locks resealed. The rest of the water was retained to become the basis of Vapaus's artificial ecology.

When the molten rock cooled, the Finns had an inside-out world about six times the size of the asteroid they had started with. The Finns were the first to try the technique with a stony asteroid. Others had "inflated" iron-nickel asteroids, but those satellites had annoying problems with magnetic eddy fields and electrical effects brought on by spinning up megatons of conductive material.

The scrap rock was dragged down into a lower orbit and the solar mirrors melted it all down into one lump of slag, which never got any other name than "The Rock." The Rock made a good base for a lot of processes that relied on zero-gee, and was also a handy orbital mine.

Joslyn and I had worked out a plan that was based on the fact that Vapaus had been inflated. It was known that the rock had bubbled in places. It ought to be possible to find a bubble, dig in through it, and reach the interior.

I hoped so, anyway. Otherwise, I was dead. I sighed. Best not to worry about that little possibility. It was going to be true of just about everything I did for the foreseeable future.

When my helmet was opaqued, it could be used as a reading screen. I had carried a few tapes along and now I put then to use, as I learned another ten new words in Finnish.

It didn't make the ride seem any shorter.

The thirty hours slid away in studying, sleeping and worrying. Riding with the helmet opaqued was tough: besides the readouts and telltales inside my suit's collar, there was nothing to see. The blacked-out glass of the helmet was dark and featureless, inches from my face. I hung in the middle of space with only my suit between me and infinity, feeling claustrophobic. That made my worrying all the more effective. A dozen times I reached for the black-out control to lighten the helmet so I could *see*, and just barely talked myself out of it each time. The sun would have blinded me. Period. That was a convincing argument, even under the circumstances.

The torp was programmed to bring me to about 100 kilometers of Vapaus and then fire its motor not quite enough to bring me into orbital velocity. My backpack unit would make up the difference, and the torp was to fall on into New Finland's atmosphere and burn up.

I was asleep when the burn came, dreaming about flying *Stars* through a coal-black cave, trying to get to Joslyn, though she fell further and further away. I came awake badly disoriented, having a lot of trouble sorting out the dream from the reality, until I remembered it was okay to kill the black-out control now. The planet of New Finland popped into existence in front of my face, and then slowly swung away and got behind me. Its job done, the guidance system had shut down, and the torp was tumbling without gyros.

I wanted to get away from the go-cart as soon as I could; I wasn't eager to share its ride down to the surface. The backpack unit, comprised of a maneuvering jet unit and life support system, was stowed underneath the crash couch, along with other equipment I expected to need. I pulled the hose connections that had attached me to the life support unit, as they were snaked through the crash couch, wrestled myself free of the couch's straps and pulled my gear out from beneath it.

Working as fast as I could, I shoved clear of the torp, dragging the gear with me. I wriggled into the backpack unit and re-attached the hose connections, then swung down the control arms and got busy with the joystick. I found Vapaus's radio beacon, got a reading on it, waited a minute, and took another reading. The backpack's guidance system was about as sophisticated as a wet finger in the wind, but the two readings were enough to give me a general idea of which direction to fly. I hosed out some fuel and watched the go-cart drift away, headed for oblivion in the upper atmosphere. The go-cart slid away, and was lost to view in a few minutes. I caught sight of a tiny spot of light ahead, just barely too big to be a star. I flipped up the helmet binoculars: Vapaus, sure enough.

I used the helmet sextant to get a rough hack on my ground-track speed. The numbers seemed about what they should have been, and I could feel at least reasonably confident that I was in an orbit that was close to the right one.

Time to do some more waiting.

About an hour later, I could clearly see Vapaus growing slowly from a spot in a round, featureless dot as I caught up in a long stern chase. Another half-hour and I could see the dot of light grow into a shape, and then I could see its spin as the surface of the asteroid rolled its lumpy face around.

I cleaned up my trajectory a bit and got myself moving a little faster and a little more accurately toward the target.

Vapaus swelled rapidly.

I performed a trim burn that set me headed squarely for the aft end of the satellite. The forward end was supposed to be a maze of air locks, ship's bays, maintenance and construction facilities, and so on. Vapaus was a busy place. From an economic point of view, Vapaus, not New Finland, was the focal point of this solar system. Wary of polluting the planet, the Finns had put nearly all their heavy industry in space. All business was transacted at the forward end, however. So far no one had found it worthwhile to develop the aft end. It was blank, empty.

That fact was my ticket in. I hoped.

The asteroid grew to dominate the sky, a titanic grey form, a giant potato-shape in the sky. Maybe it was a small world, but any world is tremendous on a human scale.

Suddenly, I had *arrived*. I was no longer moving toward

a dot in the sky; I was in the presence of a place, a world, a mammoth *thing* right on top of me.

I couldn't decide if I was awed, or scared. It didn't matter, really. It got to me, just the same.

Subtle bumps and starts of my jets lined me directly behind Vapaus, the cylindrical potato shape foreshortening as I moved more squarely over the aft end, until I was hanging in the sky, facing the exact center of a circular field of rough terrain, half-lit by the distant sun.

It rotated slowly, sedately, in the patch of sky ahead of me, and I hung there, drifting toward it, looking for a place to land.

I was looking for a good sized bubble in the rock, a relic of the boiling stone Vapaus had been formed from. Some of the bubbles had burst, their places on the surface marked by scarring craters. Others had cooled rapidly enough to survive as bubbles, perfect dome shapes in the chaotic landscape.

I jetted a little closer, a little closer, until the surface of the asteroid was only 30 or 40 meters ahead of me—or below me, depending on how you looked at it—then braked to a halt so I could look things over. It was one hell of a big rock, grey and brown, the spin that had seemed sedate from a kilometer back now frighteningly fast, the rock whizzing past at a dizzying speed.

I found I was a bit off center, drifting a bit toward the planet side. Suddenly, I was in shadow. I was low enough for the sun to drop below the horizon as seen from my altitude. I was getting God-damned *close*!

I tried to stay calm. This was going to be a hairy ride. I looked over the piece of real estate rolling toward me. There! A bubble just over two meters across, nearly in my line of flight. I fired my jets and moved in toward the surface, at about a meter a second. Sweat sprung up on my brow, and I shook my head to clear my vision. The droplets flew off my face and dried instantly against the inside of the helmet.

I was now only ten meters above the surface, watching it rush toward me. I was seconds from my landing. Now I had to try and match my lateral speed to the satellite's spin. I had to be moving at the same speed as the bit of rock I landed on. Too slow and I'd be bowled over, and probably thrown out into space. Too fast and I might fly past the asteroid altogether, and have to try again—this time badly short of fuel.

I clenched my teeth and went in, aiming to fly slightly toward the center of the rock. I fired the jets so as match speed with the spin. The whirling rock seemed to slow, and slow more, and with my feet a bare five meters above the surface, I matched the spin. I released the maneuvering controls and pulled the spike shooter from my belt, rushing as fast as I could. I was about to hit. I shot the rocket-powered spike into the rock below me. Even as it bit into the rock, my lateral velocity began to show up again. I swung up short against the line attached to the spike and landed neatly on my feet, balancing on my free hand.

The asteroid was spinning to create artificial gravity. The further out from the axis you got, the stronger that gee force would be. I wasn't very far, but I was far enough. I felt a very slight tug *down*, and as far as my inner ear was concerned, 'down' wasn't through the surface of the world anymore—down was toward the horizon, toward the rim of the world.

Suddenly I knew in my gut that I wasn't on a slight rise in the middle of a flat plane, but hanging by a thin line from an overhanging cliff three kilometers high. A cliff that had at its top—and at its base—nothing. Nothing but empty, empty space. Just as I made the mistake of looking *down*, the sun swung around the horizon at manic speed. The photoreceptors on the helmet dimmed a bit as the sun hit. I watched, fascinated as the darkened sun sped around that gloomy plane and swept *under* me. The raging inferno of the sun was directly *beneath* me. . . .

My foot slipped.

In an instant I was dangling off the sheer face of the cliff, held only by the one length of line clipped to my waist. I was going to fall! Into the sun! My hindbrain screamed and gibbered. I looked down again to see if the sun was really there, and saw the planet, New Finland, whip beneath my feet. Closer and bigger than the stars, it seemed to move even faster. Then it left my field of view, and the empty, empty stars were there. Worse, a thousand times worse than a fall into the quick death of the sun. A million year's worth of monkey ancestors yowled in my head. I was going to fall, and to fall now was to fall forever, forever into nothing, always to fall, fall. . . .

I passed out, only for a few seconds, I think. When I came to, I took as long as I dared to calm my instincts. My throat hurt, as if I had been screaming. I tried to steady my shaking body. I breathed deeply, relaxed and tensed every set of muscles, I tried to sing a little song to myself. Above all, I did not, repeat DID NOT look down or open my eyes.

All the fears that normally protect us from foolhardy gestures—fear of falling, fear of the dark, fear of the unexpected and the disorienting, the dangerous surprise, had conspired against me. If the rope had been in my hands, where I could have let go in fright, instead of clipped to my waist, those fears would have killed me.

It took long minutes to conquer that fear.

When the trembling ceased, I slowly and carefully opened one eye, making sure to look only straight ahead, struggling to convince my inner ear that it was all right, I was only hanging in front of a very ordinary cliff that was only a half meter away. Just like in training. I waited a bit, then opened the other eye just as carefully. Okay so far.

Slowly, gently, I swung my legs back and forth, working up a pendulum motion that got me in reach of the surface.

I grabbed for handholds, and clinging for dear life, very gingerly peered down to look at the rock bubble I had been aiming for. I breathed a sigh of relief. My marksmanship had been good: I was almost directly above it, and only about fifteen meters away. The surface sloped away toward the crazy sideways horizon, and Vapaus's rapid rotation brought the sun around to hang directly beneath me again.

Everything considered—the shakes I still had, the sweat that lined the inside of my suit, the aches of being in that suit for almost two days now, the idea I got that the helmet glass just had to crack, sometime, probably soon, and you'll agree I wasn't climbing down that insane cliff under ideal—or even hopeful—circumstances. The only advantage I had was that, in being rather near the axis of rotation, the artificial gravity produced by Vapaus's spin was low. I could not possibly have made that climb in normal gravity.

Climbing, especially rock climbing, is composed of pauses and lunges. You look over the rock face and rehearse time and time again, in your mind, which limb you will move first, and which will follow. You wait, and work up the will to do it. Perhaps you try the very beginning of the move a time or two, not even moving your hand or foot from the rock, just relaxing the hold one arm has on the rock, trying to see if your other arm and your legs can hold you in place until the first arm can get to where it's going. Maybe you find the move can't work, and you sweat out the close call for a moment until you try some other way. Then, finally, when there is no reason left for pausing, you lunge, and move as quickly and smoothly as you can to the next set of handholds and footholds, hoping they will support you. Sometimes they do.

It was crawl and clamber, climb and hang, pause and lunge. Twice my handholds and footholds weren't good enough, and I fell off the inward sloping cliff, and had to swing up like a pendulum again and get back onto the cliff. Then I would cling to the rock, wait out the shakes, and proceed.

Finally the rock bubble was directly below me, half a meter away. I fired a rope spike into the face of the cliff, and shot another into the side of the bubble. I clamped the two reels short and clipped the ends of the two ropes together. I fired another short rope to hold myself to the cliff more securely. Then I took a five minute break and got to work on the bubble.

I pulled my hand laser from its holster and set it on narrow beam. I fired it straight into the bubble. It took about a second and a half for the beam to pierce the bubble's surface, and then the trapped gas that had formed the bubble jetted out, carrying with it a fine cloud of rock dust that quickly dispersed. I cut along the surface of the bubble in a rough circle with the rope spike in its center.

In fifteen minutes I had a manhole-sized piece of rock free of the bubble. I holstered the nearly exhausted laser and pulled on the line that held the manhole cover. With a bit of straining and effort, and a screeching like squeaking chalk that was transmitted through the rock and carried into my suit, the rock cover came off. I released it and it swung back and forth for a few seconds, then hung quietly off to counterspinward, held oddly off-center by the unsettling Coriolis effect of the satellite's spin.

I pulled the hose connections to my backpack again and detached myself from it. I shoved the backpack into the hole first, then crawled in myself.

I was in. I had made it this far. At least I was off that cliff. Rock under my feet, instead of off to one side.

I unclipped myself from all the lines that held me to the cliff. I used one of them to lasso—on the third try—the rope holding the manhole cover. I pulled it back in toward me. I fired a rope spike into its inside surface and wrapped the line around my forearm.

Steadying the cover with one hand and wishing I had three hands, I pulled out the can of rock sealant and sprayed the thick gunk on the cover and on the lip of the hole.

I ducked back into the hole and switched on my helmet light. I pulled the cover back into place and gave it a good hard yank to give the sealant a chance. For good measure, I sprayed another coat of the stuff around the inside of the cover.

It took the sealant a few minutes to set. I used the time to get the life support unit detached from the maneuvering backpack and strapped to me by itself. I hooked the hoses up after being off them for about five minutes; about the practical limit before you start seeing spots in front of your eyes from lack of air.

I dug one last tool from the gear bag hooked to the backpack—a rockeater. It was a simple, powerful, device, and by far the biggest gadget I had taken with me. I set it against the wall opposite the one I had come in. On the other side of that wall lay the interior of this world. I switched the rockeater on. Three sets of spinning, industrial diamond-tipped teeth bit into the rock face. The rock was reduced to a fine dust and funneled into an exhaust tube. I paused for a moment to shove the end of the tube into the far side of the bubble.

Gritting my teeth, I started up the drill again and dug it into the rock. The sound, transmitted through the surrounding rock and into my suit, was the devil's own shrilling, keening racket. It dug a round tunnel about half a meter in diameter. In spite of the exhaust tube, the dust soon managed to cover my helmet, and I had to pause frequently to brush it off.

The hole grew slowly. In twenty tooth-rattling minutes, I had dug about a meter into the rock. I had no idea how thick the walls were, and was prepared to spend long hours with that screaming machine and the rock dust.

But it was less than an hour later that the rockeater almost skipped out of my hands and the last of the rock wall collapsed in front of it. I shut it off as the interior atmosphere of Vapaus whooshed into the vacuum of my rock bubble, jetting up great clouds of dust that took a few minutes to settle. I worried that the dust cloud might be seen, but when it cleared I saw the satellite's interior was dark. It was night in Vapaus.

I pulled the rockeater back down the hole it had made and stashed it in the now rather cluttered bubble. I crawled up the smooth-sided tunnel and poked my head out. I cracked open my helmet and breathed in Vapaus's sweet air.

It was 42 days—1000 hours—from the moment the signal beacon had awakened us from a sound sleep.

Now I was inside Vapaus.

Now came the hard part.

Chapter Four

I crawled back into the rock bubble and stripped off my pressure suit. It felt remarkably good to be out of it. I had been inside the thing for nearly two and a half days by that time, and was looking forward to smelling something besides myself. I peeled down to skin and realized that I was still going to be smelling essence of me for a while. I needed a bath. I had brought along one set of coveralls to change into once I ditched the suit, and I got into them now, reluctant to put clean clothes over dirty skin.

The rock bubble was not a good headquarters. It was impossible to stand up without using one hand to balance myself. The inside of the bubble was sort of egg-shaped, with the narrower end at the bottom. It was half full of sneeze-making rock dust and the rock dust was full of abandoned gear. It was easy to fall over.

The seal around my manhole cover seemed to be holding, but I gave it an extra dollop of rock sealant anyway. I didn't like the idea of taking chances with somebody else's air supply. I had spent a large portion of my life breathing canned air, and that made me very sensitive to the problem.

A growing flood of light was pouring into the tunnel from the satellite's interior. Day was coming to Vapaus. It was clearly impossible to risk being seen climbing down the interior cliff in broad daylight. I would have to wait for nightfall. That meant I could sleep, and I needed to. I detached the legs (pants, I guess you'd call them) from my pressure suit, rolled them up into a pillow of sorts and stretched out to sleep in the tunnel.

✧ ✧ ✧

Toward evening, I woke, as stiff as a board, and retreated to the bubble to do some setting-up exercises as best I could. Then I prepared to leave.

I set a steel spike in the roof of my tunnel and attached a line which ended in an electromagnet to the spike. The electromagnet was switched on and off by a radio link switch. I gave the button a test. The magnet and the line attached to it fell away from the roof. I caught them before they could go over the edge, reset the magnet, set it back in place, and gave it a good hard tug. It would hold.

I had climbed the outside of the cliff the night before. Now I got ready to start climbing down the inside of the same wall. I left behind my pressure suit, backpack, the rockeater and all the other gadgetry, and took just the coveralls and what was in their pockets. Before I went down, I looked out across the face of Vapaus.

Dusk was just setting in that great cylindrical plain. Light was provided to the interior by a powerful spherical "sun," made up of thousands of individual lamps, which hung at the exact center of the world, floating in the zero-gee zone at the axis. It was anchored to the fore and aft cliffs by strong cables, which did not support its weight (in the axial zone, it had none), but simply kept it from floating off the centerline. This interior "sun" was dimming now and was the red of a true sun seen at dusk. Houselights were coming on in the plains below.

I was surprised by how easily I accepted this inside-out world. Maybe this was because I had seen photos of other such places before, but I think it was more because it *looked* right, and natural. The scale was too vast to think of it as man-made. It was just as magnificent a vista as the Grand Canyon or Valles Marineris, but far more hospitable.

The greensward girdled Vapaus completely. Gentle hills were covered with lush grasses and graced by the hint of color lent by flowers too far off to be seen. Trees grew in profusion below my feet, in a sweeping arc of forest that climbed the sides of the world and continued unbroken over my head.

Rivers flowed in the sky as well, one directly above me. I could not see its origin, as it was shrouded in cloud, but I traced its progress toward the sea which wrapped itself around the middleground of the satellite's interior. Twin bands of clouds, which, like the central sea, ran clear around the world, hid the ground level from view at either end of the plain. These cloud bands started flat up against the fore and aft cliffs and extended about a quarter kilometer in toward the middle of the cylinder, steely grey boundaries to the green and blue splendor they framed.

As I started down the aft cliff, this band of cloud was below my feet. These clouds, and the gathering darkness, were enough to shield my movements from observation.

The fore and aft walls, or cliffs, were hollow dome-shapes. Measured along the axis of the world, Vapaus was about eleven kilometers from end to end. Measured at the base of the cliffs, it was about ten klicks. This meant that the climb down the outside had been against a constant overhang, but that climbing down the interior wall brought me down a steadily gentler slope. By the time I reached the end of the line, I was able to scramble down with a fair degree of confidence, even in the gathering gloom of simulated sunset.

I used the radio relay switch to shut off the electromagnet that held my line, and it instantly started to drop in the most peculiar fashion. As I've said, the apparent gravity inside a rotating cylinder like Vapaus increases from zero at the axis to its maximum at the walls of the cylinder. This meant, of course, that the top of the rope fell more slowly than the bottom of the rope. There was another odd effect as well: The spin of such a world isn't imparted to a free-falling object inside it. The object falls in a straight line toward the surface. But, to an observer on that surface, who is carried by the spin of the world, a falling object seems to sheer away from the direction of spin. These two oddities came together to give that falling rope the strangest snake-dance of a fall I've ever seen. It landed and I coiled in the line and stuffed it in a crack in the rock.

It was silly, I knew, but I felt safer climbing down the inner wall than I had climbing down the outside. It was, in some insane way, reassuring to know that if I slipped, I would tumble 'only' a kilometer or so down the inside instead of out into empty space on the outside.

It actually was fairly safe. The cliff wall was full of cracks, nooks and crevices: I had no trouble finding handholds. I quickly descended into the band of clouds that clung to the cliff wall. The wall grew clammy and slippery, and soon I was low enough for rain to start falling. The mist and rain soaked clear through my light coveralls. I noticed the air was a bit cool for my taste as I got nearer the surface. That made sense—Finns would *like* it cold. The air grew denser, too. The last 50 meters or so of the climb I just slid and skidded down the pile of loose rock and pebbles that had accumulated at the bottom of the cliff.

Finally I reached level ground and looked back up the way I had come. It is always satisfying to look back at pulling off a hare-brained scheme once it has worked, and I felt sure no one could have possibly anticipated this one. The Guardians would guard the airlocks at the forward end, but no one would think to post guards here.

I squelched my way through the rain-soaked grass at the base of the aft cliff and headed in, toward the inhabited parts of the satellite.

There is a man who lives on the end of a pleasant lane near the aft cliff who may be wondering to this day what happened to the pants, shirt, and food that vanished that night. Whoever he is, thank you. It all went to a good cause. League of Planets Survey Service issue coveralls were not the thing to wear in those parts, and the black bread was delicious. After the snack, I buried the coveralls and moved on.

Soon I found myself at a transport station of some kind. I hung back and watched the proceedings. It seemed simple enough. Brightly lit rail cars were running along a ground-level monorail, arriving about once every five minutes. They stopped, opened their doors, waited about 30 seconds for passengers, shut their doors and zipped off into the night.

Looking up into the sky, or rather at the land that hung over my head, I spotted the lights of other rail cars sliding silently along in the darkness here and there, like glowworms far off. One of the cars crossed the central sea, and its cabin lights were caught and reflected by the light, casting a soft burst of light that vanished almost at once.

At this time of night, there were no other riders at this remote station. I stepped aboard. The doors slid shut with a whoosh and a click, and the car rolled forward smoothly.

I stared out the window, eager to see as much of the strangely upside-down landscape as I could in the darkness. Other passengers got on the next stop. In the tradition of rapid-transit riders everywhere, I ignored them, and they me.

No one was waiting at the next few stops, and we drew near a cluster of lovely towers that stood by the shore of the central sea.

The car stopped, and two surly looking men in dark grey uniforms shooed other passengers away and stomped on before anyone else, swaggering with their thumbs thrust into their belts, their hands near vicious looking laser pistols.

The enemy.

Up until this moment, the Guardians had been academic, unknown. Now they were here, real, in front of me, I was sitting in the seat nearest the door. One of them came up to me and hooked a thumb toward the far end of the car. I didn't respond. Maybe I was too intent on looking him over. In any event, I nearly blew the whole game right there.

"What's the matter, boy?" the soldier growled. He spoke English with a flat, hard, clipped accent. "Don't want to share your seat?" He stepped closer, leering at me. "Huh?"

I got out of the seat and moved to the end of the car,

the other passengers looking at me oddly. The two soldiers flopped down on the seat I had vacated.

"That's a lot smarter, boy," said the one who had spoken before. He pointed at a patch on the wall of the car that partially hid what looked like a scorched laser burn. "Don't want no more holes or bloodstains on these nice trains, do we?" The two of them laughed loudly. The other riders studiously ignored the whole scene. The soldier waved the back of his hand at me in dismissal and spat on the immaculately clean carpet.

The train eased to a smooth halt at the next stop, and I got out at once, before I did something angry and stupid, something that would get me burned down in my tracks and waste all the effort that had gone into getting me there. It was close nonetheless.

A fellow passenger got off with me, and as the train pulled out, he touched my arm and spoke in rapid Finnish I had trouble following. "Be more cautious and careful, friend. Do not throw your life away over their childish mocking. Tomorrow, or the next day, or the next, will be the time to fight them. Die today and you cannot fight them tomorrow." He nodded and limped away, disappearing behind a turn in the path. The trees that hid him from view were burned and blackened, and the sidewalk was shattered before me.

Yesterday had been a time of fighting, too.

For the rest of the night and the beginning of the following morning, I wandered over the surface of Vapaus. I saw a good deal, but learned no more than I already knew. Here was a world not simply conquered, but brutalized. Soldiers were everywhere, shoving past pedestrians, sauntering down the walkways, cursing and insulting the Finns. Vapaus's night life centered around the cluster of towers by the side of the central sea, and here the soldiers were out in force, grabbing produce from street side stalls, "impounding" and guzzling stock from a liquor store, shouting vulgarities after young women.

The soldiers never travelled alone. From the hatred I

saw in the eyes of the Finns, I doubted if even the soldiers who travelled in pairs were all that safe.

I took a look at a map posted at one of the rail stations and found that the hospital was in a tower near the central sea. The next part of the plan Joslyn and I had cooked up called for being near a hospital, so I rode the train one last time, crossing the central sea as the artificial sun started to brighten directly overhead. The water was a fantastic sight from the bridge. From a perfectly flat plane below me it swooped into the sky like a single titanic wave frozen over the curve of the world. All along its coastline were craggy inlets, small sandy beaches, and narrow fjords. Here and there were the wrecks of brightly colored pleasure boats, but the sea itself was empty. I left the sea behind and walked from the train to a spot about a hundred meters from the hospital, in the burned-off remnants of a small park.

I took the tiny tranquilizer capsule from my pocket and swallowed it. I walked on as casually as I could, waiting for the pill to hit. It did, like a load of bricks. I fell to the littered sidewalk.

The drug was a depressant as well as a relaxant. It dropped my body temperature and slowed my heart to a crawl, enough to scare the hell out of anyone who came upon me.

The pill wore off a few hours afterwards, but I slept on. The snooze I had had in my tunnel the night before hadn't been very restful.

I awoke in a clean, private hospital room, according to plan. The nurse who watched me was tall and slender, with short blonde hair and grey eyes. She saw I was awake and pointed a pocket laser at my forehead.

This was not according to plan.

She spoke good English, with a slight lilting cadence. "You are a very bad spy, did you know? No Finn is allowed to carry a laser, but you won't have a chance to report my having this one here. Your drug was so obvious it made our doctors laugh. Your head Guardians think you can get into the hospital without our noticing things like that? What did you think getting here would do for you?"

There was one bright spot. As Joslyn and I had figured, the hospital staff had been allowed to remain at work after the fighting, in the face of the many casualties. We had hoped to find a staunch group of underground workers here, both because it was one place that Finns would be allowed to remain in an organized group, and because the doctors and nurses would get a firsthand look at the Guardians' murderous handiwork.

It seemed we had figured right. Now all I had to was convince my nurse here not to drill a hole in my skull.

I asked her a question, in very bad Finnish, trying to keep calm. "Is this room bugged?"

It startled her. She replied in Finnish that was too fast for me to follow easily. Don't believe the ads for the hypnotape courses, you don't become fluent, no matter how long they tell you to stay under. Especially Finnish.

I waved my arms to stop her. "Please! Go slow. My Finnish is not good."

Her forehead furrowed, and she repeated herself, talking more slowly. "What do you care if the room is bugged, Guardian? It would be *your* friends listening. She grinned malevolently, an unpleasant change for her pretty face. "As a matter of fact, they *think* they are listening to this room. We changed a few wires here and there, however. They will be listening to what they think are your noisy snores."

Good. At least I could talk freely. But something occurred to me. "How do I know you're not a—a Guardian?"

No one under a hundred years old should be able to look that angry. Her finger got a little closer to the trigger. "Okay, okay." I had slipped back into English. I switched to Finnish and said "Never mind. I'm convinced."

She sneered at me. "*You* don't convince *me*, fool. If you want to spy on us here, at least send someone who speaks Finnish like a good Finn."

"I'm not a spy! I work with your side."

"Nonsense! We have no record of you. You are not from here. I'm beginning to lose patience with you, spy."

If this was her version of patience, I was in deep trouble when she got annoyed. "I'm from the League! The League of Planets! They sent me!"

She snorted. "And your starship is docked at the airlock complex next to the Guardian troop transports?"

"Terrance MacKenzie Larson, Commander, Republic of Kennedy Navy, attached to LPSS 41, *Joslyn Marie*. ROK Navy ID four niner eight two four five."

A hint of doubt showed in her and the laser lowered just a hair. I thought she was beginning to believe me. "You lie," she said after a moment's hesitation. Well, maybe not yet. "If you are from the League, why didn't you show yourself three months ago when these monsters descended on us?"

"I have been in this world—or on it, or whatever you say, less than twenty hours."

"What did you do to get in? Use your own private airlock?"

I began to lose patience myself. "As a matter of fact, yes."

At that, she burst into laughter. "Spy, you are very bad," she said through the last of her giggles. "You are very, very bad at whatever it is you are trying to do."

I sighed and flopped back down onto the bed—and noticed the view out the room's large picture window. Spread out before me was the rearward end of Vapaus: I could see the cliff I had descended, and had the feeling I could pick out my route down.

I turned to the nurse, who was still smirking at me. "Could you bring me a pair of high power, oh, what is the word . . . binoculars!"

That almost set off the giggles again. "But, spy, don't most spies carry their own?"

"Look, lady, you can sit there and laugh at me, or you can get the binoculars. If you get them, I will show you my private airlock. If you don't, you won't get to see it."

"You are wasting my time. But so this nonsense will stop, I will humor you and call your bluff. Then we can get to what it is you are really doing."

"Fine. Great. Just get the field glasses."

Keeping the gun pointed at me, she stood and pushed the talk button on the room's intercom and spoke rapidly and quietly into it. Then she sat back down and we waited without speaking for a few minutes.

A big, burly man in an orderly's uniform came in carrying a pair of binoculars. Without a word, he handed them to the nurse, who gave him the laser. He pointed it at my heart instead of my skull. Not much of an improvement.

She tossed the binoculars onto the bed. I reached down and handed them back. "No, you look."

Coming no nearer than she had to, she picked them back up. "Where do I look?"

"Do you know where Roos Place is?" That was the street I had walked onto when I got to the bottom of the cliff. I congratulated myself on remembering the name.

"Yah."

"Good. Now, find it with the field glasses, then look directly behind at the aft cliff. Okay?"

"Yes."

"Move straight up the cliff until you're about half way between the cloud cover and the axis." She did so, and I watched her as she looked over the cliff, stopped, and moved back down a bit, as if she had seen something worth looking at. "Now. What do you see?"

"Some sort of hole in the Rear Cliff. Right at the top of it is some sort of glint, like off metal." Her voice was shocked. I seemed to have convinced her.

"My private airlock. If you wait until tonight, and send your raiders or commandos or what you might call them, you can look at my hole there. You'll find it leads to a rock bubble that has a hole cut in it and then patched shut. Also, a standard League issue long-duration pressure suit, a worn-out laser and some other gadgets. My ship is hidden on the far side of your sun."

"Are you truly from the League?" There was amazement and hope in her voice.

"Truly."

"We never really dared to think you'd come . . ." A sudden thought came to her. "How many troops do you have?"

I thought of the experimental matter transmitter. "If we're lucky, about five thousand."

She rushed out of the room. I could tell I had made her day.

There was a general bustle of activity, during which my orderly calmly kept the laser aimed straight at my chest. Someone came in to photograph me and take my fingerprints. I never did find out exactly why.

My nurse seemed to be trying to get someone in charge to pay attention to her. She was in and out two or three times, pacing indecisively and trying to figure out if I was telling the truth.

Finally the door swept open and a very dignified, calm sort of medical man came in. Clearly, Someone In Charge had arrived. He shooed the orderly out and drew up a chair alongside my bed. "Nurse Tulkaas has said some extremely interesting things about you, Commander," he said in very precise English. "Where are these troops you spoke of?"

"About four light weeks away, I'd guess."

He didn't bat an eye, but I could see Nurse Tulkaas's face collapse in disappointment. The doctor said, "You are not aware of the missile system?"

"We should be able to get our troops around it."

"How?"

I hesitated. "Doctor, could I get out of this bed and discuss this at a table? One with a big lunch on it? This is a bit complicated, and I haven't had a real meal in days."

"Of course."

"Great." I hopped out of bed—and hopped right back in. Finnish hospital garb does not include pants. The doctor almost smiled at my discomfort. "Nurse, could you get Commander Larson a robe out of the closet?"

The nurse got one and performed some maneuver with it that got me into the robe without getting me out of bed. Long practice, no doubt. I tied it around my waist and got out of bed again. "One other thing," I said. "Could you have a hypnotist join us? I didn't dare carry any paper or film, but I have a lot of information. If I was caught by your Guardian friends—we wanted to make sure I didn't talk. The information is blocked from my conscious by about three separate post-hypnotic commands. You'll even have to put me in a light trance to get the keying words out of me."

"I'll have Mr. Kendriel attend us." The doctor led me out into the hall.

"This is the final keying, Commander. When I speak the appropriate word, you will awaken with full conscious memory of the information you have been carrying."

I could hear the voice from far away, but it didn't seem to mean much to me.

"I will count backwards until I reach one, and then speak your key word. Five, four, three, two, one—Mannerheim. Now, then. Do you remember it all?"

Of course I did, I thought dully. "Yes."

"Good. Now, I will count forward to three and tell you to awaken. When I do, you will awaken and still remember everything. Ready? One, two, three—wake up!"

My mind switched back to the ON position and I opened my eyes, somewhat out of it for a moment. Then I blinked and turned to the hypnotist. "Could I have paper and pencil?" He handed them to me, and I scribbled down a long column of numbers, writing quickly before I had a chance to forget anything. Antenna position, power levels, that sort of thing. Then a condensed box diagram of the receiver unit's auxiliary equipment, from which a good electronics engineer could build the required circuitry.

"Commander, if you could explain what all this is about?"

"In a moment, Doctor. I have a lot of details to remember.

Please hand me that map of the planet's surface, if you would."

The last thing in the hypnotic memory had been the coordinates of the point where the receiver had to be built: latitude and longitude. I examined the map for a moment, then ran one finger down the right longitude line and another down the right latitude.

Then I did it again.

And again.

The coordinates were wrong. 45°W 15°N was under water.

I sat and stared at the map. I closed my eyes and concentrated. Yes, I had remembered the coordinates properly. I checked the map again. Said a few choice phrases. Bit my nails. But it was still under water, nowhere near shore.

"Commander! What is the matter?" the doctor asked.

"This map is accurate." I didn't even bother to make it a question.

"Yes, of course."

I turned and faced the doctor—who still hadn't given me his name. "This will take a moment to explain. The League developed, very recently, a matter transmitter. It is still experimental. But they had enough confidence to take the chance of using it. My ship was intercepted by a drone that carried the key components of the receiver unit. I was ordered here. The transmitter is a much more precisely designed system, and requires a great deal more power. The United States Space Craft *Mayflower*, which has the transmitter itself aboard, has used it to beam five thousand troops and their equipment toward us at the speed of light. They were transmitted from far outside this solar system. They were aimed to be received at 45°W 15°N on the surface of New Finland. They *must* arrive at that point, or they cannot arrive at all. That point is underwater, nowhere near land."

"There is no Finnish shipping. The Guardians control it all."

"And no ship could be big enough for five thousand troops," I said.

"This is amazing! They have really transmitted those men toward us?" He turned and asked the hypnotist. "Is that truly possible?"

Mr. Kendriel shrugged. "In theory, yes. The idea has kicked around since the invention of the C^2 drive. It would be an application of the same principle. To oversimplify, the effect that puts a ship into superlight speed is rotated through 90 degrees, producing a normal C^2, except that it is static in space, or more accurately, adjacent to every point in our space. The stumbling block has been to find a way to lock on to that bubble, track it, and pull it back into normal space in a controlled manner. I imagine that they've licked that problem." Mr. Kendriel had done some reading, it seemed.

"Remarkable. What a wonderful invention . . ." The doctor seemed to consider the possibilities for a moment. Then he came back to the problem at hand. "But why can't they arrive anywhere else? Is the beam that carried them that tight?"

"It isn't the width of the guide beam that is the trouble. It's the doppler shift. The point from which the guide beam is sent and at which it is received *must* be dead in space to each other. Exactly so. The point 45°W 15°N will be moving at exactly the right speed at the moment the radio signal arrives at New Finland. The rotation of the planet around the sun, its revolution around its own axis—even the perturbations caused by this satellite—were all accounted for precisely. If the signal is at all distorted at reception, the troops will be—distorted."

Would they appear as giants? Pygmies? Inside out? With sine waves imposed onto the cells of their corpses?

We couldn't receive them. I shut my eyes and wondered what it like to step into a machine, expecting to magically appear on a new world . . . and never come out. A quick and painless death, but one that was, in a frightening way, unknown to those who died. Would they be truly dead, frozen for a moment of subjective time that would last for all eternity? Or just—gone?

Nurse Tulkaas knit her fingers into each other and stood, staring at nothing. "We had hope for a brief moment. Now it is gone. Your League must learn to read maps before it sends men over radio waves."

"Karina, that is unfair," the doctor objected. "It was the coordinate shift that did it. It's quite simple, Commander. When we first mapped this world, we assigned a rather arbitrary set of coordinates to it. When it came time to build, one of the prime city sites lay square on what would have been the planetary date line. Rather than give up the site, it was seen as a better solution to shift the assigned lines of longitude. Your troops are targeted to what is no doubt an excellent site—as located on an old map."

"And now the men are as good as dead," I said.

Nurse Tulkaas suddenly burst out. "Why have you done this mad thing?"

I looked up from the table I had been trying to stare a hole in. "Huh?"

"Why didn't you mind your own business instead of coming all this way to raise false hope and kill so many with a stupid mistake?"

"Because, Karina," the doctor said testily, "the Commander is an honorable man sent by an honorable League of which we are members, and this Commander and that League are sworn to try and rescue us. As for stupid mistakes, it was we who made whatever erroneous maps they worked with—and we who lost this war long before he arrived."

"But we screwed up," I admitted. "We should have known about the map. That's the sort of thing they needed a Survey for. Since we didn't bother setting up until six months ago, the war is lost and those troops are dead. A lot of dead men have died without knowing it."

The doctor was about to answer when a forgotten voice cut in. "Those men are *not* dead." It was Kendriel, the hypnotist. "From what I know of the theory, and what I can see from the diagram you have made, it is obvious that once the radio signal has locked the receiver into the C^2 bubbles that hold the troops, they can be pulled out of C^2

at our leisure. We do this by hooking the signal-capturing device up to the rather simple receiver you have sketched out. Your *ship* can match velocity until it is, as you put it, 'dead in space' relative to the guide transmission. The signal can then be received without distortion, and the signal stored within the receiver. Then we can carry the capture device to wherever we wish to receive the troops."

There was a dead silence.

Short, balding Mr. Kendriel smiled shyly and spoke in English for the first time. "You see, Commander Larson, I have the hobby of electronics."

Chapter Five

With that, we were back in business, and the Finns got to work. For an underground, they were a pretty slick outfit, and seemed to operate remarkably free of interference from the Guardians.

The doctor finally broke down and told me his name was Tempkin, and admitted he was the leader of the underground. I think even at that point, his people were only about ninety percent convinced of my bona fides. Everything I had done *could* have been faked, but the saving point for me was that there wasn't any clear motive for such an elaborate deception. Even so, I was sure that they were perfectly prepared to make me disappear if I slipped up. Whether I was a plant or legit, Tempkin could be sure I wouldn't talk to anyone on the other side. That made him willing to describe how they had managed to deceive the enemy so completely.

"First off," he explained, "the hospital was a natural focus point for loyalist activity. In the same building are the administration and executive offices for the whole satellite. Fully thirty percent of the interior of this building is given over to electronics of one sort or another: computers, communications, the usual sort of things. Fortunately for us," he said with a smile, "one microcircuit looks like another. We have placed a great deal of clandestine equipment here in the control center. Mr. Kendriel is not our only electronic hobbyist by any means. We have tapped their taps, bugged their own facilities, and misdirected their own surveillance.

"Also, when it became clear that Vapaus would fall, every map, building directory, transport diagram and information service was 'revised.' There is a good deal hidden from the Guardians, simply because their computers have not told them it is there. I won't go into details at this point, but there are quite a number of large installations they don't have a clue about. Some are ready to fight when the time comes, some are already at work.

"I'll trust you far enough to give you one small example. There is a perfectly normal pedestrian tunnel under this building, that once led in a perfectly straightforward way to nearby buildings. It still leads to them, but by doing a bit of masonry work and taking down a few signs, we have made it vanish from sight. It is often very helpful to us."

I had been escorted back to my room. While we were talking, clothes suitable for a well-to-do Finn were brought to me, and I changed. Tempkin soon went off on some errand, and I had little to do but wait until he returned. I clearly wasn't yet trusted enough to get to see such things as that hidden tunnel.

In fact, I was more or less politely left to wait until the following morning. I suspect that the delay was put to use sending some climbers up the aft cliff to check out the hole I had poked in the satellite. By morning, they should have had a genuine rockeater, Republic of Kennedy pressure suit and League issue laser with a near exhausted charge in their possession, and my entrance tunnel disguised (at least I couldn't find it with binoculars later). In any event, the Finns seemed more satisfied after keeping an eye on me for a day.

The next morning Tempkin guided me to an office that we entered through the back of a broom closet. It was the radio room. Tempkin, the radio operator, and I spent several hours in a three-way, two language discussion on how to hit *Stripes* with a message laser, and what the message should say. It took a bit of computer time, some patient translation by Tempkin, and a ream or two of scratch paper, but the communications officer seemed satisfied that he could find *Stripes* with a beam once he knew where to look.

I asked Tempkin how they managed to hide the message laser from the Guardians. and he explained. "Because Vapaus is spinning, and ships were constantly flying through the vicinity, with the chance of interfering with the beam or, worse, crews being blinded by the beam, the message laser had never been kept here at all, but was always kept on The Rock. We have merely camouflaged it a bit better. The Guardians have searched for it many times, and we have let them think they found it once or twice, but so far it is safe.

"We have used the laser constantly to contact our people down on the planet. In fact, they already know about you. Unfortunately, they have no easy method of talking back. We have also a number of small relay transmitters hidden on the exterior of Vapaus. A few of these have been found, as well, but we haven't been put out of contact altogether . . . so far. As you know, it is impossible to detect a laser beam in vacuum unless you are directly in its path. This has helped a great deal."

I spent about another hour putting our message to Joslyn in a standard League code, on the very long chance that the Guardians did intercept it, somehow. As briefly as possible, it told her what needed to be done with the signal capture device, and instructed her to stand by for further word as to how to get the capture device to Vapaus.

With that, the ball was in Joslyn's court.

After a bit of thought, it was clear to me that the five thousand League troops could not be 'received' on Vapaus. There were only four thousand people living there as it was. There simply wasn't any way the satellite could provide housing, food, or even air to the troops. Also, there wouldn't be much employment for them in space. They could certainly knock out the garrison that held the satellite, but then what? The Guardians on the planet would nuke the satellite and be done with it, that's what. Or they could simply shoot down any ship that left Vapaus, not permit any supplies to be launched from the surface, and wait until everyone on the overpopulated satellite died of asphyxiation or starvation. No, the troops would have to get to the surface of the planet, that was clear. How wasn't so clear. The Guardians controlled everything that moved in space. Worse than that, no Finn was allowed to fly through space except for reasons of great importance to the Guardians, and then only under extremely heavy guard and with examinations that didn't stop at stripping down to skin. They searched with X-rays and microscopes.

The Finns had tried smuggling tiny ships and cargoes back and forth from space, but the Guardians, whatever else you could say, were excellent shots. They knocked down every aircraft and spacecraft that flew without their authority. Nothing escaped.

It all boiled down to the fact that the capture device would have to ride a Guardian ship down. It was also pretty clear that someone would have to ride down with it. I was the logical candidate for that job.

From that starting point, it wasn't a long trip to the plan we ultimately adopted. We were going to get the Guardians to build the receiver for us.

Step one of the plan was to get me woven into Vapaus's population. Someone did some skillful kiting of computer records and built up the fictional identity of Dr. Jefferson Darrow, recent immigrant from the United States. Darrow had married a Finn and had followed her here when she had immigrated. She died soon afterward, but Darrow remained on Vapaus. He worked in his own lab on various communications projects. Dr. Darrow was a highly skilled electronics technician, quite uninterested in politics—a fact which made him rather unpopular with his neighbors. He was, in point of fact, a recluse.

In short order, I was installed in a prefab bungalow near Forward Cliff, a picture of my deceased wife on a side table, the furniture wounded with a few old stains and spills, and, for the benefit of anyone who looked, a pair of underwear lodged under the dresser that had clearly been there for months at least. I was left on my own with the job of making the place looked lived in, and pretending to putter about in the electronic lab that took up one room of the house.

No one knew exactly when the Guardians might take

an interest in me, but they were confidently expected to do so. Communication workers were high on their list of useful subjects, and there would be some question as to why my file had only come to the surface now.

So I rummaged around and waited for the enemy to spot me, getting the kitchen properly dirty (work which Joslyn would confirm is right up my alley) and taking it as easy as I could.

For ten days both Finn and Guardian completely ignored me. Tempkin's organization vanished completely. I don't know who told them what, but even my neighbors pretended I wasn't there.

Then, one day, things began to happen.

I came back from a walk around the neighborhood to find the Guardians waiting for me in the living room.

There was a head man and a couple of hoods in uniform. The boss sat in my best chair, flanked by the two goons.

I saw him, and knew I looked on the enemy. He was blatantly overweight, so obese it had to be a declaration of his penchant for high living, an obscene proof that he ate and drank more than others because he had a right to more, a right to all he could take.

His hair was iron grey and cut so short it couldn't fall flat. His eyes were dead and old until he locked his gaze with mine. Then they came to life, murderous, hateful life. Those eyes were nearly lost in deep folds of fat, but they gleamed from their depths like deadly jewels. His wide, lipless mouth was very slightly open, as if it were ready at a moment's notice to gobble up anything of interest that came into its owner's path.

His uniform was not the standard grey, but a deep, brooding scarlet with death-black epaulets and pockets. The bright colors of his chestful of ribbons took on a malignant cast against that background. He stood, glared at me, and spoke in English with a typical Guardian accent, harsh and nasal. "I am Colonel Bradhurst, Special Interrogation Branch. Your records say you are Jefferson Darrow. We find that you have rather belatedly appeared on the list of skilled subjects of the Protectorate of New Finland." He paused for a moment, then spat out a sudden question. "Where has the computer kept your name up to now, cretin? Did you just appear out of thin air?"

"I—"

"Quiet!" He stalked across the room to the window and glared at the lovely view, as if he were angry with it. "How long have you been in the New Finnish star system?"

"I arrived with my wife about ten months ago—6000 hours or so."

"Very poor timing on your part, wasn't that? Your wife died, too, and left you quite all alone . . . such a pity." He turned and glared at me again. "One thing we have learned about this noisome people of yours is that they are excellent gossips. No one knows anything of you. What do you hide?"

"I just—just keep to myself. I'm not hiding anything. In fact I've been waiting for you to find me."

"Of course you hide nothing. No one ever does." His face hardened. "For long. Not from me. Waiting for me to find you? Why? What are you working on, here by yourself, Darrow?"

I decided Darrow had better play this as a coward. It was going to be pretty easy to act scared. The trick was to concentrate on feeding Bradhurst the bait instead of standing there being petrified.

"I'm . . . wor-working on a special transmitter, very advanced, that can—"

"You lie! This place has been searched top to bottom in your absence. Your lab is full of meaningless toys, nothing of any real use. 'Very advanced' devices? Nothing! You all try so very hard to impress your new masters. Trying to earn favor, clamoring over each other to gain special privileges and steal what is left for yourselves. Yours is not a loyal people, Darrow."

"These aren't *my* people!" I said. "My wife was a Finn, I'm not. I don't owe these people a thing, and they can't do anything for me. But you can."

"So why didn't you come forward?" Bradhurst demanded.

"You said it yourself—the Finns are gossips. If I went to you, and didn't convince you of my claims—they'd cut me to pieces as a collaborator. I have not dared do any new work, for fear of their seeing it. My new transmitter is up *here*." I pointed to my forehead. "But I can't get any equipment, or computer time to test things, or any chance to design or build. I don't have the resources to do it, but I *know* I could build a working, practical matter transmitter!"

He suddenly looked suspicious in a new way. It seemed I might be of value. "Matter transmitter? What are you talking about?"

"A device that could move material objects through space from a transmitter to a receiver using radio waves." That was bait enough, I thought.

He stopped. Not just stopped talking, but all of him stopped. His face lost all expression, and in his opulent uniform and stiff posture he looked more like a machine than a man. I thought I could almost see the gears turning. *Matter transmitter! That would be quite something, if he is telling the truth. Delivering such an invention to our use would be greatly to my credit. And I can test him at low risk. If he is lying he can be killed by my men, so none need know I was fooled. I can gain but can't lose.*

"Can you prove your claims? You will work with Guardians to do so?" he demanded.

"Yes," I said, my heart pounding. "Just give me a place to work. And see to it I get the credit, the reward, for my work."

"Of course we will." He stared at me thoughtfully. Cooperation is something a tyrant rarely sees. "If you are not lying. I will send some of our technicians. You will describe this transmitter, and the principles involved. If you are attempting to fool them, or trick us, you will be killed very slowly and painfully. If you are telling the truth, and if you can build this device, there will be credit and benefit enough for all. The Guardian is not ungenerous to those who contribute things of value." He made ready to leave. "But there is one more thing. It is *possible* you arrived here ten months ago. I will waste no time interrogating you now. If the record lies, you will have had a hand in it and will pay the penalty. We shall examine you most carefully now, your present and your past. If we find you are lying, you will die, transmitter or no." And he left, moving quickly for a man his size, escorted by his two goons.

I slumped down on the couch in a pool of sweat. The con game was on.

Chapter Six

"Hey, be careful with that!" The grey-suited private had grabbed up a delicate metering device as if it were a hand grenade. Jefferson Darrow, Ph.D., was moving, with a little help from his friends. I had insisted that, without actual tests, there was no way I could safely compensate for the extreme Coriolis effect on Vapaus. Of course, the spinning of New Finland on its axis created the same effect, but not as strongly. There, I could compensate. It was all nonsense, of course, but my keepers believed me, and so the test device would be built on the planet's surface. After ten weeks of conning the people who passed for scientists among the Guardians, without actually giving anything away insofar as the *way* it worked, I had satisfied them that the transmitter *would* work. Fortunately, the Guardians hadn't sent their first string research people along with the invasion fleet.

The con had been helped by the fact that the public had been aware for decades about the possibility of a matter transmitter. There had been a lot of loose talk of splitting of the atom in the 1930s, long before it happened. Back then, once people had heard of the idea, they were prepared to believe in it. My ground had been prepared in the same way. With that support, my explanations and proofs could be pretty vague, to say nothing of misleading. While I was out to build a working receiver to a matter transmitter, I certainly didn't want the Guardians to know how it was done. By the time my theories got to trained people on the invader's home planet who could spot the fallacies, it would be too late, if our side was lucky.

It had been a long ten weeks of deception. The computer forgers of Vapaus were true artists, and I sometimes thought they were going to give the banks a real headache if and when this was over. In any event, by the time Colonel Bradhurst began his inquiries, my past was put together with near-perfection. Not absolute perfection, for that would have been suspect. But the holes in the information were artfully made and easy to explain. The obscenely fat Colonel Bradhurst was by profession and inclination a viciously suspicious man, and he gave me a few bad afternoons. As a hungry dog will chew on a bone rather than search for fresh meat, so Bradhurst kept himself busy bullying me over minor inconsistencies, without ever hauling me in for the sort of full-bore interrogation that might have blown my cover.

It had been ten weeks of learning, and of growing revulsion. In bits and pieces, from tight-lipped and embittered Finns, from boisterous and sneering soldiers, I learned the story of New Finland's defeat.

It had not been as easy for the victors as they had expected. The plan had been for a small fleet of ships to enter the system, bomb a few minor towns, laser targets in the larger ones, and have the craven civilians capitulate without further resistance. The ships had come. The bombs were dropped on three towns, and the lasers had burned a dozen buildings and plazas in Mannerheim and New Helsinki down to slag. The surrender demand had been made.

The invaders had expected an unarmed world. But the Finnish memory is long, and the Finns recalled the long, long centuries with an enemy always at the border, and foreign soldiers always near. They had fought the Russians, the Germans, the Swedes, the Danes, and even, in the dim past of the 13th and 14th centuries and beyond—each other. Their past did not let them trust to light-years of vacuum as a sufficient defense.

The Finns waited until the occupation troops had begun to arrive. Few of the first wave survived long enough to land, and few who did land lived long on the planet's surface. But the Guardians were too great in strength; they had kept coming and coming. They took the planet's surface.

But, in space, the Guardian ships suddenly found themselves being cut to pieces. The Finns had been far better prepared than their invaders had ever dreamed. Finally, the Guards resorted to terror tactics: nuclear weapons were exploded in space a few kilometers away from Vapaus, and the satellite, with its high civilian population, was threatened with destruction. The satellite had controlled the orbital battle, and when it was forced to surrender, the planet's last hope was gone. The Guards almost succeeded in preventing word from reaching the League. Once the Guards arrived, no crewed ship escaped the New Finnish system. As best I could learn, the only craft of any sort that had made it out was the drone that had summoned the League.

But what should have taken ten days, a week, to accomplish had taken three months by the time it was over. The last insurrection occurred days before I arrived at Vapaus. "Light casualties" had grown into slaughter on both sides—on the ground, in the air, and in space.

But the Finns had gained time. Vapaus had become a mass of hidey-holes, secret tunnels, disguised arms factories. Taps were placed on computers and communications, reports and data banks were erased or falsified. An explosion was faked on The Rock, and a convincing show made the Guardians think it was reduced to a radioactive deathtrap. They steered well clear of it, and the shipyards there went on working, slowly, very quietly, to make the ships needed to fight, someday.

Even in defeat, many Finns had refused to surrender. The Guardians believed that fully a third of Vapaus's population had died in the riots, carnage and reprisals that followed the garrison's arrival. But the confusion was used to full advantage by the defenders. More than half the apparent casualties had gone underground, their deaths faked. They were out of sight, working on a hundred projects toward the day when they would fight back.

But not all the deaths were faked. From my windows I could see a black scar on the land half-way up the curve of the inside-out world. Overhearing a conversation at the local store, I learned that the entire family, save one son, of the satellite's administrator—Dr. Tempkin—had been wiped out in a single bomb blast. The corpses of the wife and the children were identifiable, but Tempkin's corpse was nothing but a charred cinder.

I wondered if I would have had the nerve, the courage needed to come home to a blazing ruin, see my family murdered, and yet find in myself the cunning and gall to take advantage of the situation and vanish. Could I have worked a grisly piece of subterfuge, found a dead man and thrown him into the flames to take my place? Tempkin had seemed such a gentle man. What nightmares did he have?

The invaders had not permitted "Tempkin" and his family to be cremated, and guards stood over the ruins of their home night and day. The stench that came from there was the perfume of barbarism.

It had been ten weeks completely in the dark. There was one day I noted in my head—the day when, if all our plans were to have any hope, Joslyn would have flown one of the auxiliary ships—*Stars*, probably, because it used less fuel than *Stripes*—and positioned the capture device at the right point and velocity in space. If she had succeeded in receiving the troops' signal and if she could get the capture unit to the Finns, somehow, we still might win through.

I had constructed a device the size and shape of the real capture unit, wondering if the switch could be made for the real thing. One evening I left the fake on the bench with its back panel off. The next morning I walked into "my" lab to find the genuine article. I took a screwdriver and replaced the back panel. The power light was on. I didn't know if it had indeed made the capture, or how Joslyn had gotten it to Vapaus, or how the Finns had collected it, or how it had gotten into my well-guarded lab.

The Finns were good at what they did. Maybe cloak-and-dagger was natural to their temperament. I don't know. But they were a bit over-mysterious for my tastes.

Long before I had taken on my part as Darrow, Tempkin's staff had decided on an exact moment for the troops to be deployed, and for a general uprising to occur at the same moment. Now, not only would the five thousand League troops arrive, but a planet and satellite's worth of hell would break loose, a vast underground ambush. The Finns would concentrate on crippling the enemy's transport. An army that can't move can't fight. It was vital that I stick to the agreed-upon timetable, and that was what chose the moment I would announce I was ready for the "experiment."

And so the thumb-fingered privates were loading my equipment, some of it vital, some of it window dressing. Finally everything was packed and I rode a passenger lift to the docking port of my transportation: a Finnish ballistic shuttle rocket painted over in the Guardian colors of black and red.

As I entered it I saw that the civilian passenger fittings had been pulled out and military-style interchangeable pallet clamps put in. It was a sloppy, hurried job. Sharp projections, poor welds, scratched paint and stripped bolts were much in evidence. That was the way the Guardians always worked. They were cut-and-cover engineers, shoddy workmen. Everywhere I spotted hints of overextension, a hollowness behind the conqueror's shining facade. Privates wore uniforms made of half a dozen materials, none of them very durable. A patched pair of pants was common on anyone below the rank of sergeant. The Guardians preferred the confiscated weapons of the Finns to their own. Few officers wore anything but a Finnish pistol. The guards on my house had complained that their issue lasers couldn't hold a charge more than a week.

Guardian repairs to war damage were rough and uneven. Rebuilt walls were crumbly, and the work on one bridge over the Central Sea had to be done over twice.

But they had won. So far. Even as I boarded the shuttle, which bore a strong family resemblance to *Stars*, *Stripes* and *Uncle Sam*, I didn't have a precise idea where I was going. The problem had been foreseen, and the Finns had assured me that I could expect—or at least hope for—help at any of the bases I might arrive at.

I rode down under extremely strong guard, and any service *I* was willing to fly with would have grounded that ship's pilot without hesitation. We lived through the landing, but a number of my guards were too busy making a mess of the bulkheads to bother about me.

I came out of the airlock to find a dozen troops pointing laser rifles at my head. There were times it was easy to play the part of a coward like Darrow. I froze, utterly shocked. They had found me out, and for some reason had waited until I was on New Finland to arrest me.

But then I saw a figure in an lieutenant's uniform striding calmly toward me, a smile on his face. He came up the passenger ramp with his hand outstretched. I numbly stuck out my own and he took it. "Dr. Darrow. Welcome to New Finland. I am Lieutenant Grimes. I am to escort you to Base Demeter." He shook my hand warmly. "Will you come this way?" He led me down the ramp and toward a jeep that had just pulled up. The laser rifles stayed trained on my head.

"Is it safe to . . ." I started to ask, my voice trailing off.

"Oh, the honor guard? Quite safe. They won't fire without commands. Orders, you see. A great many of these Finns tried to escape as they came out of the hatch. It was felt a show of force was needed. But you've nothing to worry about, I'm sure. Come now, this way."

He led me to the jeep and we drove off.

We rode away from the landing pad and out the base gates, headed north. We traveled for about four hours. Finally, we came to the gates of Base Demeter. The gates were hastily opened, and we headed down a wide, unpaved road that ran the length of the central camp. We took the second right down a narrow road that doubled back slightly, then made two more right turns into a single lane road that ended in a circular court about 30 meters in diameter.

The court was ringed with massive, hangarlike buildings painted gunmetal grey with camouflage-green roofs.

Grimes's driver drove us directly into the largest building through large barn-like doors. Its interior was utterly empty and gave the feeling of never having been used. It was of rough prefab construction, unventilated and unheated: it was meant to keep the rain off, nothing more or less. It was cubical, thirty meters in every dimension. There were no windows.

Grimes turned to me. "Well, Darrow, this is to be yours. We'll set a cot for you in the corner, and meals will be brought to you. There is a latrine across the court, which you will be taken to no more than three times a day. The materials you requested, and the cargo from your landing boat, will start to arrive within the hour. My commander expects a demonstration of your machine within ten local days." There was no cordiality in his voice now. These were orders, to be obeyed, no questions. He turned to leave.

"I was promised two weeks!" I protested. "I'll need at least that much time!" But it was too late. He was gone. The two weeks was a lie, of course. I expected to be ready within a week, and the attack was set for then, but greater speed than promised seemed like a good idea for keeping the brass happy.

The doors clanged shut, cutting out the daylight. I was alone with a duffel bag, two dangerous looking guards, and a nutty scheme that seemed likely to be my obituary.

I slumped back down against the far wall of the building from the guards and sighed. Time to do some waiting.

It was not one, but three hours before my equipment arrived. Two corporals with patches identifying themselves as being assigned to 135 CUSTOMS AND INSPECTION CORPS rode a cart into the building, towing a trailer full of my gear. One of them hopped down and handed me a clipboard. "Sign all six copies. This amount of luggage is far in excess of what is normally permitted. Clearance and inspection were quite difficult." He reminded me of the librarian at the orphanage back on Kennedy. The old fossil had been convinced that in a *properly* run library, no book would ever leave the shelf. I signed the forms willingly enough, and smiled happily at all the regulations he saw fit to remind me of. I was determined to be cheerful and cooperative enough to spoil his officious little day.

There were plenty of forms to rustle through, too. Receipts, acknowledgements, statements of declaration, waivers, denials of visible damage, a chit for mileage on the shuttlecraft and all ground vehicles.

There is something beautiful in the routine lack of imagination a bureaucrat brings to his work. To such a person, beauty is order, as pure as an untouched and fragile flower. Muss the slightest corner of one regulation and the bloom is gone forever.

The beauty was still there for the 135 Customs and Inspection Corps. All the forms were filled out, every single regulation had been complied with, every buck passed perfectly. In spite of all the difficulties, the "luggage" had been delivered properly, including the capture unit, its power lamp still glowing.

Never mind that I had just become the first person in history to smuggle five thousand fully armed and equipped troopers past customs. It said right over my signature I had nothing to declare.

There wasn't much point in unpacking what I had brought from Vapaus. It represented the last stages of the job, the delicate electronic work. Before any of that could be done, I had to get the big structural part of the receiver built. However, the man who was supposed to meet me at this end hadn't shown yet. More hurry-up-and-wait.

Along toward sunset, I was awakened from a light doze when the barn doors swung open and another wagon rolled in, dragging loads of steel and a number of electronics racks. I got up from my seat on the floor with a crick in my neck as a good-looking, cheerful, slightly pudgy young man hopped down from the driver's seat and walked over to me with a light step. He reached out and offered me his hand. "Dr. Darrow. George Prigot. The big brass seem to think you're on to something pretty big."

"I might be at that." I took an instant liking to George.

He was of medium height, with a thick mop of shaggy brown hair. His eyes were calm, almost sleepy, and yet with a bright spark hidden in their depths. His handshake was firm and solid, and his hands would have done a surgeon credit; big, long fingered, and used with a graceful economy of motion.

This was no military type, uniform or no. It barely was a uniform he had on. The insignia was faded, the shirt was rumpled and washed to the point where it was a completely different shade of grey from the pants, which were too long, almost making him trip over his unshined shoes. Every outfit has one of George's kind in it; the tolerated talent, too good at what he did to be done without, and therefore given more freedom, more license, than anyone else.

"A matter transmitter," he said. "I used to hope I'd get the chance to work on one. I gave that up when they sent me here. Not much research on this planet for a while."

"Well, you'll work on it now. Did you get a look at the blueprints they transmitted down from the satellite?"

He pointed to the cart full of girders and sheet metal behind him. "That's it, right there. All prefabbed. We just finished up the last of the cutting an hour ago. In fact, my plan is to get the basic structure up tonight, while you get caught up on your rest. You look pretty done in. Where are you billeted? I'll run you over."

"Short trip. I'm not supposed to go further than the privy, three times a day. They're bringing in a cot."

"Brilliant. You can't do design work sleeping on a piece of canvas in the middle of a machine shop. Heinrichs!"

"Yessir?"

"First thing on the agenda is to get the doctor here a place to lay his head. We'll build him a soundproof cubicle over there in the corner. Get some soundproof wallboard and so on. I want it up inside of three hours. Pound the quartermaster over the head until he issues you a decent bed and bedding. Also, we'll need working tables and chairs. Brass didn't think we'd need any office space to do this. Got it?"

"Okay. Do I check with you if I need anything else?"

"Use your judgment. Better still, use Steve's. He knows what we can get away with. Learn from the master."

"Yo." Heinrichs neglected his salute, but George didn't seem to expect one. Heinrichs hopped back into the wagon, and drove off.

"That should settle things. Oh! They think to feed you?"

"Nope."

"And I forgot to eat myself. Tell you what. You get freshened up a bit and I'll find us some food." And George was gone.

The privy detail marched me across the courtyard. By the time I had my shower, shaved, brushed my teeth, and generally gotten closer to feeling human, Heinrichs and a few others were already putting together my bunkroom. George appeared bearing a pair of stacked trays, and, as George put it, "some of the boys" started to rig work lights.

The lighting was stark, cross angled, like searchlights in a dark field. Brightly lit figures would scurry in front of a light and then vanish completely into huge shadows. Great misshapen beings would appear in silhouette on the walls and then transform themselves into normal humans as the original stepped closer to the wall and straightened up.

There is a magic about a rush job at night. The barn doors were left open as men came in and out after tools or a sandwich from the mess hall, and cool night air spilled into the brightly lit hangar. The previously untouched room lost its virginity. Men were at work, and litter appeared on the floor—scraps of paper full of rough sketches and calculations, sandwich wrappers, bits cut from pieces of steel that needed a trim, tools strewn about and cables snaking everywhere in entangling webs.

In the center of it all, the shell of the receiver grew like a ruin coming back to life. The first bracing appeared, and the wide curve of a half-cylinder grew across the floor. Parts were welded together, and each join was closely scrutinized by George. He was a tough man to please, and no job was done until it was done over and done right. Soon, the skeleton of the beast was complete, and we started putting the skin on.

Sheets of narrow-gauge steel were flush-bolted to the inside of the frame, and the pieces joined with a precision Finnish laser welding unit. I ran my hand over one of the seams and could not feel the join.

This was a proud crew, a tight crew. George ran them hard, but they knew how good they were. The lowest ranked laborer had just as much of a chance of winning a technical argument as his superior. Here the job was important, and to hell with the paperwork, we'll patch up a story later.

The Guardians I had been up against so far had been robots, or sadists, or barbarians, or simply boors. Here I was part of the team, since I could handle a screwdriver, since I could help Get The Job Done. After all the long weeks of isolation, starting the moment I set foot aboard *Stars*, this was just what I needed.

I nearly forgot whose side they were on, and the strong chance that this machine would result in their deaths. It's easy to rationalize killing the bad guys, but here was George offering to loan me his music system for the duration, and I might be arranging for him to be lying in a pool of blood in a week's time.

One line of thought could have cheered me up as far as that went. The plan might fail. The transmitter could go blooie. Guardian intelligence might catch up with me. I might blow the schedule. Could I speed up the work, or stall, if need be?

The great shape grew and solidified in the middle of the hangar, spotlit and backlit now and then by the welders. They were down to finicky alignment work by the time exhaustion caught up with me, and I crawled into my bunk, morning just peeping in the door. I slept long and well.

Outside my comfortable little room, a machine of death and salvation slowly grew.

Chapter Seven

"Jeff, if this thing works, things are really going to change. I mean *really* change." George downed a big gulp of New Finnish vodka and grimaced at the strength of the stuff. He handed me the bottle and I took a slightly shorter pull off it. I nodded a somewhat hazy agreement.

"Cars, planes, hell, even intersystem spaceflight—all of it obsolete. Push a button and there you are!"

"And then once you're at the other end someone hands you a bill for a gigawatt or so of electricity."

"Just a question of efficiency."

"Think it can be made efficient?"

"Sure. I think you can make it efficient."

"Me. Hmmmm."

"You. Jeff—why is it you always talk about it as if it wasn't *your* work?"

"I dunno." I realized I was on thin ice again and tried to retreat. "I guess the idea has been floating around so long I can't take credit. Or else I don't really believe it will work."

"Oh, it'll work." George was no more a theorist than Terrance MacKenzie Larson (alias Jefferson Darrow) was. His opinion, no, his *certitude* was based on faith. Faith in me, good ol' Doc Darrow. I took a longer hit off the bottle.

Judas. I felt like Judas. George so clearly liked me, respected me. I had found it harder and harder to play the part of Dr. Darrow, prize chicken and quisling, around him. Here I was, posing as the brilliant inventor of the gadget he had dreamed of as a kid in the children's barracks back on the Guardian's planet, Capital. And I was to betray him.

We were sitting in my little private room, and the boys from George's crew—more formally, the 9462 Construction

Battalion—were throwing themselves a little party to celebrate the completion of the basic structure. From here on in it was finicky work with oscilloscopes and test calipers. One of the boys opened the door, stuck in a rather red nose, yelled "C'mon! Th' party's ou' here!", and nearly slammed the door on himself as he left without waiting for a reply.

George grinned and sipped at the bottle. I shook my head at him. "You sure don't seem the military type, George. How'd *you* end up here?"

"Hell, Jeff, on Capital, *everybody's* the military sort. There isn't anything else. That's the whole point."

"What's the idea of calling it Capital, anyway?"

He shrugged vaguely. "They figure it's going to be that. Someday. The Capital. Capital of everything, everybody."

"Everybody? Earth? Bandwidth? Europa?"

"I guess."

"Jesus H. Christ! *Why?*"

"Thought you didn't care about politics."

"Politics, no." Booze, and my guilty friendship toward George loosened my tongue a bit. "But you guys have killed a lot of people here. There'd be a lot more killing if you take on the others."

"Yeah, they have killed a lot . . ." He grunted to himself and smiled grimly. "And I know what you're thinking, and you play too fair to say it: 'Why do you always talk about it as if it wasn't *your* work?' " He laughed without any humor behind it. He looked through the wall in the direction of the matter transmitter's receiver. "And what work will *we* do with *that*?"

"Hell of a machine, isn't it?"

"Hell of one." George noticed I was starting to get a little fuzzy. He slapped me on the back and stood up. "You get into that bed and get some sleep. Lots of work tomorrow."

Lots of hangovers the next day, too. *Mine* was impressive, anyway. I had been hanging around engineers too long: I felt a strong urge to disassemble my head and fix whatever the hell was the matter with it.

We went on with the work.

Then, one day, tomorrow was *the* day. I had been fooling with phony circuits for a day and a half by that time. Now it was time to quit stalling. All the modular gear lashed together on Vapaus, all the impressive blinking lights, were in place. Most of George's men were back at other work again. Just George and Heinrichs were still assigned to me.

I closed down the inspection hatch I had been diddling with and sauntered over to one of the guards. "If you would, please get a message to the base commander. Tell him we'll be ready for a demonstration at 2000 hours tomorrow."

"Yes sir!" This *was* a big moment: the first time any of my guards had called me "sir"—or anything at all, for that matter.

By now, a hundred plans were being put into effect around this world, and in Vapaus. With luck, by the time the League troops arrived, the Guardian's forces would already be half crippled. A host of mysterious flat tires, shorted out engines, strange cases of food poisoning, delays and problems from civilian suppliers. A rash of fires.

The Guardians' intelligence units were going to notice the flurry of activity. Chances were someone had been picked up and interrogated already, someone who knew more than he should have. Conspiracy is a highly skilled profession, practiced only by amateurs. There was sure to be some warning that something was up.

Would someone make the connection between my bogus machine and the sudden outbreak of nuisance attacks from a population that had seemed subdued?

Time started to drag toward deep night. I felt alone and afraid.

The remaining guard watched me closely, but allowed me to step through the doors of the hangar and breathe in the fresh cleanness of the mild autumn weather.

I looked out to the crystal clear sky, the old familiar stars, seen in strange new places from a different world. Not for the first time, not even for the hundredth, I thought of Joslyn. She was out there, somewhere, and only if I lived would I see her again. That alone was reason enough for this fight. I thought back to those good days, before the drone came into our lives with its frightful news, and further back than that, to the days of training, before the *Venera*. How had I come from all that to this sorry place? How had it come to me to try and break the yoke the Guardians had hung on this world?

I realized that I never had a choice, that I *did* have to come. The thought that, even for a moment back in the comfort of the *J.M.*'s wardroom, I had thought it might be understandable to cut and run . . . No. This was my fight, now, by right of duty, honor, and anger. For what they had done to Tempkin's family, if nothing else.

And Joslyn. She was in this fight too. There was a hell of a reason. If we won, she would be safe.

The fate of a world was more or less in my hands that night, but it was Joslyn I thought of.

I looked at the stars, and loved her with all my heart.

I spotted a portly figure in a greatcoat marching toward me in a studied sort of hurry, leaving a jeep behind him. He walked through a light, and my blood froze. Bradhurst. Intelligence. He walked straight toward me. He opened his lipless mouth, with a sort of basilisk's smile. He spoke.

"Good evening, Commander Larson."

Oh my god.

Poker face. Ignore it. You are in it *deep*! I stood there and looked at him. "Hmmm? Bradhurst? It's me, Darrow. You've got the wrong guy." My heart was pounding so hard I thought I could hear it.

"I have the right man, Commander."

A dead, silent moment passed between us. He stared at me with those vicious, dead eyes and all I wanted to do was run.

"I don't know what you're talking about. I'm Darrow."

"Of course you are. Come along, anyway." He gestured

to the guard that he was taking me for a stroll. "The guard seems to trust you, letting you stand in a open doorway like that."

"No reason not to trust me. Besides, where would I run?"

"Precisely." Bradhurst was enjoying this, a cat playing with a bird who can't get away, letting it try, anyway.

Bradhurst slipped his hands into his pocket and drew out a pair of fine leather gloves. He carefully pulled them onto his fat fingers. "Imagine my position. Thanks to me, a man is put in a place of trust, put in charge of an important new weapon. The weapon is excitingly useful, very tempting. The man's records are satisfactory. Very convenient, isn't it? Especially since this man simply popped out of the woodwork, no explanation of why he was missed before." Bradhurst smiled at me, a hungry gleaming of teeth. "There is, however, a flaw. If something goes wrong, things have gotten out of control to the point where *I* might be blamed. So I checked. And I checked again. Most slowly. Most carefully. I even check a memory file that includes a listing of the personnel of the League of Planets Survey Service. The records, and the fingerprints, were of interest."

Even in that moment, I could not help but think on how current their information was. My brevet rank of Commander was only a few months old, and the promotion of a junior naval officer could not be considered high priority information. How had that little tidbit gotten back to Capital—and then on to New Finland—so quickly?

"I don't know how you got here, Larson, but you are here. That machine in there—I don't know what it is, but I know what it isn't. And it isn't here to do the Guardians of Capital any good."

Bradhurst stopped and turned toward me. I thought of running, but he was right. Where could I run?

He glared at me and kept talking. "There seem to be an untoward number of accidents and problems with the locals tonight. I wonder if you know anything about that? But it doesn't matter now. We've walked far enough. We go back now, and tear that machine to pieces—we'll find out what it *really* is. And then, after we have shredded every single fact from the remains of your brain, you will die."

No matter how long the odds, I had to try to get away in the dark, circle back, try and activate the transmitter early. I had no chance, but I had no choice, either. I shifted my feet to run—

"Don't try to escape, Larson." Suddenly, his voice was as hard and cold as granite in a cave. I backpedaled a bit. I *had* to try.

He pulled out his side-arm. "I'm warning yo—"

A ruby beam sizzled through his neck, slicing through the flesh, and he collapsed against me, gurgling, already dead, and I staggered under the weight.

A pair of boots came crunching up, and a dim figure appeared, a laser pistol in its hand. "I had to stop the transmitter," said a nervous, edgy voice. "I couldn't let 'em keep killing. I was—I was going to kill *you* until I heard *this* guy talk." The speaker stepped out of the shadows, his laser pistol still in his hand.

George Prigot. He grabbed at the body and pulled it off me, shoving it to the ground. I gulped and wiped away the splash of blood that had struck me in the face. I looked down at the broad, puffy face. A thin line of blood oozed up from behind its lips. Now the face was as dead as those glassy, murderous eyes.

"He's no loss," George said, his voice flat and hard. He looked at me sharply. "No turning back for me, now, though."

I looked at him, and saw the wild look in his eye. "No," I said, none too sure what to think. "I don't suppose there is." *But what are you heading toward*? I thought to myself. "Why did you do it?" I asked.

George didn't appear to have heard me. He knelt down and looked at the body, his expression flat, guarded. "That night we were drinking," he said, "I realized that Capital isn't a good place. We have a better life here in this stinking *camp*, just being away from Capital, just being a little nearer people who *used* to know peace, and freedom. I couldn't help it spread. Not anymore. I started thinking about that machine, what it could do. So I decided to kill you. And then . . ." His voice trailed off, and he looked up at me, looked at me as if he were seeing me for the first time. "You really from the League?" he asked.

I remembered to breathe, gulped air, let myself go to the shakes. It had been that close. "Yeah. Yeah. Terrance MacKenzie Larson, ROK Navy. The League."

"Good." He stood up and prodded the body with the toe of his boot. "What do we do with the body?"

"I don't know," I said.

"Wait a minute. I know a place. Give me a hand." We each grabbed one of Bradhurst's arms and pulled the still-warm body up. We dragged it about 50 yards through the dark to a toolshed. George leaned the body against it, fumbled with a bunch of keys and opened the lock. We shoved the body inside. I ran back the way we came and did what I could to scuff up the gravel where the body had bled and where we had dragged it. No one who wasn't looking for blood would find it. I hustled back to find George waiting in the shadows of the toolshed.

"Now. Talk," he said. "What the hell is going to happen when we push that button?"

"Not what," I said. "Who. It really is a matter transmitter. The League is beaming five thousand troops at us."

"My God. Is it going to work?"

"I have no idea. I hope so."

"Jesus! But how are—never mind. Later. For now, what we do about Bradhurst?"

"Let me think," I said. Things were moving too fast. "Look. Call the hangar. Tell them to tell his driver you're discussing security for the demonstration with him and you're going to drive Bradhurst back to his quarters. All we have to do is stall them until the test. Afterwards, it won't matter, one way or the other."

George seemed about to protest, but then he nodded. He had killed a superior officer. He was probably in greater danger from his own people than from the League. "I suppose that's the best we can do," he said. "I'll be back. Don't go anywhere."

"Where have I got to go?" I asked. But George was already lost in the shadows. I sat in the dark for a long time.

George returned. "Okay, I think they bought it."

"Good. Let's get out of here and find a place to talk." I wanted to get away from the corpse.

George led me to an empty building at the end of camp. He seemed to know how to avoid the sentries. George. What was in it for him? How much was this costing him? Could I really trust him, or would he change his mind again by morning? Could anyone ever completely trust a turncoat?

But there was no doubt in him that night. He asked me questions and we made decisions. We planned and schemed, made plots against the lives of the men he had eaten breakfast with that morning.

"It's a lot to ask of you, George."

"I know, but you're not asking. I'm doing. I've had it. I've wired up plenty of our nasty little killing gadgets. I went past the far end of camp this morning. A firing squad. I recognized one of the soldiers on the squad, and his gun. I had fixed the power feed for him the day before. And they were shooting a twelve-year-old girl who had wandered in looking for her daddy. She thought he might be with soldiers. She didn't think about whose. They shot her for spying."

There was nothing I could say.

It was too much, too fast, too close to the end. If, if, if was all I could think. No one had any idea what would happen tomorrow. The best we could hope was that Bradhurst hadn't told anyone what he had learned, and that Guardians would know less than we did.

All I knew for certain was that tomorrow, some of us would die.

Interlude

The ghosts were with me that night. I dreamt in a pool of sweat, surrounded by faces that stared at me, unsure of me, doubtful I could fulfill the trust forced upon me.

I could clearly see only the *eyes* of the ghosts. Their faces and bodies glimmered, became nearly sharp, almost distinct and real, only to fade away again.

A dirty, mudcaked GI with a baby in his arms, a Cherokee watching in the night for the villains who savaged his world, a frightened, tiny slip of a girl trapped in a bombed-out subway, trying to calm the children imprisoned with her, singing them nursery rhymes, telling stories; half an ear listening for the sound of digging, scraping, the sound of rescue on the way, humming the little tune and wondering if help would ever come . . .

Forgotten heroes peered at me, pointed and prodded, asking if I would fail in this, *my* task.

But, toward dawn, I think, Joslyn appeared among them. She took my hand and smiled at the dead protectors.

They nodded, once, each, slowly, and faded into the gloomy mists, to guard at another gate of danger, to peer into another part of the darkness that must of definition surround free people.

Part Two
War on the Ground

Chapter Eight

When I finally woke the next morning, it took me a good long while to realize that the night was finally over, and that this was indeed, *the* day. I dressed quickly, and, for the last time, went through the daily ritual of the trek to the latrine, closely followed by my two armed guards.

I returned to my room and put on an official-looking white lab coat over my coverall. I dug under my mattress, pulled out Bradhurst's laser, and shoved it into a coverall pocket, hoping the lab coat would hide the bulge.

I ate breakfast—or at least went through the motions of eating it. About three bites actually got down—and barely stayed down. Well, there was plenty to be scared of.

I shoved back the tray, tried to compose my face, and walked out into the hangar. All the debris of our frantic activity had been cleared away, and folding chairs set up in preparation for visitors. I knew there were going to be some observers for the test, but not that there'd be so many. Another worry, and not one I was prepared for.

The watch on my wrist grew bigger and bigger, and the numbers on it took longer and longer to change. Hours seemed to go by as I stood over my control board, checking and rechecking the switch settings, double-checking procedures I knew by heart.

Finally, the moment was near. One grey uniform decked with braid, then another, and another, strolled in, found their places, and sat down.

I worried over Bradhurst. Was he expected this morning? How long until he was missed? How long till I was suspected? Had he reported on finding this Commander Larson to anyone on his staff?

The grey men continued to file in, the clock crept toward

the appointed hour, and I hoped a nervous scientist acted the same way a nervous spy did.

Again and again I asked—Was George to be trusted? He wasn't here yet. Did he have cold feet? Was he already talking to the secret police?

Fifteen minutes before the test, he appeared—the only man from his shop to come. He was in full dress uniform, the first time I had ever seen him in it. It was a formal affair, but that uniform also gave him a chance to wear his officer's side-arm. He nodded to me and tipped the side of his peaked cap with a large cylindrical map case. Poker faced.

I began to have the presence of mind to think like a soldier. Half of the audience wore side-arms of some kind, and my two guards stood by the door, stiff and rigid, saluting everything that moved. Their boot tops gleamed in the afternoon light. With luck, they would be too busy with the spit-and-polish routine to be of much help in an emergency. However, they carried heavy firepower—laser rifles that could burn holes in steel plating.

Okay, hit them first, *then* the officers, in the few seconds between activation of the transmitter and the materialization of the first League troops.

The League troops were a completely open question as well. Assuming they had been transmitted, and assuming the capture device had done its work, and hadn't been wrecked by some fumble-fingered private in the Guard's transport service, I still had no idea what sort of soldiers had been sent, or how they would react. All I could hope for was that they were ready for trouble.

At the time the League had sent the drone out to find the *J.M.*, the League's military planning staff hadn't had a chance to get a force together. The reports sent with the drone said that we could expect a combined force made up of troops grabbed in a hurry from half the member states. Since the ship which was to carry the troops to the transmission point was to be launched from Earth, we were told to expect a large proportion of Earthside troops. Political realities, it was broadly hinted in the report, would require a number of small units, token contributions from member states who didn't have the time or money to offer more.

My worrying was interrupted when General Schlitzer, the base commander, arrived amid a flurry of saluting from all sides. Lieutenant Grimes escorted Schlitzer over to me, made introductions, and left us to talk. Schlitzer shook my hand. "Good day, Doctor," he said. "Are we ready to go forward with the demonstration?"

I gulped and tried to smile with my heart in my stomach. "I think so, sir."

"Good. Let us hope this is a grand day for us both." He stood and looked over the great machine. "Tell me," he went on, "why is the receiver so much larger than the transmitter cage?"

Damn! He *would* ask that one. The bogus transmitter cage was barely a meter square, while the receiver was ten times that size. "Well, sir, the transmitter is a much more complicated device, and must be built to exact tolerance, while the receiver simply has to be at least large enough to accept whatever it is sent. So as to save time in later tests, we built one large receiver cage, which will be able to accommodate any and all of the big transmitters we hope to build later." I hoped he bought it.

"I see. Well, I suppose we can leave that sort of thing to you technical people." He nodded curtly and turned to face the audience, his back to me. Which killed him, a few minutes later.

The other brass noticed he was waiting for their attention and quieted down. Schlitzer proceeded to give a little speech.

"Gentlemen. You have all heard the basic idea behind this device. If it is successful, it will be capable of transmitting matter over radio waves. The improvement in our ability to strike faster, harder, and more effectively are barely imaginable. In a few minutes we may know that our next conquest shall not only be greater—but bought far more cheaply. We see the transmatter today. Tomorrow, a dozen worlds will see it, worlds that will not be able to face us, except in death. Doctor?"

I nodded, swallowed hard, and started pushing buttons. I energized the system and heard the loud, satisfying *clack* of big relays coming on line. The lights in the room flickered and dimmed for a moment as the machinery absorbed more and more power. Pilot lights and meters came to life. Then there was just one button left to push to start the automatic sequencers. I looked out beyond the sea of faces to the only one that wasn't staring intently at the transmitter or receiver cages—George. Moving very slowly, he had gotten himself directly behind the oblivious guards.

I hit the switch.

The lights dimmed again as power rushed into the capture device. Now we were committed. From here on in, the transmitter operated automatically.

Queep! The first of three audio warning tones. System ready. I slid my hand into the lab coat and felt the butt of the dead man's gun. George had his hand on his holster.

Queep! Capture device engaged.

George killed one of the guards, a silent laser beam boring the life out of his skull.

QUEEP! Receiving objects . . .

A blast of wind slapped across the audience as the air in the receiver was forced out by the materializing effect.

I pulled out my gun and shot the general. He turned in shock, screaming, and felt his spine opening up under my laser. He dropped like a stone.

There was a flash of light from the receiver, that left an after-image, no, a solid reality of—men!

They were here.

I turned and fired into the crowd of officers. George shot the other guard through the heart. He grabbed the guard's rifle, turned and played the rifle over the crowd, wounding, blinding, killing half of them in a sudden terrible moment. The Guardians were aghast, shocked. Two thirds of them were dead before one of them thought to fire back at us.

I crouched behind my console—which wasn't heavy steel by accident—and looked at the troops that had arrived. They were here, real. It had all worked. But this was a hell of a surprise welcome for them.

Some of them dove off the receiver stage and took cover, not sure who to shoot at, if anyone. The rest stood there, dazed. It must have been a hell of a surprise.

Queep! The next cycle of troops would be here in ten seconds . . .

I stood up and yelled "Get the hell off that platform! Clear out! Clear out!" They came, and I recognized the uniform. Well armed Republic of Kennedy marines!

"Clear out! Clear out! Get out of that thing! Move it!"

They moved. One of them had the sense to throw something at the people I was shooting at. A loud flash and a boom, and where there had been people, the enemy, was gore and a sudden stench. A few laser shots zipped across the room, and the last of the survivors went down.

Queep! QUEEP! More on the way.

I holstered the gun and stripped off the lab coat. "Soldier! You! Get over here!"

She trotted over and saluted. "Sir!"

"Who knows when there's some artillery coming?"

"Kaplan, Corporal Kaplan has a printout of who's due when, sir."

"Kaplan!"

"Yo!"

Kaplan was in front of me, already fumbling with a thick sheaf of paper. "Kaplan, when do we get some artillery?"

"Just a sec, sir . . . ah . . . elements of 107th Light Artillery. British Army. Fifth outfit to arrive. Sir, what the hell happened?"

"Later. Stick by me." I looked up from the printout to see George. "Oh, boy. Hang on, George. It's gonna get worse." George dropped his rifle as if it had turned into a serpent in his hands. He looked bad, very bad. "George! Listen! Artillery. The fifth outfit to come through. Brits.

You've got to get them out to the courtyard and show them those targets. Okay?"

"Oh, God. Yeah, okay." He was nearly in shock. Suddenly, he shook himself and he answered again in a stronger voice. "Right. I'll do it." He strode, a bit jerkily, to the receiver.

Kaplan and the first private I had talked to were standing with me, just watching their fellows appearing out of nowhere and coming out of the receiver cage.

The first private said "Pardon me, Commander Larson? Ah, where are we, sir? Weren't we supposed to land in an empty plain?"

"The main office made a mistake. The original site is underwater. This is one of the enemy's main bases. We had to improvise. Oh, and it's also mid-October, Earthside. You've been held as sort of a recording for about a month."

She swallowed suddenly and her eyes went pop. "My goodness. How are we getting out of here?"

"Very carefully."

Queep! Queep! QUEEP!

From the hardware on the shoulders, this was the load that carried the heavy brass. These were no desk jockeys; they had the look of field soldiers. I checked their insignia and spotted the commander. He was a big, solid man in a British Army brigadier's uniform.

This time I trotted up and did the saluting. "Commander Terrance MacKenzie Larson, ROK Navy."

He looked around himself, at the smoky hangar, the mangled corpses in high-ranking uniforms, and the mob of soldiers trying to get themselves sorted out. Then he saluted back and said, "Report!"

"Error in cartography, sir. Original landing site was actually underwater. The Finns and I worked out a way to hold your control signal as a recording, then we received the signal in free space and smuggled it to the surface, fooling the enemy into assisting in the construction of the receiver. We were forced to construct it in the middle of one of their largest army bases. Much of the camp brass was here thinking they'd see a demonstration of a matter transmitter . . ."

"And we've certainly given them that. They got shot up, and so the base doesn't have anyone to give it orders, and perhaps we've got a minute or two to ourselves."

"Yessir."

"Can we get out of here?"

"Maybe. If we can steal enough trucks from their motor pool." I nodded toward George. "This man can show you where it is on a map of the base."

"Roberts! Figure out where it is, take a couple of squads, and get those trucks!" He pointed to Kaplan. "You there! Stand by the transmitter and explain what's going on to the troops as they come through." The brigadier turned back to me. "What about help from the locals?"

"They should be hitting the Guardians—the enemy—on the planet and on the satellite Vapaus, a lot of little dustups, right now. Everything acting as mutual diversions."

"Very well."

Suddenly I spotted men pulling what looked like a midget howitzer behind them in the receiver cage. I nudged George and pointed. He finished up quickly with Roberts and took the rather bewildered-looking Tommies in tow, leading them to the courtyard.

The brigadier watched it all rather phlegmatically. "It looks quite a bit like we're in a right old mess. By the way. Brigadier Taylor, British Army."

"Sir."

A loud *crump* came from outside, and a moment later an ear-splitting series of explosions came from the south end of the camp. "There goes the ammo dump, I expect." Taylor said.

"They'll hit the armory next. Then work over the barracks and the rest of the camp," I said.

Another series of blasts came from the east, a sharper, staccato series of reports. Taylor looked up sharply. "That's not the shells from our artillery."

One of the Kennedy troops came rushing in from the courtyard. "The camp's perimeter fence just got blown up, a long section right in front of us!"

We all rushed out into the rapidly filling courtyard. It was a disorganized mob. Taylor grabbed the first officer he saw and yelled, "Clear these men out of here! Blow the locks off the hangars and put the troops there. We need this road clear! Lieutenant Roberts is coming back any moment with the trucks we're riding out of here. Fast!"

He strode out into the courtyard, followed by a small crowd that included myself. The fence was down all right, across maybe 100 meters of the perimeter. Men carrying weapons were running toward us. One of them carried a flag—

New Finnish flag! "Hold your fire!" I yelled. "That's our side!" I found my gun in my hand, reholstered it, and rushed out to meet them. I came up to a thin, wiry man of about fifty dressed in a worn old uniform. He saluted as some of his troops gathered in a little knot around the two of us. "It is that we do have trucks and a train," he began in very laborious English.

"I speak some Finnish," I cut in.

He breathed a sigh of relief and switched languages. "Good. We have some trucks and there is a train waiting on its tracks about twelve kilometers from here. We can take some on the trucks and get the others on the train. We heard from the higher-ups that there would be a lot of soldiers here that would need to be evacuated."

"That's for sure. Come this way." I took him to Taylor and explained the situation to the Brigadier.

Taylor nodded and pulled a small communicator out of his belt. "Freiling. Get all the troops you can moving through the break in the fence. The locals are ready to move you." He shut off the communicator and turned to me. "Ask him how many troops he can move."

The Finn understood and answered in English before I could translate. "We can do about two million."

"Two million!"

"Thousand! I'm meaning two thousand. Sorry."

"If you had more lorries, could you handle more troops?" Taylor asked.

"Lorries? Oh, yes, trucks. Sure, all you want."

"Good." He talked into the comm unit again. "Major Kavanos! Yes, I can hear you, too. Now get some of your men together and follow Roberts to the motor pool. Steal as many lorries as you can. Load them up and head for the break in the fence. Take another detail to make sure we can hold the motor pool. If we lose it, the party's over."

Before he could put his comm unit away, it beeped for attention. "Yes. I see. Well, keep shooting back, try and figure out where they are, and see if our artillery can take them out." He spoke to me. "These Guardians have finally gotten organized enough to start shooting back. We'd better get back to the courtyard."

It was bedlam. The transmitter was still pouring out troops and there just wasn't room for the ones that were already there. Taylor shook his head. "If they have the sense to hit their own camp with artillery, we're sitting ducks."

The first of the trucks was struggling into the courtyard, inching past the masses of troops. Taylor shouldered his way through the throng and jumped up on the running board for a moment. "You! Stop this truck, load it up right here and back it out of here! You men in the brown berets!"

"Sir!" their officer said.

"Get your men into that truck and out of the way!"

"SIR!"

Taylor grabbed a US Army sergeant by the collar. "You! You're now in charge of crowd control as of now. Get this madhouse organized, smartly!" The sergeant got to it.

"You there! Get the road clear!" He pulled out his communicator. "Taylor here. Attention all officers in command. Get your troops into orderly columns and as close to the edge of the courtyard as possible. We need the roadway clear. Get dispersed. One good big shell could wipe us all out. Corporal Kaplan, if you would be so good as to relay those orders to the troops coming through."

There was a good sized fire-fight to the northeast of the courtyard. The artillery, the 107th, was still pounding the hell out of the rest of the camp. The courtyard was covered in heavy smoke every now and then as the wind kept shifting. I made my way to the center of the courtyard, where the 107th had set its guns. George was still there, working the map with cool precision, his mouth thin and determined. The howitzers were kicking up the clay of the yard, and dust covered the men. George especially had been covered in a dirty white pallor.

"George!" The guns thundered again, preventing conversation for long seconds. "How are we doing?"

He shook a layer of dust off the map and indicated parts of the map covered with blood-red cross hatching, representing about two thirds of the camp. "We've been bracketing the whole place block by block, and this is what's, well—gone. Not much left but the mess tents and some of the barracks."

One of the artillery men tapped me on the shoulder. "Are we to expect Brigadier Taylor to send out"—WHAM!—"patrols to secure the areas we've hit?" A shell was fired in the middle of his sentence, but he went on as if it wasn't there.

"No, I doubt it. We don't want to hold this ground, just get the hell out."

"Very good, sir."

"Sergeant—can you spare me Mr. Prigot here?"

"Oh, I expect"—WHAM!—"so, sir. We've got the hang of the map now. One of my lads can fill in."

"C'mon, George. We've got to get you out of that uniform."

"Mmm? Oh, yeah."

The sergeant looked over George more closely. "That what the other side looks like, sir?"

"Yes," I said.

"I thought so. Bit of infiltration?"

"Something like that," George said, his voice devoid of any emotion, as if his insides were frozen. I pulled him to his feet and we shoved our way through the throng to the receiver's hangar.

"We'll get you changed in my room," I said.

The crowd inside had thinned out a bit, and Kaplan seemed to have things more or less under control. As we came in, he was giving yet another outfit a rundown on the situation.

I waited until he was done and asked, "How many more to go?"

He glanced down at a long list that was rapidly getting dog-eared. "Let's see—that last group was from the Army of the Sixth Republic, the French. After them—just about half way through, about forty or so to go."

"Make sure this thing is blown to hell and rubble as soon as the last ones step through."

"Already seen to it, Commander. Oh, and there's several shipments of weapons to hand on to the locals toward the end."

"Good. They're right outside, ready to take 'em, I'm sure."

"Yessir." With a *QUEEP* and a flash another group popped into existence on the receiver stage. Kaplan got back to his work. "All right, who are you people? Europa Federals? Right. Now listen up, fellas, and those of you who speak English pass it on to your buddies. Okay. Things have gotten screwed over but good . . ."

We left him to it and arrived at the room a few of the boys had made soundproof so I could sleep nights. I shut the door on the war outside and we sat down on my bunk.

George let out a deep sigh. "My God. How did I get into this?"

"George. You can get out now. You've paid your dues. Go. Take off. A man can't be expected to calmly go on killing his own people."

"No, Jeff. Or Terrance, or MacKenzie, or whoever you are."

"Call me Mac."

"Mac—don't you see? Yeah, I've maybe, maybe paid my dues for that twelve-year-old. Except she's still dead. But *how many more did I help kill*? I don't care how long I worked with the guys I've betrayed. They're *killers*. Murderers. How many more people were murdered by the cheap guns I fixed and the machines I designed? If I go my whole life, I can't pay that back."

He stared into space for a moment. Suddenly he shook himself and started peeling off the heavy uniform. "Let's get moving." He changed into some of my clothes—a poor but serviceable fit—and motioned me toward the door. "Let's get the hell out of here and see what's going on."

We walked past the receiver as Kaplan was explaining things to a 101st Airborne Special Operations Commando Unit and went on into the courtyard.

That sergeant must have whipped someone into shape. The trucks were rolling without any trouble, loading up with men and women from I don't know how many military outfits. It seemed like every member state had sent some sort of force to New Finland. About the only thing missing were the Swiss Guards from the Vatican.

The 107th pounded away at the rest of the camp, but the smoke from the fires they had set was already too thick to see if they were doing much besides stirring the rubble.

I spotted Taylor in the middle of the courtyard, talking into his communicator again. "Taylor here. Fine work so far. Keep them moving on." He turned to us as George and I came over. "The Finns have gotten the first troops into their train." He looked over the organized chaos of what used to be an army base and shook his head. "We are going to come through this. Amazing. You and your Finnish friends have done quite well."

Army bases aren't designed to be safe from attacks from inside themselves. We had wiped out the majority of the commanding officers in the first thirty seconds. The first warning most of the enemy had was the destruction of their own ammo dump. I didn't want to calculate how many men had been slaughtered in the sneak attack, how many had died without any hope of defending themselves. The landing field was a cratered ruin, and the comm center was wrecked, the entire camp brought low and dead.

Kaplan trotted up to me and said "Get ready for a loud noise."

"Is the receiver about to—" BLAM!!!

"It sure as hell is!" Kaplan said. "Good God almighty, I am never going to tell anyone what's going on or where they are again. I did a *lifetime's* worth today."

Trucks were starting to come back from their first trips to the rail line, picking up more men. Taylor spoke into his comm unit again. "All commanders. Lorries on the second trip. Pick a road and keep moving! Just stay in comm range. But disperse. If the enemy knocks out the rail line, let's have some eggs in another basket."

More than just trucks started appearing from the motor pool. Jeeps, half tracks, even a giant dump truck. They all stopped off, filled up, and moved out through the gap in the perimeter fence.

Random sizzling noises from high-energy lasers and an occasional ricochet were the only hint of any real fighting.

We had done it. We had actually gotten those troops here, and out of here, against all the odds. And they were going to make it, would survive at least long enough to fight.

The trucks rolled on.

Chapter Nine

The trucks ran, rolled, flowed and ebbed, their electric motors humming as they carried the soldiers away from the ruined camp.

Taylor and I watched the procession as the crowd of soldiers shrunk from thousands to seven or eight hundred. Still there was no real opposition, and the Guardian assault we expected didn't come and didn't come.

Taylor had held back one intact unit; the U.S. Army 1st Battalion, 75th Infantry, a ranger unit. They were posted on the rooftops and along the outer perimeter of the area we controlled. Taylor looked from the rangers on the roof to the crowd on the ground, shook his head dolefully, and looked back toward one of the rangers on the top of the receiver's hangar.

He extracted a rather shabby pipe and got started lighting it as he spoke. "When their reinforcements come, we will be caught with our trousers down. We've got a mob, not a fighting unit."

Except for the rangers, the soldiers left behind were stragglers, cut off from their units. Many units that had gotten away were split up. Even once they got away, they had no idea where they were going.

"Maybe they won't come before we get away," I said. "The Finns are supposed to have sabotaged most of the enemy forces by now. According to Tempkin's plan, all the Guardians are out of it for the moment."

Taylor didn't move his gaze from the ranger as he spoke. "No battle ever went according to plan. Have you ever heard of the American raid on the Ploesti oil fields in the Second World War? Tree-top bombing. One of the first times it was tried. But all but one flight of bombers missed the target and had to double back to find it. Hundreds of planes came in over the targets from three different directions at once. Sheer hell. The defending commander, on the ground, thought it had been planned that way; all he could do was watch what he thought was perfectly planned orchestration. No one in the air had the foggiest idea what was going on."

"So what happened?"

"The Americans lost over half the planes." Taylor was quiet for a long time. "Someone out there"—he pointed vaguely with the stem of the pipe—"went ahead and attacked early, or got caught after curfew and was shot full of truth serum. Someone failed to sabotage something. One of the Guardian officers wonders what happened to his friend at this camp and sent a plane over when he couldn't get through on the phone. They'll be here. With amazing luck, we might be out of here by the time they arrive."

"Then what?" I asked.

"I have no idea."

The sun crawled toward the horizon, flirted with the tops of the strange New Finnish trees at the end of the clearing, and slowly left us in the dark. There were only a few hundred of us left by then.

Suddenly Taylor's communicator beeped. I could hear the tiny voice piping out of the little speaker. "Sir, they're here! I'm at about 500 meters due east of you. Spotted them on infrared. I count ten, no, here's a second line coming around the bend. Twenty vehicles, including maybe 10 tanks."

"How much time do we have?"

"Five, maybe ten minutes to the camp, then whatever it takes for them to find us."

"Which won't be long. Keep me posted."

"Bayet!" Taylor called.

"Sir!" A tall, gangly looking woman with frizzy black hair threatening to escape from her helmet jogged up. Lieutenant Colonel Louise Bayet, commanding 1st Battalion, 75th Infantry.

"Louise, a skirmish line 100 yards east of here, if you please. Direct your snipers to expect targets from that point."

"Sir!" She got to it and within moments her troops were scrambling to new positions.

Taylor got back to his communicator. "Roberts! Get everything you can this way, and get all your men aboard a truck, including yourself. I want you here in two minutes. In three minutes I want you leading a line of trucks over the western horizon."

He cut off the little radio and simply hollered. "All ranks not of the 75th Infantry. The last trucks are on their way. *Get on them*! If there is no room in them for you, run like hell on foot toward the west! Do everything you can to stay with your unit. Good luck!"

I spoke to Taylor as a new flurry of activity began. "Brigadier, with your permission, I'd like to stay behind and do what I can."

"As you wish."

"Thank you, sir." I grabbed an orphaned laser/projectile rifle and scrambled to join a group of rangers headed to the east.

One of them grabbed my arm and said "Hold it a minute. Saunders is about to—" BLAM! A stretch of ground 15 meters long suddenly jumped into the air and left a trench behind. "Line of burrow mines. They dig themselves a hole and make it bigger with a shaped charge. Put 'em in a row and they dig a trench like the one we're jumping into." He was a burly, big, deep-brown black man with a gentle, almost childish face. "You're Commander Larson, aren't you?"

"Yup."

"Thought so. No one else around here with a good reason for being out of uniform."

"Krabnowski!" Bayet called.

"Ma'am!" my trench mate yelled back.

"Spotter says between those buildings, three trucks coming in about 30 seconds."

"Yo." Krabnowski loaded a mean-looking clip of ten

centimeter rockets into a shoulder-held launcher. He dug the stock of the launcher into the lip of the trench and peered through the sight. The first of the trucks appeared, but he let it come. The second came through the gap, and he ignored it. The third poked its nose in and he fired straight for the engine. The rocket whizzed dead in, and the whole cab went up in a sheet of flame. The third truck stopped dead, bottling up the line of retreat for the others. Krabnowski slammed two rockets into the lead truck, and another pair into the middle one. Screaming men leapt from the burning wrecks and tried to run, only to be shot down by the rangers in the trench and on the roof tops.

And by me.

"Krab! Tanks coming, left of where the trucks were."

"Okay, Bob." Krabnowski slapped in a load of thin, needle-pointed armor-piercing rockets into the launcher. "How many?"

"Don't know. Sal said at least five, then she was busy running. S'getting hot out there."

"Sure hope she makes it back," Krabnowski said.

A furious explosion shook the ground a few meters behind us, throwing dirt and rocks into the trenches, filling the air with dust.

"Here they come . . ."

The tanks appeared through the smoke, moving ponderously across the field of battle. Krab didn't fool with trying to bottle them up. He fired and hit the lead tank. It kept rolling straight for us, the main gun's barrel swiveling toward us.

He fired into both the right and left treads and they blew off, but the tank kept coming, rolling off the treads onto its wheels. I shot one, two, three of the infantrymen trotting toward us behind the tank, and brought them down, and the tank came on, with the gun's muzzle pointing straight at us.

Krab fired one last shot, squeezing the trigger gently to hold his aim. The rocket hit where the gun barrel joined the turret, where the armor was hinged and complicated, weaker.

The barrel blew almost clean off the tank in a roaring double explosion, twisting around in a crazy angle, and hanging uselessly bent to one side.

"I'll be good and goddamned," Krab said. "I set off the shell right in the barrel."

Another round smashed into the ground behind us, even closer this time. I could hear Bayet's voice. "Pull back! Pull back! Back to the courtyard!" We didn't have to be asked twice. With the tanks literally at our heels, we ran like hell for the courtyard.

The last truck full of League troops was rolling out. Roberts was standing on the tail gate, not looking at all happy about leaving. Taylor watched it go, not looking at all happy about staying. "We bought as much time as we could, Commander Larson. Everyone but the 75th got away. Now we find out how the Guardians treat their prisoners."

Bayet stood watching for the tanks. "And how long the Guards can hold them." That made me stop and think. Generals and Brigadiers aren't supposed to let themselves get captured. Maybe he didn't expect to stay captured long.

Or maybe he had gambled and lost.

We used one of the sheets from Darrow's bed as a white flag.

I felt ready to cry.

A march under heavy guard that lasted half the night brought the captured League troops to another camp, where we were loaded aboard trucks and driven off into the night. About ten hours after the last shot had been fired, we arrived at what seemed to be a former civilian minimum security prison. I wondered if the Guardians had let the Finnish criminals loose on the population or had simply shot them.

They shoved us in two to a cell and collected dogtags. I didn't have one, of course. They demanded my name and I didn't see any point in giving a phony one. I hoped George

Prigot had had the sense to ditch his tag and give them an alias. I got a cell with Krabnowski. He was friendly enough, but I felt very, very alone.

The day had been a pretty depressing success. The League troops had gotten here, and had flattened an enemy base. But men on both sides were dead, and any day that ends in prison is not all good.

We were there about an hour or so when a precise looking corporal unlocked our cell door and yelled "Larson! Come with me!"

"Lucky me. See you, Krab."

"Good luck, Commander."

The corporal was joined by a surly private at our cell door. The two of them took me into what looked as if it had once been the prison's visiting room. It was a large room with a glass wall dividing it in half. All the original furniture had been stripped out of it, and all that replaced it on my side of the glass was a bare wooden chair, spotlit by fierce, bright lights. There were no other lights on my side of the glass.

A strange device, a set of articulated probes of some sort, sat in the corner. It was a collection of well-elbowed arms that looked like an upended two-meter spider on wheels. Just the sort of thing the Guardians would leave lurking in the darkness.

On the other side of the glass wall I could see nothing but a pair of silhouettes shown up against other bright lights that shone straight into my face. I was shoved into the chair and tied down rather sloppily.

"Let's get straight to it, Larson." The voice came, flat and tinny, over a speaker in the ceiling. Dazzled by the bright lights, I couldn't even tell which of the silhouettes was doing the talking. "We had reports a few days ago that a Jefferson Darrow was to perform some sort of experiment at Demeter today. A Colonel Bradhurst, of Intelligence, was working on a theory that you were Darrow, and you match Darrow's description so closely we won't even bother with fingerprints. The two of you are one and the same.

Now then, we are going to ask you some questions, and we're going to get the answers.

"How did those League troops get here, and how many are there?"

"Terrance MacKenzie Larson, Commander, Republic of Kennedy Navy, four niner eight two four five."

He sighed. "Don't play games with us. We don't play by your rules. And if you want to play by some limp-wristed antique like the Geneva Convention, I understand that back when anyone took it seriously, a soldier captured out of uniform was legally a spy, and it was considered traditional to shoot him."

Another voice, the other silhouette, spoke for the first time. It was more tired, more sympathetic, far gentler. "Commander, please, let's be reasonable. Name, rank and serial number we already have. You and I both know that we have ways of getting the answers, and I promise you, we don't waste time making them pleasant. So: How many troops, and where did they come from?"

"Terrance MacKenzie—"

"Yeah, yeah. We get the idea," the first voice cut it. "Now knock off the hero routine. If I decide to do it, in ten minutes I could have you wishing you *had* been shot as a spy."

I didn't reply. I was too scared.

"Last chance, Commander."

I said nothing.

"Okay. We start experimenting. Corporal, if you please?"

I heard some vague noises behind me, and suddenly I was jabbed in the butt with a needle.

In a few seconds, my head started to swim and my eyes lost their focus.

The ROK Navy had put a lot of emphasis on resisting interrogation, up to the point of actually using truth drugs on the midshipmen. The teachers had shown us the ways of resisting, and I prayed now that I remembered them.

Even as the drug started to affect me, I began *using* it to defeat itself. A "truth drug" doesn't make you more truthful; it makes you more literal-minded and passive, more open to suggestion. So I *told* myself to be passive, to ignore the outside world, to listen to nothing, to *hear* nothing. I told myself to climb into its navel and stay there for the duration. I could feel the drug making me helpless, and I made one last try to hide the truth behind the dreams and the tortuous web of free association my forebrain constructed.

The teacher wanted me to recite the preamble to Kennedy's Constitution. I shifted my feet and began, but it came out wrong, it wasn't right at all—

You are old, Father William, the young man said,
And your hair has become very white,
And yet you incessantly stand on your head—
Do you think, at your age, it is right . . .

The class devolved into a chorus of laughs and catcalls, and the teacher, suddenly wearing a grey uniform, slapped me hard. . . .

. . . My lips were dry and cracked. Someone was trying to tell me a riddle, but they kept giving the answer and wanting me to reply with the question, "How many men can fit in a suitcase?" But somehow, try as I might, I couldn't say it . . .

. . . I thought at first the world had gotten bigger, but then I remembered that I was a child. I walked down the long hallways of the hospital where Mom and Dad were doctors, looking for them. I wondered why all the beds were empty, because they had been full of sick people before. I touched my face—I had a surgical mask on. No one could recognize me with that on. That made me feel good. No one I didn't like would know me with the mask on. I walked on and on up and down the barren hospital, but it was empty through and through. I got more and more tired, and finally I sat down in a corner to cry. After a while, I noticed sharp little footsteps coming near me. I looked up and saw an ugly old man in a grey uniform. I got so scared I tried to wish him away. He changed into a pretty nurse, and I looked up and saw it was Joslyn, come to tell me to be quiet and not say anything, just be quiet and it would be all right . . .

. . . But where were Mom and Dad?

I sat in the ejection seat, waiting for the thing to fire so I could get out of it, that way if no other. Let the next trainee into the damned thing. But the control booth seemed to be having some trouble with the gear. They were rolling in some massive piece of test equipment. I knew then that I'd be stuck there most of the day, and decided to quit complaining, button my lip, and wait it out. I tried to reach and shut off the intercom but my arms were stuck to the god damned ejection seat . . .

. . . seat? The hard lines of the glassed-in control booth shifted, blurred. The ejection seat shape-changed; it was a wooden chair and I was tied to it. Only the test equipment stayed the same, and I recognized it as the wheeled spider-thing that had been sitting in the corner of the interrogation room. Now the arms were unfolded and surrounded my head. At the end of each arm was a blunt-ended probe and a red guide lightbeam, the beams pointed at my head. I had a splitting headache and my nose was filled with mucus and blood.

A man with bags under his eyes and uncombed hair stood in a rumpled uniform, watching as technicians fiddled with the machinery. He spoke, and I recognized the voice of my second interrogator. "It seems as if you've given us a very long night." He nodded at the spider machine. "While you were coming to, we injected a very small, in fact microscopic, device into your bloodstream. It floated up into your brain. This oversize hat rack is here to get it aligned *exactly* where we want it. Oh, don't worry, the thing is small enough to go straight through any blood vessel, and it will simply dissolve in about nineteen hours or so. You won't have any physical brain damage. On the other hand, you won't enjoy the next few hours. I expect you've heard of direct brain stimulation? Well, we've refined it a little."

He turned his back on me and walked away.

A moment later he rejoined his partner behind the glass wall. The first voice came over the speaker, heavy with exhaustion and annoyance. "In a minute, I assure you that in about one minute you will want to beg for the chance to answer our questions—but you may have a little trouble saying so."

"He's telling the truth, Commander. Before we go any further, once again, where did those men come from?"

"Terrance Mac—" The world exploded.

My hands, my eyes, my brain, burst into billowing sheets of flame. The world was pain, and fire. The room roared with flames and gave off thick, stinking smoke. The guards, standing at rigid attention, burned brightly, the fire sweeping up and down their uniforms.

I looked down and saw my chest aflame, and the smell of roasting meat leapt into my awareness. My *eyes* burned, and burned, and I could feel the lids wither away with the awful, searing, killing, heat—

And it stopped.

I stopped screaming without realizing I had begun. I flopped back against the chair, whimpering. I was unharmed. In body.

"What we can do once, we can do many times. The device in your brain has been carefully placed where it will stimulate the part of you that feels *fire*, and *pain*." The first man's voice had a murderous pleasure in it now. "Tell us what we want to know, or you will *burn* and *burn* until you wish the fire was real so it could hurt you, kill you, and the pain could end. But it can't end, not ever, unless you answer us. Where did the troops come from?"

Maybe I wouldn't have answered even if I had been capable of speech. As it was, there was silence.

And then there was flame.

It shouldn't have been as bad, since I knew what to expect, but it was worse, far, far, worse.

My insides were on fire. I could feel my heart, my lungs, my guts and stomach shrivel up into cinders in the heat.

My legs were twin slabs of roasting agony, pulsing shafts of pain that should have ended in death.

Inside my skull, the fires raged, my brain and eyes reduced to black cinders that burned on and on after they should have been ashes—

And stopped. The interrogators must have said something, but I didn't hear them. My hindbrain was in charge, screaming in terror and demanding I escape! survive! But I was tied to the chair—

And the world burned anew. Agony gave me a manic strength and with a convulsive spasm I snapped the chair to splinters. The knots that held me unraveled and I jumped from the chair, screaming.

I stumbled and fell to the floor, landing on my hands, or what my pain told me must be the blackened stumps of hands, and the impact was new and more violent pain.

I cried out, screamed, yelled, moaned, constantly without stopping for breath.

I rolled to my feet and saw the guards, twin towers of flames, moving slowly, so slowly, toward me.

Snarling in animal hatred, I sprang toward them. I grabbed the first by his throat and *pulled*. His neck snapped under my manic strength. I pulled his laser away from his corpse and played it over the other guard, sweeping the beam back and forth over his body again and again as he fell, wanting to know that one thing, at least, truly burned.

Two grenades on his belt clip went off, throwing the body into the ceiling and smashing a hole in the floor.

I turned and fired through the glass wall. The interrogators dove for the floor, but I followed them down with the beam. The beam sliced a junction box, and the lights, which I saw but dimly through the flame that engulfed all, flared and died.

Clutching the gun, I staggered through the door I had come in, and came upon another flaming soldier. He died where he stood. I ripped his laser from his holster and tore the grenades from his belt, wondering that holding them in my burning hands didn't set them off.

Two more guards, and I blindly cut them down.

The flames went on and on, pulsing and flaring across all I saw or felt. By now I was bathed in sweat, and the *sweat* burned, my sweaty clothes burned. Blood from a cut on my hand burned.

Lurching and screaming, barely knowing or caring what I did, I caromed off the walls, stumbling down the corridor. Something moved and I fired at it, not stopping to see if I hit it. The corridor grew longer and longer, a hideous tunnel of flaming oranges and reds, like the monstrous gullet of some hell-spawned nightmonster that had swallowed me whole.

Something was in my way, wouldn't let me pass. The cellblock door, I realized. I first thought to hold a grenade against it and blow it up, but I remembered in time that it would kill me to try it.

I had to get out, escape. I thought of the laser, and used it to slice clean through the lock. The door swung open. A guard was on the other side, in my way, on fire and reaching for his gun. I killed him with mine.

I saw another locked door in front of me. Burn it open, like the others? But it was already burning. But it might be the way out! I had to get out! I cut through the lock.

"Hey, are you crazy—Jesus Christ, it's that guy who was with us!"

"Never mind that, he cracked the damn cell block!"

They were coming toward me, so I am aimed the gun at them—

—There was a blow to the back of my neck and I fell to the ground, cringing at the contact with my seared flesh. Why didn't it stop? Dimly I knew I was still conscious, but I gave it up and writhed in my pain. It was too much, why didn't it stop, just let me *die*? But still I heard the voices, they wouldn't go away.

"He fried the guard! Grab the lasers and the grenades and let's break this place!"

"Open up over here!"

"Use the keys, you pyro!"

"Go! Go! There's dead guards all over! Move it, while the power's off."

"That's Larson! My God, what did they do to him?"

I didn't care. Pain is exhausting. It will not go away, let you rest. My body was twitching, quaking, every muscle straining. I couldn't faint, but I could sleep. And dream.

Of fire.

I awoke in the middle of a cold night, delightfully void of warmth. My legs, feet, arms, were masses of cramps and spasms, but they were whole, and wonderfully cold.

Hands lifted me, and carried me, gave me over to other hands. Guns and lasers fired unimportantly behind me, and I was carefully placed in the splendidly stinging cold of a metal truckbed.

Chapter Ten

"I said put him down, not drop him!"

"Easy there."

"He's got the shakes again."

Voices. Light and darkness, too indistinct to be called sight. Skin rubbed raw and tired. Muscles in knots. Thirst.

"Hey, his eyes moved. I think he's waking up."

"Good. Then maybe I can ask some questions." It was a voice with a gravelly accent.

They were talking about me. A glass of water was put to my lips and I drank automatically. Then my thirst awoke and I gulped at the water frantically.

"Enough for now," said the gravelly voice. An arm in a white sleeve drew the glass away from me. "Strong enough to talk?"

"Ehhhh—yes."

"Good. But we will go slow."

"What happened to me?"

A face formed out of thin air at the end of the arm. The browns and greens of uniforms, rough-hewn figures inside them, came into being behind that face, scuffling their feet and looking at me.

A smile. "I was about to be asking you. I think our Guardian friends have been using their brain machine, yes?"

"Yes." That was it, they had made me think of—fire flame forever and I burned, the flames grew in my mind and I bit into the blood of my lips to quench them to put the smoke and stink away from me—

—SLAP "Stop!" SLAP "Stop thinking about it! It is the brain implants again. The implant itself, that is gone by now, but men have laid where you are and died of the memory. They show people death, and no man can see that long and live."

A sting in my arm was a syringe. "A tranquilizer. It will relax." I drew in a deep, shuddering breath, nodded, and thought of cool and quiet.

"If you want to pay them for the implant, first you must rest." Another glass of water at my lips, and I tried to lift my hand to it. A restraining strap held my arm in place. "Relax. Rest. You have earned it. Later, I will teach you how to do the forgetting of these things."

A long time later, I awoke with a ravenous appetite. It was the middle of the long New Finnish day, by the look of the light streaming into the sunny room through expansive bay windows. All was white, or golden sunlight, or pastel green in my room, calm and protective and warm. I lay back in bed, thinking.

Thinking of two things, one very good, the other a torture. It was great to feel the direct responsibility for five thousand lives off my shoulders. Now they were here, and their own agents. I could take a back seat in the war now; the pros could take over.

But this was balanced against viciousness, the two teetering on the point of a cruel knife, each rising and falling in my mind.

Yesterday, I had killed at least a dozen men.

There were a dozen families somewhere, waiting for the call, the letter, the visitor in uniform, that would tell them their son or brother was dead, that a stranger had killed him.

I had learned why people shouldn't be soldiers.

The door swung open to fresh hot coffee, buttermilk pancakes, sausages, and the doctor who had been with me before. "A few of your army friends said they were from your world. They made a breakfast they said you would like. Lots, isn't it?"

It *was* a lot, but that was fine with me.

I gobbled down everything in sight. It seemed like months since I had eaten, and my stomach wanted to make up for lost time. Finally, I chased one last sausage around the plate, and leaned back with a mug of the best coffee on three planets. "Feeling better?"

"Fantastic."

"Good. Now, then, brace yourself. I am going to do something that will upset you, frighten you. Try to be ready." He pulled a cigarette lighter out of his pocket. It was an ornate, heavy thing, the color of dull silver. He pulled back his thumb and sparked it.

Fire!

I stared into the flame, fascinated. It turned from a friendly yellow to a blood-curdling red, and it grew. It leapt from the tiny lighter and licked the ceiling, poured down to burn the sheets and burn at my legs, my arms, shriveling them down to—

SLAP!

My cheek stung suddenly, and the burning of the sheet vanished as suddenly as the lighter's flame. "That, my friend, will happen whenever you see flame, or fire of any kind. A candle, a campfire, a rocket blast, perhaps even the beam of a laser or seeing the Sun in the sky. The Guardians, they like using fire-thoughts. It may go away, it may not. The Guardians abandon those they use the brain implant on, because they are usually insane. Many are brought to me. Your general made a question of our people and brought you here. You are strong, and have been well trained, they tell me, and you escaped early on in the torture. So with luck, it is not so bad. We can hope.

"But it will take a little time, perhaps a day or so, perhaps a week, or a month. If you do not take the time until I think you are cured, then you will die, and it will be the most horrible death I can be thinking of. You will frighten yourself to death. I have been able to cure those who did not die that way first.

"So. We hypnotize you. Lean back, relax, and look-look at the ray of sunlight coming in the window. See how the tree branch outside makes it jump and dance, up and back, up and back . . ."

"And up and out of it . . . Good! You have the luck to be a *very* cooperative subject. Tomorrow we work more." The little man rose to leave. At the door, he stopped, turned around, and smiled almost shyly. "And, for all here . . . thank you for all you have done."

There were twice-daily sessions with the doctor for the next three days, and in the back of my mind, a flame-colored monster gradually lost his hold on my soul.

Beyond that, not much happened to me. I was left with a lot of time for thinking, and a lot to think about.

I worried about the Guardians reinforcing. They had certainly been hit hard when the League troops showed up. It hadn't just been the League forces, though. The Finns had revolted all over the planet, and had done so with at least short-term success in many places. The enemy had his hands full with them.

The dispersed League troops were engaged in various commando raids, and were having good results, according to what reports we got.

But it would all go for nothing if the Guardians could reinforce and we could not. As long as the anti-ship missile system lurked in the outer reaches of this solar system, cutting New Finland off from her friends, we had lost.

The converse was true: as soon as the missiles were out of commission, the League would have won. Not much was known about the Guardians, but it seemed clear they controlled only two star systems; New Finland's and that of their base planet, Capital, wherever that was. It might be a long and bloody battle, but if our side cracked the anti-ship missiles, then the League's tremendously greater resources could be brought to bear, and that would be it.

The missile system. That was the key. Obviously, it had to be controlled from some central command station. Otherwise the unmanned missiles couldn't be warned of scheduled arrivals of Guardian ships. They had to be under negative control, told *not* to shoot at certain targets. Unless the missiles were programmed otherwise beforehand, they would go after anything they spotted. The speed of light was too slow for any other mode of control; if the missiles waited for a command from base that might take an hour or a day at speed-of-light, the target ship would have time to spot the missiles, defend against them, maneuver, or blip into C^2 again and get away.

No, it had to be a hair trigger, negative control system. So there had to be a central control point.

Take it, control it, use it to deactivate the missiles, and the war was won.

Should we fail to take it the war was lost.

We would lose even if we simply destroyed it. The Guardians had to have had the sense to set things up so they could signal the missiles from outside this star system. Even if the signal took a month to cross the void, they could still time the entrance of a ship carrying a replacement local control device. Until the replacement was ready, the missiles would still hit anything that moved without prior warning.

I was sure the Guards couldn't get away with having only an extra-system controller, and no control system inside the New Finnish solar system. There had to be some way of defending against jamming, phony signals, or malfunctions.

So far, my logic seemed good. Now all I had to figure out was the location of the control station, and the house of cards would be complete, my logic-castle launched into the air . . .

Castle in the air. It hit me.

Vapaus. The control system had to be on Vapaus. And that meant trouble, maybe disaster.

I found my pants and left my sickbed. I had to speak with Brigadier Taylor. I managed to escape the nurse on duty with only a minor skirmish.

Someone had loaned me a set of ROK army uniform fatigues. which fit me as well as most clothes I borrow. Twenty minutes after leaving the doctor's house, I was cooling my heels outside Taylor's office, in a requisitioned school house. My heels were easy to cool, as were my ankles. My borrowed pants didn't make it past my shins.

After a shorter wait than I had any right to expect, I was ushered into the Brigadier's presence.

We got through the pleasantries quickly enough and I got to the point. I ran through my train of thought about the existence and nature of the missile control station. None of it was news to him, nor did I expect it to be; he was paid to figure these things out, and indeed he rather gently pointed out that the planning staff had come to the same conclusions before the League forces had stepped into the transmitter.

"I thought as much, sir, but it can't hurt to confirm these things."

He nodded politely and his hands moved back toward the paperwork I had interrupted. "Was there anything else, Commander?"

"Well, sir, I know where the control center is. Or at least where it ought to be."

That got his attention back. "Where?"

"Vapaus."

"I see. Why ought it to be there?"

"Well, sir. Look at it this way. If we've got the nature of the control center figured out properly, that means that, in a last ditch, catastrophic situation for the Guardians, all they have to do is knock out the control center and sit back and wait for reinforcements—and only their side could reinforce."

"And Vapaus is a big, lovely target you could track from any inhabited point on the planet. Even the smallest ship could carry a bomb that could crack it like an egg. Clever."

"One other thing, sir. I think we were meant to figure this out."

"Eh?"

"So we won't be tempted to try and take Vapaus. We're supposed to realize that, if we attack, four thousand would be killed the moment they realized we were searching for the control center there."

"My dear boy, we've *already* retaken Vapaus. The inhabitants of the satellite overcame the garrison there the same day we arrived. They were always capable of knocking out the garrison. It was the fear that the Guardians would reinvade that deterred them. When hell broke loose all over the planet, the Vapaus leaders decided the risk was lowered enough to try it. I understand the biggest problem the Finns had was keeping the prisoners alive. The guards tended to look the other way when lynch mobs appeared."

"Then I respectfully submit that Vapaus, and our only hope of winning, are both in the greatest danger. The moment one Guardian commander feels his side has its back to the wall, he will destroy Vapaus."

That gave him pause. "If what you say is correct, the only chance we've got is to knock out every remaining enemy aerospace field capable of hitting Vapaus, before they can launch that attack."

"While signaling Vapaus to begin a very cautious search for the control station. It could be hidden in something the size of a broom closet."

"True. Commander, my respect for the League of Planets Survey Service has just gone up yet another notch. I think I'd better get my staff to work on this theory."

"I could be wrong, sir."

"Yes, you could be. But I'd be a damned fool to assume it. You've shown a remarkable knack for staying alive so far, Commander. That requires luck, or clear thinking, or both. I'm inclined to believe it's your thinking. If you can find your own way out, I think I'd better have a good think myself."

He was extracting his pipe as I left the room.

Taylor was a good commander. That much he had proved in the evacuation of Camp Demeter. He had chosen the 1st Battalion, 75th Infantry to cover the retreat of the rest of the force. The 75th was the lightest armed force, and, as rangers, were superbly trained in individual initiative and independent action. I think Taylor had expected the 75th to be captured, and had expected they'd break out.

The speed with which they exploited my very random attack showed just how ready they were. Ten minutes after

I burned through that cell door, troops were already capturing trucks and nearly all the prisoners were freed.

Four days later, well planned raids against the Guardians' supplies and help from the Finns had almost completely re-equipped the 75th, and all of it done so quietly that our base was still unknown to the enemy.

Taylor's staff soon proved it was good, too. The Finns had put together a strong intelligence network, and Taylor's people were using it to good effect.

The first thing we learned was very good news: For the moment, the Guards had only one aerospace base capable of launching a ship toward Vapaus: Base Talon, which the League command codenamed Hades. All the other aerospace bases that were operational at the time of the League's arrival were small airfields, little more than clearings equipped with fuel storage tanks. These were wiped out by the simple expedient of blowing up the fuel tanks, or cratering the landing field. Some had been former civilian fields, and of this number, one or two had been captured. However, the enemy still had good surface-to-air missiles and strongly held airfields (which could only operate aircraft, not spacers): the Finns had gotten a few ships shot down and given up spaceflight for the moment.

Unfortunately, whatever the Guardians lacked in number of aerospace fields, Hades made up for in quality. And size. It was huge, and well defended. Without any explanation of why the League was interested in Hades, the Finns were ready to give it a go. With the fighter and air defenses based at Hades out of the picture, they could control their planet's airspace, and launch safely to and from orbit.

The League and the Finns had at least a fighting chance to hit Hades and knock it out. There were problems, though. Our troops were widely scattered and would have to be brought to bear. They would have to move in secret. We would have to accept heavy casualties. But it should be possible to deal Hades a crippling blow. And if the League and the Finns controlled Vapaus and controlled the air, the war on the ground would be quickly won. There were still plenty of Guardian forces out there, many of them in pretty good shape. But if we held space and air, if we held the high ground, they wouldn't have a chance.

It was beginning to look like hitting Hades was the way to win the war, even if the missile control station didn't exist. Taylor changed his mind and decided not to inform anyone about our theories concerning the control station. Too many spies, too many taps on communication.

There was a map of the planet on the wall of the schoolroom Taylor used as HQ, and now geography started to make itself felt. Aside from large landmasses at the North and South Poles, New Finland's land was nearly all in the western hemisphere. There were three small continents there, mainly on the northern side of the equator. Only the largest of the three straddled it.

On a geologic timescale, these three landmasses had broken apart from each other quite recently, and they were rather close together, divided by narrow channels of deep water. The coastlines were rough and contained many fine bays.

The smallest, least settled, and northernmost of the continents was New Lapland.

Both Hades and the League forces were on the largest and most populated of the three, Karelia. The remaining continent was Kuusamo.

Karelia held the largest cities, and probably about 90% of the population. For that reason, the Guardians had put their largest bases there, so as to have forces on hand to control the populace.

The cities were nearly all on the seacoasts, and so the Guardian camps were in the interior, both to keep the troops away from un-Guardian influences, and to command the air and land transportation lines.

Karelia's terrain was rough, hilly, and for the most part, covered with forestland: it was not easy to put roads through. Before the war, air transport had been very important. Now the Guards controlled the air, but were spread too thin to cover the roads very well. The heavy forest cover made surveillance hard. At least we hoped it would.

We began to pick up information on the rest of the League troops. Pins sprouted wherever they found themselves. A pattern grew, a rough circle centered on the ruins of Base Demeter. Finn and League troops were all over the map, on all three continents, and on nearby islands. We were far and wide, there was no doubt about that.

Taylor's staff decided which groups were worth moving, which would do more good fighting where they were, which would do best joining the fight for Hades. Many forces, both Finn and League, which could have been of great help, had to be left where they were: they simply couldn't get to Hades in time.

Speed was vital. Bayet said her 75th Infantry needed another three days to rearm, and that it would take three nights for them to march to Hades.

Taylor took that six days as his cut-off. Anyone who could make it to the gates of Hades by then, alone or a thousand strong, was given the order to march.

Surprise would be our first line of defense. Preparation must be fast, undetectable. We had to hit them before they decided to launch an assault on Vapaus.

The days wore on in a complication of decisions that were almost totally inexplicable. Guesses were piled on guesses, chains of logic metamorphosed into rat's-nest reasoning, and sheer exhaustion made clear thought a rarity.

But, bit by bit, piece by piece, Taylor and his staff made sense of the situation: where everyone was, when they were to leave, how they were to travel, what point in Hades they were to attack.

At the end of the second day since my talk with Taylor, the lights were dimmed in the little school room. The floor was covered with papers, the air was rich with the odor of too many people in one room drinking too much coffee. But for one sergeant asleep in a chair and an occasional courier looking for a lost piece of paper, the room was empty.

The map of Hades supplied by Finnish intelligence (at the cost of brave men's lives) was covered with optimistic plastic markers of various shapes and sizes and broad grease pencil lines pointed straight to the heart of the camp.

Fifty troops to take the power room . . .

Twenty troops to cut fences from perimeter 500 to 610 . . .

One hundred troops to stand by with hand-held anti-aircraft weapons until plus ten hours . . .

Two hundred fifty troops to seek out and destroy orbit-capable craft . . .

Estimated total League and Finnish forces, 4,300.

Estimated total opposing forces, 6,000.

An idle gust of wind came through an open window and blew a few of the markers off the map to clatter on the floor.

Chapter Eleven

Taylor didn't know what to do with me. He asked me what I should do, and I said, "Scout."

He told his aide that, and the aide told me "Team Five." I checked in at the ops tent. They told me to wait, Team Five was supposed to be showing up. It turned out that it was Krabnowski who showed up, along with three other troopers.

"Morning, Commander. Sir. Just heard from HQ you were with us."

"Hey, Krab. Call me Mac. I don't know what Navy rank means to you guys anyway. So I guess you're Team Five?"

Krab looked surprised. "Yup. Hey, Bob. Goldie. Joan. This is Commander Mac."

Bob looked at me with bleary eyes suspended under bushy black eyebrows. "So?"

"Hiya, Mac," Goldie said. Goldie was short, stocky, but even in U.S. Army fatigues, gorgeous. Her eyes were big, blue, wide, and clear, with no makeup and not needing it. Her hair was a warm honey-blonde. She had an ample bust, a slender waist, nice hips.

Joan might not have been as openly decorative, but she was beautiful while Goldie was pretty. Tall and cool, with dark brown hair cut very short, slender and languorous. Her eyes were grey and quiet, set in a smoothly sculptured, high-cheeked face.

"Hi, Mac," she said. "That's a private's uniform. What's the gag with Krab calling you 'Commander'?"

" 'Cause I'm a commander. ROK Navy. No one brought me a Navy uniform."

"And you can't shoot up the bad guys in your skivvies," Krab put in.

The other three suddenly looked very unnerved. "Oops. Sir. You're a *real* officer?" Goldie asked.

"Pretty real."

"Oh, boy. Sir. Sorry about the 'Hiya, Mac.' Sir. You just get into the habit of reading insignia. Sir."

" 'S'all right. I'm not going to be too much on giving orders. I'm just along for the ride."

"Well, okay, sir." Goldie said.

"Mac."

"Mac, sir."

"Skip it."

Goldie turned to Krabnowski. "So why didn't you tell us the man joining us was an officer?"

"Figured you'd have the same brains I did and recognize him," Krab said.

Goldie peered intently into my face, subtracted the grime and the three-day growth of beard, and it seemed a light went on. "You're Commander *Larson*! Terrance MacKenzie Larson! The man who got us here!"

"That's right."

Joan whistled and poked Krab in the ribs. "Krab, how do you make friends in high places?"

"Charm, Private. Charm."

"And *you* were the one who got us sprung," Joan added, "And got the brain implant."

"For that, man, we're really going to hunt Guardians. Those sons of bitches. Sir," Goldie finished.

"So let's get this show on the road and give you the chance."

"Groundcar's right outside."

Ten minutes later, the MP and the Finnish town policeman waved us through the perimeter.

A fair dusting of snow covered the ground as we moved out of the town. All was white, and quiet.

Our job was straightforward: watch for Guardian patrols and forces that might spot the League forces heading toward Hades. Stop them if we could, warn those who followed if we couldn't.

We crammed into one liberated Guardian groundcar, which mounted a heavy machine gun amidships. That made it a little tight for five, especially when two of them were Krab and myself, but we managed.

There was something that had been confusing me and I decided to ask about it. "Hey, Krab. Maybe you can explain something to me," I said. "Why is it you guys don't have all kinds of fancy gear here? Seems like the brass shipped you off without any of the goodies."

"That's not cause they were cheap," Krab replied. "That's cause it makes sense. Notice what we're driving here?"

"A stolen Guardian groundcar."

"Right. A groundcar. Not a hovercraft, or some fool walker with articulated legs. A car, a nice, simple machine. A motor in the hub of each wheel. Battery pack under the rear seat to power them. The Guards thought it out the same way we did."

"Which is how?"

"Both armies are on the ends of really long supply lines. Light-years. So this jeep ought to be simple enough to fix with a minimum of parts. Also, it's the best machine for the job. This is rough terrain; this road goes up and down more than straight ahead. A hovercraft would just sort of fall off the side of the first hill it tried to climb. H-craft are damned noisy, they make great targets on infrared, they aren't very stable—like if the wind is blowing they drift, and if you have to get moving in a hurry you can get your head missing waiting for the ground effect skirt to inflate. They're a *lot* more complicated and more fragile than a car."

"Okay, that makes sense, but why did they send you off with such primitive guns? No self-seeking ammo—"

"Self-missing ammo," Goldie corrected. "The stuff picks *a* target, but it might not be yours. Also, don't get used to it, or it's just too bad when you run out. Think anyone here could manufacture it if we run out? Besides, the rifles we were issued can't fire it anyway."

"There you go again, badmouthing the LUIW," Joan said.

"I am not!" Goldie retorted. "That's just a plain fact—it can't shoot self-seeking ammo."

"Wait a minute," I cut in. "What's a Looey?"

"This is," Bob said, patting the stock of his rifle. "The League Universal Issue Weapon. LUIW. All the rifle troops sent here are carrying them."

"And if you insist, I will badmouth it," Goldie said cheerfully. "You can keep the self-seeking rounds, but the LUIW has too low a fire rate. Only eighty rounds a minute on automatic."

"C'mon, get serious, Goldie," Krab replied, with the air of someone who has had the same argument before. "When you fire on auto, 99 times out of 100 you aren't really aiming to hit anything anyway; you're firing to force the other side to take cover so they can't aim at *you*. If the thing fired 250 rounds a minute, they wouldn't duck any faster, but you'd run out of ammo four times as fast—and do you want to lug half your weight in ammo just to piss it away?"

"Couldn't they just make the ammo lighter weight?" I asked.

"Wouldn't make any sense. The weight of a round is what gives it momentum, range, accuracy, penetration, so it can make nice big holes when it hits something." Krab said. "Lighter rounds get slowed by air resistance, get blown away by a light breeze—no good. I like the LUIW," Krab went on, thoughtfully. "Nice, mechanically simple. Doesn't jam. Just wish they'd trade the laser unit for an extra 100 rounds of ammo."

"What we really have here, Commander, is the LUIW/L—second L for Laser," Bob explained. "Krab here feels it's just gadgetry, not worth the extra effort of lugging the powerpacks."

I was beginning to wish I hadn't started the conversation. Soldiers can get pretty opinionated about their equipment, I guess. My four companions were soon arguing fiercely over the merits of the LUIW, among other things.

But they all agreed that the LUIW had merit as a lowest

common denominator, and if everyone got the same gun, you were a lot better off than if every outfit went for a specialized weapon no one else understood.

Still, high tech hadn't been banned from the battlefield: for one thing, there was the Iron Maiden. Bob took the first shift with it. The Maiden was a baby combination radar, sonar and infrared set that fit over the head and let the wearer watch the world through a pair of video screens about a handsbreadth from his face. The Maiden was pretty much a guarantee of a headache after more than a hour, and so we switched it off every thirty minutes.

My turn came second, and it took some getting used to. A cheerful little idiot of an imaging computer converted the radar pulses to two parallaxed side-scan images; the result was something like looking through electronic binoculars.

The set usually did a lazy scan of about one rpm—as if my head were spinning slowly around and around on a pivot. Tongue switches let me select radar, sonar, or IR viewing, and also let me override the auto scan if something interesting came up. The Iron Maiden was a royal pain, but a very handy way to keep tabs on things.

We drove on.

Joan took over on the Maiden, and I concentrated on getting the spots out from in front of my eyes. Goldie sat curled up like a kitten under the machine gun mount. "Hey, Commander. You know how to play Ghost?"

"Play what?"

Krab shook his head. "Watch it, Commander. She's a killer at this one."

"Shut up, oh corporal mine, or we won't let you play. Okay, Commander, the first one up picks a letter. Each person goes, and adds a letter to the word. You've got to be spelling a real word, but if you finish a word over three letters you get a letter. First G, then H, and so on. The first one to get 'GHOST' loses, and you keep going until all but one person is left. Bob, you go first."

"Let's see . . ."

✧ ✧ ✧

"Now what kind of word starts out M I S O R I?"

"It's a perfectly good word."

"You're bluffing. Go ahead, Bob, challenge her."

"If you're after 'Missouri,' you're way off. Besides, it's a proper name."

"M I S O R I—it's a perfectly good—"

"Krab! Get off the road!" Joan grabbed at the outside of the Maiden, worked the hand controls.

Krabnowski dove the groundcar into the underbrush of the forest, skidding to a halt in the snow. Even as the groundcar was still in motion, the rocket launcher was in his hand. Krab had taken that back from our prison keepers personally. "Where?" he asked.

"Bandit! Coming in low, dead from Hades! Call it—south southeast. Course—say 190."

Krab tossed off his helmet and slapped a rocketpack into the launcher. "Bob, raise HQ. Get 'em off the road if they're on it. We'll try and keep the heat off them."

"Scout Five to HQ Comm. Scout Five to HQ Comm. We read a bandit, headed your way, bearing about 190. Possible picture taker."

Goldie was on her feet, the machine gun undogged and loaded.

"Goldie—can that thing pierce aircraft armor?" I asked.

"No, but it'll sure as hell get his attention while Krab's getting a vector on him," she said tersely. "Joan—how long?"

"He's low and slow—call it about 80 seconds. And make that bearing 195—right through that notch in the hills."

"Yeah, he's flying for pictures, all right," Bob put in. "HQ acknowledges. They're under the trees already."

"Lot of good that'll do them on infrared," Krab said, fiddling with the rocket launcher. "Joan—he following the road?"

"Looks like it."

"Goldie, let 'em know we're here."

She let loose a few rounds of explosive bullets in the air. They blew up at the apex of their trajectory.

"He took the bait," Joan said. "Coming in. Visible in about ten."

We could hear the howl of the jet engines now.

"Comin' on in," Joan reported. "Thinks he's gonna burn some local with a pop gun. Give 'em another goose, Goldie."

The jet appeared over the horizon, bearing straight for us. Goldie threw another volley into the air.

The jet suddenly accelerated and screamed in right over us. He dropped a bomb, which went in about a hundred meters away from us. The ground beneath us shook as it exploded, and the air was suddenly full of smoke and bits of burning wood.

Joan shouted out, "He's turning! Gonna barrel right back down the road, from the north." Goldie whipped the gun around and zeroed in on a piece of empty sky right over the road.

The scream of the engines faded for a moment, then roared in our ears louder than ever.

"He's dropping another load! Should fall shor—"

The ground ripped itself apart fifty meters from the groundcar, redoubling the stink of high explosive in the air. The jet screamed directly overhead, Goldie dumping bullets onto the fuselage, where they exploded like firecrackers.

Krab jogged out onto the road with the launcher. "One more pass! Joan, when he's at 1500 meters, call out. That'll give the heat sensors time."

"Got it. Goldie, I think you screwed up his tail surfaces—he's turning real wide, might be headed home—no, here he comes—"

"Spotted!" Krab yelled.

"One Five Zero Zero—MARK!!"

Krab fired six rockets at once, and they flared aloft, burning like Roman candles, twisting and turning in formation as they chased the jet. One missed the tight turn, but five roared dead into the target; a fireball blasted into violent being where the jet had been, flaming into an orange and black mass of roiling fire. It dropped suddenly into the forest, and hit, exploding, throwing us out of the groundcar and lighting the sky with blood-red tendrils of smoke that left behind a shattered pile of wreckage and a sheet of flame.

It was suddenly quiet.

And it was back with me. I could feel it. This was *real* fire, true fire that killed and consumed. Horrified, fascinated, I stared for long seconds. This was real, and right here, and it would burn a long time. In some perverse way, I wanted it to.

Suddenly, I realized that *I* was not in flames. It was outside me.

Or nearly so.

With a wrenching of my will, I got to my feet and dusted myself off.

Krabnowski came back to the groundcar, kicking a few burning twigs out of his way. Bob spoke quietly into the radio and hung up the mike. Joan took off the Iron Maiden and shook her head, blinking rapidly. She set the Maiden in her lap and rubbed her eyes.

Krab handed Goldie the launcher. She stowed it, reshipped the machine gun, and Krab started the groundcar. We rolled on.

Ten minutes later, Goldie and Bob were arguing over whether "MISORIENT" was a real word. Behind us, a column of death-black smoke climbed into the clean sky.

We made our camp sixty kilometers from the plane crash site without further incident.

The night was cold, sharp, crisp, dark and quiet. It was my watch, and I sat up in the groundcar, a blanket around me, thinking.

I felt, somehow or another, *safe* for the first time since I had found myself in this war. Here, tonight, the dangers were crystal clear, obvious, seen far off, as if on the horizon of a vast plain. A man or a machine could appear, and try and kill me. If the attempt succeeded, I would die. Nothing else. No subterfuge, no scheming, no bluff and counter-bluff, no tactics or strategy or wondering who to trust.

All I needed was caution, and the higher parts of my brain could sit back and take a rest.

I suddenly felt I understood the quartet I traveled with, and the way they had fought with such calm precision that afternoon.

There can be a moment when a struggle becomes a simple, obvious choice of YES I will survive or NO I will not. The choice is elemental, automatic. Even a suicide is careful crossing the street on the way to jumping off a building.

Make the right choice, choose the right path, and you live. Otherwise, you die.

I cradled my rifle in my arms and calmly watched over the cold night.

Two days later, the dangers got complicated again.

We were driving down that same road, enjoying the day and watching for trouble when Krab suddenly pulled off the road and drove into the brush.

"What—" I began. He cut me off, motioning for silence.

I shut up, and heard the high buzzing of a groundcar's electric motor coming from up the road.

With sharp hand signals, he urged Joan, Bob, Goldie and me into positions behind cover. The moment we were set he jogged about twenty meters back the way we had come from and made rare use of his laser rifle to slice through a tree trunk. The tree toppled across the road with a loud crash.

Krab pounded back and dove into the brush near me.

We waited.

About fifteen seconds later, we had company. A groundcar, the twin of the one we had stolen from the Guardians, zipped up the road. The two occupants had heard the tree's crash and had their weapons at the ready.

They stopped the groundcar a few meters back from

the downed tree and started to step from the groundcar, cautiously searching out whoever had done it.

They never made it out of the groundcar alive. I nailed each of them with a slug in the chest.

No one moved for a long minute. I had shot without thinking, and done it right. Now I felt sick.

We crept out from the brush carefully, wondering if the dead Guardians had any friends following behind.

"Nice shooting, Commander," Krab said.

"Yeah, just wonderful," I said bitterly.

"Bob, radio this in on our next report," Krab said, shouldering his rifle.

Soon we were putting miles behind us in two groundcars. We were ahead of schedule, and that wasn't good. There was very little point in reporting a stretch of road "clear" and then leaving it unswept for 48 hours. With that in mind, Krab decided to set camp early.

We made camp at the top of a gentle hill that looked out over a broad valley. Not only was it a nice view, but we could see anyone who was coming. We camped in the center of a wide hollow near the brow of the hill, which kept us out of the wind.

Being warm in the middle of a cold night is a satisfying thing. The five of us huddled close to the fire and relaxed over our meal. Goldie was officially on watch; she ate with her laser rifle across her lap. The Iron Maiden was set to give out a frantic beeping tone if anything awoke its idiot radar brain. We were covered.

Bob finished his meal and strolled over to the Guardian groundcar we had grabbed in the fight earlier that day. He came back with a bulky canvas sack which landed with a heavy thud when he dropped it.

Krab peered at it across the fire. "*Now* what?"

Bob squatted in front of the bag, picking at a clamp on the bag's drawstring. "Mail call."

Goldie suddenly looked interested and started to help him. Joan sighed in exasperation, a kindergarten teacher whose charges keep spilling the fingerpaint—on purpose.

"Commander, I *was* hoping your presence would put at least a slight damper on those two. Just tell me whether this rates a dishonorable discharge apiece for them."

I grinned. "I haven't the faintest idea, but a D.D. sounds about right."

Bob spoke with a tone of injured dignity. "We are *not* snooping. We're scouting, aren't we? Well, here's a whole bag full of intelligence to go through."

"Plus we won't have to search for firewood the rest of the night," Goldie put in.

"Now, we can't go destroying evidence," Bob said.

"Hey, Commander," Goldie said, "if we find any checks or money or anything, can we impound it?"

"Bright, Goldie," Bob said absently. "Just stroll into the First Bank of New Finland and ask to cash a Guardian payroll check. They'll be happy to take your head off at the door."

"Yeah, I guess you're right. What else we got?"

"Not much," Bob said as he shuffled through the letters. "Hmmmm. Boring. Boring. God, the Guards get dull mail."

Krab had a thought. "Hey, any care packages in there?"

"Good question," I said. I pulled out a small box, about ten centimeters on a side. I cut it open with my knife. "Paydirt! Chocolate, cigarettes, some kind of cookies . . ."

Bob and Goldie immediately gave up on the letters and checked for more packages. In a few minutes, the two of them were surrounded by a pile of food, cigarettes, some cold soldier's long johns, and a collection of pornographic novels printed on lightweight paper—"packaged especially for space travel to save *you* money" it said on the box. Bob decided he was on a streak and kept digging.

"Hey, now this looks interesting."

"What you get, Bob?" Krab asked.

"Military pouch or something. Says TOP SECRET."

"Watch it, Bobbie. Might be booby-trapped," Goldie warned.

"Just a sec." He pulled out his pocket flash and clasp knife. "Hell, if they think I can't get past *that* . . ." He started to work on the pouch's lock, holding the light in his mouth. After a minute or two of jiggering, Bob twisted the blade of his knife slightly to the left and the pouch unfolded itself with a click.

Bob smiled to himself as best he could with the light in his mouth and started to rifle through the papers inside.

He started to read, flipping through the first few pages, then slowing down, going back to the beginning, reading it slowly, carefully. I watched his face, lit by the firelight, and saw the color leave his face. He set down the papers, swallowed hard, and spoke. His voice was low and quiet, but the tone of his voice was enough to silence the rest of us. "God's own holy shit. We're going to die. Commander, Corporal Krabnowski, we had best damn well say to hell with the schedule and break radio silence right now."

"Why?" I asked. "What is it?"

"There's—there's a ship coming," he said. "A hell of a big one. One that can come through space and enter an atmosphere. It's some kind of aircraft carrier, or spacecraft carrier. The damn thing must be the size of an asteroid, and the *guns* it must have . . ."

I reached over, dug into the military pouch and found a piece of paper, and a number. I read it out loud. "Ship's complement: two thousand men."

There were other numbers, that I had to read out loud, that said hope was lost. "Service facilities for supplemental support of eighty Comet space-going fighter craft, fifty Revenger multi-entry aerospace fighters, and forty Tornado aircraft are required."

There was more, much more. It was an information kit for the dead commander of Base Demeter. Schlitzer. I had killed him myself. The package was sent to advise him of what services might be required of him.

Bob fingered one of the documents nervously. "They call her *Leviathan*."

"Commander! Groundcar coming!"

"You sure that's the one from HQ?" It was still night;

New Finland had a long one. I trained a pair of IR binoculars on the bend in the road.

Krab patted his rocket launcher, loaded and ready in his lap. "If it's not, I've got a reception planned." But when the groundcar popped out from behind the trees, the League's Flame, Ship and Star ensign was flying from its gun mount. There were two people in it, a woman and a man. I recognized George. The woman must be the intelligence officer Taylor had sent us when we transmitted a coded report on the *Leviathan* information. HQ had sounded as alarmed as we were.

The groundcar pulled to a halt.

"My God! George!" He looked like death warmed over, wan, tired, spent.

"Hello, Jeff." His voice was flat, laden with exhaustion. When had he slept last?

"Krab! Get over here!" Krabnowski yelled to Joan to take sentry and hurried to the groundcar and helped me lift George from the seat.

"George, what happened to you?" I asked. Krab and I held him up. I was sure he couldn't stand on his own.

"J-just can't sleep. Haven't eaten. Dunno."

I turned to the woman. She stepped down from the driver's seat, shaking her head. "*Bonsoir*, Commander. Lieutenant Marie-Francoise Chen, Army of the Sixth Republic of France. 899 70 12 28. I do not know why they made this man travel. Expert on Guardian technology or not, he is not well enough to do so. I am sorry."

"I quite agree." Damn it, war time or not, they couldn't expect to squeeze any more use out of George when he was in this shape. "George. You've got to eat. We're going to get some food into you and get you to sleep."

"Don't want to eat. Tried sleeping. Can't."

"You eat, like it or not. Goldie—get some chow whipped up. And dig up some sort of sleeping pill from first aid."

"Right."

Krab and I half-led, half-carried George to the campfire. Goldie was already busy getting food together. Bob and

Lieutenant Chen grabbed some gear from the groundcar and followed us. Chen started looking over the material while we got some food into George. Goldie got a powerful sedative down with the last gulp of soup she had heated from freeze-dried stores. Soon the drug took hold in spite of him and he slept, fitfully, through dreams that should have wakened him a dozen times, but for the strength of the drug.

"Why don't you sack out too, Commander? Everyone else got at least six hours last night. You didn't sleep at all, and we've still got some waiting to do," Krab suggested.

Chen looked up. "Yes, Commander, do so if you have tiredness. It will be several hours before I have any results."

"You talked me into it. Goldie—let me see one of those knock-out pills." I couldn't afford to waste sack time lying awake worrying.

"Commander. Wake up." Joan shoved a cup of coffee under my nose and broke up my dream. I took the coffee and downed it in one gulp, searing my tongue in the process. "Arrgggh. Thanks. How long have I been out?"

"About three hours."

"How's George?"

"Sleeping like a baby. He finally quit tossing around and settled down."

"That's something, anyway." I had slept in my clothes except for my shirt, belt, and shoes. I wriggled out of the sleeping bag and put these on, getting into my clean shirt a bit reluctantly; it had been "clean" for the better part of a week now.

"Chen got anything yet?"

"She says so. That's why I woke you."

Joan retreated from the tent's entrance and let me out. We walked to the fire. Lieutenant Chen sat by it, not even noticing she was shivering slightly. She had wrapped a blanket around herself, a mug of tea by her side. She had fine, delicate, oriental features on a round, high-cheeked face. Her hands were long-fingered and graceful. She moved quickly, precisely.

The night was cold, and clear, and quiet. The slightest hint of light in the east warned of the still-distant dawn.

As I approached, she saw me, stopped her reading, and closed her notebook. She sat, staring at nothing, chewing on the end of her pencil, for a long time. Then she rose, and saluted me. She spoke quietly. "Commander Larson, I have completed my first analysis."

"Well?"

She hesitated. "Let us step away from the camp for a moment. Come."

I followed her as she led me away into the darkened clearing.

She began. "Technically, I suppose I should be making this report only to General Taylor. But, I think you and your friends have the right to know. Forgive me if I cause you to tell them. This is very difficult, even just to one person. I have learned most of what I can about the enemy ship, *Leviathan*. The good news is that it was launched from their planet, Capital, long before we attacked. It is chance that brings her here now, not a counter-attack. They will arrive expecting a subdued, peaceful, planet. I do not know exactly when she will come, but soon, soon.

"I have considered the state of our own forces, such as they are. I have balanced this with what is known of the enemy's other bases.

"*Leviathan*, she is awesome. On the face of it, she could defeat us all, easily. But there are flaws in the giant's armor. Indeed, I think much of the armor is not there at all. There is hope, a slender thread of it, for us. There is a slight chance that we can win through and defeat this *Leviathan*.

"In my profession, I deal in numbers, in facts, in probabilities. Sometimes to remember that those numbers are people of flesh and blood and souls is a most difficult thing.

"But I force them to be numbers, in my head, because then terrible things are not as terrible. But this time, for me, now, it is impossible to think of them but as people who laugh and cry.

"It will be most difficult. It will require great luck and nerve. But, perhaps, we can beat *Leviathan* and win this war.

"But, in that effort, it is all but certain that most of us will die."

Chapter Twelve

At first light we again contacted Brigadier Taylor. He ordered us to stay put: by now we were within a few hours drive of Hades. There was little point in risking the information we had gained by getting much closer.

By now the positions of League and Finnish forces were in the shape of a rough half-circle around the northern side of Hades. Little incident had marred the approach of our forces. With luck, the Guardians wouldn't spot us until it was too late.

So, now, we waited. When George awoke, I suggested that he and I go for a walk and stretch our legs a bit. We needed a chance to talk. He looked better than he had the night before, but he didn't look good.

"Jef—I mean, Mac. What's going to happen?"

"I don't know, George." The two of us sat down on a fallen log.

"If you—if we—if the League forces win—what will happen to me?"

"Whatever you want to happen, George. You've got skills, talent, and there's a lot of room out there."

"I've been with those American soldiers, mostly. They told me a lot about Earth. Do you think I could go there?" He blew out a great puff of air, and watched his breath swirl for a moment in the cold air. "I'd like to see Earth."

"It's something to see."

"They used to talk about it a lot back on Capital, but it sounded all different. The Americans talk about big cities and all kinds of different kinds of people in one place, and on Capital, they tell you about all the evil, corrupt people and how disorganized it all is."

"Well, I suppose they're both right."

"But, don't you think I'd have trouble there, being from Capital and the Guardians and the war?"

"Yeah, probably." I looked out over the valley. Ahead, there, somewhere, lay Hades. "You're a good man, George, and I've got to be honest with you. I don't know where it'll be easy on you."

"I know. I also know no one has the slightest idea what will happen after the next twelve hours or so."

"I will promise you this. I'll get you off the planet, out of this star system. Maybe I can talk to Pete Gesseti, a friend of mine. Get you Kennedy citizenship. They're terraforming a moon called Columbia. Maybe they could use a good technician."

"Hmmmmm. That'd be nice. If I live to get there."

I didn't have any answer to that one.

We sat quietly, looking over the peaceful valley.

"Commander! They're here!" Goldie ran up to us. "Joan spotted the column headed this way!"

By the time we got back to camp Taylor was there with Lieutenant Bayet, and a tall, redheaded male officer wearing a British Army uniform. Behind them, soldiers marched and vehicles rolled down the road. Taylor acknowledged my salute with a nod. "Commander. Lieutenant Chen here tells me that it might be possible to defeat *Leviathan*."

"Yes, this may be. But only from space," Chen said. "From the ground is hopeless. And those in space need the information we have here."

The British officer I didn't know spoke. "We can't possibly transmit it by radio. The Guardians would be sure to listen, and know exactly how much we knew about this thing."

"Do we have message lasers with us?"

"Nothing powerful enough to hold a good, tight beam to Vapaus without worrying about detection. Every time Vapaus reports, we hear about new spies and snooping equipment the Guardians left behind."

"And we have a great deal of information here," the Briton went on. "We have no encoding equipment, no video equipment. We'd have to *read* that encyclopedia to them. It would take the better part of a day, even ignoring line-of-sight problems. The Guardians would track the transmission long before we'd made a good start. No. We must send it by post."

"Very well, Stanley. You've convinced me," Taylor said unhappily. "Oh, excuse me, Commander. Major Deforest, this is Commander Terrance MacKenzie Larson, ROK Navy. George Prigot, who has been of great help on technical matters. Major Sir Stanley Deforest, commanding a detachment of the Royal Regiment of Fusiliers."

"Delighted to meet you," Deforest told me. "Heard a great deal about you, all good. Now then. We agree we must send it by post. By hand. That means we must hijack one of the aircraft we intend to smash."

"I agree," Chen put in.

"Mmmmm. Mr. Prigot. What types of craft that could reach the satellite are at Hades?"

"Well, of course I don't know what aircraft are where, but the only Guardian ships that could reach orbit are the Revenger ballistic ship or the Nova class attack ships. The Novas launch more or less like a normal plane, then fly to appropriate altitude and launch themselves from midair into space."

Chen spoke up. "According to our Finnish informants, of those two, only the Nova is at Hades. No Revengers."

I objected. "I was under pretty tight wraps at the time, but I think it must have been Hades that I landed at when I first came to the surface. What about the ballistic job I came in on? It was a converted civilian ship."

"No. That would be one of the *Kuu* spacecraft," Chen said. "All are accounted for. Some recaptured at Vapaus, others, blown up or sabotaged. There are none at Hades. That leaves only the Nova."

"Pity it couldn't be one of the ballistic craft. You say this Nova takes off and lands like a normal aircraft?"

"Yes, horizontal launch."

"Then what we must do is hold a runway while we get one of them in the air, carrying some of our people to Vapaus."

"How much would that add to our other problems?" I asked.

"Not a great deal, I think," Taylor said. He spread out a chart of Hades on the hood of a groundcar. "This is our most up-to-date information on the place, Lieutenant Chen?"

"Yes."

"Then the Novas are almost certainly in these hangars aside the longer of the two main runways. The hangars are dispersed pretty widely, one every quarter mile or so, to prevent one lucky hit from us wiping them all out. Now our current plan is to come in from the north and sweep straight across the base, blowing up anything that looks worthwhile. Then we simply keep going and run like hell out the south side of the camp, praying the enemy is in no shape to pursue. A raid. Now what this hijacking idea requires is that we contain the main garrison and thus hold that runway clear long enough to get the plane off, and *then* run like hell."

"We just sit there and soak up casualties until we get a signal that the ship is away?" Bayet asked.

"Yes. I agree it is a pretty grim circumstance. But unless we get that ship off, get the information on both *Leviathan* and the missile control center to Vapaus, we have lost, and the Guardians will simply kill us sooner rather than later. It is our only chance to win, and go home."

Bayet clearly didn't like it. "We don't have any pilots with any hope of flying that thing."

"On the contrary, Lieutenant," Deforest said. "Firstly, Commander Larson here is an experienced spacecraft pilot. Mr. Prigot is an expert on Guardian technology, and their way of doing things."

"And, included in the forces that came with us are thirty Navy fliers," Chen reminded the group.

"What Navy fliers?" Bayet asked.

"Thirty fliers from the U.S. Navy. Experts on flying unfamiliar aircraft. They were brought along in the event of just this sort of case, or unless the Finns needed more pilots."

"So they were, Chen. My memory is going. Find them, and get them here. Or at least enough of them to fly that plane," Taylor said, and then turned to me. "Commander Larson. We must do this, though none of us like the idea. I am afraid Deforest is right: *you* must be aboard the ship we hijack. Not only as a pilot, but as the ticket in. The Finns on Vapaus know you. They will trust you, listen to you. Mr. Prigot, if you are willing, I must ask you to go along. And Lieutenant Chen, you will act as the actual courier. You are our resident expert on *Leviathan* now, and I imagine the Vapaus Finns will have more use for an intelligence expert than we in the days to come.

"And you'll need help getting to that ship, obviously. Not too large a force, no need bringing attention to this project. I think the scout force you've been with has proved its ability." Taylor went on. "Commander Larson, I leave it in your hands. It is up to you."

"I'll do what I can, sir."

"I think that will be enough. Good luck. Do your best, and while you're doing that, I've got to manage the rest of this war. Stanley, Bayet, let's not keep that driver waiting."

They crossed the clearing and got into the major's groundcar. They returned a last set of salutes from our little force, and drove away.

I wondered if I would ever see any of them again.

The troops continued to pass through, sometimes in large numbers, sometimes the flow of soldiers reduced to almost nothing. We waited for the fliers to show.

Two hours later a quartet of young officers in blue uniforms arrived in the clearing, looking not quite sure of where they were supposed to be. Goldie waved them over to us. "You must be the flyboys," she said.

The one woman in the group grinned ruefully. "Yeah, we're the flyboys. Captain Eva V. Berman, United States Navy, Deep Space Special Forces Detachment. This is Lieutenant Commander Randall Metcalf, Lieutenant Commander Robert Emery, and Lieutenant Edward Talley,

United States Marine Corps. That Lieutenant Bayet said you had a job for us?"

"Well, for two of you."

"And two for backup. Our crew is so hungry to fly, you're lucky all thirty didn't show up. We drew lots. These three won, and I cheated."

"I thought so," Metcalf said. He spoke with a slight drawl. He was tall, lanky, with a thin face, wiry black hair, and a pair of bushy eyebrows that made him looked surprised. "I counted about twenty slips in the hat with your name on them."

"Quiet, Randall," Berman said. She was toward the short side of a pilot's height. She had chocolate-colored skin and dark brown hair, cut short, and a smart-aleck twinkle in her honey-colored eyes. "Pay him the slightest attention and you're lost. Just let him be first into the bar, let him fly a plane once in a while, and keep him fed. Now then, what is it we've got to do, and when do we do it?"

Long hours later, well after dark, we were at our jump-off point, half a kilometer from the base perimeter, and about three times that far from the nearest hangar that could hold a Nova, according to George. We were a motley crew: Bob, Joan, Krab, and Goldie, U.S. Army; Metcalf, Berman, and Emery, U.S. Navy, Talley from the Marines; Chen, French Army; me from the R.O.K., and George.

Metcalf and Berman were the prime pilots for the job. If they didn't make it, Emery and Talley were it.

Attack was timed to start about three hours before the late rising of New Finland's large natural satellite, Kuu.

"Commander. It's getting close to time," Krab whispered.

"We ready? Both groundcars okay?"

"Enough juice to make it. We're ready. 'Bout five minutes."

"Okay." The signal for the attack was an opening barrage of artillery, which would be followed immediately by the launching of blindingly bright flares. The League troops were supposed to know to look the other way. The flares were expected to dazzle a large number of the defenders for the first minutes of battle. The blind-lighting would last two minutes, then drop to a useful intensity.

We waited, sitting in the two groundcars.

Then—BLAM; BLAM; BLAM; we shut our eyes and hunkered down. Seconds later, we felt the silent burst of light from the flare through closed eyelids. Even without looking, it was awfully bright.

They must have known *someone* was out there—there was return fire immediately. Too immediate; they couldn't possibly have taken time to aim.

Bob was listening, too. "What the hell do they think we've got—bombers? I hear anti-aircraft fire!"

"Well, they're throwing high explosive, too," Krab said.

A shell landed behind us with a *boom*. "Yeah, Krab, but artillery fired *blind*?"

"It can kill you just as dead."

Suddenly it got darker inside my head. "Flares dying! Let's move it!"

But we were already rolling. Krab drove the lead groundcar. Goldie, Berman, Talley and I rode with him. Bob drove the second groundcar carrying the others.

Krab put the lights on, and the perimeter fence sprang into existence not thirty meters away. He got us a bit closer and slammed on the brakes. Joan and Goldie were out of the groundcars and moving toward the fence, carrying flexible bangalores. They unrolled the charges, shoved them down at the base of the fence, set the timers, and ran for the groundcars.

The fence went up and over as they regained their seats. It landed, and the ground exploded underneath it.

"Mines, dammit!" Already the roar of the battle around us was loud enough that Krab had to yell. Explosions and shouts filled the night. "Goldie! Saturation fire, fore and past fenceline!"

Goldie took up the groundcar's deck machine gun and sprayed bullets into the ground around and beyond the gap in the fence.

Three more mines went up, and we were through the fence before the ground had settled.

The hangar we were looking for was on the farther of the two parallel runways. We were coming in from the northeast corner of the base, and the runways ran east-west.

Krabnowski killed the lights the moment we were through the fence and drove straight south into the darkness, careering wildly, bounding through potholes and hummocks in the rough ground.

Here and there in the darkness on either side of us, we could see other parties moving forward, toward the center of the camp.

League mortar and artillery was starting to make itself felt. Ahead of us, buildings started to go up, the noise of the individual explosions lost in the roaring noise of the battle surging forward around us.

Krab slammed into the paved runway and the groundcar nearly flew out of control as the tires hit their first decent traction of the night. We overshot completely and ran over the far side of the pavement. Bob saw it and moved fast enough to swerve hard and keep his car on the pavement. Krab cut the wheel hard and got us back on the runway.

The flares had given a lot of light until now, but they began to gutter out. In the flickering half-light thrown by the flames of battle fire, I spotted the cross-turn on to the south runway, and pointed it out to Krab. We took the turn on two wheels and jounced down hard on four coming out of it.

"There!" I yelled. The hangar was dead ahead. As we came closer, the lights died. Someone had had the sense to cut the power.

Goldie and Joan lay down covering fire with the deck guns as we squealed to a halt outside the hangar. Krab and I were the first to reach the buildings on foot, running like hell. We were in front of the open roll-out doors. And there she was. From what George said, that had to be a Nova. A laser cut through the air and reminded me I didn't have time to look. But Krab nailed the guy before I could take a bead. I spotted a second on a catwalk and cut him down with my rifle.

Movement at the back of the place. Krab and I both fired at it, and heard screams in return.

"Hold your fire! Clear at the back!" A crash of heavy boots on a sheet metal door, and Bob had kicked his way in the rear. "We blitzed three of the bastards out back."

I kept moving. There was a steep open staircase, almost a ladder, halfway down the left side wall, that led to a loft overhead. I charged straight up it before I could give myself a chance to think, firing slugs wildly to cover myself. I heard a noise and shot at it. A thudding noise told me I had hit. They cut the power back in from below, and I saw I had killed him.

Moving fast, I checked the rest of the loft. Clean.

Time. We had crossed the perimeter 10 minutes ago.

I got back down and counted noses. Emery was gone.

"Where's Emery?" I asked Metcalf.

"I looked next to me in the jeep and he just wasn't there," Metcalf said. "Must have plain bounced out of the seat on one of the bigger bumps."

"Damn!" For some reason, it suddenly struck me I didn't remember his first name. "Jesus, I hope he makes it back to our lines. Bet he's safer out there than we are in here."

"Don't remind me. So let's work on getting out of here."

"George! Is this the bird we want?"

"This is it." Something of the old George was in his tone of voice. He was near a complicated machine again.

"Then let's get busy. George. There's offices upstairs—"

"Tech manuals."

"Right."

He headed up the steep stairs.

"Commander, aren't you a little worried about showing so much light?" Julie asked.

"Yeah, but we need it to work by. Besides, I don't know if light or dark will attract the most attention. Look, I want you four to post some sort of watch. But keep close, keep low, and don't do anything exciting."

"Don't worry."

"Chen, Berman, Metcalf, Talley—let's get to it." We looked for a hatch into the ship and found one over the starboard wing. The Nova was a big, black, mean looking beast, a hulking mass of brute streamlining. It had no grace, just power. We went aboard.

Metcalf got in first and found the lights. He looked around with a disapproving expression. "Well, it's home, but it's not much."

"Thing must fly like a lead brick," Talley put in.

"Look, if the thing gets us into the air and stays there, I've got no argument with the design," I said.

"What design? Brute force and a set of fuel gulpers. You could put those engines on the hangar and it'd fly just as well," Metcalf said.

The three of them were already in command seats, looking over the controls. Berman had taken the pilot's seat. She flicked up a series of switches and the control panels came to life. The cabin was full of whirring and clicking as machinery woke up.

"Pretty lights," Metcalf said. "Hope they're attached to something."

"Can you people fly this thing?" I asked.

" 'Thing' is the word, but I think so," Metcalf said. "Controls are more or less standard. Give us a little bit of time to look it over."

Suddenly, the whole plane, the whole building, rattled as the battle moved our way for a moment. Another load hit even closer a few seconds later. "Well, get on it, and I'm going to see how they're doing out there," I said.

Talley shook his head as he toggled a few switches. "No sense worrying about them, sir. If they don't make it, we won t be far behind."

"Well, somebody get a seat warm for me. I'll be back."

I got out of the plane and met George as he was climbing up on the wing. His arms were full of thick volumes with boring titles. I patted him on the back and kept going.

I headed toward the entrance of the hangar. Abruptly, it was lit with the brightness of a lightning bolt. A roaring explosion deafened me for a moment, and I was thrown to the ground.

As I scrambled to my feet I saw Krabnowski hunkered down by the corner of the doorway. "Krab!" I went over, squatted down next to him and looked out over the night.

"Getting hot out there," he said.

"They gunning for us?"

"They're gunning for *everybody*. Damn, it's cold. Here we are freezing our buns off waiting to see if we get burned alive."

"How long we got?"

"No idea. Ten minutes, fifty years. Depends on how well they manage to contain the Guardians down the other end of the base. If the Guards can counter-attack, they'll do it right down our throats."

"Jesus."

"So you get back there and get that ship in the *air*. Maybe we can't beat 'em, but we can fade away. Time is what we're up against."

Two minutes later I was back in the ship, doping out the navigator's station. Could we fly it?

If Chen and the Navy fliers could figure out what all the buttons did. If I could get the computer to figure an air-launch program that would get us to Vapaus. If the dials weren't lying and it really was fueled and powered.

I got to work on the nav station. George and Chen were helping the others by cross-checking the controls against the tech manuals.

The navigation system wasn't that different from what I knew, and I got it chugging along after a fashion. Vapaus was a pretty standard mission, so there was plenty of data in the computer to play with.

No, the machinery wasn't so bad. But the numbers . . . I liked what I saw less and less. The window—the slice of time and the piece of sky we had to hit to make rendezvous with Vapaus—was awfully tight, and fuel consumption was outrageous.

It was tighter than I had ever dreamed it might be. I struggled to lay in a solution. I finally got one, but I didn't like it. Not with an amateur crew and hostile airspace all the way. Still, we might make it . . .

Krab shoved his head through the hatchway behind me. "Commander! If you're not out of here in ten minutes, you're not going! Damn it, we're three klicks away and I could *see* our lines get broken."

Berman yelled "Tow cart! Get the damn tow cart hooked up or we're not getting out of the hangar! Talley, you and Larson. C'mon, Randy, let's get it lined. We'll skull out the rest in midair."

Krab, Talley and I rushed out of the hatch. It took a nerve-wracking three minutes to find the tow cart. If it had been taken out for maintenance, that would have been it. The only way the Nova could move under its own power was jet or rocket power—and firing up inside the hangar would have caved it in on top of the ship like a puff of wind knocking over a house of cards. But Talley found the cart parked just outside the hangar in the darkest corner.

The battle was headed this way, our side in fighting retreat. The fight would move right through this spot, and soon. The flash and roar of the firefight grew closer and closer. "That's one hell of a nice mess," Talley said.

"And getting nicer," Krab said. "Let's haul it, man!"

We didn't argue. Talley jockeyed the cart around and we got the tow bar hooked up to the forward landing gear.

And the war reached us. Talley's chest dissolved into a red pulp and he fell clear of the cart. Bob appeared out of nowhere and was in the driver's seat, gunning the engine as he poured fire into the darkness. But the uniforms he was shooting at—

"Is that our side?" I yelled.

"It doesn't matter, damn it!" Krab screamed. *"Get that ship in the air!"*

A shell, stray or aimed, sliced the rear wall off the hangar.

Krabnowski dropped to the ground. Bob was screaming at me. "Go! Go! Get the hell out of here!" He raked the ground ahead of him with fire as the Nova started to roll out onto the runway. Goldie and Julie were ahead of me, hugging the ground, returning the hail of fire that came out of the darkness.

I jumped onto the wing and dove through the hatch, bullets clattering past me. I slammed the hatch and sealed it.

"Tow bar clear! God bless you, Talley!" Berman called. "Rolling free! Main air engines start, one, two, all engines."

The powerful jets exploded into life. "Engines, full power, mark," Metcalf said. "Watch the nose-up on this sucker, Eve."

I saw it out the nav station window. Three tiny figures, already a hundred meters back, firing into the darkness.

They all died that night. They must have. God knows how many of us did, all told.

"I christen thee the United States Commandeered Spacecraft *Bohica*!" Metcalf yelled.

Berman sang out "Full throttle—and—we—are—AIRBORNE!"

We flew out of the wreck of Hades toward the line of dawn, out of burning night into the day.

I allowed myself a moment's silent prayer for all of us before I started work at the nav station.

Interlude

That moment. It all changed then, for a very brief spark of time. So many people died that night, and I moved to a new place and a new fight so suddenly, that it was as if the people I had known weren't dead, but simply somewhere else. Not dead, just gone away.

That moment. As our fugitive ship scrabbled into the sky, I felt the fire again. Just for an instant, it returned. And now I was its master. Inside me, I had conquered that monster. I knew it was to be a capricious and dangerous servant. In my fancy, the flames beneath and behind me saluted my departure.

Death unreal, and fiery destruction my slave. The pure warrior. Then that moment was gone, and I belonged to myself again.

Part Three
War in the Sky

Chapter Thirteen

"Altitude 10,000 meters, climbing to cruise at 100,000 and steady on course. Keep her pointed that way, Randall," Berman said as she unstrapped herself and climbed from her couch.

"Will do, boss." Metcalf guided the big plane with a careful delicacy; by no means did he trust this ship yet.

"Commander Larson? Could you come forward a moment?" Berman asked.

"Just a moment." By my board, Metcalf was barreling us right down the line; there wasn't much for me to worry about at the moment. Still numbed by the horror on the ground, I was moving slowly, almost feebly. I climbed out of my crash couch and moved forward to Berman. She was crouched in front of the weapons control station, where Chen sat. George was seated in the comm officer's station, across the tiny aisle from Chen.

"What is it?" I asked.

"She must have been hit by a ricochet. Creased her scalp. I don't think she's going to make it."

Krabnowski hadn't made it. Was anyone I had left five minutes ago still alive?

"Commander?"

"Mmmm? Sorry. Let me take a look." Berman moved out of the way, and I knelt down in front of Chen. She was pale, limp. A thin line of blood dribbled out of the corner of her mouth. A vicious broad slash marked the path of the slug across her forehead. Could the bullet have caused a concussion? Could it have cracked her skull a little bit? What of the blood in her mouth? Another bullet through her lung? I opened her mouth and probed with a finger. No, it looked like she had bitten open the inside of her cheek. Probably a spasm had jerked her whole body around when the bullet hit.

I wiped her blood off my hands onto my coveralls and opened her left eyelid. I moved my hand to shade light from the pupil, moved it away. I tried it again. Her pupil didn't react, didn't expand or contract. "Christ, I think she's concussed."

"What do we do?"

"How the hell do I know! I'm no doctor!" What did they all want? What was it I was supposed to do? "For God's sake, leave her alone!"

"But she might die!"

"And if we clean the cut and put a god-damned band-aid on her forehead we could dislodge a hunk of bone right into her head and watch her brains squirt out her ears! Strap her in as best you can, leave her be, and get back to flying this thing—or we're *all* dead!"

Berman shot me a venomous glance and tended to Chen. I stalked forward to the cockpit and sat down next to Metcalf. Why had she asked me? She should be in command, she outranked me. Ah. I was in the Survey Service. I was supposed to have extensive medical training, I guess. She had wanted medicine, not commands.

"Damn it," I said aloud. "I don't remember the last time I ate or slept."

Metcalf's eyes scanned the controls and the skies, and he spoke without looking at me. "What happened on the ground?"

"They're all dead, Randall."

His jaw muscle worked. "Praise God in Heaven. Praise almighty God, but sometimes I wonder if He's paying the slightest damn bit of attention. Better get Eve back up here. We're coming up on the coast, and there's supposed to be some sort of Guardian airbase down there. Could be a problem."

She heard him. "Coming, Randall!"

She and I brushed each other in the narrow aisle. Her pretty face and hands were smeared with unnoticed blood.

She glared at me, hurt and angry. Neither of us said anything.

She strapped into the seat I had just vacated and took the controls. "Now at 14 minutes into the flight. Passing coastline in approx 90 seconds." Her eyes were cold, her hands and knuckles white with their grip on the control yoke.

I sighed inwardly and felt more tired than ever. I trudged the few steps to my nav station, set the belts around me, and looked into my radar screen. Adrenalin shot through my system. Three of them!

Metcalf called them first. "Commander! Bogies, six o'clock low and climbing fast!"

"I got 'em, all right, but there aren't any bogies up here; just bandits! George! Can you pick up any radio from them?"

"Just a second. Not sure of this rig ye—"

George threw a switch and a hard voice blared out from the overhead speaker. "—peating, this is Skycoast leader to Nova Fighter, acknowledge. You have no clearance. No clearance. Respond or be fired upon."

"Well?" George asked doubtfully.

"For Christ's sake get on the horn!" Berman shouted back. "Kid 'em along until we get out of range."

George fumbled with the control panel for a moment, then hit the right button and pulled a headset out of its niche. He put it on. "Call—calling Skycoast Leader. Come in Skycoast Leader."

"Skycoast Leader. Identify yourself!"

George looked out the window and read the number on the wing. "This is Nova 44-8956NF, 44-8956NF. We are attempting escape from attack on Talon Aerospace Center. We have sustained damage. Bad damage." Talon was the Guardian's name for Hades.

The voice from Skycoast was still very suspicious. "What sort of damage? Can we assist?"

Metcalf turned around and mouthed *landing gear* to George. George nodded and spoke. "Landing gear jammed—we were fired upon while trying to fly the ship out."

Now the trio of Guardian jets were visible in the infrared

TV pickup in the tail of the plane, three tiny dots rapidly growing. I put on my own headset and cut in the intercom. "Navigator to pilot. Can we put on any speed and leave them behind?"

"Negative. Not and reach rendezvous. We can't afford the fuel. Besides if we try and hightail it, no way we could outrun a missile at this range."

"Terrific." The *Bohica*, or whatever Metcalf had named it, had launched unarmed.

George was still talking with the enemy pilot. Now he switched to intercom and told us—"They're coming in for a fly-around to inspect our damage. They've instructed us to cease climbing, level off and match speed."

Metcalf swore under his breath. "Well, boss?"

"Do it, Randy. They've got the guns," Eve said.

Guns, I thought. *There was a gun right by my side* . . . I spoke into the intercom. "Does everyone have a side-arm, a laser?"

"Yo." Metcalf.

"Yes. So what?" Berman asked.

"I don't," George said.

An idea was coming to me, but damn it, it was a long shot. "Okay, Metcalf and Berman—who's the better shot?"

"I only qualified Marksman," Berman said.

"I made Sharpshooter," Metcalf said.

"Okay, Metcalf. You get your pistol out, set to laser, fullest power, tightest beam." I did the same to mine. "And switch seats with Berman."

"Just what the hell have you got in mind?—sir," he asked as they traded seats. The ship burbled in flight for a moment and settled down.

"We wait for the right moment, when at least two of the fighters are in range, then you and I fire our laser pistols direct at the pilots, at their faces, and blind them."

"You're kidding," said Berman.

"Only if you've got a better idea," I said.

"No, but I wish I did," she growled. "I'll be ready to give it the gun on your order. Unless you *are* kidding?"

"No such luck," I said. "It'll work, won't it, George?"

"It ought to," he said nervously. "The laser beam will go clear through the glass in our portholes and their windscreens. If you can get them full in the face, yeah, it'll work."

"All right," I said. "Just be ready to floor it and head for orbit."

"Just one thing," Randall put in. "On our original flight plan, we still have seventeen minutes and 1000 kilometers to go before air-launch."

"I know. Launch sooner and we can't possibly reach rendezvous with Vapaus. But if we don't shake these guys, we're not going anywhere. Let's stay alive, get into some kind of orbit and worry from there. One thing at a time."

"They're closing for the fly-around," George reported.

I looked at my radar. "Two are, anyway." One plane, the leader, probably, was hanging back, holding station two klicks back. The other two planes scurried forward. They were dull black, with angular forward-swept wings and windscreens like dark, massive insect eyes. "George, you know that ship at all?"

"Not one bit. New to me."

"Two fighters coming up."

George cut in. "They request you attempt to cycle landing gear."

"At these speeds?"

"We weren't planning to use the gear, anyway." Metcalf was always ready to be helpful.

"Okay, I'll give 'em a show," Eve said. She flipped the landing gear switches back and forth, so the gear would go in and out fitfully.

I watched the screen. "One of them had to see it. One of them is now directly above us, one below. George, patch the radio into the intercom."

"—isible damage, Nova fighter. No visible damage."

George gulped and spoke again. "Believe it's in the hydraulics somewhere."

"Possible, Nova fighter. But we see no leakage."

"Boss, slump back or something! If they see a woman flying this thing—" Metcalf said.

"God, Randy, you're right." Berman pulled in from the window, trying to keep herself small and still reach the controls. Our uniforms weren't exactly regulation either, but there was no help for that.

"Commander! My bird's in the slot!" Metcalf said.

"Nothing on my side—he's coming down from on top of us—" I replied.

"Now my plane's drifting forward, easing back in a bit."

Metcalf and I watched our targets sidling in and out of position on either side of the *Bohica*.

"He's coming in . . . okay, I can fire—" I said.

"He's drifting back. C'mon, you bastard, look this way!"

"Can you fire? This guy's sitting there waiting for—"

"Almost—almost—FIRE!!"

We fired at the same moment. From my viewport I could see the thin line of ruby cut through the sky.

The beam slapped at the pilot's face. Instantly his visor began to melt and flow. He reached for his ruined eyes in a spasm of pain, and suddenly his jet dropped away, out of the sky and into the sea.

"Now!" I shouted. "Gun it!"

The big engines throttled up hard and we clawed for sky. "Metcalf—did you—"

"Yeah, I got him."

I watched the radar. "One still on our tail." I looked into the IR from the rear viewscreen. Far behind, two contrails plummeted down, down, down in crazily twisting spirals. Between them, an angry black speck was growing behind us.

I cut the radio back in. "This is Skycoast Leader. In pursuit of renegade Nova fighter. Sanders and Hampton are downed by Nova. Renegade bearing—" and the radio began to squeal and chirrup meaninglessly.

"He kicked in his scrambler. We won't hear anymore." George reported.

"We've heard enough," I said.

"Commander Larson," Captain Berman said, "we cannot

achieve rendezvous with Vapaus. We'll overshoot the entrance to the launch window."

"I know, I know." Daylight grew stronger. We had flown into the sunrise quickly. I killed the IR view and went to normal vision from the video screens. The sky was bright, but the sea below and land behind were in darkness. We still climbed, and now we could see the curve of the globe at the horizon.

"We have to try for orbit, any orbit," Eve said. "There isn't an airfield held by the League that could handle this crate, anyway. And if we turned back toward land they'd shoot us down for sure. We don't have the jet fuel to try for anything else *but* orbit. It's that or fall into the sea."

"A rock and a hard place," Metcalf put in.

"More like a wet one," Berman said. "Randall, watch the radar. Larson's got to bollix up some sort of course."

It couldn't take long. Minutes before we were shooting for one tiny piece of sky. Now I would count us lucky to hit any orbit at all. I started to crank out the numbers for a minimum orbit, lowest energy delta-vee, no change of orbital plane, never mind the sunlines—

"Missile fired! Two missiles!"

I cut away from the nav system and checked on my own radar. Maybe thirty seconds had passed since we had hit the two downed fighters. I cut back to nav. The computer had solved the problem, such as it was. "Pilot! Let's get out of here! Heading 98 degrees, Yaw zero, Pitch 35 up, roll zero!"

She swung the ship's nose hard, snapped into the heading and pitched the plane up, making it climb. "At heading!"

"Fire orbital insertion burn, full power fusion engines, at altitude 50,000 meters."

"Orbit engines, full, 50,000."

I cut back to radar. "Missiles closing." Dammit, Chen was unconscious in front of the weapons control station. The radars for this sort of job were there. I upped the magnification.

"Holding heading 98, 0, 35 pos, 0. Altitude 25,000

meters—mark!" Eve's voice was hard and cold, but now fear was behind the calm.

"Missiles closing—range 14,000 meters. Closing at 650 meters a second."

Metcalf's voice cracked. "Altitude, 30,000 meters."

Eve spoke. "Larson—call out missile ranges. Randall—give me a countdown to air launch altitude."

"Ten seconds," Metcalf said.

"Oh my God . . ." Almost forgotten in the fight, George stared at the video pickup, his hands balled into useless fists.

"Range, 11,000, meters," I said.

"Eight seconds."

"Ninety five hundred meters." Now, out of the rear TV pickup, I could *see* the missiles, tiny white circles of fire with dark points at the center.

"Eight seconds."

"Stand by for airlaunch," Eve called. Would Chen make it? How many gees could she take with that wound?

"Seven seconds."

"Seven thousand meters." My voice was high and weak over the roar of the engines.

"We won't make it."

"Shut up, Randy—give me data!"

"Forty-two hundred meters," I said. He was right. We weren't going to make it.

"Sweet Jesus, five seconds."

"Missiles at 3000." Suddenly one of them slowed, fell back, and dropped off the screen. "One missile out of fuel."

"Please, sweet Jesus. Four seconds."

"Second missile closing faster. Twelve hundred meters."

"Three seconds."

"Five hundred meters!"

"EVASIVE!" Eve yelled, and wrenched the ship into a deep, shrieking dive that snapped my jaw shut. I tasted blood. An explosion slammed after us, shaking the ship, and I heard the scream of metal shearing away. Eve pulled out of the dive and began to climb again.

"We're hit. Lost some rudder control, and we're leaking somewhere," she said.

"Yeah, but my God we're alive," Randall said. "Thank your Aunt Martha it wasn't a nuke."

"We've got a yellow light on the orbital engines. Randy, can you read it?"

"Fuel leak."

"Can we make orbit?"

"MISSILE ON SCREEN!" It came out of nowhere, the moment I switched back to low magnification.

"Randy! Altitude!"

"Forty eight thousand meters!"

"Missile impact in three seconds."

Eve pulled back on the yoke, brought us to a dangerously steep climb. Somewhere in its guts, the ship shuddered and there was a dull thud.

"Forty nine thousand meters altitude."

"Impact in two!"

"Fifty thousand meters—"

"AIR LAUNCH!"

The huge motors exploded into ravening life. On the rear video screen, I could see a ghostly image of flame reach out and touch the missile. The missile vanished, vaporized.

The noise was fantastic. The whole ship was shaking frantically. George seemed to say something to himself, but it was impossible to hear. He seemed to shake with a reaction more violent than the ship's.

Through the headset, I could just barely hear Berman and Metcalf.

"Red light on fuel leak now, boss."

"I hear you, Randy. We gotta cut our mass."

"Passing Mach one." The shaking, the vibration remained for a moment, but now the roar of our flight faded away. Then, as we came out of the atmosphere, the vibration faded too.

"Okay, pumping fuel from wings to main tankage."

"Eighteen seconds into burn."

The tension had broken, vanished completely. We were still alive.

"Fuel leak looks worse than I thought. We might have trouble hitting even minimum orbit," Metcalf said.

"How bad is it?" I asked.

"Look out your port."

Here, above 90 percent of the atmosphere, the wingtank hydrogen vaporized immediately. There was a stream of thick, ropy vapor spewing from a hole the size of my thumb at the base of the wing.

"Jesus," I muttered.

"You said it," Metcalf agreed. "I'm pumping the wing tanks into the onboard tanks as fast as I can, but I gotta pump from both wings at the same time to keep the ship balanced."

"Will we make it?"

"I never try to predict a leak."

"Thank you, that's very helpful."

The cabin was quiet for a moment, then a tiny, weak moan came from Chen. She was still with us, for the moment. But how long could she take 3 gees?

Now it was 3.5 gees. As the ship burned fuel and thus lightened itself, the rocket engines could push the lightened load faster and harder with each passing second. We would hit peak acceleration of about 4 gees and a whisker.

"Sixty seconds into orbit insertion burn. Commander, have you taken a look at dropping the wings?" Metcalf asked. "Once the wing tanks are pumped dry, it'd be nice to dump the weight. Can we get away with it, or would it louse up our trajectory?"

"What trajectory?" I said. "We've settled down to the right heading schedule, but we didn't start that way. We ought to hit *an* orbit, but I have no idea which one. Let's see. Why don't you run the pumps ten seconds after the tanks are dry, just to be sure. Then shut them down, kill main engines for two seconds, blow the wings and throttle back up?"

"Why not indeed?" Metcalf said. "We're not going after

the precision flying award, that's for sure. Eve, can you handle that?"

"I can," she replied, "but I don't know if this heap will hold together."

"If it doesn't, we all hit the drink," said Metcalf. "With that leak, we definitely don't have the fuel to make orbit carrying the wings."

"Hasn't been one of our better flights so far, has it?" Eve said unhappily.

"No, boss-lady, it hasn't," Metcalf agreed. "Should have the wing tanks pumped dry at 120 seconds into the burn."

"Okay, stand by for two-second engine stop at 130. Randy, I'll do the flying, you make with the bolts on the wings. Blow 'em clean."

"I've got the safety off already. Just one button to push."

There was a sudden whirring sound as the pumps ran out of anything to pump. Just then, the ropy jet of vapor from the wing sputtered and vanished.

"And there go the wing tanks, bone dry at 105 seconds into the burn," Metcalf said.

"Okay, stand by for wing and tail jettison," Eve warned.

"Okay, Eve, all explosive bolts armed and ready. You hold onto this sucker when I blow the wings and tail. It's gonna want to spin out in ten different directions."

"I'm on it. Let's get it lined."

"George, you and the Commander call the wings when they're well clear. I'll watch the tail through the rear screen," Metcalf said.

"Stand by," Eve called. "125 seconds. 126, 127, 128, 129, SHUTDOWN!"

There was a leaping-off of pressure as the engines cut out. Then, out my port, I could see brief flashes of light. There was a squeal of metal on metal, and then the wing drifted silently away, sidling off into the sky.

"Port wing clear!"

"This one's clear too," George said.

"Tail assembly clear. At least this ship works properly when you want to blow it up. Gun it, professor!"

"Engines restart!" We were kicked back into our couches, harder than ever. We were topping 4.5 gees. Was Chen going to make it?

"Mac, do you have any idea where this orbit is going to take us?" George asked.

"Which orbit? The one we were supposed to hit, the orbit we tried to launch into, or the one we're *actually* boosting into? We were coming out of evasive action when Eve hit Airlaunch. I don't even know which way we were pointed then! Eve corrected and got us pointed the right way, but I've got no way of figuring the effect of those first seconds on our flight path, or what losing our wings will do. Should put us higher, but I don't know by how much."

"Makes things a little tougher to figure," Metcalf commented.

"But we are going to make orbit, aren't we?" George asked.

"Oh, probably," I said, "but it won't last long—two or three revolutions maybe—we'll be so low in the upper atmosphere that we might even have been able to use the wings, a little. Not enough for it to be worth it."

Berman and Metcalf were pilots. They had worked this out already. George, however, was distinctly uncomfortable. "So we get this far and wait to fall down?"

"Just hope someone up there is willing to pick up hitchhikers," said Metcalf. "We won't be within two thousand klicks of rendezvous with Vapaus."

"Oh." George sat there, bewildered for a minute. "So why is everybody so calm?"

"When we courageous flying types get *really* calm, that's the time to start worrying," Metcalf explained. "Personally, I wet my pants when that first missile went half way up our tailpipe."

"C'mon, it wasn't *that* close!" Eve said with a smile in her voice.

"So why are my pants wet? 245 seconds into burn."

A few seconds later a buzzer went off. "Dammit! Ten

second fuel warning. Burn time 250, 251, 252, 253, 254, 255—past this it's all bonus time—257, 258, 259—"

The engines bucked once, twice, growled, flickered, and died. We were weightless.

"Engine stop, 259 seconds. Maybe a hair more with that last rumble. Commander, are we going to stay up here?"

"Gimme a few minutes." The only things I knew I could handle without spending two hours with the manual were a sextant and an altitude radar. I got a rough ground speed with the sextant and bounced a series of pulses off the planet with the radar. Then it was a matter of fiddling with scratch paper. "I make us doing 7400 meters a second, roughly, at 162 kilometers, and it looks circular. We made it, just barely."

That rated a ragged cheer.

"George," I went on, "Get on that radio and give Vapaus a call. If you can convert from Guardian settings, they're on UHF channel two."

"Piece of cake. Ah, Lieutenant Metcalf, what was it you named the ship again?"

"United States Commandeered Space Craft *Bohica*. It's a long story."

"Be careful or he'll tell it," Berman warned. "Commander, let's see to our patient."

I unstrapped myself and guided myself over to Chen, Berman right with me.

Chen was still out, completely. Now, in zero gee, the oozing cut in her forehead hardly seemed to bleed. Instead of pouring down her face, the blood ballooned from her face in a tiny sphere that trembled with her breathing. Eve kicked past me into the rear of the cabin and returned with a compact first aid kit.

"This is the United States Commandeered Spacecraft *Bohica*, USCSC *Bohica* calling base station Vapaus. Come in, please. We are derelict and carrying wounded. Come in Vapaus. This is the USCSC *Bohica* calling . . ."

George's thin, cheerful voice droned on in the background as Eve and I tried to tend Chen. I gently sponged the blood away from her forehead and gingerly tried to clean the cut. It didn't seem too deep or too bad.

There was a small flashlight in the first aid kit and I tested her pupils again. This time they responded, a little. She coughed and a few drops of blood gurgled out of her mouth and floated out into the cabin. Eve corralled the blood between her hand and a sponge. That cut in the mouth was still nasty. In zero gee, the blood could pool up and block her lungs—she could drown in it.

"Mac, you must be exhausted," Berman said. "I'll do what I can with Chen, and you take it easy. We'll need you to be sharp when we talk to Vapaus." She started to bandage the forehead cut.

"Ah, actually, Commander, if you could spell me for a minute before you take a break, I'd like to step to the head," Metcalf said. The *Bohica* was a long-duration ship, and had a tiny washroom.

"Okay." I climbed into the copilot's couch and Metcalf headed aft. The legs of his pants were darkened and an acrid smell followed after him.

George paused in using the radio. "I thought he was kidding about wetting his pants."

"Not a hot pilot anywhere who couldn't use a diaper now and again," I said. "Some parts of my training were a little messy too."

Metcalf returned in a few minutes, his pants wetter but cleaner after being rinsed.

"Randall, maybe you'd better see if we can't keep our nose through our direction of travel." Already, the *Bohica* was beginning to tumble. Tenuous though it was, the atmosphere was still with us, and if we could keep our cross section small we'd last in orbit a lot longer.

I didn't need to tell Metcalf any of this. He took once glance out the port, saw the planet's surface roll past it, and whistled. "I'm on it."

"This is the USCSC *Bohica* calling base station Vapaus. We are derelict, and have wounded. We request aid. Dammit. This is the USCSC *Bohica*, calling anybody. Help. Over."

George went on and on. I tried to sleep. I'd had about four hours sleep in the last fifty-two hours. I tried to doze for about an hour, but I was too restless. I gave it up and went forward to see how Metcalf was doing.

"How's it look?" I asked as I settled into the copilot's seat.

"Not so good. The gyros are from some bargain basement somewhere. Pitch is okay, but the yaw isn't much and the roll is nothing at all. They must have been ripped up by that near-miss."

"So what're you doing about it?"

"Hosing it out the attitude jets and waving our fuel supply goodbye. Thank God the bozos who built this crate at least gave the att jets a separate fuel source, or we'd have lost them when the main engines ran out of juice."

"What about the jet fuel?"

"What? We can't burn that up here. No air to burn it with."

"No, but there must be some way to vent it."

"So?"

"So, if you vent it, you cut the mass of the ship, and—"

"With less mass to push around, the att fuel will hold out longer. We'll, let's see." He pulled out the pilot's manual George had rescued from the hangar. "Vents, air—fuel. Page 456. Hold it, diagram, page 444. Hmmm. Well, that's something. If they haven't bent all out of shape, the vents are positioned so the thrust from one venting cancels out the thrust from the other. Probably still get *some* tumbling from it, but what the hell." He checked the manual for the appropriate switches, then punched some buttons. There was a far-off *whoosh*ing and suddenly the *Bohica* was surrounded by a cloud of white vapor that dispersed instantly. The ship started to roll around its long axis, but Metcalf let it ride. "I'm just going to worry about holding that cross section. A roll doesn't matter. Thanks for the idea."

"Any other problems?"

"Well, I think we've got a battery problem. Power seems to be draining pretty quick. I'm going to have a few words with the ground crew about that when we get back. In the meantime, maybe you could power down stuff we're not going to need."

"Do what I can." Which wasn't much. I shut off lights and powered down boards we weren't going to need—mine and Chen's, for starters. But these were the most trivial uses of power. The real crunch came where we couldn't do anything about it: the radio, the life support system, the attitude control system. I cut back the thermal controls a bit, but even being a bit colder wasn't going to help much.

It was a dark, cold, quiet ship that fell through the sky around the bright planet, the war planet that spun silently around the ports. Soon, we again entered the shadow of the world.

"This is the USCSC *Bohica*, calling anyone, calling anyone. We are derelict and have wounded. This is the USCSC *Bohica* calling . . ."

We drifted on through space. George's voice gave out, and I spelled him for a while. We came out of the planet's shadow, and then, dead ahead of us, the bright star that was Vapaus rose above the swelling curve of dawn on New Finland. It was lovely. As the light poured into the now-cold cabin, it seemed a new warmth, a new hope came to us all as we looked at that shining point of light.

I switched from the broadcast antenna to narrow beam and aimed the squirt antenna straight at Vapaus. "This is the United States Commandeered Spacecraft *Bohica*, calling base station Vapaus. Come in, Vapaus base. We are derelict and carrying wounded. Please, come in, Vapaus base."

There came, finally, an answer. I couldn't understand the words at first, until I realized it was Finnish.

There was expectancy in the faces around me.

"Well, what did they say?" George asked.

"They told me to surrender or be fired upon."

"Oh, my God."

I hurriedly took up the mike again. "This is *Bohica*. We are a League ship. We're on your side!" I said in bad Finnish.

"Surrender or be fired upon."

Suddenly, on either side of us, there were bright flashes of fire-yellow light, and a clicking on the hull. Explosive shells had gone off very near us and small fragments bounced off the ship.

"That was a calculated miss," Metcalf said.

"Yeah, a shot across our bow—but they had to have fired those shells before they radioed us," said Eve.

"This is *Bohica*! Vapaus base, we request you cease fire! This is an unarmed ship! We are unarmed—carrying wounded!"

The star that was Vapaus flickered at its edges for a moment. "They're firing again," Metcalf said.

Long seconds later, more flashes of light, brighter, closer, and this time it was the sound of steel smashing through the hull. The ship began to tumble, skewing end over end. An alarm sounded.

"We're losing air!" George cried. He shut off the alarm.

"Vapaus, your fire has punctured our hull! Please cease fire! We surrender, for God's sake!" Now the bulk of the satellite was beginning to swell as our orbit overtook hers. There was no reply, but no fire either.

George scrambled for a bulkhead and grabbed a red box out of a cubbyhole. A patch kit. He pulled out an aerosol can and sprayed a grey smoke into the cabin. It hung there, pulled nowhere, then slowly drifted toward the ventilator. He shook his head. "If the leak was in the cabin, this stuff would suck toward it in a straight line. It's somewhere else in the air system, where we can't get at it."

Eve watched the growing shape of the satellite. Now it was close enough that we could see its spin. "Why don't they finish us off? What are they doing? Those shots bracketed us perfectly. If they had wanted to destroy us, they could have had us on the first shot."

"I don't understand." I paused for a moment, then transmitted again, speaking Finnish. "This is *Bohica*. Calling Vapaus. We are derelict. We have wounded. We are your friends. We stole this ship to escape the enemy. Please do not fire. Please respond."

The speaker remained silent.

Slowly, the satellite crawled across the sky as we overtook her in our faster, lower orbit. Then she drifted behind us to fall behind the curve of New Finland.

We were in sight of the great satellite for over an hour, with no more words and no more attacks.

But then something came to me, an idea that I had blocked into the deepest part of my mind. I examined the radio's frequency controls and shifted them to a new setting. Then, hardly daring—for some reason even afraid—I broadcast again.

Deep in my crawling fears I thought I knew what had happened: somehow, the Finns on the satellite had been overthrown a second time by the enemy. They had attacked, then examined our orbit, found it would decay in a few hours, and decided not to waste effort to destroy us.

In that case, if she had survived this far, there was still one person, one ship, who might be able to save us.

"This is Commander Terrance MacKenzie Larson, aboard the USCSC *Bohica*, calling the League of Planets Survey Ship *Joslyn Marie*. We are derelict, carrying wounded, and under fire from the satellite. If you can respond safely, come in, *Joslyn Marie*." I paused and bit my lip. "This is Mac. Joz, are you there? Please, Joslyn, are you there?"

But there was only silence. Vapaus drifted below our horizon.

We kept trying. There was little else we could do, other than curl up and die. Marie-Francoise Chen seemed near that anyway. Eve had long since run out of anything that could blot up the blood from her mouth. Now she was using a small sponge, blotting the cut in Marie-Francoise's mouth, then wringing out the blood into a plastic storage bag to keep it from floating out and spattering around the cabin. She had not been entirely successful; the area around Marie-Francoise was covered with splashes of blood—some dry, some still shiny and sticky-black. Eve seemed unaware that there was far more blood on her face than on her patient's.

The cut on Marie-Francoise's forehead had stopped bleeding, but Eve was forced to impede the clotting in the mouth in order to sponge up the oozing blood. Even so, the cut seemed to be closing slowly.

It was something like three hours since we had launched. We transmitted again and again, both to the satellite and to the *Joslyn Marie*. There seemed little hope in either, but no hope at all elsewhere.

"This is Terrance MacKenzie Larson aboard the *Bohica*, calling Survey Ship *Joslyn Marie*. For God's sake, Joz—answer. Mac to Joz, come in, please. . . ."

Randall was staring moodily off into nothing. The *Bohica* seemed to have stopped tumbling, at least. He had nothing to do, except watch the batteries drain, watch the air gauge show our air slowly vanishing out some pinhole, and stare at the sky.

"This is Mac Larson, calling the LPSS *Joslyn Marie*. Joz, can you read me? Come in. Callin—"

Suddenly Metcalf yelled out "Radar! Something coming up on us retrograde—and fast!" I kicked in my radar, and saw two tiny pinpoints slide out of the east, climbing over the curve of New Finland.

They were coming fast, damn fast, retrograde, flying the opposite direction from normal orbit. An immense amount of power was needed to hit retrograde orbit—at least ten kilometers a second delta-vee.

"They must be doing eight gees," Randall said.

"Missiles. God damn missiles," Eve said hollowly.

It was too much. To make it this far and be blown out of the sky by our own people. "They think we're a bomb, a nuke," I said. "They think we're a booby-trap and they waited until we were on the other side of the planet from them to shoot us down."

The two fierce knives of light drove toward us, rounding

to hard dots of brightness as the missiles arced over toward us.

"Two blips, closing at like 500 kilometers a second, accelerating."

"George—Eve—Randall. Thank you. You all did your best. As Marie-Francoise did," I said, very quietly.

Eve looked at me sadly, intently. Her face was covered with bloody splashes. "Goodbye, Commander."

All was quiet for a moment. "Two blips still accelerating, dead for us. Thirty seconds to impact," Randall said. "We're going to die."

We could see the missiles plainly. No escape.

—And then there was a bright shaft of light that gleamed but dimly through the thin air there at the edge of space. It lanced to one missile, and the missile blossomed into incandescence. The laser reached for the second bomb, and it too vaporized. The blobs of expanding light rushed past us in weird silence, into the blackness of space.

A third blip came speeding over the side of the planet, from the same direction as the missiles.

The radio burst into life. "Mac, are you there? For God's sake, are you there? Mac?"

I began to laugh and cry and my muscles began to shake all at once. It had worked. She had been there. We were going to live. She had done it. The others were frozen where they were, still not understanding. I switched on the mike.

"Joslyn," I said, "I have always admired your sense of timing."

"Oh, Mac! Thank God!"

Chapter Fourteen

Joslyn wasn't going to be able to help any more for the moment, but it had taken some real heroics for her to get as far as she had. And she had saved our lives. Certainly that was enough.

The *J.M.* had been docked at Vapaus for some weeks now, as quietly and secretly as possible, and Joslyn had heard just a few seconds of one of my transmissions to the *Joslyn Marie* through the repeater pick-up she carried when away from the ship. It was, thank God, enough to convince her.

They *had* thought we were a bomb. The great satellite we thought was ignoring us was on full alert, everyone in pressure suits in case the supposed bomb did major damage.

Joslyn had taken about half a second to decide what to do, and then broken all records getting through Vapaus airlock control to the *J.M.* She had undocked *Uncle Sam*, our cargo lander, just in time to see the missiles launched into retrograde orbit.

She launched in pursuit without waiting for clearance, without a glance at her fuel gauge. To catch the missiles she had to perform a velocity change of more than 24,000 kilometers an hour, and that meant something like five minutes at eight gees. It was a hell of a ride, but finally the missiles came above her horizon, and that was that.

Now *her* tanks were dry, and she was just as stranded as the *Bohica*. A very apologetic Vapaus command was sending a tug to each ship.

The catch was that the tug headed for *Uncle Sam* planned to be able to get back. Instead of the brute-force flight Joslyn had followed, the tug was launched on a trajectory that would take 15 hours each way to match between the two orbits. No reunions just yet.

We couldn't even really talk. Her orbit put her above our radio horizon about four minutes an hour. And an open radio channel used with three or four other people in the room isn't really my idea of privacy.

A tug came for us inside of four hours. Metcalf used the last of our att fuel to kill our tumble, and the Finns docked with our ventral airlock, came in, got Chen on a zero-gee pressure stretcher, hustled the rest of us out, and slammed the hatches shut in ten minutes. Then the tug backed off about thirty klicks and shot a missile right into *Bohica's* hapless self. That was one bad luck ship.

Our entrance to Vapaus was more routine than the first time I had arrived. The tug docked at the central docking collar at the axis of the satellite. From there mechanical arms grappled the ship and guided it along a tracked entrance system to a vast airlock chamber about a third of the way down the axis. Instead of bothering to pressurize the lock, the ground crew extended an accordion-pleated flexible tunnel about four meters in diameter. This was set up around the tug's side hatch and inflated. We disembarked, walking gingerly in the reduced gravity of the dock areas. A doctor and orderlies were waiting to transport Marie to the hospital center.

Dr. Tempkin himself was there to meet the rest of us. He greeted us politely and hurriedly, and then led us through a maze of corridors to an elevator which carried us down to the central cylindrical plain of Vapaus.

The elevator had a glass wall, and at one time the view of Vapaus's interior must have been beautiful, magnificent. Now it was the picture of a near-ruin.

The vast greenness was scorched to sullen brown. The lawns, the trees, the parks were all more than half-dead. Here and there were patches of green that seemed to be fresh and new, as if the plants were staging a struggling return. But this was more a dead place than a live one. The central sea was no longer a sparkling blue, but a ring of dark, murky, greenish-brown. No pleasure craft could be seen. Here and there, stolid, dark trawlers plied its surface. Clambering up from points every 90 degrees around the interior, straddling the central sea with broad legs on either side of it, was a giant construction of open girders, the whole unit symmetrical, each pair of legs supporting a long central arm. The four arms met at the exact center of the world, the midpoint of the axis, four giant 'Y's upturned and joined in the center by their bases. In the center of the vast thing, along the axis of Vapaus, we saw what looked like great, gimballed turbines.

"What in God's name is *that*?" George asked.

"That," Tempkin said, "is 'Hydra.' The entire unit is there for the purpose of holding the gyroscopes you see at the precise center of the world. It took five days to assemble it, using every man, woman, and child we could spare."

"*That* was assembled in five days?"

"It was long ago designed, built, disassembled, and stored in case of just such an emergency as we now face. It was intended for rapid assembly. And do not forget we are a major shipyard, with many automated construction machines to help us."

"What is the emergency?"

"The Guardians launched a bomb against us a week ago. It failed to destroy the station, but it nearly cracked the shell of the satellite. It was a near miss. We spotted it and it set itself off prematurely to prevent our deactivating it. Even so, it had enough force to throw a tumble into Vapaus's spin. The whole satellite is wobbling. Shrapnel thrown by the bomb impacted with tremendous velocity. Nearly enough to crack us wide open—and more than enough to set us tumbling.

"When Vapaus began to tumble, we lost much of our power network, and the temperature control scheme was thrown awry. There were great, sudden rains, which washed much of our topsoil down into the central sea. All this, and our green plants died. Of course, we rely on them to exchange CO_2 for oxygen.

"We have done all we could to refresh our oxygen, but our reserves are near gone. We have seeded the central sea with algae to produce oxygen while we recover. The trawlers are working to recover the topsoil."

He paused for a moment. "Also, there was fighting, burning, sabotage, as we overthrew the Guardian's troops. This, too fouled the air, and repair machinery was badly damaged.

"We will most likely survive, but it will be no small matter to restore this world."

We rode the elevator down in silence.

As we left the elevator, I noticed a low, intense humming that seemed to pervade everything. It was the gyros, whirring and humming high above, working to wrest this world back into its proper rotation.

The air smelled of smoke and dirty soot. It was stale and stuffy.

As we walked, the people looked at us with mild curiosity, but their expressions all seemed dazed, shocked, tired. As Tempkin led us to the administrative center, we passed burned-out buildings, charred fields, smashed and broken places.

At Tempkin's office, the debriefing began, all of us from the *Bohica* barely able to keep our eyes open, wishing we could change our clothes. A recorder was set up, and we sketched in the story of the war on the ground. I emphasized George's role in all that had happened. Tempkin was tremendously suspicious of George anyway, and insisted, gently but firmly, that his fingerprints and photograph be immediately "sent down." Midway through the debriefing, an orderly came in with a slim file folder. Tempkin examined its contents and nodded to George, saying "Well, you don't seem to be on any of our lists, and the Commander is willing to vouch for you. Welcome." He didn't seem very happy about it.

I described the discovery of the mailbag, and what was found in it, and our deductions concerning the existence and location of the missile control station. I described the decision to bring the information to Vapaus, and our escape to orbit. Tempkin interrupted with a question now and again, but for the most part, he listened quietly.

Finally, the story was finished. Tempkin sat in thought for a while. "I am stunned," he said at last. "From orbit, we watched the destruction of the spaceport you call Hades, thinking that it meant we had won. With Hades gone, the Guardians could be starved out. We thought nothing was left but the mopping up, the setting to rights. Then the supposed second bomb came—which turned out to be you. We thought this time they were trying to be clever and fool us into inviting the bomb into our home.

"Already, we have assigned technicians working on ways to punch holes in the missile system. It is thought it might take years, but we are patient, and self-sufficient enough.

"Now, this mighty ship, *Leviathan*." He stopped, and shook his head.

"But, Commander Larson, Lieutenant Metcalf, Miss Captain Berman, Mr. Prigot. For now you have done our part and more. Little more can be done now except to study the information you have brought. Take the time to rest." He stood up and led us from the office.

Vapaus had been a garden world, and perhaps would be again. Now it was a grey, dirty ruin. Having seen it more nearly whole, it was worse for me. But I knew my companions were saddened by the shattered, grimy look of the wounded satellite. I invited them all to be billeted away from the sad landscape, in the *Joslyn Marie*. There was room and to spare. The *J.M.* had been built for a crew of nine.

It was good to get there. That ship was home.

The four of us had a quiet meal together, refreshed ourselves, and retired to bed. George, Randall, and Eve settled down for the night in a stateroom apiece. I entered the captain's stateroom—our room—Joz's and mine. I got into bed, looked around the peaceful room. Home. I luxuriated in the comfort of clean skin, a full belly, and zero gee to sleep in.

The room was warm, cheerful, and cozy. I could see

Joslyn's clothes, her hairbrush, I could smell her scent. Not just the smell of her perfume, but her own special, private scent, a delicate hint of fragrance that reminded me of clear blue skies and love in peaceful springtime.

A thousand times I had imagined our reunion, picturing us rejoined upon the wreckage of a battlefield, or in the deep green coolness of a secret corner in Vapaus, or in the depths of space. But never this way. Reunited with a Joslyn still missing, a joining with what seemed her ghost, surrounded by hints of her existence, Joslyn herself gone.

A horror I had kept locked away from myself as best I could in all that time slithered its way to the surface of my brain. She was dead. I had never dared admit to that fear, against all the risks and flames of war, that she might have been killed in some battle here in space. I was exhausted, I was drained of all emotion, facing a grim future darkened by the coming of *Leviathan*. There, in the darkness, formed the conviction, cold and certain, that Joslyn *was* dead, that she had sacrificed herself in the rescue of *Bohica*, that the tug had failed to pick her up, that her ship had crashed, that disaster had overtaken her in the complicated dance of the orbits.

It is hard to cry in zero gee. The tears don't *go* anywhere, they simply well up in your eyes and turn your vision into a shimmering cloudiness. I shook my head and the foolish tears were flung from my eyes.

It was reaction to too much danger, too many fears, too many close calls. Here, now, safe for the first time in uncountable days, I collapsed into horrifying tremors of fear and sorrow, caught between wakefulness and nightmare.

Awareness ebbed from me. Gradually, I descended into my nightmares, my memories—of my mind and body and world on fire, of cold nights of fear, of broken and bloodied bodies, friends destroyed by unseen murderers before my eyes, of always running, always nearly trapped. Always the vision of Bob, Julie, Goldie, Krab as I last saw them, as they were eaten up by the war and the darkness.

Thus Joslyn found me, and came to me, and understood, far into the night.

"Mac, what have they done to you?" Joslyn held me in the darkness, shifted her arms and held me tighter. She could see the clouds and the fire still between us, the darkness of the war inside me. "Grim, frightened, so fierce. Oh, Mac. Please. It's all right. It's all right. I do love you so."

I shook my head and kissed her, barely able to speak. "Oh, Joslyn, thank God for you."

"And for you." In the dimness of the stateroom I could barely see her face, but her expression was clear and indescribable. Love, passion, desire, relief, confusion, trust contended in her eyes, the set of her mouth, her knitted forehead.

Finally we slept.

I knew that night that Joslyn had saved my life many times before she shot down the missiles aimed at the *Bohica*. I knew that I had remained as whole as I did, all that time we had been apart, only because I knew she loved me.

"Welcome to breakfast, oh mighty Commander," Randall said.

I sailed into the wardroom and smiled ruefully. "Hello, folks." Joz was playing hostess and serving up an English breakfast to Eve, Randall and George. "Somebody sure let me sleep." By my watch, about 13 hours.

"You needed it, Mac. Hungry?"

"You'd better be," George said. "Mrs. Larson, ah, Lieutenant Commander Larson, I mean your . . ."

"Call me Joslyn."

"Thanks. Joslyn sure doesn't do cooking by half."

"Oh yes, she does. Tomorrow is my half. My turn."

Joslyn said, "And the day after that, and after that, and after that, and—"

"What?!"

"I've been doing the cooking for this ship ever since you jumped overboard in *Stripes*. You've got a lot of catching up to do."

I laughed and made a rude noise. Then my stomach woke up and I discovered I *was* hungry. Joslyn's cooking at breakfast can take some getting used to, but I had done that long ago. Joslyn had clearly been dickering with someone for fresh food from Vapaus's surviving farms. I faced a "good British breakfast" of bacon, sausage, baked beans, fried eggs, strong black tea, orange juice and thick-sliced ham. It vanished quickly, to Joslyn's obvious delight.

While I was still eating, the others had gotten to the coffee and chat stage. Randall was fiddling with the viewscreen controls. After a bit, he managed a view from our sternward camera, nestled between the *Joslyn Marie*'s main engines. The *J.M* was docked to Vapaus by an airlock on the side of the ship, so that the stern cameras had a clear view, unobstructed by Vapaus. The curve of the planet was plainly visible to the rear of the screen, and here and there tiny ships could be seen drifting through the maze of stars that entangled the sky. "Nice view," he said. "But where is *Leviathan*?"

That was the question we lived with for two months. There was no clue anywhere as to when *Leviathan* would arrive. It might be tomorrow, or today, or next day. In the meantime, we tried to get ready, in the sky and on the ground. The troops that had hit Hades had taken about 30% casualties. We had wounds to bind. There was enough work to go around.

With Hades out of the picture, it was possible to fly somewhat risky missions back and forth between Vapaus and the planet's surface in the *Kuu* class ballistic transports the Finns used. These ships could go in, pick up personnel or supplies, and get the hell out fast. The Guardians were still a serious enemy, still had an air force, still fielded more soldiers than we did. The *Kuu* missions were dangerous, and we lost a few of them. But we needed them. They lifted the remainder of Eve and Randall's group of fliers to orbit. Their commander didn't make it, which left Eve in charge.

The *Kuus* brought in needed repair equipment, technicians, information to Vapaus, but they were also invaluable for getting our people to where they were needed on the planet.

Vapaus was the acknowledged headquarters of the Finnish and League forces. With our ability to observe any point on the planet, we could know when to hit, when to fight, when to protect what was left of our forces. But ground fighting was almost an incidental in those days, limited to small skirmishes and isolated firefights. Neither side was in shape to do much more.

The repairs to Vapaus went forward, and the satellite slowly healed. There was a half-day of celebration when the wobble had been worked out of Vapaus's spin and Hydra could be shut down. However, Hydra was not taken down—it might be needed again. To see that huge structure still there, every day, was a constant reminder that the war was not over, that danger was still close.

But ahead of all other work was the preparations for meeting *Leviathan*. Marie-Francoise recovered quickly and worked endlessly with the Finns to squeeze every drop of information out of the documents we had. The Navy pilots and the Finnish pilots trained together and made frequent trips to The Rock, where the major shipyards were located. There, frenetic efforts were being made to mass-produce orbital fighters.

There were a thousand strange schemes for space-battle weapons; exotic acids, clever limpets, robot mines to be placed in orbit, drone ships and so on. There simply wasn't time for them all. The engineers set out a rigid series of priorities of what could be done in what amount of time.

George and I worked on battle tactics. I think we mostly got the job because the Finns didn't know what else to do with us. We were given a fairly free hand and a large auditorium with a big hologram tank in it to play with. I think we surprised them by actually accomplishing something.

We were so badly stuck for a while there, I think we surprised ourselves. The first thing we did was program the hologram display to present New Finland's globe, Vapaus, The Rock, New Finland's natural moon, Kuu, and so on. Then we taught the computer what the performances of our fighters were, what the abilities of *Leviathan* were, what we thought would be the likely performance of the fighters *Leviathan* carried would be.

George took command of the League forces, and took control of the Guardian ships until we knew our forces well—then we switched to get a feel for fighting against them. Which orbits benefited which craft? What traps and decoys could we lay for them, what tricks could we anticipate and avoid from their side? All of this was of use, of course, and we passed a lot of information on to the people who could use it.

There was one problem, however, which no one could figure out: *Leviathan*'s reentry. Obviously, the thing was expected to enter the atmosphere and there perform as a gigantic armored airship. Yet there seemed to be no possible way the great ship could hope to survive entry into New Finland's atmosphere.

There had to be a way. Otherwise, the ship was useless. But *Leviathan* hitting atmosphere from orbital speed would be like asking a soap bubble to survive a hurricane. Any ship intended as a lighter-than-air craft had to be far too lightly built to be able to hit atmosphere at eight kilometers a second.

One night, when we had gotten that far and no farther, we were sitting in the auditorium, each of us with a portable computer terminal in his lap. The holo tank was frozen into one moment in time, the planet, moons, and ships locked into that one moment. I felt good and damned tired of playing space games. I decided it was time to come back to the central problem.

"Dammit, George," I said. "There's an answer and we're not seeing it. They've figured it out. They've *got* to have some stunt maneuver, some brilliant trick to get them into the air. If we can dope it out, we can be sitting right on top of them when they try it."

In the presence of a whole new set of gadgets, George had staged a major recovery of his former spirit. He was taking a lively interest in the coming battle, not because it was an event that might decide the fate of a world, but as a fascinating puzzle to be solved.

He thought over the *Leviathan* problem again. "All right, they have to enter atmosphere. They can't do that from orbital speeds. So they can't be entering from orbit."

"That's perfect, George. What does it mean?"

"Beats the hell out of me," he said brightly. "That's as far as I've gotten."

"Terrific." I sat and thought for a bit. "Maybe *Leviathan* is an elaborate hoax. Maybe the mailbag *was* a plant."

"Makes sense. All the Guardian generals got together and decided to concoct a phony weapon that would scare the enemy into setting new records for producing fighters and weapons."

"I see your point. So let's take what you said, and work it from the other end. If they attempted reentry, they'd be torn to pieces. So: what is the maximum velocity they could deal with and hold together?"

George worked with his computer terminal. Finally he said "If you're waiting for things to make sense, keep waiting. With the best materials at hand, careful flying, real precision, and amazing luck—they could just about manage Mach 2 without leaving the vertical stabilizer behind. Also the wings. And that is a very optimistic upper limit."

"It's *got to* be a fake!"

"But it doesn't make any sense as a fake, either."

"Let's take a break," I said with a sigh.

"Sold." George punched some buttons and the images

of New Finland and vicinity vanished as the house lights came up.

We left the theater and headed back to the *Joslyn Marie*. We found a note from Joz in the wardroom: *Visiting Marie-Francoise. Back soon.* George shrugged. "Does that mean we risk your cooking again?"

"It's my turn tonight anyway."

"Easy on the garlic this time, okay?"

"Spoilsport." I started digging out cooking pots and latching them to the stove. Cooking in zero gee is no trick once you get used to it. It isn't hard, just different. "So, what is it we've got hold of here?"

"A ship that can't land, can't re-enter, but has to pop into the atmosphere and float there."

"*Could* it do that? Sort of a matter transmitter with no receiver?"

"Yeah, right," George said. "If they could do that, why bother building the ship? They might not even need aircraft, let alone a carrier."

"Okay, it was just a thought. Where's the soy sauce?"

"On everything when *you* cook," a cheery voice said from above us. Joz floated into the wardroom head-first from the upper deck. "How can you put that stuff on every piece of food you get your hands on?"

"Same way you can serve three kinds of pork for breakfast." She spun herself around to be right-side up and I gave her a kiss. "How's Marie-Francoise?"

"Getting on quite well. They won't let her out of hospital for a week yet, but she's turned that hospital room into an office. Papers and computer gear everywhere. And the view from there! even with the whole inside of Vapaus ripped up, the window looks out on—"

"The whole satellite. Remember how I got into this place the first time?"

"It's no good trying to tell *you* anything. I shall have to talk to George. George, what did you clever lads manage today?"

"Well, we made the League's ships show in blue and

the Guardian ships show in red, but then we decided we liked it better the other way and switched it back. Then Mac finally got the scoring system to work properly. I took all five hands of gin during our lunch break, and then we decided to show the League ships in yellow, but non-propelled facilities, like Vapaus and relay satellites, in blue. Before we knew it, it was time for dinner."

Joz gave us both an odd look. "That's certainly giving your all for the war effort."

I clipped the lip on my pan of peas and sighed. "What George is trying to say is that we're stuck. We've got the display system down perfectly . . ."

"Well . . ."

"Okay, almost perfectly. Battle Control on the Rock will be getting a duplicate program to display the real thing, when it comes. But now that we've got the system, we can't run any realistic simulations until we know how *Leviathan* is going to approach the planet."

"I'm starting to think we won't figure it out till the real one shows."

"The rate we're going, you're right. Dinner in twenty minutes."

I fussed over dinner, the problems still spinning around in my head. It was a riddle: how can something be next to a planet in space without being in orbit around it, and yet be practically dead in space relative to the planet? Put it another way—what has exactly the same orbital characteristics as a given planet in a given orbit . . . "Son of a bitch! I've got it! Joslyn, you mind if I put dinner on hold for a while, maybe all night?"

"What for?"

"I know where that damn ship is going to come from! At least I think I do! I want to get back to the Battle Theater and see if it makes sense."

We were there in 15 minutes, and I immediately began working the computer keyboard.

A diagrammatic view of the inner New Finnish Star System lit up the screen, the planets in exaggerated scale—

otherwise, they could not have been seen at all. "Okay, great," I said. "Now, this is a dynamic display. I'm going to speed up the time scale." The tiny specks of worlds started to zip around the bright point that represented New Finland's sun.

"*Now*, I'm going to tell the computer that New Finland no longer exists. Watch what happens to Kuu, the moon."

Abruptly, the blue and white marble of New Finland vanished. The grey dot Kuu burbled briefly, then continued to follow the same orbit about the sun that the planet had.

"So what does that mean?" George asked.

"We've been forgetting that *New Finland* is in orbit around its sun."

"We accounted for solar gravitation in our programs."

"I mean the big picture. Look at Kuu! It doesn't give a damn whether New Finland is there or not! It's the *orbit* that matters, not what is *in* the orbit."

Joslyn stared at the display, "So that means *Leviathan* has to end up being in exactly the same orbit as New Finland, thrusting in some very precise way to compensate for New Finland's gravity, and come in on a trajectory that lets them match the planet's velocity exactly—"

"And they'll just float down into the atmosphere—"

"Since they're matching its velocity anyway."

"It's crazy!" George protested. "No parking orbit, no margin for error, if they go wrong by a tenth of a percent, they'll either plow right into the side of the planet or roll right off into space again."

"I wouldn't want to be the pilot," I agreed, "but it ought to be possible. They do have some fairly heavy maneuvering engines."

"Jesus," George said, staring at the display.

"Okay," I said. "Let's work out the details." This was it. It had to be. It made sense, if a fairly desperate sort of sense. It felt *right*.

"It's a terror weapon. It's incredibly inefficient most ways, but it sure would scare the hell out of me. Just imagine the damn thing *parked* right over the capital, blocking out the sun, not letting anything else fly, or even move, without its permission," George said, hours later, late into the night.

"Yeah, but it's more than that. It's an extension of power. It can go anywhere to dominate any place over land or sea and sky. It's part of a grand plan. One *Leviathan* to a world, and that world is under your thumb. It can't revolt without the site of the rebellion being smashed to rubble. Also, according to what Marie-Francoise has figured out, it's half offices inside. An flying office building. A capitol building, an administration center."

"The soldiers conquer and move on. *Leviathan* moves in and controls," Joslyn said.

I set the holo tank back to the view we had built up of how *Leviathan* might enter. The tank became a tangle of ellipses, hyperbolae, and parabolae. The basic requirement was that *Leviathan* achieve New Finland's *precise* orbital velocity *exactly* at that point in the sky that the fringes of the planet's atmosphere occupied. That didn't eliminate as many possibilities as one might think: we had limited things down to four families of approaches, but each family had at least twenty major members; there was an infinity of variations overall. But not all the variants made tactical sense. We started asking ourselves—which was the best way of doing things from a *military* point of view? My guess was that the Guard would do what we had done—dive out of the sun. It was a fast approach, it kept them hidden from the planet for the longest possible time, and if they were coming from any other direction, we should have spotted them by now.

Twelve hours after I forgot dinner, we left the Battle Theater. We had made a lot of progress: it seemed possible that *Leviathan* would want to sneak up on the planet, with as little warning as possible. That had to mean—almost literally—diving out of the sun, on a tight, hard hyperbolic or parabolic course that whipped in close and hard to the sun, getting lost in the glare and the radio noise a star throws. In that way, there would normally be almost no way to detect the ship. But once the Finns knew where to look, it would be a different story.

Day after day we plugged away at the simulator. George and I were there ceaselessly, and Joz split her time between the Battle Theater and working with Marie-Francoise. Marie-Francoise was more or less mended, though still woozy at times. She ignored that, working every moment she could on finer and finer evaluations of *Leviathan*. Joslyn shuttled back and forth between Vapaus and The Rock, where the fighting ships were being built with frenetic haste. She talked with Eve, Randall, and the other pilots. What tactics made sense? *Leviathan*'s defensive fighters did such and such a thing this or that way. Was that a weakness? Could it be exploited? Then the pilots usually said well, maybe. Could you run a simulation? Then Joslyn would come back to us asking for the sim.

The fighters that came off the Rock's production line were ugly, mass-produced, cylindrical tin cans of space. The standard type was called a Hull Three by official Finns, and a "Basic Fighter Vehicle" by the fliers. Basic Fighter Vehicle became "BFV," became "Beefie." Other pilots decided the things were better named for their shape, and tagged them Lead Pipes, which led to some strange names being painted on the hatches: *L.P. Cinch*, *No Moving Parts*, *Down The Tubes*. Some of the Beefies got names no one dared write down.

There were some variants, two of which were important. The Basic Fighter Vehicle, Stretched Tankage. BFV/ST: The Beast. Beasts were the long-duration ships, trading more fuel, more air, and more food for somewhat lower performance. There was also the communication ship, the eyes and ears for Battle Control: the Attack Tracking/Recon/Control ship. AT/R/C. *Hatrack*. We had two of them. The Hatrack also earned its name by virtue of all the antenna hanging off it in all directions. Hatrack had better radar, better radio, better computers than a normal ship would need. It was supposed to be able to run the battle and help fight it at the same time. To make up for the mass of all the extra hardware, Hatrack had two sets of the modular main propulsion system set up in tandem, and a set of stretch tanks off a Beast.

God, were those ships ugly.

All carried powerful lasers and missiles. A few had specialized weapons carriers welded on top of all the other modifications.

At the same time, New Finlands's existing craft were made warworthy. Some of the *Kuu* class ships, which had already done heroic service, were armed more heavily. The space tugs were armed with lasers, drones were turned into robot kamikazes.

Except for skeleton groups of shuttle and maintenance craft, every ship was rebased at The Rock. If it was at all possible, not a shot would be fired from Vapaus. The Rock was just that, a solid mass of stone. It made much better armor for itself than the fragile, spinning shell of Vapaus ever could.

We could not afford to lose either satellite. If we won through, they were vital lifelines between New Finland and the remainder of mankind. If we could not smash *Leviathan*, the satellites might be the last bastions of free people in this star system. If need be, they were the launching places, should we be forced to retreat and hide in the depths of space, vanishing into the dark orbits of the outer planets.

But for all of us, those who knew exactly what was expected of the enemy, and those who knew only that danger was on the way, there was one thing we did over and over again. People looked to the skies, with eyes, with view screens, with radar, with telescopes and asked, *When are they coming?*

It was two months after my second arrival on Vapaus that the company of the *Joslyn Marie* was awakened suddenly in the middle of the night.

From almost the first moment the crew of the *Bohica* had arrived at Vapaus, the search for the control center had commenced. There were teams crawling over the entire satellite, searching with sonar and radar, sharp eyes, record checks, and hunches.

Tremendous preparations for battle had been made since Dr. Tempkin was disheartened by the news of the great ship. Our ships were ready and the crews were eager to fight. Deep inside the sheltering mass of The Rock, Battle Control was operational, the crews trained, the computers up and running. The wounds of Vapaus were not healed altogether, but her hurts had been greatly eased, and precautions taken against the dangers of wartime. New weapons appeared every day, it seemed. It was possible that we had an actual chance to beat *Leviathan*.

The *J.M.* was almost getting to be a crowded ship: Marie-Francoise Chen had accepted our invitation of a billet on board. Randall Metcalf and Eve Berman slept there when they were on Vapaus. George Prigot, Joslyn, and I were permanent residents. We were settled into a life that seemed happy and comfortable in the face of the urgent work we were all engaged upon.

All six of us were aboard the *J.M.* the night the intercom buzzed to life next to Joslyn and me.

" 'llo?"

"Commander Larson!" It was Tempkin, sounding very excited. "We have found it!"

"Found wha'?"

"The missile control center! Bring that Prigot and the French officer. Rauman Park station, on the red transit line. Have your party wear their pressure suits." He broke the connection.

"Pressure suits?" Joslyn asked sleepily.

"Don't ask me, I just took the message. Let's get this crowd moving."

Eve and Randall invited themselves, of course. Fifteen minutes later we were aboard one of the transit cars moving through the strange darkness of Vapaus. Here the lights in the sky weren't stars, but streets, houses, people carrying flashlights. It was eerie for what you had unconsciously decided was a star to commence swinging back and forth with the easy motion of a night-walking stroller.

There were few other passengers aboard, and that perhaps was lucky. It is generally considered gauche to wear pressure suits in a habitable area: not only do they attract stares and tend to crowd up a place, as they are rather bulky, but a person in a pressure suit is a sight to start rumors about leaks . . .

There was a car waiting for us at our stop. The driver urged us to hurry and we lumbered aboard. He immediately started off at a great pace through the darkness, driving on large balloon tires over the countryside, ignoring the roads. After a few minutes, I could see the dim outline of a large tent, lit from within. We pulled up and the driver urged us inside.

Dr. Tempkin was there in his own pressure suit—which had been put on over his pajamas. "Good evening to you all. We have indeed found what we were looking for." He gestured to a knot of men clustered around the center of the tent. "There is a hatchway there, cleverly sealed. They are working to open it. There is a vertical tunnel beneath it, leading straight through the bedrock of Vapaus. We sent a tug to examine the area from the outside. At the end of the airlock tunnel is a well-camouflaged platform, open to space. On it, racks of equipment and radio antenna. It *must* be there to control the cursed missiles. It was found when a nearby resident remembered seeing Guardians working here. Sonar soundings located the tunnel precisely."

A murmur of conversation from the knot of men was followed by a brief smattering of applause. The hatch was open.

Tempkin locked his helmet in place and we heard his voice over our suit radios. "Let us go take a look."

Floodlights were brought to bear, pointing straight down the tunnel. It was square in cross-section, about a meter on a side. Bolted into the bare rock on one side was a metal ladder. Tempkin went down first, and I followed.

"The airlock at the bottom here is really tiny. Better take it two at a time," I said.

Tempkin and I shuffled into the lock and cycled through it.

We cracked the exterior hatch and moved out onto the platform. We stepped out of the hatch onto . . . something.

Our feet, our sense of balance, the utter silence, all told us that we were on solid ground that was perfectly still beneath our feet. But that ground was a wide-mesh metal grating. Below us the stars, the sun, the planet and the sky wheeled.

The platform was welded to heavy I-beam girders at its four corners, the beams set into the solid rock. All was painted the exact dirty grey of the surrounding rock that was Vapaus's exterior.

I imagined how it must look from space—a tiny patch of hard-to-see rectangularity, whizzing past the eye in a moment as the world spun by. No wonder it was hard to find.

In the exact center of the platform was an elaborate two-operator control system, locked inside a wire cage. Just outside the door to the cage was a featureless rectangular solid, the size and shape of a coffin.

"Ah! The antennae hang through the grating beneath it," Tempkin said, kneeling to look through the floor. "We can hang an atmosphere bubble around this platform. Then we can work on it more easily."

George and Marie-Francoise came through the lock. George stopped and looked hard at the coffin-shaped box. "Mmmmph," he said. "I know this machine, the big box outside the cage. I helped design it. It's a shield box, an entrance control. It's a standard device for protecting valuable machines that must be left untended."

He walked over to it and pushed at an unmarked, featureless point on it. The front panel swung open smoothly. Inside was an array of unmarked heavy-duty switches, each with a safety cover. Above the switch array was a single, larger toggle switch. George pointed to the lower array.

"One hundred switches. When they are set to the proper combination of on and off, you flip the top switch and the cage door opens nicely."

"If you set it wrong, or if you try and force the cage door or something, what happens?" I asked.

"Dunno. Depends on what kind of bomb they put in it. Might just melt down the machinery, might crack the satellite open. But I can open it safely. I'll need tools. Induction meters, very sensitive. Radiation checkers, so maybe we find out about the bomb. Screwdrivers, wrenches, magnifiers, work lights, micro tools, labels, note paper . . ."

George was soon hard at work. The bubble crew came with their rappelling gear and started climbing over the rock to put the pressure bubble together. Tempkin and I returned above ground and Randall and Eve went down to take a look. The above-ground site was being turned into a full-fledged worksite. Tents were going up, more portable lights were going up, and there was a comm station being hooked up. Someone had set up a mobile canteen. Joslyn and I wandered over to it to scrounge a cup of tea. I hadn't gotten through half of mine before a message came through that George wanted to talk to me. I resealed my suit and returned to the control platform. Strange to be drinking tea one minute and standing on a metal grate with the universe spinning under my feet the next.

"How is it going, George?" I asked.

"Not good," he said, without looking up from his work. "This is not fun." He traced a circuit painstakingly as he spoke. "You know the old bit about the guard dog who was trained to attack anyone who came near his master's place? Well, the guy goes off and comes back, and there's his dog, just laying for him. I helped design this system, maybe five years ago. They wanted a *real* safebox no one could get past. We thought of all sorts of crazy, complicated ideas. So complicated they could be fooled, or broken, or gotten around. So we came up with this nice, simple idea instead. But we did put one gimmick on it, though. An inductance sensing detector. This is one hell of a weak inductance field I'm using. A few less gauss and it wouldn't register at all. A few more, and up it goes."

"Wonderful."

The bubble crew finished up and I shooed them off the platform and back up into Vapaus. I closed both airlock hatches after them—and toyed with the idea of following behind them. George had never said exactly why it was he wanted me. Maybe he just wanted someone to talk to, in order to keep himself calm. Maybe he just wanted me as a good luck charm. Whatever the reason, it was an honor I would have been happy to forego.

With the bubble ready, I opened an air tank and the slack plastic soon billowed out from the platform. I cracked open my faceplate. George took off his helmet and gauntlets.

Finally, George sat back on his haunches and sighed. "That's it. All circuits traced. The switches are set properly. Unless those bastards booby-trapped it, or someone is playing games. Here we go."

"Wait a second," I said. I jacked my suit radio into the airlock comm panel. "This is Larson," I said. "We're going to try the cage door control now. Seal the upper hatch. I'm going to get the lower one open, just in case we have a problem." I watched the telltales, and reopened the lower hatch as soon as the panel indicated the upper hatch was sealed. I yanked my comm jack from the panel. "Okay, George," I said. "Let's give it a try."

George nodded and threw the switch. The control cage door opened smoothly. "Very nice," I said.

George grinned happily. "Sheer luck." He clumped over to his pile of gadgetry. "Next up." He carefully cut two wires leading from a fat cylinder just inside the cage door. "That's the self destruct unit," he said. "In other words, the bomb the entrance control operated. Harmless now."

Just then the access control panel lit up like a Christmas tree. George looked up in alarm. "My God. That thing just tried to set off the bomb!" he said.

"You mean if you hadn't just cut the wires—"

"Yeah. But I got the combination right. It can't have set it off!"

"Maybe there was a delay circuit."

"No. There wasn't. I told you, I helped design this thing. The only way the system can come alive after the panel's deactivated is if it gets a signal from the outside!"

"The outside?" George and I looked at each other, both of us suddenly understanding, suddenly horrified.

"George! Below you!" I yelled. There, beneath our feet, a high-gain control antenna was slowly swiveling to a new heading.

"My God!" George said. "*Leviathan* must have sent the destruct signal! She's here! Let's get the hell off this platform!"

George rushed for the hatchway, and I was right behind him, slamming down my faceplate as I followed.

There was a deep, rumbling roar in the rocks above us. I dove through the airlock.

The rocks above us rumbled again, and jets of fire lashed down from the girders which held the platform to the satellite. Then, incredibly, the platform itself sheared away from the girder attachments and fell out into the depths of space, brushing past the plastic bubble as if it wasn't even there. Our air exploded away into space—and George's helmet and gauntlets had just sailed off into space with the platform. I grabbed a handhold and held on, but George was pulled, feet first, half out of the lock. His face was alive with terror, and he grabbed for the lip of the hatch, his legs hanging out over emptiness. The last of the air blew out the lock, and we were in vacuum. At least that meant I could relax my grip on the handhold and reach for George.

But George was already unconscious, stunned by the pressure drop. He let go his hold on the lip of the hatch and started to slide out the airlock. I dove for him, and caught him by the suit collar. I braced my feet inside the lock, grabbed him under the arm with my other hand and dragged him into the chamber.

I swung the outer door to, dogged it shut, and threw open the spill valve. Air blasted in to fill the lock chamber. About a quarter of an atmosphere. George gurgled and started breathing. His nose was bleeding. I opened my helmet—and heard Joslyn calling for me over the airlock's intercom. "Mac!" she cried. "Are you there? Are you there?"

"We're both here, and more or less all right," I said. "We're okay, inside the airlock. Get the upper hatch open and we'll come on up."

"Commander. This is Tempkin. We've just received reports of—"

"Of a gigantic spacecraft appearing from behind the sun. We know." I paused for a moment. I was dazed, short of breath, and my arm hurt. "*Leviathan* sent a signal to the control station here, the second she came out from behind the sun. George had already cut the cable on the bomb that would have melted the platform, but they had charges in the I-beams, too. Those went off and they cut it all loose. The whole platform just fell out into space."

"What do you mean? What has happened?"

"I mean *Leviathan*'s commander took over the missile control system the first moment he could, and why the hell didn't we figure out *that* part of it? They're here."

Chapter Fifteen

Four hours later, the group that had swarmed around the tunnel shaft was scattered. Marie-Francoise had demanded that Joslyn attend her to help in the gleaning of new information on *Leviathan* from direct observation. The ship was still not much more than a dot on a radar screen, but at least the intelligence types had something tangible to work with for the first time.

George and I were hustled off to the hospital. My arm had a greenstick fracture, and George had a mild case of vacuum shock. Neither of us was seriously hurt, but the doctors wanted us kept overnight. They weren't worried about our recovery; they just didn't want to take chances with personnel valuable to the war effort.

I didn't fight it. I was short on sleep and they even gave me a private room.

Soon after the doctors and nurses left me to my own devices, a soft knock came on the door. "Come in," I called.

Eve came in and rather hesitantly took a seat by my bed. "Hello. How they treating you?"

"Hello. I'm okay. I'll be out of here tomorrow morning. What's up?"

"They gave me the fighter command."

"Oh." There wasn't much past that I could say. Eve and I had started off on the wrong foot on the *Bohica*, and things had never improved past the peppery stage.

"None of the Finnish naval officers past the grade of Lieutenant are still alive. Executed by the Guards or dead in action. They decided they needed someone with command experience," she explained.

"Why come to tell me?" I asked.

She blushed slightly, her deep brown skin darkening,

and she looked away. "I thought you might figure you deserved it."

"Nope. As you said, you're the senior officer."

"I've got a feeling the Finns could patch together a brevet command under some League regulation if they wanted to."

Had she come just to rub it in? No, if anything, she seemed embarrassed to be here. "Eve. I don't want it. I never wanted it."

"Dammit, Larson, neither did I!"

Bingo. "I see."

"I'm a fighter pilot, not a strategist. I could spend the next ten years over in Battle Control, and I'd *still* be a fighter pilot."

"I sympathize. But I ask you again. Why tell me about it?"

"Because you are the only other officer remotely qualified for the job. Joslyn's good, but she's a grade below you—and she's got the same problem I've got—she's got a pilot's point of view, not a god-damned chess player's. If I could refuse the appointment in your favor, I'd do it in a second."

"No." That much I was sure of.

"Why not?"

"I could ask you the same question. Eve, I've taken whatever they handed me in this war since way back when I was minding my own business. I've faked it. I've winged it. I've improvised. I could take what they gave me, because I was the only one for the job, but I can't take your fight. *You're* the one that's got the training, the rank, the fliers who know you. This is your ticket. Not mine."

"Dammit, Larson! Mac. Don't you get it? *I can't send my kids out to die!*"

"No? Neither can I. But you have to. So you will. If I thought I'd be a better fighter commander, that I could keep more of them alive, I might be tempted. But I don't think that. And I can't take it just so you could sleep better nights. I've already got my own nightmares."

No more words. She rose, turned and stalked out the door.

I killed the lights. I didn't sleep well *that* night, anyway.

✧ ✧ ✧

A few nights after Eve offered me the command, I still worried over it. Joslyn and I talked it over. "As far as I can see it, Mac, you were offered the chance to make a bad situation worse. Her making the offer hasn't gotten around, but if it did, it would certainly be pretty rotten for morale. Worse if you went through with it. I wouldn't want to fly for a reluctant commander."

"But could I have said yes? Should I have said yes?"

"I don't quite see how. There isn't any way your taking command would make matters better. What scares me is that she made the offer at all. She must be so afraid. It doesn't make me expect brilliant command decisions. But so much damage would have to be done to the morale of the fliers if they knew she was unwilling . . . You'd have to be good enough to overcome that. Mac, you're not. You couldn't be. If you were, you'd be thirty years older and an admiral instead of an explorer."

"I know. I guess the offer scared me, too."

"One other thing, my love. Remember that even if our ships are held in reserve, we're some of the 'kids' she has to send out to die."

The Finns managed to send a space tug after the missile control station and retrieve it. When it was examined, it became clear that if George hadn't cut that last set of cables, the thermite charges would have incinerated everything on the platform before the girders were blown to throw it into space. As it was, we recovered the control station virtually intact. The controlling software had all been wiped clean. There was no hope of recovering the control commands and taking command back from *Leviathan*. The hardware was intact, though. The Finns immediately got to work tracing the circuitry and learning how to run it. Inside a day, we knew which button was supposed to do what, even if the buttons didn't work anymore.

It was valuable information, for a terrible truth was upon us. We could no longer simply defeat *Leviathan*: we had to board her. She now controlled the missile system. If we had located the Vapaus control point just a day or so earlier, we might have had a chance to hash out the code needed to order the missiles to self-destruct. One thing we learned from the recovered Vapaus control station was that the missiles would indeed remain on patrol, still attacking anything that moved, indefinitely, if their owners could no longer control them.

The only way to do that was to get aboard *Leviathan*, get to the control station, and use it to tell the missiles to blow themselves up.

That wasn't going to be easy. It called for a redrawing of all our plans on very short notice. Now that *Leviathan* had been spotted and tracked, we could tell with a great degree of certainty what her course would be. From where she was, there was only one path that led to a safe arrival in the air of New Finland. She would reach the useful range of our fighters in 360 hours, and arrive at the planet in 500.

One thing was a great help. George was utterly certain that the control station aboard *Leviathan* would be completely identical to the one we had. The Guardians tried to standardize people; they certainly didn't custom-design machinery. Working with speed and determination, the Finns hooked up the recovered control station to a simulator and set to work training teams of two in the use of it. The controls were on two panels four meters apart and set up so the two operators stood back to back. It was impossible for one person to work it alone.

Joslyn and I were one of the teams they trained. If and when we got onto *Leviathan*, each of the teams was to head for a certain part of the ship. There were about six areas of the ship that Intelligence (in other words, Marie-Francoise with Joz kibitzing) thought might hold the control station. There were two teams for each site. We'd be lucky if one made it. There wasn't time to train three sets of teams: *Leviathan* was on the way.

Joslyn and I got to the point, after long, weary hours being drilled by the Finnish simulator team, where we could have run the station in our sleep. At times, I did.

✧ ✧ ✧

Waiting was tough, but after a long time, it ended. *Leviathan* was in range, and the first of our ships could go after her.

Joslyn and I were overseeing a Finnish crew that was stripping the *J.M.* for battle as the first attack started. The *J.M.* had to be made lighter, her weapons had to be prepared. *Stars* and *Stripes* were off-loaded to lighten the *J.M.*, but *Uncle Sam* was left in place, both as a lifeboat, and to provide independent firepower if need be. There were lots of details to be worked over, but all work came to a halt when the audio started coming in from the first attack, and we listened in as the fighter team approached the enemy.

"—ord, that ship is big."

"Oh, my God! It's too big. We can't fight that thing."

"We already are. This is Able Archer. I am being fired upon by laser. No effect on fighter at this range."

"This is Able Baker. I'm getting it too."

Eve's voice came in. "Jesus, they're eager. Archer, Baker. Fire a Redeye missile each. Hatrack, give them miss vectors. Let 'em think we're screw-ups. We need to see how they'll react. Hatrack, launch sensor probes in their wake."

"This is Hatrack. Missiles and probes launched on near-miss. Boosting toward target."

"Bandit! I see bandit launch, from the port side."

"How many?"

"Hard to read, radar is pretty jammed up. Visual poor at this range with the sun at their backs. I count one, two, three craft."

"This is Hatrack. I have tracking on bandits. They are ignoring missiles and headed for our fighter group."

"Battle Control here. Flights one and four, lateral flank maneuver, space to 100 kilometers, ecliptic."

"Able Baker. They are firing on the Redeye missiles. Lasers from the main deck. Archer's Redeye is homing. Baker's is sliding away. Looks like you didn't put enough miss on it, Randall."

"How about that?" Randall radioed from the lead ship.

"Battle Control. We are receiving from five good probes, but not for long. Four is overheating, laser damage. Four is out."

"Hatrack here. One fighter still heading for us. Other two turning to hit the probes."

"Able Archer here. That un-miss of mine is heading straight for their main laser array, looks like. The Redeye's shielding worked, I guess. And *whambo*! That didn't do that laser cannon any good."

"Hatrack. That fighter nearly in range. Permission to engage?"

"Battle Control here. Negative! we have to draw out more than three lousy ships."

"Hatrack here. You just got 'em. Here come—oh, lordy lord, eighteen blips, half to a defensive shell, the other half heading our way."

"This is Baker. I can scope the defensive shell zapping the probes and the other Redeye."

"Hatrack. Another flight launching. I count at least ten blips."

"Dammit. This is Battle Control. Withdraw. If they chase you, let 'em. Don't hit the fighters so near the big ship."

"Well, that was exciting."

"Stow it, Lambert. All according to plan, and you know it."

"Oh Jesus. Maybe not. There are five of the bastards on intercept with me. Eve, I gotta fight it out. Going into firing pass—and there we—"

There was dead silence on the feed for a moment. Then "Hatrack! This is Battle Control. What the hell is going on!"

"Nothing, anymore, Batcon. But Lambert got two of them, first. All other fighters withdrawn safely."

The Guardians gave chase, and the first wave of our fliers withdrew. The word was passed to the second wave to trim up their orbits, and as the Guardians came in behind the first wave, the second wheeled out from behind the planet and pounced on their rear. They were cut off from their main ship, and she was too far off to offer assistance.

None of the Guardians escaped. Four of our fighters didn't make it. And that was the last thing that went right, the last piece of tactical planning we followed through on.

No one ever saw that battle. There could be no eye witnesses. Only by sheer chance did anyone actually see his opponent, and then only for split seconds as two warring ships whizzed past each other. This was a battle of distance and speed, of long hours of boredom, brief moments of mind-wrenching action and danger sandwiched into them at random.

Those who directed the battle watched symbols and numbers and orbit projections, translated into holographic displays. Joslyn and I watched, when we could, on the repeater monitor receiving from Batcon. The whole affair seemed a large and elaborate game. In the center of the hologram was the planet, represented as a plain, featureless ball, or actually two balls, one centered inside the other—the inner showing the physical planet, the outer showing the practical limits of the atmosphere.

The planet was shown as transparent: one could see the tiny midges of light that displayed the fighters as they whirled behind the bulk of the planet.

A great, blood-red arrowhead bore in on the planet, slowly, ponderously: *Leviathan*. Two blue ovoids, Vapaus and The Rock, ambled round the planet in a stately dance, Vapaus orbiting three times each time The Rock orbited twice.

The midges, the fighters, were the color of their bases. A gossamer thread held each object, to show its present orbit.

Now and then, the flashing dot that represented a missile would sprout from one ship and move to another, and the second ship might wink off the screen. A voice would call "Nailed the bastard!" or "Jesus, they've torched Edmonds."

✧ ✧ ✧

I was shocked by *distance*. It made no sense—I had traveled dozens of light-years to get here, and these little ships were flying but a few hundred thousand kilometers. But in spite of accelerating constantly at one standard gee, and building up incredible velocity, these ships took long hours to reach each other.

The Guardians sent a second wave of their own after us. Our attacks had been carefully planned long in advance up until that moment, but sooner or later, something had to break. The Guardians' ships cracked our formations. We still did well, but not as well. We destroyed another eight of their ships, but lost another four of ours.

Eve seemed afraid to risk the forces needed for whatever challenge was at hand. She sent two ships where five could do the job, or one instead of a pair. Out of fear, she was letting us lose, letting us die, a little at a time. The battle degenerated into one-on-one slug fests between pairs of ships, or three ships against two, a battle of stragglers and predators.

Patterns started to develop. Both sides learned, paying for knowledge with the lives of their pilots. The enemy ships were lighter, smaller, shorter duration ships than the Beefies. Their very lightness gave them an edge in acceleration over the short term. Crudely put, they put bigger engines on smaller, flimsier ships.

Their lightly built ships would lose in a laser duel, but had a better chance of outrunning a missile. But the Beefies and the Beasts carried a lot more fuel and breathing air.

I watched the display as a Beast chased a bandit up out of orbit. By then we knew very precisely how much fuel the bandits could carry, and thus how long, all told, they might fire their engines.

I guess the pilot of the Beast worked it out in his head. He chased the bandit at his top acceleration, 2.6 gees. The bandit could do 3.1, and he started out 1000 kilometers ahead of his pursuer, gradually edging farther and farther ahead. But, even if he had wanted to, he couldn't have turned back; the Beast would have had him.

After three quarters of an hour at 3.1 gees, the bandit was moving at a speed many times faster than the planet's escape velocity. The Beast turned around and headed for home at an easy 1 gee. The bandit was as good as dead. He didn't have the fuel in his tanks to get back.

He tried. He not only had to shed his speed, but shed it fast enough to get back to the planet, where he might hope for rescue. Maybe his engines finally melted to slag, maybe his tanks dried sooner than they should have. He didn't make it. He's still out there, somewhere.

A bandit and a Beefie chased each other into opposing orbits, the Beefie only 50 kilometers below the bandit. One traveled east-to-west, the other west-to-east: every 42 minutes they made a pass by each other. Their closing velocity was nearly 60,000 kilometers per hour. They ran out of missiles first. The missiles' tiny on-board computers couldn't maneuver quickly or accurately enough to make a hit at those speeds.

Then it was lasers.

The two ships flew past each other, having about 10 minutes line-of-sight on each other every half orbit, every 42 minutes. The two beams lashed out at their opponents, both ships heating and overheating as the ships bore down on each other, each tracking the other. Then the two would have a half hour to cool, to check damage, to recuperate and watch the readings on the battery gauges.

Then another pass, another half-orbit's rest, then back at each other, the two ships gradually dying as they were cooked. The radios died as the antennae melted off. The ships tumbled as paint bubbled off and safety valves vented, causing tiny side thrusts. Low on fuel, the pilots ignored the tumble. Both ships had tracking devices for their lasers, so the beam could be aimed no matter where the ship was pointed.

The batteries drained, the lasers grew weak.

In the middle of a pass, the Beefie's laser overheated and blew up. The ship itself survived for the next pass.

The bandit must have thought he had the kill. The two ships came back at each other. The Beefie pilot used the last of his fuel to very slightly raise his orbit, and then fire his engine once again—with the bandit passing straight through the fusion flame. The bandit came out a puddle of metal. The Beefie's orbit went unstable. He reentered.

He hit atmosphere over the night side of the planet, when, by chance, the *J.M.*, docked at Vapaus, was almost directly overhead. A field of darkness, then suddenly a spot of light, then a long fiery tail careering through the night, then the darkness undisturbed again.

Death and the threat of it were everywhere I looked, watching the tiny sparks circle the battle monitor, watching relayed transmissions from the cameras on the fighters, on Vapaus, and The Rock.

A fighter out of fuel, out of weapons, its pilots capable only of watching the missile coming toward him from an orbit just barely faster and higher than his, the missile just *waiting* there for long hours until it drifted close enough. The pilot could *see* the missile fifteen minutes before the end. He aimed his camera at it, a tiny dot that grew larger and larger in the screen, and then the picture went dead.

A bandit's power system must have died suddenly: he was headed back toward *Leviathan* at high velocity. He reached the point where he should have put on the brakes to make a safe docking. Instead, he kept going, falling like a rock straight for the ship. *Leviathan* fired on her own fighter with a great flurry of missiles, and the bandit turned into a cloud of dust that swept past *Leviathan*.

Space was littered with broken machines, derelict ships and missiles, debris, clouds of vapor that dispersed into vacuum from broken fuel tanks, and the broken bodies of dead warriors. Some hit the atmosphere, and New Finland was graced for many days with the pretty sparks of more shooting stars than usual. Others drifted out into distant orbit of the planet's sun, or out of the system entirely, to be lost forever.

It was carnage in slow motion, hours or days of struggle for advantage, climaxed by death that came in the blink of the eye.

And we were losing.

I could see it when I tore myself from one little part of the picture, from some small, fascinating horror, and look at the whole battle at once.

Whoever had ships left, when the other side was wiped out, would win. For each two ships of ours that died, three of theirs were killed. But the Guardians had more ships than we did, and their commander was cautious. He held his ships back deep in the holds of *Leviathan*, as the great ship bore inexorably down toward the air.

Eve couldn't do it. Maybe it was a hopeless situation, maybe a wiser or older commander could have kept us out of trouble.

She tried. But all her machinations and provocations had failed to strip *Leviathan*'s flight decks.

So she played her hole card.

Us.

"Berman to *Joslyn Marie*. Please come in. Over."

"This is *Joslyn Marie*. Come in, Battle Control. What have you got for us, Eve?"

"Stand by, Mac. We're piping numbers to your computer. Okay, call up file *Bushwhack* and slave your monitor to my computer."

I typed in the commands, and the battle model vanished from the hologram generator. *Leviathan* appeared.

"Okay, Mac, Joslyn, this is our best information on *Leviathan*—what Marie-Francoise and Joslyn cobbled together, plus watching through the scopes, plus guessing.

"You guys get to attack her," she said.

"Y'know, I had a feeling you'd bring that up."

"Sorry, Mac. But listen. We can't get the ships up from the hangar decks to kill them—so we have to bottle those ships up. Now, here are the targets." Four spots on the hologram started blinking red. "These are the launch sites for the fighter craft. A pair forward, a pair aft, port and starboard, out of the hull itself."

"Nothing off the main deck?"

"Nope. We figure the topside is for use in atmosphere. They fly fixed-wing right over the side, and we can see what look like ballistic launch cradles, for use in gravity. Okay, we've logged this course into your onboards." The image of *Leviathan* shrunk to a tiny dot. The planet reappeared, and *Leviathan* was faced away from it, thus directing her engines precisely toward the planet for braking. A looping red line popped into existence. It leapt away from where the *J.M.* was now, shot toward *Leviathan*, crossed her stern, flew by the ship's port side, then petered out, headed nowhere at all.

"That's goddamn hairy, Eve. What thrust levels?"

"Six gees the whole way. That's why you're it. No other ship has enough jump in the engines to fly that long at those power levels. You're the only ship with the delta-vee to get in and out fast enough with a chance to survive."

Joslyn stared at the plotting thoughtfully. "Captain Berman. Could you include the jets of *Leviathan*'s thrust in the image?"

A pink plume a hundred kilometers long popped into the image. It cut directly through our course.

"My God!" I said. "Eve, you're sending us through a fusion flame?!"

"Dammit, I know that! I know, I know, I know. But there isn't a single other damn way to do it. The fusion flame creates a gigantic plasma shadow their detection gear can't see through. It provides the cover for you to get close enough to hit them."

"What is our time in the plume itself? And what temperatures can we expect?"

"We figure the time at between four and ten seconds. We're trying to keep you to the edge of it, where it's a bit cooler. In the fringes, the temperatures are no more than 6,000 degrees absolute. The plasma particles are thinner there too—lower density."

Joslyn's voice was flat and hard. "We cannot survive that."

"With *Uncle Sam* docked in place, using *Sam*'s heat shield to protect the nose of the *J.M.*—"

I whistled softly. This was insane. "That will help, but not enough. The heat's way too high to handle."

"It's not just heat. It's more like flying into a nuclear bomb as it goes off," Joslyn said.

"Let me finish. We're going to insulate you. You'll make it, probably. You have *got* to smash the launch stations. *Leviathan* hits air in 58 hours. My kids are too hard pressed. The way this fight is going, I won't have a fighter left by then. *Leviathan* will hold the sky—and then they can deal with Vapaus whenever they want. They'll win. If those launch sites are wrecked, we'll still be in this one. And you're the only ship with a ghost of a chance."

"Eve, it can't work! Why not have us fly through the sun, for God's sake?"

"Mac—Commander Larson. Lieutenant Commander Cooper. You have your orders. The insulation crew is to start on you right away. I suggest you get your ship cooled down as far as possible. You launch in three hours. Berman out."

I pointed to the thin red line that showed our course. "Notice something, Joslyn? They didn't even bother plotting a course back for us."

"I know, Mac. But that bit I'll attend to right now. Hell. Right about now I'm wishing we hadn't agreed with each other quite so much about doing our duty."

"Tug captain here. Please now undock your ship and take up station-keeping 100 meters from satellite."

Joslyn did so. Then we waited. We heard scratches and thumps on the hull, and then silence. "Tug captain here.

We have done the attaching of the end of the mylar to your ship. Please, using gyros only, no thrusters, commence to be rolling at half revolutions a minute."

The *Joslyn Marie* began a long, slow roll along her long axis. We watched the view from a camera on Vapaus. Hanging beside the *J.M.* was a stubby cylinder. It held what looked like a giant roll of aluminum foil between two of its work arms. As the *J.M.* rolled, the foil paid out. The tug moved itself along our ship's axis, so that the foil was wrapped over the ship. Normally, mylar was carefully bonded to the side of a spacecraft slated for work close to the sun. There was no time for careful work now. The mylar was rolled right over the attitude jets. If we *had* used them, the stuff would have been blown off into space.

Finally the entire ship was covered. A tiny spacesuited figure who had been watching calmly from a perch on one of the tug's arms used a machete-like knife to cut through the mylar as it continued to roll off the reel. The cut was sloppy, but he managed to cut it free. He grabbed onto the end of the strip that wrapped around the *J.M.* and hung on. He picked up the spin of the ship. He used a sprayer to squirt adhesive all over the end of the mylar and then used his backpack jets to push him down onto the hull, dragging the foil with him. He set his feet against the outside of the film. When the end of it hit the hull, it stuck and he bounced.

"Remind me never to try that," I said.

"I doubt you'll have trouble remembering," Joslyn said.

"Next step," I said. The tug captain touched up his attitude fussily and then moved the tug slowly back down the length of our ship. A thick stream of goo spewed from a hose held by another arm. The goo fizzed and bubbled as it hit vacuum, then spluttered against the mylar over the ship's hull and hardened into a foam casing for the ship. It was ablative shielding material, used to beef up heat shields. Heat would dissolve it away, but the ablated shielding would carry the heat along with itself.

It was a cockeyed, haywire solution to flying into a fusion

plasma, but it was comforting all the same. It was an ugly jury rig, but the shielding upgraded the mission from "suicide" to "risky."

Except for a single radio aerial and the main engines, the entire ship was sealed in. That aerial was expendable—the fusion flame would vaporize it anyway. All our other communication and detection gear was stowed away.

"Cooling system shunted through engine bells and on full," Joslyn reported.

That was important. We needed to start cold. Heat was generated constantly by a working spacecraft. The shielding made excellent insulation. By routing super-cold liquid hydrogen from our fuel tanks into the cooling ducts of the ship, and then through the engine bells, we could pull the temperature way down. The bells were cold now, and made good radiation surfaces.

Once we lit up the fusion jets, there would be no way to cool the ship until the shielding blew off.

If we lived long enough for the shielding to blow off.

Chapter Sixteen

The clock went to zero.

The *J.M.* launched herself away from station-keeping at an easy one gee, and we throttled up to six gee in about three minutes. We could hear the creaking and groaning of the ship's structural members as they took up the load.

Faster and faster, Vapaus fell away from us. Joslyn and I were crushed into our acceleration couches more and more deeply. The couches had been adjusted to high-gee configuration, which basically meant they were now sacks of viscous jelly inside thin, very flexible membranes. The jelly was some exotic organic compound, and the membranes tended to be very slightly permeable. As a result, the cabin soon stank to high heaven. I didn't cut in high power on the ventilation system, though: it would get a workout soon enough.

In fact, the temperature was already rising. We had cooled the entire ship down to 4 degrees C. Now, though the engines were isolated so as not to contribute much heat to the system, there was plenty of other heat inevitably produced by running the ship, and no way to get rid of it. It started to warm up again. Slowly, but we'd have to watch it.

Our velocity increased at a frightening rate. In less than three minutes after hitting six gee, we had passed New Finland's escape velocity. If the flame under our tails decided to go out, or the astrogation system went blooie—well, we weren't coming back. We'd fall into the sun. Of course, the plan was for us to fall into something very like the sun in any event: *Leviathan*'s fusion plume.

We had no cameras outside the shielding to see it, but there was another glowing point of light between us and the sun. Much smaller, much closer—and much brighter. From here, it would be a sloppy point of light to the naked eye. *Leviathan*.

Six gee was wearing, to say the least. By the end of this day, in spite of all the protection and cushioning we had, Joz and I were going to be covered with bruised skin, capillaries popped and broken. Both Joslyn and I were awash in various drugs and vitamins to bolster our bodies against the killing pressure. And if it did kill us, the *Joslyn Marie* would go on as a robot and try and carry out the mission on her own, with two corpses along for the ride.

I *felt* like a corpse already. I couldn't turn my head to look at Joslyn, but each of us could see the other through the ship's camera system. She looked like someone had dropped a ton of bricks on her face, which wasn't so far from the truth. She moved her eye toward the camera and flicked the corner of her mouth in a attempt at a smile.

On we roared into the depths of night. This was no close, safe orbit. This was out into the great emptiness.

Five hundred seconds: 7,350 kilometers from launch point. Velocity: twenty-nine kilometers a second.

Seven hundred seconds: 14,406 kilometers out. 41 km/second.

Nine hundred seconds, the halfway point in the initial burn: 24,000 kilometers from launch point. Fifty-two km/second—190,000 kilometers an hour.

Now the gee forces were getting noticeably higher as we lost the mass of our fuel. Ship's programming accounted for this. At 1,000 seconds, the first of several throttlebacks occurred.

Faster and faster we fell deep into the sky on a roaring tower of fusion flame, atoms dying and aborning in the violence of our passage. My body was already exhausted with nothing more than the effort to stay alive. Each breath was a struggle to my body that suddenly weighed 600 kilograms, but my soul reveled in the awesome power of the skybeast we rode, a blazing torch in the empty black. The power, the might, the incredible velocities were no longer frightening, but enthralling, invigorating to my spirit. My wife and I rode a mighty chariot through the skies to wreak vengeance on our enemies and tormentors.

That last must have been partial oxygen starvation; *Leviathan* massed about 1,000 times as much as the *Joslyn Marie*.

But, damn all that's holy, she was a *good* ship. Her engines didn't falter, she held true course, she streaked across the skies.

Twelve hundred seconds into the mission: 42,000 kilometers from launch, 70 km/second—over 250,000 kilometers an hour. Our speed itself was a shield. We were moving too fast for any but the most sophisticated radar to have the slightest chance of tracking us.

We flew blind, on into the deep.

Fifteen hundred seconds, 25 minutes into the flight: over 66,000 kilometers from launch, roughly 30,000 klicks to fly. 88 klicks a second.

Sixteen hundred seconds. The numbers stopped meaning anything. Now it was time to get ready to fight. The exterior cameras were still inside their protective nacelles, but powered up. I got the radar system ready, but not switched on—the mylar shielding would have fried its brains.

Joslyn and I worked the controls carefully, barely speaking, moving as little as possible. Lifting an arm in six gee required as much effort as a full chin-up on Earth.

Eighteen hundred seconds. Course true. One half hour from launch. Velocity relative to target, 121.21 kilometers/second, bearing zero two zero.

Then: engine shutdown. Zero gee. Camera three on, nacelle open, camera remaining under shielding.

We suddenly floated at our ease, the engines stopped, our hearts wildly pounding against the terrible pressure that wasn't there any more. Then our stomachs did flip-flops as the gyros whirled into action, rotating the *Joslyn Marie* to the safest attitude, placing our nose dead ahead.

Head first, we fell into the fire.

Camera three showed us the darkness under the layers

of mylar and shielding. Then the darkness was suddenly dark no longer, but a dull, sullen red that grew violently in intensity and brilliance, finally exploding into nothingness as first the shielding, and then the camera, vaporized.

An alarm clanged shrilly.

Joslyn called out "Skin temperature 500 degrees and rising."

"Emergency cooling system on and full."

"Skin temp 600."

"Okay, coming up on weapons launch!" I called.

"Attack computer launching weapons, cycle begins, launch torp 1, 2, 3, 4, 5, 6 away, cycle to load, launch 1, 2, 3, 4, 5, 6—torps clear!"

"Joz, I see all external thermocouples ablated—no reading."

"Right-o. Last of shielding gone. Hot spots in stern bulkheads, cooling at 95 percent capacity."

"And rising. We got problems."

"Skin temp now 1,200. Damage lights on, more coming."

"Cooling overload!"

"Now seven seconds inside plume."

"Cooling overload, all units, all units over maximum."

But then we were out of it, clear of the plume.

The computer grabbed at the ship, spun it on thrusters this time, pitching the multi-megaton ship through 100 degrees in half a second.

The interior of the *J.M.* was a hellburning hurricane as the cooling system hauled out the superheated air, full of the smells of burnt insulation and melted plastics and the stink of sweat. The air temperature briefly hit the boiling point of water and dropped quickly again as the heat pulse moved through the ship. The cooling system was pumping liquid hydrogen from the fuel tanks through the emergency cooling coils and boiling it off into space. The temps came down quickly.

We didn't even notice. The camera clusters came out, and, at that moment, we saw *Leviathan*.

Gigantic. Huge. Monstrous. No machine, no spawn of

man's hand could be that vast, that great, that *awesome*. It had to be a monster, a *thing* of nature, some nightmare child of a dark sun, a great beast the shape of a hunting manta ray.

It was a mass of brooding metal, getting closer, growing larger as we as gaped at it in shock, stunned by its brutal, grotesque massiveness.

The ugly monster swelled as we rushed closer, then vanished and reappeared in the rearward screen as we flashed past. By the numbers, we were alongside her less then a second, but surely it must have been longer.

But then we were past, and the cameras zoomed in closer as we flashed away, skewing away under an easy one gee thrust at 90 degrees from our former course. Bursts of light flared against the side of the great ship. One, two, three . . .

"I count five hits," Joslyn said.

"Coming up on second firing sequence."

"Torps fire: 1, 2, 3, 4, 5, 6 . . . recycle to load—1, 2, 3, no four, no five, 6 fires."

"I read four and five as misfires."

"Disarming and jettisoning misfires on manual. Duds away."

Flares of light appeared in the screen and shrunk to nothing as the torps blasted away from us and zeroed in on *Leviathan*.

The great ship's lasers opened up on them, but we counted three more hits.

"Can you spot any launches against us?"

"Hold, monitoring . . . negative. Oh, Mac, my darling, we're clear!"

"Hot damn! Are we on the line for your escape-and-return course?"

"Certainly are, dearie. All set to crash into Kuu!"

"I'm afraid to ask if you're kidding." I looked at her. The grin was too pleased with itself. "No, you're not kidding. Okay, stand by to crash into New Finland's Moon."

✧ ✧ ✧

With the ship directed to a new heading, the engines roared back to six gees, and we were squashed back down into the acceleration couches. After the brief respite, the crushing agony of that thrust seemed worse, if anything.

When Joslyn had worked out a course away from *Leviathan*, she knew she couldn't head back the way we had come—*Leviathan* wouldn't be surprised a second time, and we weren't on her blind side anymore anyway. So we had to get away from the ship, which was directly between us and New Finland. However, we also had a hell of a lot of velocity to shed: we had to decelerate. Joslyn fired our engines to accelerate us 90 degrees away from our previous course. We were still moving out, but now we were also moving sideways. Once this sideways motion had gotten us well away from *Leviathan*, we could put on the brakes.

However, we were simply moving too fast and our tanks were too nearly empty. We had to have help slowing down. We were flying toward Kuu aft-end first, the engines firing—but the engines would need help.

That was were Kuu came in. We would fly around it in a tight curve, using its gravity to brake us, or, more accurately, to send us moving in the opposite direction at the same speed.

This sort of maneuver had been used for over a century, but the catch for us was, that to get redirected, we needed to come frighteningly close to Kuu's surface—about 13 kilometers. That was close enough to be called a crash if we were off course by more than .01 percent.

Kuu wasn't much, just a ball of rock, a small and useless world. But there's no such thing as a small world when you're dropping toward it. Every detail of that low-budget planet swelled disturbingly in the view screen. It was cratered to saturation; any rock that dropped wouldn't add to the number of craters; the new crater would simply erase an old one. There might have been mountains and valleys and plains at one time, now there was nothing but the cratered rubble of their destruction. It was the dead, ugly bones of a world, without the benefit of distance or atmosphere to soften the harsh cruelty of that landscape.

We sweated out *Leviathan*'s revenge on us, but no attack came. Perhaps we had crippled her launch cradles, perhaps we had been moving too fast to be caught, perhaps they were too hard pressed in the battle with the League fighters.

The harsh black moonscape swept ever closer. Our radar told us we'd miss by zero, but the distance we hoped to miss by was smaller than the margin of error the radar had at this range.

"Mac! Camera five!"

I switched over to five, and swore under my breath. *Leviathan* was launching. One, two, three bright sparks popped away from the ship. A fourth spark came into being, but suddenly turned into a fuzzy patch of brilliance.

"Something went up on the launch cradle!"

"We didn't stop 'em, but it looks like we slowed 'em up." No more sparks jumped away from the ship.

I flicked back to the main view camera and saw Kuu dropping in like a boulder on an ant. The sphere grew even as we watched, and I had to jog back the magnification to pull the whole globe into view.

Radar showed us still 30,000 kilometers out and closing. We watched the dead planet grow, its image wavering now and then in the plume of our exhaust.

By the time we were 10,000 klicks out, our headlong rush had noticeably slowed. By 8,000 we seemed to be barely crawling. All was relative, though; we'd still need every gee of thrust we had to get out of this. Kuu's gravity took hold of us and pulled us in. We gained velocity again.

Now we seemed not only to be moving toward the moon, but around it, the surface sliding along underneath as our trajectory led us around the limb of the world. The *J.M.* kept her engines pointed dead at the landscape that rolled forward beneath us. It seemed as if we were in a long, steep glide now, swiftly sailing down in toward the rubble of the crater field below us.

I told the computer to bring up the impact predictor

program, call up data on Kuu from memory and show it on my main monitor. The program gave me three displays.

One was a simple meridian grid map of Kuu. A tiny red "x" rolled slowly over it. If the engines crapped out right *now*, that x would be the site of our very own crater.

The second was a number, now up from 0 to 15,350—our peripoint in meters over the average radius of the planet.

The third was a burbling black line, which shifted and flickered from moment to moment—it was a radar display of the visible limb of Kuu; a cross section of the landscape ahead of us. It answered the question—seeing how our peripoint is 15 kilometers, are there any 16 kilometer high mountains in the way?

Peripoint would be almost exactly at the center of the farside of Kuu—the area which was most poorly mapped.

If the engines held out, and we lived to the point where the red "x" vanished, it would mean that, *if* Kuu was a perfectly round body with no mountains or valleys (which it wasn't), and *if* its gravity field was uniform (which it wasn't), we would miss the satellite's surface.

Then the peripoint figure started to drop. 15.3 km, . . . 15.25, . . . 15.15. "Damn it!" I said. Kuu's gravity field wasn't uniform, all right. Below the surface we passed over was an area of greater density, and hence with a stronger gravitational pull than the average for Kuu. It was pulling us down.

Now there was no sense of sailing, of a long glide—we were falling, no two ways about it.

Kuu's ugliness whizzed past our cameras.

That burbly line got more burbly. "We are coming up over a highland area," Joslyn remarked. That was a neutral way to put it. "Ohmigod, we're about to pile into a mountain!" would have done just as well and been just as accurate.

"All right, Mac, I'm taking manual control. Give me countdown to peripoint and peripoint in meters."

"Twenty seconds. Peripoint 12,500. Nineteen seconds. 12,400. Eighteen. 11,900."

Joz was glued to her own displays, watching the engines, the limb radar, and the TV pickup of the real estate below.

"Fifteen seconds," I went on. "11,900. 14 seconds. 12,000. 13. 12 seconds. Holding at 12,000."

"Cut! Go to digital, climb altitude maximum," Joslyn ordered.

"Maximum elevation, 10,500 meters. Rising . . . 10,600 . . . 11,800—scramble! No data!"

"It's all right, Mac. We're through. The radar's trying to read empty spa—"

WHAM!!

The lighting died for a moment and I remember thinking it made no sense, if we had hit there would not have been time to notice we were dead. Emergency lighting came on and the readouts unscrambled themselves. Suddenly I realized we were in zero gee.

"Joz—what—"

"Shut up!" she yelled, urgently throwing switches.

I sat there in the middle of the air when I should have been weighing six times too much, waiting for the hot pilot in the next chair to save my skin and explain.

The lights flickered again, and the ship lurched sickeningly as the engines relit under us. The ventilators brought a new odor to the sweaty ooze we had long ago forgotten—the smell of burnt insulation and melted wire.

"I've got some control back, Mac, but I think we've lost engine number two—and we're riding the idiot backup computer. See if you can get the prime computer back on line."

I was already keying in the start-up commands. The prime system was back on line in ten seconds.

"Okay, Joz, see if you can get it to take commands."

"Laid in. Whew! When things go wrong!"

"Are we out of it yet?"

"I think we'll hold together, more or less. Engine two is right out and gone—I believe the bell isn't there at all anymore. Cooling failure, and the poor thing went poof."

"What happened?"

"I think the last tall ridge we passed over made the computer think we were going to crash. It ran an automatic evasive maneuver, throttled the engines up full, then decided we weren't going to hit, and dragged the thrust level back down again, hard. All in about half a second. These engines have had a bit of a time of it already. They were hit with this super surge and it was just too much for them. Engine two blew, and that caused a *second* power surge that had circuit breakers cascading out through the whole power loop—including the propulsion system. Out go engines one and three.

"I've brought one and three back up, and gimballed them to compensate, but as soon as I can, I'm throttling them back down to about two gees, from six. They probably aren't feeling too well either. The cooling situation isn't very good at all," said Joslyn, concluding with a masterful understatement.

"But can we get home at two gees?"

"Oh, yes. We lost the engine, not the fuel. But it will be a longer trip by some hours. And of course, *Leviathan* is still out there."

The *Joslyn Marie* swung out from behind the dead world that had so nearly claimed her, and headed back down toward her base, her friends, her enemies, and her fate.

Part Four
Leviathan

4 Thine enemies roar in the midst of thy congregations;
they set up their ensigns for signs.
7 They have cast fire into thy sanctuary, they have defiled by
casting down the dwelling place of thy name to the ground.
8 They said in their hearts, Let us destroy them together:
they have burned up all the synagogues of God in the land.
13 Thou didst divide the sea by thy strength: thou brakest
the heads of the dragons in the waters.
14 Thou brakest the heads of leviathan in pieces, and gavest
him to be meat to the people inhabiting the wilderness.
18 Remember this, that the enemy has reproached, O Lord,
and that the foolish people have blasphemed thy name.
20 Have respect unto the covenant: for the dark places of
the earth are full of the habitations of cruelty.
23 Forget not the voice of thine enemies: the tumult of those
that rise up against thee increaseth constantly.

—The 74th Psalm

Chapter Seventeen

Our limping ship came up from around the far side of Kuu and fell down toward the inner orbits of New Finland.

Joslyn worked quickly to decide on a new orbit for us. With one dead engine and two questionable, she was not going to try any grandstand maneuvers.

She settled on a highly elongated near-equatorial orbit that brushed The Rock's orbit and rolled ten times further out from the planet, to a 50,000 kilometer apopoint. "If we got stranded in that orbit, someone from The Rock or Vapaus ought to be able to come and get us, sooner or later." Joslyn explained.

"You're forgetting *Uncle Sam*," I said. "She'd make a pretty good lifeboat—and she can fight."

"I'm sure *Sam* could take care of us, but my interstellar namesake here is a valuable piece of hardware and we should be sure she's kept handy. As it stands, I want to get us into that orbit and settle down to do some damage checking before we go one bit further. This is a good ship, but the poor dear is likely to blow up on us if we ask too much more of her without a chance of repair."

"Which I suppose I should get on with." I got busy with the damage control diagnostics. Most of the diagnostic work that needed doing I could do sitting at my computer console. The computers checked out the ship's dozens of systems and hundreds of subsystems. When something didn't come up to the standards set for it, the computer presented the situation as best it could to me. I would note it for later manual repair, or do a visual once-over, or tell the computer to switch over to a back-up system. Many of the problems were so clearcut the computer simply informed me of switchovers—the primary was in a hopeless mess.

It seemed as if there were no obviously lethal problems. There were dozens of minor breakdowns, though, and that could be just as bad. Usually disaster in space isn't the result of one overwhelming failure, but a series of small, related failures that combined in unexpected ways.

That was why the *loss* of an engine was so nearly fatal, even though the *absence* of an engine wasn't. The designers of the ship had included an excellent collision avoidance system. Quite reasonably, that system hadn't counted on anyone trying to get that close to a planet at such velocities.

It wasn't that we were in danger of crashing. It was very close, but at the moment all hell broke loose, we weren't actually about to hit. The margin of error was simply too close for the anti-collision system. Avoiding collision is important, to say the least, and the system has a very high priority over ship control and a very inflexible margin for error when guarding against a hit.

What was nearly deadly was the intercession of this very good system at exactly the wrong moment, under unforeseen circumstances. What was dangerous was the throttle-up, with the engines already straining; that throttle-up being caused by the anti-collision system panicking. When the engine blew, that caused the ensuing power surges which set up cascading power and control failures throughout the ship. *That* series of failures was what nearly got us.

We weren't going to let something like that happen again.

When I finished at the computer, I started on my inspection tour of the ship. Several trips to the parts storage compartment later, I had replaced many of the units the computer hadn't trusted.

Even after I was done, long after we reached orbit, the control boards showed that our ship was at war. What should have been in the green was in the amber, or even the red.

Outboard cameras rolled out on telescoping booms and looked at the exterior of the ship. They sent back a picture of a badly cooked hull. The shielding for the pass through *Leviathan*'s flames had been barely enough. There were a dozen spots where the hull had discolored and deformed.

Leak meters showed we were losing air. I sealed the hatches leading to the after decks and depressurized them. No sense letting air leak out of cabins where no one was breathing.

The thrust bulkhead camera had failed when the engine had. We managed to guide a camera on a boom down to take a look at the main engine compartment.

There was a mess. Engine two wasn't broken down—it was gone. The fusion flame must have vaporized the engine bell and most of the innards of the thing within milliseconds of the cooling failure.

One and three were still there, but with some unnerving dents and dings in them. The engines were meant to withstand such a disaster to one of their fellows, but it had obviously been close.

Neither Vapaus or The Rock contacted us for long hours. We squirted several brief ID codes over our comm lasers, essentially saying "We're here!" We got back automatic responses from the communications computers, that said "So are we." It seemed that the people there were too busy to deal with us just yet.

Space was largely quiet. We didn't use radar, so as to avoid detection, but IR, radio, and long range cameras could tell us something. Few engines burned, few lasers fired, few warheads exploded. The battle seemed to have worn both sides down to the nub.

By this time, all of the repeater satellites that relayed information between ships and satellites was gone, all of them long ago shot down. We were down to line of sight.

If Battle Control wasn't interested in us for the moment, that suited us fine. We worked at getting ourselves—and the ship—set to rights. Clumsy but effective zero-gee showers got the greasy residue of the high-acceleration bags off our skin, and stowing the bags themselves was a welcome chore. With the shape our main propulsion was in, there was simply no possibility of the *Joslyn Marie* accelerating hard enough for us to need them.

Both of us were covered with blotchy red rashes; high-gee thrust bruises capillaries. The rashes were more uncomfortable than painful, and we stocked an ointment that helped a lot, though it made fresh flight suits a little sticky.

We didn't bother with cooking, but simply shoved some quick-rations down our throats. That, protein supplements, and heavy-duty vitamins pills made dinner.

We took sleeping in shifts, four hours each while the other watched the boards.

It was fifteen hours after we bombed *Leviathan* when Battle Control finally contacted us by laser. I was on watch and quickly roused Joslyn when the cue light came on.

"—is Battle Control. Come in, *Joslyn Marie*. Do you read? Over." I didn't recognize the voice, but it sounded tired past the point of collapse.

"This is the *Joslyn Marie*. We read. Over."

"Stand by for instructions." There was about a half-minute pause. Then—"This is Berman. Listen to my orders, transmit in five minutes to confirm that you can carry them out." Her voice was utterly dead. There was not the slightest humanity left to it. "You are to clear and kill every available bank of the *Joslyn Marie*'s computer memories. No regard for later restart or operations. Only programs utterly necessary for maintaining the ship inert in orbit, as well as fullest radio control and minimal life support, are to be maintained. All ballistic, maneuvering, and record keeping functions are to be killed. All memory sets and computer files not needed to keep the ship barely alive are to be eliminated. You will then stand by to receive and record data transmissions from this location, and you will then assume the function of Battle Control. We will transmit a repeater of the current tactical situation in fifteen seconds. That is all. Confirm in five minutes. Berman out."

"Bloody hell. 'Assume the functions of Battle Control'! What in the world is she thinking of?" Joslyn said in astonishment.

"That, I think. Retaliation," I said, pointing to the screens. The visuals on the tactical situation appeared in the central hologram tank. It was there to read. A line of three missiles were homing on The Rock. No ship, anywhere, could possibly intercept.

I asked the computer for the status of The Rock's defenses.

The computer searched the data just transmitted to us and put the news on the main screens. ALL LASER STATIONS OUT OF COMMISSION. DEFENSIVE MISSILES REMAINING: 1.

The simplest math. Three missiles incoming, 1 intercepting missile left. The Rock was doomed. Thus *Leviathan* revenged herself against the attack we had made on her.

"Damn it, we should never have flown this raid!" I said.

"We had no choice, Mac. We had to take the chance."

"Chance, hell. They were bound to retaliate!"

"I know. And Eve knew. And she gave the order."

Joslyn sighed. "Now she has given another one," she said. "Can we do it?"

I thought for a moment. A long one. The *J.M.* was a good ship, and had good computers . . . but she wasn't a command center. We didn't have enough radio channels. The computers weren't big enough to store all the data on all the ships, friend and foe, let alone track them all. Our radar wasn't up to that, either. We'd have to rely on reports from the fighters. The task was impossible for the ship to perform.

But there it was.

I hit the transmit switch. "This is the *Joslyn Marie*. We are beginning erasure of our computer memories. Please prepare for data transmission."

Well, what else could we do? They were going to *die*. We could at least try to keep fighting.

The ship handling programs, the ballistics-to-maneuvering routines, the food-prep and inventory programs, the interface programs for contacting the aux ships, the diagnostics, the attack tracking system, real-time damage control—all of them to be erased, made dead, vanished. The *Joslyn Marie* paralyzed, mute, and lobotomized in the bargain. The ship lost attitude control, as the *Bohica* had so long ago (or was it truly that long?), and we began to tumble.

I had the line printer run out a copy of the ship's log before I erased it. If there was a future, someone might find it interesting.

We were stealing the brains of the ship. Just as a perfectly functional arm or leg can be rendered useless by a blow to the head, so was our ship losing, not her capabilities, but the means of controlling and using them.

Joslyn and I worked in a numbing fog. We had to make a hopeless idiot of the ship that had kept us alive, the ship that had been home. We knew it probably meant our deaths as well. Oh, yes, we could escape in *Uncle Sam*, but to where? The Rock would soon be pulverized. *Leviathan* would soon settle into the atmosphere. They would have won. It would only be a matter of time before someone thought to send a missile out into this lonely orbit.

Life support. Kill the sensors in the after decks. Shut down the sensors and the back-ups forward, for that matter. What point in an alarm system when there was no longer a way to deal with an emergency?

It seemed as if there ought to be a way to do these things by hand, to monitor the dials by eye and go throw a switch or twist a knob. But the sensors and the dials and the switches and the knobs were all linked to the computer system. The computers themselves were backed up by duplicate, triplicate, and quadruplicate machines that could take over—but we needed *their* memories as well.

Within ten minutes, Battle Control started piping data to us over every channel we had.

The single most important program was an emulator routine that let the *J.M.*'s computers cope with programs written for Battle Control. That one they transmitted twice and had us run a comparison drill to make sure the two transmissions were identical.

Our machines had to be able to play the part of their big brothers on The Rock—otherwise, they would have been unable to deal with any of the data coming in on all channels.

And there was plenty of data. Ship positions, fuel and

power reports on each one, reports on enemy fighters, on *Leviathan*'s status. A recording of the holographic representation of the battle up to now, in the hope that we might learn something of the enemy's tactics—and, for that matter, *our* tactics.

The job wasn't as bad as I thought it would be. For one thing, there was the grim fact that there weren't as many ships to keep track of as there once had been. Secondly, someone at the other end was weeding out a lot of things it might be nice to know, but which we would never have the chance to use. A few of the blanked-out programs and files came through as titles and nothing else—FIGHTER PILOT ROSTER AND BIOGRAPHICAL . . . THIRTEEN DIGIT PSEUDO RANDOM NUMBER GENERATOR . . . LAUNCH TRAJECTORIES AGAINST PLANETARY TARGETS FROM ROCK'S ORBIT . . . and so on. There were other, more subtle cuts. I noticed there were no programs for operations above *Leviathan*'s current altitude. We weren't going to have to go that high, anyway.

The most important data was on the enemy. What did they have left? What sort of shape was *Leviathan* in? What weakness had been exposed? What sort of chance did we have, and what was the best way of exploiting it?

At least it was clear that our attack on *Leviathan*'s launch stations had done some good. It seemed as if they hadn't launched a manned ship since we had hit them, only missiles.

Our side, however, was down to a bare 18 Beefies and Beasts. Both Hatracks were gone. Other than that we had *Uncle Sam*, *Stars*, *Stripes*, and a number of ballistic landers, plus a few tugs, drones, and other non-combatant ships.

We got a giant holographic memory of all that was known of *Leviathan*, and her current condition. Joslyn patched in everything our cameras had recorded as we passed the great ship.

There was a torrent of information. Then it began to slow to a flow, then a trickle, then nothing.

There was more, much more, that could have been sent, but already there was more than we could possibly use.

Our computers were full to the brim with data, every usable byte of storage space filled. There was room for the data that would come in from the ships, and nothing else.

All the comm lines were given over to the computers, and there had been no chance for us to talk with the people at the other end at the Rock. Those that could and would escape had already done so, some in slow moving tugs unsuited to war, some in pressure suits hoping to be picked up. Some of these made it. Others were never found.

Now The Rock was on a skeleton crew, waiting the last few minutes until it had to die. Eve was there, and George, and dozens of others I would never get to know.

Marie and her intelligence crew had already been ordered off The Rock and sent to Vapaus, where they were to continue the job of guessing what the Guardians would do next. Marie-Francoise made doubly certain that George came off with her crew. He was the best source of information about the Guards she was likely to have for a long time—and she was a bit worried he might decide to stay behind, try for a clean death that would let him escape all his doubts.

I don't remember how I said goodbye to Eve. I can't recall what I said, or if I said anything at all, or what they said to me.

All I can remember is seeing her face in those last few minutes as the video cameras beamed their images to us. She looked so *tired*, so wearied, that it seemed at first that there could be no other emotion in such a face. But it was not so.

I saw the elements of anger, determination, and perhaps a hint of the warrior's lust for battle blended in her face. She had no fear, no time or desire or need for fear. Then the first missile came, then the second, then the third, and in the flame of purest destruction, then did they die.

The video screen showed us the fusion bombs guttering down to death. The Rock broke up slowly, and tumbled apart. New Finland, Kuu, and Vapaus all weathered a few strikes from new-born meteors. Then it was over.

"Mac. Vapaus reports a missile exploding *exactly* ten kilometers from its forward docking area," Joslyn said. "That's a pretty clear message—keep the battle control center off Vapaus or we destroy it, too."

"Which makes us the ace in the hole. *Leviathan* probably thinks we crashed into Kuu," I replied thoughtfully.

"I doubt they can find us. They won't look here, and they need their radar elsewhere. It's up to us, Mac. The knowledge aboard this ship is the absolute, utterly and totally last chance our people have got." She paused. "And, you, sir, command this ship. We are, all of us, in your hands."

It sunk in at last. The chain of command had gotten each link snapped and cut—Taylor, Berman, and now it cut down to me.

It was all mine. It was up to me. In my hands. I suddenly realized I was *looking* at my hands, intently, as if they could tell me what to do, how to save us from this last extremity. I lifted my hands to my head and cradled my face in them for a moment. I sighed deeply and looked at the screens, straightening my back and getting hold of myself. Some tiny part of me believed that I would certainly die. It was not fear, it was a conviction, too strong to be called by any other name than knowledge, that I was doomed.

Yet with it came the determination to go out as the others had, with a firm grip on the job, and advancing, as best I could, with the last flicker of life I held. Patriotism, fealty to my oath, even self-preservation were gone from me, for at least the time at hand. All that I had was the desire to go out fighting.

Somewhere in myself I found the secret of command. Out there, scattered in space, were men and women who *demanded* leadership. Circumstance left them with no one but myself, and their vast, inchoate, and unarticulated voice instilled in me the power of command.

"Joslyn. We've got to win this one."

"Yes."

"Which means we still have to knock out that anti-ship missile system, so our side can bring reinforcements to bear."

"Right. Which in turn means we have to get to and *use* the missile control station."

"Which is in some very secure place in a ship the size of an asteroid. We have to board *Leviathan*."

"That's the sticky part, all right."

"Well, I may have the beginnings of an idea. But first I want to talk to Marie-Francoise."

A big part of what Battle Control had given us was the control over secure communications. Everything possible was sent by laser, and even then it was encoded. In theory, no one could "read" a laser message that wasn't directed at them, but theories had been wrong plenty of times, and there had been plenty of spies in history. We were very careful, for which I was now thankful, as annoying as it sometimes was. If we had been using straight radio traffic I would never have dared called Vapaus, in the fear that a lot of communication traffic with it would finger it as a military target.

As it was, we were reasonably certain that we were not endangering our remaining orbital base. Marie-Francoise was on duty when we got through to the intelligence center. Her face on the video screen showed a certain tired surprise when she saw who was calling. "I thought you were dead by now."

I swore under my breath. Morale was going to hell—and I could have wished to inherit a better informed intelligence chief. Then I remembered that Vapaus had just come up from behind the planet—with the relay satellites out, there was no way she could have known what had gone on in the last 45 minutes or so.

"Mac," she said after a pause. "What do we do now? We have lost our commanding station. We have some fighters left, but no way to guide them. I don't dare use this place for a commanding center. They'd bomb us in earnest."

"Marie-Francoise," Joslyn said, "The Rock passed the command data to us before they died. *We're* Battle Control now."

A tiny gleam of hope showed in Marie-Francoise's eye.

"Enough of the data? Enough so you know all that will happen?"

"Yes," I said, wondering if I were fibbing. Yet as I said it, my idea was shaping up. "Marie-Francoise, you've got to know *Leviathan* better than her captain by now. Based on what you've got, what is the maximum velocity relative to atmosphere *Leviathan*'s going to face?"

"Mmmmmm. By the time they reach the true, thick air, no more than 550 to 600 kilometers an hour."

"How far outside the atmosphere when she stops braking? Distance and time."

"Give me a moment on this . . . if she to follow optimum path—turn over maneuver, to get to glide attitude—no less than 100 kilometers, twenty-five minutes, maybe 120 and thirty minutes maximums."

"Do you have up-to-date data on our fighters? We should show eighteen operational."

"That is right. With The Rock out, I have no further updates, though."

"Right. Now, this one I'm giving to you and to Joz here at the same time. It's tricky. Factor in facilities at that end. I want every fighter to disengage, retreat, and return to Vapaus. Assume that we use the mass of the planet to hide the maneuvers from *Leviathan*. How fast can the last one get back to base? Can Vapaus handle all the ships at once?"

"The last I know, the answer for now—yes."

"Good. Both of you get cracking on that. I'm going to run a battle simulation, working on the assumption that you both get good news answers."

"Shall I issue the recall order?" Joslyn asked.

"Not yet. Another thing. Marie-Francoise—find someone with nothing to do and get 'em in charge of rounding up everything that can survive a ballistic reentry with people on board. Don't worry if it can get back *up*—down is all.

"Then get me a breakdown on how many able-bodied types are available for extremely hazardous duty. Volunteers only, and without taking both parents of a child, that sort of thing. Can you run that one fast?"

"Yes, easily. But what is it that you are planning? It would make it easier to know."

"I promise I will. Just let me flesh it out a bit first. It needs it. Get back to me. I've got to do some thinking."

I cut the connection and stretched out—even being back in zero-gee, my muscles hadn't gotten uncreased yet. Six gees takes it out of you. I reviewed my thinking.

It was respect for the dead to call Eve's tactics a plan of battle, but not accurate. I had found myself wondering more than once if I *could* do better. Now I would find out.

She had tried to peel back *Leviathan*'s defenses, without any clear idea apparent of what to do about it once they were peeled back. She had consistently been afraid to commit a sufficiently large enough force to do the job, with the result that smaller forces suffered murderous losses.

That was the situation I had inherited. There was one advantage we had: pilots. We had more pilots. Large as *Leviathan* was, it wasn't large enough to carry spare pilots for its ships. Each ship that died killed the pilot. *Leviathan* carried aircraft as well as spacecraft. It was all but certain that her pilots doubled up, one man expected to fly both a spacegoing fighter and an air fighter.

Therefore *Leviathan* could have a hold full of air fighters and no way to use them—if the ship was short on pilots.

Leviathan's space fighters and missiles were completely unaerodynamic. Her aerial fighters could not fly in space. Her Nova class aerospace fighters, such as the lamented *Bohica*, would be of no use until the ship was well within the atmosphere for a very tricky reason: they were too slow.

That's a funny thing to say about a Mach 4 fighter that could fly itself to orbit, but consider: *Leviathan*'s entry to atmosphere required her to match the rotational velocity of the planet *exactly*. It was a very small needle's eye that ship had to thread. *Leviathan* had to be moving tens of thousands of kilometers an hour slower than orbital velocity, or else she would be torn to pieces.

The Novas were a compromise between air and space, and thereby not too efficient in either. Loaded with weaponry and carrying fuel enough to reach orbit, the Novas left the runway able to do no more than 2.5 gees—better as they burned up fuel. The Beefies could take them at launch like shooting fish in a barrel, if the Guardians were foolish enough to launch them. The situation was worse for the Novas if they found themselves at high altitude and low speed: they could get no use out of the wings and the fusion engines would gulp fuel trying to hold altitude.

What it all boiled down to was this:

Leviathan carried no planes that could defend her in the borderlands of space, where there was not air enough for a jet engine to breathe or for a wing to grab, and no spacecraft that could defend her when she was too close to the planet, moving too slowly, for a space fighter to get away without disaster.

In the borderlands. When *Leviathan* arrived there, *that* was our window in time. Hit her there, when her missiles could no longer hit Vapaus, when her space fighters would be stranded in orbit if they were away from *Leviathan* when the big ship hit the air, when she was vulnerable. Pull her pilots up off the decks and don't let them back down. *Then* it might be possible to board the ship without being blown out of the sky.

It made sense. My ideas could work. I started on the simulation.

Fifteen minutes later, Joslyn brought me a fresh bulb of tea and a sheaf of printout paper. She set both of them into restraint niches and watched my work from behind me. Though I absently noted her presence, it took me a minute to come out of my work and acknowledge her.

"Hello, there," I said.

"Hello there yourself. Drink your tea and tell me what this grand plan is."

"I will. Just give me a minute to unjangle my nerves. How's the ship holding up?"

"It looks like we've a bit of an air leak somewhere. Some impervious seam gave up the ghost or such. We're tumbling a bit, though fairly slowly. Don't try any aerobatics. The far wall will have moved by the time you get there. The tumble will also be a bit of a bother in holding cabin temperatures. Sun angles. We'll have heating fluctuations. The air-cleaning is basically all right, but it may be a trifle murky and damp in here after a bit. I don't want to try and fix it until it's impossibly bad. Without parts, I might make it worse.

"Of course, there's no hope of actually *flying* her, but she'll keep us alive a while longer."

"How long?"

"A week, if your standards aren't high. Ten days if you want to live in a pressure suit—but we'd be in sorry shape by then."

"Can she be repaired?"

"Oh, lordy, yes! Just needs some time in a shipyard, parts, and her computer programs replaced. The poor thing is essentially sound. Just a bit at the end of her tether."

"As are we all."

"Mac?" Joslyn asked, a hint of firmness in her voice.

"Yes?"

"I won't surrender her. I won't leave her derelict and have those murdering bastards patch her up to go shooting people somewhere else."

I looked at my wife. She looked like hell. Her face was blotchy patches of red where high-gee had broken capillaries. Her eyes were bloodshot and puffy. Her lips were dried and cracked. Her voice was strong and calm, but there was a note of brittle anger beneath that.

"This is not just my ship, Mac. This is my home."

"This is my home, too, Joslyn. Joz—I have an idea, a plan. I think it might work. If we try it, we'll have to leave the *J.M.*, but only for a while. I promise you, they shall not take this place. We'll set charges and blow her sky-high, if need be."

She hugged me, and I hugged back, hard. "Thank you, Mac. I know I didn't even really have to say it, except for myself. One gets very careful of a ship, in it for a long time. And I was alone with her all that time you were away. I could not let those monsters have her."

"They aren't going to take her," I said. "They aren't going to take anything. I think I've found the way to beat them."

She pulled back from me to look me in the eye, to see if I was in earnest, if I truly had some hope to offer. Then, at last, she smiled, and suddenly she got beautiful again. "Oh, Mac. It's about time someone did. How?"

"You ever hear the first law of offense?"

"Some ghastly Americanism, wasn't it? 'Hit 'em where they ain't'?"

"Change that rule to '*when*' they ain't." I keyed in commands to the computer, instructing it to show *Leviathan*'s entry course. "This is based on the best we've got on *Leviathan*. The maneuver she's got to fly into the atmosphere is complex and must be incredibly precise. Watch the dotted blue line—that's her tracking line, relative to the planet. Unless they crash, or abort the entry, and head back into deep space, they have to follow something within a half percent of this plotting. Okay. Now, here. The engines cut out. At this point, *Leviathan* is actually moving slightly *away* from the planet. She's got to balance her own motion very carefully against both the planet's gravity and the fact that New Finland is, essentially, creeping up on the ship.

"*Leviathan* is in a very slightly faster orbit, just one planetary radius plus a hiccup closer to the sun. It is just at this very delicate point in time that she *cannot dare defend herself*.

"The ship has to flip end over end. She's been keeping her stern pointed toward the planet so her engines were pointed toward it to decelerate. Once she needs to fly in air, that means getting her wings faced in the right direction. She's really one big wing, of course, a lifting body, but she still has to be pointed the right way.

"That ship is *big*, and can't maneuver all that fast; the planet is *close*, and getting closer. Before they perform the flip-over, they must have every fighter on board and battened down, unless they want them slammed against the bulkheads when the ship goes base over apex. With the ship first whirling around in space, and then immediately hitting atmosphere, it'll be dammed hard to launch or recover anything, anyway.

"Once they begin turnover, that's it for space-going fighters. Any not yet aboard aren't going to get there."

"They'll still have the laser cannon."

"Yeah, I know. But we may be able to get around that. Somehow. Okay, keep watching the simulation in the holo tank. *Leviathan* completes her end-over-end maneuver and lines up for entry. She hits air, more or less in a dive. Her speed is about 500 kilometers an hour. Immediately, she starts to pull out of the dive, going into a long, gentle glide down into denser air. She's got to keep her nose well up to do this, holding right to the edge of a stall. She needs to sink into air she can grab quickly.

"Once she hits the dense lower atmosphere, she can bring her nose down and come to her cruising speed, about 200 kilometers an hour. Okay?"

"Right," Joslyn said.

"All right. Once she's at that speed, she's basically just a big, fast-moving dirigible. But *until* she's at that speed, I am willing to bet she can't launch anything. Not in a nose-up attitude at 500 kilometers an hour. The planes would either roll off or get blown off."

Joslyn stood silently, looking at the holo tank. She used the controls to jump back to the beginning of the display and run it again in fast forward. *Leviathan*'s tiny double shut off its engines, flipped end over end violently, dove precipitously into the atmosphere, belly-flopped its way down to about 5000 meters, and settled down to cruising flight.

"Mac. What you're saying is that from the moment she starts entry maneuvers to the time she's stable in the air she's completely defenseless."

"Except for the lasers, yes. What do you think?"

"I think you're right. My God. We should have held back every ship until right now, attacked en masse and thrown our whole force into the fight at once. We could have forced every spacecraft and every pilot off the ship. They would have hit air without a pilot still on board."

"I know. So why didn't we think of it three weeks ago?"

"Never mind that. The question is, do we still have the ships to force the Guardians up off the decks at the right moment?"

"I bet we can pull this off. I *know* we can. Let's talk to Marie-Francoise and Randall and make plans."

Chapter Eighteen

"Mac, you give us some fire control and some decent orbital data, and we'll razzle-dazzle those laser cannon right out of business. Leave it to us," Metcalf said from the cockpit of his fighter.

"Can you rotate all your pilots through Vapaus and get your ships refitted and patched up in time without *Leviathan* spotting us?"

"No problem," Metcalf said. "The Rock's orbit is full of debris. We've got to fly carefully, but all we do is fly through where it used to be, then do the transition to Vapaus on the far side of the planet from the big ship. No way they'll be able to track 18 little ships through that rubble field. They might suspect, but they won't know."

"And Mac, don't forget we've still got fusion bombs if they take Vapaus out—and they know it," Joslyn reminded me. "They'd pay a price."

"Okay, I guess we've got to take the chance," I said. "Otherwise it's all over anyway. Go get your refits."

"We don't even need 'em. Our limiting factor was personnel, not ships. There's a spare Beefie for every pilot but two. Vapaus shipyards are getting them checked out now. Including some modifications I ordered."

"You've got something in mind?" I asked.

"Sure. I'm going to lead the first boarding party," Metcalf replied.

"Say again? Is it you or the radio that's crazy?"

"I said I'm leading the boarding party."

"You can't fly that ship in air," I protested. "You'd crash."

"That's why we do it in space," Metcalf replied calmly. "It's possible—I think. If not, we abort, take some pot shots. And leave it to you."

"You on the level, Metcalf?"

"Never more so, boss man. I owe those bastard knuckle-draggers one. Look, we're gonna lose line of sight in a sec. Metcalf out."

I shrugged at Joslyn and cut the line from our end. He had his orders. I knew he'd carry them out. If he wanted to put some embroidery on them, fine. I figured he could give *Leviathan* a good-sized headache if he wanted to.

Marie-Francoise had kept her staff busy. What I had wanted was every ship that could carry troops and drop out of the sky onto the deck of *Leviathan*. What she gave me just started there. She also reported that 80 percent of the population of the satellite had volunteered for unspecified hazardous duty. That came to about 2500. All the ships fit for duty could carry maybe 200 troops.

Then Marie-Francoise came up with a wild card: One-man escape shells.

Escape shells are one of the simplest and scariest ways to get out of space. About all they amount to is someone in a spacesuit inside an ablating heat shield, plus a moronic guidance system and a retro rocket. If you're stuck in space, you wriggle into the thing and push the button with crossed fingers.

The guidance gizmo points the retro in roughly the right direction, and with luck the retros fired properly, you get kicked in the direction of the atmosphere, the heat shield melts away, maybe without cooking you. You press another button and explosive bolts blow the re-entry shell either away from you or through you and then a chute pops open, which, more than likely, deposits you in the ocean, where you drown.

They weren't *really* all that dangerous, I suppose, but there were people who rode them as a *sport*. In my line of employment I've been close to killed enough times trying to do a job that I don't see the point of risking my neck for fun.

About 200 escape shells had been stockpiled on Vapaus while it was being built, for the use of construction workers in an emergency. This official stockpile had never been used, and it still gathered dust in a storeroom somewhere.

Marie-Francoise also found a club full of overconfident idiots who called themselves The Meteors, which I thought was all too well-chosen a name. They had held regular drops before the war, and had manufactured their own shells. They hadn't been able to make any drops, or any new shells, since the war began, but they had had their eyes on the old official stockpile for a long time.

The club president insisted that The Meteors could land on the open flight deck of *Leviathan* if they were dropped from orbit accurately. They planned to use grappling hooks and count on plenty of padding in their suits. I hesitated before agreeing to let them go, but we were going to need every overconfident idiot we could get our hands on.

From every side it was the same—everyone wanted to fight, everyone wanted to go, everyone wanted to grab that ship. Marie-Francoise told us Vapaus was a beehive stirred up. Every workshop was full, every gun was loaded, every ship was ready to fly.

The pent-up frustration of cowering inside a hollow moon while others decided your fate, the hatred for the enemy, and perhaps most of all, the nerve-shattering *waiting* to find if you'd ever live free again, or if you'd be killed by a fusion bomb, had been turned into a sudden manic sense of hope, born of a chance to do something, anything.

Meanwhile, Joslyn and I had our hands full staging the withdrawal from the battle that still filled the sky. Carefully, we ran a fighting retreat so as not to leave our rear unguarded. We got our few ships back to base without further loss.

From the enemy's side, it must have seemed that the smashing of The Rock had done what it was supposed to do. There were no more sorties against the Guardian fighters, there were no more strafing attacks of *Leviathan*.

We worked out a tight schedule of cycling all our pilots through Vapaus, getting them showered, fed, rested and put into their new ships.

Maybe *Leviathan*'s captain knew that ships were going back to Vapaus—maybe he lost tracking on them when they hid out in the rubble of The Rock. What mattered was we didn't have any ships coming *out* of Vapaus. I crossed my fingers and I hoped that they were satisfied that we were calling it quits.

On our side, the accidents of fate had left me the ranking officer in the line of command. Because of that, people I had never met, people born fifty light-years from my home, who didn't speak my language, who had nothing to do with me, were calmly and confidently being handed weapons so that they might take their parts in a half-baked scheme that was probably the result of too much caffeine and not enough sleep.

But the schemes didn't stay half-baked. The amazing thing about command is that it *works*. I handed out vague general instructions on some phase of our attack, and back to me came word that preparations were underway, computer simulations had been run, soldiers briefed, and all was in readiness. Everyone snapped to—with a vengeance.

I wondered about *Leviathan*'s commander. How much did he know about us? Presumably he had managed to contact some little band of surviving Guardian ground troops holed up somewhere. We at least had to assume that. He must have monitored general broadcasts. Had he spotted his own upcoming moment of weakness as he entered the atmosphere? Had he found some way of countering our moves? Had he closed our window in time? What was he?

All I knew for sure is that we'd give him plenty to think about soon enough.

It started. The first phase of our plan was to raise merry hell on the launch and recovery decks just before entry, trying to prevent the launch or recovery of spacecraft. Marie-Francoise agreed that the space-going fighters almost certainly had been meant for delivery to an orbital base. They'd be worse than useless, doing nothing more that adding weight to *Leviathan*'s hull once she hit air.

Leviathan's commander would be facing some tough choices. If indeed he *could* afford the significant weight penalty of twenty-odd spacecraft, *should* he?

Leviathan might be a flying machine, but she was not a fast or graceful one. Could he afford a helm that responded sluggishly? Could he settle for a faster entry and a lower cruising altitude due to extra ballast? If he did jettison the ships, could he leave them in a parking orbit and risk our capturing the ships? Believe me, we were ready for that contingency. Or would he decide to drop them into the atmosphere to crash and burn? We set out to further complicate his problems.

From our makeshift control center, Joslyn vectored the Beefies against *Leviathan*'s fighter screen, sending them in to engage the enemy, but also to draw the fighters away from *Leviathan*. It was a delicate cat and mouse game: we wanted to present tempting targets to the enemy, but not actually let them hit any of them.

One thing that helped was the mass of knowledge we now had concerning the enemy ships. We knew how many gees the Guardian fighters could do, how quickly they could react, how accurate their weapons were.

The crew on The Rock had compiled such detailed data that we had fifteen or twenty clear "signatures," patterns that certain pilots seemed to follow. We knew that one hotshot who gave his ship about an extra half-gee gun at launch was very conservative about using his lasers. One fellow kept a very poor eye on his rearward radar.

We used this information, and all our skill, and all the skill of our pilots to herd the Guardian ships away from *Leviathan*.

It worked pretty well. The hologram tank stopped showing the little pinpoints of light drifting at random. Gradually, *Leviathan* was left nearly alone in the sky, the fighters being teased further and further away.

Whoever was running the show on *Leviathan*'s bridge could see the pattern, too. He started to call in the fighters, and so we upped the pressure, trying to balance our provocations and attacks against the urgency of their attempts to return. The closer their fighters got, the hotter we made it for them. The pressure of time was finally starting to work for us. Our fighters took more chances than I told them to, and played a little rougher than I planned. I didn't mind. I wanted them to be aggressive. For the first time, we were calling the shots and the enemy was responding to our moves.

But if I was learning fighter pilots were a pretty unruly lot, so was my counterpart aboard *Leviathan*. Long after Joslyn and I had spotted the first movement toward a recall, his force was still widely scattered, engaged in a dozen indecisive shooting matches. Metcalf was ready to tell me about it.

"Boss man, we've got those cowboys so trigger-happy they're liable to shoot themselves," he reported by comm laser.

"If they do, keep out of it."

"I've been good so far—three times I could have smeared one of them."

"I've been watching the tank. I notice the third one suddenly got missing."

"Okay, so I'm trigger-happy too. Or do you want me help the Guards look for the guy?"

"Oh, no, have your fun. But if you can hold yourself back just a little bit, I can promise you a real turkey shoot in about eight hours."

"This had better work, Mac. I have an overwhelming urge to paint more little spaceships on my hull. However, I promise to dedicate the next one to you."

"Well, I can't ask for more than that. Get some shuteye. You're out of range of everybody, and you don't need to maneuver for two hours."

"Okay, but put in a call if you want me. Metcalf out."

For long hours it went on, as we sent our fighters to harry the invader, guiding them in long looping orbits that popped them over *Leviathan*'s horizon briefly and then out again, chasing this fighter, leaving that one behind. We sent our little ships skittering in between and through and around as best we could, trying to keep the Guardians up off their flight deck.

Joslyn and I settled down to hour after long hour of voices buzzing in our headphones, worriedly switching through the frequencies, trying to read numbers that grew fuzzy through bleared eyes. Too much tea and coffee, not enough food, no sleep.

Around us, the *Joslyn Marie* continued to die. The air slowly grew damp and musty, with a tinge of old, burned rubber to it. Carbon dioxide built up slightly. We had not the time, the energy, or the need to attend to it. Soon we would board *Uncle Sam* to do a job, heading for one fate or another.

And two tiny, shrinking fleets of ships continued to do battle.

Our window in time was beginning to open. Our deadline was that moment *Leviathan* would have to cut her engines. The hours crawled down into minutes, and then the moment came, and then the flames that marked the great ship's passage faded from the sky.

I keyed in the laser link with Metcalf. "Okay, Randy. Give 'em grief!"

"Way ahead of you, boss man. We're already closing for the planned full-blown attack, by the numbers. We are now firing the beam-riding Redeye missiles from all ships."

"They going to have something to ride?" I asked.

"Oh, I imagine so."

The Redeyes were missiles designed to home in on a laser cannon, following the beam down to the laser itself. The Redeyes were swathed in extremely heavy ablative shielding that could bear up under a tremendous amount of heat and light energy. Metcalf's fliers had loosed a great volley of them, expecting a few to get through while the huge enemy lasers zapped the rest of them.

But the Redeyes needed a laser beam to ride down, and *Leviathan* provided that. Our fighters popped into sight from behind the planet, the Redeyes coming on ahead.

Leviathan's lasers opened up on them. This was the crucial moment for us.

"Beam riders tracking," Metcalf reported. Suddenly the banter was out of his voice. His own craft, and two or three others, were in the focus of the lasers. The Beefies had been coated with the same ablative shielding that the *J.M.* had used to survive the run through *Leviathan's* flames.

"I'm picking up some heat now." His fighter dodged in and out of the beam as the enemy tracked his weaving course across the sky. "They sure know how to aim that thing. Looks like Vaajakoski's in it too—and there's Takiko in a beam. Some real heat now. The ablatives are helping, but they aren't going to last."

The missiles swarmed to their targets.

"I gotta get out of here. Cooling system in trouble." Metcalf swung his ship around to gun out of range. One of the missiles exploded in space, cooked by *Leviathan*. Another went out. Then one found its mark, and the heat was off Metcalf.

"Whooey. That was some cook-out. Turning now, closing again. Vaajakoski and Takiko still under attack . . . make that Vaaj only. And now she's clear. Three laser cannon fired, all silenced."

"Randall, there are supposed to be *four* laser cannon on *Leviathan*," Joslyn reminded him.

"Yeah, I know. Either it's still out from three days ago, or they are pretty goddamned cagey bastards down there. We're headed in."

The Beefies closed, trying to take and hold the piece of sky between *Leviathan* and her fighters.

"The big ship has ceased fire," Metcalf reported. "If they miss us, they'll hit their own ships at our backs. Hey, boss man, just a note. That hull of theirs can soak it up. The 500 kilogram missiles don't even dent it. Glad the laser stations weren't that tough."

The main body of Guardian fighters were now seventy kilometers from *Leviathan*, with Metcalf and his team dead in between them. The enemy was badly caught—they were close to where they needed to go, short on fuel, and yet unharrassed only as long as they didn't try to go there.

The Beefies only opened fire if the Guards tried to move nearer *Leviathan*. They were welcome to move further away, but they couldn't afford to. They might not have the fuel and they certainly didn't have the time.

I checked our estimated schedule for the big ship and confirmed that *Leviathan* was delaying her rollover to glide attitude. She *needed* the pilots.

All the battling ships were, by this time, drifting toward, or more accurately, *dropping* down toward New Finland. They were all well under orbital speed.

Leviathan was on her planned course. The Guardian fighters had to stay with her or miss their last chance to get aboard. If the Guardian fighters boosted up to orbital speed, they could never return to base in time.

Leviathan's captain had to wait out our fighters. Would we pull our Navy pilots' fighters out of their crash-landing trajectories in time for the Guards to recover the fighters?

We gave them a yes on that one. Metcalf's little force suddenly withdrew toward orbit.

Instantly, the Guardian fighters formed up to recover, jockeying to establish an orderly, compact formation to get aboard *fast*.

Then we changed our minds. Metcalf's forces doubled back and dropped toward the Guards.

The turkeyshoot began.

The Guardians could not maneuver, or they would never be recovered. They were forced to hang there, defenseless.

The Beefies soared to the attack with every laser cooking, every missile with a target picked out. *Leviathan* tried to shoot back, but her own people were between her hull and our fighters. Two Guardians ships were blown up by *Leviathan*'s fire. Space was filled with pinpoint explosions and wheeling debris.

"Skipper, you were true to your word. This is the best shoot-em-up I've ever been to until yet. That's three so far."

"Just don't get zapped yourself."

"Yow! That last big laser is back in business. Oh, God. They've got Greenblat. All ships! Keep below the plane of her topside deck! That last beamer is still with us."

The battle went on, and *Leviathan* sunk slowly toward New Finland.

"Mac, they've got the formation broken. The Guardians that aren't on board are dead. Pull 'em back!" Joslyn said.

"You're right. This is the *Joslyn Marie* to all fighters. You've broken them! *Leviathan* has to start pitchover any second now. Pull back and get to orbit."

"This is Metcalf. I request formal permission to attempt boarding."

"Metcalf! Is that for real!"

"Yes, sir! Permission granted?"

"What about that last laser cannon?"

"They can't bring it to bear on their own deck! Mac! For God's sake, yes or no! We've got about 90 seconds max to pull this off!"

This was desperate madness. Something in Metcalf's voice told me he knew that too. "Permission granted . . . and God be with you," I said, whispering the last.

"Metcalf out. See you on the down side, *Joslyn Marie*!"

There were still Guardians' fighters in the sky, but the Beefies ignored them—the Guards could never return to base now. We let the Guard pilots decide for themselves whether to re-enter and burn, or try for orbit and take their chances surrendering to the rather unsympathetic Finns of Vapaus.

The Beefies gathered themselves into a tight formation, banked out from beneath the big ship and grabbed for some sky. They shot across *Leviathan*'s starboard wing down toward the planet, a mere flash across her view ports as they raced toward the distant ground.

The great, lumbering ship sailed on through the sky, as if all the battling midges that had sparked and died around her meant nothing to her fate. But New Finland's gravity field reached out and grabbed with gentle, impalpable fingers at the great beast in the sky that now gave itself up to the planet. *Leviathan* fell. She moved not only toward her skyfall in the air of New Finland, but toward her tormentors as well. The Beefies fired their engines again to slow themselves and let *Leviathan* fall toward them.

The ship began her turnover. With amazing speed for such a giant, the massive craft wheeled end over end and lined up her wings with the winds below.

She came upon the Beefies. Her last laser cannon reached out at terribly close range and touched, once, twice, among the tiny fleet and where that finger touched, ships died.

But then the Beefies fired their engines again and leapt toward her decks as hawks would swoop on their prey. The tiny ships matched speeds with the great one, using their main engines to brake themselves, matching velocity.

From each ship, slender cables shot out toward the flight deck. At each cable's end, canisters of vacuum-bonding cement split open and instantly the glue turned hard as iron. They reeled themselves in with power winches.

Now I understood the modifications Metcalf had ordered for his replacement ships. The cable assemblies were standard equipment for asteroid prospectors who wanted to catch hold of a piece of skyrock. Obviously, the rig worked just as well for catching a ship.

Fifteen ships survived to attempt boarding. Two more were blasted by *Leviathan*'s lasers. Another pair had cable attachment failures. They made it back to orbit and eventually got picked up. Takiko brought his ship in all right, but he hit the deck too hard. He lost cabin air and suit pressure and died fast.

But that left ten sets of lasers, and ten sets of eyes and ears and brains on the enemy deck. The Beefies lasers were meant to cook ships across the reaches of space. With the power of those, we could hold the deck.

"This is Metcalf. Might be my last call for a while. We're down and alive, ten of us. I've already set off glue bags and I'm pasted in here pretty firm. It should be a hell of a ride."

"Metcalf, that was some sweet work there. We're setting you all down for a Distinguished Flying Cross apiece."

"I'll pass that along to the gang, but if you make it a unit citation you'll save on postage. I've gotta button this can up for the ride down. Metcalf out."

"All right, Joslyn, that's our cue. Get *Uncle Sam* powered up and I'll make sure the lights are out here." I started powering down what systems were still in use aboard the *Joslyn Marie*. The fighters were finished with their work, and the *J.M* was of no use as a battle control center.

Now, *Uncle Sam* was needed. I used the comm laser one last time. "LPSS 41 *Joslyn Marie* calling Vapaus control. Prepare all boarding craft. We expect to dock in one hour."

Within minutes, the *J.M.* was powered down, an inert hulk. A radar transponder and acquisition lights were left to guide us back to her, eventually. That, and self-destruct devices hooked to batteries and a radio-link were the only things drawing power.

More quickly than I would have thought possible, we were ready to evacuate the vehicle, as the regulation book would term the procedure. *We* called it leaving home.

Joslyn and I watched the screens aboard *Uncle Sam* as we pulled away. The *J.M.*'s acquisition lights blinked every two seconds, and would until someone went aboard and shut them off, or until the *J.M.*'s power cells failed in thirty or forty years. Beyond that, she was dark and dead and lifeless. I held Joz's hand in mine and watched the shrinking, tumbling ship slide away from us.

I couldn't promise myself we'd be back; I wasn't sure of it.

But then there was a course to lay in, and a job to do. It felt good to be in a living ship again, where the ventilators whirred and the helm answered crisply under your pilot's hand.

Next stop was Vapaus, where a boarding crew and weaponry awaited us. Joslyn gave *Sam* the autopilot course and we tried to get ourselves in some sort of shape to fight.

First and foremost, we shared a shower—there wasn't

time to take turns, and neither of us was willing to go second, anyway. Once again, we had spent days in the same clothes without benefit of hot water, and there had been a lot of reasons to sweat. I can promise that getting clean was the only thing on our minds. Then, more rich protein foods and vitamins, and fatigue killers to hold us together through the next few hours.

But nothing could keep us away from the view screen for long. Korsky had been one of the fliers to make it onto *Leviathan*'s deck. She had managed to use a broadcast antenna to transmit pictures from her nose camera, which was pointed straight forward at the bow of *Leviathan*. The Finns picked up the pictures, beamed them to us, and sent along their own images from cameras aboard tugs sent out with the specific job of recording the entry of the great ship from orbit.

Even had it not been the skycastle of the enemy, even if our people had not been uninvited guests aboard, even if our fate was not wrapped up in hers, the flight of *Leviathan* was a spectacle worth watching.

Chapter Nineteen

You get used to things being big in space. Fifty years ago they were building power satellites bigger than Manhattan, and things had gotten bigger since. Vapaus had many times the mass of any ship of sky or sea ever built. In space, *big* made more sense than *little*—if for no other reason, than perhaps to give humanity some intermediate scale between itself and the vast emptiness.

But, in the air, in the real sky, beyond a certain size, *big* loses its meaning, no longer gives a sense of scale. *Leviathan* went beyond big and huge and gigantic and every other word for large. No superlative could take it in. Nothing *that big* could possibly fly.

But fly *Leviathan* did. Never was there such an entry, never such a flight. "Hitting air," for a spaceship, is all vast speed and violence, the velocity of orbit converted to the red of glowing heat shields and speeding plunges down to a rate where aerodynamics meant something.

Leviathan entered New Finland's atmosphere at aerodynamic speed, and seemed, from the cameras on the orbital tugs, to float in as gently as a leaf.

From Korsky's camera, *Leviathan* rode the maelstrom. The great ship had her prow pointed square at the planet. And she was falling. There was no mistaking that.

Leviathan was a huge manta-ray shape with a swollen belly. Inside her huge delta wings and inside that belly were the large lift cells, full of either helium or hydrogen. Sandwiched in between the cells were decks for men and ships and equipment. Between the two wings was the main body that contained the office decks and workshops.

Along the sides of the main body, at the middeck levels, were the launch and recovery cradles for the spacegoing fighters. These had been the targets of the *Joslyn Marie*'s attack run.

At the topside stern was a huge fin, a vertical stabilizer, which served double duty as a control tower for flight operations.

The main aircraft deck was laid out before the control tower. Aircraft were launched straight over the edge of the bow. Our fighters had pinned themselves down in the middle of the flight deck area, blocking the runways.

Six large cone-shaped spoilers stood out from the bow of the main deck, forcing the air flow away from the deck so that people and machines could stand on the flight deck without being blown over the stern of the ship as *Leviathan* coursed through the sky at hundreds of kilometers an hour.

Korsky's camera took in a wide expanse of flat deck that cut the world in twain. The forms of two tiny Beefies could be seen in the distance. Korsky zoomed to one of them and we could see a flicker of movement—the pilot waving.

The giant air spoilers started to buck and quiver against the sudden slap of air as *Leviathan* finally reached her appointment with New Finland. Her great size and high speed caused a great pressure wave ahead of the ship, a large shock zone that the ship had to punch through.

Wild, violent eddies of air slapped down hard on the decks. We could see the Beefies buffeted by them and see the view from Korsky's camera scramble and clear as her little fighter was rocked back and forth.

Then tortured wraiths of cloud vapor started to whip and swirl along the decks. *Leviathan*'s passing was heating and concentrating the minute traces of water vapor into sudden clouds at altitudes where clouds had never been.

Like a view of hell, the too-sharp horizon formed by *Leviathan*'s bow began to glow a dull, sullen red as ablative paint started to vaporize and whisk itself away.

Leviathan dove straight down, right for the planet, seeking the levels of air pressure that would support her wings, gathering as much air speed as she could before pulling out.

New Finland ceased to be a disk and grew to a rounded

body in space, and still she swelled, until she commanded every inch of sky not cut off by the ship's deckline. There came an indefinable point where one sensed that the camera was no longer rushing toward a place, but already *there* and traveling *through* that place. *Leviathan* became part of the planet, a member of her sky.

The buffeting grew worse and worse, until there was rarely a moment with a clear view for us. The Beefie pilots must have come close to having the life shaken out of them. The planet, stained hell-red by the heat of reentry, grew visibly as we watched.

Korsky's broadcast antennae sheared off, and we lost the picture. Metcalf, sounding as if he was getting pretty rattled himself, reported Korsky's ship was still holding together.

A picture from an orbiting tug cut in. The long-range lens zoomed in toward the struggling ship. She was beginning to pull out of her dive, leaving a trail of storm-eddies behind her as she fought to bring her nose up.

I swore under my breath. With a long, lazy period, as the movement flowed from wingtip to fuselage and back, the kilometer-wide manta wings were—*flexing, bending.*

"Mac . . . The wings!"

"I know. My God, do those bastards know what they're doing?"

Joslyn forgot whose side was conning that ship and talked to it, pilot to airplane. "Come on, you great bloody beast. Pull out! Get your nose up. Dear lord, I think they're losing the port wing. No, thank God, it's still together. Come on, steady on, easily, you great oaf, or you'll have a wing off for certain!"

It ceased, for a time, to be the flagship of our hated enemy. *Leviathan* was truly a great beast, one of the air, struggling against her wounds and the wrath of her element, fighting to live.

With a crawling in my gut, I remembered that if *Leviathan* didn't make it down, neither would the missile control center. If that went, all would have been for nothing.

Again and again, my hands reached for an invisible pilot's joystick. Some deep-seated love of things that fly wanted to grab that struggling beast and guide her to safe haven and calmer air below.

Slowly, ponderously, with the tortured magnificence of embattled greatness, the beast of the air slowed herself, pulled herself up from a dive into the abyss toward a strong, sure, coursing glide. Gigantic contrails and tiny whirling storms formed in her wake. The ship surged ahead and steadied itself as the air-breathing engines came to life, and the flying aircraft started to cruise.

Leviathan arrived.

Joslyn killed the view from the orbital cameras and suddenly the docking complex on the forward end of Vapaus popped into existence on our forward screen. Joslyn had piloted us in on instruments even as she watched *Leviathan* enter.

As Joslyn warped us in, I changed into my combat flak suit—basically a fairly bullet-proof, fairly laser-reflecting coverall with plenty of pockets—and then went to the feelgood cabinet and found another set of pills for us to down. Super powered vitamins, over-achieving amphetamines that had a label warning about trying to tear walls off, another anti-fatigue number to suck up the exhaustion elements that clog the blood of a tired man, psycho-depressants to counter the monomania the other drugs caused, and a witch's brew more. I downed a set myself and brought Joslyn's dose to her. Neither of us liked taking the things. They sure as hell weren't good for you, and they were no substitute for a decent night's sleep and proper food—but if they kept us awake and alert today, they might be what kept us alive for tomorrow.

She winced as she swallowed her share of the little ghastlies, and chased then with a gulp of water from a drinking bulb. "Urg and argh. We shall pay for these indiscretions in tomorrow's dawn."

"If there is a tomorrow. Are you quoting something, or did you make that up, and are we docked yet?"

"I made it up, I think, and our guests are already arriving

and I'm not even dressed. Could you see to them while I slip into something more lethal?"

I opened the hatchway to the lower deck as the drugs started to hit me. Suddenly, I was more awake than I had been in weeks. I glanced to the metal handrail to see if I was grabbing it so hard it bent. I wasn't, of course, but the surge of artificial endurance helped a lot. More than a few hours that hopped-up could put me in a hospital, but for a little while I could feel normal and then some.

As I reached the deck, the inside of the airlock cycled open and men started to pour through it. A pressure tunnel had been linked to Vapaus's interior, so they could get on board without having to wait through airlock cycles. The first one in wore a second lieutenant's insignia. Of the rest of the men and women, some were army, but many were in civvies—some of my high-risk volunteers. They knew where they were heading, and they were spoiling for a fight. All wore heavy flak jackets and were loaded down with equipment. They carried a pistol and a rifle each. Many also carried a number of vicious looking throwing-knives.

I gestured to the second lieutenant. He was a short, peppery little man with an unruly shock of white-blonde hair and a wicked gleam in his eye. It looked like his nose had been broken at least once. Under it hung a droopy, insolent, moustache. He gave me a snappy salute. "Second Lieutenant Raunio, sir."

"Welcome aboard, Lieutenant. We've got about fifteen minutes to get your people ready for acceleration. Get all your gear into the storage bays, then flatten down against the padded sections of the lower bulkhead here, and try not to drift off. There are hold-down straps to grab on to, so use them. We may have to do some maneuvering, so don't get started getting your gear on until after you hear the all clear from us. All right?"

"Yes, sir. That is fine. All of these fellows have done plenty of spacing before today. They know what they are to be doing."

"Good, I hope I know what I'm doing once we get down there."

He smiled wolfishly. "I bet that you do."

I chalked up that ambiguity to translation trouble, saluted again, as he seemed to expect it, and left him yelling orders in Finnish, seasoned with a choice string of obscenities.

Joslyn was already "dressed to kill," as she put it, when I got back above deck.

"How does *Sam* look?"

"Nice green bird, so far. Vapaus Port Control set records topping off all our tanks, and all systems ticking right along. We'll be ready to boost in plenty of time."

I sat down at my console and put in a call to Marie-Francoise. "How does the situation look?"

"So far, not bad. The escape shell team is on station. There are fifteen ships of one sort or another ready to follow you down. Metcalf and his pilots haven't been bothered too much yet. Nothing that can get past their shipboard lasers. Good weather down there. *Leviathan* is following a due-west ground-track, headed toward the coastal town of Vipurii, and sunlight is about at local noon where they put her down. Joslyn already has the projected target area logged in to her navigation systems. The others will follow your beacon down."

"Any change in our target?"

"No. You'll still head for the main radio room. So have the radio direction finder ready."

All the assault teams were to carry a "black box" that was keyed to electronic "noise" of the sort the control station from Vapaus was found to give off: the *Leviathan* station should give off the same noise.

"Good luck, Mac."

"And to you, Marie-Francoise. *Uncle Sam* out." I cut the connection. There was an unnatural sense of calm aboard the *Uncle Sam*. The dangers were once again clear and clean. Our skins were on the line, the outcome was sure to be decided soon, and for all time. In a few hours we would be living winners or dead losers. It was even a strange and frightening sort of comfort to know that my wife and I would die together, if at all.

Then Joslyn pushed some buttons, and we went in.

The instant the engines lit, calm was forgotten. I could feel my heart start to race. The battle was joined, and I found my hands over the laser controls without willing them there.

But there was an atmosphere to punch through first. *Uncle Sam*'s engines roared in the silence of space, and the ship dropped toward the planet far below. Finnish crews in other ships followed in formation, the ships separated by several kilometers.

Stars, *Stripes*, and a dozen ballistic landers, mostly of the *Kuu* class, lit their jets along with us. The pilots were tug captains, merchantmen without battle training. They were all we had.

If every ship made it down, we could put 200 troops aboard *Leviathan*.

Joslyn took us in at a steady one-gee boost, spinning the ship end over end to start braking as we neared the planet. At constant boost, the trip to the edge of the atmosphere took brief minutes.

At the very fringes of the atmosphere, Joslyn cut the engines. We rode in zero-gee for a few seconds, and then an almost imperceptible tugging from below grew to a gut-crushing force that slammed me into the acceleration couch. I discovered four new places where a combat suit could cut into you. We had hit the air.

Joslyn was taking us in hard and fast, using the steepest possible re-entry angle to get us there soonest, to give *Leviathan*'s radar as little time as possible to look us over.

The acceleration eased off gradually as we shed our great speed. Our formation had floated off a bit during reentry, and the other ships skittered in closer to us and dove toward our target. This part of the job the tug commanders knew well, and the stragglers zipped back into their slots quickly.

We fell deeper and deeper into the air.

"Okay, Joz, I just picked up *Leviathan* on radar. We're over her horizon."

"Right, Mac. I've got her. Right where she ought to be, give or take a kilometer. We're on course."

High cloud cover was between us and our prey. I tried to raise Metcalf on a radio frequency.

"*Able Archer*, this is *Uncle Sam*. Come in, please."

"This is *Able Archer*. Come on in, we're holding your seat. It's getting a little hot, boss man, so step on it if you please. They're trying to get fighters airborne, but we've cooked three as they came up from below deck. Some kind of troops on deck too, but we've got 'em sort of under control. Korsky's laser is just about out of juice, and the rest of us aren't far behind. Take the heat off us and maybe we can recharge our power cells. And hold just a sec—*something* scrambled past from below decks just now. They've gotten a fighter off somehow."

"Yeah, must be a drop-launch rig on the underside of the ship. We track the bandit—make that two—headed for us. Can you give us any visual?"

"Maybe. You're at extreme range, but camera on anyway."

A swirl of static filled the screen and settled down to a steady, but snowy picture of *Leviathan*'s main deck. As we watched, a blur zipped past and a third bandit appeared on our screen. We were still five hundred kilometers from *Leviathan*, but closing very fast.

The enemy fighters were gunning right for us. I picked them up on our own long-range cameras. I jockeyed around the laser cannon and fired. The first bloomed into a fireball within seconds. I nailed the second just as quickly. The third peeled off suddenly and dove for the ground, then came up from below, straight up our tailpipe.

Our stern lasers were still stowed in the hull. The stern was right in the airstream. If I unlimbered them now, they'd be torn off before I could shoot.

"I'm on it, Mac," Joslyn said calmly. "All ships, break formation and land at will." She wrestled *Uncle Sam* out of glide and fired the fusion engines. That killed the third bandit.

"Nice shooting, you guys. I think I've got you on visual now," Metcalf radioed. "Wave at the camera and smile. And here come three more of the little devils—no, make that two, and chalk up a bandit to Gilbert."

Our ships scattered as the pilots started thrusting. The view from Metcalf's camera showed a hazy sky full of tiny points of light that were moving in fast.

We broke through the cloud layer and there was *Leviathan* laid out below us, an island in the sky, an island under siege.

From Metcalf's camera, we saw *Uncle Sam*, the proud stars and stripes painted on her hull clearly visible, leading our little fleet in, sailing on toward battle. Dull patches of light lit up the cloud layer, growing brighter and brighter until *Stars* and *Stripes* and the Finnish craft broke though the cloud layer, each ship on its own pillar of gleaming flame. It was a splendid sight, that armada of the sky coming to seek revenge on the invader.

But there was no time to look on such things. The two fighters Metcalf had called rose toward us and then died under my lasers. No more followed them.

Leviathan lumbered majestically through the sky, here and there fires burning on her deck, which was spotted with the burned-out hulks of ships the Beefies had cooked as they tried to launch. The great ship resembled some great monster of the sea as she came boldly on, a satanic magnificence in her lines.

"Shifting to aux engines," Joslyn reported. *Uncle Sam* lurched for a moment as Joz shunted power to the chemical rockets from the fusion engine. The fusion job would melt most deck plates to slag, and slag is hard to set down on, and even harder to walk on. The chem engines gulped fuel more quickly and used it less efficiently, but the temperatures were a lot more reasonable.

We headed for a landing.

And the whole outside world turned red before the camera died.

"Boss man! That last main laser! In the control tower."

Joslyn cut our engines, we dropped like a stone, and in a

few seconds were below the great ship. The laser could not hit us without chopping through *Leviathan*'s own deck plates.

"That was too bloody close. Mac, can you hit that tower with a torp?"

"I can try. Gun those jets, while they're on another target." Directly above us, the ruby beam refocused on a new victim, one of the Finnish ships. Her captain tried to boost out of there, but the laser moved faster than he could. The little merchantman went up in a mushroom cloud of fire. I felt a sick feeling in the pit of my stomach.

Joslyn slammed down the manual engine controls, and we sprang back into the air over *Leviathan*. She killed the main jets and hit the attitude jets to bring our nose over until we were exactly upside down, falling straight into the ship's deck, bringing the nose launching tubes to bear directly on the control fin. I fired every tube at once, dead at the still-firing laser cannon. In the split-second before Joslyn maneuvered again, I could see four tiny beams from the Beefies on the deck firing at the tower as well. Joz let the torps get away, then spun us around through ninety degrees and fired the engines again to get out of the way of the deck as it seemed to rush up from below us.

Again we fell past the deck of the enemy ship and fell toward the planet's surface.

"Randall, how'd we do?" I radioed.

"They're out of business for sure, now. Come on in, Mac. We've got the red carpet out."

"Just a second, Mac. As long as we're down here, let's get that ventral launch tube," Joslyn said.

"Do it."

She braked our fall, more gently this time, and held us in a hover with *Leviathan* directly above us. I spotted a long, tunnel-like extrusion that ran down the centerline of the ship, open at both ends. "That's got to be it, Joslyn." I loosed another flight of torps. I flew them by remote control and scooted them down the tunnel. Bright orange explosions thundered and belched fire out each end of it.

"That ought to hold 'em for a while. Let's get to it."

Joslyn bumped up the engines and took us up over the deckplates.

Three of our ships had landed. Two more came in as we watched. Joslyn jogged the maneuvering jets and we swept out over the giant deck. It was as if we had come to fly over a great, flat plateau, a mountain in the clouds. Here and there across the great plain our ships were coming in to land.

We settled down onto the deck of *Leviathan*. Joslyn brought us in as gently as she could, easing out the landing jacks and coming down smoothly, the hydraulics softening the touchdown.

"Well, we made it."

"So far. Let's see how our passengers took it all." I turned on the below-deck cameras. "Lieutenant, we're on the deck. All clear. How are your men holding up?"

A groggy Lieutenant Raunio wobbled to his feet and waved at the camera. "Not too badly to be, sir. Two or three got the air-sickness, but I will make them do the cleaning up later."

"Sounds fair to me. For now, get them ready to move."

I watched the nose cameras, now panning the deck below us, out of the corner of my eye as I talked, and then switched my full attention to the exterior. "Metcalf, what's going on down there?"

"Hiya, Mac. Welcome aboard. Things have been sort of quiet for a while, but they pulled down a deck elevator a few minutes ago, and I think it's headed back with a reception committee. Call the bow twelve o'clock, and it's about four o'clock, two hundred meters from your position. We lost Gilbert a few minutes ago. Someone got in close with a grenade, it looks like."

"Okay, I see it. I'll keep a beamer on it. Joslyn, go ahead with the ground coolers, and let's get that crowd outside."

Joslyn hit a switch and opened the liquid nitrogen valve. The super-cold liquid poured out onto the rocket-heated deck plates and boiled away into vapor, crashing the deck temp down hundreds of degrees. We sat tight for a minute or two, waiting to see if the deck plates held up to the strains of the sudden temperature shift. But nothing cracked and collapsed under us. We unbuttoned the ship.

"Mac! Here comes that elevator!" Joslyn called.

I fired the laser cannon. A jet fighter exploded into flame as it rose into view. The elevator lurched to a stop a few meters short of the deck line. The nose of the jet was lined up on *Uncle Sam*. They would have used the fighter's guns and missiles on us right from the deck.

Another elevator, half a kilometer away, rose into view, a fighter on the platform. As soon as the plane reached deck level, its guns opened up on one of the Finnish ships. Incendiary bullets found the hydrogen tanks, and the Finn exploded. I put an air-to-air torpedo to use ground-to-ground and the Guardian fighter followed its victim into annihilation. "Jesus, how many of those elevators have they got left? Metcalf? Metcalf! Come in!"

I spotted a figure jogging across the deck toward us. I lowered the lasers on it. "I *will* come in, if you get the damn hatch open!" I heard over the radio. There was a sharp explosion from a way off, and the figure—Metcalf, of course—threw itself flat on the deck and covered its head.

The fires of the explosion settled down, and Metcalf got up and started running again. Joslyn popped the inner and outer hatches at the same time, and thirty seconds later Metcalf was past the Finns on the lower deck and in the control cabin, gulping air, leaning again the cabin wall. "Okay, so I cut that a little close," he said.

"What did you do, blow your own ship?"

"Right. We've got to get through that deck and get below. I wanted to knock a hole in it. I overloaded everything and set off all my ammo, too."

I looked at the screen and shook my head. Where Metcalf's ship had been was nothing but a few scraps of smoking metal, and a smooth, undented, perfect expanse of deck.

"Damn! That stuff is *tough*. Their own troops weren't afraid to throw grenades at us and hit their own ship's deck."

"We'll have to take one of the hatchways."

"And they'll be waiting for us."

"Mac! Radar!" The screen was lousy with blips. "What the hell?"

"That's the escape shell troops!"

"Yeah, *some* of the blips," Metcalf said. "But the big guys are bogies. Shoot first and ask questions later. Call 'em bandits and zorch them."

I reached for the laser controls, hesitated, then kicked in a radio frequency we hadn't used yet. A torrent of Finnish thundered down at us before I could reach the volume control. "If those are bandits, they're awfully good actors." I slapped the intercom switch to the lower deck. "Lieutenant, get your man with the best English up here on the double."

"My English is damn good enough, sir!" Raunio announced as he came through the deck hatch.

"Fine. Just get on the horn there, doctor. It looks like we've got Finnish jets out there and—"

My words were drowned out by the roar of a jet zooming overhead on a strafing run. "Give me taking the microphone," he said. Raunio talked urgently with the flier. They seemed to come to a quick understanding and the Finnish aircraft pulled out to fly a wide patrol circle around the ship. "Now he knows who's who," Tempkin said simply.

"Here come the parachutists," Joslyn said. Tiny parasols dotted the sky and rushed toward us as *Leviathan* cruised toward the piece of sky that held them.

Raunio said, "One of the Finnish to be saying some sort of troops forming up near over by the base of that big control fin."

"Out of line-of-sight for our lasers. This is what they call all hell breaking loose," Metcalf said morosely.

"Well, it's time we contributed. Randall, I hope you've got a gun."

I went down the ladder to the lower deck. The Finnish soldiers were just about ready to go, checking each other's equipment. I grabbed my own weapons, including a rocket launcher, a scaled down version of the one Krabnowski had died carrying. I checked over the direction finder that had been keyed to the control station's noise pattern. There was no chance of a reading out here on the open deck, but I could see that the power light came on. I shoved it into my backpack.

"Lieutenant!" I called. "Over here." We went over to the hatchway. "Here is the situation. The deck is too tough to blow a hole in it. There's a deck elevator stuck halfway up the shaft, with a blown-up jet burning on it. That elevator's our way into the ship. Get a squad to get in close in enough to put that fire out. We've got foam bombs on board."

A ballistic lander like *Uncle Sam* tended to set a lot of brush fires; foam bombs that would smother the flames and get rid of the heat were standard gear.

"Okay. Leave it to us doing it," Raunio said. He shouted at his troops, a squad of them grabbed the foam bombs from the racks and then he stepped to the open hatch, fired a few covering rounds, and jumped to the deck of the ship. I followed out, scrambling down the hatch ladder and dropping the last meter or two to the deck of *Leviathan*. Metcalf and Joslyn came down the ladder.

That scene, more than any other, is etched completely into my mind. There was a crystal-clear air of unreality about what I saw, all the colors brighter, all the distances bigger, all the strangeness of what I saw more alien than it should have been.

As we stepped out of *Uncle Sam*, *Leviathan* came out from under the cloud cover that had blanketed the sun, and everything stood out in bold, clear relief. To the stern, the control fin stood 50 meters high, its apex blasted into twisted shards by *Uncle Sam*'s torpedoes. The wreckage of the control tower and the laser station atop it burned. Finnish and Guardian ships scattered across the broad expanse of the deck were still aflame. The brilliant orange flames stood out against the dark grey hull metal. Inky black smoke poured forth from the wrecks and floated almost lazily up a few meters. There, beyond the protection of the spoilers at the bow of the ship, the smoke was suddenly smashed into wild tendrils that snarled into fantastic knots before vanishing completely behind the fast moving ship.

As our troops descended from *Sam*, the last of the Finnish ships set down and dropped its cloud of nitrogen coolant. Small bands of soldiers were beginning to come out from the ships. We heard the chatter of automatic weapons.

There was nothing but ship and sky; *Leviathan* flew too high and her topside was too wide for us to see the ground from the deck. The swift ship had left the clouds far behind. The sky was now a bold cobalt blue, laced with thin traceries of perfect white clouds. There was nothing but orange flame, black smoke, grey deck, blue sky and white cloud. A universe of elemental colors.

Into this world came those who had fallen from heaven to the attack. The ship rushed beneath the vanguard of the parachutists. As they passed over the deck, they fired glue bombs on cables, smaller versions of what the Beefies had used.

Twenty of them came over the deck at the same moment. Of those, one or two failed to get their cables fired off properly and they simply sailed over the stern of the ship to land below on the surface of the planet. The rest caught the deck properly and their parachutes were suddenly great kites as the cables came taut and brutally yanked harness and chute, dragging the chutist forward with the speed of the ship.

Three or four must have been killed by that savage pull, their necks broken, as they did nothing to save themselves, but merely hung in the wind, macabre decorations suspended in the sky.

The others survived to activate the small power winches at the ends of the cables and pull themselves out of the sky safely down to the deck.

More of the chutists came on. Some were too low and their chutes vanished under the keel of the ship. The riders must have been smashed flat by the impact with the hull of the ship, pasted there like bugs on a windshield.

Some of those who came too high landed safely on the

planet. One sailed through the billowing flame at the apex of the control fin and kept on going, a human torch aflame. He hung from his chute writhing in pain, until the flames that cooked him melted the chute's shroud lines. He dropped away suddenly, and the speed of his fall instantly extinguished the flames. Just before he vanished under the stern, I saw a reserve chute pop open. I never found out if he made it to the ground alive.

Two hundred men and women had ridden escape shells from orbit toward the deck of *Leviathan*. As best I could estimate, something less than one hundred actually made it to the deck in one piece. But, God, did we need that one hundred. We needed every piece of covering fire we had.

It took less than two minutes for *Leviathan* to pass through the whole of the parachute force. Raunio by that time had his team ready to take care of that burning jet. He led four men toward the elevator at a dogtrot. They got within 10 meters of it when someone below deck started taking potshots at them. They hit the deck instantly. Raunio lobbed a grenade, there was a thud and a puff of grey smoke, and the shooting stopped. Immediately the five men got up and started heaving the foam bombs into the burning wreck. The bombs reacted quickly in the intense heat, expanding into a dense purplish foam that fizzed up over the flames, dousing the fire.

A second team jogged out carrying small tanks of liquid nitrogen. They tossed them onto the elevator stage and shot a few holes in them. The nitrogen boiled out onto the stage and vanished in a cloud of steam as it contacted the intensely hot deck plates. I hoped that would cool the elevator stage down enough to walk on in insulated boots. Raunio turned toward the ship and gestured *come on*. Leaving five troops behind to hold *Sam*, the remainder of our force ran across *Leviathan*'s terribly exposed deck to the jammed elevator.

The thing had stopped about a man's height short of the main deck, leaving a wide gap for us to enter the ship by.

Raunio posted two guards outside and the rest us jumped down to the still-hot, but bearable, elevator stage. Someone tossed down a pile of rope ladders which we hooked over parts of the foamed-over wreck of the jet on the stage.

The ladders were about 10 meters long, which was just about enough to reach the deck below. We climbed down. I saw our sniper. Raunio's bomb had splattered him a little.

The plane had obviously touched off a fire down here when it exploded. The deck was a charred disaster. Five other fighters, in various states of ruin, stood like boggle-eyed monsters in their bays, burned and scorched. I caught a whiff of cooked meat, and my stomach almost rebelled. It had been a flash fire—white hot for a few seconds, then gone. Hydrogen fuel, probably. The sniper must have come in after it was out. No one who was here when it happened was still alive. No one could be.

We were inside the skin, if not the belly, of the beast. We posted a guard to hold our exit and went on.

We were on the port side of the ship, about halfway across the wing. Our team was to try for the most likely location of the missile control system: along the centerline, under the big vertical stabilizer and control fin.

We moved. I set Raunio in the van with the same men he led to the hangar, then put myself next along, with Joslyn, then the rest of the Finns and Metcalf in the rear.

It took a minute or two with a flashlight to find an exit in the gloom of the charred hangar deck, but then we spotted it and got set to go through it.

Raunio planted himself in front of the closed hatch and gestured for one of his men to open it. Raunio stood with machine pistol drawn and face set as the door whipped open.

Nothing there.

He dove and rolled into the corridor, jogged down to the starboard cross corridor, then signaled to the rest of us waiting at the hatchway.

He gestured us on, and we moved silently into the ship. We headed down a corridor that led to starboard, toward the centerline of the ship. We started out at a cautious walk, carefully checking each cross corridor. This part of the ship seemed deserted, untouched, pristine. Yet in the emptiness was something that unnerved, that made our feet move fast, that made us start to hurry, almost running, along the corridor. The brightly lit ways seemed haunted, watchful. We could hear the muffled thumps and bumps, the far-off clang of alarm bells, the muted sounds of shouts and gunfire. Somehow the distant sounds only made the quiet in the corridor all the more unnerving.

We got moving. On and on we went, making the best speed we could, sometimes slowing cautiously, sometimes racing ahead.

The corridors were numbered at each cross-corridor in severely stenciled characters. The signs put us on B deck, corridor 36. The cross-corridors were numbered P-16, P-15, P-14, and so on. I took them to mean portside, x number of corridors from centerline.

A sudden, sharp, explosion from nearby put us back in the shooting war. I almost walked up Raunio's back as he dropped to his belly and sighted sternward along the next cross corridor. He fired at something, there was another explosion, further off, and he was back on his feet, moving again.

We rushed on our way, always toward starboard and the stern.

"Behind!" I heard Metcalf yell, and the corridor we just walked past was lost in a swirl of fire and explosion.

We took cover as best we could and shot back until whoever it was stopped shooting. We left two dead, and kept moving.

Again we were fired upon, this time from dead ahead. I realized that the fire had to be coming from the main corridor through the ship's centerline. There the Guardians were set to repel boarders.

I pulled my rocket-thrower out of my backpack and loaded in a set of incendiaries. I fired three of the vicious little things and they spurted away. A brief moment later the concourse billowed with flame—then darkness and silence. Somebody behind me tossed a smoke grenade into the dark, and we moved.

The smoke hung there for a long time. We moved into the main corridor, the muffled sound of other fire-fights coming from far off.

Joslyn jabbed me in the ribs and nodded off to the right. There was a broad companionway, a ship's stairway, leading belowdecks. Hand signals moved down the line of soldiers and we headed down it deeper into the ship. "C" Deck was quiet. Raunio left two men as a posted guard. Down, in the preternatural silence, to "D," "E," "F," leaving two guards at each level. Raunio didn't like dispersing his force, but it was the best guarantee of our getting back.

We paused at the top of the companionway to "G" deck, and I took a look at the direction finder. The vertical plane indicator was still pointing slightly down; at least one more deck to go.

Whiffs of gunpowder, tendrils of smoke, the burnt-rubber smell of cooked insulation drifted through the air. Off in the distance was the popping chatter of small arms fire, and every now and again, a deep rumble that gently vibrated the deck as a larger explosion went off somewhere. But here, around us, it was quiet. As quiet as a trap about to be sprung.

Raunio peered down the companionway to "G," then tossed a smoke grenade down it. The smoke billowed forth, oozing down the corridor and up toward us. As it spread, small arms fire began, closer, harder. Explosions went off, and a laser hissed somewhere.

Raunio pointed to a faint beam of light betrayed by the smoke. It was at about waist-height in the companionway, half way down. Joslyn made a snip-snip motion with her hand and took off her backpack. She got a set of wire cutters out of a compact set of tools. She lay face up in the corridor and gestured for me to grab her ankles. I did so and started to slide her down the companionway. Her helmet scraped over the steps. With tiny, fluttering motions of her free hand, she told me how far to slide her down. When she was under the booby trap, she gestured *stop* emphatically.

The wire cutters went click, click, and the faint beam of light died—and the lasers with it.

I was about to pull her up when she gestured to be slid further down. Another one, and another. Then the third trap was clear and the entrance to "G" deck was open.

Now we knew what to look for. Three other photo-beam gadgets were easy to spot as we moved down the corridor.

I checked the D/F unit. No vertical component; we were on the right deck. The thing pointed out a hell of a source, straight back to sternward. We were getting close.

We moved toward the stern. Raunio posted two more guards, and we were down to twelve men. Probably just as well; more would have gotten in the way down here.

Now were we deep, deep within the belly of that beast. For the first time in my life, I began to understand claustrophobia. We were *inside* the enemy. He was before us, behind us, to port, to starboard, above, below. He could come for us from any direction at any moment.

Now, at each crossing of a corridor, Raunio went through an agony of care, kneeling to the deck, sticking his pistol out before his head, holding a throwing knife at the ready in his other hand, checking both directions with a quick, sudden shake of his head back and forth, then again, both ways, before he was satisfied.

On and on it went, stopping our quiet progress every few dozen meters to go through the routine again. Then, finally, there came a time when Raunio stuck his head out and retracted it instantly to look at a bullet ricocheting off the piece of deck where his head had been.

He scrambled to his feet, gathered himself for a spring, leaped across the intersection, spraying the air with fire from midjump. There was a dull thud. I dropped to the deck and fired blindly down the corridor in both directions There were bodies down on both sides of the intersection. Raunio ran to one, put his pistol to the back of the head and fired, then did the same for the others.

I wondered if he was mutilating the dead or killing the wounded. I doubt if he knew, or cared: he simply wasn't taking chances.

I didn't have time to mull it over—I found myself shooting at something without stopping to think. I heard Raunio curse and the whir of a knife flying past my ear. I dropped to the deck and kept firing. One Guard was down with a knife in his throat, another kept shooting back. I reached for the rocket-thrower and blipped three more of the brutes at them. Too late I remembered I had it loaded with incendiaries. A half second later the corridor was full of the stomach-churning stench of burning human flesh. There was a great wailing scream that stopped as Raunio fired into the flames. A wall of heat and flame rolled down toward us, reaching close enough to shrivel my eyebrows and eyelashes before it shrunk back. There was nothing beside people in the corridor that would burn, and the flames guttered quickly down to nothing.

This was the place. I could feel it. Booby traps, the guards . . . I pulled the D/F unit out again, and it pointed straight as an arrow down the cross corridor.

"This is it. Come on." My words broke a silence that, but for cursing and gunfire, had lasted for what seemed like hours. We had been inside the ship 23 minutes.

I led the way and Raunio grew eyes in the back of his head as he took up the rear. I tried to step over the still-smoldering corpses without looking, or smelling. Or thinking. The demons gibbered at the base of my skull.

Joslyn raised her pistol and fired as a bullet pinged off my helmet and rang my head like a bell. I felt a numbing shock to my chest. Stunned, I looked down at myself. A second bullet had slammed into my flak suit and flattened into a shapeless mass embedded in it. Without thinking I reached to brush it off and burned my fingers on the slug, still hot from the gun barrel and the impact. I stuck the burned fingers in my mouth and sucked at them, wincing at the pain. As I sat there, some part of me yelled to get up, keep moving, get shooting. Suddenly I felt a good swift kick in the rear, and Metcalf grabbed me by the collar, pulled me to my feet, and got me moving.

"C'mon, boss man. He's dead, not you." He nodded to the corpse Joslyn had made as we passed it.

"Thanks, Randall."

"Forget it. All part of the service."

And I pulled him down as another gunner popped into view. We fell to the deck with a jarring slam. The gunner had nothing but a gun, a hand, and an eye visible as he peered out from the cover of the next intersection. My pistol was in my hand. I settled myself into the approved prone firing position and carefully squeezed the trigger twice. On the second shot, that eye died, and the hand dropped the pistol.

I glanced down at the D/F. It was going crazy, whirling its pointer around and around, every light lit. We were right on top of the control station. I walked forward a few meters to an unmarked door.

We were there.

Joslyn handed me a blob of plastic explosive. I jammed pieces of it to the hatch handle, the four corners, made a guess as to where the hinges were and slapped blobs there too. Joslyn followed me, jamming tiny radio control fuses into each glob of the stuff.

We signaled the others to flatten themselves against the bulkhead that the hatch was in and did so ourselves. Joslyn hit the button on the radio trigger and KABLOOM happened. We were all deafened by the blast. The hatch leaped out of the frame and slammed into the opposite inside wall with a resounding *clang* that was the only thing loud enough for us to hear. A cloud of dust and smoke jumped out of the hatchway.

Raunio stepped through and fired three times. I went in second and found three dead men. I saw a flicker of movement and blasted at it. Four dead men.

The smoke cleared away quickly.

This was it.

Here, in this compartment, were the transmitters that

controlled the anti-ship missiles that lurked in the outer reaches of this star system. Here, if the commands the Finnish technicians had come up with were correct, we could order that system to self-destruct, tell the killing missiles to die. The League ships that waited on the fringes of interstellar space could pour into the system, and the war would be won at a stroke.

This was it.

Joslyn and I knew what to do. We had trained on the recovered Vapaus unit dozens of times. Elsewhere in the ship were other teams that had trained just as hard, were just as ready. But we were it. One other team besides us had been sent to this location. It was never heard from.

I tried to talk to Joslyn, to say, "Let's get started." But I could not hear myself. Joslyn's lips moved, and I heard nothing. I was deafened. It sunk in. So was Joslyn. So were the others. That was bad, that was very bad.

The two control panels were set with their backs to each other, so the only way to synchronize the commands was by calling them out so the following operator could know what the lead operator was doing. If we couldn't hear, the job was impossible.

We spent a long, harrowing ten minutes, first trying to get the Finns and Metcalf to understand the problem, and then yelling our heads off until we could hear each other over the ringing in our ears, while an increasingly edgy Raunio kept watch over the corridors.

Finally, with our throats raw and our ears still sore from the beating they had taken, Joslyn and I got to work.

The Vapaus technicians had provided us with skeleton keys based on the locks on the station recovered there, but there was a more reliable source for keys at hand. We took them from the dead bodies of the two Guardian operators.

We engaged the system.

"Key one in," Joslyn called.

"Key one in," I confirmed.

"Turn key one to first position at my command," she called. "Ready, steady, go!"

We flipped the keys over one click and a green light came on over my board.

"Key two in," Joslyn said.

"Key two in."

"Turn key two to first position. Ready, steady, go!"

A second light came on.

"Key one right hand," she called. "Key two left hand. Key one and key two to second positions simultaneously. Ready, steady, go!"

Two more lights appeared and a panel slid open before me. Inside, a new set of controls. Then, off in the distance, I heard gunfire.

"Now grasp Mode Select Switch. At my signal, turn three notches to Full Manual Override. I will count off each click stop. Stop one—now. Stop two—now. Stop three—now." Joslyn's voice came more and more clearly to me, pure and sure in its calmness. Again, in the distance, was the clatter of gunplay. It seemed louder.

"Left thumb over Mode Activate One. Right thumb over Mode Activate Two. Depress both simultaneously on my signal. Ready. Steady. Go!"

Suddenly, a loud, recorded voice boomed out in a harsh nasal accent. "You have activated the Full Manual Override system. You have thirty seconds to lay in a correct command. If no correct command is received in thirty seconds, the controls will lock, this compartment will seal automatically, and poison gas will be introduced. Thirty seconds—mark."

Joslyn's voice came from behind me, as calmly as ever. "Release safety cover over self-destruct command button. Ready, steady, go. Three inner switches are revealed."

"Twenty seconds, mark," said the recording.

"At my signal, depress leftmost switch. Ready, steady, go. Rightmost switch. Ready, steady, go. Final switch, the center switch, and cross your fingers with your free hand, my love! Ready, steady—GO!"

The control panel in front of me lit up like a Christmas tree. A new recording boomed away in the same old voice. "You have set the anti-ship missile system to self-destruct.

If no countermand is laid in within five minutes, self-destruct commands will be radioed to anti-ship missiles. Five minutes, mark. Thirty seconds after self-destruct transmission, this control system will automatically clear all its memory space and operating systems if no countermand is laid in. Four minutes, 45 seconds; mark."

With a whoop of joy we were in each other's arms. Then there was a roar of gunnery, very close. Metcalf yelled to us, "Not so fast, kids. We may not get that five minutes. We have to hold this place and keep the bad guys from getting back in."

Raunio and George were firing in both directions down the corridor from inside the hatchway.

I snarled and slapped a load of high explosive rockets into the launcher. I stuck the launcher out into the corridor and fired once, each way. The explosions knocked us all from our feet, shook us to our bones, and redeafened us all.

I looked out the hatchway. Not only was there no one left in the corridor to shoot at us, there wasn't much left in the way of corridor.

And we waited through the longest five minutes of my life. Toward the end of it, we could hear again.

"Ninety seconds, mark," said the recording.

I toyed with the idea of putting a bullet through that speaker.

Guns and lasers came from the corridor again. Raunio and his men returned the fire. That was going to be a tough way to get out. I decided not to try it. We still had a few meters of ribbon plastique left to play with. The stuff was "directionalized" and color coded, yellow and blue. The force of the explosive went in the direction of the yellow side. If you wanted a plain old any-which way explosion, you kneaded the stuff into a homogeneous green lump.

I climbed up on a stool. I took all the directional I had left and rolled it out with the yellow side against the overhead bulkhead, forming a circle about a half-meter around. The overhead was aluminum, not the super-tough material used on the outer hull. We'd get through it. I shoved four of the radio-fuses into it and hopped back down.

"Sixty seconds," the nasal robot voice announced.

One of the Finnish volunteers spun around and fell to the deck with her forehead missing.

"Christ," Metcalf said. "C'mon you damn recording, get that signal sent or we all end up goddamn hamburger!"

I pulled the stool out of the way of the coming explosion and watched the fighters at the door. There was no room for another gun there. All we could do was watch the moments die.

"Come on, Mister Machine, tell us about thirty seconds," Metcalf muttered.

I coughed and spat out a mouthful of gunpowder-flavored slime. I noticed my hands were badly cut up and wondered when it had happened.

Finally, the good news came: "Thirty seconds, mark."

"Thought it had broken down on us," Metcalf said.

"Not yet, and you just hope it doesn't for thirty-one seconds," I replied.

Raunio tossed a grenade in each direction down the corridor. Smoke belched in the door and filled the compartment.

"Fifteen seconds."

"Raunio! We're going out through the ceiling! Be ready to fire your last rounds."

"Ten seconds."

"Get in here!" I yelled to the Finns. Raunio shoved his machine pistol into his holster, lobbed one more grenade in each direction and backed away from the hatchway. He turned and grinned at me. His face was blackened with grime, his hair singed half away, and three long slashes bled freely from his left ear to his chin. "Okay, Mister Larson, sir, get us out of here!" he yelled as the grenades bellowed from the hallway.

George holstered his pistol and scrambled to his feet. He nodded to me and leaned back again the wall, exhausted.

"Five seconds."

"Four."

"Three."

"Two."

Joslyn had her finger on the radio fuse detonator.

"One."

Then there was no sound but the gunfire in the hall. A pause longer than any life.

A click.

The nasal voice returned. "All anti-ship missiles have been radioed to self-destruct. Signals will reach missiles in four to ten hours. Control system will shut down and erase in thirty seconds."

We had won.

We had won the war.

Joslyn pushed the trigger and the charge went off with a wild roar that engulfed the room anew in smoke. For long seconds it was too dense to see anything.

Finally it cleared to show a slab of aluminum hanging from the overhead bulkhead by a single crazily twisted shred about the size of my finger. I pulled out my laser and slashed it down. It swung down to the deck with a clanging thud.

Bullets spattered the bulkhead opposite the hatchway. A half-dozen guns fired as one and an enemy soldier dropped into the compartment, a bloody ruin.

Metcalf and Raunio poured fire through the hatch as I grabbed the stool and set it under the hole in the overhead. I grabbed Joslyn and half-shoved, half-threw her through it. George followed, then the Finnish privates.

"Metcalf! Raunio! You!" I fired my own pistol into the hatch. Metcalf was through the hole in less than two seconds. Raunio was on his heels, and I was on his.

I looked around me. We were in what looked like an officer's cabin. Then I saw the officer. Very dead. Joslyn had put a bullet between his eyes before he could lift his pistol from his side.

Raunio kicked open the hatch into the corridor and we got the hell out of there.

We tried as best we could to follow the path we had

used on "G" deck, one level down, but it seemed "F" was laid out differently.

We were lost in record time. Raunio was in the lead again, wasting no time in caution now. He careered around every corner with his gun blazing in case anyone was there. I looked up at the corridor numbers and swore. We were headed the wrong way. I yelled for Raunio. "You maniac! That's the wrong way!"

We turned and headed back toward the bow.

I turned us to starboard and then back toward the bow, so that we were in Starboard Corridor One. I figured Centerline was most likely to be held in force. We hauled down S-1. We needed to get to Forward corridor 36; F-36 and centerline being where we had left our guards posted.

I remembered something important and pulled out my radio. "All League and Finn troops! Code word PAYDIRT. PAYDIRT. Mission accomplished. Retreat, escape, save yourselves, mission accomplished and pass the word." I tossed the radio at Raunio and told him to repeat that in Finnish. We kept moving.

The air was acrid, carrying the smell of fire and sweat. F-50. Fourteen more to go.

There was a section of collapsed bulkhead blocking S-1. We jogged starboard to S-2 and kept moving, shifted back to S-1 four intersections down, at F-42.

On and on. I turned us to starboard and then back toward the bow, so that we were on starboard corridor 1. And we found the intersection of Centerline and Forward 36.

Two surprised Finnish guards almost blew us away before they recognized us. We yelled for the guards left on "G" deck and swarmed up the companionway, leaving them to follow.

"F" deck to "B" deck. Four flights of stairs, or companionways, or whatever. That might not seem like much, but try it after the day we had had. The guards from each deck joined us as we passed. By the time we clambered up to "B" there were spots in front of my eyes and I was heaving my lungs to grab all the air I could.

We were lucky up until then. But Centerline, "B" deck, was the site of a pitched battle. We were pinned down by fire coming from the direction of the bow.

Five meters forward of us I saw a companionway leading to "A" deck; topside, the flight deck, out. A short cut. If we could get up that way, it would save us an endless—and quite possibly deadly—run through the labyrinth of corridors that led back to the aircraft elevator we had come in. It was damn tempting. But we couldn't stick our noses out of the companionway without getting blasted into hamburger.

Ten meters the other way was the corridor we had come down from the elevator, less than one long hour ago.

I sat there, trying to decide. My force and I were panting with exhaustion, and exhaustion decided me on which way to go. I knew we could not make it down to portside and then run all that way back on the flight deck. Time was against us. We had to go for the short cut.

And we had to go *now*, if we were going to live. I slapped the last clip of incendiaries into the rocket launcher. "Raunio," I said. "Signal your men at the elevator that we're not headed that way. We're heading straight out that companionway ahead." I kept my head down and put the launcher over my head, over the lip of the companionway.

Instantly bullets twanged against hull metal. I pulled the trigger, firing blind, and the first little missile whooshed away.

A bolt of flame lashed out a moment later. I leaped out onto "B" with a war-cry in my throat and stood with my feet planted, the launcher grasped before me in both my hands. Before me was an inferno, a corridor wreathed in fascinating hellfire.

A writhing figure, cased in flame, collapsed to the deck I fired straight into it and it exploded into flaming horror. Burning human gore splashed onto my hands, my face, my chest.

The fire, the flames, the red-orange monster. I fired again and again with the launcher, doubling and redoubling the havoc to no purpose.

My little band of fighters ran for the "A" deck hatch as I covered them, remembering other fires, so long ago. Again and again I fired, unaware that the launcher was empty. Look at the fire, exult in the carnage!

"Mac! Hurry! Please!" Joslyn called.

And then I heard the *click, click, click* of the emptied launcher firing nothing as I pulled the trigger. I realized what I was doing, dropped the cursed thing, and ran for "A" deck. I jolted up the companionway to the flight deck, to the broad expanses of *Leviathan*'s topside.

There, too, was carnage.

Two more of our ships were blasted away. Dozens of tiny pitched battles raged on the great flight deck, opponents pinned down behind pieces of wreckage, firing at each other.

Uncle Sam still stood intact, her proud red, white, and blue paint job looking awfully damn good—and damned far away. There had to be a half kilometer of open deck between us and our ship. Further off still, I could see the stars on *Stars* and the stripes on *Stripes*, still bold against the Finnish sky.

Leviathan was moving slower, flying lower, listing slightly to port. Now the planet's surface was visible from the deck. Fires burned in a hundred places on *Leviathan*'s deck.

I got my radio back from Raunio and broadcast again. "All troops! All League and Finnish troops! Codeword PAYDIRT! Mission accomplished! Withdraw, withdraw, withdraw. This is recall. Get the hell off this ship and save yourselves! Relay this message." I handed the communicator to Raunio again. "Repeat that. Raunio, repeat a recall to those guys guarding the hangar entrance and still below. Let's get out of here before someone notices us."

The exhausted soldiers followed Raunio in one last run for their lives. One young kid stopped running suddenly and fell to the deck with his chest holed. A stray bullet.

From every point of the vast deck, soldiers were headed toward the landing craft. I saw two or three parachutists simply run to the stern and jump overboard, trusting to their reserve chutes. The rest were doing what we were doing, a fighting retreat. Twice we practically ran over Guardian troops who were busy blazing away at our troops with their backs to us. They didn't last long. Raunio ran out of throwing knives.

Uncle Sam seemed to grow no closer as we ran. My heart was pounding, my head was spinning. I dumped my backpack and dropped my rifle. It had all been too close-in for that. I tossed away my helmet and did all I could to force one foot in front of the other.

Slowly, so slowly, we came toward the lander. A Guardian jet roared across the sky a little ways off, a Finn on his tail. The Guards had gotten that ventral launcher back in service fast. A missile blurred across the distance between them, and the Guardian blew up, the wreckage slamming into the control fin and bouncing around the deck before it fell off the stern.

Uncle Sam was suddenly close, seventy-five meters. Fifty meters. Closer. And we were there. Joslyn was first in the hatch and first to the lander's flight deck, but I was a damn close second.

Exhaustion. It was so tempting to take off, get out, get away, and call it over. But we had come this far, and maybe we could end it all.

The view screens showed the battle below us and the Finns scrambling into the lower deck. Joslyn cast off her battle gear and dropped into the pilot's chair. I skinned off my own flak suit and let the rest of my guns clatter to the deck. I wiped a bloody sleeve across my face and got to my flight station.

"Joslyn, go to T minus five seconds before lift off and hold. There'll be stragglers. Power up both chemical and fusion engines. I'll want 50 percent of hover power from the fusion side for as long as you've got it."

"But not power to take off on?"

"It's time to finish this thing. I want to see if a fusion jet can slice through this hull metal of theirs." I hit the intercom. "Lieutenant Raunio! Up here, if you please. I'll need some good Finnish spoken. Randall, we may need a spare pilot."

They came up to the flight deck. "Doctor. Get on the horn to all ships. Let them launch the moment they have everyone they can carry on board. *Stars* and *Stripes* I want to hold a while longer. We're going to try and punch through this deck and do some damage." Raunio relayed the orders. Metcalf dropped heavily into the empty flight station and started to help Joslyn get *Uncle Sam* ready to move.

I sneaked a peek from the hatchway camera. Nothing moved out there at first, then a sweating soldier staggered into view and threw himself into the ship. Another followed.

The first Finnish ship took off from the bow and headed for any touchdown site she could find. I watched her grab for sky. Below her the New Finnish landscape sprawled out grandly. On the horizon, coming up fast, was the seacoast.

Another Finn launched. The last pair of Guardian fighters in the sky tried to go after him, but the Finnish fighters chased them away.

Another Finnish lander got away.

"*Uncle Sam* is at T minus 5 seconds, and holding. Fusion and chemical drives at the ready," Joslyn reported. She leaned back in her crash couch with a tremendous sigh. "My God. Mac, we pulled it off."

"So far, anyway. Lieutenant Raunio. What status for *Stars* and *Stripes*?"

He called the two ships and reported. "All systems go for launch immediately. They both request to take off."

"Denied," I snapped. "We're going to try and nail this beast for good. Let's damn *finish* the job."

"I quite agree, Commander."

"Boss man, there goes the last of the merchant ships."

"Good. Everybody, scan the decks on every camera. Anybody see anyone still out there?"

"Nothing."

"No."

"All clear."

I prayed they were right. It looked that way. "Button her up, Joslyn."

"Hold it!" Metcalf called. Three figures were hurrying

forward as fast they could with their hands on top of their heads. Guardian troops, surrendering. "Oh, hell. Let 'em come." I hit the intercom. "Lieutenant. Three prisoners surrendering and coming aboard. Try to keep your men from killing them." The three climbed aboard very carefully, keeping their hands in view at all times. Through the hatch camera I saw Raunio come into view, give each of them a hard punch to the stomach that dropped each to the deck. He grabbed them by the collars and threw them through the inner airlock one by one, then waved at the camera.

I wondered to myself what sort of work was going to be available to a fellow like Raunio in peacetime. Alligator wrestling, or the local equivalent, perhaps.

"So let's button this crate up," I said. "Half-hover power on fusion jets." The deep rumbling of the fusion engine below us came to life. "Relay same to *Stars* and *Stripes*." From the base of both of those ships a tiny violet-white pencil of light lashed out and flattened itself against the incredibly tough material. For a long time, nothing happened.

Metcalf let out a low, deep whistle. "That deck should be vaporized after five seconds of that."

Ten seconds, twenty seconds, and still the hull held out. But then something seemed to waver and sag beneath *Stars*. At the same moment, the rumble of our own drive fluttered and then deepened.

"*Stars* reports that *Uncle Sam* has pierced the hull," Raunio said. I glanced at him and saw the light in his eye, the thirst for final victory his voice betrayed.

"Okay, Joslyn, give us hover at ten meters."

The rumble grew louder and *Uncle Sam* lurched into the air. The fusion flame sliced through the normal material below the outer hull like butter, vaporizing the aluminum instantly. A demon's brew of chemical smoke suddenly sprang out of the hole in the hull and spurted up around *Uncle Sam*, blinding us. "Twenty meters, and give us about a meter a second headway toward the stern," I said.

"Lieutenant Raunio, order *Stars* and *Stripes* to do the same at half a meter a second as soon as they burn through."

Uncle Sam's drive sliced through the exterior hull metal nicely once the first piercing was made. She cut a trench in the flight deck out of which spewed the smoke and fire of hell. First *Stars*, then *Stripes* floated gently into the air and started to burn their own slashes into the skin of *Leviathan*.

Now came the real assault. "Joslyn, take us out over the port wing."

Sam upped her speed suddenly and zipped out over top of the port wing. "Okay, hover right here at 15 meters until I give the word. Get ready to bounce out of here at maximum boost."

Joslyn nodded, and our ship took up its new station.

"Mac, we've got to be right over the lift cells here. If that isn't helium down there . . ." Metcalf said worriedly.

"I know, I know. But it sure as hell ought to work."

"*Stars* and *Stripes* both report two minutes of fuel. They request permission to try and land."

"Damn it. Okay. Granted."

Instantly, the two smaller ships popped away.

"Mac, they'll have to ditch. We're well out to sea," Joslyn said. "We haven't got great lots of fuel ourselves," she added mildly.

The two little ships reached for sky and cleared the deck. They fell toward the sea in formation, engines braking their falls, with no thought of trying for shore, now at least 10 kilometers away. They eased themselves gently toward the sea. The fusion jets touched at the seawater and it exploded into live steam, hiding the two ships from view for long moments.

Raunio listened over his headset and reported. "Both ships now landed okay," he said. He grinned proudly. "My son piloting *Stripes*. He fight real good, I bet. He safe, now."

Uncle Sam hung above the wing of her great adversary, the lone ship left in the skies above *Leviathan*, but for a few skirmishing fighters long kilometers away. Her drive flame bore in on the unseen piece of hull beneath us. Our ship burbled slightly and Joslyn corrected. "Mac, I think we just hulled her—"

BLAM! A great slap of force threw us high into the air above the ship, flinging us clear of the explosion.

The Guardians had trusted their tough hull too far. They had filled *Leviathan*'s lift cells with hydrogen, the lightest, most lifting, most flammable gas possible.

Joslyn gunned the engines and bounced us high over the burning ship. The port wing was surmounted by a wall of flame. *Leviathan* lurched and shuddered violently. A great piece of the wing broke clear off and dropped lazily down into the sea. *Leviathan* went out of control, and swung about in a great spiraling curve toward the shore, losing altitude and forward speed steadily. We kept station on her, watching the death of that great beast, that great ship, that terrible enemy.

Lower and lower she fell, more quickly now, coming in over the coastline barely 600 meters up. Another explosion ripped off a great multi-ton piece of the port wing and it fell to the ground, a fireball. The control fin seemed to fold up and collapse. It fell away sternward, still attached to the kilometer-long ship by twisted remnants of girdering. It slammed into the earth, throwing up a great shower of soil and sand, trees and boulders. It dug a long, deep furrow in the ground before it dragged the rest of the ship into collision with the planet.

Leviathan crashed with a concussion that shook the land, the sea, and even the sky for a great distance.

Like a mountain unleashed from its moorings to the land, *Leviathan* rolled and bounced and broke apart in billowing sheets of flame that reached kilometers into the sky. Pieces that seemed small by comparison with *Leviathan*, each larger than the *Joslyn Marie*, split off and crashed to the ground.

Slowly, gradually, after many minutes of agony, the last pieces of the tortured monster came to rest and collapsed in flame. The flames spread out and the grasslands, the trees, the very soil burned in the fabulous heat. The fires would burn for hours more.

We watched in horror, in disbelief, in victory at the carnage we had wrought.

We had won, utterly.

I leaned back in my crash couch and stared, in my mind's eye, through the blank bulkheads of the good ship *Uncle Sam* at the clean skies above.

We had won.

"Put her down, Joslyn," I said quietly. "Put her down and let's get some rest."

Chapter Twenty

Joslyn and I walked hand in hand toward the sea, along the quiet shore. Out in the further reaches of the harbor, we could just pick out the outline of *Stripes*, now being towed into shore. *Stars* floated at dockside a few kilometers down the coast, waiting to be lifted from the water.

It was late evening in the long day of New Finland, and the sun was casting a rich warn glow over the water ahead of us. Joslyn spotted a familiar silhouette a short distance away, and we walked toward it, watching the sky.

The first silent, distant flash came just as we reached George. There it was, high in the sky over the fading sun. George stood staring at it gutter down to nothing as we came nearer. He nodded to us without speaking.

The three of us stood there. Vapaus came over the horizon and moved over us, a friendly watcher in the night. I turned and looked back toward the land, where *Leviathan*'s wreck lay huge and broken across the burned-out meadowlands.

The nearby town, Vipurii, was shot up and scarred and still there. A few cities—Mannerheim, New Helsinki, were gone forever, at least as they once were. Tomorrow was time enough to begin the rebuilding.

Hundreds, thousands, tens of thousands were dead, and many more horribly wounded. Heroes and cowards alike had fallen—most to be forgotten, a few to live forever in death. A world was scarred, and bent, and bloody, but unbroken.

It was over.

It might be said that the thousands who were dead had lived as much as it was needful for them to live, had contributed to the victory and gone on. One could say that, once again, the tree of liberty had been refreshed with the blood of patriots.

But it was hard, now, to think of a victory, or a defeat, or a war at all. All I could feel for certain was that I was still alive, and free, and just barely unafraid.

Another light flared suddenly, quietly, in the sky, and Joslyn took my hand. The radio waves carried the invisible commands from a machine that was dead, and the anti-ship missiles, killer robots in space, were dying. Suicides all—the last resort of the insane.

George sighed, and fumbled at nothing with his hands, as if the engineer in him was looking for something to fix, or build. "There go the prison walls. I helped build them and thank God I could help tear them down. Soon the rest of your people will be here, and then you'll—no, then *we'll*—be off again to fight them on Capital. And there are a lot more people back home who would be glad to see our side—the League side—win."

"We'll win."

"Mac, Joslyn. This little planet was damn lucky it was you two who came. They'll be naming things for you when it comes time to rebuild. If it had been someone else, instead of you two, the Finns might have lost for good."

"We would have won, George. The Guardians would have attacked some other world, stretched themselves even farther to conquer. They might have won two worlds, or three, for a time, but the threat they posed was the very thing that made the League stronger, and less afraid, than they could ever believe it could be."

"Maybe. But you two saved a lot of lives, and kept this from spreading to a lot of worlds."

"That's good enough for us, anyway," Joslyn said. She squeezed my hand in both of hers and smiled.

"And then they'll be beaten, for good," George said, and I could see how much it cost him to call the Guards "they." He was trying, but his soul was not yet free of their claim on him.

"No, they won't be," I said. I dropped Joslyn's hand and

walked toward the tideline, and let the cool waves lap at my feet.

"The sky is very large," I said, "and as long as humans travel there, and are free to do what they want, a few will want to rule and conquer and be mighty and greedy. This time, we beat them. And as long as there are men and women—even just a few—who care more about each other than themselves—people who'll die to see a baby live—we will be able to beat then again."

I thought of Pete Gesseti and his thoughts about our missing comrades, the crew and passengers of the *Venera*. They were out there, on the Guardians' base planet, Capital. I was sure of it. They were waiting for us to find them, to track the Guards down to their home world and free our comrades. The job wasn't done yet.

walked around the machine, and let the [illegible] drop at my feet.

"The sky is very large," I said, "and as long as humans travel there, and are free to do what they want, a few will want to rob and conquer and be mighty and greedy. This time, we beat them. And as long as there are men and women—even just a few—who care more about each other than themselves—people who'll die to save a buddy's life—we will be able to beat them again."

I thought of Pete Cornish and his thoughts about our missing comrades, the crew and passengers of the *Lancer*. They were out there, on the Guardians' base planet, Capital. I was sure of it. They were waiting for us to find them, to track the Guards down to their home world and free our comrades. The job wasn't done yet.

Volume II
Rogue Powers

For Mom, who shared her love,
taught me self-confidence,
and gave me the world's
greatest middle name.

Chapter One

Aboard LPS *Venera*

The ship stank. And Lucille Calder was getting tired of it.

The *Venera's* ventilation system, shot up two days after the hijacking, was barely working. The system had taken the damage when the Survey Service students had tried to get the ship back. The students had failed, of course. They were armed with only a few side-arms the Guardians hadn't found, while the Guards controlled the ship, had all the heavy guns, had all the advantages. The Guards had killed a few more Survey personnel, taken the side-arms, spaced the bodies, confined the survivors to their cabins, and that was that.

But the Guards had been stupid enough to fire heavy ammo through life-support equipment. Now, twenty-one days after the hijacking, the air pumps wheezed and shuddered instead of humming. The scrubbers weren't working properly and the whole ship was rich with the smell of bodies and fear and burned-out machinery. Everyone had a headache, which probably meant that the carbon dioxide count was going up. And the water was starting to smell like the bottom of a pond. The few members of *Venera's* crew who were still alive could probably have patched things up, but they were confined to quarters, two to a cabin, like everyone else. Either the Guards couldn't do the repairs or they didn't care how bad things got.

The Guards spoke English. None of the Survey students had seen anything but white male Guardians. That was about all anyone knew about them. Somewhere, somehow, out among the uncharted stars, the Guardians must have gone off to settle their own world and hide from the rest of humanity. At least that was one theory that made sense. The Guards themselves didn't explain anything.

Lieutenant Lucille Calder, Royal Australian Navy, was locked up in her cabin, but she was a good enough pilot to *feel* the clumsiness in the way the Guards handled the *Venera's* controls. She knew how much fuel the *Venera* had carried. She had made a point, these last three weeks, of carefully timing the burns the Guards made and estimated how many gravities of thrust they used. She kept a rough running account in her head of how much fuel this thumb-fingered crowd of barbarians was wasting as they corrected and over-corrected and re-corrected their errors.

Bad piloting wouldn't kill them just yet—there was still a fair amount of fuel left. On the other hand, the fouled air and water might be enough to do them in very soon. For the sake of Guardian and prisoner alike, *Venera* had to get somewhere fast.

But Lucy and the other survivors of the hijacking had no idea where *Venera* was being taken. The view screens were shut off, so there were no stars to look at—whatever good that would have done—and there was no real way of telling if they had remained in normal space or made one or more jumps into C^2 space. Lucy knew nothing, could do nothing, could see nothing. She didn't like it.

She stared across the tiny cabin at her bunkmate, Cynthia Wu. Ensign Wu was from High Singapore's tiny Defense Force, an outfit with little more to do than track the endless stream of cargo ships that called on the huge Earth-orbiting city. She was used to waiting, to dull patches. Lucy wasn't so lucky. The Deep Space Fleet of the Royal Australian Navy had trained her for command, for quick decisions and independent action. She needed to be in control, to have some effect on what happened to her. She needed a viewport to see out of, an idea of where they were going, an idea of why they were being taken there. She wanted to know who these surly men were who called themselves the Guardians. She had to know what they wanted with the *Venera*—and whether or not she would live through it.

And she wanted a shower. Lucy's mother was an Australian aborigine, and her father the descendant of British stock. They had raised her on a huge range station, a sheep ranch, at the edge of the desert, where the sun baked down and made a person sweat and smell. Both her mother and father had come from families who kept showerbaths outside, so you wouldn't bring that odor into the house. And now Lucy had been indoors with the smell of many unwashed bodies—including her own—for the better part of a month.

Lucille Calder was a short, stocky woman, dark-complexioned with short-cropped, brownish-blond hair. With a pug nose and a hint of a double chin, she would never be called pretty, but she didn't much care about that. Pretty wasn't her job.

For the thousandth time, Lucy looked across the cabin and watched Wu calmly turn over the page of her book and continue reading. For the thousandth time, Lucy overcame the urge to grab the book out of Wu's hand and heave it at the bulkhead. But even at the moment she was ready to commit mayhem against her cabin-mate, Lucy knew Cynthia Wu was probably the best person she could have been locked up with. Wu had patience, and faith in the power of logic and the careful examination of the possibilities. Those were things Lucy had to learn from somewhere.

Lucy wished the ship was under spin so she could at least pace the deck. It was hard to expend nervous energy in zero-gee without literally bouncing off the walls. She undid the restraint line that held her to her bunk and pushed herself toward the hatch. There was a peephole in it that let her see out into the corridor. Not that anything was ever out there but another grey bulkhead. Floating in mid-air, she sighed and peered out the hole. Still nothing there—

Quite suddenly, she found herself pasted to the deck, a roaring noise filling the cabin. The goddamned Guards had fired the main engines without any warning again. Lucy swore to herself and got up off the deck. She hit the stopwatch function on her wrist-aid and began timing the burn. It felt like a shade under a standard gee and a half this time.

Wu didn't even look up from her book. Lucy wondered which of the two of them was being more foolish: Wu, for doing nothing at all, or she herself for fussing over thrusts and burn times that wouldn't really tell her anything useful.

But *this* burn went on a long time. By Lucy's timing, the engines fired for twenty minutes and a few seconds. In the ringing silence after the roar of the engines, she worked the resulting acceleration out in her head—about eighteen kilometers a second. *That* meant something. No reasonable flight between two points in a star system would require such a big change in velocity. On the other hand, eighteen klicks a second was a fairly modest relative motion between two stars.

It had to mean that the *Venera* had indeed made a C^2 jump. *Venera* must be matching velocity in a new star system.

"Cynthia," she said quietly. "We're here."

Wu looked at her sharply. "How do you know?"

"That was a burn to match velocity between two star systems, and if you're trying to hide where you're going you do that after you get to the new star. Besides, that burn must have just about emptied the tanks. They wouldn't risk running out of fuel unless they were in range of their own people."

Wu closed her book. "God, Luce, I think you're right."

But there was arrival and arrival. Getting to the target star system was one thing, but in from the outer regions of system, down to planetary orbit, was quite another. It was another day and a half of confinement before anything else happened.

Then, in the middle of the ship's night cycle, they were awakened by another main-engine burn, no more than a minute or so at about a gee. Then came a series of bumps and jumps from the attitude jets as the Guardian pilot fine-tuned his course. For a long time, there was no sound but the complaints of the over-strained ventilation system. Finally, more bumps and stutters from the trim thrusters and then, far-off and faint, a series of dull thunks and clanks.

"Docking collar," Lucy said. "My God, they must have done the C^2 jump damned close to a planet to get us in this fast."

"If we are close to a planet," Cynthia said. "Maybe we've just docked with some station in free orbit of the local sun." There was a series of sharper clacking noises. "Well, maybe we'll find out soon. There go the capture latches."

There was no question of sleeping any more. The two of them got up and got dressed.

They could hear voices now, bellowing, yelling, the sounds of every gangway crew that had ever brought a ship into port and secured her in a berth. The air changed, became cleaner, sweeter, as the ship's air mingled with the atmosphere of whatever it was they had docked to.

They heard the rattle of keys and the sound of angry, urgent voices. Finally, the hatch to their cabin slammed open, and a man in battle-armor hung in the hatchway. "Get your stuff and move," he barked, his voice made deep and booming by the suit's speaker system. "Head to the main sternward hatch and through the airlock into the station. Do what any Guard tells you to do and you might not get hurt." He turned, grabbed at a handhold, and pulled himself down to the next cabin without looking to see what Lucy and Cynthia did.

Lucy had a mad impulse to race after him, to smash the faceplate on his suit, to demand an explanation, to run like hell, to do something, anything—and then she turned to see Wu calmly packing up her few belongings into her duffel bag. Lucy pulled herself to her locker and did the same. She would have to learn patience, if she wanted to live.

The stern airlock was a knot of chaos. Guardians in battle-armor took no nonsense, answered no questions, did nothing but grab at their prisoners and heave them through the hatch and down a connecting tunnel. There was a viewport by the airlock, and Lucy managed to get a quick peek through it. She caught a quick glimpse of a fair-sized orbital station of some sort. The Guards were still grabbing anyone who didn't move fast enough to please them. Lucy decided that she didn't need some metal-clad goon groping her, and got through the tunnel unassisted.

She emerged into a large hemispherical loading bay, surrounded by baffled, angry, frightened classmates. Her fellow prisoners were still coming through the hatch, set in the center of the base of the hemisphere, that communicated with the *Venera*. Lucy tried to count the people in the bay, to see how many of her classmates had stayed alive and made it this far, but they were still in zero-gee. It was impossible to keep track of all the men and women hovering or drifting in the air long enough to tote them up.

Prisoners were still straggling through the airlock tunnel. A scuffle of some sort broke out across the loading bay. Lucy couldn't see much through the tangle of floating bodies, but she could hear shouting and meaty thuds. Then three small, perfect, globes of bright-red blood sailed quietly past her and splattered onto the bulkhead in slow-motion.

"AW RIGHT, SHUT UP!" An over-amplified voice boomed through the bay. "SHUT UP! Make your way down a bulkhead and set your feet on the flat deck of the bay. There are handholds all around the edge of the dome at waist height and I want each of you to grab one and stay put. I'm gonna get a head-count, and nobody is going anywhere until I do, so clear the center of this bay, get off of the dome wall, and get down to the flat deck. Line up around the edge of the dome. Move it!"

Slowly, with a lot of muttering and grumbling, the prisoners did as they were told. Lucy spotted Cynthia Wu at the base of the dome and headed over toward her, towing her duffel bag.

"Hey, Luce. There you are. Now maybe we get some answers," Cynthia said.

"At least we're out of that cabin. And into some cleaner air," Lucy said.

"Give thanks for small favors. We won't see any big ones."

"PIPE DOWN!" The bay was just about clear, and now they could see the speaker, a heavy-set man in his forties, standing on the flat deck of the bay. He was in full battle-armor, his faceplate open. He wore magnetic boots and clomped to the center of the deck, holding a clipboard. What looked like sergeant's stripes were painted on the arms of his suit. "Awright. Now, I'm gonna do a roll call, and you'd better cooperate, because nobody's going anywhere until everyone is accounted for. Call out when you hear your name. And say whether you were crew or passenger on the *Venera*. I gotta split this out into two lists later. Ackerman, Daniel."

"Yo!"

"Passenger or crew, Ackerman?"

"Passenger."

"Right. Amoto, Dwight."

"Present. As the senior surviving member of *Venera*'s crew, I demand—"

"Shuddup, boy. You ain't where you can demand anything. Calder, Lucille."

"Present. Passenger."

"Danvers, Joseph."

"Present. Passenger."

"Desk-Desk—"

"Deshophsky, Dmitri. Present. Passenger."

"Okay. Right. Entin, Robert. . . ."

Lucy waited out the roll call with the rest of them, keeping count herself. Two men turned up missing, and there was a twenty-minute delay until it was discovered they were still locked in their cabin aboard the *Venera*. Finally, it was over. Five crew and fifty-three passengers were in the bay, still alive. Twelve crew and sixty Survey Service personnel had set off from Bandwidth.

"That does it. Now stay put and keep it down." The sergeant hit a stud on the arm of his suit and spoke into a helmet mike. "Captain? All present, accounted for. We're ready for you in Bay Three, sir."

✧ ✧ ✧

Captain Lewis Romero pressed the mike key on his desk intercom. "Thank you, Sergeant. I'll be there directly." Romero's office was in the outer deck of the station's spin-section, and thus under the 1.13 gees of the Guardian home world, Capital.

As befitted the commander, it was the largest and most luxurious office in the orbital station. As befitted the commander of a small post located in a backwater rear area of an over-extended military, Romero was an ignoramus. Competent officers were too much in demand to waste one on what amounted to garrison duty.

But Romero's back was straight, his uniform was pressed and cleaned at all times, his jackboots—which were more than slightly incongruous on a space station—were gleaming, and his black hair and moustache were neatly trimmed. On a station like Ariadne, that was really all that was required of him.

At the moment, his sallow face bore its usual expression—a patently synthetic look of friendly interest. He spent a lot of time in front of a mirror, rehearsing facial expressions. Romero saw himself as a reasonable fellow, ready to listen, who led by gentle persuasion and example. He was proud of the effort he put into appearances. After all, if one didn't look the part, how were the troops to know who the leader was?

He pressed the call button on his desk, and within a minute an answering *beep* came from the console. His escort was ready. He stepped out of his office to find four surly-looking troopers in full dress uniforms, two on either side of the doorway. They formed up, two ahead and two behind him. "To Bay Three," Romero said. They escorted him to the lift. Romero, so concerned with appearances, would have been horrified to know how foolish the men of his station thought the whole idea of an escort squad was.

The lift car arrived and the five of them squeezed into it. Without waiting for instruction, two troopers knelt down, a bit awkwardly in the tight space. There were small studs set into the heels of Romero's boots, and each trooper pressed the one on his side. That powered up the electromagnets in the boots, making them suitable for walking the corridors in the zero-gee section of the station. Romero had had them made up specially. They looked a great deal better than standard mag work shoes, which clashed horribly with his jet-black uniform.

The elevator door opened, and there was a slight pause while the escorts changed into standard mag boots there. Finally they made their way to Bay Three. The head of the escort detail opened the hatch, and they ventured out into the center of the large deck, stepping most carefully.

The first thing that struck Romero was the stench. Well, these poor devils couldn't help that. Lieutenant Henry had taken their ship quite a while ago, and a ship under guard had little time for sanitary questions. Still, perhaps he ought to have a word with Henry about keeping CIs cleaner in future. The smell was quite ghastly. Romero did not allow any reaction to the odor to cross his face, but held to a stern-but-fair expression that seemed quite suited to the occasion. He took a good look at what was going to be the replacement technical staff. Damn shame that Ariadne's whole tech crew had been shipped out to the Main Strike Fleet for the coming attack on New Finland, but such were the needs of the times.

But what of their replacements? A motley bunch. Every color of the rainbow, but then that was true of practically every gang of CIs ever taken. They seemed to have no idea about the foolishness of mixing the races. And their women! Women not only in the military, but outranking men, if he followed the insignia. Lieutenant Henry had reported that a woman—and a black one at that—had been *Venera*'s skipper, before he shot her.

He stared hard at one or two of the white men they had bagged in this haul. How could they bring themselves to take orders from some blackamoor female?

Finally, Romero completed his inspection and spoke. "Good day to all of you, and welcome to Guardian Orbital Station

Ariadne. My name is Captain Lewis Romero, commander of G.O.S. Ariadne. Let me start straight off by clarifying your status. You are not prisoners of war, or technically prisoners of any sort. You are under the jurisdiction of the Guardians of the Planetary Commonwealth of Capital. Under Guardian law, you are Conscripted Immigrants—CIs—and have the rights and obligations of any other sort of immigrant." Romero didn't mention that there *were* no other sorts of immigrants. They'd find that out soon enough.

"Now you were brought here to work. Work well, pay attention to your duties, and many of you may well prove eligible for Guardian citizenship. Sloth, inefficiency, or refusal to obey orders will gain you nothing and could cost you dearly." He paused meaningfully, then went on in more cheerful tone. "But, I'm sure there won't be any such difficulties. You are here to work. Work hard, and you will be treated well. I think that about covers it. Sergeant Mosgrove here will arrange for you to be escorted to quarters and—ah—cleaned up. Then we can see about explaining your duties to you." Romero turned as if to go when a high, clear voice called out.

It was Cynthia Wu. "Excuse me, Captain, but just so I've got this straight. It sounds like you've prettied it up, but we've been kidnapped and brought here as skilled slave labor. Is that about right?"

Romero flushed angrily. The insolence! And from a tiny little doll of a Chinaman's girl. He chose to ignore her. No response at all seemed best to him. He calmed himself and said, "Sergeant Mosgrove. You may commence with the processing of the priso—of the immigrants, Sergeant." With that, he turned and left the compartment, his escort keeping in perfect step with him.

Mosgrove saluted Captain Romero and watched as the commanding officer and escort turned to leave the bay. The sergeant glared at Romero's back with undisguised contempt. The girl had talked back to the station commander—and Romero hadn't done a damned thing to her! No doubt about it, Romero was all spit and polish and no backbone. In a *real* outfit the little Chink slut would be a dead and bloody pulp by now. *That* was the way to set an example. But if the Captain wanted to ignore insolence, the Captain could deal with the results. "Aw right. Now I'm gonna take you in groups of six for cabin assignments. The sooner we're done, the sooner you can wash and eat."

Time passed. The Survey Service prisoners began to learn about their new home—their new prison.

Ariadne Station was a fairly standard design. It was made up of three cylinders linked together through their common axis, like three fat tin cans stacked end to end. The three were simply called A Drum, B Drum, and C Drum. B Drum, the center cylinder, was spun up to simulate one Capital gee, 1.13 Earth gravities, at its outermost deck. The two outer cylinders, A and C, were zero-gee work areas.

Ariadne was a communications center and a space traffic control station, tracking the orbital tugs and other craft, assigning orbits to spacecraft moving in orbit around the planet below.

The station was a gloomy, uncomfortable place, or at least the parts of the station the Survey Service prisoners could get to were. As with all such spun-for-gravity systems, the closer to the axis a deck was, the weaker the force of simulated gravity. Lucy and Cynthia found themselves assigned to a small, bare, austere cabin with four other women on Deck Three, the living area nearest to zero-spin. All the "Conscripted Immigrants" were on Three and Four. Decks One and Two were nearer zero-gee, but housed the command and communications centers. Deck Six was farthest from the spin axis. That was split between officer's country, sick bay, the commissary and some engineering and exercise areas.

The CIs' barracks decks were painted a uniform gunmetal grey, and the lighting was kept dim to save power. The cabins were tiny, cramped, and stuffy. Nothing folded up into the walls to make more room. The beds were welded in place, and the one chair, which was bolted to the deck, was bare aluminum and usually too cold to sit on. There was no storage space, and the only way to keep the place at all tidy was for each of them to stuff all their possessions back into their duffel bags. The duffels themselves took up a large part of the cabin. The six women settled on the convention of keeping them on the bunks during the day and stacking them in the corner to sleep.

The Guards wasted no time in getting some work out of their new "immigrants." It seemed the CIs were to replace a Guardian crew that was being shipped out to other duties. The Survey Service prisoners were hurriedly trained to do the technical work of the station, often literally with guns to their heads.

Cynthia might have gotten away with speaking up in Bay Three, but the CIs quickly learned that was an exception. Several of the Survey students protested their treatment and were beaten severely. That, at least, the Guards didn't try to make mysterious. They were quite happy to let the CIs know what would happen if they didn't cooperate. There were further protests and further punishments, but nothing changed the situation. The Survey Service CIs were on Ariadne Station whether they liked it or not. Escape was clearly impossible, and Guards controlled the guns, the food, the water.

The CIs were expected to run the station's communications center, operate the space traffic control system, manage the station computer system, and generally do routine technical work. Failure to cooperate got them nothing but another beating. The Guards made that simple to understand.

The League of Planets Survey Service had chosen the brightest young people from the military services of every League member and trained them to be skilled pilots, ready to adapt to new situations. The CIs—they were already learning to call themselves that—mastered their new jobs quickly. It helped that the equipment was more or less familiar, as if the Guardians had begged, borrowed, and stolen whatever old and new designs they could get their hands on, and copied them.

The CIs tried to protest, to sabotage, to avoid work. Until Wilkie was shot. Wilkie hadn't done anything. They shot him because Leventhal had refused work, wouldn't cooperate. Romero had strutted out to talk with them all the next day and announced that Wilkie's death was not an accident—it was policy. "Shirk your responsibilities, and it isn't your life you risk—it is your friend's, your cabinmate's, your comrade-in-arm's. I was reluctant to take extreme measures, but you have left me no choice. Each of you is hostage to the behavior of the others."

Leventhal tried to kill himself by slashing his wrists the next day. They got him to sick bay in time.

But that settled it. They did the work. They cooperated. "Bide our time, wait and see," Wu had said, and they did.

No one told the CIs anything. No one explained what the Guardians were, or where they were, or what was going on. But that did not stop them from finding things out.

Lucy drew a regular shift in front of a communications console. It took her only a day or two to confirm her vague impressions of what was going on. Most of the signals were encrypted, but enough was in clear for her to find things out. She compared notes with the other CIs, and they quickly came the same conclusions. Ariadne wasn't in orbit around Capital, but circling another planet, called Outpost.

Much of Lucy's job was in relaying data and voice communications between at least two dozen ships in different orbits. Ariadne relayed any traffic for ships that didn't have line-of-sight on each other.

Lucy's console, and nine others, were in a large compartment on B Deck. As she and the other CIs worked, two well-armed Guardians watched them, sullen-faced and bored. Slave labor Cynthia had called it, and that was close enough. And Lucy told herself that no half-abo Aussie from the Outback was going to be a slave. Not for long, and not without revenge.

Another signal was coming in from the big ship in high

orbit. *Leviathan*. *Leviathan* was using the same code as the planetside stations, and she wanted to know that code for her own reasons. She hit a few keys on her console, and a copy of *Leviathan*'s signal went into a very private computer file she had set up. Lucy was learning.

Chapter Two

Aboard G.O.S. Ariadne

First Lieutenant Johnson Gustav, Guardian Navy and Executive Officer of G.O.S Ariadne, did not like his post or his duties. Still, it could have been much worse. By rights, he should be dead, should have been found guilty and shot through the heart for the crime of filing a treasonous report. Being transferred out of Headquarters Intelligence to be the executive officer of some unimportant orbital station wasn't much, but it was better than being dead. And being out in a backwater post gave Gustav all his off-duty hours to reflect on the concept of the truth being treason.

His report had been erased, shredded, burned, purged, eliminated in whatever form in which it had existed but one. It was still in his mind. Gustav had the feeling that Captain Phillips had arranged to keep Gustav alive so that one last copy of the report, up there in his brain cells, wouldn't be "erased" as well. Which meant that Phillips knew Gustav was right, Gustav told himself as he checked over the daily reports. Phillips was a good man—so why didn't Phillips forward the report instead of wiping it out of existence and shipping its author to some tin can orbiting Outpost? Gustav had gone over it in his mind a thousand times, but he knew he would go over it a thousand more before it was over.

He didn't forward it because Captain Phillips knew that doing that would get us both shot without accomplishing anything, Gustav told himself. Phillips was like that. All the good officers in Intelligence were. They had to balance the necessary against the possible. Odd phrases like that cropped up in Intelligence a lot. Phillips had sent Gustav off to Ariadne with another one: "Pay more attention to politics and less to reality. Until the times change."

Well, the times were about to change all right, but not to anyone's benefit. It was all there in the report.

The trouble was that Intelligence trained its men to be objective in analysis, and it was the only branch of the Navy that sent its men out of the Nova Sol star system to other settled worlds. People trained for the objective analysis of reality were not likely to do well in Capital politics.

It had been easier before he had been trained to go out. He had heard what every kid heard growing up, from the school books and the Political Orientation lecturers: That the Guards had threatened the established order on Earth and had been driven off the mother planet by the plutocrats, cleverly leaving misleading clues as to the part of the sky for which they were bound. That the League of Planets had been formed with the sole purpose of tracking the Guardians down and smashing them, that the League would never stop searching for Capital, the one world that threatened the League's utter domination of human space, and that Capital must be prepared, well armed, disciplined, ready to fight.

Then Gustav had been approved for Navy Intelligence, started his training, and learned a whole new story, one he hadn't really believed until he had shipped out in a tiny one-man ship with a phony Liberian High Free Port registration to wander the League worlds gathering information for Capital.

He had gone out and come back in a score of times. He had stolen designs and collected technical journals that would end up in Guardian labs. He had fingered likely ships for the CI "recruiters." He had read news services and passed back political reports. He had traveled. He had seen.

Gustav had been to Kennedy, to New Asia, to New Finland, even to Earth. He had seen Capital's "enemies" and discovered that the plutocrats and hedonists and demagogues and bloodsuckers of grade school P.O. were just—people. Worse, they were people who had never even *heard* of the Guardians, and it took a day of digging in the

New York Public Library datafiles to find more than a passing mention—and the truth—about the Guardians.

The schoolbooks' hundreds of thousands of heroic Guardians of the Atlantic Front turned out to be a few hundred rowdies scraped up from the LaRouchists, the Birchists, the Afrikaners in Exile, the National Front, something called the Ku Klux Klan, and a few other groups. And the *Oswald Mosley* hadn't narrowly escaped destruction by the space fleets of Earth's criminal nations. Earth's nations didn't even *have* space fleets at that time. The *Mosley* would have been permitted to leave peacefully, and good riddance, except Thurston Woolridge and some of the other Guardian leaders had been sprung from jail in raids that had killed. some people and freed a number of dangerous criminals. As it was, the *Mosley* got away only because the British and the Americans didn't have ships available to chase her. Once she had left the Solar System, no trace of the *Mosley* was ever found—but then, no one had ever looked very hard. She was missing and thankfully presumed lost with all hands. The Guardians weren't a heroic page in history; they were a grubby little footnote. No one remembered or cared about a nut group from a century past.

To discover one's hated enemies to be by-and-large civilized, decent people was disquieting. To discover them to be completely unaware of one's existence was galling. To discover the legends of one's people to be the glorification of a seedy little bunch of political thugs was humiliating. But to discover those hated enemies had a combined military potential a thousand times, ten thousand times, greater than one's own planet was bone-chilling. Earth certainly had space fleets now. So did Britannica, and Europa, and Kennedy and Bandwidth. The League was big.

However, Supreme General Officer Jules Jacquet, Tenth Leader of the Combined Will of the Guardians of the Planetary Commonwealth of Capital, and head of a rather shaky government, needed some sort of external crisis to divert attention from other problems. And it couldn't hurt to grab some technology and skilled laborers at the same time. Jules Jacquet decided to attack the League.

Then-Commander Gustav had done what he had seen as his duty and filed that damned report, and had ended up busted in rank and posted to a pesthole named Ariadne.

Now he had other duties, the day-to-day jobs of running a space station, a job that included the task of watching the CIs. And that was a complicated game of cat-and-mouse, one that Gustav worked to win—but not by too much. He did not dare press his advantages too hard.

The Survey students were smart enough to assume their cabins and work stations were bugged—and they were getting better and better at finding the mikes. They "accidentally" sabotaged a tap now and then, and Gustav usually let it go, simply repairing the damage after a day or two.

After all, the CIs were prisoners in fact, whatever they were in name. They could never escape, they could never contact the outside universe. Gustav therefore allowed them their secret meetings, their conspiracies to collect information. Nothing could ever come of them, and the more energy they expended on the plots he knew about, the less effort they could put into ones he had missed. He was impressed by their efforts. They had only been here six weeks or so, but they clearly gotten themselves very well organized in that short space of time.

In a way, that was good news. Another of his duties was keeping the CIs sane enough to work. They needed the chance to grouse and complain and talk their situation out with each other. Everyone needed a way to let off steam. Plots and schemes fit the bill very well.

Gustav never forgot that his CIs were soldiers. If he had ruthlessly crushed every attempt to circumvent the authority of the Guardians with an iron discipline, his CIs would probably have rebelled violently—and died pointlessly, perhaps wrecking Ariadne and thereby hurting the war effort in the process. Gustav stopped the train of thought right there, before he could ask himself if hurting the war effort was such a bad idea.

So he didn't erase the CIs' many "secret" databanks. If he had, it would simply cause them to start over, hiding things better the next time, perhaps in some memory section he couldn't find. Gustav didn't stop Schiller from using the station telescope and spectrograph to try and identify the brighter stars. Even if Schiller succeeded—which was most unlikely—the twin star system of Nova Sol was one hundred fifty light-years from the nearest League world. What was Schiller going to do? Walk home? Use a message laser to send an SOS that would arrive in the middle of the next century?

Gustav sighed and glared at the desk he was stuck behind. Paperwork and playing footsie with the slave labor. A fine situation for a soldier to be in.

The damn fools around Jacquet! Why couldn't they *see*? A system that put a joke like Romero in command of a station and then used kidnapped spaceship pilots to run the place was in trouble, terrible trouble. Why the devil couldn't the Central Guardians *see* that?

Cynthia Wu moved carefully around the storage compartment, checking the deck, the bulkheads, the storage racks. She had rigged her "bug-sniffer" out of parts stolen from an old pressure suit radio and from some other odds and ends, but it worked, for all of that.

Finally she shoved the device back in her pocket. "Clean, as best I can tell. Unless Gustav is playing the game a new way. But none of the standard issue bugs are in here."

Lucy and a half dozen other CIs relaxed slightly. Lucy pointed at Dmitri and nodded toward the door. Dmitri nodded back and headed out into the corridor to watch for Guards. "So maybe it's safe to talk," Lucy said. "So we talk. Schiller, any luck?"

"Yes and no." Sam Schiller was a tall, dark, clear-eyed farm boy from Iowa, USA, with a thick mop of deep brown hair and a quiet, serious manner. As a kid in the corn fields, he had loved to look at the stars, and had joined the Navy and signed up for the Survey just for the chance to see them up close. He had been in the Navy Astrocartography Command, and was the obvious choice to look for home amid the points of light. "No really solid idea of where we are yet," he went on, "but I've got a program running right now: Every time the high-gain antenna is out of use, I've got it checking a different piece of sky for radio sources. I'm not just after artificial sources of course, most of the signals that transmitters and radars and so on put out are too weak at interstellar range—and I think we're too far away for most of them, anyway. But there are natural sources—pulsars, hot gas clouds, that sort of thing. I've got eight mapped now. None of them are strong enough for me to get a really good signature with our gear, but sooner or later I'll nail the galactic center. That'll give us a lot."

"What about visual?" someone asked.

"Not so great," Schiller said. "I'm working with gear that's supposed to spot incoming ships, not read spectra of stars. Without spectra you can't really tell one star from another reliably—especially when you have no idea of the distances to the stars in question. All I can say for sure is that we're a long way from home: at least one hundred light-years from Earth. I need a star catalog. Has anyone found anything like that in the computers?"

"Not a thing," Wu said. "They've got what looks like a bootleg copy of a standard databank reference encyclopedia, but it's been edited—censored, more like. I cracked into it. Almost no history left, something on a few of the sciences, but everything on stars and astronomy and astrogation is gone. Nothing left but the titles of the articles."

"That makes sense," Lucy said. "If you were trying to keep your home world hidden, you'd make astronomy a state secret."

"But how could you keep it secret? All you have to do is look up at the sky!" Amoto objected.

"That's just it," Schiller said. "If all you've got is eyes, you'll never get anywhere. To tell one dot of light in the sky from another, you need to measure spectra and radial velocity and Doppler shifts—and if you're doing what I'm trying to do, trying to find some signposts in the sky to point you home, you've got to plot the apparent positions of the stars in the sky against their true positions in space, in three dimensions. That takes either a properly programmed computer or years of counting on your fingers. And I don't have a computer programmed for astrogation."

Schiller rubbed his face for a moment and went on. "But I *can* tell you a bit more about the star system we're in. I *think* it's a binary star system, but with a weird geometry I haven't worked out completely yet."

"How come you're not even sure about being in a binary system?" Cynthia asked. "No offense, but that seems so obvious."

"If it *is* a binary system, the other component—the other star—is pretty distant, and to the naked eye it doesn't show a disk. It just looks like a very bright star. I'd be more sure about things, except the geometry is so crazy. The planet we're in orbit of is called Outpost, we all know that. The usual thing would be for all the stars and planets of a binary system to be moving in the same plane. Well, there's one very bright star on the local sky. It has a extremely high proper motion against the background of the sky—measurable over a period of days, even with the equipment I've got. But it's way the hell out of the plane of Outpost's orbit. It's moving so fast across the starfield that it's *got* to be in a mutual orbit with *our* star. The evidence says a rare type of binary system. But everything I've ever learned about binaries says there shouldn't be planets in such a system. Which I guess means the theories are wrong. Wouldn't be the first time."

"That's for sure," Lucy said.

"One other thing," Schiller said. "There's lots of very strong radio sources associated with that star, all sorts of noise on all sorts of frequencies. I haven't checked with any of you in Signals, but I'll bet that radio source is Capital, circling the other star of whatever the hell this two-star system is called."

"I picked up some in-the-clear traffic that called Outpost's star Nova Sol B," Lucy put in.

"So presumably the other star is Nova Sol A. At least we've got a name," Schiller said.

"But Sam, will you ever find Earth?"

"I've had six weeks, and I've had to dodge the Guards and run the space traffic center at the same time. Give me six months, or a year, and I'll find it, well enough to navigate in the right direction and refine our course between C^2 jumps."

"Okay," Lucy said. "What about a ship?"

"No chance," Wu said, "at least in the short run. Nothing larger than a tug ever calls here, besides the atmosphere landers. Nothing with a C^2 unit aboard, you can bet that."

"What about the *Venera*?"

"They undocked her the day after we got here," Stana said. "My guess is she's already got a new name and that flame-and-delta Guardian flag painted over the Survey Service symbol."

"Any chance of building a C^2 unit ourselves?" Schiller asked.

"Out of what? With what tools? Anyone memorize the plans of one?" Wu said.

"Somebody in this crowd must at least know the principles," Stana objected. "And there are parts and tools."

"With Guardians sitting on them," Danvers said. "And those are warships in orbit around us. With guns. Cynthia's right. And even if we did make a C^2 unit and plugged it into a ship, remember we're talking *light-years*. The thing's got to move a ship with a minimum accuracy of one part in a million. What do we calibrate it with? And what about a power source?"

No one spoke for a long time.

"At least we know where we stand," Lucy said. "Sooner or later Sam will come barreling down the corridor with the news that he knows where home is—and just as important, where *we* are. And then, somehow, we've got to grab a ship and launch it. Only one person has to be on it, or it could even be a drone. Just so long as it carries the message that we're here—"

"—And that we're not alone. We're not the only CIs," Stana said. "We can't be. I bet there are lots of CIs back on this Capital place."

"She's right," Amoto said. "They've got a whole bureaucracy set up for it. I saw a form that said 'Office of Conscripted Immigration' on it. And one of the troopers posted on duty in my section told me it wasn't so bad—one of his *grandparents* was a CI."

"My God. How long have they been grabbing ships?" Stana said. "Why hasn't anyone ever caught them?"

"And why do they want all these people?" Schiller demanded.

"C'mon, Dwight," Cynthia said. "If that were true, why didn't the League find 'em years ago?"

Amoto held up his hands, palms out, in front of him. "Hold on a second. Think it through. When a ship is lost in interstellar space, you never *expect* to see it again. And given the choice between believing ships blow up now and again, and believing that pirates from beyond the stars have been kidnapping people—"

"Yeah, I suppose," Schiller said.

"You realize what that means," Wu said. "When we were back on the League worlds, *we* never heard a hint about hijacked ships."

"So?" Schiller asked.

"So the League doesn't know such things happen, or that these people, these Guards, even *exist*. So the League thinks we're *dead*, and that *Venera* was lost with all hands."

The room was silent for a moment before Cynthia spoke again. "They won't come looking for us. We're on our own."

"Not for long. Something's up," Lucy said. "That's why we're here. The immediate reason we were put on Ariadne was to allow them to transfer its crew elsewhere. And I've picked up a lot of traffic from the big ship, *Leviathan*, the one that arrived in orbit about twenty-five days ago. They're still having trouble filling billets even after 'recent transfers of comm personnel.' Which I figure means the men from here. And what does it suggest to you when a big ship rushes around to fill all billets? Plus there's more general radio traffic everyday. They call the ships orbiting Outpost the Main Strike Fleet. The Guards are going out on some sort of military mission."

"You're saying they're going to attack someone," Schiller said.

"And who is there to attack but League worlds?" Lucy replied. "Unless there's another mystery planet, which I doubt. And if the Guards attack the League, the League will find out there are such things as Guards, and the League will come looking for 'em. Our job is to do our work, gather as much information as we can, be good little boys and girls, and watch for the chance to get the hell off this station and back to the League carrying a roadmap with Capital on it."

Two weeks later, there was a sudden increase in radio traffic. Ship orbits started getting shifted more and more often. The CIs were kept busier than they had ever been, patching calls and tracking ships. Then, one after another, the ships left orbit altogether, heading away from Outpost to deep space, to a point far enough distant from Nova Sol B to allow a safe C^2 jump. As Lucy watched her board, the realization sank in: the Main Strike Fleet was leaving. Lucy wanted to jam the calls, send bad messages, whatever she could to stop them, but she knew all the effort would get her was a bullet in the back of her head. Besides, once they were clear of the planet, whose bulk had served to block signals most effectively, the ships had perfect line-of-sight on each other. Their messages bypassed the relay station altogether.

One ship was left behind. *Leviathan*. Lucy had never seen her, but the scuttlebutt from the Guards and the radio channels was that *Leviathan* was the biggest starship ever built, the first of her class.

Why the hell would they leave the big ship behind?

Curious, Lucy glanced over her shoulder to see if the Guard on duty was watching carefully. No, thank God, they were talking with each other about last night's poker game. She tapped into the signal traffic from *Leviathan* command channel directly and listened on her earphones. With luck they'd be using one of the codes she had broken.

"—long, Carruthers. We'll see you in a few months."

Lucy's eyebrows shot up. They were talking in clear! No encryption. But it wasn't the first time. The signals crew on *Leviathan* seemed to be out to lunch half the time.

"I suppose, Johnny. You go and have your fun while I try and get those pinheads on Capital to send me some fighters. Or maybe even the rest of my crew. I'm still only half-manned."

Lucy got more interested. This sound like two commanding officers talking, saying goodbye.

"Come on, now, they're only 6000 hours behind schedule."

" 'Only' he tells me. Listen, seriously, you guys be careful. Main Strike shouldn't be flying without *Leviathan*. We shouldn't divide our forces."

"Yeah, I know. Bollixed up the whole battle plan. But orders are orders. 'Main Strike Fleet is to depart on schedule, and no debate on this point will be heard.' "

" 'Any ship not yet prepared will join the Fleet later,' " the other voice said, completing the quote. "But look on the bright side. They were going to send us with you as we were."

"But *Leviathan*'s nowhere near ready!"

"I talked 'em out of it. Pounded my fist on the table at the Admiralty and showed them what was what."

"Bloody fools."

"But it's going to be all ri—"

"Calder! Quit staring into space and get back to work!" One of the Guards had finally noticed that Lucy had stopped pushing buttons.

She came to herself and cut off her tap on *Leviathan*'s radio.

Whatever it was the Guardians were up to, had begun.

Chapter Three

June, 2115
Aboard G.O.S. Ariadne

Romero could barely contain his excitement. "You know, Gustav, to be utterly frank about it, I was worried that the departure of the Main Strike Fleet would mean that Ariadne would get rather pushed to one side. But this. This! Suddenly Ariadne and Outpost are vitally important. More so than ever. It will look good for both of us, I'm sure of that."

Gustav's eyes were on the paperwork, and it was all he could do to nod stiffly and mutter some sort of commonplace as a reply. The universe had just changed, changed completely, and this fool could see nothing in it but good odds for promotion. "Yes, sir. I can see that."

"It's all been top secret," Romero told Gustav. "They've sent in all their experts twice now, and that hasn't worked. They can't afford to try that again—not in the middle of a war—but the job needs doing. It certainly needs doing. And we are on the scene."

"Yes, sir," Gustav said as he read the report. The information in it was incredible. Utterly incredible. "That's putting it mildly. But as regards personnel—"

"That decision has been made," Romero said, his voice suddenly stiff and formal. "Unless you want your record to reflect the refusal of an assignment?"

"No, no sir. Of course not. It will be a privilege to go. It is the question of the translator for the job."

Romero made a well-rehearsed frown and nodded sagely. "Yes, that was a difficult choice. The hardest of all the personnel selections. You are ex-intelligence, and experienced in dealing with—ah—un-Guardian situations. As to the pilot and troopers, I merely chose the men with the best service records. But as to the translator, I must admit that I hesitated long and hard before deciding on a CI. The security problem is obvious—but you will be along to keep a eye on her. Besides, you haven't reported any major infractions among the CIs—and our whole ideology is based on the fact that such rabble will come to see things our way, the right way, once they are exposed to the truth. Besides, she is the best qualified."

Ideology? He made the decision based on *ideology*? "Excuse me, sir. I don't understand. I assumed that Headquarters had made the choice. *You* chose the personnel?" Comforting that HQ had not made this big a mistake. But frightening that HQ was so blinkered that it would assign such a low priority to the event. Even the war should have taken a back seat to this.

"Yes, of course," Romero said. "That's normal procedure, the commander making crew assignments."

"Yes, but sir, this is far from a normal circumstance. And I can't really say that with any certainty that skill in a few languages has any bearing—"

"That will be all, Lieutenant," Romero said, with the touchiness of a man tired of his competence being questioned. "My decision is final. You may go."

"But—"

"You may go," Romero said again. "Now."

Gustav came out of his meeting with Romero covered in a cold sweat. The news was stunning. Incredible. And they had handed Ariadne the job of dealing with it. *Romero* in charge of it! That damn fool wasn't competent enough to tie his shoes without consulting the manual, and they handed this job to him because Ariadne was in charge of Outpost sector communications! Brilliant logic. Obviously no one had any idea how big this was. And to send a CI, not a loyal Guardian, to do the job—how big a fool could Romero be? How could he think the CIs were truly pacified.

Gustav knew he had made a mistake—a big one—in not reporting every trivial infraction and major scheme the CIs had launched. But if he had, Romero would have come down like a ton of bricks, and the station's work would have ground to a halt.

And how could he have ever dreamed that *this* would have happened?

Lucy thought she was being arrested when the call came. Gustav *had* bugged the meetings, knew what was going on, knew that she was tapping the comm lines. But the Guard who came to her work station said nothing beyond ordering her to the executive officer's office. None of the CIs had dealt much with the XO yet, and Lucy had little idea of what to expect. She pushed the buzzer at the entrance to his office.

"Come in," a tinny voice said through a speaker. She opened the hatch and entered. Gustav looked the way he always did: too young for his job, dark-haired, with deep, intelligent eyes and a face that would have been handsome smiling—if Gustav ever did smile. He was of medium height, or slightly above, in good shape, though his midriff seemed in the first stages of going to fat. A good field officer recently trapped behind a desk.

"Lieutenant Calder. Have a seat."

She took a chair and sat down. "Thank you."

"All right, let me clear the air of the easy part. I don't know and I don't care about any and all of your conspiracies and plots and plans and meetings, and that's not why you're here. Your people are prisoners—and I'll call you that even if it's against policy—and you can never ever escape. Period. You're too far from home and have too few resources. I don't care about your plots because they can never do you any good, or me any harm. You are here for the rest of your life. So as long as you do your work, we don't care. Or at least I don't, and as far as you're concerned, it's the same thing."

Lucy swallowed hard. "I see."

"That's all unimportant now. Something has happened, and you are a part of it."

"I am?"

"Yes," Gustav said. "Yes, you are. Against my better judgment, you are. You have drawn the assignment. There's a, ah, *group* on Outpost, and we need a linguist. The files on you we took off the *Venera* say that you are one. Close enough?"

"I know some languages. French, Russian, a few Australian aboriginal dialects, Chinese, but I'm—"

"Then you're better qualified than anyone in fifty light-years. No one here has spoken anything but English for a hundred years. One or two in Intelligence have been taught a few Western languages, but that's it. We need someone to learn a whole new language, and you know how to do that."

"But what lang—"

"I don't know. Nobody knows. We found them four weeks ago, and so far no one knows *anything* about them."

"But who is it I'm to talk to?" Lucy asked. "Where are they from? And how could their language be unknown?"

"They're from right here," Gustave said. "Outpost. And it isn't a *human* language you'll be learning. Your teachers will have six legs."

And Lucy could do nothing more than stare at him.

On Approach to Outpost's Surface

The lander came down, a strictly routine sort of flight of a completely unremarkable craft. The lander was a fat, rounded cone-shape, a standard design for a ballistic lander; she could have come off a production line anywhere in the League—and perhaps she had. Lucille didn't even know the lander's name. The Australian Navy's space fleet had always had a superstition about such things—if you didn't know the name of a ship, it was bad luck to fly in her. Lucille didn't have much truck with superstition, but it didn't make her any more comfortable.

Gustav had been assigned to the mission. A sergeant named McKenna piloted the lander, and there were two troopers along, Carlton and Mansfield. McKenna brought them in carefully, setting down in the center of a large clearing in a temperate-zone forest. The moment the landing engines shut off, Lucille heard an oddly familiar thrumming noise on the hull. It was raining out there, making the same noise on the hull that it had on the tin roof back home on Earth, in Australia, during the all-too-rare rainstorms of the arid Outback.

The lander had four viewports. Lucille cautiously unstrapped herself from her crash couch and stepped to the closest one. That was no desert out there, but a dark, dank wet field and forest. She could see two circular burned spots in the clearing, the signs of other landings here. Lucille carefully rocked back and forth on her feet, heel-to-toe and back. She felt rather light, say perhaps eight-tenths of an Earth gravity.

Gustav rattled off a chain of statistics without looking up. "Before you can ask, I did my homework and converted the figures to scales you know. Surface gravity .83 Earth gees. Atmospheric pressure 110 percent Earth sea level value. By percentage, much more carbon dioxide and water vapor, much less nitrogen, slightly less oxygen than Earth. The carbon dioxide makes it unbreathable. Possibly we can get by without full pressure suits, but right now I'm not taking any chances. Local environment in landing zone: dank, murky, cold, but somebody calls it home."

"Thanks for the travelogue. Now what?" Lucille asked.

Gustav joined Lucille at the port, then turned to one of the troopers. "Go below to the galley and get us some coffee, Mansfield. What we do now is wait, Lieutenant Calder. We wait. Our friends will have heard and seen the ship coming down, of course. We wait, and we hope the rain lets up. Our friends don't seem to like it, though that's just a guess."

"How did you first find them?"

"It was a scientific mission, of all things. We don't go for that sort of thing, but someone managed to get a grant from Capital University, get the use of a military landing craft. In all the years we've been here, it was only the seventh or eighth expedition to the surface of Outpost. They were doing a survey of temperate-zone plant life on this planet.

"Anyway, the Outposters appeared and our people ran like hell, back into the ship. Thought they were just a herd of some sort of animal that was large enough to be dangerous. But they watched through the ports and the Outposters had *tools*. All the cameras and viewports were half-blinded by mist and fog, but the crew saw that much. They radioed that little tidbit back to HQ, and were ordered to withdraw at once. Get back to orbit. Smart move. It let both sides think things over for a while, gave us a chance to put together a team."

"And the second landing?"

"Oh, they launched direct from Capital. All the heaviest scientific brass. They had all the cameras and recorders and whatever along, everything waterproofed and hooded against rain and so on. A lander this size, and three times as many people on it. They landed, and then sat here for two weeks until their supplies ran out. And of course, since the second group was ready for rain, there wasn't any. They were just about ready to give up and try a search from orbit when the Outposters came out of the trees again. Our people got all excited, went out in their pressure suits for the First Contact—and the rains came down. Heavier than this, heavier than ever. Couldn't see three feet. Our people were suddenly up to their knees in mud, and the 'Posters vanished."

"Never to be seen again?"

"That's right. The powers that be decided they couldn't afford to keep all that scientific talent waiting around. Not with the war on. Budgets are tight. I think they got nervous about putting all the big brains in such a dangerous situation. Anyway, the orders came down two days ago, and here we are, the smallest practical crew with the most supplies they could cram in a lander."

"And we sit here until Hell freezes over, or until the natives show?"

"And then we put the one linguist in the star system in charge. We don't try anything else this time until we can talk. Our job is to make contact, or die of old age waiting to try."

"What you're telling me is that I'm going to do humankind's First Contact with another intelligent species," Lucille said. "Me, a prisoner, a slave laborer."

The troopers and the pilot looked up sharply at that. "Relax, all of you," Gustav said warningly. "She's telling the truth. She is what she says she is, and we all know it, no matter what we're told. It's just us followers here without any leaders. No one to pretend in front of." He turned back to Lucille. "Yes, you're here to do the contact. You *are* the closest thing to a linguist we've got, and you're expendable. As are the rest of us. And let's not pretend about that, either."

"I wouldn't think your people would want a lowly CI to be that visible in the history books."

"Oh, don't you worry about that," Gustav said. "You won't even rate a footnote, more than likely. You can *do* whatever you like, but we can *write* the history books to suit ourselves."

The trooper came up from the lower deck, carrying a thermos and coffee cups. He poured for Gustav and Lucille. "Thanks, Mansfield. Get at ease and stay there. We could be cooped up for a while. Might as well take it easy or we'll be at each other's throats." Gustav handed Lucille a cup and the two of them returned to the viewport. "We don't know anything about them," he told her. "We don't have any decent close-up photos of them, we don't know if they're a high civilization or sitting around in mud huts. There's no way to be certain they're really *intelligent*, in our meaning of the word. Apes use tools, and some insects organize well—but the photos we've got seem to show them carrying things made of worked metal. Working ore into metal sure as hell suggests intelligence. But we don't *know*. We don't know if they are nomads or have vast cities. No one has ever bothered to map the planet properly. You've seen the cloud cover from orbit. Solid cover over ninety-five percent of the planet. It hasn't helped. Our charts are barely more than outlines of the continents. We've never taken much interest in the planet itself. The temperate zones are as you see them here—*this* is as attractive as Outpost gets."

Lucille said nothing. First Contact. Very old words for something new, something that had never happened. And it was hers.

The raindrops drummed down on the hull.

They waited. The sun went down in the middle of the driving rain, and Gustav gave up watching at the port. He dug a book out of his kit and began to read.

The pilot and the two troopers went belowdecks to their bunks, but Lucille stayed at the porthole, too caught up in it all to do anything but watch and wait. Never had she seriously considered the possibility of making the First Contact. Oh, she had dreamed of it, talked it up in the bull sessions with the other Survey students, in a time that seemed far removed from being a CI and a prisoner to the Guardians. No one who ventured into unknown space could help but think on the possibilities. But this was *real*. The myriad possibilities had focused down onto one actuality, and that was Lucille Calder, the half-abo rancher's daughter, about to be the first human being to converse with an alien race. Except humans were the aliens here.

She turned and looked at Gustav. He was leaning back in his crash couch, reading a novel he had borrowed from Cynthia Wu. Gustav was not simply one of the few Guardians interested in the books the CIs had carried for pleasure reading, he was the only Guardian who would think of politely borrowing—and later actually returning—books, rather than simply taking them.

"You know, Gustav," she said, "try as I might, I can't make you look like the enemy."

Gustav looked up at her, lay down his book, and gave her a wry half-smile. "That was exactly the thought I had when I first saw your people on your worlds."

"I thought Guardians didn't travel outside the Nova Sol system."

"They don't, except for spies."

"Ah." Lucille didn't quite know how to answer that.

"Or, to use the more correct phrase, Intelligence Operatives," Gustave went on. "And I guess I should thank the luck that got me kicked out of Intelligence to be XO on Ariadne—or else I'd have missed the chance to see whoever it is out there."

"What got you kicked out of Intelligence?"

"Telling the truth. I filed a report saying it would be a disaster to launch a war against the League."

"And has it been a disaster?"

"Too soon to tell. But numbers don't lie without help. My numbers might have been the first un-jiggered statistics the big brass had seen in generations. And those honest numbers said we don't have a chance against you."

"Why are you telling me all this?"

"I suppose I don't really count on coming out of this alive," Gustav said calmly. "The Outposters could be hostile, or there could misunderstandings. Too many variables, too many things to go wrong. I'll consider this mission a success if we can radio back a basic vocabulary for the next team to work with before we die of whatever this planet uses to kill people.

"I've been to Earth, I've been around the League, and I don't like the idea of attacking you. I feel as if I ought to apologize." Gustav paused for a moment. "And I suppose I don't want the woman who's going to talk to the aliens to think that *all* our people are barbarians and fools. We're not. There are good people on Capital. Honest and decent. But the situation is out of control."

And again, Lucille knew no way to answer him.

The hours and days slid past. On the third day, the rains ended. The sight of blue sky and fleecy white clouds perked everyone up. Carlton, Mansfield, and McKenna were watching out the portholes, enjoying the chance to at least see something besides rain.

"Sir, can't we at least take a little walk around the clearing?" Mansfield asked.

"No," Gustav said. "We stay here, we wait here. Passive. We play it safe and wait. It's hard on our patience, but we let them come to us. We don't want to seem threatening."

"*Are* you threatening?" Lucille asked.

Gustav sighed. "*I'm* not. And I doubt the Central Guardians want to be. If you want to know if we plan to conquer Outpost, no, we don't. Up until a year ago, when the Main Strike Fleet operation began, we didn't even bother landing on it. We could tell from orbit it wasn't much good for human use, not particularly habitable. It's not land we need, it's people and skills and manufactured goods. The 'Posters are safe from us. So look on the bright side, Mansfield. You've got a nice soft duty. You could be out with those poor bastards in the Main Strike Fleet. God knows where they are."

"Sir, even you don't know the invasion target?" Mansfield asked.

"Nope. I think Romero knew, but that one they kept very tight."

"Sir!" McKenna shouted. "They're out there!"

Lucille rushed to join the three enlisted men at the port. "Can we transmit to Ariadne?" she asked.

Gustav shook his head as he switched on the outside cameras and started all the recorders. "No. The station's below our horizon and there's nothing in line-of-sight with us at the moment. We'll tape it and transmit it all the first chance we get."

Lucille grabbed a hand recorder and started it. If something happened, if they got eaten or couldn't get back, she wanted a record, something besides video tapes to send back. Eyes saw things cameras didn't. "Contact. We see them! Four, five, six individuals crossing clearing from the treeline toward the lander. They are dark brown in color. They are bilaterally symmetrical, but they do not appear to be six-legged. No, they're centauroid. The main length of the body carried horizontally, like a horse, but the forward part is rotated up to carry the chest and head upright. Their heads are raised on long, flexible necks. Too far off to see many details of the head. Getting closer."

She swallowed hard, and tried to calm herself before she went on. "They have two forelimbs, arms we should call them, set at the base of that long neck—the shoulders, I guess. They have two pairs of rather heavy, stocky legs, so they walk on four legs and have those two arms besides. Better compromise than ours, bipedalism for hands. Can't see the walking legs too well through the brush. They have long, thick, heavy tails that might be used for balancing somehow. Some have their tails raised to point straight out behind them. Two are just dragging their tails. They seem to be carrying various kinds of tools or weapons in their forelimbs, their hands. Still too far off to get a clear look at the hands or head."

Lucille kept talking, barely stopping for breath. Her heart was hammering against her ribs. This was *it*! "They seem closer to reptilian than to mammalian, but that doesn't mean anything. There won't be true reptiles or mammals here, of course. I say reptile, but I guess I say that because they don't have fur, their skin is naked—and by that standard, humans are reptiles.

"They aren't clothed, though some of them seem to have belts and wraps and bracelets on. I can't say why exactly, but none of it looks like decoration. All functional-looking stuff, tools and equipment. There's definitely worked metal there, a lot of it.

"Scale. Hard to say precisely, but I'd call their body length at about a meter and a half, plus another meter for the tail. And the head on those shoulders comes to about the height of a man. They're bigger than we are.

"Okay, they're maybe fifty meters away now. I've got the binoculars now. Can see the head better. The head is elongated, front to back, shaped sort of like an egg lying on its side. The neck attaches at about the center of the head, the balance point. I'd say the head is about thirty centimeters long, back to front, and maybe fifteen from top to bottom and side to side.

"I see eyes. All of them have dark eyes, black eyes, no white to be seen, just shiny round black spots. All of them look very much alike. It's a first impression, but it seems to me they would be very hard to tell apart except for the things they wear. But back to the heads. The eyes are set very far forward in the head. They probably have binocular vision like ours. I don't see anything we'd call a nose or ears, but there's something, some sort of low structure, on the top of the head, toward the rear. A mass of flesh with a complicated fold structure. It's moving with a breathing sort of motion, and as they get closer I can see what could be earholes on it.

"The mouth. Hard to see from this angle. It's small in proportion to the rest of the head. The jaw is hinged very far forward. Can't see any of the dentition, or even if they have teeth in the first place.

"They've stopped. They are standing close to each other, clustered together, about twenty meters from here. One of them, the one in front, is making some sort of gesture with his right arm. Those arms look very strong.

"They're waiting for us."

Lucille pulled herself away from the port and turned to look at Gustav. His face was pale, excited, and he seemed short of breath. "It's time for me to go out there," she said. "And I think the best way to do it is alone. You said we don't want to seem threatening."

Gustav opened his mouth as if to protest, but then nodded. "Dammit, you're right. McKenna, I want this ship at launch-ready. If we need to run, make sure we can do it. Mansfield. Carlton. Suit up. No weapons, period. We don't defend ourselves. You two and I will stand in the lock while Lieutenant Calder descends to the surface. Let the—the natives see you. We'll make sure they know Calder didn't come by herself, but we don't leave the ship unless she's in trouble. Don't you leave the ship *until I give the order*. Lieutenant Calder—you realize that I might be forced to leave you out there. The information we've got already is more valuable than any of us. If I have to leave you to get it home, I will. And if they kill you, all we dare do is stand and watch. I don't intend to start a war, or get them started hating humans, whatever the provocation."

Lucille nodded stiffly. "I know. It's the only way you could do it. I'd make the same call in your place. We've got no choice but to take the chances." *And I don't know if I'm doing this for Humanity with a capital H, or curiosity, or glory, or the thrill, or to show I'm not scared, or to score points with the god-damned Guards to get the CIs a better deal. It doesn't matter. This is bigger than all those things.*

"Then let's go," Gustav said. His voice nearly cracked.

There was more than being unfamiliar with Guardian suit design that slowed Lucille down. Her fingers shook, her mind wouldn't concentrate on the job of getting the clamps clamped and the seals sealed. Gustav and Mansfield finally had to help her after they were in their own pressure suits.

The four of them crowded into the lock. Gustav hit the buttons that ran it through the decontamination cycle. The inner hatch slammed to, and the air in the lock was pumped into a holding tank. Lucille could feel her suit swell up slightly as the lock's pressure reached a vacuum. The flash heaters came on, and the lock's interior was briefly above the boiling point of water. A poison gas was pumped in, held in the lock for 60 seconds, and then pumped back out. The procedure was intended to kill any bacteria or other microbes that might have been in the air or on the suits. No one was really sure it worked. Maybe cross-contamination was impossible between Earth and Outpost microbes. Maybe there wasn't a need for pressure suits either, and they could get by with breathing gear. Now wasn't the time to find out.

Their helmets misted briefly as the cold, wet air of Outpost was introduced into the lock. "Pressure balanced," Gustav announced. "I'm opening the outer hatch."

Sunlight flowed into the lock. Lucille shuffled forward cautiously. She saw the world through the thin glass of her bubble helmet.

Suddenly, a long-forgotten memory burst into her mind. This place, these colors, all looked familiar. As a child, Lucille had often visited a cousin's house on the verdant southern coast land of Australia. The deep blue skies and dark, wet greens of Outpost's forests and meadows brought back thoughts of long-ago cool spring mornings, the fresh-scrubbed moments when all things seemed possible. No hint of Outpost's air came through her suit, but she recalled the rich, clean odor of a new-mown lawn, the heady fragrance of fertile soil after a good rain. Lucille breathed deeply and found only the soulless scent of sterile, sanitary canned air. Try as her frightened subconscious might to convince her otherwise, this wasn't home.

"Okay, everyone move up a bit so we can be seen," Gustav said.

"Where are they?" Mansfield asked. "McKenna, can you see them through the ports?"

"Just a second." McKenna's voice came through the suit radios. "Yeah, they were waiting around the other side of the lander. They must have heard the lock opening—they're circling around to find you."

"There they are!" Carlton said, pointing.

"Everyone take it easy, move slowly, calmly," Gustav said. The Outposters came into view around the side of the lander. They saw the hatch and stopped, swung around to face it, and waited.

"Here I go," Lucille said. Her voice sounded weak, young, reedy, even to her own ears.

One of the landing legs was directly below the airlock's outer hatch. There was a small platform atop the leg, and a set of ladder rungs bolted to the leg. Lucille stepped out onto the platform and slowly, carefully, made her way down the ten meters of the ladder. She stared hard at the polished metal of the ladder, watched her own gloved hands moving from rung to rung with a fascinated stare. The details of the gloves' stitching, the wrinkling and un-wrinkling of their fabric, the movement of shadows in the bright morning sunlight as she moved her hands, all seemed incredibly complex and important. She grasped for every mundane detail, memorizing it, cherishing the known and accepted as she went to meet something that was neither. There was a meter-and-a-half drop between the last rung and the ground. Lucille got to the bottom of the ladder and let herself go.

She forgot to allow for the mass of the suit and hit the ground heavily, nearly stumbled. She flung her hand out and balanced herself against the solidity of the landing leg. She turned out away from the lander, faced the natives.

There they were, a few meters away, separated from her only by the tall grasses.

Something was wrong. It was too quiet. No outside noise reached her. She kicked in her helmet radio with the chin switch. "Gustav! I forgot something! Does this suit have external mikes and speakers?" Lucille's stomach knotted in needless panic as she imagined crossing to the aliens, standing close enough to touch them, but unable to speak or hear.

"Yes, dammit, I meant to tell you. The switches are on the left arm of the suit, marked 'MIC' and 'SPK.' Hit the one marked 'REL' too. That will transmit the outside speakers to us. I'm starting the recorder. We've got cameras on you and the Outposters, and the lander's external mikes are running too. We'll get it all, sight and sound."

Lucille lifted her left arm and found the switches. She carefully pressed the three buttons, her movements made slightly awkward by the suit.

Suddenly the rustle of leaves, the small cries of far-off animals, the thousand small sounds of a living world, were in her ears.

She stepped forward toward her hosts. The grass was taller than she had thought, over a meter high, and the ground was wet and muddy. More and more, she felt divided out from her surroundings by the suit and the fragile glass bubble of her helmet. Would they think the suit was her skin? Could they see her head through the helmet, and know she was the living being instead of the suit?

She walked slowly, deliberately, toward them, avoiding any sudden motion. Fifteen meters, ten, five, three away from them. She stopped.

The Outposters shifted their stance nervously, and looked at her through their black doll's eyes.

Lucille looked back at them. Their heads seemed huge and faceless. The eyes seemed expressionless, the mouth too small and unimportant. She noticed for the first time that the skin around the eyes and atop the head seemed to be moving, constantly and rhythmically. Perhaps it had to do with breathing. That structure on top of their heads seemed involved with the movement. It might be their version of a nose.

They seemed huge. Lucille decided they were about the size of a small horse or pony. Their skin was indeed naked, and leathery.

The nearest one gestured with his right hand. The fingers were strange. There were four of them, all mutually opposable, like four very flexible thumbs.

He—she, it, something else? Call them "he" and "him" for the moment—"he" made sounds. Deep, booming sounds that had odd timbres and tones. Lucille thought she heard what sounded like vowels and consonants, but nothing distinct enough to be noted as words. Was he shouting, making a speech, singing, or yelling because someone had stepped on his tail? Was he welcoming or warning?

Lucille spread her own arms wide and opened her hands to show they were empty. She hesitated, searching for words, finally saying the best and simplest thing: "We come in peace." She stared hard at them and remembered the Guards and their fleets. *At least, I hope we do,* she thought.

The Outposter who had spoken came closer, and the work of meeting each other began.

Interlude

Main Strike Fleet went out, and conquered New Finland, and the news trumpeted on every street of the cities of Capital. Bands played, soldiers marched, and holidays were declared. Even on as remote an outpost as Ariadne, there were celebrations—though not all aboard chose to join in. Leviathan *followed after the Fleet, not long after, to consolidate the victory, and rule the new territories, and that too was an occasion some residents of Ariadne saw no need to celebrate.*

But neither Fleet nor Leviathan *ever returned. One day, after* Leviathan *left orbit, the gloating, feverish reports of the great conquest simply stopped. From that silence, the Conscripted Immigrants of G.O.S. Ariadne drew grew comfort.*

Slowly, grudgingly, news and rumor spread through the station, and no one knew quite what to believe. A League army had arrived out of nowhere, said one story, and torn the Guards to pieces. There had been a great running battle in space, and in the skies over New Finland, and Leviathan *had been destroyed.*

The CIs aboard Ariadne had no way of learning more. But in the silence, in the sudden absence of reports from New Finland, they drew hope.

For the Guards had shown their hand, had revealed their existence. Sooner or later, the League would come. A full year and more had passed since they had first been captured. But now the League would hunt the Guards down. They would come. They would come.

And yet, some among the CIs warned, it might well take time. For even if the League had won a great battle, it was often true that a war's victors had their own wounds to bind. . . .

Chapter Four

March, 2116
Navy Castle
The Planet Kennedy

Pete Gesseti followed a step behind as Commander Terrance MacKenzie Larson, Republic of Kennedy Navy, turned the knob, opened the door, and stepped into the courtroom to face his court-martial. *He should have known it would come to this*, Pete thought. *But he did know, and it didn't make any difference.*

The court was a high-ceilinged, old-fashioned, somber sort of room, the walls and floors of polished oak, cut from Kennedy-grown trees. The judges waited behind the massive judicial bench, heavy red drapes behind them, the flags of Kennedy and the Navy ensign set to either side. The wall paneling was intricately carved into friezes, scenes of heroism on the seas and in the sky, the proud moments in the ROK Navy's history. The courtroom was a deadly serious place.

Pete followed Mac Larson and his chief counsel, Captain Brown, into the chamber, and looked over the friezes. *They should be carving one for Mac,* Pete thought, *but instead they want to nail him to the wall in person.*

Mac Larson didn't like to hear it, but he *looked* like someone who belonged in a historic scene. Tall, blonde, tanned, handsome, lantern-jawed, muscular, a very imposing figure in the jet-black ROK navy uniform.

Peter Gesseti, Republic of Kennedy State Department Assistant Undersecretary for League Affairs, was short, had a few wisps of brown hair left, and was a round-faced sort of man on whom all suits looked rumpled. His profession and his own poor skills of deportment had taught him the importance of looks. Pete was certain that Mac's appearance would be a help in the case: Mac certainly didn't look like a traitor. Pete also believed in playing every card: He had urged Mac to wear all his decorations. It never hurt to remind the court of the defendant's reputation.

Stern-faced, walking with a firm, measured step, Mac approached the bench, saluted the court, removed his side-arm from its holster and laid it in front of Rear Admiral Louis Leventhal, the presiding judge.

"Commander Terrance MacKenzie Larson reporting as ordered, sir."

"Thank you, Commander. Sergeant-at-arms, if you would be so good as to accept receipt of the defendant's weapon. Be seated, Commander." Leventhal straightened some papers on his desk and looked away as the sergeant bore the gun away. Pete watched, but he himself did not much care for watching Mac's shame.

An ancient ritual, the surrender of the defendant's weapon. Putting that gun in the safe was a good way of asking: Was the accused worthy to bear arms in the name of the state? Was he guilty of a crime, or, of equal importance to a military tribunal, had he betrayed his trust? The gun itself was meaningless. It was certainly unloaded; perhaps it had never been fired. But it was a symbol of what the state put in the hands of its young men and women. Starships, for example, were powerful things, powerful weapons. Was Terrance MacKenzie Larson to be trusted with one?

Pete Gesseti considered the chief judge, the man who would have to decide that question. He was an old man, old enough to have been stuck on-planet for twenty years, and old enough to have served on dozens of courts-martial. He was almost entirely bald, and his face was worn and solemn. When he had had hair, it had hidden the fact that his ears stuck out. Now he was old enough, respected enough, known enough, that no one dared think his stuck-out ears looked funny. He had a wide, thin-lipped mouth that fell easily into a frown that was not of anger or sadness, but of concentrated thought. His eyes were as clear as ever, and of a deep, penetrating grey.

Pete knew that drawing Leventhal was a big plus. The Admiral's kid had been on the *Venera*, had been a classmate and friend of Mac's. Mac and the Admiral even knew each other slightly. Pete had dickered and dealt hard to snag Leventhal. He hoped it was worth it.

"Mr. Gesseti," Leventhal said.

Pete rose. "Admiral."

"Are you involved with this case? I was not aware that the State Department was taking an interest."

"It is not, your honor. I have requested and been granted a leave of absence to serve as assistant counsel to the defense. I hold a law degree and a reserve Navy commission." *And if State wasn't taking an interest, I wouldn't have been let within ten kilometers of this place, and you know it, Admiral.*

"I see. Might I ask what school and what rank?"

"I was law school class of '98 from New Amherst College, and hold the reserve rank of captain." *But don't ask to see the commission because the ink's still wet.* It had taken a few more deals to get the military rank, but Pete had wanted to be damn sure Mac had a friend in court.

"You are aware that these proceedings have been classified as secret?"

"I hold a higher clearance from State, Admiral." *And leaking this farce to the press would raise some merry hell indeed,* Pete thought. *"Navy Brass Puts Hero On Trial." Don't tempt me to use* that *weapon, Admiral.*

"Very well, Captain Gesseti. Thank you. The clerk will read the charge."

"Republic of Kennedy Navy Judge Advocate's Office proceeding in a general court-martial against Commander Terrance MacKenzie Larson, ROK Navy, this 9th day of Fifthmonth, year 97 Kennedy Calendar, March 19, 2116, Earth Standard Calendar. The Honorable Admiral Louis Leventhal, presiding judge; the Honorable Captains Benjamin Stevens, Eric Embry, David White, and Sandra Tho, associate judges. The defendant, Commander Terrance MacKenzie Larson, is charged under Article VII section iii paragraph 3 of the Uniform Code of Military Justice: 'public utterances detrimental to an alliance to which the Republic of Kennedy is a signatory,' and paragraph 6, 'public utterances detrimental to the prosecution of Naval operations,' both charges raised from a Class IV to a Class III violation under the provisions of Article I section ii paragraph 4, 'the Republic being in a state of War, each charge shall be considered to be one Class higher than described in this Code of Justice.' Charges are brought in regards to the following allegations, to wit: numerous public oral statements by the defendant in opposition to the deployment of RKS *Eagle*, USS *Yorktown*, and HMS *Impervious*, the three large space-going carrier craft available to the League of Planets in the prosecution of the present war against the Guardians."

"Captain Brown, how does your client plead?"

"Not Guilty, your honor."

"Then let the record show a plea of Not Guilty. Captain Tsung, if you would proceed for the prosecution."

"Your honor, as the facts themselves are not in dispute, and by prior agreement of opposing counsel, I elect to forego my opening remarks and reserve my evidence until the defense has concluded its own case."

"To the defense, then. Captain Brown."

"Thank you, your honors. I will be as brief as possible in my opening remarks. As Captain Tsung has remarked, the defense will not dispute the facts of the case, which are well known. The defendant did indeed make statements and comments and allow himself to be interviewed at the times and dates and with the persons itemized in what will be the prosecution's exhibit A. Our case will instead turn upon an entirely different point of military law and tradition.

"It has been said that the sublimest word in the English language is 'duty.' Duty is service, and military service especially. Duty above self-preservation, duty above honor, duty above even the orders of a superior. Any sailor or soldier of this Republic would be liable to arrest, court-martial and punishment for obeying criminal orders—orders, for example, to massacre civilians. Under such circumstances it is the sworn duty of our military personnel to not only question, but refuse, their orders.

"The Navy of the Republic of Kennedy traces its traditions back hundreds of years, to the ocean-going navy of England that defeated the Spanish Armada and the American wet navy that held the sea lanes against Hitler. It looks back to Task Force One, the three U.S. Navy starships that made the first journey beyond Earth's sun a century ago. Since our race first left the Solar System, we have come to be more and more spread out among the stars, and so communication has become more difficult, slower, less reliable. At the same time ships have become faster, more powerful—and thereby, potentially—more dangerous. For this reason, independent judgment, the ability to react to a changed or entirely new situation not covered by orders, has been a vitally needed skill in our Navy.

"Also for this reason, no Kennedy naval officer is trusted with a ship until and unless he or she is thoroughly indoctrinated into our traditions, until the events carved into these walls are etched as well into the psyche of the officer, until that naval officer has learned the many things a ship *can* do that it *must never* do. Our defense against the might of our own weapons is and always has been the quality and integrity of our people.

"Obviously, the refusal of orders is a serious thing. It cannot be done lightly, and in all but the most drastic of cases—such as the hypothetical one I have offered—the commanding officer must be allowed the benefit of the doubt. Obedience to orders is the due of a commander.

"A sailor or soldier must be prepared to obey orders that will result in his or her own death, in the destruction of his or her unit, in the loss of all that is held dear, just as an officer is expected to give orders, if need be, that will kill that officer and destroy that officer's own command. Clearly, such sacrifice must be made to a purpose. No person in our military is expected to die uselessly. He or she is expected to die and kill willingly *if it is needful*.

"It is an assumption inherent in all this that there is a

higher good than survival. That higher good is the preservation of one's family, one's people, one's society, one's beliefs. Defense of these higher goods, perhaps at one's own expense, we call 'duty.' But when a sailor or a soldier or an officer knows, with certainty, that obedience to an order will accomplish the destruction of men and materiél sorely needed in the fight to come, and will accomplish no other thing, then duty lies with disobedience. Such, we will prove, is the present case. Terrance MacKenzie Larson was ordered to remain silent. With full knowledge of the consequences of his actions, he spoke. As he expected, this resulted in the present court-martial.

"As I have noted, duty is above honor, and Commander Larson has willingly risked the shame of imprisonment and conviction to do *his* duty. It is now the *duty* of this court to see that justice is done, and to see that Commander Larson is held blameless for his actions, released from custody fully vindicated, and returned to his unit with his reputation intact."

Pete leaned over and whispered to Mac. "Now *that's* some kind of speaking. You might get out of this yet."

"I didn't get in to get out, Pete," Mac whispered back. "That twenty bucks still says I lose."

Brown turned his back on the court and winked at Mac and Pete as he collected a sheaf of papers from the defendant's table. Then he turned to the bench and said "The defense calls as its first witness Terrance MacKenzie Larson, Commander, Republic of Kennedy Navy."

The prosecutor rose and spoke. "For the record, I wish to insert a correction. The defendant's rank was conferred by brevet, and was not even conferred by a ROK Navy officer. His permanent rank is second lieutenant."

"Your honors, I object!" Brown shouted. "My client's brevet rank—conferred at the discretion of the U.S. Naval officer under whose command he serves in the joint operation known as the Survey Service—is every bit as legal and binding as a conventional promotion—and I defy the prosecution to suggest that it was undeserved. The only effect the brevet promotion has had upon my client has been the denial of the pay and benefits of a commander. He continues at the pay schedule of a second lieutenant. I thank the prosecution for reminding us of yet another injustice done my client."

The five judges conferred briefly and then Leventhal spoke. "Objection sustained. Captain Tsung's remark will be struck from the record. Commander Larson, you may take your stand."

The clerk swore Mac in. Brown went through the usual preliminaries of identification, and then began to question him.

"Commander. For the record, and for the information and with the permission of the court, could you repeat the opinions that got you into this situation?"

"Yes. As I have said publicly on many occasions, I believe that the deployment of the *Eagle*, *Yorktown*, and *Impervious* would be potentially disastrous to the Republic of Kennedy and to the alliance, the League of Planets."

"And why is that?"

"These carrier ships are the largest men-of-war ever built by the League. Their function is analogous to that of an ocean-going aircraft carrier: They carry fighter and attack spacecraft, and deploy these fighters in battle. The idea is simple: The carrier serves as a forward base. The fighters and attack ships can return to the carrier rather than to home base, and can thereby be shorter-range, lighter, faster, and carry less fuel and more armament than a fighter forced to travel from a distant base."

"But this sounds as if the carriers are ideal for space war."

"In theory, they are. However, like the old ocean-going carriers, including the namesakes of the *Yorktown* and the *Impervious*, these carrier ships are extremely tempting and vulnerable targets. Because they are so large, their fusion rocket engines must be very powerful and of course a fusion engine emits a lot of energy across the electromagnetic spectrum. The *Yorktown*'s engines, for example, would be detectable at least a light-year away. Beyond that, of course a large target is easier to pick up on radar than a small one. For these and other reasons, it's easy to find one of these ships. The enemy, having found such a ship, will certainly try to destroy it, both because it is a great threat to him, and because destroying it will remove such a large fraction of our war-fighting capability.

"There is an additional problem with the three ships in question. They are old—of old design and old construction.

They have been more or less mothballed for decades. Upgrading a forty-year-old engine or attempting to retrofit a modern system into these old hulls is far more difficult and expensive than starting from scratch on a new ship."

"We are all naval officers here, Commander, and all have no doubt heard these arguments before. What made you pursue your views so vigorously, so publicly, all but forcing a prosecution, risking damage to your career, or even a term in the brig?"

"My experiences in the New Finland star system soon after the League-Guardian War began."

"Could you elaborate?"

"Objection! The prosecution must object in the strongest terms." Captain Tsung no doubt had been waiting for this, and dreading it. He had to try to cut this line of questioning off. "The defense is attempting to bring in extraneous side issues. How the defendant came by his view is irrelevant. For that matter, the defendant's views are themselves irrelevant. The defense is attempting to build a case on the altar of duty. This, too, is beside the point. The only issue here is whether or not the defendant did indeed violate the Uniform Code of Military Justice by making certain statements. The defense admits he did indeed make such statements. As this is the only point on which the case turns, I respectfully request the bench to instruct defense to rest so we may proceed to the prosecution."

Pete looked on admiringly at Tsung. The old snow-em-with-everything routine. Every possible argument for ignoring side issues. Not a bad gambit. If the judges bought just one bit of Tsung's argument, they'd have to buy the whole thing. If they did that, the defense was dead.

Pete and Captain Brown had been expecting this, and Pete was ready to do his bit. It would require a little sarcasm, and better for assistant counsel to be snotty than let Brown himself get in trouble with Leventhal for being disrespectful.

Pete stood up slowly. "Your honors, I must raise a number of counter-objections. Captain Tsung knows damn well he's stuck with the unpleasant job of trying to throw an interstellar hero in the brig, and he's doing his best—doing *his* duty, if you will. Fine. But don't let him tell you how to do *your* job. If you wish to cut off the defense, you can decide that on your own without his help. Furthermore, five minutes ago my learned friend was foregoing his opening statement and reserving his case—and now he wants to shut down *our* key witness after five questions! Your honors, I submit that entertaining such a motion, permitting such a strategy, would deny our client's single chance to defend himself. As it is, he will be heard only in a secret proceeding. Allow him at least that."

"It seems to me, Captain Gesseti, that we now have the choice of being instructed by either the prosecution or the defense," Leventhal growled. "We shall confer." The five judges bent their heads together and whispered briefly. Finally, Leventhal addressed the court. "In this matter, we overrule the prosecution. We find that it is conceivable that reasons could exist that would compel the defendant to act as he has. Therefore, the search for such reasons in the experience of the defendant is not irrelevant. Defense may proceed with the current line of questioning."

"Thank you, your honor," Pete said as he sat down. It had *definitely* been worth all the trouble to get Leventhal on the court.

"Let me restate the question, Commander Larson," Brown went on. "What were the experiences in the New Finland system that led you to your views?"

"I came to my opinions as a result of our fight against the Guardian ship *Leviathan*.

"*Leviathan* is—or rather was—basically similar to the *Eagle* and the other carriers, except for three major differences. One, she was much larger than our ships. Two, she was designed to enter an atmosphere; she could operate either in air or space. The third difference was that *Leviathan* was a lighter-than-air craft. *Leviathan* used a combination of aerodynamics and the lifting power of hydrogen gas to keep her in the air.

"However, the points central to this court-martial are these: *Leviathan* was by a factor of a thousand the most powerful ship in that system, but she could have been destroyed at any time by a single nuclear weapon. Our side did not do so because the controls operating the anti-ship missiles were aboard her. If we destroyed the control system, there would be no way to tell the missiles to let a ship past."

"In other words," Brown put in, "had not circumstances made the League and Finn forces hostage to the continued existence of *Leviathan*, she could have been destroyed easily."

"Perhaps not easily, but there is no question that we could have blown her. However, our forces were able to board *Leviathan* and take over the missile control center long enough to send a self-destruct to all the missiles, and that left the way open for League ships to enter the system. *Leviathan* was then attacked by small landing craft using their fusion engines as weapons. When their fusion flames finally burned through to the lift cells, *Leviathan* was destroyed by explosion and fire."

"You have touched lightly on your own part in all this. Did you not in fact take command of all the League and Finn space forces when all the more senior officers had been killed?"

"Yes, I did."

"Did you not in fact plan and lead the boarding operation, and *personally* use the missile control system to send the self-destruct? Furthermore, was not your lander the last ship to leave *Leviathan*, remaining there at great risk and at your specific orders to pick up any survivors and ensure that the enemy ship was destroyed?"

Mac hesitated. "Yes, that is correct," he said.

Pete smiled. It was hard to be a modest hero under oath. Brown wanted to make sure the record showed what sort of man they were putting on trial.

Brown went on. "I have here a list of decorations awarded to you. Have you not in fact received the New Finnish Gold Lion, the U.S. Legion of Merit, the British Victoria Cross, the Britannica Order of Honor, The League High Cross, the Finnish Hero's Medal, the League of Planets Survey Service Stargrid, as well as the Republic of Kennedy's Purple Heart, Silver Star and Medal of Honor, as well as many other honors and citations?"

Mac shifted uncomfortably. "Yes, that is correct."

"Commander Larson, where is your wife? Have you seen her recently?"

"She was reassigned to the Navy Yards at Britannica. I haven't seen her in some months."

"Was she not in fact transferred away from the Survey Service Base shortly after you first spoke out against deploying the three carriers?"

"She was ordered back home within thirty-six hours after my first statement."

"Has it ever occurred to you that the two of you were separated as a punishment for your statement, punishment without benefit of trial or appeal? Was this not indeed persecution and harassment of a heroic man and woman because of your—"

"Objection!" the prosecutor shouted. "Counsel is clearly not questioning the witness, but making a speech. I request that this leading and biased so-called 'question' be stricken from the record."

"I withdraw my last question," Brown said smoothly. Good, thought Pete. Getting the judges to hear it was enough, on the record or no. And it didn't hurt to tweak the opposition before turning Mac Larson over to him. "Your witness, Captain."

Captain Tsung was clearly rattled enough for Brown's purposes. He rose uncertainly and approached the defendant. "Ah, ah, Commander. I'm certain that no one in this court questions your courage, or your contribution to the war effort . . ." Tsung's voice trailed off for a moment. "But that is not what is on trial here. Commander Larson. You base your assumptions on the vulnerability of the three carriers on the fact that you were present when the *Leviathan* crashed."

"Yes, that is correct."

Pete bounced up. "I'd like to clarify the answer to that question. Commander Larson did in actual fact command the ship that wrecked *Leviathan*, and the larger ship was destroyed by his command and according to his plan. Excuse the interruption," he said brightly, and sat back down.

Captain Brown leaned over toward his assistant counsel. "*That* wasn't approved courtroom procedure," he whispered to Pete.

"No, but why let Tsung make Mac seem like he was standing around watching the world go by when a giant spaceship just happened to crash in front of him?" Pete replied. "Mac came as close as anyone ever has to winning a war single-handed."

"Except the war isn't over yet. No one's found the Guardians' planet."

"Don't remind me."

Tsung seemed more and more unhappy about the job of prosecuting Mac. "Ah, Commander. Conceding that you did indeed destroy *Leviathan*, how does that bear on the vulnerability of the League carrier ships? After all, *Leviathan* was destroyed in large part by fire, in an atmosphere, while flying as an aerodynamic vehicle, under circumstances wholly different from those the *Eagle* and the other carrier will experience. Our ships are, after all, incapable of entering an atmosphere, and certainly do not carry large lift cells filled with hydrogen gas."

Mac smiled slightly. "Forgive me, Captain, but I don't think you've done your homework. I was debriefed very carefully after the missile system was destroyed. In that statement, which I can see on the prosecutor's table, I reported that the *Joslyn Marie* at one point attacked the *Leviathan* using space-to-space torpedoes."

For the first time, Mac's voice and manner showed some emotion, some passion. Even talking about the carriers here, in court, got him visibly angry. "As I noted in the debriefing, the *Joslyn Marie*, although perhaps a thousandth the mass of the *Leviathan*, was able to make several direct hits on the big ship. As I have stated already, we could not risk the destruction of *Leviathan*, and so the torpedoes were armed with conventional explosive. If we had armed the *J.M*'s torps with nuclear warheads—which we could have done easily—there is not the slightest doubt that the *J.M* could have taken out *Leviathan*. Those hits made by conventionally armed torps prove that a ship the size of the *J.M* could certainly destroy the *Eagle*, and the people and equipment aboard her. And I might add that the Guards know all this as well as we do. They have learned it the hard way. They foolishly put all their eggs in one basket. We must profit from the enemy's error instead of making the same fatal mistake ourselves. The secret we are trying to keep is no secret to the enemy—it is secret only to our own people and the men and women aboard those carriers."

Tsung knew when to quit. "Thank you, Commander. No further questions."

Pete popped up again. "The defense rests its case at this time, your honors. By prior agreement with opposing counsel, we will waive our concluding statement. The prosecution may now proceed with its case if it so chooses." *In other words, we're quitting while we're ahead,* Pete thought.

Tsung had the sense to request a recess for lunch after Mac's testimony. He needed time to collect his thoughts and get his notes in order, time to relax and plan, and he needed to give the judges time to forget a bit of Mac's impressive bearing. So far nothing had gone his way, and he was determined that would change.

After lunch, Tsung began his case by quoting Mac's statements and showing a recording of one of his interviews. The message was the same one, but put in far less respectful tones.

Mac and Pete watched the screen impassively as Mac's image spoke. "The carriers are deathtraps. They are sitting ducks. We are told that the ships were built 'to interpose powerful forces across the spacelanes in times of crisis.' Those ships were never needed for that, in all the years they were on active duty. They were mothballed because modern weapons and tactics—and the absence of a major war—made them useless.

"Their true purpose, the true reason that these ships were built, the true reason that they are now being recommissioned, is that admirals like to have big impressive ships to fly around in. Every cost-effectiveness calculation, every war game, every strategic plan, has shown that these ships are as much liabilities and targets as they are advantages and weapons."

Tsung stopped the recording. "That, your honors, is what Commander Larson had to say to the public last week. That statement was carried on Kennedy's largest video network. It was widely quoted. Commander Larson has said the alleged peril these carriers face is a secret—but that peril is no secret, thanks to him. Fortunately, none of his statements have gotten into the off-planet press as yet, though that is but a matter of time. No doubt ships are carrying copies of our war-hero's opinions to every major world in the League.

"And what effect will that have on the war effort? Commander Larson gave up his efforts to discuss his views through normal military channels, and instead went public. How will it serve morale, fighting spirit? Can it serve but to discourage the men aboard those ships? Can it but give aid and comfort to the enemy for him to hear that we regard our own ships as admirals' toys, sitting ducks, deathtraps?

"Your honors, I will present no witnesses. I could exhaust us all with a stream of experts on strategy and tactics who would confirm what I have said, and then the defense would dredge up its own experts to refute me. I could call Captain Josiah Robinson, the commander of the *Eagle*, and he would be happy to tell you the high state of readiness his ship is in, and how his men are reacting to Commander Larson's statements. But you are all naval officers, and you know all these things.

"The one witness I would call, if I could, would be a naval commander—a *Guardian* naval commander. We must assume they have their spies here on Kennedy, watching us. The Guardians, on their hidden planet, Capital, perhaps have already viewed the recording we have just seen. If I could put a Guardian naval officer on the stand, under oath, I would ask him: Did Commander Larson's statements reveal weaknesses of which the Guardians were unaware? Did he make *their* forces more confident? Was what he said good for *their* morale?

"We have heard a great deal about duty today. We have been told that Commander Larson felt it his duty to speak, a higher duty than that he had to Navy regulations. Was it not a higher duty still to keep silent? He has hurt our perception of our strength, our morale—and aided that of the enemy. He has told us of a danger that it seems only he can see. Assuming the danger exists at all, has he not made that danger greater by pointing it out to the enemy? But speaking out on this 'danger,' has he not increased all our other dangers?

"This man has displayed courage, enormous courage, both in battle and in coming forward to say what he has said. But has he displayed good judgment? I think not. Your honors, I ask you to demonstrate your own judgment and find for the prosecution. In the old days, the wet navy days, they said that 'loose lips sink ships.' In our present day, loose lips might serve to *vaporize* ships. Do not encourage the practice of loose talk by letting this man go free. Yes, he is a hero. But heroism is no excuse for making a terrible mistake of judgment.

"Your honors, the prosecution rests."

Leventhal banged down his gavel. "Very well. This court-martial is adjourned. The court will withdraw to reach a verdict. This court-martial will reconvene at 0900 hours tomorrow morning."

Captain Brown and Gesseti joined Mac for breakfast in his cell the next morning. If you could call it a cell. Maybe Mac was confined to quarters in the Navy Castle, Pete thought, but at least he was confined to comfortable, if not downright imposing quarters, on a high floor of the Tower. The rough-hewn walls of the semi-circular room were hung with paintings of great ships and admirals, the furniture was from the captain's cabin of an old U.S. wet Navy battle cruiser, and the floor was covered in a rich, solemn burgundy carpet. Pete was pleased by the room. They only put high-class prisoners here.

The Navy Castle had not been built by some romantic architect to look like a fortress—it *was* a fortress, with stone walls three meters thick at the base, internally reinforced with steel and modern graphite composites. The walls would defend against mobs and most conventional attacks, and the bomb shelters drilled into bedrock a kilometer below could hold out long after the Castle proper had been vaporized. The Castle was designed to do more that just survive an attack, of course. It could fight back, with an armory full of rifles and side-arms and supplies for a siege. There were other weapons tucked away inside the great building, which no one talked about much.

The Navy Castle had been built seventy-five years before, in quiet and peaceful days—at least they had been peaceful days on Kennedy. The ROK Navy was busy back then, as it was now, frequently being dispatched in answer to League requests: police actions, rescue missions, and even the transportation of riot police from one star system to another. The League had been formed largely in reaction to the economic and political disarray on far too many of the settled worlds, and it fell to the navies of the strongest powers to effect and enforce the League's decisions.

The ROK Navy had been there in the evacuation of New Antarctica, literally on day one of the League's existence. The Navy had flown relief supplies, bombed one side or another in the midst of revolts, arrested arms runners and drug smugglers, done too many dangerous things to trust much to days of peace. Only now, in the fight against the Guardians, did the ROK Navy find itself in its first war, but it had experience enough of fighting.

So headquarters was built inconveniently far from town—near but not at the spaceport, in sight of but not on the coast, on the brow of a hill in the middle of a large and carefully tended clearing. It wasn't due to chance that the view from the Tower was superb, nor due to the prestige of the unit that the First Marine Battalion was stationed there.

There had been scoffers who laughed at the egos that needed such a huge building, and a few Army types pointed out that the Castle cost more to build than most of the Navy's ships. Then the Fast Plague came, and madness literally became a contagious disease. When the cure was found, and the riots were over, the Castle was still there, with only a nick or two and a few scorch marks to mar the outer stone facing. The Army's gleaming, modern, downtown HQ Center had to be torn down and rebuilt altogether.

The builders of the Castle were more far-sighted than they were optimistic.

The view from Mac's room was spectacular. Mac couldn't seem to eat much. He was too drawn by the view, the things to see. The coastline, the skyline of Hyannisport, the broad plain of the spaceport, were laid out in a magnificent panorama. But it was the spaceport that Mac stared at. As he watched, a ship, a small winged job, made a horizontal launch into the perfect blue morning sky and rushed for orbit, the dull yellow of its airbreathing engines suddenly flaring into sun-bright specks as it shifted to fusion power.

Pete could guess what was going through his young

friend's mind. He was watching the ship climb to orbit, to space, to the dark between the suns. Perhaps toward Joslyn, Mac's wife, once again so far away.

"I should be out there, Pete," Mac said at last. "There's work to be done and I'm one of the best qualified to do it, and I'm cooped up here."

"You'll be out there soon, Mac. The judges will pass their verdict, this whole farce will be over, and you'll be back at it. Besides, you're only locked up here because you had a job of talking to do that you thought was pretty damn important. And you were right."

"Maybe you even did some good, though I doubt it," Captain Brown said, carefully refilling his coffee cup, "And Pete, we gave it our best shot and did pretty well, but I've never had much hope of getting Mac off. The regulations are pretty clear, and I can't see Leventhal and company being thrown by a lot of verbal flourishes."

"Why do you doubt I did any good?" Mac asked.

"Because you're a lousy politician, and you didn't know the right people. Oh, I don't think you had much choice, and you did get your case heard, but all that accomplishes is getting the brass with their backs to the wall. They can't lose face by admitting you're right. They want to prove *they're* right—"

"And the only way to do that is to deploy the damned carriers. But I had to try, Captain Brown. For all the reasons you talked about in court."

"Yeah, I suppose," Brown said, clearly not convinced.

Suddenly Pete was angry, though he couldn't quite explain at what. All he knew for sure was that Terrance MacKenzie Larson was not the sort of man who should be hung out to dry. It was only the higher ranks, the admirals who loved their big ships too much, who felt the need to punish him. They had left the dirty work to the Tsungs and the Leventhals, honorable officers honorably and reluctantly doing their duty. Right now, Pete felt he never wanted to hear the word duty again.

There was a polite knock at the door and the very

respectful white-gloved marine informed them that the court-martial was ready to reconvene.

They descended in the sleek, silent-running elevator, and were led the familiar way to the courtroom by the marine guard.

There was shuffling of papers, and rising for the court, and finally it came, unwilling, from Leventhal's lips.

One word.

"Guilty."

Chapter Five

March, 2116
Guardian Contact Headquarters
Outpost

The day dawned as most of them did in this clearing, with a mist-shrouded sun easing its way through the knotted, roiling cloud, and the tangled limbs of the surrounding forest. Two camps, one human, one Outposter, stirred and began their morning routines as the sun burned off the mist and the clouds, and the dew dripped off the plant life.

C'astille opened her eyes, uncurled her legs from beneath her long body, flexed her tail, and stepped out of her field shelter into the clearing. She sucked in the fresh morning air through her blowhole. The morning air smelled good, invigorating. She stretched her arms and flexed her long fingers. It would be another good day. She went to the camp kitchen in search of breakfast.

On the far side of the clearing, inside one of the humans' pressurized huts, Lucy Calder slapped at the alarm clock with somewhat less enthusiasm for the day. With the dim thought of a shower and coffee, she stumbled out of bed. She had been up late again the night before, working on her notes. And Outpost's day was only nineteen hours long. It took getting used to. And C'astille would beat her to the Crystal Palace, as usual. She had given up trying to be early for their meetings—C'astille would simply be earlier still the next day. Calder liked her counterpart, and even felt in some strange way that she had something in common with her, but a little less enthusiasm for early morning work wouldn't be amiss. Coffee. That was the main thing.

◇ ◇ ◇

Neither side was consciously aware of it, of course, but each had done the same thing, or had at least arrived at the same result: Young, open-minded, highly intelligent, and quite expendable individuals represented both species.

The Guardians hadn't made any immediate, deliberate decisions to put Johnson Gustav or Lucy Calder on Ariadne at the moment of First Contact. However, human traditions of exploration and military service, formed by decisions made and lessons learned over thousands of years, favored the practice of using young, still-flexible minds with few immediate dependents to lead expeditions to the unknown or the unpredictable. It seemed to be what worked best: More explorers and soldiers came back when the leaders were young and smart and had few attachments to the outside world. Given that tradition, persons like Gustav and Calder were the most likely to be thrown into situations where a First Contact might occur: for example, on board a station orbiting a largely unexplored world.

But fresh, sharp, and flexible minds did work best, and not just for humans. C'astille's mind fit that description just as well. She had long dreamed of being the finder of a new thing. As a youth, she had at times worried that the world was too well known, that there would be no discoveries or explorations or new things to learn. All that had changed now, of course, and certainly there were now to be strange new things to fill more than a lifetime.

She found the humans themselves the most interesting. Even now, long after she had first set eyes on them, the sight of humans, especially walking in their bizarre bipedal gait, fascinated her. The sight both mesmerized and repelled practically any Outposter not used to it. A human parallel to this reaction could be found in the unpleasant, creepy thrill some humans got out of touching a snake. A nastier, more accurate, and more compelling analogy might be the giddy, horrified, stomach-knotting reaction humans often have when they see a member of their own species, unfortunate enough to have both legs amputated, forced to walk on hands instead of feet.

To the Outposters, the humans looked mutilated, a front half of a creature chopped from the whole. Given the cultural and biological background of the Outposters, the very sight of a human brought a whole constellation of unpleasant things to mind.

It *took* a flexible, educated psyche like C'astille's to accept the fact that these were natural, whole, and healthy creatures, probably evolved in a process similar to that which produced C'astille herself, and not monsters.

From what C'astille could understand of what Lucy said, the humans had an advantage without realizing it: they were used to the idea of seeing a creature that walked on four legs, and even had a comfortable, familiar, and not unpleasant legend—something called a centaur—to help them get used to the shape and movements of the Outposters. The Outposters had no such comforting images. To C'astille and her fellow Low Assistances, the humans did not bring to mind a more or less friendly sort of mythical beast. A very mild analogy to what humans reminded them of would be the front half of Frankenstein's monster lurching off the laboratory slab.

Humans took some getting used to, and the older Outposters happily left direct contact with the halfwalkers to the younger set.

Her meal quickly finished, C'astille cantered across the clearing from the Outposter camp to the Talking House. The halfwalkers had built their part of it first, not long after C'astille had first met the human Calder. The human techniques of building had puzzled the Outposters. The methods seemed highly inefficient, but the human structures went up quickly enough, and, after all, results were what mattered.

Dressed in a light-weight pressure suit, Lucy walked the paved path from the human camp to the Crystal Palace. C'astille was there, her tail flicking with eagerness to begin.

Calder grinned and waved. Every morning it was the same; the moment she saw the young Outposter, she was caught up in the other's unflagging enthusiasm for their work. She hurried through the lock cycle, stripped her suit off, and sat down at the field desk inside the Palace.

The Crystal Palace wasn't much to look at, but it worked. A Guardian Army engineer's platoon had built the thing. They had poured a concrete slab foundation, assembled a rather large prefab hut and bolted it to the slab. The hut was meant to keep the rain off and nothing else, and the slab to keep the hut from sinking into the soggy ground. They installed a quiet-running generator and hung lights. No effort was made to make the hut airtight, but inside it, a more sophisticated structure went up. The engineers made a room-sized clear plastic box with an airlock on one side. It took up about a third of the interior of the prefab hut, and it *was* airtight. The makers added a few conveniences outside the box, on the slab: racks to hold equipment, a hose-down station to get the mud off a suit before entering the airlock, that sort of thing.

The whole interior of the box was always visible from the outside, except for a portable toilet which could be hidden behind a screen when in use. Lucy had quickly named the plastic box the Crystal Palace, and was delighted to have it. Learning and teaching a wholly novel language was rough enough without having to stand in the middle of a soggy field in a pressure suit to do it. Gestures, expressions, movement were essential to learning, and all were infinitely easier out of a suit.

Of course, there was no practical limit to how long a pressure suit could be worn if survival was the only criterion. But the suits were heavy, tiring, restricting, they limited vision, and the speakers and mikes were only so good.

In the Palace Lucy could relax, pace, even take a nap or go to the head between language sessions, grab a snack from the compact refrigerator or make a cup of coffee. Far more important, she could see and be seen. Pantomime was often vital to making sure she understood what a word meant, and it was a hell of a lot easier to have the props of language-learning—a drawing board, objects you wanted the names of, notepads and recorders and so on, safely under weatherproof conditions, and it was a double pleasure not to have to handle a pencil through a pressure suit's gloves.

C'astille understood the advantages of getting in out of the rain as well as anyone, and once she had gotten an accidental whiff of what the humans breathed for air she understood why they needed to stay in a suit or a glass box. Unlike humans, the Outposters could smell and taste carbon dioxide and nitrogen. It seemed human air had too little of the former and too much of the latter. She too was glad to get her drawing and writing and recording things out of the rain, and even took the human lead in making the Outposter half of what she called the Talking House as comfortable as possible. She and the other Low Assistances brought in work tables, lights, rest couches, and their own food stores and portable power sources.

Not long after the language lessons had started, it had become clear to both sides it would be wise to concentrate on teaching the humans C'astille's language. Things simply weren't working going the other way.

The Outposters had so much trouble learning English that at first Lucy Calder thought their language was hard-wired into them. It seemed possible that Outposters inherited their language genetically, and were no more capable of learning an alternative to it than a human was capable of learning an alternative to the sense of smell. Lucy would have been pleased if that idea had been correct; it would have meant one language would be usable across Outpost.

But the Outposters weren't the problem; English was. The Outposters just couldn't seem to get the hang of it. Calder concluded the problem lay in the structure of English, the parts that tone and sound played in meaning. She had a hunch that the 'Posters would do better learning

Chinese, but there was little point in teaching them a language wherein Lucy was the only one else in the star system who understood it—and Cynthia Wu, of course. Might as well teach them one of the Australian aborigine dialects. Come to think of it, Calder had a feeling C'astille would do pretty well at those. But not at English.

So Lucy did the learning, slowly, gradually. More of it today, and she had some questions to ask.

She cleared her throat and forced her voice into the odd resonances of C'astille's tongue. "Your presence is sensed, C'astille," she said. It made as much sense as "hello," and meant as much.

"And yours is sensed as well," C'astille said. "Talk starts?"

"Talk starts. But word-learning remains deferred," Calder said. It was the passivity of the language that was the most difficult and bewildering. It was hard for her, and hard for her human students of the language, to bear in mind that action must be placed away from the speaker, or better still, removed entirely and the verb used to describe a state of being rather than an action. "Absence of knowledge continues for my Guidances. And yet word-learning and word-puzzlement are at its center. A thing is pointed to—this structure, my clothes, our vehicles, our path to the Talking House—and the humans say they got there by being made, or built. Sometimes the Outposters have things pointed to and it is said they are grown. Your recorders, your structures, your couch are called 'grown.' Is it that verbs 'grow' and 'make' or 'build' are the same, or are so many of your things formed from live things?"

" 'Grow' is not 'build.' My couch is grown, my house is built from walls and other parts of a material grown in sheets. But walls not *precisely* grown. Never living, but made by living things not of my species. Species are caused by my people, and these species are makers of much of our things."

That was tangled, but Calder thought she had the gist. "And the new species that are caused. How many—" Lucy quickly checked her dictionary. No, she didn't have the word for "generation." "How many cycles from parent to offspring between the old species and a perfected new one?"

C'astille pulled her head back on its long neck, an involuntary gesture of surprise. "Why, none, or perhaps accurately one. The old form is taken, the changes are made on its—again, the word is not yet given to you. It is *lasut*. Do you have the concept of small structures that are controllers of what a live thing is?"

"Humans have known of this concept long years."

"Here they are called *lasut*." Calder noted its phonetics down, had C'astille repeat it so she could record it and practice it later, and the conversation went on. Both were used to such circumlocutions and pauses by now.

C'astille continued. "The *lasut* are changed, and the next thing to come from them is what is wanted."

"That is not our way," Lucy said. "Human skill with changing these *lasut*—called genes by us—exists, but I have suspicions it is quite modest when compared to yours. Much time, many tries, many cycles of parent and offspring between first effort and success. Also, humans seek not to bring forth a wall-growing life form, but just a stronger animal, a plant that will give more food."

"So are all your things made, as has been seen?"

"Highly close to true. A human is the maker, or the maker of a machine that is the maker of nearly all our things."

"Even your *secu werystlon*?"

A tricky term. Literally, it translated as "outer memories," and seemed to cover both sound and sight recorders, computers, perhaps some other gadgets, perhaps even pencil and paper. It occurred to Lucy that the term was a bad fit. It was their name for a class of things that had some equivalence to computers, and recorders. "Yes, if I understand with precision," Lucy said carefully. "These are not grown, but are themselves machines."

"Many of ours live."

Lucy had the sudden and ghastly vision of a disembodied brain inside a glass jar, hooked up to wires. No, it wouldn't be like that. But the image wouldn't fade. *You learn something new every day*, she thought, and the two of them got on with the language lesson.

The days passed, and both sides learned.

Gustav pounded away stolidly at the keyboard.

Alien Contact Status and Action Report 137

General Summary:

Once again, no major changes since last report. CI Lucille Calder continues to make gradual progress on Outposter-1 language. The Outposters have confirmed her earlier understanding that there are any number of different languages spoken by the Outposters, many of them mutually unintelligible. Previous theories to the contrary must be abandoned. Orbital examination and mapping of the surface continues to be hampered by cloud cover, but orbital work has located about 100 probable city sites on the planet, in widely scattered locations. Recent low-altitude atmospheric overflights, launched from Orbital Station *Ariadne*, of many of these sites have located definite small settlements. Many appear to be abandoned. The largest of these seems about as large as a human village of a few thousand. We at Contact Headquarters once again urgently request that these overflights be suspended, as they must be disconcerting to the locals. We do not wish to adversely affect relations with Outposter groups we have not yet met, and these overflights can tell us little more than they already have: that the Outposters have very many small settlements.

Specific Summaries:

Language: Calder has done excellent work, and has now established a reliable basic vocabulary of Outposter-1. At my instruction, she now divides her time between learning more O-1 and teaching what she has learned already to the trainees sent from Capital. These trainees are already capable of some conversation with the locals. She is also involved in the effort to get a computer to serve as a translating device. All of these efforts will eventually succeed: Calder will become more fluent in O-1 and she expects to be able to talk in related dialects; the trainees will learn the language as well; and the auto-translator device will be perfected. However, I must emphasize once again that all of these projects involve the most gradual and painstaking effort. By the very nature of the work—in large part patient trial-and-error—breakthroughs simply are not possible. With all due respect, the work cannot be rushed, and I can assure everyone involved that we at Contact HQ are as eager for more results as anyone. But patience is required. We will be learning the subtle points of O-1 for the next generation at least. Calder deserves nothing but praise for her efforts.

Culture and Technology: I am forced to make the same report I have made so many times before: The levels of culture and technology are undetermined but high, and probably higher than thought at the time of my last report a few days ago, particularly in the biological sciences. Apparently, the Outposters can "custom-tailor" the local equivalent of chromosomes on a rapid and routine basis. What would seem a staggeringly difficult job of genetic engineering to us, they can do with casual ease.

At this point, I feel compelled to repeat a caution I have made many times before: It would be a great mistake to assume the Outposters are primitive because we locate no huge cities from orbit, or because they appear semi-nomadic, or because we do not detect powerful radio or electric power generation. We have by no means begun to understand these beings, but I can at least offer a theory.

Humans have always assumed that cities, preferably large cities, are the centers of culture, and humans have always assumed that cities are permanent. The Outposters make neither assumption. I believe this is a key dividing point in the development of our differing cultures. Insofar as the connection between culture and technology, I submit a statement that should have been obvious before we found the Outposters: There is no such connection. To cite but one example: The ancient Greeks certainly had a lower technology than many subsequent civilizations, but certainly they had a higher culture than most . . .

There was a muffled *thud, thud* on the bulkhead, which was what passed for a knock at the door of a pressurized prefab hut. Gustav, glad of the break, hit the *lock cycle* button and spent the next two minutes straightening up the papers on his desk. One nice thing about airlocks—it was just about impossible for anyone to barge into his office.

A long series of thumps, clumps, and bumps further heralded the arrival of a visitor. "Hey, Johnson," Lucy said, her voice muffled by the breathing helmet, as she came into the room.

"Hi, Luce. How's the day so far?"

"Good," she said, pulling off her helmet. "I get two kinds of days—the kind where I wonder why it's taken us so long to get so little, and the kind where I'm amazed at how much progress we've made in so short a time. Today," she said with a grin, "is a Type Two day. The Outposter voice-recognition program seems to have most of the bugs out of it, finally, and that's progress."

A strange thing had happened since the day the two of them had landed on this world. Conscripted Immigrant Lucille Calder and Lieutenant Johnson Gustav had become friends. It shouldn't have been able to happen—but it had. There were still boundaries, very hard-edged ones, about that friendship. They did not discuss the war, or speculate what had happened out there, once New Finland was no longer reported in the news as a new Guardian province. Something had happened. Something had gone wrong for the Guards—and the Guards were suddenly busy with complex preparations for some new effort. That much was clear from the rumors that drifted down from the newly busy G.O.S Ariadne. Both of them were burning with curiosity. But they could not, would not talk about it in front of each other.

"So," Lucy said. "Making out the next report?"

"Yup. The top brass still want us to hand them a perfect auto-translator instantly, and can't believe we can't just pull it down from the shelf. I'm sticking my neck out to explain why it can't be done in slightly firmer and less oblique language this time."

"Damn bureaucrats. Yours are the same as ours."

Gustav grunted and said nothing. Lucy was still like that, probably always would be. She could not or would not identify herself as a Guardian. Even wrapped in all the excitement and challenge of this wonderful chance find, even granted all the privileges and freedom she needed to do the job the Guardians wanted of her, she refused to forget she was a prisoner.

It made things tough for Gustav, because it threw both their motives into question. He knew himself to be just as much a prisoner of the Central Guardians and their endless, desperate ambition. He knew things back on Capital could only be getting worse, with the war news as bad as it was. When, as he frequently did, he asked himself why Lucy went on, he was forced to ask at the same time why he himself went on.

Because it's an incredible opportunity, not to be refused. Because the dream of meeting the Alien is what makes kids join the navy in the first place. Because we're doing it for our species, not for whatever grubby party goons are living in Capital Palace at the moment. Because to say no would be suicide. Because someone else would do it for them anyway, if not as well. . . . And from there on down the reasons got less convincing, more uncomfortable. Though Gustav couldn't answer why he went on, he thought that Calder might be able to. Which meant there was a limit to how far he could trust her. Gustav didn't like that, because Calder had become what no Intelligence officer could afford, even an ex-Intelligence officer: a friend in the enemy ranks.

Gustav broke the silence at last with some comment about his report. They chatted about the routine affairs of the camps, and the progress of various language trainees, and the need to shut down the overflights that damn fool Romero insisted on making. At last they found themselves, as always, coming back to the central and endlessly exciting topic: the Outposters.

"I like them, C'astille especially," Calder said. "Using that damn language is like trying to wrestle wet noodles, but she and I can communicate, and either I'm getting better or she's learning to explain better."

"What does the language itself tell you?" Gustav asked. "I mean about the 'Posters?"

Calder just shrugged. "I'm no xeno-psychiatrist. I'm not an ethnologist, or even a real linguist. The two glaring differences are the sound structure and the bias toward making passive statements. You've seen my translations. They are awkward because O-1 is clumsy for statements of action. English is clumsy for passive statements. Where we'd say 'she came through the door,' they might say—" Lucy shifted to the local tongue and said a few words. "Now that can be translated to English as 'The door was at the location passed through by the person,' and that's a mess. But the *way* of stating that very passive concept is very direct and succinct in O-1. The verb form is all one word with the proper prefix and suffix and intonation to give just that meaning. To state it in the typically very active voice used in English or most human tongues is very close to impossible."

"And you don't think that says anything about our local friends?"

"It does, I'm sure of it, but I simply don't know *what* it says. It would be real easy to hand out some guff about their being 'at one with their world' and not divided out from it. Some of the kids back home make that distinction between the aborigines and the Europeans. Mom's the aborigine and Dad's the Brit—they *both* laughed at that one. I have the distinct feeling the Outposters manipulate their environment for their own convenience just as much as we do. But their needs and methods are both different from ours."

"That's a long winded way of saying 'I don't know.' "

Lucy Calder grinned. "Or, to translate from O-1, 'The absence of knowledge is retained in my mind.' "

"Oh, shut up," Gustav said. "Let's get some dinner."

Chapter Six

April, 2116
The Planet Bandwidth

With a moody, methodical air to his actions, as if he had been planning it a long time, Commander Randall Metcalf, United States Navy, pulled the bartender's head off.

George Prigot shifted uncomfortably on the next stool and looked around nervously. "Randall, I don't think that's allowed."

Metcalf ignored his friend and carefully set the head down on the counter. It resembled an oversized doll's head, with slightly glazed eyes, waxenly pink skin, and slightly over-perfect rosy cheeks. The handlebar moustache looked as if it had been stamped out by a machine—as indeed it had.

"I have been," Metcalf said, pulling out a small tool set, "stuck on this automated hell-hole for over six thousand hours. I have had my hair cut and my food cooked and my pants pressed and my pizza delivered by robots. I have been given exactly accurate directions to and fro by robot cops." Metcalf pulled the wig off the bartender's head, found an inspection plate, and began unscrewing screws. "I have been asked how long I will be gone by parking meters. I have been spoken to by doors, walls, taxis, airplanes, showers, clocks, and elevators, all warning me to use care, not to be late, not to forget, to be sure and look both ways before crossing."

Metcalf pried the plate off and peered inside. "I have spent whole days engaged in conversation, without once talking to a human being. Every time I make a purchase my receipt tells me my remaining balance, to four utterly meaningless decimal places, not only in the U.S. dollars paid into the account by the Navy, but in Bandwidth CashUnits and six other major currencies, based on the exchange rates as of a millisecond before. Every morning and night the damned mirror in the head in my hotel room reminds me to brush my teeth." Metcalf selected a set of wire cutters. "I," he said, snipping the leads to the speaker behind the bartender's smiling mouth, "have *had* it with all the nag, nag, nag, nag, nag."

"I dunno," Prigot said, still a little nervous, trying to soothe his friend. "I kinda like it. Attentive service, everything works."

"You, old pal, are an engineer. The damn robots don't bother you. You *like* machines—but would you want your sister to marry one? That's the only damn thing they haven't automated here—so far."

"I don't have a sister."

Metcalf looked up from his work to stare pityingly at Prigot. "Then, to paraphrase the immortal Marx, she's a very lucky woman. You don't get the point, do you? At least here, in the bar we come to every day, I want a machine that will shut up and just pour the booze and leave me alone."

"Ten C.U. says the maintenance machines have it repaired before you can order your next drink," Prigot said.

"You're on. Because I have also just cut the maintenance request caller inside this gizmo's head." Metcalf closed up the inspection panel, replaced the wig, stood to reach over the counter top, and shoved the head back down on the bartender's neck-pivot.

The bartender's body twitched once as the head's circuits linked back up with it. The head swiveled through 360 degrees, then the eyes seem to lock and track. The bartender turned, and its arm came up to shake a finger at Metcalf. A deep bass voice rumbled up from its chest. "Pppllllleazse uzzze cayrrre inn future, sir," it said, its voice needing a moment to get up to speed. "If not for the back-up speaker in my body cavity, I could not now talk to you, and thus could not serve you properly."

Prigot roared with laughter as Metcalf glared at the robot. "Tomorrow," Metcalf said. "Tomorrow I come in here with a shaped thermite charge and melt you down. Now go get me a double scotch."

"Draught for me," Prigot said cheerfully. "On your tab. Gotta start spending those ten C.U."

"Thank you. I will get your orders, sirs." The robot rolled down to the other end of the bar.

"Damn it, George." Metcalf stared into the mirror behind the bar. "Damn it, George. *Nothing's* going right."

The robot delivered their drinks. Prigot reached out a graceful, long-fingered hand and took up his tankard. "That's another thing I like about Bandwidth," he said. "You got a really good-sized beer here." Prigot carefully sucked some of the foam of the head, caught Metcalf's eye in the mirror behind the bar, and grinned as he raised his glass to him.

George Prigot was the shorter, chubbier, more relaxed of the two. His brown hair had been bleached almost to blonde by Bandwidth's sun, and he had put on a kilo or two. He had grown a beard, too. It was an improvement, and gave his face a maturer look, hiding the almost childlike delight that lit up his face whenever something interesting happened. He wore a rumpled old coverall covered with pockets and zippers and velcro. He seemed relaxed, comfortable. "Come on, Randall. It's not that rough."

Metcalf hadn't fit into Bandwidth as well as Prigot, to say the least. He had the air of a man forced to hurry up and wait, who needed to check the time every three minutes. He was tall, skinny, pale-skinned, with black hair and bushy black eyebrows. His fingers drummed on the counter top, and he leaned his bar stool back on two legs, threatening to overbalance and crash to the floor. He wore his undress tropical khaki uniform, with a line of ribbons over his breast pocket that would have deeply impressed anyone who knew what they all meant. "I take it you haven't heard the latest, then," Metcalf said. "I got it through the Navy scuttlebutt. I doubt it'll hit the news services for a day or two. They convicted Mac."

"My God."

"Busted him back to lieutenant commander, confined him to base at Columbia at the Survey Service training center. He's going to be a prisoner and an instructor there at the same time. *He* suggested the sentence *himself*, of course, as the best way he could still serve the war effort while doing his time."

"But why did they do it?"

"We've been through this. Because Mac said they could blow the *Eagle* the way we took out *Leviathan*."

"I know what the charges were. I just can't believe they'd really do it."

"That's something you've got to learn, George. You want to think we're all angels in white at this end. Well, you keep telling me there are decent people among the Guardians, and I believe you, because you're one of them. Here's proof that we've got some flaming bastards on our side."

George Prigot grunted and sipped at his beer. Suddenly his good cheer was gone.

George was a Guardian, born and bred on Capital. He had met Mac Larson on New Finland, become his friend, fought at Mac's side, against his own people, when the brutality of the Guards became too much for his conscience. Randall liked George, and knew how much George *needed* to believe in the rightness of his choice. That made it difficult for him to accept that League people could pull a rotten stunt like throwing the book at Mac. Illusions died hard with George.

Metcalf sipped at his scotch. He had been on New Finland too, had earned his Distinguished Flying Cross there. He knew Mac, could very easily understand George's loyalty to the man—because he felt it himself. Mac had saved them. The League forces and the Finns had wanted to curl up and die then, but Mac—Mac had found the way to pull them all together, had found the reserves of courage and hope that hadn't even been there before Mac went looking for them.

Without Mac, they'd both be either dead or Guardian prisoners right now. Metcalf felt a strong urge to *do* something about Mac, help him in some way. But there was nothing he *could* do. Except maybe fight the war. And there was no war to fight—and wouldn't be until the bright boys found Capital.

Supposedly, George and he had been shipped to on Bandwidth for reasons that had something to do with the search for Capital. No one had quite known what to do with George after New Finland, and Metcalf half suspected *that* had much to do with why the two of them had found themselves on Bandwidth.

The whole thing was a military jury-rig. Certainly there was value in questioning prisoners, and there were any number of Intelligence officers from across the League right here on Bandwidth, very happily doing just that. Whatever prisoners of war from New Finland that could be pried loose from the Finns were here. But there hadn't been many prisoners to start with, and the Finns, as the party most aggrieved by the Guards, were reluctant to give many up. But here the available P.O.W.s were. And so George was here. Perhaps there was even value in having George around as a tame expert, catching the P.O.W.s in lies and suggesting questions that might be asked of them.

It might even make sense to have Metcalf there because he had experience of Guard battle tactics and might have something to contribute. Metcalf rather suspected he was really there because there wasn't much call for fighter pilots at the moment and because the higher-ups wanted some around who could keep Prigot company—and keep an eye on him. George, after all, was a turncoat, and he might turn again. . . .

However, George Prigot didn't seem to need much watching, though he was glad of Metcalf's company, and glad to have a familiar face around. But there wasn't much for Metcalf and him to *do*.

Metcalf took a long pull at his drink. They had been cooling their heels, with little to contribute, for close to ten months now. The war had dragged to a halt for lack of an enemy to fight.

And all they had to work with were the prisoners, and the prisoners didn't talk much. When they did talk, it turned out they didn't know much. The Intelligence officers didn't seem to mind. As far as Metcalf could see, most of them saw interrogating the prisoners as a career choice with good job security rather than as a temporary assignment. They went gaily on, asking the same things again and again, charting responses, correlating results, writing summaries of evidence that were longer than the evidence itself. Metcalf could almost sympathize with the Intelligence team. These were the only enemy troops they were going to get their hands on for the foreseeable future, and they were going to milk the chance for all it was worth.

But all that to one side, there was no progress whatsoever on the central question: *Where is Capital?*

The Guardian leadership, very wisely as things turned out, had practically made astronomy a state secret. None of the prisoners had ever seen a star chart. None of them even knew there were grid reference systems to locate stars relative to each other. None of them knew that stars *were* differing sizes and colors. It made asking where their sun was, or what mass and spectral class it was, a stunningly futile undertaking.

As Metcalf was fond of pointing out, rarely had so few who knew so little been asked so much by so many for so long. When he said that to George, George replied, "So what?"

Metcalf didn't have an answer for that. He signaled the damned robot over to order another double scotch.

Chapter Seven

Chralray Village, the Current Nihilist Camp
The Planet Outpost

D'eltipa had a great desire to be found anywhere but where she was. But it was this village, that they had tarried in for far too long, and this hall, and this time, and she had no choice but to meet with her First Advice, Nihilist M'etallis. D'eltipa found irony in M'etallis' title. As Primary Guidance of the Nihilists, she had never accepted a syllable of M'etallis' advice. And now M'etallis would succeed her. M'etallis would be the one to deal with the halfwalkers.

The aliens, strange as they were, strange as they had to be, represented so much change and renewal to come—they were hope itself—and yet they could not have brought their remarkable flying-carrying machines down out of the sky at a worse time. Even without the halfwalkers, the situation would be explosive.

And the halfwalkers, weird creatures that they were, represented infinite complication. No one had made sense of them yet. The aliens seemed to have no desire to *go* anywhere. And they did things in such strange ways. D'eltipa found herself forced to believe the reports of the learners, but she still found it fantastic that such a complex thing as a spacecraft was *built* and not grown.

Perhaps, the learners suggested, it was actually impossible to grow one, or grow the parts of one to be assembled. Something about stresses and pressure and heat. The halfwalkers could build those things and yet seemed to have no skill of biology at all. Strange indeed.

She felt her mind straying, and almost allowed it down the side path. But the *humans*, as they called themselves, were not the central problem, though M'etallis no doubt had schemes already that involved them. M'etallis herself was the problem, a problem just waiting to happen. No, that was too gentle. M'etallis was a disaster, *impatient* to happen. And D'eltipa could see no way that would keep M'etallis from the post of Primary Guidance.

D'eltipa had even given up her hopes for a splitting of the path, of disciples of *her* Guidance being there to start anew down the correct course after she was a suicide or had been Divided from her people. And that time would be soon. She understood fully that she should have surrendered Guidance and taken her own life long ago, but she had remained, desperately hoping for some other inheritor than M'etallis. But D'eltipa's nearest followers were all dead, suicides, the kindly, dignified, death Nihilism had been founded to grant. And D'eltipa hung on, past all hope, until it was too late, until she herself felt the coming of Division. And, for the founder of the Nihilists, that was an irony far too cruel.

M'etallis! Nihilism would be so perverted under her that it should not be called by that name. Murderism, or Annihilationism, perhaps. But there would be no peaceful endings, no aid for the fearful under the next Primary Guidance. The upstart was not interested in easing the way out of life. She looked only for power. And soon she would have it.

That last point was one of the few on which M'etallis would have agreed with her Primary Guidance. The old fool was headed straight for Division—and undoubtably knew it. M'etallis felt a sudden acute shock of her chronic impatience. All the cantering about in circles, all the subtle—and unsubtle—suggestions to certain Nihilists that their proper time to die had come, all the agreements formed and broken, all the efforts meant to put her in her present place, all of it was at last to pay off.

M'etallis was certain to take control. She would at last be able to set about turning this absurd little sect into something worthwhile. And now D'eltipa courted the final humiliation, for no other possible purpose than to hold things back from their inevitable resolution.

M'etallis blew an angry snort through her blowhole at the thought. All the time that had been wasted! Why couldn't the old spread their wings and give over to the young without all this interference?

M'etallis paced back and forth down the long, low halls of Chralray's Second House. It was almost time to go and meet with D'eltipa at Guidance Hall. But wait. Delay a moment. Let D'eltipa fidget a while too. Time was on M'etallis's side, and it might as well be used.

She trotted out to the south windows, that looked toward the meadow and the halfwalker's camp. Plain old bad luck that it had taken so long to clear the vermin out of the area when the humans first arrived. The humans had very prudently stayed in their carrier—*ship* was one word for it, and *lander* another—until their hosts could wipe out the more energetic—and hungry—animal life. Hunters and beaters still worked endlessly to keep the perimeter clear. M'etallis wondered if the halfwalkers appreciated the trouble it took to keep such a large clearing safe. Perhaps they did. The humans seemed to be making a very permanent job of that camp. They remained, and built as if they intended to stay forever. There was no sign of their looking toward the Road—but then the Roads they traveled across the sky must be long enough indeed.

M'etallis stamped her left forefoot. *She* could do with a bit of travel now. The Nihilists had stayed too long in this place. Time to strike camp, time to find an empty village or build a new one for the next season. She couldn't remember any Group spending this long in one village. Chralray might even spring up into a permanent city, fate forbid.

But the aliens were too great a chance to pass by. It had been M'etallis herself who had heard third-hand from a sojourner that some big metal shape had come down from the sky and come to rest near Chralray, stayed a bit, and then left with a great noise, that some odd creatures had been seen around it. That was why M'etallis had chosen Chralray Village for the season. M'etallis was not one to let new things slip by.

But now it was well past time for the meeting with D'eltipa. The skin around M'etallis' eyes crinkled in the Z'ensam equivalent of a gleeful smile, and she galloped off toward Guidance Hall.

The Z'ensam were the descendants of migratory herd animals, and like most migrators, were not a territorial species. The concepts of personal property, and money, and trade certainly existed among them, but did not hold anywhere near the emotional importance they did for humans. They were important only insofar as they helped to establish rank, a pecking order.

Their property was generally portable, for the very good reason that it had to be. The Road would call, the eyes would yearn for new vistas, and it would be time to move. It took the strongest discipline and the most compelling of reasons to keep the Z'ensam in one place for long. But the halfwalkers seemed prepared to stay where they were indefinitely, and *that* qualified as a compelling reason.

To the Z'ensam it was natural to abandon a village and move the Group to a new site—either an existing village some other Group had abandoned, or a virgin site where a new village would be grown. Indeed, the villages were more for the sake of protecting property from the weather and keeping Groups organized than they were for the comfort of individuals. The Z'ensam evolved in a fairly harsh temperate zone. They were therefore better adapted than humans to extremes of cold and heat and rough weather, and tended to bother far less with heating and cooling.

M'etallis walked straight into Guidance Hall without a knock, a pause, or the slightest formality. A great deal of human etiquette and ceremony and law deals with the circumstances under which one can and cannot or must or must not admit or deny another to one's home territory, but such questions simply did not enter into any Z'ensam society.

A human second-in-command, especially a rebellious one, would have been stopped by an underling and announced, delayed, be made to wait, perhaps even led through guards and fortifications—symbolic or functional—before arriving in the presence of the Leader. If such things had been absent in a human meeting, there would have been a great show *made* of their absence, a demonstration that the visitor was welcome and trusted in the Leader's territory.

But the Z'ensam lacked the trappings of the territorial imperative, along with the imperative itself. M'etallis simply trotted through the doorway of the Guidance's hall and wandered about until she found D'eltipa impatiently pacing down one of the corridors.

The older Z'ensam pulled herself up short and glared at her subordinate. At which moment M'etallis had to physically restrain herself from rushing outside to gallop around the building and crow with delight.

D'eltipa actually had a long red *welt* down the length of her back! She was already *in* the first stages of Division. She was practically ready to keel over then and there! M'etallis held her emotions in check and contented herself with a merry flick of her tail.

"Your presence is sensed, Primary Guidance," M'etallis said, in what she hoped was a calm and neutral voice.

"And yours, First Advice. Nothing can be hidden at this point, I know my condition as well as you. You need treat me with the dignity due to wisdom only a little while longer. But I still have time for talk. Come, let us be found in the garden."

"As your Guidance is pleased," M'etallis said. The garden was surrounded by a low wall. They would be unseen there—and that was just as well; D'eltipa's appearance was not suited to being seen in public. M'etallis was surprised to find herself concerned that the Guidance not be humiliated. She twitched her tail, and realized she still had feelings for her old teacher. She felt a sudden twinge of guilt that she had driven D'eltipa to the extremity of accepting Division. But the change must come. New thoughts must lead Nihilism, and D'eltipa of all Nihilists must accept that each person choose her own mind's way out of the world. But it was sad that things had reached such a crossroads.

M'etallis could not admit it herself, but she was unnerved to find principle, and tenderness, and regret at unfortunate necessity, still to be found in her soul. She had sought power so long that she had almost convinced herself that power was all she cared for. Perhaps one day it would be. She would by no means be the first seduced away from a goal by the means of achieving it.

The older Nihilist led the way into the garden. It was a lovely spring day. "So, M'etallis, soon you shall be called by a different name. Are you practiced, so you will answer when someone calls for D'etallis?"

M'etallis choose not to respond to such needling. "Not as such, but I have trust that my new name will be familiar to me."

"Yes, you are practiced, then. And you have been ready for a long time, as well. But you are not called here for teasing, but for schooling, and warning. This has been said before, but hear it again: Change is like any tool; not good, or bad, but only a thing which can be suited to many purposes. Use it, but wisely. I fear you will not."

"Guidance. Let us not have platitudes or wasted time and words. Years ago, when I ended my sojourn at your side, you left with me the knowledge that the curse of our people was in knowing their fate. All other living things, plant and animal, wild-evolved or guided and bred by us down a path of our choosing, did not know of their doom. Even the animals whose life cycle parallels our own do not experience the loss we do. Only our kind, the Z'ensam, have ever known the pride of having a full name—and so only our kind are haunted by the fear of losing it—"

"Gallop on, say it. I know my fate. Losing it to be Divided out from thought and knowledge. But you have taken that teaching to extremes, leaving it perverted. I had only the goal of aiding those who so wished a chance to pass from life painlessly, with mind intact, still bearing a full name.

But each must choose for herself. You would have us *all* swept away. Can you not see the paradox you find drawn around yourself? You have used the power of your own mind to reach the conclusion that sentience—the power of mind—is an abomination! You seek the extinction of your own people."

"I seek the perfection of nature," M'etallis said primly. "All life is beautiful. Death is ugly. Therefore the *knowledge* of death is ugly. And, that knowledge of our own doom is ours alone. The heritage of all other living things is to grow and live and prosper and multiply—until death, unknown, unseen, unlooked for, takes one life to replace it with another. A flower, a bug, a cartbeast, have no realization that they will die, and so for them the ugliness of death does not exist. The heritage of all the Z'ensam is a grim and terrible choice: to move toward an early death, or to let the cycle of life debase us—" M'etallis drew up short. "Guidance, pardon. The heat of my feeling, I did not recall your circumstance. . . ."

"I find relief that you can still feel embarrassment. There is kindness still in your soul. But it only strengthens my question: You seek the *power*, the capacity, that could destroy us all: but would you set it to use? Would you truly be the causative center in the extinction of your own kind?"

"What is the better alternative? We are trapped. We might go on and on, yes—but to what end? What goal? That the unborn generations can grow to find the ugliness of Death or Division to snatch at them? I would have the melancholy of the Z'ensam over and done, not drawn out over endless generations. And, Guidance, I must add a further point. New events have brought new insight to me. My goal widens with its opportunity. It is not my own kind I would be the cause of destroying. It is *mind* that perverts nature and life with the knowledge of death and the end of things. It is *mind* that should be removed, mind wherever it is, wherever it comes from, mind that should be made gone by any means possible.

"You call me cruel, cynical, jaded already. Therefore what

I say next will merely seem in character. It will require power to wipe out the Z'ensam, and we cannot get power by killing those we would have power over. A grand paradox. But now we are presented with a far easier, far more palatable way to kill our way into great power."

D'eltipa looked at her successor in stunned silence. There was a dull, rumbling roar from the meadow. Both of them turned to watch the human's lander rise into the grey, roiling cloud of the perfect spring sky.

Chapter Eight

Guardian Contact Base
The Planet Outpost

Captain Lewis Romero was a dangerous man with an idea, in the way an unskilled pilot was dangerous with a spacecraft. Only a bad pilot would head out without a good idea of what his ship could do. Romero hadn't thought his idea out past the end of his nose.

Romero was also ambitious. Ariadne station was a busy place these days—new battle fleets were forming and training, and they made much use of the station's communications and supply capabilities. Ariadne was also charged with supplying the contact base on Outpost and handling the scientists' ever-growing demand for communications and information. Romero's command was doing useful work, his people were accomplishing things—but it wasn't enough.

Romero had finally come to the realization that he had made a serious tactical error sending Gustav down here. He had known from the start that the Outposters were more than just of interest to the scientists, that they were a golden opportunity for career advancement. But it was *Gustav's* career they were advancing.

Well, Lewis Romero had been a good little sailor long enough. None of the excitement going past was doing him any good, and it was time to change all that.

That was why he had come down to Outpost. Ostensibly, it was a courtesy call, a chance for Romero to see after the supply situation, make sure that all was going well, a chance to listen for complaints or suggestions. All that would do as an excuse. Romero had to admit to himself that Gustav seemed to have things well in hand. The camp was in excellent condition, clean, well laid-out, and the enlisted men, officers, and civilians all seemed quite satisfied with the physical conditions they worked under. Romero strolled the camp, watching humans and Outposters working together. He had never seen a native in the flesh before; they seemed quite surprisingly large. Romero was upset to see everything working smoothly, good progress being made everywhere.

Damn! He should *never* have let Gustav take command of the contact base—though with Gustav's Intelligence background and the shortage of personnel, there had been very few other choices, and there was no way Romero could have relinquished his command of Ariadne to do the job himself.

More galling still was the way Romero's job on Ariadne was suddenly so much more difficult with Gustav gone. Officially, Gustav was still the station's executive officer, on detached duty, so Romero couldn't put in for a replacement XO. The personnel shortage again. But there was so much *work* to do with Gustav gone! And he, Romero, had handed him a prize like First Contact! *He'd* be promoted, *he'd* be in the history books, and Romero would be stuck on Ariadne for 20 years! Jealousy was not an emotion unknown to Lewis Romero.

Romero needed to talk directly with the Outposters to get his plan started. He needed *all* the credit. If Gustav got his nose into it, no one would ever notice Romero at all. So Romero had fussed and fumed and waited until the computerized auto-translators were ready. He had been one of the main sources of pressure for getting them done—though he had been very back-room about it all, very careful to see to it that no one realized *he* was eager. He had never personally urged the techs to finish fast, but had gotten others to do that for him. If the Outposters were the biological geniuses everyone claimed, Romero knew he was a made man.

But how to get in touch with the Outposter leaders? Romero had worried over that point for endless hours, and had never come up with anything better that stopping the first native he saw and handing out that centuries-old saw, "Take me to your leader."

Which is exactly what he did with the next 'Poster that went past, and the black box of the auto-translator blatted and hooted out his meaning in O-1.

C'astille, the native most used to humans and their ways, was still greatly confused by the human who had come to her and asked to see her leader.

The humans said they had grown to but little knowledge of the Outposter social structure, but the Outposters had had just as little success understanding human rules for living. But both sides had tried, and Lucy Calder had explained military ranks and insignia as best she could, even using a wall chart to show which was higher and lower.

The insignia this human had painted on her pressure suit denoted a higher rank than any a Z'ensam had ever seen. Perhaps *this* one should be addressed in the senior mode. C'astille decided to play it safe and use the D' prefix.

She could tell this human was new here: the auto-translator could barely make sense of the human's words. It took a while for the halfwalkers to understand the limitations of the device they had built themselves.

A new human, and one of high rank. Only after she had considered all that did she think on the actual request the human had made. Certainly if this was a human Guidance, come at last, M'etallis—no, *D'*etallis now that Eltipa had divided and no longer had a full name—D'etallis would want to see her. C'astille decided she had best cooperate.

"Our Primary Guidance, D'etallis, would be honored," she said. She spoke in careful Australian-accented English, startling Romero. "I feel certain that she would wish to know you. May I have knowledge of your name?"

"Romero. Captain Lewis Romero," he said.

"Honored D'Romero," C'astille said, "you shall soon be with D'etallis. The Talking House is unused at present. If you would accept waiting there, I would bring D'etallis, and thus both sides could talk in comfort."

"That would be good."

"Then D'etallis shall soon be there. The two of you shall sense each other soon." C'astille nodded her head to the human and hurried off to find the Guidance.

Lewis Romero's heart hammered in his chest as he watched the Outposter heading off into the brush. It shouldn't have been that easy, but he wasn't going to argue. The first hurdle was cleared. Maybe his idea would actually work.

D'etallis was delighted with the news that a senior human was eager to get right down to talking. The Z'ensam had been impatiently waiting for something of substance from their visitors. Chains of command, orders from above, the inertia imposed by a large organization, the delays of distance; to D'etallis, all these strange concepts were mere excuses, stalling tactics. Now, finally, it seemed, the humans had sent someone who could do more than hold language lessons. Finally, someone in charge was here. Maybe this D'Romero wouldn't have to wait for orders from above—a concept the Z'ensam were just barely beginning to understand—before he *did* anything. Leader to leader, directly, immediately, that was the way the Z'ensam did things.

Now maybe they would get somewhere. She hurried to the Talking House and found this D'Romero in the boxy transparent room that held the human air, folded up in their strange way into that support thing they called a chair.

Romero saw the Outposter approach and stood up. Unsure of the required etiquette, he offered a slight bow. The Outposter nodded its head back at him.

"D'Romero," it said. I am D'etallis, Primary Guidance of this Group. Your presence is sensed."

"And yours as well." *That* much etiquette he had learned, anyway. "I come to ask questions, and perhaps to offer trade."

"Good. There are items you make that we would have."

"And the reverse might well be true. There are things you *might* be able to make that we would have."

"I have no understanding."

"Let me see if I can explain. I have put several things on the table on your side of the pressure wall." Romero pointed to the table. There was a swatch of material from a League pressure suit, a section of plastic bulkhead cut from the *Venera*, some samples of League electronic equipment, a few other things.

D'etallis turned and looked. "I sense them."

"Good. Now then. Here is my question. I am told that your people are very wise in the life-sciences. That you can cause living things to breed and grow as you desire."

"Certainly."

"Very good. Now then. Can your scientists create living things that can eat any or all of those materials, live on them, breed and grow very quickly?"

D'etallis went over to the table and barely glanced at the things on it. It picked up the suit and set it down almost at once. "Absolutely. They could be bred in a few weeks at the most. Eaters are used to dispose of unwanted things already. Simple modifications of these beasts would suit your need."

"Wonderful!"

"We would want things in return."

"Of course." Romero waited for it. If they wanted something he couldn't promise. . . .

"But let me understand clearly before you hear my bargain. I have toured one of your *landers*"—D'etallis used the English word—"and I have seen of what they are made. I am told that you have much larger vehicles, *starships*, that are so big they cannot leave space to land. All these pieces you show me seem to be from a lander or a starship. If properly bred Eaters were let loose on a starship made of such materials, they would wreck it in days, perhaps hours."

Romero hesitated. "Yes, that is true."

D'etallis flicked its tail. "You seek living weapons, then.

You seek such simple things because you humans know all but nothing about life-science, and your enemies, familiar with your other ways of fighting, would have no defense against such things."

Romero found himself in a cold sweat, but he could see nothing to be gained by lying. This D'etallis saw the whole thing. "You are correct."

D'etallis' face wrinkled in an expression that Romero was told indicated pleasure. "I face a similar problem, halfwalker.

I want *your* weapons. I have seen the ones your people carry, and I am sure our comparable devices are crude and powerless in comparison."

Romero almost fainted with relief. He was going to pull it off! His future was assured. Now all they needed to work on were the details. He ran a supply depot. Weapons he could supply until he had enough bioweapons to show the brass—and once they saw bioweapons wrecking a ship, they would back him all the way.

"I am sure then, that we can come to a very favorable agreement," he said.

The two leaders, human and Outposter, Z'ensam and halfwalker, talked for a long time, and then departed, each eager to move the bargain forward.

And Lucille Calder didn't discover that she had left the Crystal Palace's voice-activated recording system on all night until she ran the tape next morning.

Chapter Nine

Guardian Contact Base
The Planet Outpost

Lucille Calder was sitting in Gustav's office when he arrived the next morning, her face strained, her skin pale. He had never seen her as tense, as frightened.

Without any preamble, she rose and spoke as soon as he was in the door. "Johnson, I'm about to take a terrible risk. And I might be putting you in terrible danger. It might even be treason. I don't know. But I don't see any choice. You're the only person I can trust. The only one who might be able to do something about it," she said, holding up a recording tape. "You've got to listen to this. I left the Crystal Palace voice-activated recorder on by accident overnight, and—and it picked something up."

Johnson Gustav didn't know how to react. He was having an increasingly hard time knowing how to deal with Lucy. Technically, he was the officer in charge of this CI, the warden of her prison, or to put it in less prettied-up terms, her slave master. But he was also her partner in an exciting piece of research, her chief scrounger in the constant fight for equipment, the assistant coordinator of all the projects she was involved in. And whatever had brought her here this morning didn't seem likely to simplify matters. He sighed and asked, "What's going on, Luce?"

"Something that could make the war worse. Spread it to the Outposters. Johnson, I know you and I never discuss the war, or politics. But I know neither of us wants the killing to spread. And it might, and I need to talk to you, and you have to listen to this goddamned recording!"

The Guardian ex-Intelligence officer looked over the Conscripted Immigrant. It was hard, even impossible, to think in those terms about Lucy. He looked again, harder. There was barely-controlled fear, even horror, in her face. Whatever this was, it was bad. And he was her friend. That much he knew, whatever the rules told him. "Okay, so I'll listen to it. You aren't the sort who'd put both of us at risk for no reason. I'll trust you."

"Thank you, Johnson. I hope you don't regret it." She pulled a portable recorder out of her equipment bag.

Gustav went through the motions of filling the coffee pot and getting a pot started as Lucille fussed with the recorder, finding the right spot on the recording. Finally she found what she was after and let the playback roll. Gustav froze when he heard Romero's voice. He turned away from the coffee machine and looked at Lucy. He wanted to tell her to stop, to go no further, not to draw him in. But then he saw the look on her face, and knew that he could not do that.

He sat down behind his desk, and listened carefully, the color draining from his face. When the playback was over, and Lucy hit the stop button, he shook his head and spoke in a whisper. "No wonder he wanted to make this damn fool inspection trip. Jesus Christ, Romero. You idiot. You stupid, stupid idiot."

"Johnson," Lucy said, her voice quivering on the edge of hysteria, "*those bioweapons are to be pointed at my people.* If Romero's idea works, I'll have helped kill them! I can't go on with my work here and tell myself that learning to talk to the Outposters is for all humanity if the result is a fool like Romero and an alien megalomaniac sitting around planning massacres!"

She stopped, breathed in and out deeply for a moment, making a visible attempt to regain control of herself. She straightened her back and looked at Gustav, straight in the eye. "Lieutenant Gustav, on your honor—*tell me the truth*: Was Romero speaking for himself, or was the deal he offered Guardian policy? If the bloody Central Guardians are behind that horrible plan, *you have to tell me.*"

Gustav felt sick inside. The last of his faith was gone.

The whole thing was rotten. He could give her a precisely truthful answer, but he knew the scuttlebutt, he knew what had been going on, he knew what manner of men had survived the purges and the shake-ups. And he knew how they would respond to Romero.

He shut his eyes, cradled his face in his hands. "It is not Guardian policy," he said, his voice muffled by his hands. "Not yet. But it will be. You and I never talk politics, but I guess it's time to start. It's time to say what I know.

"The bloody stupid bastards were wiped out on New Finland. The invasion failed. *No one* made it back. And every source we've got says the League is out looking for us in force. They know we exist now, and they're scared of us. That changes *everything*. They know we're out here, they know we've killed a lot of people, and everything they've got will be put into finding us. It means they *will* find us. Our leaders have finally admitted that to themselves, and they're in a panic."

He paused for a long moment, and then went on in a bitter, angry voice. "And our courageous, idiotic Leader of the Combined Will, General Jules Jaquet, who got us into this mess, also got himself into some very big trouble. There was a quiet little coup attempt and he just barely hung onto power. Now he's got to show he's tough and capable and ready to fight the defensive war he's forced on us, or else he's out on his ass. And the people he has to impress, the admirals and the generals and the pols, are brutal, crude. Barbarians. Jaquet and his crowd shot all the decent men still in the government, or threw them in jail. Most of the better ones resigned long ago."

"But what happens now?" Lucy asked.

"Romero's probably already en route to Capital. He'll talk up the idea of bioweapons at anyone who'll listen, and the brass are desperate enough that they *will* listen. Jaquet will *love* the idea. There is no way we can stop them. They have the auto-translators, and people who know O-1. The situation is completely out of our control. Oh, I could hand you some piece of nonsense that maybe the government wouldn't stoop that low, but the Centrals are scared silly, they'll try anything." Gustav suddenly slammed his fist down onto the desk. "The stupid, stupid, *fools!* We have no idea about these Outposters, what they are, what they think, what they want—and the higher-ups want to give them lessons in how to kill humans and wreck ships!"

Lucy stared at him. She knew, and Gustav knew, that he had just crossed a point of no return. He should have had her arrested for spying, had her confined already, the recording destroyed. "Thank you for telling the truth, Johnson. And thank you for having the decency to be horrified."

"I wish I wasn't so easy to horrify," Gustav growled. "I'd sleep better. But wait a second—is there any hope on the other end? Is there any chance that the *Outposters* can't do it? That they can't deliver?"

Lucy thought hard for a moment and shrugged. She felt very tired. "I don't know, and I don't think any of your technicians or scientists could answer that—"

"And even if the techs could tell me, I couldn't risk asking them. Loyal Guardians all, no Settlers here, thank you. Besides me, I suppose."

"What's a Settler?"

"People back home on Capital who want to plant some crops there instead of trying to conquer the universe. Not important now. But the point is we can't ask the techs."

"I trust C'astille," Lucy said suddenly, firmly.

"How? Why? Isn't she one of these Nihilists or whatever that religion of D'etallis' is?"

"It's not a religion, or a philosophy. And C'astille isn't one of them. She's a sojourner."

"Say again?"

"A sojourner," Lucy said. "I don't quite understand it all myself, so I can't explain it very well. Nihilism is a Group, and a Group is sort of a small nation, or sub-nation, except territory isn't involved, and I have no clear ideas about what the supernation is that oversees it all."

"Go on," Gustav said.

"Anyway," Lucy said, "let's say you didn't like your Group, that you didn't agree with the ideas the Group shared. You'd leave and get on the road and find another Group. Easy to do.

"They have excellent roads, and communications are good. You know they have radio, and the equivalents of books and maps. If you find a Group you agree with, you can drift into it as it travels the road.

"If you disagree, you vote with your feet again and find some other Group, until you're traveling with a crowd that thinks the way you do. And they certainly travel. All the phrases and sayings about roads and journeys show how important movement is to them. It's very unusual for Outposters to stay in one place as long as they have here, incidentally; we're *important* to them. And since the Nihilists have *us*, that makes the Nihilists important, and they've attracted a lot of new members who are curious about us. And lost a few who just got restless and hit the road again."

"But you were explaining why you could trust C'astille," Gustav said.

"Right, I'm getting there, but it takes so much background. I know it seems silly for me to give you a lecture on Outposter society at a time like this, but you have to *understand*. More or less in what corresponds to late adolescence, a young Outposter is expected to wander off from his Group and spend time traveling with other Groups. Sort of exchange students, I suppose. A wanderjahr. They aren't expected to join the other Groups, though they can if they wish. Usually you finish your sojourn and go find your birth-Group.

"C'astille speaks of her Group, which is north of here at the moment, as if she still wants to get back there someday. She definitely has no interest in being a Nihilist. And before you ask, as far as I can make it out, a Nihilist is someone who believes in committing suicide before going mad, or suffering senility, or something. Apparently there's a high incidence of mental disease among the elderly. They don't like to talk about it much, and when they do it's pretty oblique stuff, even for Outposters. C'astille very strongly does not believe in Nihilism. She was more or less just passing through when we landed, and she stayed around out of curiosity. I might add that she seemed worried when the old leader died and this D'etallis took over."

"So you think we could talk to C'astille? Play her the recording, ask her if such bioweapons were possible?"

"Yes—and more than that. I think we owe it to her. Don't forget, in exchange, D'etallis wants human weapons to attack Outposters. The other Groups have to be warned."

"Then let's find her," Gustav said, rising.

"Good," Lucy said. Suddenly the brittle calm that had sustained her seemed to collapse. She looked afraid, more afraid than she had been in all the time he had known her. "Johnson? If it's true—what can we do about it?"

Johnson Gustav looked at the coffee maker. He had forgotten to switch it on. "I don't know, Lucy. We need time to think. But we're in this, even if we don't like it. Let's get suited up and find our friend."

They found C'astille without too much difficulty. The young Outposter was fascinated by all things human, especially construction, and she was developing into a highly qualified sidewalk superintendent. It had been getting more and more difficult to find a place to land supply craft as the Contact Base grew, and so a team of Guardian Army engineers was pouring a reinforced concrete landing pad in a nearby clearing. Suspecting that the native would take an interest in the proceedings, Gustav and Lucy drove a jeep over to look for her, and sure enough, C'astille was there to watch the engineers at work.

C'astille was clearly glad to see Lucy, and surprised to see Gustav. For his part, Gustav was just as glad to find C'astille well away from the main camp and prying eyes.

"C'astille! We need talk with you," Lucy called in O-1 as she jumped from the jeep. She stumbled just a bit as she hit the ground—she had never gotten exactly *graceful* in a pressure suit, even in one of the light-weight models they had finally gotten. A few of the Guardians engineers went without suits at all, and just used respirators or air helmets. But Outpost smelled a lot worse than it looked. That incredibly rich moldy odor crept past any respirator seal, and permeated any clothing worn outdoors. Even with airlocks and filters, enough Outposter air leaked into the mess hall to make it smell like a pile of steaming compost.

C'astille waved—a habit she had picked up from the humans—and trotted over to Lucy.

"Hello, Lucille and Johnson. I am glad to see you," C'astille said carefully. She was justifiably proud of the English she had learned. She did better than any other Outposter. Lucy was by this time convinced there was no single cause for the problems the 'Posters had with English. It was a combination of the sounds they could produce, and language construction, and viewpoint, and who knows what else. Lucy often wondered how bad her own O-1 accent was, though now wasn't the time to worry about it. But C'astille's Aussie-flavored English was an odd touch of home.

"C'astille," she said in the native language. "You are sensed. M'Gustav and I are here for talk. He does not have many words of your tongue, but of course can hear and talk through the translator machine he carries." She paused. How to explain? "We have accidentally learned a thing, and it is most urgent that we know if it is true or not. Come take a little walk with us."

C'astille looked at the two of them. "Something is strange," she said. "Is it that you have something to say you wish no one else to hear?"

"Yes," Lucy said.

"Not even other humans?"

Lucy glanced at Gustav. "No," she said. "Not even other humans."

"This is most interest making," C'astille said, excitedly sweeping the ground with her tail.

Lucy could not resist a smile. She should have known C'astille would love the idea of hearing a secret. "I am glad that is so for you," she said.

"The forest is safe of Hungry Ones for a good distance," C'astille said. "Let us be in the trees."

Lucy began to speak as the three figures moved into the brush. "We want you to have hearing of a recording of talk between your Guidance and ours. The recording happened accidentally, no one *sought* to ah, hear this, but it happened, and when it was heard by us . . ." Lucy found her voice trailing off as she ran out of excuses.

"It happened. It doesn't matter how it came to be," C'astille said.

Lucy shrugged. If C'astille didn't mind, she wasn't going to argue. She wasn't even too surprised that C'astille wasn't upset at a case of spying on her leader. It fit with the Outposter viewpoint, somehow. "So, listen," she said. She unslung her equipment bag, dug out the recorder, and punched the play button.

C'astille bent her head forward to hear better and stood, stock still, while the voices of human, Z'ensam, and the translator machine talked.

Finally the recording ended. She gave a low snorting noise, shifted on her feet, and said, "I have heard. What more would you know?" Her voice was suddenly flat and nasal, her whole body seemed strangely stiff and unmoving.

"Can your people make such creatures, that will eat such things?"

She wobbled her head back and forth on its long neck, a nervous fidgeting movement. "Yes, we can. As D'etallis said, it would be easy to change them from creatures we already have. This does not mean we *should*. Your people have no experience of our fighting. There would be great destruction."

Lucy thought of nuclear bombs, lasers, automatic weapons. "The same could be said of your people facing our weapons."

"D'etallis seeks power and control and the expansion of her Group," C'astille said. "She is a dangerous person, and I do not doubt that she would be willing to have the use of any weapon she could get at, against anyone she could find.

If she gets a weapon from D'Romero, she will not hesitate to turn it on Romero. What drives your Guidance to do this foolish thing?"

"In all accuracy, we must call him M'Romero, for he is no true Guidance, no leader," Lucy said. "He will go to those in power, and seek power from them in exchange for the living weapons."

"This should not be what occurs." C'astille said.

Lucy couldn't tell if C'astille was simply speaking in the normal passive voice of O-1, or if she was deliberately speaking ambiguously, trying to learn what the humans felt before she gave too much away. "M'Gustav and I agree. But we do not know how to stop it. M'Romero is gone, and has already spread his message—and D'etallis will already be at work, preparing her half of the bargain."

"Yes. She would not wait," the Outposter agreed. "Then we must cause warn to others. I must be with my Group and cause them to know this. But I have no understanding of you two. Is not M'Romero of your Group?"

Lucy paused again. How to explain? There wasn't time for the complicated truth of the League and the Guards and the CIs and Gustav's Settlers, whoever they were. But she couldn't lie. Not to C'astille. "We do not share the words for me to make all clear, and accurate. But this is close to truth: I am not of M'Romero's group, the Guardians. I am a sojourner, like you. I traveled here against my will, and was delighted to find your people, all chance, at the end of my road. I have helped these Guardians to speak with you, because I was curious and sought knowledge, but I can do so no longer. These weapons will be used against my Group, and so I have hurt my own people. I must stop."

"I am of the Guardians," Gustav said, his translator's words carrying none of the complicated emotion Lucy could hear in his own voice, "but I must take a new road, try and stop what the Guardians would do. Lucy's Group is at war with mine. If my Group attacks her with terrible new weapons, that will only make *her* side strike back at *my* side the harder. No good can come of making that war bigger. And there must not be war with your species helping to kill mine, or my species helping to kill yours. Begin that now, and humans might be trapped into hating your kind, being afraid of you. And they might decide to kill all of you," he said, and then hesitated. "Which they could do."

"I believe you, human. But I have often sensed that you think us not as clever as you, because you can do things we cannot, or because you choose to do things we choose not to do. I understand your people are spread across the sky, and our astronomy is good: I know how vast the sky is. *But our machines are living things that grow, and breed, and reproduce.* If we have the making of two, we have the making done of millions.

"Know too that D'etallis has a strange vision of Nihilism. The idea has been passive, she would make it active. Again, you and I do share not words to say *why*, but she seeks to kill all Z'ensam, all Outposters. When she had only the weapons and the knowledge of Z'ensam, she was no great danger. The other Groups could counter her moves. With human machines behind her, she will walk far down that killing road. But do not imagine you are safe in all your worlds. You *must* understand, and believe, hard though it might be. If she became the leader of all the Z'ensam, and decided her ideas called for the death of humans, she could have the death of you all."

The two humans were silent.

"I have belief of you, C'astille," Lucy said at last.

"That is good. But what is to be done?" C'astille asked.

"I have to stop my work here, today," Lucy said.

"Could the two of you fake things?" Gustav asked. "Create confusion with bad translations or something?"

"No," C'astille said. "There are too many others who would have finding of the mistakes too soon. M'Calder is right. All we can do is stop. And then I must leave for my Group, warn them."

"That'll have *you* safe. But what about M'Calder?" Gustav asked, the machine adding the honorific to Lucy's name in translation. "I can cover for you for a few days, Lucy.

Maybe you could fake being sick, or something. But then what?"

Lucy shifted her feet, tried to scratch her nose, and bounced her fingers off the pressure suit's helmet. She wished they could sit down comfortably and think and talk. But the only place where all three of them could be comfortable was the Crystal Palace, and that wasn't safe. She shifted to English, and let Gustav's translator keep C'astille up to date. "I think I have an idea. Can I pretend to be sick enough to be pulled back to Ariadne?"

Gustav shrugged. "I suppose. We don't have a real doctor down here. But what's the point?"

"Well, you said that the League was bound to find us, sooner or later. When? How long do we have?"

Gustav made a vague gesture with his hands. "Tomorrow. Ten years from now. They've got a lot of ground to cover. But now we've given them a reason to make the effort."

"I've had most of the morning to think on this. Suppose we gave C'astille some sort of homing beacon. Something that would give out a signal we could track on a frequency the Guards aren't likely to monitor. Something so she could go off with her Group and we could find her later on."

"That's simple enough. But then what?"

"So when the League arrives, they're going to want someone who can talk to the Outposters, and they'll want some Outposters to talk to. I could be the League's link, their ticket in."

"What good would that do?" Gustav asked. "Besides helping your side win the war?"

"It might keep the League from *starting* a war with the Outposters. If they get hit by bioweapons that are as bad as what C'astille says, and they find out they come from here—they might decide they have to exterminate the Outposters in self defense. The Guardians' alien allies—if the League decides that's all the Outposters are, things could get very, very bad."

"I suppose," Gustav said. "But what could you do?"

"If I could get to the League when they get here, I could

put them in touch with the other Groups, let them see D'etallis isn't the only game in town. I *might* be able to keep the war from spreading."

"Maybe. But how do we do it? How do we get you away? Have you figured *that* out?"

"We could say I got caught without a helmet and got carbon dioxide poisoning. I'd get sent to Ariadne, deathly ill. The doctor there would look me over, and poke me and prod me and make me feel better. When I recovered, I could steal a lander and make a break for it. We could make it look like I was shot down. I land near C'astille's beacon and wait for the League. When they come, I contact them."

"How?"

"If the lander's still functional, I fly. If not, the lander's radio, or the 'Posters have radio."

"But what about life support? For years and years, probably?" Gustav asked. "You can't eat Outposter food. You'd die of carbon dioxide poisoning if you tried to breathe their air. You'd have to live in the ship, or a pressure suit. And they'd give out, sooner or later."

"Pauze," C'astille said, having a little trouble with the English word before she shifted to O-1. "If I have understanding, there is no problem. Our people could provide air and food that would suit you. Be sure of it."

"There you are, Johnson," Lucy said "Do you think I could get away? Don't forget, Ariadne's radar operators are all CIs."

"Mmmph. I had almost forgotten that. With *that* working for you, and if we timed it just right, you'd have a chance, though God knows you could be shot down for real."

"I almost don't mind that. I just want to be safely dead in the eyes of the Guardians. I don't want them to come looking for me to get more out of me."

"And suppose you really end up dead? Will you feel better then? Getting yourself killed won't undo what's happened."

"I know that! But I—"

"Lucy, listen to me! *You did not deliberately hurt anyone.*

You were trapped here, in our star system, with no way out, ever, and you lucked into an exciting chance that should have had *nothing* to do with war. You were learning a language, and it's not your fault what is said in that language. You weren't telling me where League bases were, or building bombs—"

"Johnson! Stop it! I know I didn't do it intentionally, but facts are facts, I must live all my life knowing that my people are going to die because of what I did in all my innocence. I betrayed my trust—"

"Then you are not alone," C'astille said in O-1. "Here and now I come to choose you grotesque aliens over my own kind, and side with you against the leader of the Group that protects me. And M'Gustav deliberately comes to choose betrayal of *his* Group. You are the lucky of we three: You betrayed by accident. M'Gustav and I know what we are doing before we do it. But we are all traitors."

"And all the pretty speeches and ethical standards and codes of honor and ideas about right and wrong won't change that," Gustav said. "C'astille is right, and I suppose we all have to face that. I'm sorry. I think your plan might work. You know what you're asking of yourself. You could easily get killed or be marooned somewhere on Outpost and watch your air run out. But I think we have to try it."

"But where does it leave you?" Lucy asked.

"I don't know. They might catch me and shoot me. If not, I'll still be here, running things, or on Ariadne."

"Run things, then. Stay alive. I'm burning all my bridges. One of us should keep some options open."

"You're pretty easy on me."

"Gustav, you are my enemy. We are at war, you and I. But I want you alive, and well. I'd feel a hundred time worse a traitor if I got *you* killed."

C'astille looked on in confusion as M'Calder took M'Gustav's hand in hers and squeezed it, for the briefest of moments, before she let it go. The two humans looked at each other in a most peculiar way for a moment, then drew apart, seemingly very upset about something.

"It can't be, Lucy. But God, I—no, I can't even say it."

"Neither can I, Johnson. Neither can I. We'd better get back before they miss us." The humans said their goodbyes to C'astille, arranged to talk with her the next day, and went back to the jeep.

C'astille, watching the two humans go, could make nothing of it. But there was something about that moment when the two humans touched that seemed perverse, as if the two of them wanted to—but C'astille couldn't think *that*, even to herself.

Alien or not, they couldn't be monsters. And there was something else that disturbed her greatly. The translator hadn't been able to make complete sense of the English-spoken conversation, and she had to take that into account. Yet she had gotten the strong impression that the humans were discussing medicine—and not as a bizarre, horrifying, and dangerous thing, but as something quite normal and routine.

She started back toward the clearing where the engineers were still hard at work. Every time she thought she was used to the humans, had finally made sense of them, this sort of thing happened.

Only in the last few weeks had she become certain that they were all one species, instead of a vast number of related species that worked together. But they varied so much, in height and size and color and shape, and in a hundred details. No animal species on her planet had such a wide range of variation. She had thought for a time that they were all mutations from some true breed, and she had worked out a complicated social theory to account for it, of a race that got some use out of its mutants and sports by sending them on risky jobs of exploring and so forth. But that hadn't made a great deal of sense, and all the humans seemed far healthier than mutations usually were. There was a lot to learn about them, and learn from them.

If D'etallis didn't wipe them out first.

Chapter Ten

Ivory Tower
The Planet Bandwidth

It was only when he was behind the door of his office that Randall Metcalf felt really safe. The Navy had assigned him an overly automated hotel as a billet, and there was little he could do about the hyperactive robot service there, but in his office, inside *those* four walls, *he* could call the shots and choose the equipment. There was no machine more complicated than a pencil there, no technology higher than an electric light. He could be alone with his reports, could slog through another day of flying a desk, sift through another stack of transcripts of interrogation. He could search in peace and quiet for some morsel, some clue, that would be of use in the fight to come. If they ever found anyone to fight.

But today, as usual, there was nothing in the reports. The prisoners had been squeezed dry, long ago. But orders were orders, and reading the interrogations was the job at hand. It sure as hell killed the day.

Randall was therefore very glad to hear George knock on his door at quitting time. He eagerly closed up his work and they left the office together. George was as bogged down in busy-work as Metcalf, sitting in on interrogations that went over and over the same ground again and again. The Intelligence types had theories about long questioning sessions being the most effective.

The two of them headed out of the office. It turned out to be a pleasant evening, with a freshening wind blowing in off the Straight Straits, and Metcalf had had enough of the corner bar for a while, so they decided to grab some carryout from the robot in the lobby and eat in the park.

Ivory Tower, the largest city on Bandwidth, was a forest of tall buildings set in generous parkland; towers and pylons and skyscrapers in every imaginable architectural style all caught the eye. It was a far more mature city than it should have been, but robots could build fast. Twentieth-century-style glass boxes shared the skyline with gaudily baroque piles based on medieval cathedrals, scaled-up pagodas and copies of the Eiffel Tower and the Washington Monument and the cliff-dwelling blocks that were the latest style on Earth. It kept the eye busy.

Smaller buildings, more modest in scale but equally varied in style, were set along the wide boulevards. Trees, grasses, and flowers imported from Earth were planted in the parklands, and real, honest-to-God ducks quacked and fussed and paddled around the ornamental ponds and lakes. Metcalf liked to sit on a low hill in Unity Park, near the League HQ tower, and look out over it all. Even he had to admit that Bandwidth had spent its riches well.

It was a perfect evening, the sun still reddening the sky, a hint of the enticing spicy odor of the Sea of Ness in the air, the stars just coming out in the purpling east. Lounging back on the grass, staring out over the park and the skyline, munching on a kosher hotdog that would have done New York proud, and with his beer still cold, Metcalf concluded that Life was Good.

It was on a night like this, back home, that he had decided the sky and the stars were for him. He looked up at the sky, and a familiar thrill ran through him. "Just look at those stars, George," he said in a near whisper, all the usual bantering tone gone from his voice. "They're so damned far away—and there're *people* out there! We've crossed that distance. Makes me feel proud. Proud and small, all at once."

"I know what you mean."

"Maybe ten years after they got the C^2 drive running, they flew a ship to Rigel and radioed back, just in case they couldn't get home. That radio signal won't reach Earth for more than another century! Jesus, it makes me proud.

Humanity's not just some bunch of geeks standing around on street corners. We can reach the *stars*."

Neither of them spoke for a long time. The sky grew darker, and the stars came out in all their glory. Meteors zipped across the firmament. Lights came on across Ivory Tower, subdued enough not to disturb the splendid skies, but artfully placed and aimed so as to set the great buildings off from the surrounding darkness.

"The stars are different here," George said.

"*That* much, we know," Metcalf replied with gentle sarcasm. None of the Guardians had recognized the night sky as seen from any League world, which would at least seem to suggest they weren't from any place nearby.

"You know," Randall said, "I remember back at Annapolis, back on Earth. I had put in for Space Fighters the first moment I could. Tonight reminds me of the night the word came through that me and a bunch of my buddies had gotten it. We all went down to the shore and pointed out the stars to each other. We kept telling each other—'see that one just to the left of the Big Dipper? I'll be there!' "

"The Big Dipper?"

"One of the constellations as seen from Earth."

"Okay, I'll bite. I forget what a constellation is."

"Whoa. You're kidding. You know, connect-the-dots between the stars and imagine a picture there."

"Oh, okay. That's right. Mac explained that, and the intelligence guys asked me about 'em once."

"Wait a minute. You guys don't even have *constellations*?" Metcalf asked. *Every* culture made up constellations. How could anyone with a normal imagination avoid finding patterns in the sky and naming them?

"Yeah we did. We just don't call 'em that. Called 'em sky pictures, I guess. Never had a real name for 'em. We didn't have any *official* ones, of course, but all the kids made up their own."

Metcalf grunted. That made sense, in a twisted Guardian sort of way. If you didn't want people to learn astrogation, you didn't teach them astronomy. If you didn't want them to learn astronomy, you didn't encourage people to make up pretty pictures in the sky. But they'd do it anyway. Who could enforce a rule against looking at the sky?

"Doesn't really matter, anyway," Metcalf said. "Stars is stars, and stars is pretty."

They were both quiet for a while. A meteor flashed across the sky, arcing slowing from east to west before it vanished.

"I wonder if that's what got the Lost Star story started," George said at last. "Or maybe it was a comet, or one of the outer planets."

Metcalf suddenly sat bolt upright. He had the feeling that George had just said something very important. "What do you mean, George? What's the Lost Star?"

"Oh, just an old story that floated around the children's barracks. Once upon a time, there was one star that was brighter and bigger than all the rest. One night, it decided it didn't want to stay in the same part of the sky with the same stars all the time, so it broke free, and flew off by itself. It sailed clear across the sky, proud of how special it was—and then it got lost, because it did not listen to the ruler of the sky, and did not go in the proper direction. It vanished into the northern lights, never to be seen again. And the moral of the story was to always be part of the group. Never go off on your own, or question authority—or you might vanish too."

"Lovely story to tell children," Metcalf said.

"Oh, yeah," said George. "Really sweet. There were a lot of versions of it floating around. Enough so I've always thought it had some basis in fact. Something that everyone saw, like a comet or a big meteor. Something that moved across the sky and disappeared into the northern lights."

Randall frowned. "Hold it. *Northern* Lights? You said everyone lived in the southern hemisphere of Capital and the north was unsettled."

"Right. So?"

"So you said you had northern lights. That'd mean lights coming from the *equatorial* sky, and that doesn't make sense."

"Why not?"

"Northern and southern lights are aurorae linked to the magnetic poles. Charged particles are pulled in from outer space by the planet's magnetism and sucked in toward the poles. The charged particles zip into the atmosphere, and hit an air molecule, and that sets off sparks of light—the aurora. If there were enough charged particles hitting to set off a glow at the equator that could be seen in the south, then the whole planet would glow in the dark—and so would the people. The radiation would kill everything."

"I could say you're glazing my eyes over, but I'll leave it at a simple 'huh?' "

"Sorry. Trust me, equatorial aurorae don't make sense."

"Whatever you say, but on a clear night back home, lots of times you could see a glow of orange light, all along the northern horizon."

"Always the same brightness?"

"Pretty much. The light gets hidden by weather, of course, but it's more or less always the same."

"Hmmm. That's not an aurora, anyway. Aurorae aren't constant, they come and go, change color, flicker for a few hours or days and then fade."

"Fine. Now I'll know aurorae when I see them. Why are you all excited about this stuff?"

"Because it all sounds very unusual. It means there's something odd about the skies of Capital. And that means there might be something odd, maybe even unique, about Capital, or space around it—"

"And that might help us find Capital."

"Right. So let me ask a dumb question," Metcalf said. "How do you know for certain that north was north and south was south. Couldn't they switch the compass directions on the orders of the Grand Wazoo or the Imperator of the Grand Bugaboo—"

"You are referring of course to the Most Honorable Leader of the Combined Will, long may he lead us, etcetera, etcetera. Did you get the last pickle?"

"Yes, sorry. Whatever you call him. Couldn't he or some

guy a hundred years ago have decided to fool all of you and tell you south was north, just to confuse the issue if you tried to help us barbarian hordes find your home?"

"Well, Mr. Barbarian Horde, they could have, but they didn't. I did a lot of instrument design, and I can tell you flat out that Capital has compass-standard and spin-standard local planetary north." There were two way of defining a planet's local north. North was either the hemisphere wherein the planet's spin was counter-clockwise when viewed from a point over the rotational axis, or the hemisphere contains a magnetic north pole. Spin standard was the normal test—virtually every planet spun, but lots of them had missing reversed magnetic poles. "And the birds fly north, toward the equator, when its gets cold. My mouth was all ready for that pickle."

"Sorry about that. Well, they couldn't have fooled the birds, I guess. So let's see: We've got a glow in the sky toward the equatorial horizon and a legend of a Lost Star that vanishes over the northern horizon, never to be seen again."

"Except some versions of the story say the Lost Star will come back out of the north when it's learned its lesson. But that's folklore, Randall. Nothing more."

"You were the one who said it had a basis in fact—and my guess is whoever saw something move across the sky, way back when, could tell a star from a planet or a comet or a meteor. All in all, I'd say it was weird enough to rate comment. It gives me an idea—but I'm no expert." Randall stood up. "Come on," he said.

"Where are we going?" George asked.

"To find an astronomer, of course. Someone who might know where to look for lost stars."

George led Randall back to his office. Compared to the barren cell Metcalf hid himself in, George's workshop was a jumbled madhouse. George fell in love with every gadget, and put all of them to work in his office. The chairs were self-adjusting, the lights came on automatically, a grabber was ready to find any book on the shelf and hand it to George. There were keyboards and terminals hooked into a half dozen computer grids.

Old coffee cups and plates with sandwich rinds and sheafs of printout were everywhere. Metcalf had often suggested that George should get himself one more gizmo: a cleaning robot. But George was convinced he'd never be able to find anything if the place got cleaned up.

But before Randall could even shove the magazines off the chair and sit, George had dipped into the professional directories and retrieved a list of the astronomers with security clearance currently on-planet, in the city of Ivory Tower, and cleared to do consultations on military topics. A hard copy of the list in hand, they were ready to go looking.

A Dr. Raoul Morelles was the first name on their list, and when Randall called, he was more than a trifle surprised that Morelles was willing to see them. But all it took was the slightest hint that they were involved in the search for Capital. Randall told himself he should have known better. Capital was a tempting enough mystery to draw in practically anyone.

This Metcalf person probably didn't realize it, Morelles told himself, but on any other planet but Bandwidth or Earth, the fellow would have been lucky to find an astronomer at all. It was depressing in a way.

Very few astronomers were *on* planets anymore. The opening of interstellar space had hurt astronomy in unexpected ways. The discipline had become fragmented and specialized. The traditions of the old science were that of the utterly passive observer, cut off from the object of study by tens, or thousands, or millions of light-years, forced to glean every scrap of information from whatever miserly number of photons his or her instruments could capture.

Not anymore. People interested in planet formation or atmospheres didn't become astronomers at all—they went out and found a planetary system forming or an atmosphere that they could study. Stellarists interested in a particular star would load their instruments onto a ship and launch for the object of their interest. Scientists were widely scattered, and communications weren't good enough. Results were frequently published long years after the work was done. Many results were lost altogether, along with the experimenter. Astronomers tended not to be good ship handlers, and they had an unfortunate tendency to get "just a bit closer" to some rather dangerous objects—stars, for example.

The scientific establishment of Bandwidth couldn't do anything about vaporized stellarists, but it could correlate results, and the computers were there for number crunching problems where the number of variables was itself a large but variable number.

The field astronomers looked down on their ground-based colleagues, the theoretical astronomers, a bit, and harbored a suspicion that they were little more than computer programmers and librarians. But, sooner or later, all the data ended up at the dirtside research centers.

Dr. Raoul Morelles liked to think of himself as a spider at the center of a web, with all the threads leading back to the center. Bandwidth and Earth, there were the two places the data came, and maybe Earth has computers as good—but try getting at them. Too crowded, too congested. Bandwidth was the place to work. Interesting problems cropped up all the time.

Morelles didn't look like a spider. His appearance was closer to that of a praying mantis. He was tall and thin, with a shock of white hair that stood straight up from being endlessly shoved out of his large, serious eyes. He had long arms and legs, with delicate, almost frail-looking hands. He seemed always to be deliberately holding himself very still, as if he were concentrating on something that might vanish if he looked away. His clothes were worn and spare. Tonight he wore the old workshirt and the khaki trousers that he found most comfortable, a pair of slightly shabby slippers on his feet.

When he answered the door and he found two slightly

embarrassed young men, he had a hunch that he was about to find himself in the middle of a very interesting problem indeed. He had received one or two queries from the people searching for Capital—but never at this hour of the night, and never from two such unofficial looking visitors. Brimming with curiosity, he let them in.

In short order, they all got the introductions out of the way, Morelles ordered the kitchen to make coffee and deliver it to his study, and they sat down to talk.

"It's this way, Dr. Morelles," the young Commander Metcalf began. "As you might know, there's a lot of effort being put into finding the planet Capital, where the Guardians come from."

"I don't follow the war news much, but I have heard something about it, yes. Do go on."

"Well, George here is from Capital, but he's working with us. He and I were talking tonight, and something he said got me thinking that we've been going about it all wrong. The intelligence teams have been waving star charts at the POWs and asking about spectral types and so on, but it doesn't do any good. The prisoners they're interrogating don't *know* any of that stuff.

"Anyway, I was talking with George, and he got to describing the night sky of Capital, the way the people there actually see it. What I want is to work backwards. I want to figure out what must be in the sky for it to look and move the way George says it does. Like the ancients figuring out the Earth is in orbit by seeing the Sun rise. I want to find the pattern to fit the facts, instead of just casting blindly about waving star maps at the prisoners."

"It would have to be a very unusual sky for that to work," Morelles said doubtfully. "It would have to have some remarkable feature indeed for your idea to work—a close-in nebula, for example. I would expect someone would have told our people about such a thing by now."

"I know," Commander Metcalf said. "But what we've got hold of is a feature of the sky that's remarkable for *not* being seen. Tell him about it, George."

George, with plenty of interruptions from Metcalf, and many questions from Morelles, described the strange behavior of his planet's night sky.

"Hmmmm. All right," Dr. Morelles said. "I see your point. If that isn't strange enough to give us some clues, then it certainly ought to be. I must say, though, that the strangest thing is that none of this came out from all that interrogation you mentioned."

"Well, maybe the powers that be were smarter than anyone thought in putting me on this damned planet," Metcalf said. "I'm the only pilot, the only person who makes his living—and *stays* alive—by looking at the sky and wondering what's out there. The intelligence teams are trying to backtrack by figuring out the travel times and the number of C^2 jumps the prisoners experienced between Capital and New Finland. *That* won't do them much good. I think that if we can figure out what all this stuff about equatorial lights and vanishing stars *means*, what sort of objects moving how in the sky are required to make things look that way, we can dig through the computer files and maybe find a system that matches it."

"Yes. I see. You may have something there. Please help yourself to more coffee. Let me work on this." Morelles started to think.

Fifteen minutes later, George Prigot felt more than a little out of his depth. Morelles was a rather odd character, to say the least, and he felt increasingly unsure that he was the man they should be talking to. For starters, Morelles had stopped talking—or moving—at all. When Morelles had said he was going to work on the question, George had expected he would go to a computer terminal and start tapping in queries, or at least pull some huge book down from a shelf and mutter to himself as he flipped through it. But Morelles had simply leaned back, propped his elbows on the chair arms, cupped his chin in his hands, and stared at the ceiling. The astronomer didn't move but to breathe or blink—and then he shut his eyes, and his breathing became very shallow. George was beginning to think Morelles might have had some sort of silent stroke and died.

"Were any formal star charts made by the people on Capital?" Morelles asked, interrupting the long silence so abruptly that both George and Metcalf jumped. "Did anyone keep permanent records?"

"Ah, no," George said, still a bit rattled. "It wouldn't have been allowed. We aren't supposed to make up stories about the sky in the first place. The Central Guardians ruled that folktales and superstitions were misleading and time-wasters and declared them illegal."

"That sounds like the most unenforceable law I've ever heard," Morelles growled. "Either your leaders were very sensitive about such things, or they know nothing about psychology."

"I suppose, sir," George said uncomfortably. It was okay when Randall kidded him about home, but he still squirmed when a stranger sneered at the Guardians like that. The evidence of his own eye had forced him to decide the Guardians *did* bad and foolish things, but he couldn't admit they were bad, or foolish.

"Do you have any rough idea of the average life-span of people on your planet?" Morelles asked.

This guy Morelles must have learned to ask oddball questions the same place Metcalf had, George thought. "Not really. Not more than 70 or 75 in Earth years, I guess. It's news when someone reaches the equivalent of 85 or 90."

"I see. Then allowing for childhood forgetfulness, we can take perhaps 80 years as the basic upper limit for the survival of knowledge about one certain patch of sky. Do you see why that's important?"

"No, sir," George said.

"I think I've got it, Doctor," Randall said. "Stars don't just appear and disappear. They're permanent. There must be some cyclical pattern of motion of Capital's sky that took this Lost Star out of sight—assuming the Lost Star isn't just a legend. But if no one now alive actually remembers seeing the Lost Star, a human lifetime gives you a lower limit for how long that cycle can be."

"Exactly. That 80 years gives us a lower limit for whatever sort of cycle we are talking about."

"Oh, I get it!" George said. He was smart enough, plenty smart enough, to understand the motions of the sky, and once he thought about it, it was obvious that stars didn't just vanish. It was just that he never *had* thought about it. Just as the Central Guardians intended, he had never really believed that the points of light in the sky were mighty suns.

"So what *is* that cycle?" Metcalf asked.

"I should think that would be fairly obvious."

"So call me stupid, Doctor," Metcalf said evenly. "What is it?"

"I would say that Capital's sun is one of a binary pair."

"But I know what a binary sun is—two stars in orbit around each other," George protested. "But no one back home has ever seen another sun—or even a particularly bright star."

"Oh yes you have. What about that glow coming from the North, from over the equator?"

"That's from another *sun*?"

"I expect so. Does all this make sense to you, Commander Metcalf?"

"Yessir." Metcalf nodded and thought it through. "Capital's north pole must be pretty much pointed at the other star right at the moment. That's the only way the other star would never be visible from the southern hemisphere of Capital."

"You're quite right. And that *does* suggest a rather odd structure to Capital's star system," Morelles agreed. "But I don't see anything else that fits the facts."

"Sir, if you don't mind my asking," George said, "what sort of odd structure are you talking about?"

"Let me see if I can sum it up. Capital's sun—what do you call it?"

"Nova Sol."

"There must be a dozen stars with that local name in the League," Morelles muttered. "People aren't very original. Very well, Nova Sol is in a binary relationship with another star: The two of them orbit around each other, or more accurately, around an empty spot of space midway between the two of them, where the gravitational attraction of the two stars is exactly balanced. That central balance point is called the barycenter. The two stars revolve around that point other in no less than 80 years. Do you understand that so far?"

"Yes. But I can't see how the other star would be hidden all the time."

"Wait a minute, Doctor," Metcalf said. "I think I've got it. Capital's orbit—not the planet, but the *orbit itself*—is on edge to the other star. Right now the orbit is face-on toward the other sun."

"Precisely!" Morelles grinned with delight.

"Wait a second," George cut in. "Could you explain that again?"

Morelles sighed, in the manner of a man who has dealt with too many slow students over the course of a lifetime. "Let me see if I can explain." He got up suddenly, went into the next room, and returned with a big sheet of stiff posterboard paper, a pair of scissors, and a marking pen. Morelles shoved everything else off his big round coffee table, and George and Metcalf rescued the coffee cups just in the nick of time. Morelles lay the sheet of posterboard down on the table.

Morelles sketched rapidly on the posterboard. "Now then," he said. "The usual thing for a solar system is for everything to move in the same plane. I've sketched some of the major elements of Earth's solar system here. If you want to represent the orbits of all the planets, except for Pluto, you can just draw them on a flat piece of card as I have done. Within a degree or two, all the orbits are in the same plane. Pluto is the exception that helps explain the rule. Pluto's orbit is, oh dear, what is it? Oh yes, about seventeen degrees away from the plane of the others. If I wanted to show *its* orbit accurately

I'd have to take a loop of wire or something and poke it through the cardstock so half the wire loop was above and half was below my flat plane, and then I'd have to set that orbit—that loop of wire—so it was at a seventeen degree angle to the paper representing the plane of the Solar System. Does that give you an idea about the planes of orbits?"

"Yes, I think so," George said. He was beginning to understand, and beginning to be annoyed at the teachers who hadn't shown him this. George, a lover of gadgets and machines and machinery, was getting his first introduction to the greatest clockwork toy there was—the complex and orderly dance of the skies.

"Good," Morelles said. He had clearly taken on his classroom persona, and all his words and movements became exaggerated, as if he were talking to a whole room full of slightly puzzled students. His voice got a bit louder, his enunciation more careful, and his hand gestures were suddenly broad and expressive. "Now, since we've got a large enough piece of card, I can draw a whole other solar system on it over here, with a star and planets and satellites and so on. Notice it's all still on one flat piece of paper, everything still moving in one plane. Now I've drawn in the orbits of the planets around the second sun. Let me draw in one more orbit."

He started his pencil on one of the two suns and drew a wide circle that went through it and the other sun, so that the two stars then were 180 degrees away from each other on the circle.

Directly in the center of this big circle, he drew a dot. "That dot is the barycenter. It is, quite literally, the system's balance point, where the gravitation of one star exactly cancels out the gravitation of the other. It is the center of gravity, the balance point for the whole system. Now, imagine the two suns orbiting each other around that barycenter, and the planets orbiting their respective suns, everything in the same plane."

"Okay," George said, as Morelles clearly expected some sort of reaction.

"Good. Now, this sort of arrangement is what most binary star systems look like. That's clear enough to see. But here's where we get to the unusual features of your Nova Sol system."

Morelles took his pencil again and marked one solar system *Alpha* and the other *Beta*. Then he took the scissors and cut along the orbit of the outer planet in each. He was left with two circles of cardboard, each with a sun marked by a dot in the center and the planetary orbits drawn around the sun. He picked up the system marked Beta in his left hand and Alpha in his right. "Now we work in three dimensions instead of two."

Morelles held Alpha perpendicular to the floor and turned the Beta system this way and that. "You can see that I can put the plane of the Beta *solar system* at any angle to the plane of *Alpha's* solar system, and it will have nothing whatever to do with the plane in which the two *stars* revolve about each other. Now I'm holding the Beta system at 90 degrees to Alpha, now 45, now parallel, now 135 degrees. No matter how I turn it, you can still imagine a circle, a mutual orbit, joining the two suns. They can go around each other no matter what, and don't care about the planes of the planets' orbits."

George nodded. "I see it."

"Good!" Morelles said, beaming. "Normally, everything *will* be in one plane, but something could change that. An impact, a momentum exchange during a close encounter with a passing star, even a capture event that caused two unrelated stars to fall into a mutual orbit. Clearly something like that happened here.

Now, we have one last step."

Morelles stopped for a moment, and stared into space. "How to proceed?" he asked himself. "Ah! I see the way." He dropped Alpha and Beta on the top of the round coffee table, and stood up abruptly. He ran back to his office and returned with a rather sharp looking cut-all tool and a pair of thumbtacks. He scooped up the Alpha disk and shoved a pin through its center, through the dot that marked the sun. Then he crouched down by the coffee table. "The round tabletop can represent the plane of the orbit of the two suns," he said. He lay the Alpha system card flat on the table, near one edge, and mashed the thumbtack through into the table.

The table was a lazy-susan arrangement, and Morelles spun it around on its pivot until Alpha was on the far side of the table from him. He poked another pin through the Beta system's sun, and shoved that pin into the *rim* of the table, so that Beta system's orbital plane was perpendicular to the orbit of the star around the coffee table. He gave the table top another push, and it spun round and round.

Two disks of cardboard, directly across the diameter of the table from each other, one flat on the surface, the other held perpendicular to the tabletop, whirled around and around. As each went past him, Morelles reached out his hand and set the disks spinning around their pushpins.

"Not quite accurate," he said. "There is one more detail. I have only shown you the situation when the Alpha system is face on to Beta. In that circumstance, only one hemisphere of a planet in the system will see Beta. An observer on that hemisphere will see this one bright star, far brighter than any other, perhaps bright enough to be seen in daylight. That observer will see the star move across the heavens, year after year, until it moves below the horizon and is lost to view."

"Sound familiar?" Randall asked George, a broad smile on his face."

"From the *other* hemisphere, Beta will be hidden from view, for decades at a time. But not forever." Morelles stopped the table's spin and pulled the Alpha system out of the rim of the table. He pushed the table a quarter-turn forward, and used the cut-all to slice into the rather handsome wood of the table, cutting straight from the edge toward the center. He cut out a notch of wood a millimeter or two wide and about ten centimeters long—and then slid the Alpha system card into the notch. "Now Alpha is edge-on toward Beta. In this position, Beta is visible to both hemisphere. One hemisphere sees it slowly setting, creeping toward the horizon, year by year—while the other sees it rising."

Morelles looked at his chopped-up table and smiled. "There you have it, gentlemen," he said. "A first crude armillary, a mechanical representation of Capital's star system. The two stars, which are represented by the pushpins, revolve around each other in their mutual orbit, the circumference of which is the rim of my coffee table. The planets orbit around the stars, the pushpins, in the planes of motion represented by the two cardboard disks. One orbital plane is in the plane of the star's mutual orbit, while the other is perpendicular to it. Both are firmly attached to the rim of my coffee table, and move as it moves."

"Hold it," George said, staring at the model. "If I've got this straight, that means that, in real life, the *northern* hemisphere of Capital is currently pointed at this other star? The other star is visible from there? And the southern, populated hemisphere is pointed away from it—which is why we never see it?"

"And the northern lights are like a dawn that takes years to happen," Metcalf said. "The other sun is just below the horizon." He gave the table a spin, and stood up. "Think of that, George," he said. "You lived your whole life in a binary star system and never even knew it. Gotta hand it to the Guardians. What a beautiful job of misdirection. They never told you, so you couldn't tell us, and so the League hasn't been able to find you. We've only been looking at single-star systems, because that's what you *thought* you lived in." Randall shook his head in wonderment, and then looked up at their host. "Doctor Morelles, I thank you. You might have just solved a big problem."

Morelles got to his feet with a smile. "It has been a pleasure. But, may I ask—what will you do now?" he asked.

"Start a search through all the catalogs, I guess," Randall said. "We'll look for pairs of distant binary stars where one of the stars is the right mass and temperature to support life."

Morelles smiled. "That is *my* proper work. With all due respect, I am sure I could do a far more sophisticated search than a non-astronomer. Please allow me to do the job. I'd be delighted to do so—and before you say it, I know they'll slap a Top Secret on this at least, and that's fine. I have clearance. I'll get started on it right now."

"Doctor, it's urgent but it isn't *that* urgent," Metcalf said. "It can wait until morning."

Morelles smiled. "You're forgetting, Commander. Astronomers always work nights."

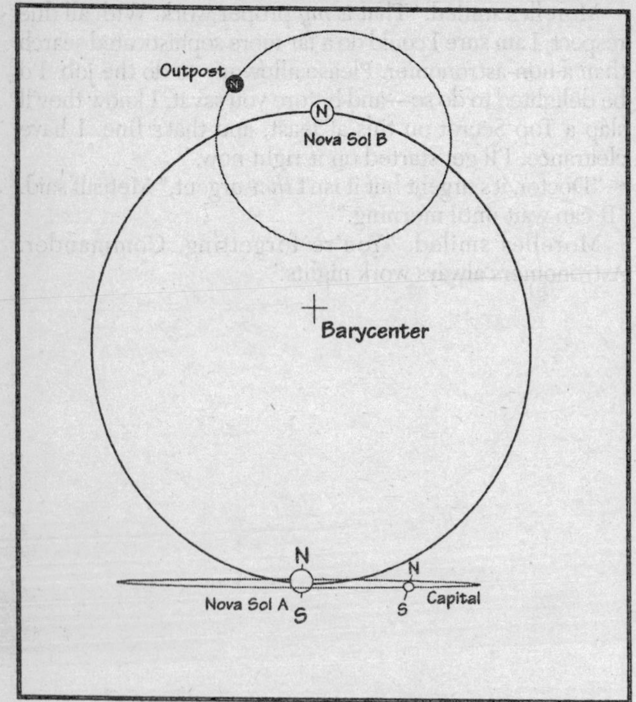

THE NOVA SOL SYSTEM
(uninhabited planets deleted for clarity)

Nova Sol B, with Outpost in orbit around it, orbits the system's barycenter in the normal manner, with the plane of the star's rotation, the plane of the planet's rotation, and the plane of the planet's orbit all in the plane of the orbits of the two stars about the barycenter. Here we look down on the North Pole (indicated with "N") of both Outpost and Nova Sol B. Nova Sol A's plane of rotation, the plane of Capital's orbit, and Capital's plane of rotation, are all rotated 90 degrees away from the plane of the two stars' rotation about each other.

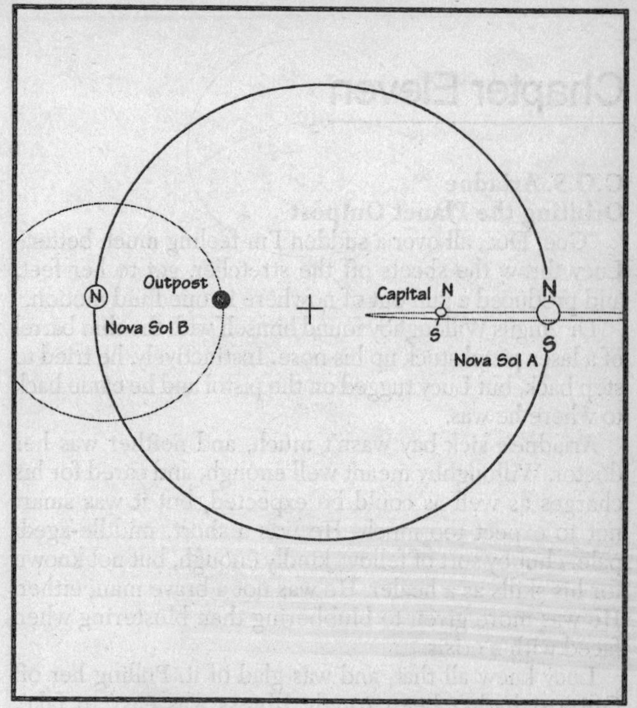

THE NOVA SOL SYSTEM

In the previous illustration, Nova Sol B would have been hidden from view by anyone on the southern hemisphere of Capital. Now the two stars have moved one-quarter of the way around in their 130-year orbit. Nova Sol B is now visible from the southern hemisphere of Capital, and will be so for another half-orbit of the two stars about their barycenter. Note that, as Outpost orbits in the plane of the stars' mutual orbit, Nova Sol A is routinely visible from any point on Nova Sol B's surface.

Chapter Eleven

G.O.S. Ariadne
Orbiting the Planet Outpost

"Gee, Doc, all over a sudden I'm feeling much better." Lucy threw the sheets off the stretcher, got to her feet, and produced a gun out of nowhere in one fluid motion.

Dr. Angus Willoughby found himself with the slim barrel of a laser pistol stuck up his nose. Instinctively, he tried to step back, but Lucy tugged on the pistol and he came back to where he was.

Ariadne's sick bay wasn't much, and neither was her doctor. Willoughby meant well enough, and cared for his charges as well as could be expected, but it was smart not to expect too much. He was a short, middle-aged, pale, chubby sort of fellow, kindly enough, but not known for his skills as a healer. He was not a brave man, either. He was more given to blubbering than blustering when faced with a crisis.

Lucy knew all that, and was glad of it. Pulling her off Outpost hadn't been rough; illness was easy to fake, especially with Gustav to back her up. Getting rushed to the infirmary was straightforward, and Willoughby was easy enough to scare. But if he had been made of sterner stuff, there could have been problems.

And Lucy had problems enough as it was. But one thing at a time. "Okay, Doctor." She pulled a pressure syringe out of her hip pocket. "You get a double dose of some feelgoods, and I'll be on my way. Roll up your sleeve."

"But I ah—ah—"

"Do it, or I clean out your nasal passages." Did that sound dumb to him, too, or was he too scared?

Willoughby pulled his shirt sleeve up without further

debate, Lucy slammed the hypo down and the powerful narcotic forced itself through his skin and into his bloodstream.

He dropped a little faster than Lucy had figured. Maybe he just fainted.

That was square one. She stood in the tiny room, waiting for long moments. No sound. She opened the door a bit and peeked out into the corridor. The stretcher-bearers were gone, back at their regular duties. Enough cases had come up from Outpost, cuts and burns and carbon-dioxide shock, that it was all pretty routine to them. Pull the casualty off the lander, get the stretcher to the doc, and then back to work.

She locked the door and peeled her CI jumpsuit, revealing a Guardian private's uniform underneath. She shoved her laser pistol into her belt, and checked on dear old Doctor Willoughby. He was folded up in the corner, gently snoring, out of the game for quite a while.

Now started the tricky part. The sick bay had a standard terminal station, hooked into Ariadne's computer systems. The CIs had been working over that computer system for quite a while now. Lucy powered it up, requested the calculator, tried to figure the square root of negative 43, then asked for the base-8 equivalent of her parent's phone number back on Earth. Then she typed in

Operate Gremloid

There was a brief delay, and then the computer responded.

EXPOSE YOURSELF

Sydney Sally

ALIAS?

Ned Fine

PROVE IT—WHERE WAS YOUR FATHER BORN?

Liverpool, Pommieland

WE'VE GOT YOU LINED, SAL. WHAZZUP?

The whole Gremloid system was like that, with the computer handing out and expecting slang and inside jokes. Gremloid was buried deep inside the computer system, and only after one of several cuing routines would the computer system even admit it existed.

But even if Gremloid was buried deep, he could reach into lots of places.

Lucy typed in

Looper Snooper: Straitslace Sue

SHE BE LINED.

Good. Straitslace Sue—more commonly known as Cynthia Wu—was at a terminal somewhere, working. Now to get Gremloid to send her a message. So far no one aboard Ariadne knew who had been aboard that medical shuttle. Lucy had to let Cynthia know what was up.

Gremloid, C.Q. Straitslace Sue

IT'S IN THE HOPPER—COOL YOUR JETS

There was a brief pause, and then a new line popped on the screen.

S.SUE RESPONDS: WHO AND WHAT IS IT?

Gremloid had cut into the regular operations of Cynthia's terminal, told her someone on the Gremnet wanted to talk to her, and sent her reply back.

Lucy had no time to jigger around with the usual jargoned-up lingo of the Gremnet. She had to get some very precise information across.

Cyn—this is Lucy. No time to explain why, but I came here to steal a ship, and land it on Outpost. Once there, I will use a beacon set at a frequency at hertz equal to your MMDDYY format birthdate, Earth calendar, divided by three. No time for questions. I'm in sickbay. Where is closest prepped lander and can you create diversion to draw sentries from same? There was a longish pause. It might have been Cynthia thinking, or a Guard asking her what was going on, or Cyn carefully checking the computer files to see what landers were where. Lucy didn't know or care. She just prayed for Cyn to hurry.

Cynthia Wu felt the bottom drop out of her stomach. The Gremnet always had that effect on her, as if she was talking to a ghost, a disembodied voice, but this was worse than usual. Lucy was supposed to be a thousand kilometers away, straight down, on the planet's surface. Cynthia was at her regular post in the radar room, monitoring the comings and goings of ships. It was a lonely post, especially during the night watch. No one else was on duty, just Cynthia and her keeper, a Private Wendell.

She glanced up at him, then looked back at her console screens. What the hell was Lucy doing here? But it wasn't time for questions. She used Gremloid to call up the sabotage and surveillance files. The S&S files were the most carefully hidden part of the CI's underground computer net. The names, the call-up procedures, the security techniques, were constantly being changed. That was part of how they maintained its security. Hiding things had gotten a lot easier since Gustav had gone down to the surface. Romero was not exactly known for running relentless security checks. Thank God for small favors.

Lucy had been away far too long to know how to use the current incarnation. Come on, come on—ah, there we go, a lander nice and close in Bay Three. Cynthia keyed in her reply, willing that her sentry stick to his comic book for another five minutes.

THERE IS A HERO-CLASS LANDER AT LOCK 6, BAY THREE FUELED AND AT GO. I WILL INSTRUCT COMPUTER TO WARN OF FUEL LEAK AND EXPLOSION DANGER IN THAT COMPARTMENT IN TEN MINUTES. GO NOW. GOOD LUCK.

Lucy breathed a sigh of relief. *That* was why she had tried Cynthia first. No gush of questions to slow things down. She was just ready with what was needed when it was needed. Level-headed common sense taken to an extreme state.

God bless you, Cynthia. I'll explain some day, if I can, Lucy typed.

I KNOW YOU WILL. GO NOW. HURRY.

Lucy cut the power on the terminal and slipped out into the corridor. It was the night-shift on Ariadne. All the corridor lights were dimmed, and the constant background noises of the station's machinery was subdued. All was gloomy and still. Quietly, quickly, going by side corridors and ducking out of sight whenever she heard a noise, she made her way toward the docking bays in the zero-gee section.

A Hero-Class in Bay Three. And the sentries ought to be scared out of there in about seven more minutes. That only left a few problems—like operating the Guard controls—she had seen them, but never run them—and making a landing someplace where C'astille's people could find her. And convincing the Guards that she was dead and not worth going after. There was a way, but it was tricky. Dangerous. But grabbing a Hero would help. The Guard pilots had nicknamed them Neros, because the ships had a tendency to burn. No doubt that was part of why Cynthia had chosen a Hero for Lucy.

Through this corridor to the elevator banks—good! There was a car waiting. She rushed from a shadowy corner into the car and punched the button for the zero-gee section. The door shut and up she went.

The elevator traveled up to the zero-gee section and the doors opened. The lights were dimmed here, too, and Lucy felt a cool, metallic tang in the air, as if she could sense the vacuum held back by the airlocks. A silly idea. Her head seemed to be full of them tonight. She had just about three minutes to get herself inside Bay Three before Cyn's bogus explosion warning would scare everyone out. No time to hide and skulk in corners at the sound of a voice now. She had on the right sort of uniform. She'd just have to trust to the gloomy lighting and hope that she didn't run into a Guard who would recognize her face.

Lucy rushed along the corridors, swarming along the handholds at top speed. She hadn't been in zero-gee for months, but it all came back to her now. Like riding a bicycle, or so went the expression. Lucy hadn't ever learned to ride a bike.

Bay One. Bay Two. Bay Three. Here. In here.

Lucy stopped herself and hung in mid-air at the personnel hatch to the bay. Bay Three. This was where the CIs—no, they had still thought of themselves as Survey Service back then—this was where the Survey Service group had been put aboard Ariadne when they were taken off *Venera*.

Well, if this was where she got on, it was also where she got off. And no way to sneak in. There was a small viewport set in the hatch, and Lucy cautiously peeked into it.

The interior of the bay was in darkness. One small light shone in the corner—the two sentries playing gin rummy, being very careful of the cards in zero-gee. Good. Their eyes would be adjusted for light, not dark. Lucy took as good a look as she could at the dim interior. When the *Venera* survivors had been piled in here, the vast storage and transfer space had been completely empty, stripped bare. Now there was cargo stored everywhere, in crates and cases and pressure vessels lashed down and stacked and secured on every inch of deck space. It was a maze of hiding places.

The hatch was closed but not dogged shut. Slowly, with exquisite care, she opened the hatch. It creaked just a little as it swung outward, a bare little chirp of a noise. She swung the hatch open just far enough to let herself slip through it. Hugging close to the deck, she pulled it shut behind her. Floating noiselessly through zero-gee, she pulled herself along the deck and hid herself behind a convenient stack of cases.

Now it was time for Cynthia to come through.

At that moment, Cynthia was in a cold sweat, doing her best to have a pleasant chat with Private Wendell, who had suddenly tired of his comic. He was a nice enough kid who probably had a crush on her. She blanked her terminal's screen the moment he had come over to talk about the movie that had been shown the night before, a rather pedestrian Guardian comedy that had proven humor was incompatible with censorship. Wendell had loved it, which probably proved that taste was likewise incompatible.

She tried to shut him up politely, get him back to his reading. "—Listen," she interrupted gently, "I've *got* to watch my screens, or else get shot when some pair of ships crack up out there."

"Huh? I thought things were pretty quiet tonight."

"They are, but I want to keep it that way. And with one thing and another I've barely had a chance to monitor. I've really got to pay strict attention for a while, until I know what's going on out there. I need to get caught up."

"Okay. Could I maybe get you a cuppa coffee? It'd gimme something t'do."

Please, please do, you silly kid. Anything to leave me alone, Cynthia thought. But she couldn't seem eager. "Isn't that against regs? You're supposed to be keeping an eye on me."

"Hell, you've been here close to a year and you've never tried anything. I'll just go to the galley and back. Stretch my legs. Be back in five minutes."

"Wellll—how about tea instead?"

Wendell displayed a grin full of buck teeth. "Sure. I'll go get it."

Cynthia called up Gremloid before he was out the door. What the hell was Lucy doing back on station? Where had she come from? And what the devil did she need to steal a ship for? No time for that. Cynthia hurriedly instructed Gremloid to slip the bogus emergency to the main computer through the ship's environmental monitor circuits.

Lucy was probably in or near Bay Three by now—the sickbay was close to the elevator banks, and Luce was fast in zero-gee. But Cynthia didn't dare stage a phony alert in the time Wendell was gone. Too suspicious. She told Gremloid to run the fake in ten minutes. That would give Wendell plenty of time to spill the tea, mop it up, make it again, and bring it to her.

Lucy knew how slowly time moved for her when she was waiting, but this was ridiculous. Though it was too damn dark to check her wristaid for the time, she was sure more than ten minutes had passed. There was nothing she could do but wait in the dark, and mentally rehearse the moves that would get her to Lock Six. As best she could remember, Six should be on the opposite side of the deck.

"Here's the tea," Wendell announced in a loud, clear voice as he came in. Cynthia nearly jumped half out of her skin.

"Oh—you startled me," Cynthia said, trying to regain her composure. She took her tea and smiled at him. "Thanks."

"No problem. So how's it look out there?"

"Very quiet. No one changing orbit, so far as I can see."

"Good. So I guess we can talk a bit, then, now that you're caught up."

That was exactly the last thing Cynthia was in the mood for, but it would cover for her when all hell broke loose in a minute or two. "I guess so," she said, smiling. She was just beginning to strain her imagination, trying to think of a topic she could possibly discuss with him, when a shrill *beep, beep* came on at the radar room's security console.

"Oh, hell," Wendell said as crossed to see what the alarm was.

"What is it?" Cynthia asked. Either they had caught Lucy or Gremloid had just tossed his diversion into the main system.

"Hold on a sec—I'm not that good with this thing. Ah—oh, no big deal, not our section. Fuel leak in the zero-gee section. Happens all the time. They'll get it fixed."

"Oh."

"So, anyway," Wendell said cheerfully, "y'know what I really liked about last night's show?"

"Tell me."

The alert might not have bothered Wendell, but the two sentries in Bay Three got pretty excited. It was more than a *beep, beep* to them. A huge voice shouted down at them, "Evacuate and seal off this compartment. Explosive fuel leak detected. All personnel evacuate this compartment." A siren started, and the booming warning voice repeated again and again. The two of them were out the personnel hatch in nothing flat.

Lucy watched the two of them get out and dog the hatch behind them. Then she pulled herself up from behind her packing cases and kicked off toward Lock Six. Everything going well so far—

There was a clank and a thud as the personnel hatch was pulled back open. Lucy grabbed at a handhold and pulled herself down, taking cover behind a pressure vessel. The main lighting came on, dazzling her eyes.

"We saw you, whoever you are. You should have remembered that hatch has a viewport. Come on out."

"Sergeant Mosgrove, that could be a real leak warning. It's still repeating. Let's get out of here."

"Shut up, Sammy. Whoever is in here jiggered that alarm to get us to leave our posts. You want to steal a ship? Go ahead and try, you lousy CI bastard. I knew you creeps couldn't be trusted."

"How do you know it's a CI?"

"Who else would be after a ship?" Mosgrove growled. "Come on out, 'cause we're coming in."

Lucy's heart was pounding fit to break through her ribs, and she found her gun in her hand. She pulled herself along the ropes and cables that held down the cargo, peering around the packing cases, trying to get a sight line. The booming voice repeated its warning. Soon other sentries would come, to check on their comrades. She didn't have time to fight these guys. If she could get to Lock Six. . . . It should be a small lock, its hatch set flush with the deck. There. Ten meters away, across open deck—

She spotted one of the Guards and fired before she could think. A young kid, maybe nineteen, and he screamed as her laser chopped his hand off.

Mosgrove, a sour-faced man of indeterminate age, came up behind the younger man, and Lucy felt a terrible pain in her left hand and caught a whiff of cooking meat. Mosgrove had fired and hit her. She fired her own weapon right in his face, and her enemy became a corpse before he could lift a hand to shield himself.

Lucy forced herself to take their guns. She might need weapons where she was going.

Ninety seconds later she was cycled through Lock Six and strapped into the pilot's chair in a Hero-Class lander.

She thought of two men, one dead and one maimed, and she didn't feel very hero-class herself. Then she started flicking switches and trying to remember what she could about how the Guards flew these things.

The radar room's comm system was wired into Launch and Recovery Control, of course. Cynthia's own radars were watching a lot farther out than the skin of Ariadne. L&R would call her, ask to confirm an unauthorized launch the moment it happened. Cynthia chatted aimlessly with the endlessly dull Wendell, waiting for the call. The comm light lit up. "Excuse me a second, Wendell." She hit the answer key. "Radar room here." She had to keep her voice calm.

"Cyn, this is Schiller over in L&R. We've got a sensor light here showing an open docking collar where a lander's supposed to be. Is that a bum sensor or did a ship really drift loose over there?"

"Hmm. Stand by. I'll have to reconfigure for a close scan. But we got a reading of a fuel leak over there."

"Yeah, we got that too. Sounds like a right nasty malfunction."

"Could be the lander's pilot cast loose to get clear of a possible explosion."

"Yeah, we thought of that. Got it yet?"

"Hang in there, Sam. The controls seem a little sluggish for some reason."

Sam Schiller wasn't especially concerned up until that moment. Little malfs like this were what he was here for. But then something strange happened. As he listened over his headset, Cynthia started whistling, badly.

Cyn *never* whistled. It wasn't in her character. Neither

was the tune, a breezy little bit of froth. Cyn was big on the classics, and on the Atonalists. But that tune sounded familiar. A very old pop song, an ancient piece, one of a series that had been dredged up by someone back at the Survey Service Training Base and played to death. One of those tunes that could get stuck in your head. But there had been some special reason for that one song being popular. What was it? Schiller remembered some of the CIs singing it to tease—

Whoa. That was it. *Lucy in the Sky With Diamonds*. They had used to kid Calder with it, back on the *Venera*.

And Wu was no kidder. Schiller had been, once, but living in the enemy's lap had drained that from him and left a residue of paranoid imagination. "Ah, Cynthia. I've got a lot of what sounds like room noise on the line. Please switch to your headset, and I'll do the same."

"Stand by." There was a click. "On headsets now."

Schiller plugged the tiny speaker into his ear. "Okay, if I keep my voice down we're private at this end. You trying to tell me something?"

"Affirmative."

Great. Some Guard was breathing down her neck. At least the L&R sentry was across the room. "Understood. Something's up, but you can't tell me because of our babysitter. He can hear what you say, but not what I say."

"Affirmative," Cynthia's voice said, a strange, false lightheartedness in her tone.

"So who the hell is on that lander?"

"You'll have to trust the readings I just gave a bit longer, Sam. Let's just take our time and do it right, so we don't lose one."

"Okay, Calder's on that thing, somehow, and you want me to stall. What the hell is going on?"

"No info yet, Sam. Stand by." There was a long pause. "I have some sort of very close-in radar contact. We might need to put in a call to Search and Rescue."

Sam Schiller wasn't very good at this sort of thing. He was glad Cynthia could think fast. Search and Rescue was one banged-up old cargo ship and whichever two Guard pilots who wanted a chance to catch up on their sleep. The longer it took to rouse them, the longer it would be until someone figured out there was an escape in progress and called Fighter Command. And the way Cynthia was running things, there wouldn't be anything on the record to show the CIs had aided the escape or impeded the Guards.

Unless they were tapping the intercom, in which case Schiller knew he was going to be shot. Schiller reached for the S&R phone and swore to himself. He didn't *want* to be good at this sort of thing.

At least laser wounds didn't bleed much, though this one hurt like hell. It really didn't look too bad, a slash of angry red along her wrist and her pinky. There were already signs of some nasty blistering, though.

There wasn't time for painkillers or first aid. She had to get this tub out of here, below the radar horizon. And this was the second time she had ridden a Guard ship without knowing the vehicle's name. If Hero-class boats even rated names. Might just be a number.

She had kicked free of Ariadne with maximum thrust of her maneuvering jets. Now she spun ship and set up for retro fire. Get down, get away, then worry about fancy stuff.

She punched some buttons and brought up the inertial tracker, then punched in a set of ground coordinates. It had taken hours with C'astille to figure out the coordinates of Lucy's landing site. The Outposter had some trouble with human mapping conventions, but nothing compared to the trouble Lucy had had with the native's charts. C'astille wanted her several hundred kilometers north of the Guardian contact site.

Lucy knew that if she missed that landing site by too much, she was a dead woman.

With any luck, the landing site would be on the far side of the planet from her current position, with the bulk of a whole world to hide her movements. There hadn't been any way to time it out. She swore a blue streak when the navigation computer showed her that the landing site was, at the moment, almost directly beneath her lander. The Guards would have perfect line-of-sight on her all the way in if she made a direct approach. So much for luck.

Okay, it was bloody well time to work with what she had. A minimum power reentry would land her about 180 degrees away from where she was now. She checked the map display in the inertial guidance computer. There was open ocean on the opposite side of the globe. That was a start. Two minutes later the nameless lander fired her engines in retro-fire.

Twenty minutes. Cynthia Wu felt the sweat coming out of every pore in her body. Twenty lousy minutes was all she and Sam had been able to buy for Lucy. Now all hell was indeed breaking loose. One dead, one badly injured in Bay Three. Fighter Command, up on Nike station, had jumped in with both feet four minutes ago and would have their fighters scrambled in another two. They had patched into the radar feed from Ariadne, and Cynthia had no way of cutting the feed. They were running her radars by remote now, combining her radar returns with their own. All Cynthia could do was watch the radar screens and pray that Lucy could get herself lost. And fast. If she could hit atmosphere, get behind the planet, out of line-of-sight, she might pull it off.

Lucy watched her own screens. First Ariadne's beacon slid behind the planet and winked out, then Nike's. Good. Loss of signal. Over the radar horizon. Thank God. If she couldn't see them anymore, then they couldn't see her, either.

But there was something else she needed to do before she hit air. The lander was armed with four small torpedoes. As soon as she was hidden from Nike's radar, she jettisoned two of them—not firing them, just ejecting them from their launch tubes, so they tumbled slowly away from the lander. She was tempted to dump all four—but she might need some armament if the day ever dawned when she flew this thing out of here. Once they hit air, the torpedoes would burn up, maybe even explode. They would put some debris on Guardian radar screens, once they scrambled fighters. It might even be enough to throw them off the scent.

Or maybe not. Lucy went back to concentrating on her ride down, flying the lander. Finally the damn thing hit air. Lucy had no exterior view cameras on, but she could imagine the torps starting to tumble, starting to glow from air friction. She could imagine the plume of superheated air that was growing around her lander. The air would become ionized, and glow fiercely in the darkness as she slid into the nightside of the world below. If her luck was bad, some ship or station overhead would spot so bright a thing as a night reentry. But without good radar and careful tracking, things that only Ariadne and Nike were equipped for, the Guards wouldn't have enough to find her, especially if the reentering torps were there to confuse the issue, and if she were maneuvering in the atmosphere—something she very much intended to do.

Lucy wanted to try an old idea, dreamed up in the very beginning of space flight, or perhaps even earlier. Rock skipping. Instead of plowing straight down into the atmosphere, she would use the lander's energy of velocity to bounce in and out of the upper atmosphere several times. It would play hob with her heat shield, but she only wanted to use the thing this once.

She pitched the lander around until her conical shape produced more lift than drag and started gaining altitude once more, until she was flung clear of the sensible atmosphere. Back in vacuum, her lander again became a purely ballistic vehicle, her velocity still very high, in the thousands of kilometers an hour, but just barely suborbital. The little craft soon began to fall again, this time half-way around the world from her first entry. Lucy swung the nose around again, the conical lander in effect becoming a large, crude airfoil. Again she was flung clear of the air, but this time not so high, not so far.

She checked the situation in the guidance display. Nike

and Ariadne's orbits had now carried them well out of line-of-sight for both of them. And the decoy torpedoes and her oddball entry were probably enough to lose any fighters they might have scrambled.

The landing site was barely in range for a gliding reentry. Her lander started to fall in toward the planet again, for the last time. She was going to make it. Then all she had to do was sit tight and wait for C'astille's people to find her. She hoped they took their time. Lucy felt about due for a breather.

Fighter command never tracked her second and third entries, just the first. The computers spotted an explosion in the upper atmosphere and tracked the path of a small amount of debris that impacted on open ocean. Even if she had lived through that, somehow, a human couldn't survive long on Outpost anyway. The Guards listed Calder as died trying to escape.

But even after Cynthia Wu tuned in on the beacon frequency, and locked in on a strong signal north of the Guard's contact camp, she worried that Guards would turn out to be right after all. For even if Lucy had gotten to the surface alive, Outpost was not the sort of place people on their own *stayed* alive for long.

Chapter Twelve

Aboard HMS *Impervious*
In orbit of the planet Britannica

Commander Joslyn Marie Cooper Larson, Royal Britannic Navy, stood by her uncle in the reception line, doing her best to keep an eye on him as she smiled and shook hands with the guests that filed past.

Dear old Uncle George. She couldn't help liking the poor old dear. Oh, there was no doubt that he had a strong fondness for the bottle, and there was probably truth to the rumor that he had been posted to Britannica 30 years ago to keep his slightly drunken self as far as possible from London society and politics. But none of that mattered. Great Uncle George—or Captain Sir George Wilfred Thomas, when they were in uniform—was a most courteous, thoughtful, and hospitable man.

If the mark of a true, blue, gentleman was the ability to behave well under trying circumstances, then Sir George had proved himself to be among the truest and bluest. He was master of HMS *Impervious*, one of the carrier ships Joslyn's husband Mac had campaigned against.

Sir George had been the *Imp*'s reserve captain, charged with maintaining her in storage for the last ten Earth years. He had been active duty all that time, but he liked to joke that he had been reactivated along with his ship.

And yet Sir George hadn't held Mac's words against Joslyn, though she couldn't have blamed him if he had. Instead he had most gallantly asked her to serve as official hostess at tonight's reception. Flag-rank officers from half the members of the League were there in celebration of the *Imp*'s recommissioning. If anything, Sir George seemed delighted at the chance to twit the stuffier officers with his choice of a hostess.

Sir George himself was splendidly turned out in an elegantly tailored formal dress uniform, a chestful of ribbons for who-knows-what glittering against the sleek black of his jacket, all his braid and insignia brushed and polished and perfect. He smiled and joked with everyone as the reception line moved past, the picture of a hale and hearty old man, his tall, thin figure the natural focus of attention. There was not the slightest hint of a hair left on his smooth-polished scalp, and his snow-white eyebrows bounded up and down as he talked. The only wrinkles on his face were crows-feet and laugh-lines. Fondness for the bottle or no, his complexion was fresh-scrubbed, pink and healthy, with no trace of the mottled skin or liver patches one might expect, and the grip of his handshake was still firm and strong.

It was a festive night. Hangar One, decorated with bunting and flags, with thick carpeting rolled out, a walnut dance floor laid over the steel decks, and a Navy band playing an elegant old refrain, looked as if it had been designed to double as a ballroom—as indeed it had.

Joslyn looked lovely that night, and knew it, and enjoyed the fact. The Royal Britannic Navy didn't have a uniform for officers, female, formal evening, but instead expected its female officers to "select a gown of color, cut, and style suitable to the occasion." It was one of the few regulations Joslyn actually enjoyed obeying. She had literally let her hair down, out of the usual tight braid, and it fell in long, full, golden-brown waves down the length of her back. She wore a long, full, flowing, strapless evening gown of midnight black, woven of a sheer, glistening fabric that caught the light as she moved.

She was tall and slender, and the gown suited her exactly, adding a special grace to her every move. She wore a single strand of pearls around her throat, and matching pearl stud earrings. Her blue eyes and peaches-and-cream complexion completed the picture of a charming and lovely young upper-class woman. She was that, but she was also a skilled pilot, and perhaps the most experienced combat veteran aboard the *Impervious*. She had killed her share of Guardians, a hard fact to keep in mind as she greeted the guests with a charmingly shy and youthful smile.

Joslyn was glad, now, that Uncle George had asked her to play the part of hostess. She didn't know or care if it was some complicated political ploy of his, or if he simply thought it would be fun. Joslyn herself could have held a few grudges against a few people, but she had concluded it wasn't worth the effort. The Office of Personnel for one, but then they had only cut the orders the Britannic High Command had told them to cut, if the scuttlebutt was to be believed. She greeted Admiral Samuel Whitmore of the High Command with a smile, and thought daggers at the bugger, just in case he had been the one with the gallows sense of humor, posting her to a ship her husband said was a deathtrap.

She didn't so much mind being posted away from Mac. Oh, she missed him terribly, of course. And she was furious at Whitmore and anyone else in the Royal Britannic Navy who might have been behind the order that had yanked her home and away from the Survey Service. But she was Navy, from a Navy family, and one had to expect to be separated from a husband in wartime. That came with the territory of military life. If Mac had been a civilian, they'd probably be just as far from each other right now, for all practical purposes.

And she had the comforting knowledge that Mac was *safe*. For far too long in those dreadful months in the New Finnish system, she had been alone in the *J.M.*, waiting, never knowing from moment to moment if he was dead or alive, knowing only that he was in constant danger.

At least now she knew he lived. And they could write each other, send recordings. That should have been enough. But she loved him very much.

Yet it *was* good to be home, or at least in orbit around home. And she could catch a shuttle down to Kings Town

Field and be home with Mummy and Dad in twelve hours whenever she could wangle a pass. She felt more *British* than she had in a long time. She had traveled widely, seen many ways of doing many things, but it was good to be *home*, and be surrounded by the ways she had learned as a child. It was good to be where everyone knew the importance of warming the teapot properly, and trivets and elaborate gardens and digestive biscuits and driving on the left side of the road were quite normal, the done things, rather than quaint, charming old customs, survivals of an earlier age.

And there was work, a therapy that had always helped Joslyn. There was a lot to do aboard *Impervious*. The ship was a huge cylinder, a thousand feet long and three hundred fifty feet in diameter. Fifteen huge fusion engines were clustered on the aft end, and the circumference of the hull was a forest of detection gear, antennae, gunnery, hatches, and inspection ports. The bow of the ship was a flat disk. In its center was a large circular hole, a launch and recovery port. Even if the ship was under spin *and* under thrust, it was just about possible to bring in a fighter or other smaller vehicle there, and a system of elevators could then move the ships to the *Imp*'s circumference. Every ninety degrees along the circumference of the bow end were launch tubes for the fighters, the Wombats and SuperWombats. The bow holes of the launch tubes led into tunnels that ran half the length of the ship. The launch tunnels were normally in vacuum, but the One and Three tubes were being worked on at the moment, and were sealed and under pressure. Inside the launch tunnels were great electric catapults—linear accelerators—that could take a fighter and fling it clear of the *Imp* without either ship firing its engines. The launch tunnels could also be used to move ships much more slowly between the bow centerpoint launch and recover port and the hangar decks.

There were four hangar decks, one for each launch tunnel. These took up the entire circumference of the *Imp* amidships. Since the One launch tunnel was out of action,

Hangar One had been done over for the reception. The ship was under spin at the moment, of course, and the hangar was under about three-quarters of an Earth gravity. The hangar was high-ceilinged and went through ninety degrees of the ship's circumference. It was disconcerting to see handsomely dressed ladies and gentlemen calmly strolling or sitting on a deck that was curved about halfway toward the vertical.

The other side of the steel deck beneath the dance floor was the outer hull of the ship. There were great hangar doors, large enough to move a SuperWombat through, and Joslyn couldn't help imagining some practical joker opening the doors beneath the wooden dance floor, and all those old stuffed shirts dropping straight through into space. . . . But even the most ghastly bore didn't deserve that fate. However, if the hangar decks were in vacuum, and the ship were under spin, the fighters could be simply dropped through the hangar doors. When so dropped, they would move away from the ship at the speed the ship had been spinning. If the ship weren't spinning, the fighters would use their own maneuvering jets to get on or off the ship.

The *Imp* had been mothballed thirty years before, left in a distant parking orbit of Britannica, and more or less forgotten about until the message torp had come in from the Finns with word of the Guardians. *That* had set off a panicky rearmament program, not just on Britannica, but throughout the British Commonwealth—and the League. The *Imp* was Britannica's ship, though, and it was a Britannic decision to dust her off and get her battle-ready.

It wasn't easy. Thirty years was a very long time in the art of shipbuilding. The words "obsolescent" and "obsolete" didn't quite cover the situation. The *Imp* could more accurately be described as a fossil. She practically had to be stripped down to the hull. The computers had to go. The communications equipment was hopeless. The laser cannon and torpedo tubes had to be pulled out and replaced with modern equipment. And of course the power plant had to be radically upgraded. A modern fusion generator was half the size, was far more rugged, and could give twice the power of the old monster aboard the *Imp*. And the engines. Good Lord, from what Joslyn heard, dealing with the engine problems was more an historic epic than an engineering challenge. Modern engines of the size originally fitted on the *Imp* gave twice the power, but unfortunately they couldn't be used—the *Impervious*' hull and superstructure couldn't withstand the increased thrust stresses. But the old engines couldn't be trusted either. They had too many hours on them, and were a plumber's nightmare besides. The only people who knew how to maintain them had retired ten years ago. And no current engine model had anything like the proper thrust ratings to be a direct replacement.

But somehow it was all getting done. Joslyn was on the periphery of it all. Her direct concern was with the fighters that would be carried by the *Impervious*, and that was trouble enough. She was doing her part, making a real contribution. She had more actual experience of directing fighters in real combat operations than anyone in the Britannic Navy. From time to time it struck her that the Office of Personnel had simply done their job and put her exactly where she could do the most good. She was certainly whipping the *Imp*'s fighter wings into shape.

The last of the guests filed through, and it was time for the dinner to begin. The ship's cooks had done themselves proud, as if eager to put the lie to the old saw that the British couldn't cook. The appetizer, the soup, a lime sherbet to cleanse the palate, the meat course, the dessert, coffee, all of it delicious.

Joslyn sat at the head table with Sir George at her left. At her right was a rather handsome young officer, a Captain Thorpe-Peron of the RBN. He seemed rather young for a captain, a short, almost pudgy sort of chap, with white-blonde hair and brown eyes. He was slightly round-faced, and seemed soft all over, somehow.

Thorpe-Peron was fascinated by anything to do with the *Impervious*. What did the pilots think of their fighters?

How was the refitting going along? Were the flight deck crews ready? How much training in pressure suit work did they have?

Joslyn never enjoyed talking shop during a social occasion, but she did her duty as a hostess and chatted cheerfully enough. She didn't notice at first that Admiral Whitmore had left his seat to whisper a word in Sir George's ear. But she did notice that whatever it was Whitmore had to say seemed to upset Sir George terribly.

After Whitmore left and returned to his seat, Joslyn was shocked to see Sir George call for a steward and have a decanter of port brought out to him, long before his guests were finished with their coffee. A discreet glance around the table made it clear she was not the only one to notice his behavior.

It wouldn't do, she decided. Better to get him away from table and fuss at him instantly than let him get an early start on a drunk, tonight of all nights.

"Captain Thomas?" she said to him, standing up. "I've just recalled. There is a tiny problem concerning the choice of dancing music. I wonder if you might come with me to have a word with the musicians." It wasn't much good as a lie, but it was all she could think of quickly and it was far better than having him pass out in a dead drunk two hours from now.

"Beg pardon?" Sir George answered, his glass halfway to his lips. "Ehh? Oh, of course, of course." He rose, glass in hand, and followed her away from the table.

Where could they talk privately? Not the kitchens or the passageways. Too many people coming and going. Hangar Two, then. The hangar decks were separated by a single bulkhead. Joslyn led the way through one of the personnel airlocks. There wasn't any pressure difference between the two sides, so she didn't have to cycle the lock, but she was careful to dog both doors shut after they were through. Careless pilots didn't live long.

Hangar Two was the twin of the deck now being used as a ballroom, but where on one side of the bulkhead were gaiety and music, on the other side were gloomy, echoing spaces and the machines of war. It was crowded in there: The fighters usually carried in Hangar One were in Two so as to make room for the dinner.

"Now, then," Sir George said as he looked around the hangar. "What's all this about the dance music?" he asked with a distracted air as he sipped at his port.

"Uncle George, will you for God's sake put that stuff away!" Joslyn shouted at him. She grabbed the glass and threw it across the deck. It hit with a crash, somewhere in the shadows. "You are the *host* at this party, and I will not let you get to be a fallen-down sodden drunk by the time the dancing starts! What host has ever had booze brought to his own table while the guests were taking coffee! How insufferably rude can you be! And manners like that from the captain of the ship, no less—"

"I'm afraid I'm not the captain any more, my dear," Sir George said, very gently. "Though you are quite right to stop me drinking so soon. It wouldn't do at all."

Something froze inside Joslyn's gut. "Not the captain?"

"Oh, I suppose I still am, officially. But good old Sam Whitmore just let me know that it might be nice for me to make a toast to my successor—lovely way to let a fellow know, isn't it?"

"Oh my God," Joslyn said, all the anger washing out of her. "Oh, Uncle George, I'm so sorry. It's that doughy little man Thorpe-Peron, isn't it? I should have *known* why he was pumping me for all the information." She threw her arms around her great-uncle and hugged him. "Damn the bastards! It's just not *fair*!"

"There, there, my dear. Commanders shouldn't hug captains, even under these circumstances." Joslyn smiled, and Sir George gave her a pat on the back. "Do settle down. I must admit that I am nowhere near as surprised as you. I've been waiting most of a year for them to put me out to pasture. You give a grand old girl like the *Imp* to an up-and-comer like Thorpe-Peron, not a broken down old sod like me. Now, now! Don't say anything. And let me just tell you that our doughy-faced young captain is a fine officer—a fine, fine—"

Sir George's voice broke, and he stepped away from Joslyn into the lurking shadows of the hangar deck. "Damn the luck!" he shouted into the echoing silence. "I've been little more than a caretaker all my life, a placeholder, keeping a chair warm until the other fellow wanted it. They got me out of England because of my drinking—and they thought that putting a man on the backside of nowhere was a way to take his mind off drink. I decided to make do, settled down permanently, put in for emigration, and got it. I watched Britannica grow into a worthwhile place. And I joined up, got my commission, served for years in whatever post they could find for me where I couldn't do any harm. This old hulk was my first command. I have taken care of this ship for ten long, lonely years, since the old reserve captain cashed in his chips in his sleep.

"But I did my job right. I checked over every inch of this old girl myself, learned what was too old, what was still good, what would be needed—and I kept that information up to date, once it was done. When they asked me what it would take to get her ready for battle, a year ago, I had the answers ready, right there under my arm, in detail. My staff—all eight of them—had wondered why I fussed so hard over a ship that no one would ever use—but by *damn* she's ready for a fight a year sooner than expected, because I did my homework!

"And they're taking her away from me and giving her to some pasty-faced public-school boy so he can punch his ticket with a major command on his well-charted way up to full admiral." Sir George's voice was bitter and angry.

"Uncle George," Joslyn said. "I am sorry. So very sorry."

"And now it will happen again," he said. "I'll be posted off somewhere *else* where they think I can't do any harm. Everyone will watch, and wait for me to crawl deeper down inside the bottle—"

"Captain to the bridge," a disembodied voice boomed

out. "Red Alert. All hands to Battle Stations. We are under attack. This is not a drill. Captain to the bridge."

Sir George stopped and looked up, toward the loudspeaker. "Under attack? What the devil could they—"

The first impact was felt more than heard, a booming, shaking roar that knocked them off their feet. The lights died.

Joslyn got to her feet in the pitch darkness. She was about to call out, to shout to her uncle to see if he was all right, when she heard the sound.

The sound no one aboard a spacecraft ever wants to hear. Through the bulkhead that led to Hangar One, they heard the horrible sound of air whistling away into space, of screams and cries and alarm bells, heard the sound dying off into an even more terrible silence as the air that carried the sound vanished out into space.

"Oh my God," Sir George said. "Oh my dear God, they've hulled Hangar One." His voice was deep with shock, echoing in the absolute darkness. "They're all dead in there. My God."

Joslyn climbed to her feet—and then got back down on her hands and knees. No sense getting knocked down again, banging around in the dark, waiting for another hit. The gloomy red of the emergency lighting system flickered on, and she saw Sir George striding purposefully across the deck, toward the airlock at the aft end and the nearest way to the bridge. Now that she could see, she got carefully to her feet and kicked off her high heels. She wasn't about to try *that* balancing act in a ship under fire.

WHANG! A huge noise like the greatest of all bells being rung blared out, and the deck shivered. Joslyn fell again and got back up. Something, a missile that misfired, a piece of debris, had bounced off the hull beneath their feet. There came another rending crash, followed by the deep, roaring shout of air rushing out into space. The sound seemed to come from deep inside the ship.

Alarms came on again, pilots and personnel came rushing

into the hangar from the aft airlock. Voices began to shout, and a mad tangle of frantic activity tried to sort itself out as the hangar crew and pilots readied for combat in the overcrowded space. Joslyn was glad to see them get there fast. She was the one who had seen to it that pilots and hangar crews were billeted near their battle stations. It saved time, and right now they needed every scrap of time they could get.

Joslyn's fighter, a command SuperWombat, was across the bay. Barefoot, in a ruined evening gown, her hair streaming behind her, she made her way through the confusion to her post.

Captain Sir George Wilfred Thomas got to an intercom station and used the Captain's override to punch up the bridge. Nothing. The bridge didn't respond. Damnation! He tried the Combat Information Center. Nothing. Was the intercom out? He keyed in another code, the Damage Control officer. The D.C. officer could be anywhere in the ship, but the intercom computer was supposed to track him or her at all times. The intercom squawked and answered. "Commander Higgins, at post in aft damage control center," a perfectly calm voice with an odd, rolling accent answered. "What is your report?"

Thank God. Higgins was the man for a moment like this. "This is Captain Thomas. I am on Hangar Two. Hangar One has been hulled. I cannot raise the bridge. I cannot raise the Combat Information Center. Can I get through the corridors to the bridge?"

"Captain. I am glad you are alive. I assumed you were in Hangar One. Sir, I lost all status reports on the Combat Information Center and the bridge immediately after the first impact. I must assume they are out of commission. We were hulled twice and took some glancing hits. There seem to have been no explosions, however. I cannot be certain yet, but I believe there is no corridor still under pressure that could lead you to the bridge. I am sending runners in pressure suits to inspect."

"Very well. What sort of outside communications do we have?"

"None at the moment, Captain. Outside comm is normally channeled through the bridge. We should get backups soon, routed through the auxiliary command station, which is functional but not yet manned."

"Very well. Commander Higgins, for the moment, I have no tactical information. I am trapped on Hangar Deck One, and I have a battle to fight. Assume that the aux control crew cannot reach their posts, or are dead, and get some of your personnel there on the double. I will contact you soon, Commander."

"Yes, sir."

Sir George turned and watched the activity on the deck. Crews were sorting themselves out, looking sharp, all things considered. But where should he be? Number Two Hangar Control, he decided. That was the spot, just across the deck. Sir George quick-marched to it, keeping well out of the way of the crews prepping the Wombats.

The four Hangar Control stations were always manned, behind sealed airlocks. Thereby, in theory, their crews could get some birds launched at any time. Captain Thomas hoped the theory held up. He undogged the outer door to the Control station's lock, cycled through, and hurried up the gangway. Hangar Control was high up on the aft bulkhead of the hangar, with big quartz ports that overlooked the entire compartment and let the Hangar Boss see everything that happened.

"Captain on the deck!" a rating called out.

"As you were. Hangar Boss, report," Sir George said.

"Sir. Our Forward Launch Tunnel is out. We are at Go for radial launch. We're ready to lift and drop Wombats through the hull doors as soon as we have the hangar in vacuum. Ready to button up in three minutes."

"Very good. The other hangar decks and Central Launch and Recovery?"

"Sir. CLR does not respond. Four is at Go for radial or forward launch. Three was on standby, with no fighters in bay, with skeleton crews in Hangar Control. Fighters normally in Three shifted to Four. Likewise in One—and the crew in Hangar One control say they are the only people still alive in the hangar. They were buttoned up, behind their airlock, when the deck was hulled."

"Very well. God help us all." It was beginning to sink in that the entire Britannic fleet had been decapitated. All the fleet's captains had been at the ball, all the flag officers, all the visiting bigwigs. Dancing four minutes ago, all dead now. The fleet was under attack and under command of junior officers. Sir George realized he might well be the senior officer left in the fleet. There was little time to think. "Can you patch comm with all the fighters through here?"

"Yes sir."

"Lieutenant, instruct Hangar Four to prepare for radial launch. The *Imp* has taken too much damage to trust the launch tunnels, whatever the readouts say. The bridge is out for the moment, and might have been destroyed. I will command this ship from here. Hand over whatever operations you can to Hangar Three and clear some of your consoles for combat control. Advise Damage Control of the shift. In fact, give Damage Control a direct audio feed from here. Tell them I am here and that I expect a report as soon as aux control is manned and ready."

"Sir."

Sir George stepped back and let the lieutenant and her enlisted personnel do their jobs. There was no point in rattling off a string of commands to do this and that about the ship. The crew needed time to sort itself out and get to stations. He stared out at the hangar. Joslyn—Commander Larson—had earned her pay. That crew was sharper than it had any right to be.

Six minutes had passed since the first explosion.

Joslyn swore bitterly to herself and decided an evening gown made a rotten uniform after all. The damn thing was so tight across the hips she couldn't climb the boarding ladder. Finally she said the hell with it, bent over, and ripped open the seam from the hem to the waist. Let the hangar crew see a little leg, she had work to do. Joslyn had stashed a hairnet in the pilot's ready-box by her fighter for just such an occasion as this. She wrapped her hair up into a quick, sloppy bun and pulled the hairnet down over it. *Next thing you know I'll be going into combat wearing curlers,* she thought, and wondered what part of her mind that idea had come from.

She scrambled through the fighter's hatch into the cockpit and started button-up, wishing there was time to get into a pressure suit. Well, she would just have to hope the hell that the fighter's cabin pressure held.

Oxygen, fuel, fusion source, laser pack, missiles, gatlings, maneuvering jets, main engines, comm unit, battle computer, flight command computer, tactical computer and downlink, all backups. She checked everything, and checked it all again, and again, until a loud *clump, clump* told her the overhead grapples had latched onto her SuperWombat. She looked up through the overhead quartz viewport. The pair of huge ceiling-mounted grapples had locked properly into the hardpoints. She gave the hangar crew a thumbs-up and felt her SuperWombat lurch slightly to one side as the grapples lifted her off the deck. She retracted the landing skids as the grapple unit moved on its overhead track, carrying her toward the hangar doors.

She pulled off her earrings, grabbed at a headset, put it on, adjusted the mike and earphone, and keyed in the radio. "This is A for Albert Leader, buttoned up, grappled and hanging. I am Go for launch. Albert craft, give me status by the numbers."

"Albert One, ninety seconds to button-up. Grappled and hanging."

"Albert Two at Go."

"This is Launch Boss. Albert Three not accounted for."

Damn, Joslyn thought. Mawkly had been two tables down from her at dinner. "He's dead, Launch Boss. Pull his ship for reserve."

"Will do, Albert Leader."

"Albert Four at Go."

"Albert Five. I have a yellow on laser pack, but otherwise grappled, hanging, at Go."

"This is Albert Leader. Five, we're going to want you out there."

"Right-o, Joslyn. But don't count on my lasers. Maybe the back-ups will kick in, but not so far."

"Albert Six at go."

"Albert Leader to Hangar Two Launch Boss. Albert Three has no pilot, all other Flight Albert craft at Go for radial launch."

"This is Launch Boss to Flight Albert. All green at this end. You are Go for rapid radial launch. All birds grappled, hanging, and ready for drop. Stand by for radial launch under spin. This is Launch Boss to all hangar personnel. We will dump air pressure at combat speed in one minute. All personnel behind a pressure door or in pressure suits. Hang on against the suction during pressure-drop. Vacuum in forty-five seconds."

A new voice came in Joslyn's earphone. "This is Captain Thomas to Albert Leader and Flight Albert. Commander Larson, you will be patched through at all times to me personally. We have no information about this attack. All radio and detection gear are out. We're deaf, dumb and blind. As yet, no ship-to-ship communication. Yours is the first flight to launch. I want you to set your birds in a defensive shell around Albert Leader's ship. Commander Larson, they are to keep trouble away from you so you can find out what the devil is going on. Do your damnedest to raise any other ships you can. We have no tracking or plotting on the enemy ships. We have no intercept vectors. Nothing. You must depend on your own detection equipment, and on what ships in better shape than the *Imp* can tell you. You will have to be my eyes and ears, and that's as important as shooting down bandits. I expect you to engage the enemy in self-defense, but we need data to fight."

"Aye, aye sir."

"Launch Boss," Sir George said, "you may launch Flight Albert at will."

"This is Hangar Two Launch Boss. Section leaders report all personnel protected from vacuum. Stand by for combat emergency pressure drop. Ten seconds to air dump. Five seconds. Air dump. All air spill valves open."

There was a tremendous roaring *whoosh*, and Joslyn's SuperWombat rocked slightly on its grapples as the hangar released its air into space through half a hundred relief valves. There was a brief whirlwind of dust and bits of paper, and Joslyn saw a suited figure hanging onto a stanchion as the suction tried to pull him off his feet.

The Wombats were, like the *Impervious*, basically cylindrical. The pilot sat at the bow, surrounded by tough quartz viewports that allowed vision up and down, port and starboard, and to the fore. Cameras and monitor screens gave a view aft and could zoom in on interesting details in any direction. Three fusion engines at the aft end provided main power, and smaller chemical jets around the circumference were used for maneuvering and course corrections. Joslyn's SuperWombat was a "stretch" of the standard design—longer on its axis, with better detection and communication equipment, larger fuel tanks, and a fourth fusion engine to compensate for the greater mass.

"Hangar Boss here. Hangar at vacuum. Open Hangar Door 21. Flight Albert to start radial launch in ten seconds."

Joslyn did a last meaningless check of the major systems. It was too late to abort the launch now, anyway.

Nine minutes had passed since the first impact.

The grappler rolled forward again, until Joslyn's fighter hung over the two great hangar doors, each twenty meters long and ten wide. Hinged to open along their centerline, they swung open to the darkness of space. The last puff of air scooted out the doors, rippling the magnificent view for a moment.

The stars swept past the doors as the *Impervious* spun on her axis. The lovely, far-off blue-and-white ball of

Britannica swung into view for a moment, then vanished as the great ship wheeled on.

Suddenly Joslyn felt as if she was falling down the biggest elevator in history. The grapple had released her bird and she fell out through the hangar door, suddenly weightless, bursting out of the dim recesses of the ship to the brilliant sunlight that blazed across the darkness.

She fell away from the ship and looked up through her overhead viewport to watch the rest of Flight Albert unload from the *Imp*. The carrier was spinning once every forty-five seconds; all that was required to keep Flight Albert together was to drop one Wombat every forty-five seconds. It was a good drop, Flight Albert lined up nicely.

"Flight Albert form on me," Joslyn ordered. "Hedgehog formation, and give me two mile distancing." They moved into position crisply, no wasted moves or fuel. Good kids. "Albert Leader to *Impervious*. All birds green, in formation."

Time to take a look around. Joslyn kicked in the tactical radar. She didn't bother checking the viewports—the naked eye was of very little use. Radar and radio were what she needed.

Wherever the enemy were, they knew well enough where the *Imp* was to score at least two direct hits on her. No sense in worrying about their detecting anything. She cranked up the radar and set it to maximum power and rapid pulse. The holo tank immediately started forming an image. There were the Flight Albert birds, there was the *Imp*, right overhead. Lots of other big blips, coded red for unknowns, bogies, and a stream of much smaller, faster-moving blips. The comm computer got to work, sending Identify Friend or Foe signals. The IFFs came in, and some of the blips turned to green for friendlies. Ship names started to appear in the tank by the blips. The little ones stayed red. There were a hell of a lot of bandits out there.

"This is *Impervious* Launch Boss. Flight B for Bertram unloading from Hangar Four, C for Cuthbert ready for drop from Two."

The small blips were staying stubbornly red. No response to IFF. They didn't seem to be maneuvering, though some of them were mighty close, and on courses that threatened collision. "Bandits on screen," Joslyn called. "Altitude 121 degrees, Azimuth 291. Four bandits at that bearing."

"This is *Impervious*," Sir George's voice announced. "Flight Bertram, track and intercept."

"Flight Bertram on intercept, sir."

Joslyn forgot about the bandits. Bertram would handle them, or else her own kids would keep them out of her hair. She had to get Thomas some data. She checked her radar tank again.

There was the *Lord Mountbatten*, a heavy cruiser. Maybe they had held together. "*Impervious* Flight Albert Leader to *Lord Mountbatten*. Come in, please."

"This is *Mountbatten*. Come in *Impervious* Albert."

"*Impervious* has lost main ship-to-ship communications and Combat Control. I am relaying for Captain Thomas. Report on tactical situation."

"Stand by. Thank God you're there, Albert. Thought we had lost the *Imp* altogether. Stand by. Patching you through to our Combat Information Center." There was a pause and then a new voice came on the line. "*Mountbatten* CIC to *Impervious* Albert. Are you patched for relay to commander *Impervious*?"

"Are you receiving, Captain Thomas?" Joslyn asked.

"Yes, thank you, Albert Leader. Please patch my audio through to *Mountbatten*."

"*Impervious* patched and ready," Joslyn said. "Please relay report, *Mountbatten*."

"Very well," the calm voice said. "Eleven minutes ago there was suddenly a swarm of radar contacts. They're still coming in, though the worst damage was done in the first moments. We're shooting up most of them now. The computers report over two thousand contacts, possibly many more smaller contacts. The bandits do not maneuver, and they are very small and fast. They are going right through the fleet and have hit a lot of ships and stations. There have been some impacts on the planet. Damage control is busy on all ships. We are tracking the bandits that missed and find they have not maneuvered. We haven't picked up radio or other transmissions from the bandits."

Joslyn shook her head. *Mountbatten*'s CIC officer wasn't offering any interpretation, but then, he didn't need to. Rocks. The little blips, the bandits, were rocks someone was throwing. They were all over the place, still streaming through the fleet. As she watched, the image in the tank shrunk and new images showed up around the new, larger, perimeter. Her radar signals were still moving out, covering a larger and larger area, and the bounce-backs were taking longer and longer to arrive back at her ship. There was Wight, Britannica's larger moon, marked in red until the radar figured out what it was and marked it in the grey of a natural body. That was about the effective range of her fighter's radar. *Mountbatten* would have to do the *Imp*'s long range work until the carrier could patch herself up.

But near-space was full of bandit rocks. Joslyn didn't even bother to hope that the *Imp* was the victim of some random meteor shower. This was a softening-up attack. The Guards were out there, somewhere.

Sir George had already reached the same conclusion. But the word from *Mountbatten* was that no actual enemy ships had been detected. Yet.

"Sir, all fighter flights deployed and on station," Launch Boss reported.

"Very good, Lieutenant," Sir George said. He turned and spoke to the intercom. "Commander Higgins, are you there? If so, report."

"Yes, sir. I have a crew at auxiliary control. They have ship's conn, and are rerouting to get tactical and comm data there. The Combat Information Center is still out, but aux control says they will be ready to handle combat functions in five minutes. Sick bay reports many casualties and fatalities. Engineering and main ship's armament are green. I have runners laying comm cable to sections that are still out. One runner got to the bridge and reports it destroyed."

Damnation! "Thank you, Commander. Tell me, is there a way clear to aux control from where I am?"

"No, sir. Corridors are blocked by debris and in vacuum. I will keep you advised if we get a way clear."

"I'll put on a pressure suit now, Commander. The moment a corridor is clear, I want to know it."

"Yes, sir."

Sir George punched up aux control. "This is the Captain. It appears that I can't get there from here. I am in Hangar Two Launch Control, and will command from here at present. Sooner or later we will need to recover those fighters, and we can't count on getting the Bow Recovery Area up to snuff for a while—and I expect Damage Control would have an easier time of it in weightlessness. I want spin taken off this ship at combat-speed. And order ship secured for maneuvering."

"Aye, aye, sir."

The overhead speaker blared a moment later. "ATTENTION ALL HANDS. STAND BY FOR COMBAT-SPEED DE-ROTATION IN THIRTY SECONDS. SHIP WILL TAKE APPROXIMATELY ONE MINUTE TO LOSE SPIN. SECURE ALL LOOSE ARTICLES AND BRACE FOR DE-ROTATION."

Everyone in Launch Control grabbed a stanchion or strapped themselves in behind their console.

"DE-ROTATION COMMENCING IN TEN SECONDS."

"Hang on, lads and lassies!" the Launch Boss called. "Here's where Cook gets all his crockery smashed."

"DE-ROTATION COMMENCING."

A deep roaring noise came up through the deck and everything lurched to one side as the de-spin thrusters fired all around the circumference of the big ship. Structural beams groaned and creaked as the stresses shifted, and someone's clipboard slid across the deck to slam into Sir George's shin. He swore and kicked the thing away. It sailed halfway across the compartment. As spin was taken off, gee-forces fell and everything got lighter. Sir George felt himself getting a bit queasy, and wished for a little drop of something to settle his stomach. Zero-gee didn't bother him any more than full gravity did, but he had never enjoyed what a spin-up or spin-down did to his inner ear.

"DE-ROTATION COMPLETE. SECURE SHIP FOR MANEUVERING."

It was fifteen minutes since the first impact.

"That's done, anyway," Sir George said to no one in particular. "One day some dull little sod in a dreary little lab somewhere is going to discover artificial gravity and save us all this mucking about with spinning ships. Get me through to *Mountbatten*. And dig out a pressure suit for me."

"*Mountbatten* here," a new voice answered, younger, more nervous than the comm officer who had answered before. Sir George recognized the voice. It was Pembroke. As of fifteen minutes before, he had been *Mountbatten*'s third in command. But that had changed.

"Lieutenant Pembroke, is that you?" Sir George asked. A rating drifted over, dragging a suit. Sir George gestured for the man to help him on with it as he talked to *Mountbatten*.

"Yes sir. I have the conn. Captain Sanji and Commander Griffith are aboard the *Imp*."

"That's right. Stupid of me to forget," Sir George said cheerfully. "Well, if they've left you in charge for the moment you might as well enjoy it. We still have no radar of our own, so we're going to be hanging on your every word. But have a listen first," he said in his best fatherly voice. "I'm afraid we've taken some damage and none of the flag officers can get through to take charge of the fleet. I'm the senior line officer anyone's been able to scare up so far, so I'm afraid I'm forced to play admiral for a bit. Do you understand?"

There was a pause before Pembroke answered. "Yes, sir. You are assuming command of the fleet. Very good, sir."

No doubt the boy could guess they were all dead, but breaking it gently might keep him from panicking. Couldn't be helped. Sir George stuffed his arms and legs into the suit and pulled the seal shut. "Right, then. Let's get to it. I'll give you my hunch, Pembroke. The 'bandits' that have hit us were rocks, thrown by a catapult, a linear accelerator quite some distance away. Perhaps from outside Alexandra's orbit. Rocks small enough and moving fast enough that our radar wouldn't pick them up until they were right on top of us. And they were thrown blind long before anyone decided to put the *Imp* where she is. We've gotten our nose bloodied by a lucky hit."

"But sir, if that's so, they must have been launched weeks ago."

"True. But if they were launched from much closer, we'd have spotted the linear accelerator. Linacs are bloody big things, with huge radar images, and massive power sources and whatnot to detect. Now, they've done us some hurt, and we're using up ammo and power fending off rocks. Which means we'll have less ammo to fire at the Guards ships when they come. I need you to relay an order to fire only on bandits that are on intercept courses. The rocks can't maneuver, and we can't waste our effort chasing rocks that have missed us. Lucky for us, from that range they had to be firing blind, though they got off some lucky hits on *Imp*. What sort of damage have the other ships taken?"

"Well, sir, we're not configured for flag operations at the moment, but most of the larger ships seems to have taken at least one hit apiece. Some of the smaller ships got hit too, and they can't soak up as much damage, of course. *Hotspur* was wrecked. *Othello* is going alongside to look for survivors, but there's not much hope. Other than that, the *Impervious* seems to have had the worst luck."

"So she has. But trust in Higgins to patch her up. Which leaves us with the question of what happens next. We can detect good-sized spacecraft that don't want to be found at least thirty million miles out, which means that our friends are at least that far away. We have some time. At least quite a few hours, possibly a day or so. They had a difficult timing problem, I must say. They had to synchronize the arrival time of the thrown rocks—which, as you say, must have been thrown weeks ago—with popping a whole fleet in out of C^2 at the right moment, in the right spot. They had to arrive as close in to the sun as they dared, which would be about one hundred fifty million miles out. Which means the enemy is *here* already, somewhere between one hundred fifty million and thirty million miles out from the sun, but we have not yet detected them because we don't know where to look. But follow my chain of logic and make sure I'm not daft. They threw the rocks to soften us up, make us duck our head, force us to waste ammunition and fuel. The best time to do that is when it won't give away the 'surprise' part of their surprise attack. You know how the Guards love surprises. That means the rocks timed to arrive just as the Guardian fleet could be detected from Britannica. No sign of them yet, but perhaps they've over-estimated our detection skills. But we'll spot 'em at a range of about thirty million miles or so. They've been here a while, rushing for us."

"But why haven't we detected them?"

"Because they're just specks of metal very far off. Any radar powerful enough to watch in all directions in space to C^2 arrival range would jam every other use of radio in the system. The Guards presumably have kept radio silence and haven't maneuvered. Once they light their fusion engines, we'll see 'em! I'll grant you that the rock throwing was risky. We might have spotted it, somehow, a ship happening across a stream of boulders hurtling straight for Britannica. But we didn't. The rocks add perhaps an hour or two to our warning time—but the rocks have done damage to my ship, and others. A clever plan, and one that might be worth the extra effort, or might not. Does all this make sense or have I gotten as blotto as the fleet scuttlebutt says?"

"Makes enough sense to scare the hell out of me, sir."

"Good." *And I knew it made sense,* Sir George thought,

but if the next rock gets me, I want someone else in the fleet to understand the situation. "Then here is what you are going to do. Leave ten fast frigates behind, and then I want you to lead the entire fleet out of Britannica's orbital plane. Launch *now* at flank speed north, off the orbital plane and to sunward. Disperse in a spherical formation, pretty widely, at least five hundred miles between ships. The Guardians will be looking to find our fleet at rest in orbit around Britannica, but let's not oblige them. Use lasers for communications if at all possible, maintain radio silence the best you can—and use frequencies that the sun's natural radio noise will drown out at long range. Hide.

"Now, we'll have the fast frigates' sensors, and I expect we'll have the *Imp*'s detectors up to par by then as well. When we detect the incoming fleet, I will transmit their heading to you. You will maneuver to put the fleet right in the sun's disk as seen from that heading. That won't hide you completely, but it will give the buggers some problems.

"*Impervious*, her fighters, and the frigates will meet the enemy fleet."

"But, sir—"

"But me no buts, Lieutenant. The Guardians are here to smash the finest fleet in the British Empire. Pearl Harbor started twenty minutes ago. This is a raid, not an attempt to land and conquer the planet. They wouldn't try *that* with Britannica. New Finland was a lot more weakly defended, and she was too much for them to swallow. No, they want to knock out our ships before we can go hunting for them. My job is to defend this fleet. So I mean you to go *out* of harm's way. If they move against the planet—and they won't—we can jump on them. But right now let's keep them away from their targets. Execute your orders."

"Aye, aye, sir. *Mountbatten* out."

Sir George stared at the microphone for a moment. It was the strange sort of moment all commanders dreaded. His orders had gone out and were being acted on, all that could be done was being done—but he, the person at the center, calling all the shots, could do no more than wait. A younger officer might have worried, bothered his men, nagged at them, told them to do what they were doing already, but if Sir George had been taught one thing by his long and not-very-illustrious career, it was patience.

Sir George's ship was half-wrecked, all his superior officers were dead, a fleet of unknown power was undoubtedly bearing down upon him, and disaster was the most likely outcome. Yet he felt more alive and confident than he had in twenty years. Still holding the mike, he pulled a headset out of its niche and put it on. He shooed the communications rating out of his seat and sat down in front of the console, thought for a long moment and then spoke into the mike again, very quietly. "Commander Larson. Are you still on the line?"

"Yes, sir."

"Then cut your relay for the moment. I'd like a private word."

"We're private at this end, sir."

"And at this end." Oh, there might be a half dozen radio-detection technicians listening in, or the battle recorders might be putting it all on tape for posterity, but that didn't matter. No one around could hear, the techs and historians would be discreet, and the moment *felt* private. "Joslyn, my dear, we should both be dead with the rest of them," Sir George said, in barely more than a whisper.

"I know, Uncle George. But we're not. Call it the fortunes of war or dumb luck."

"All I know is my being alive is a direct result of your taking me to one side and bawling me out for being a drunken fool."

"Uncle George—"

"It's true and you know it. Half an hour ago I was being kicked upstairs as an old incompetent, and now I've got greatness thrust most unwillingly upon me. And I wonder how I've done with it. You heard my reasoning and how I've chosen to deploy my forces. Have I done it properly, or gone quite mad? I would value your opinion."

"Sir. I believe you were absolutely correct in your analysis.

I believe you are thinking clearly and well. I think you have responded to the situation in the best possible way."

"You've changed your tune in 30 minutes."

"And so have you, Uncle George. I didn't think you had it in you."

"To tell you a dreadful secret, my dear, I'm fairly certain I *didn't* have it in me, up until that rock hit us. Maybe I still don't have it, and I'm fooling us all with a grand old show. Time will tell. Now I've got to go breathe down Damage Control's neck and get this ship ticking along. Patch through all your radar information to us, and whatever you can get from the frigates' detectors."

"Good luck, Uncle!"

"And good luck to you, Commander! Captain out."

Joslyn smiled to herself and got down to it. He *was* an old dear. But that to one side, the main thing to do at the moment was watch her radar. There were eight flights of Wombats deployed about *Impervious*—Albert to the bow, Bertram to the aft, Cuthbert and Dagmar to port and starboard, Elton above, Farnsworth below, Gordon and Harold hovering well to the rear as reserves. Good formations, good deployment. But from what Sir George had said, it seemed likely that there would be nothing but rocks to shoot at for quite some time. Joslyn worked it out in her head. Even given a fairly close-in detection of the enemy fleet, and even assuming that the enemy, once detected, would move and maneuver faster than any ships ever had, the Britannic fleet would still have several hours warning. And they had just proven they could launch on fifteen minutes' warning under battle conditions.

Joslyn decided to make sure at least some of her crews were fresh when the Guards showed up. "This is Albert Leader to Hangar Two Boss. Lou, I think we might as well get half my flights back aboard and into the sack. We'll start an eight hour on, eight hour off rotation right now."

"Right-o, Albert Leader. Stand by just a moment. According to what I've got, the E, F, G and H Flights were just coming off duty when the fun began. Let's cycle them back in and get them tucked in while the rest of you lot patrol the dark reaches of space."

"You've been reading too many cheap novels, Lou, but that sounds good. We'll do radial recovery."

"There's a candle in the window for you."

The recovery went quickly and smoothly, all the off-duty fighters landed in under twenty minutes. Joslyn felt quite pleased with her kids. Good pilots all.

Flights Albert through Dagmar went rock-shooting, with Joslyn picking the targets. Her radar was substantially more accurate than a standard Wombat's. Her problem was mainly one of spotting targets that would actually hit something: if they shot at all the rocks, they would have run out of power and ammo in two hours. But ninety-five percent of the rocks didn't even come close to a ship.

But that didn't stop Joslyn from respecting the rock-throwing tactic: it forced the Britannic forces to stay at alert a long time, always a wearing experience. It soaked up ammo, and did some real damage to ships.

That made it all wiser to move the fleet. Joslyn watched in her radar as *Mountbatten*, *Churchill*, *Princess of Wales*, *Determined*, *Warspite*, and the lesser ships pulled away from orbit of Britannica, toward the sun and out of the orbital plane. *Hotspur's* wreck stayed behind, abandoned. Joslyn hoped that at least the dead died quickly.

Ten of the fast frigates—ships of the same class as the dear old *Joslyn Marie*—remained behind. The *Imp* and ten frigates. It seemed very little with which to meet the enemy. Then Joslyn dimpled. Mac would have cheerfully pointed out that the *J.M.* had attacked *Leviathan* all by herself. The odds were a lot more even here.

The runner had made it—barely—through the wrecked corridors from aux control to Hangar Two. Sir George followed the runner's torturous route back, through improvised airlocks and wrecked corridors and burned-out compartments. There were grim sights to be seen on the way. Sir George was shocked to see dead bodies floating in the corridors, their young, ruined, lifeless faces staring back at him from the vacuum. "Fatalities" was such a tidy, hygienic term to apply to those horrors, those hideous slabs of meat that had been alive and laughing and full of promise such a brief time before. Sir George had never seen bodies of the battle-dead before. For the first time, he began to get genuinely angry at the Guardians, and took his first lessons in hating them. Why had they done this?

War in space, battles between great fleets, had never been more than a theoretical possibility before the Guardians. Space war had been a game, a chess problem to Sir George. Neatly labeled spots of light that moved about in a display. Dead bodies floating in the corridors of the *Impervious*: That was real war, real death. Entirely too real. Grim-faced, the old officer struggled to keep up with his youthful guide.

Auxiliary control itself was in perfect shape, so clean and quiet and orderly that it seemed surreal. Technicians worked here and there in front of open access panels, talking in low tones, slapping in jumper cables, getting readings, pulling in control. The reserve bridge crew had finally gotten through the corridors and were at their stations, activating the backup systems, setting things to rights, bringing the ship back to life, superbly British and phlegmatic in the face of disaster.

The main holo tank sprang into life suddenly, showed a scrambled mish-mash for a moment, then cleared to show a tidy, precise display of the tactical situation. Neatly labeled spots of light that moved about in a display. Sir George sat down in the captain's chair, remembered himself, and shifted to the flag officer's chair. The captain's chair would have to remain vacant. Another little reminder of all the officers they had lost in the first thirty seconds. Sir George felt strangely wary, unsettled. All this studied, quiet, purposeful action, this cathedral of calm, was a fraud, a tidy lid atop the carnage of war. Dead bodies floating in corridors. He shook his head and began to take in the situation.

The *Imp's* radar and passive detection gear were back on line. At least two of the four laser cannon were operable. They had half the torpedo tubes, and fish enough to shoot through them—though the age-old slang term seemed a strange one to use for torpedoes that never got wet. The *Imp* was showing signs of life, could still fight.

The main engines were dicey. All of them were fitted and supposedly ready for action, but only the even-numbered half had been inspected, tweaked up, and approved by the Chief Engineer.

"Helm officer. Bring all main propulsion engines up to standby. Prepare to maneuver using odd-number engines. If any of them blow, abort and shift to even numbers. Let's find out the worst now instead of later."

"Aye, sir."

"Lay a course directly away from the sun, flat as can be on the orbital plane. One gee acceleration. Communications—relay same course and acceleration to escorting craft and order them to safe distances and positions for powered flight. Relay to commander of frigate group. Detach one frigate to remain behind in present orbit and link to *Impervious* through secure laser comm channel."

"Aye, sir."

"Detection. Patch in communications to the stay-behind frigate and all the orbiting stations. Order them to use active radar, powerful and frequent pulses. Maximum range and coverage. Assign pulse frequencies to all of them. Use our own active radar until we start to maneuver—then shut down and listen and watch only. Passive. Pick up any radar reflections off the pulses the stay-behinds send off. Use the optical systems to watch for the lights of fusion engines.

"Helm, come to heading and prepare to perform maneuver in four minutes."

"Coming about. Four minutes to main engines."

"Albert Five to Albert Leader."

Joslyn pushed a button and answered. "Albert Leader. Go ahead, Madeline."

"Skipper, maybe I'm dense, but I can't figure it all out. Why did the Guards throw all these rocks at us and give us warning that they were on the way?"

Joslyn sighed. "The starting point is that it takes time to move around in a star system—and you can't pop out of C^2 too close to a star or else the gravity field fouls things up and you come into normal space a zillion miles off course or inside the star or moving at a hundred times the velocity you wanted. So the Guards had to arrive in Britannica's star system at least one hundred fifty million miles out from Epsilon Eridani herself. They are out there, heading for us, right now."

"And the rocks are just a diversion, to force us to keep our heads down?"

"Right. Except they must have timed the rocks to hit about the same time we could detect them. But even after we detect them, we might have days before the two fleets are close enough to shoot at each other."

Madeline Madsen sighed, and spoke again. "It seems to me," she said, "that war must have been a lot simpler when you didn't have to travel so far to *get* to it."

"Wrong again, Maddy," another voice chimed in. "All this is just a classic version of the timing problems a mobile force has always faced."

"Ooh, Artie, don't *we* sound grand. Someone's been reading the cram notes on space strategy again, someone has."

"Oh, ease off, Maddy. At least some of us do read."

Joslyn let the good-natured bickering go on. It would let some of the tension bleed off, keep them from getting bored or scared.

There was another rock, headed straight for the *Imp*. Joslyn fired her main laser, vaporized it, and wished the battle would hurry up and get started.

Chapter Thirteen

HMS *Impervious*
Departing orbit of the planet Britannica

The *Impervious* shut off her odd-number engines. The damn things had held out. Sir George called for tea and stared at the screen. The *Imp* had taken up a stable solar orbit about seven hundred thousand miles starward from Britannica, the frigates and the frigates' auxiliary craft and the Wombats hovering about her in space.

The rest of the Fleet was lost in the glare of the sun, barely detectable even at this range, no more than a few million miles.

There was a job to do, still, that Sir George had not provided for. "Get me a secure channel to *Mountbatten*," he ordered. It took a little time. Finally the comm laser was locked on *Mountbatten*, and the answering beam had found the *Imp*.

"Pembroke here. Standing by for your response." They were far enough away that normal conversation was impossible. The laser light bearing Pembroke's words took about ten seconds to travel to the *Imp*, and it would take just as long to send a return answer.

"Thomas here. You're hard to find, which means you've deployed well. Retain this link to receive our detection information. I want a small, fast corvette detached from your fleet. She is to backtrack the course of the thrown rocks, move along that course to their launch point, and attempt to locate and destroy that accelerator. That accelerator could be a stay-behind weapon that will be harassing us until we put it out of business. It is vital that the corvette locate it, but I don't want them taking fool chances trying to destroy it. Obviously, it might have moved since it fired on us, but it still might be possible to spot it. Once we find it, we can smash it whenever we wish.

"A final point. If the *Impervious* is lost, or I am killed, the flag duty, the command of the fleet, reverts to you. I would strongly advise you start considering tactics to meet that contingency. Thomas out."

Four hours had passed since the first attack. The enemy fleet should have been spotted long ago. Either the Guardians hadn't timed it well, or they had over-estimated the Britannics' skill in ship detection. At least the fleet was clear of the bloody rocks. The units still in orbit around Britannica reported the rocks were still coming, but the stay-behind frigates and the stations were getting to be increasingly good shots. None of the rocks had scored a hit for over an hour.

"Captain, sir, we have an unidentified radar return," the ensign serving as detection officer announced calmly. Instantly aux control's constant low murmur of voices was silenced.

"Communications. Patch everything said and done in this compartment to *Mountbatten* over a secure laser channel—and send everything from the detection console as well. Detection, full report."

"Sir. Very faint return on last pulse—there it is again, a bit stronger. Coordinates: negative zero point nine EECC latitude, one hundred seventy-three point four EECC longitude. Request passive systems aboard *Mountbatten* and other ships center their search on that point and report to *Impervious* to provide parallax. Now have third and fourth pulse returns. Target is moving rapidly—toward Britannica. Velocity very high to show in so few pulses, but not yet determinable."

"Optical? Spectral?" Thomas asked.

"Sir, no optical detection, therefore no spectral readings."

"Then they haven't lit their engines yet. The fusion plumes would show, that's for sure. Communications. Order *Mountbatten* to commence maneuver at low power. Get the fleet in the sun's disk as seen from radar return.

Helmsman. Bring us about to present our bow to the target. We're a lot smaller side-to-side than we are end-to-end. Keep our smallest cross-section pointed through them. Communications. Use secure laser-comm to repeat orders for radio silence to escort vehicles. Keep it quiet. Laser communications only. And keep laser to a minimum, too. In theory laser comm can't be detected, but let's not test theory too far. Detection. Ensign McCrae, isn't it? What more have you got?"

"Sir. Awaiting data from *Mountbatten*. No significant changes in target. Range decreasing, and we'll have enough data for a Doppler check soon. Not yet."

"Sir," The comm officer called. "Secure laser signal from *Mountbatten*. They are executing maneuver, and report it a minor correction. They were almost in correct position already."

Sir George allowed himself a brief smile at that. He had done some good guessing to place the main fleet there. He punched up the flag commander's strategic display in the holo tank. Very roughly, they were all strung out in a line: *Mountbatten* and the rest of the fleet about a million miles toward the sun from Britannica's orbit, then Britannica herself, then, well starward from the planet, the *Imp* and her escorts, and then, far starward off at some unknown distance, a radar return, presumably the Guardian fleet. That's where he would have come in, straight from starward, the shortest distance from an arrival point to the planet. And that's where they had come in. Good.

"Sir," McCrae called. "Incoming request from *Mountbatten* that the high-power radar units around Britannica sending radar pulses shift from spherical search mode to a narrow beam centered on unidentified return."

"Denied. That would give us some detail we don't need yet, and tell them we've spotted 'em. Spherical search to continue. Work with what you've got a while longer, lad."

"Aye, aye, sir. We have now received parallax data from *Mountbatten*. Approximate range, awaiting refinement, thirty million miles. Velocity determination difficult because the target is moving straight for us."

"Well, 30 million miles is what they said our radar could do. It would appear that our radar is exactly up to spec." Sir George punched up the officers' mess on the intercom. "This is the Captain. Send a steward with tea, coffee, and some sandwiches. We've got a bit of a wait yet, and there's no sense going hungry."

Reports started coming from all over the ship. There were, as expected, no survivors in Hangar One. There were 157 dead there, and sick bay reported at least 100 additional fatalities, possibly 200 serious non-fatal casualties. Some forward compartments were still cut off from the ship's corridors by vacuum and there were certainly more dead and injured that had not been accounted for yet. Out of a normal ship's complement of 1100, perhaps 750 were fit, ready, and able to get to battle stations.

The damage control crews worked on. Work-arounds, back-ups, improvisations were plugged in, patched in, forced into place. Wreckage was cleared and either jettisoned or lashed down in Hangar Three for later salvage or use. Corridors were patched and repressurized. Main ship's weaponry was ready, too. The *Imp* could fly, and fight. Sir George was satisfied of that. To his mind, the rest of the Britannic fleet was now in graver danger than the *Imp*—and the greatest danger the fleet faced was the loss of its experienced commanding officers. That was a danger that a damage control team couldn't handle. It would take years, perhaps a generation, to wholly repair that catastrophe. Thank God the Prime Minister and the cabinet had turned down the invitation to the ball.

The poor old P.M., the whole government, in fact the whole planet, was sweating this one out. Standing orders were to maintain radio silence when attacked. The Guards seemed to have a hell of an intelligence service, and it had to be assumed that anything transmitted to the planet's surface would get back to the enemy, either through electronic taps or through plain old-fashioned agents-in-place. A civilian government still largely geared to peacetime, and in a gossipy capital, would be easy pickings for spies. The fleet didn't dare send news of how the battle was going.

They were probably more scared back home than the fleet was up here. At least the fleet had some idea what in blazes was going on.

Thirty million miles. It was a meaningless figure. Huge beyond imagining in everyday terms, but in the scale of interstellar travel, it was nothing, a distance traveled in less time than it took to say the words. Thirty million miles.

Even the measure was obscure. Only Earth's British Commonwealth and the world Britannica used 'miles' anymore. Even the Americans had given up long ago and shifted to metric measure. These days, few non-British even knew that a mile was, by some vague amount, longer than a kilometer.

The Britannic fleet was learning just how real thirty million miles was.

Detection nailed down the Guard fleet's velocity: 282 miles a second, or just over a million miles an hour. A pretty hellish clip, but still it would take thirty hours for them to reach Britannica, even if they didn't decelerate at all.

The watch had changed while Flight Albert had been on patrol. Albert Leader's approach and recovery was a lot less exciting than her departure, which suited Joslyn just fine. She willed the hangar crew to hurry up, get all the ships in, seal the hangar doors and pressurize *fast*. She wanted food, and rest, and sleep, and she wanted to get started on them quickly, before another alert came and put her back in her SuperWombat.

For a wonder, there weren't any foul-ups, and the hangar was buttoned up and under pressure in record time. Joslyn had the hatch undogged and was already out of the ship and on her way along the handholds when she noticed the stunned silence around her.

Only then did she remember what she looked like. Her long honey-colored hair was wadded up in a tangly ball inside her hairnet. She was barefoot. She was more out of than in the ruins of the evening gown she had ripped apart so she could get into her fighter. Her careful makeup job was undoubtedly sweat-streaked, blurred, and muddled into a fright show. She blushed mightily, then laughed at herself and went on her way. "Let me tell you fellows, it was rough out there," she told the hangar crew. She hurried on to the pilot's mess. Time for food and then some sleep!

But she had only just gotten herself around a sandwich and a cup or six of tea when the intercom squawked, summoning her to auxiliary control at her earliest convenience. Joslyn swore to herself, and headed back to her cabin. It only took a moment to change into flight coveralls, and aux control was no place for a lady to wear the remains of a party dress. She looked longingly at her bunk, and toyed with the idea of a ten minute catnap—but she knew that was impossible.

"Duty," she said to the empty air as she braided her hair back into a bun, "thy name is lack of sleep." She decided she had time to wash off the remains of her make-up first, even if she had no chance for a full shower. She sponged her face down and headed down the corridor to aux control.

"Ah, Commander. Welcome to our bridge-away-from-bridge," Sir George said. "We're a bit cramped, but managing. I want you to take a look at the tactical situation and tell me what you think your Guardian friends plan to do."

"Hello again, Captain," Joslyn said. "Well, let's see." She took a long hard look at the hologram tank and frowned. "I assume that we found them on active radar pulsed from Britannica's orbit. That wouldn't give our position away. The Guards haven't kicked out any radar pulses looking for us, have they?"

"That's right."

"Then they won't have spotted *us* yet. Not at that range.

But they'll have picked up the pulses sent out from Britannica's orbital stations. Presumably Britannica's radar has been hitting them for a while, but the signals have only just gotten strong enough for us to detect them on return. They know we will spot them soon, but they can't be *sure* we've nailed them yet."

"Quite right," Sir George said.

"Is it? Loud cheers if you're that certain. This sort of they-know-that-we-know-that-they-know always makes my head spin. But anyway, let's think it through. They'll assume that we'll have maneuvered since the rock-throwing. They know we'll be hiding, and that they will have to find us."

Joslyn thought for a second, still concentrating on the radar display. "Detection officer. If you had the best possible equipment—optical, infrared, and so on—and didn't use active radar, how far off could you detect the *Imp* if she were rigged for quiet running?"

Joslyn took her first real look at the ensign sitting in as detection "officer" as he swung around in his chair and grinned at her. Presumably the real detect officer was dead, wounded, or trapped in a compartment. The kid on duty was a fresh-scrubbed, cheery-looking lad with apple-red cheeks and black hair and brown eyes and snaggly teeth, far too young to really understand the stakes of the game he was in. "Well ma'am, I assume you mean in the present geometry of the situation. The *Impervious* has her bow pointed through their location, and so shows them a small cross-section, and that helps a great deal. And we're pretty much in the sun's glare—lots of background noise. There's a certain amount of backscatter reflection off the Britannic arrays, of course, and we're getting some of that—but not enough to read through the glare. Besides, the blips I'm getting seem to be a large number of smaller ships—they probably can't have very large or powerful detection gear aboard. I would say perhaps ten million miles at the outside limit. But why *wouldn't* they use active radar—they would have detected the radar pulse that picked them up for us—they'd know we know where they are and—"

"Spare me who knows what," Joslyn said. "But even if they've been hit by radar pulses for quite a while, we haven't been able to pick up the returns from that radar because the returns have been too weak until now. They can't know exactly when we'll detect them, so they can't be *sure* we've spotted them already. Maybe we can fool them. You've got enough data to plot their projected course and watch it optically, don't you?"

"Yes ma'am. I wouldn't actually see their ships until they started maneuvering, but *not seeing* fusion lights would tell us they hadn't changed course. That would be just as good as seeing them."

Joslyn thought for a moment. "There're still rocks coming in toward Britannica, aren't there? Suppose we order all our radar to a narrow sweep of the piece of sky that the rocks are coming from. We have a ship in that area, the corvette that's supposed to track down the linear accelerator. It seems very unlikely to me that the Guards were able to track that frigate's launch. Here we go again with the we-know-they-don't-knows again, but *they* wouldn't realize *we* are aware of the frigate's identity. They might think we think some ore freighter is one of their attack ships. The Guards will see us bouncing a radar reflection off that ship, and will see our search in that area. We can act as if we had spotted that frigate, didn't know what it was, and were tracking it intensively. *They'll* think we're expecting them to come down under cover of the rocks."

"Which will make them think *we* haven't spotted *them*, and so we'll get *them* to not use *their* radar, so *they* won't find *us*," the ensign said with a laugh. It appealed to his sense of humor. "And once they start braking—and they *have* to, sooner or later—I'll be able to spot the plumes instantly. It'd work."

Sir George smiled. "Send orders to that effect to the radars around Britannica. And don't explain it, either. Just the bare instruction to redirect the radar. If someone is listening in, that might add to their confusion."

"I'm bloody confused enough for everyone," the comm

officer muttered under his breath as he set up the transmission.

The hours crawled by, the situation largely unchanged. The Guardian fleet moved closer and closer—or at least the computer's projection of its course said the enemy was still headed for them. Ensign McCrae got increasingly nervous. He *knew* the Guards had to be where the computer said they were, that his equipment would spot the lights of their fusion plumes the moment they maneuvered, but he didn't really believe it.

Commander Larson remained on the bridge, laying plans with Sir George and watching the tactical display. According to the computer, the Guard were still hurtling closer. Twenty million miles. Eighteen. Fifteen. Ten. The numbers changed meaninglessly.

McCrae felt bored and tired and nervous and fidgety and eager and scared all at once. He wished the devil the sodding Guards'd get on with it. They had to start braking soon or they'd never stop in time. Maybe they had malfunctioned, miscalculated—

It took a full ten seconds for him to realize what the screens were showing him. "Sir! Ma'am! Fusion lights! They have commenced braking."

"There we go! You won't need active radar now, Ensign," Commander Larson said. "Details as you have them."

"Yes ma'am. I count at least fifty fusion lights. Fifty ships. A variation of sizes. We'll need readings for a few minutes before I can give you masses and accelerations. Range at engine-light: approximately 6.7 million miles."

The commander pulled herself over to the detection station and looked over McCrae's shoulder as he worked to pull more data out of his screens. There they were, right in the middle of the crosshairs. The computer had kept a damn good track all this time. And the Guards had never used their radar. The gag with the frigate had worked.

"Captain," Commander Larson said. "At the power levels they're using, their own engine exhaust plumes will jam all their detection equipment. There's a good chance we can stay hidden for quite a while yet."

"I was hoping for as much. Ensign McCrae. Tell me, in your own opinion, formed out of your own vast experience: Can they see through the plasma their exhaust plumes are putting out?"

"Sir. As long as they are decelerating, they will not be able to detect us at any distance at all," McCrae said. "Their fusion plumes will jam all their radar and visual, right through to infrared."

"What fun. Then it might be time to arrange a reception committee to greet our visitors. Communications. Get me a link to *Mountbatten*. If this doesn't work, they'll be on their own. Flight Boss, recall all fighters. Get them aboard and refueled and ready for sortie. Secure the ship for maneuvering and get me a secure laser link to commanders of the escorting fast frigates. Commander Larson. What are our visitors going to do next? Is there any lesson for us from the attack on New Finland?" Sir George asked.

"No, sir. This is nothing like what they did there."

"Your own thoughts, then."

"Well, sir," the commander said carefully, "if I were the Guardian admiral, I'd head straight for Britannica and use her gravity well to maneuver, and do my detecting while in orbit of the planet. I'd knock out our radar stations there. Maybe I'd even do a very brief, token attack on the planet—that would force our side to respond, if it had gone off to hide the way we have. That's the one flaw in your tactic of not being there when they come after us—the planet must be defended. But *Mountbatten* and the rest of the fleet are well positioned. They could be there to interdict quickly. The Guards know the fleet will have moved, and they probably have a number of contingency plans based on where the fleet has moved *to*, though I can't say what those plans would be. But there is one thing I'd love to know. How the hell are they going to get out of here? They'll have to brake in order to fight us—and then they'll have to accelerate like mad to get out of the system with us on their tails. That's a lot of fuel."

"Mmmmph. True. Very well." Sir George frowned. "McCrae. What more have you got?"

"Um, ah, quite a bit, sir. I'll be able to refine things more and more as we go on from here. But as of now we've got the target range and the temperature of the fusion lights now—those figures let us calculate the amount of power the engines are putting out. We've just gotten an optical track. That gives us a change-of-rate, and the Doppler confirms the figures. They're slowing at about one gee. Figuring one gee into the engine temperature tells us how much power the engines are putting out, and *that* tells us what we really need to know, the mass of the ships."

"You're quite right, ships' masses are the only part of all that I want to know. Well?"

"Ah, yessir. I beg your pardon. I now count fifty-five separate targets. Fifty seem to be the same mass—about twice the size of our fast frigates. Very crudely, that gives those ships a crew of about twenty to thirty, and potentially some pretty heavy armament."

"The other five ships?"

"Are a puzzler. The engine temperatures are all different, much hotter, which means the engines are running much closer to their maximum power ratings. As if much smaller engines were being used to power the larger ships—and what I can pull off the spectroscopic scanners show a lot of impurities, as if the engines are old and worn and bits of the throat nozzles are vaporizing into the fusion flame. And those five ships must have ten times the mass the others do."

Joslyn looked sharply at McCrae. "Let me have a look at those figures, Ensign."

Sir George let his younger officers fuss with the technical issues. He had was some thinking of his own to do. He intended to launch the *Imp* straight at the incoming fleet, hidden from their view by the glare and the jamming effects of their own braking thrust. It was something of a risky proposition. He could not think of any detection system that could see through the fusion glare—the League had been trying to develop just such equipment for years. And a similar maneuver had worked against the Guards in New Finland. But the Guards *might* have come up with something. And they *might* shut off their engines for a bit, just to do a bit of searching, right at a very awkward moment. And there was the risk of plowing the *Imp* right into the flame of an oncoming ship's thrust. That wasn't a great danger with a steady hand at the helm. He shrugged. They didn't pay warship commanders to be overcautious.

The real danger was that the Guards knew perfectly well they were coming in blind, and would be prepared for such an attack. Very well, they would be expecting it. That was simply one more thing to take into account. They would not know where, or when, he would strike, or with how many ships. How many he had already decided, hours ago—the *Imp*, her fighters, and the frigates would go it alone.

When was the issue, then. There were arguments for making a strike further out, and counter-arguments for waiting until the enemy was almost in orbit of Britannica. Sir George was inclined to strike as soon as possible, if for no other reason than to give his sailors a psychological boost, a chance to hit back. They had been waiting, sweating it out, feeling helpless and scared long enough.

The sooner they were busy, the better. He turned his attention to the flagplot tank and started playing with the variables—looking for the advantages of one course over another, intercept points, closing rates, fuel usage, thrust levels . . .

"Sir George, excuse me."

"Commander Larson," the old captain said with a start. "You have something for me?"

"Maybe, sir. I've got an idea that the five largest targets are fuel ships, expendable and possibly uncrewed. We've just gotten an optical reading, light reflected off the fusion flames, and the five larger targets are *huge*, even for their mass—which suggests that they are carrying a lot of something that isn't very dense."

"Such as liquid hydrogen to top off the tanks of the rest of the fleet so everyone can make their get-aways!" Sir George said. "Splendid. It makes a great deal of sense. The ships come in, run their raid, refuel, and run like hell. We ought to be able to do something with that. Give me a moment to think." Sir George rubbed his chin thoughtfully. "We have nine frigates with us," he said at last. "We'll assign two to the attack on each tanker, and I want you to get Flight Albert out there alongside the last frigate to hit one tanker."

"Very good sir, but there is one other thing: the tankers' engines appear to be running nearly at maximum temperature, and their spectra suggest they are old and worn. It's what I'd do. No sense using new engines on expendable ships."

"What are you suggesting?"

"That the tanker engines aren't as robust as they might be. We might consider firing the *Imp*'s laser cannon at the tankers from long range. With a bit of luck we'll overheat the engines and blow them—"

"Leaving the tankers with no way to slow down, so they zip across the star system never to be seen again, leaving the rest of the attack fleet with no fuel to get home on. Joslyn, you are a true member of the clan. Only someone with a drop of Thomas blood in her would have dreamed up something that nasty. We'll do it your way, and then play shoot-'em-up with the other ships."

The *Impervious* maneuvered for the second time fifteen hours after the rock attack. Sir George selected a fairly sedate five-meter-per-second acceleration, a two-hour burn, and ordered a course that kept the *Imp* out of the Guardian fleet's projected flight path for as long as possible. Sir George checked his tactical display. The *Imp* would intercept the Guard Fleet six hundred thousand miles out from Britannica. Assuming the buggers didn't spot them and run.

"Detection," he said, "I want to hear the moment you think they might have spotted us. Any course change, any maneuver." The *Imp* had one great advantage. She had had hours to track her foes, lick her wounds, carefully plan her counter-attack. The Guards would be expecting some sort of move, but they would have only seconds to analyze the *Imp*'s attack and respond.

"Aye, sir."

Engine shutdown. Back to zero gee. *Impervious* and the frigates flew on.

Sir George worked at his planning. The two fleets would pass through each other at a relative speed of about 105 miles a second. The tanker-ships were well to the rear of the Guardian fleet, which mean there would be marginally more time to hit them before the Guards had passed through the *Imp*'s trajectory. Sir George ordered the ship brought about to aim her stern through the direction of flight—as soon as the *Imp* was through the Guard fleet, she would have to start matching velocity with the enemy.

The laser cannon crews were given their targets and ordered to stand by. The lasers would be effective at a range of no more than ten thousand—and that gave them just over a minute and a half to hit those tankers. Sir George ordered all debris and wreckage thrown overboard and dispersed as widely as possible. With a little luck, one of the Guard ships would run into something, anything. Hitting a disposable drinking cup at 105 miles a second could wreck a ship.

He looked around for Joslyn—she was a comfort, one of the few people he, the Captain, could talk to. But then he remembered. She had to get to the flight deck and get her crews ready. It occurred to him that there was battle on the way, and his niece was on the front lines of it. He might never see her again—and he couldn't remember her leaving just now. Well, good luck to her. The way to make her safest was to do his own job properly. But he had already done all he could. It was time to wait again. And time for another bloody cup of tea.

✧ ✧ ✧

All eight flights of fighters sortied again, an hour before intercept. They held station on the *Imp*, ready and waiting for action. The fast frigates each deployed their three auxiliary craft. Everyone got ready.

Time moved slowly, wearing on nerves, until the moment when it began to move all too rapidly. "At effective laser range in three minutes," the weapons officer announced.

Sir George thrummed his fingers nervously on the arm of the command chair.

"Two minutes," McCrae announced. "*Impervious* and escort craft all well clear of enemy ships' fusion plumes."

Good. Now if those bastards could keep from changing course for a few minutes, the *Impervious* might not get melted down to slag.

"Sir!" McCrae called. "I have just picked up a very jammed-up radar pulse coming from the Guard fleet. They'll have spotted us now."

"How could they spot us? Is it something we don't have?" Sir George asked anxiously. If the Guards could see through a fusion plume, the League might be in very serious trouble.

"No sir. Brute force detection, that's all. They're pumping a hell of a big pulse through the radar and seeing if anything makes it back through the plume. Useless at more than this range, and at our closing velocity they don't have time to respond and maneuver anyway. It's an impact warning system, that's all."

"Good. Then you might as well crank up our active radar, Ensign, since they know we're here. Pass the refined targeting data along, obviously."

"Yes sir!" McCrae grinned. Sir George was as pleased as McCrae to unlimber the *Imp*'s own detection gear. It had been frustrating as hell to sit on top of those monster radars for all these long hours without the chance to use them.

"One minute."

"And here we go," Sir George announced. "Put tactical on the main screen." The ship's computers drew a diagram that showed the *Imp* and her allies and antagonists. Neatly labeled dots on a screen.

"All four laser cannon trained on target one. Concentrated fire commencing—Mark!"

"Detection—any effect on the tanker?"

"Temperature of target climbing rapidly. There's a brightness flare! *Something* has blown on it! Tanks, or the engines, I can't see."

"Laser crew!" Sir George called. "Shift to target two! Fire torpedo volley at target one, track it two ways, for constant thrust and for no thrust!" Sir George felt his heart pounding with excitement. This was it. This was battle well and truly joined, for the first time in his long life.

McCrae was going happily mad, watching nine kinds of monitors at once. "Range to second target much shorter. Explosion detected. She's blown already. Definitely an engine meltdown that time."

Sir George turned to the weapons officer. "Split your fire! Two cannon on target three, two on four! Torpedo volley on target two, as planned!"

"Sir!" McCrae was near a fit. "Incoming laser fire. They've ranged us."

"Intensity?"

"We can take it, and they're not holding target well. But you can bet there's more on the way. Explosion detection, make that two explosions! Third and fourth tanker blown!"

"Target five!"

The weapons officer shook her head. "Sorry sir, we're already outside effective range for five."

Sir George looked again at the tactical display on the big screen in surprise. The *Impervious* had already flown clear through the opposing fleet. "Bloody hell. *That* didn't take long. I want torps chasing targets three, four and five. Flight boss. Are escorting craft at safe distance for maneuver?"

"Aye sir."

"Helm, you may commence planned maneuver on schedule."

"Sir. Ship's attitude at thrust heading. Thirty seconds to throttle-up to three gravities thrust."

"Communications, warn all hands."

"ALL HANDS. STAND BY FOR THREE GRAVITIES THRUST OF PROLONGED DURATION."

"Detection. Damage to enemy fleet."

"Sir. Too soon to read it. Four of the five tankers are out, either wrecked or engines overheated and blown. All four are unable to maneuver. Our torpedoes still chasing them. It will take at least 300 seconds to call hits and misses."

"And the attack fleet itself?"

"No hits as yet, sir. The frigates and the Wombats are chasing them."

"TEN SECONDS TO THREE GRAVITIES."

No chance to bother with using half the engines for safety's sake now. It was a stern chase, and the engines would hold or they wouldn't. Depending on how the Guards reacted, they could be under three gees for ten minutes or three hours. The great fusion engines roared to life and slapped everyone down into their chairs. The *Imp* began to shed her velocity starward so she could head sunward, back in toward Britannica. She would catch the Guards sooner or later, but she was out of the game for the time being. Now it was up to the frigates and the fighters.

Twenty-three hours had passed since the first rock had hit the *Impervious*.

Chapter Fourteen

Deep Space
Epsilon Eridani (Britannic) Star System

Five gravities was no fun. Now Joslyn found herself wishing she *didn't* have a pressure suit. The damn thing was designed for use in high-gee situations, but it wasn't exactly comfortable. Joslyn hated high gees. She started wishing the retroburn could be over the moment it started. But the Guardian fleet was already far ahead to sunward, and it would take some chasing to catch them.

The Guardian ships were moving toward Britannica at about eighty miles a second now, still braking, slowing all the time.

The *Imp*'s fighters had started their retroburns while moving *away* from the planet at twenty-two miles a second. The fighters had to lose that speed, reverse course, and then gain speed moving the other way, chasing hell-for-leather after the invaders. It was going to be a long ride.

Joslyn watched the Guardian fleet in her radar. Now the gloves were off, as far as detection equipment went. Both sides knew exactly where the other was, and every frequency was full of radar. The Guards were holding formation for the moment—no, wait a moment.

"Albert Leader to all units. They're splitting their forces. Half the ships are decelerating at higher thrust, call it four gees. They'll match with our velocity plenty damn quick at that rate. The second half of the fleet maintaining previous thrust—including the surviving fuel ship."

"Albert Four here. Right-o Joslyn. What's the plan?"

Joslyn checked the numbers. The fighters and the frigates were still in formation together, now headed sunward at about twelve miles a second, perhaps half a million miles from Britannica. The *Imp* was well behind them, just about dead in space and starting to gather speed back in toward the planet.

"They're the ones who are short of fuel, lads and lassies. If they want to chase us, we let them do the work. All ships, shut down all engines in thirty seconds from my mark—MARK. We let them come to us, we take one firing pass through them, then we relight our engines. Then we barrel on in toward the planet to take on the second team. We should be able to reform on the *Impervious* and move in as a fleet if we time it right."

Joslyn cut her engines with the rest of them, glad of an excuse to get back into zero-gee. Let the Guard fleets get tired and worn by gunning around at high gees.

But the second team, the half of the fleet following the fuel ship . . . If *she* had been coaching the opposition, she would have ordered the second team to cut their engines altogether. Without the braking thrust, the ships would have fallen in toward Britannica—and away from the *Imp*—that much faster. And the *Imp* was worth getting away from. So why had they kept to their plodding one-gee thrust?

Aha! Because if they delayed braking, they would have to brake at a higher thrust later on, to make up for the deficiency. And that fuel ship was barely keeping up the pace as it was. And they *needed* that fuel ship. It was their last ticket out of the system.

In other words, the fuel ship couldn't manage any better than one gee. It was a fact worth remembering.

Second Lieutenant Madeline Madsen, Royal Britannic Navy, wasn't interested much in strategy or deception schemes or fleet movements. She knew only that there were twenty-five large enemy ships heading straight for her, intent on killing her.

She was interested only in her armament, her fuel, having her pressure suit sealed and ready. She wanted to stay alive, and that meant shooting her way through the Guardian fleet and coming out the other side. Simple.

In some part of herself, she wanted to get mad at the powers that be, because she was merely a pawn, a player's piece in all this—except Captain Thomas and Commander Larson were out here risking their lives too, and the P.M. and the Governor General would die just as dead if the Guards bombed the capital. Every ship's commander in the fleet had been in that bloody hangar. They paid the piper, too.

Pawns weren't the only ones dying.

Madeline watched all her screens carefully, mentally rehearsing her firing run, her targeting, her maneuvers. It was all laid into the computer, just in case something killed her but left the ship alive. Even if they took her out of the game, she'd leave the opposing side something to remember her by. Of course, a computer program couldn't improvise or react to surprises. Maybe it would be best for all concerned if she stayed alive.

She knew her job—and knew that all the schemes, the strategy, the studies, the simulations, the training, the ships, the expense, the time, the whole damn navy, had only the point of putting young women and men where they could fight. All of it, the great confusing, clanking, ponderous bureaucratic machinery, was there only so she could be here, to put a few ergs of energy or a few ounces of metal into the enemy ships.

At the moment, she would have been just as happy if the bureaucratic machinery hadn't worked. She was *scared*, actually aware that she might die, for the first time in her short life.

Time stopped meaning much. She was ready. All she could do was wait. The Guards were coming straight for the Wombats. Maddy swore to herself. They were still braking. The Wombats would be moving at less than five miles a second, relative to the Guards, when they passed through each other's formation.

And it started. Her first assigned target in range. Two torps away, and watch for incoming. There. Radar and optical were both tracking it. A torp coming right for her. Use the recoilless gatling guns, throw some metal at it. The gats fired two-ounce steel cylinders, and spread their ammo far and wide. You fired five thousand rounds and hoped one hit. One did. A flash of light, and radar said the torp had stopped accelerating.

But her IFF said someone had her lined. Time to randomize the situation. She kicked in her main engines at six gees for ten seconds, then spun through ninety degrees and fired her auxiliary thrusters to confuse the track a bit more. Another target. Close enough for lasers, by God. She opened up, gave the target fifteen seconds at full power, then shut down and gave them a dose of Doctor Gatling for good measure.

But by then the opposition had had time and a half to get her lined. Without regard for heading or targets, she fired her mains again, full open, ten gees for three seconds, then spun end-for-end and braked at ten for another three. That should get her off their screens for a bit.

Time to look around. Tally-ho! Short range—the target was braking, heading straight for her, the fusion plume actually visible to the naked eye.

She had two torps with ablative coatings that could survive, very briefly, in a fusion plume. Time to see if they worked. She loosed one of them at the plume, then maneuvered again, quartering around to get a clear shot at the enemy ship with a conventional torp—

—No need, up she goes! She wasn't sure her torp had had time to get there and hit. But good lord, that ship had been close! Not more than a hundred miles off, at most—

A jarring impact. Red light! Fuel tank two, damn, she was venting hydrogen, bleeding like a stuck pig. The auto damage control took over, pumped to the other tanks, shut it down. Still alive.

Maddy didn't stop to worry about how close the call was. Time to move. For all she knew, she had just flown right into her own gatling gun fire, or hit a random fragment from a blown ship—but she had to assume that a bandit had her lined and was ready to nail her.

Ten gees again, at a crazy skew to her current course, twenty full seconds, and she wanted to black out and throw up at the same time.

Another target—no, the radar's IFF said it was an aux ship off one of the frigates. She pulled her hands back from the weapons panel and left the aux to its own devices. No radio calls on targets in a fight like this—though there had never *been* a fight like this before—but ships were too far apart, the complexities of ship-to-ship combat too much to worry about to allow time for calling in a bandit at twelve o'clock high.

And Maddy wondered where the hell she was, and where she was going—oh balls and bastards, she was headed straight out of the system, practically in formation with the Guards. Time to move. Two more bandits, two more torps apiece, and another rip from the gats. She took ten seconds out to take a proper bearing and slammed her engines into gear again, bringing her back to original course and heading in one violent, twisting corkscrew maneuver.

On the radar, dead ahead. A Guardian ship. A straggler. Derelict. Dead in space. Easy target. Was the ship already wrecked, all hands lost? Were they willing to surrender, prisoners to interrogate? Were they making repairs right now? Would this be the ship that made the direct hit that blew the *Imp* when she passed this way? No time to find out, or even think. Only time to decide.

Maddy gave it thirty seconds with the lasers that ripped the hull open from stem to stern.

And then she looked up and space was clear. So that was battle. She didn't know it would be that easy. And suddenly she was thinking again, a human being and not a trained ship-killer. She looked to the radar, where the derelict still showed, well behind her now. That was the only ship she was absolutely certain *she* had blown. Would they have surrendered? Battle. She didn't know it would be that hard, either.

✧ ✧ ✧

Sir George frowned at his screens. Ships lost: two frigates, three frigate's auxiliary ships, six fighters. And twelve Guard ships blown.

That left thirteen Guardian ships waiting in the *Imp*'s path. And these Guardian ships were clearly designed for battle against big ships. They might have had trouble with the fighters, but they could out-maneuver the *Imp* easily.

A pincer. If the escort fleet was up to it. "Communications. Can we get a secure link to Commander Larson?"

"I'll try, sir. The Guardian ships are right between the *Imp* and Albert Leader. They might pick it up."

"That's what scramblers are for, Lieutenant."

"Yes, sir."

"See what you can do. Ah, another thing. Do we still have the link to *Mountbatten*?"

"Yes, sir."

"Patch it through to my headphones, if you please. This is Captain Thomas calling Lieutenant Commander Pembroke. Awaiting your reply." The laser beam would have to carry the message across a million miles of space, and then it would take a minute to get Pembroke on line. More waiting, and very little else to occupy Sir George's attention in the meantime.

He suddenly felt very old and tired. He hadn't slept since the night before the reception, over thirty-six hours now. It seemed more like a century before. This was a young man's game. And would have been, if the Guards had held off for a day. Young Captain Thorpe-Peron would have had the conn, with a full flag staff to run the battle with him, instead of one broken-down old remittance man.

But Sir George knew he had done well. The Guards should have won the Battle of Britannica in the first thirty seconds. But it seemed he had a sporting chance to turn a disaster into a victory. The Guardians were in trouble now.

"Pembroke here. Awaiting your reply. From what we're receiving on laser-link, I offer my congratulations, Captain."

"Thomas replying. Thank you. But it might be time for you to do your bit. We've split their fleet. There are twenty-six ships headed your way at one gee. This will take some timing, but we are going to try forcing them to move faster—right into your gently grinning jaws, if we can manage. The twenty-sixth ship is their fuel ship, their ticket home. We think it can't *do* more than about one gee. Knock that ship out, and our visitors can't get home. They won't have the fuel to run far, and we can hunt them down.

"Now let me be honest enough to tell you what you've already guessed. One very good reason that I left the rest of the fleet behind is all your commanding officers are dead. They were killed in the first moments. The junior officers commanding the ships I left behind are all we have. When we were facing an unknown enemy coming from an unknown direction at unknown strength, I could not risk His Majesty's ships in untried hands.

"The odds are better now. We've gotten a look at the Guard ships and what they can do, and I think if we use you properly, we can bounce the Guardian fleet to pieces. So far, to quote, 'We have scotched the snake, not killed it.'

"And I must ask you a question. The lives of your crew, the survival of the Britannic fleet—and the safety of Britannica itself—rely on your answer. *Can you young fellows handle those ships in battle, completely on your own?* I will not be able to help you. The *Impervious* will have her hands full. Say no, and whether you are wrong or right, the Britannic fleet will survive, and these Guard ships will escape, and possibly destroy a ship or two of ours. That will be a small price to pay for the survival of the Fleet as a fighting force. Answer yes, and be wrong, and we face disaster. I order you to think before you answer, to confer with your fellow acting commanders, and consider well. Answer on your honor, not on your pride. That is all." Thomas cut the contact.

"And it's bloody well enough," he said half to the comm officer, half to himself. "But sometimes you've got to trust in untried judgment, or you might as well pack up and go home. You need a little faith in people."

"Yes, sir." *You've proved that*, the comm officer thought. *I never would have risked my neck to your judgment if I had a choice. But it's sodden-drunk old Cap'n George that kept us alive.* A light glowed on the comm console. "Sir, we have a secure line to Albert Leader."

"To my headset, please. Thank you. Commander Larson. We have some tactics to discuss. . . ."

Ten minutes later *Mountbatten* sent a signal: " 'Let our just censures attend the true event, and we put on industrious soldiership.' "

Sir George grunted and said nothing for a moment when he heard it. Did Pembroke know his spacemanship as well as his *Macbeth*? Well, a sense of history never did anyone any harm, though Sir George felt, on the whole, he would have preferred a simple 'yes.' "

He transmitted his instructions to Pembroke, and decided to switch from tea to coffee. Black. Strong. He wished for a little something to brighten it up, but brandy wouldn't do at the moment.

The *Impervious*' engines roared into life, bearing down on the thirteen Guard ships to starward. The Wombats and frigates turned to harry the Guardians as the *Imp* brought her firepower to bear on the enemy. *Mountbatten* led the rest of the Britannic fleet in an all-out assault on the twenty-six inbound Guards, intent on blowing the tanker at all cost.

Sir George, still wearing a pressure suit over a much-wrinkled formal dress uniform, sat in his borrowed flag officer's chair in his back-up bridge, surrounded by half-trained junior officers doing their best.

This was it. The Guards were in trouble, but either side could win. If the *Imp*'s lasers were powerful enough to thin the enemy ranks before the *Imp* was within their range—

They were. The lasers killed three of the Guards.

If the Wombat pilots weren't too shaken up and exhausted, if they had fuel and ammo enough to fight—

As per the plan, they herded the Guard ships practically right into the *Imp*'s torpedo tubes, and accounted for a few more kills themselves.

If the *Imp* could hold together, survive the inevitable battle damage—

She could. Commander Higgins reported only a few more hits, from fairly small and slow-moving armor-piercing missiles of an unknown type.

Strangely, the missile warheads didn't explode. The things just bore into the ship, crashed through a few bulkheads, and came to rest. Sapper teams were taking a look at them.

And, the biggest if, *if* the *Mountbatten* and the other ships were skippered by *wunderkinden* and not cocky fools—

And oh, thank God, they were, they were.

Pembroke led them in a classic interdiction maneuver, making masterful use of the bulk of Britannica to hide his ships, boring straight in for the fuel ship, ignoring all other targets until that one was gone, then chasing the attack fleet, fragmenting it. The assault cost two large Britannic ships, and two more frigates.

A few smaller ships reported hits by the same strange slow missiles, but no one paid much mind to them. Probably some sort of failed experimental munition.

Once the main Guard attack collapsed, and both Guardian formations were broken, the battle degenerated into a series of one-on-one shootouts as Britannic ships chased down the stragglers. None of the Guard ships seemed interested in pressing home their accounts, once they had managed a hit or two with their strangely ineffectual torpedoes. All of them simply cut and ran.

Within eight hours, the Guards lost twenty-one more ships, including the last tanker. Ten Guardian ships were unaccounted for. Probably all or some of them managed to slip through the debris and confusion of battle, get far enough out to jump to C^2. The remainder were chased down, pursued until they ran out of fuel, overtaken and destroyed. Several Guardian ships were invited to surrender. All refused. Not a single Guardian prisoner was taken.

There was something strangely anticlimactic about the way the battle ended. The Guardians folded too suddenly, too completely, there at the end. Something about that bothered Sir George.

But who was he to look a gift horse in the mouth? He had won a great victory, and kept his fleet intact. The Britannic Fleet had lost one cruiser, four corvettes, five frigates, and eight Wombat fighters.

Historians no doubt would call it a British victory, but both sides were bloodied, and the British had dead enough to mourn, and holes enough torn in the chain of command. Fending off a raid is never a triumph.

But there was time to rest, and heal, and sleep, and patch up the ships. For the survivors, that was victory enough. At least it was over.

Except, of course, that it wasn't.

Aboard Impervious, Warspite, *and* Mountbatten, *the sappers worked on the odd missiles, and were baffled to find no warheads there to disarm. Only some odd off-white pellets, of various sizes, packed in what seemed to be sawdust, that spilled out and floated around in zero gee. Some of them were small enough to get sucked into air vents, others got caught in odd places, nooks and crannies of equipment.*

By the time they thought to x-ray the pellets, and found they were eggs, the first of them was hatching, deep inside Impervious' *air system. The shell cracked, and, in the darkness, a pale, frail, worm-like thing writhed and twisted mindlessly to get free. It crawled away from the egg, clinging to the wall of the air vent with hair-like cilia. It found a plastic coverplate over an airpump.*

It began to eat the coverplate.

It lay its first eggs two hours later, without pausing in its feeding.

It died shorting out the pump.

Chapter Fifteen

Survey Service Headquarters
Columbia, Kennedy's Natural Satellite.

Pete Gesseti opened the door to Mac's cabin without knocking, switched the light on, saw Mac in his bunk and tossed the oversized, bright red envelope marked *Secret* to him before Mac had time to do more than wake up.

Mac's reflexes snatched the envelope out of the air and he sat up in bed. "Pete, what the hell—"

"There are two reports in there, and they change everything," Pete said. "You're going to have two questions, so let me answer them before you can ask. Yes, Joslyn is safe so far as I can gather, and no, you didn't give the frigging Guards any ideas. They had to have planned the raid long before you said a single word."

Mac felt the bottom fall out of his stomach, and he ripped open the envelope. Two loose-leaf folders.

Naval Action Report: Guardian Attack on Britannic Fleet, aka "Battle of Britannica." That was bad enough, but the second was worse.

Report on the loss of His Majesty's Ships Impervious, Mountbatten, *and* Warspite *to Guardian Attack*. "Oh, my God," Mac said. He rubbed his face, trying to wipe the sleep out of it, swung his legs out from under the covers, and sat on the edge of the bunk. "Oh my God, they got the *Imp*."

"These two reports came in to State and the Navy Castle fifteen hours apart," Pete said, "and they wouldn't have gotten to Columbia until like next year if they had gone through channels. But when they hit the higher-ups, all hell is going to break loose, and the big brass is going to need this base. My boss put me on a high-gee shuttle to get these to Driscoll soonest so she could know what's coming. I sort of got two copies instead of one because I thought you'd want one. Shove that one under your blankets by accident for now and read it later. Get dressed because I'm on my way to kick Captain Driscoll's door down now and I want you with me.

"Oh, and as soon as my office saw these we put in a call to the Judge-Advocate's office and it just so happens that your conviction was reversed and your permanent rank boomed up to captain about thirty-eight seconds after they knew we had heard about the *Imp*. They're going to look bad enough as it is without you rotting away in a training job for warning them. The power of the threatened news leak."

It was too much. Still half asleep, Mac decided that when Pete Gesseti brought the word, the news was *always* too much. Shocked by the news, groggy and unshaved, relieved that his wife was all right, Mac changed into a work coverall, put on socks and shoes, and followed Pete out into the corridor.

"I always get lost in this underground maze of yours," Pete complained. "Lead the way."

Mac nodded and turned down the corridor. There were a hundred things he wanted to ask, but Pete talked on before he had a chance to say a word.

"Our Navy is going out of its tiny little *mind*. If this could happen to the Brits, we could be next," he said, following Mac through the corridors of Survey Service Base. "HMS *Impervious* and two other major combat ships were eaten by *worms*. Not the steel hulls apparently, but every kind of plastic, pressure suit fabrics, graphite structural supports, insulation, you name it. Also any foodstuff—and corpses," Pete said, wincing at the thought.

"Eat the ship interiors? How is that possible?"

"I don't know," Pete said. "All I know is the worms would eat through something, and lay eggs, and the eggs would hatch and eat something and lay eggs . . . One malfunction, then two malfs, then twenty, a hundred at once. And the cute little buggers excrete some kind of slime that reacts with oxygen and foams up. *That* eats up ship's air, so pretty soon there's none left to breathe *and* the blobs of foam block air vents and feed pipes and what have you. There's some sort of poison gas, too, but no one is sure if the worms produce that directly or if it's a byproduct of the reaction that locks up the oxy in the foam. People dying because the worms eat through reinforced fabric and their pressure suits were swiss-cheesed. Ammo going up because the fucking worms eat through the *trigger safeties*. Airlocks shorting out and opening pressurized interiors to space. Fuel tanks rupturing. And the worms breed incredibly fast. It took about 36 hours for them to wreck the *Imp*.

"Captain Thomas is going to be an Admiral by about next Tuesday. Not only is he a hero, he's all they've got left. There were one hundred fifty senior Brit officers killed, and some from other planets, too. Thomas finally realized it was hopeless and gave the order to abandon ship. They started taking crew off and the worms got aboard the rescue ships before anyone figured out what the hell was going on."

Mac had been walking more and more slowly, listening to Pete's hurried words. Now he stopped dead and turned to look at the older man. All those people dead . . . and something popped into his mind. "Pete—wait a minute. It just registered. You didn't say Joz was okay. You said something like you *thought* she was okay."

Pete tried to look Mac in the eye, and couldn't. "Yeah. That's right. I *think* she's okay."

"Pete! What the hell does *that* mean?"

"Well—" he shrugged, "—the casualties were real bad, and survivors got shuffled to a half dozen places, a lot of them without ID and in bad shape, unconscious. They won't have a complete accounting of personnel for a while yet. But she's not on the casualty list, and there was a specific mention that three Wombat pilots were killed. I found three pilots' names in the casualty list, and Joz wasn't one of them. I dunno, Mac. That's the best I can tell you. Believe me,

Mac, I tried. I tried like crazy. But she wasn't listed as dead, and that's all I could find."

Mac restrained an urge to grab at Pete, shake him, as if he could squeeze more information out of him. Mac felt a terrible emptiness open up inside him. Joslyn was supposed to be safe, at home, in the midst of a great fleet deep in friendly territory. And now she might be dead—and he had no clean, clear report of exactly how it happened when he was prepared for the news because he knew of the danger. No. Mac looked forward into the days—or weeks or months—when she would be missing, and feared dead, but the news never certain, an agonizing time when he dared not hope because he was a navy man and an astronaut and he knew what the odds were, and yet could not help but hope because he loved her, but still not *knowing* until the last corpse had been accounted for. . . .

"Mac. Mac. Stop. This isn't the time. We have to see Driscoll. Now."

Mac blinked sharply, and suddenly realized he *had* grabbed at Pete, had his hands clenched around the diplomat's shoulders, gripping him hard enough that it must hurt. He let go his hold, and tried to breathe deeply, calm down. "So let's go. But for God's sake tell me everything you know."

Pete let out a deep sigh, and fell into step beside Mac. "Thomas got out okay, but there were hundreds dead. There's nothing alive aboard the *Imp* and the other ships but the foam worms. They wanted to tow the *Imp* out of orbit before the worms shorted out an engine control and maybe rammed her into the planet, but they're afraid to get near her for fear the eggs can survive vacuum and one egg might float into an airlock. For a while there was a rumor that the eggs could survive *re-entry*. Not true, but the people on-planet are going nuts for fear that the worms might get loose on the planet.

"And now the ROK Navy brass has to admit you were right, quit pushing papers around and get on with the war. Except that you were warning that a big ship could be killed just as dead as a little one by a nuke—substitute 'worm' for 'nuke' and you were dead on target. If a few frigates had been wormed, we'd have lost nine people per ship and a pretty smallish ship at that. Easily replaceable. We lost the *Imp*, and that's a significant fraction of the League's naval power and personnel wiped out. Now they *have* to go to smaller ships. But now there's not time to *build* smaller ships."

Mac grunted. "And all this time I was hoping I was wrong."

"You weren't alone in hoping that, my friend. And here we are." They came upon the entrance to the Captain's quarters, and were stopped by the ROK Marine on duty. "Sorry, sir, the Captain—"

"You'll tell me that the Captain can't be disturbed," Gesseti said in a calm voice, speaking rapidly, "and then I'll wave my credentials and this pretty red package marked *Secret* at you and show you the sealed letter from the Kennedy Secretary of War and you'll let me in, right? Wrong. Instead of wasting five minutes on that little scene you'll let us in *now*."

"Ah, well, yessir, but the Captain isn't in her quarters."

"It's three in the morning local. Where the hell is she?"

"In her office, with two other gentlemen."

"Who the hell is she meeting with at this hour?" Mac demanded.

"I don't know, sir."

"Easy to find out," Pete said. "Lead the way, Mac."

The marine looked uncertain about what he should do, and stepped toward Mac as if to stop him. "Hey, wait just a second, ah, sir, she's not to be—"

Pete grinned evilly at the marine. "Stay put, soldier. You're not to leave your post, remember?" Mac and Pete headed down the hall to the Captain's office.

Mac was thinking more clearly by this time, and there was an obvious and frightening question. "Pete, those worms can't possibly be some natural breed the Guards found growing under a rock. Not and eat shipboard plastics."

"No," Pete replied, his voice flat and hard.

"And no one in the League can breed things like that."

"Nowhere near it. Been trying for a long time, too."

"And if the Guards can do that, what else can they do?"

"Don't make me think about it. I saw shots of the *Imp*'s interior and I'm already having nightmares." They arrived at Captain Driscoll's outer office door and went in, to find another marine sentry on duty, sitting behind a desk. "Good evening, Private," Pete said in an aggressively cheerful voice. "We need to see the Captain most urgently."

"But she's extremely—"

"Not any more, she's not," Pete said, neatly stepping around the desk and opening the door to the inner office before the marine could react.

"Hey!"

"It's all right, Eldridge, let 'em through," Driscoll said, her voice coming from behind the door. "I know that voice, and when Gesseti wants in, he gets in. Law of nature, and we might as well cave in gracefully to it."

"Yes, ma'am," the marine replied, more than a little bemused.

The two of them went in, and Mac saw who Driscoll's visitors were. "Randall! George! You guys are supposed to be on Bandwidth looking for the Guards."

"Not anymore. We *found* 'em," Randall said. "I wanted to rouse you when we landed two hours ago, but George warned me you like your sleep—"

"You found 'em? The Guards? You found Capital?" Mac asked.

"Near enough," George said happily. "We got hold of an astronomer and the three of us doped out what sort of star system Capital had to be in—and we're here to hand Captain Driscoll a search list, all the possible systems."

"And the odds look damn good," Driscoll concluded, grinning. "You can salute me any time you're ready, Lieutenant Commander Larson."

"Uh? Oh, yes ma'am." Mac saluted and then caught the twinkle in Driscoll's eye. "Sorry about that. Ma'am."

"Forget it," she said. "Who can remember salutes at three in the morning?"

"Well, we have got to break the boy of the habit," Pete said. "His conviction has been overturned and he's been bumped to Captain his own self. That's the one piece of good news I've got. The rest is all . . ." Pete looked around and stopped talking.

Driscoll followed his glance. "Oh, yes, you might not know these gentlemen. Commander Randall Metcalf, U.S. Navy, and George Prigot. . . ."

"Of no fixed address," George suggested. "No one has ever quite managed to figure out my status."

"George Prigot. Yeah, Mac told me all about you," Pete replied slowly.

"Relax, Pete," Mac said. "They're family. Randall and George have security clearance for Secret, Top Secret, and Very Unlikely, even right up to Ridiculous. And they're in on this."

"Okay, so I bend a few more security rules," Pete said blandly. "But here's the reports my boss wanted you to see, Captain," he said, handing the red envelope to Driscoll. As she opened it and started reading, he pulled a tape cartridge out of his pocket. "Is there a—"

"In the cabinet against the far wall," Mac said. "Here, I'll set it up." Mac took the cartridge, opened the cabinet, and switched on the playback unit. "I'll throw it on the big screen." He crossed back to Pete and handed him a remote control unit.

"What's on the tape?" Randall asked.

"Real bad news," Pete said flatly. "Captain Driscoll. Have you read enough so you'll know what you're seeing?"

"Yeah. Jesus Christ. I've read enough so I don't want to see anything."

"I can't blame you. My stomach hasn't been right since I saw it the first time. But let's see it anyway." The lights went down and a meter-wide view screen on the side wall came on. After a warning that the contents were Top Secret, a line drawing of the *Impervious* came up on screen. "Okay, this is the way the *Imp* looked a week or so ago. Big cylinder. Here's a phantom view. Note the four hangar decks that take up the whole outer circumference amidships."

Suddenly, one of the hangar decks turned black, and a thick line of black bored straight through to the heart of the ship. "Blammo. A rock, launched from a linear accelerator that has since been captured, hits the *Imp* at extremely high velocity. A big rock, moving very fast. Hulls the hangar deck and keeps right on going, ripping deep into the ship, opens the bridge to vacuum and a lot of compartments in between. Kills people, wrecks equipment, tears up the ship's internal communication and life support real bad. They lose more people before they can get backups going. And practically every Britannic line officer ranking captain or above was at a ball in that hangar. Plus many distinguished guests."

"Including Ortega, my executive officer," Driscoll said grimly.

Pete Gesseti hung his head for a moment and sighed. "I'm sorry. I didn't know. We've taken so many losses and there's no time to grieve over any of them. There were no survivors from Hangar One. But by sheer chance, Captain Thomas and Commander Joslyn Larson, his chief fighter pilot, weren't in the hangar at that moment. Anyway." More lines of black bored into the image of the *Imp* on the screen. "More rock impacts. None of them do anywhere near the damage of the first. It seems like it was chance, not planning, that made the first strike so bad. The *Imp* wasn't even in her present orbit when the rocks were launched, weeks before. The Guards just threw a lot of rocks to soften up the Brit fleet and got lucky. Crippled the *Imp*. The damage control officer, a Commander Higgins, has been recommended for the Elizabeth Cross for his work in getting her back in shape to fight. A posthumous recommendation.

"With all his superiors dead, Captain Thomas, quite correctly, took command of the fleet and led a brilliant defense. The enemy ships only got in a dozen shots or so at the larger Brit ships before the Guards were destroyed or chased off. A long, complex battle. And Mac, the report makes clear that Joslyn was okay to this point. Afterwards, we just plain don't know. I'm sorry.

"As I was saying, the Guards only managed to get off a few shots at the Brits. But some of those shots impacted on target, and they carried these little wonders, or rather eggs that hatched and grew into these bastards." The meter-wide screen was suddenly filled by the image of a foam-worm. Its body was a glistening, sickly pinkish-grey, the color of meat that had started to rot. It was covered with thousands of stubby hairs, cilia. It had no eyes, no apparent sense organs of any kind. "That nightmare is really only about four centimeters long. It can crawl. It has a toothless mouth that secretes God knows what, but it can dissolve practically anything. It has an anus that excretes nightmares. That's about all we know. That and the fact that it can lay eggs. God can it lay eggs. Asexual. It comes close to laying before it's finished hatching from its own egg. A generation about every two hours. No one can figure out how it can have that fast a metabolism without literally burning up. They sent a robot camera aboard the *Imp*, and it radioed back these images before the worms ate the camera."

The scene shifted again. It was a zero-gravity charnel house, an abattoir, the signs of death all around, lit with the reddened gloom of emergency lighting. A blob of what might be machine oil, or blood, or something else, drifted into a wall and splattered there. Corpses and wreckage floated through the murky, poisoned air. The eye looked for signs of movement, life, in the bodies of the dead that drifted past the camera, and seemed to see it, strangely distorted, until suddenly it was clear *what* that movement was. Everything, everywhere, was covered with a writhing, twisting, mass of tiny grey-pink bodies that crawled and slithered and fed indiscriminately on human dead and plastic wallboard and clothing. The camera moved in on a swollen, horribly distended corpse, its skin roiling, knotting and unknotting, moving with the horrid mass of things that had eaten their way inside. The camera turned to look up at the overhead bulkhead. Blobs of the worms' foamed excrement had accumulated over and in an air vent, clogging it hopelessly. The camera found a junction box, and looked at it, its cover eaten away, the wiring inside sparking and melting, shorted out by the corpses of dozens of the worms. And live worms were feeding on the dead. One of the ghastly little destroyers lost its hold and drifted off the pile of its fellows, came floating straight at the lens, wriggling, struggling in midair to find a foothold, turning end over end, closer and closer, until it landed square on the lens, blacking out the scene—

The tape ended, the lights came up, and Mac was suddenly aware of a gagging noise coming from the office's head. George was crouched over the toilet, being hopelessly sick. Randall's skin had turned a greenish-white, and he looked close to joining George. Driscoll stared, grim-faced, at the blanked-out screen.

Pete retrieved the tape from the play-back unit. "The camera lens was plastic, so the worm ate it." He shoved the tape in his pocket, turned, and faced the others. "Now imagine how happy and relaxed they are on Britannica right now. It might be an official secret, but trying keeping *that* kind of disaster quiet. The Guard fleet didn't get within three quarters of a million kilometers of the planet itself, but suppose, just suppose, *one* missile with those things aboard was fired at the planet, or that *one* egg got out of the *Impervious* and re-entered somehow, or got aboard a ship that landed and came out on someone's clothing—how doesn't really matter, but suppose those nightmares got loose and started breeding on the planet. . . . Hysteria is barely the word for it. And the one piece of good news that makes that impossible is also the worst news. They've found out the things can't survive except in zero-gee. They caught some worms and put 'em in sealed glass containers to study in one of the orbital stations. As soon as they carried the worms into the spin section, they died. They've checked it other ways: The *eggs* can survive massive acceleration, but the worms die in anything but weightlessness."

"Why is that bad news?" Driscoll asked. "It means Britannica is safe."

"Because it makes it even more certain that these things are artificial."

"The Guards *bred* them?" she asked.

"Not bred," Mac said. "Manufactured. Invented. Jesus. Those aren't animals. They're *weapons*. Bioweapons? I don't know what the term would be."

"I don't follow you," Driscoll said.

"The old tired joke about designer genes," said Mac. "They decided what they wanted, drew up some blueprints, and either created a whole new creature or vastly modified an existing one. We can modify, say, a cow's genes enough so that it can digest Kennedy's indigenous plant life. That's about it. We managed to grow K-cows, but it strained our abilities to the limit—and killed a lot of cows before we got it right. Something like these worms is as far beyond what we can do as faster-than-light drive was beyond the Wright Brothers. And if they can grow things that *only* live in zero-gee, they can grow things that endure gravity as well as we do. Or breed an entirely different kind of creature that can attack us in a completely different way."

George rinsed out his mouth and staggered back from the head. "Artificial life is absolutely brand new, so far as I know," he said. "I never heard the slightest hint of any such thing. And if they had those horror things a year or two ago, they'd have used them at New Finland."

"Pete. The genes of these things. Are they Earth-descended? DNA, RNA?" Mac asked.

"No. A completely unfamiliar genetic structure. Not Earth-based, or from any other planet we've ever got data from.

Brand new. They got this far starting from scratch. Real smart guys."

"This is all obviously very important," Driscoll said. "But why the big rush to see that *I* knew about it?"

"I suspect the same reason that Commander Metcalf and Mr. Prigot are here," Pete said. "Some set of powers-that-be decided to hand the project of physically searching through Mr. Prigot's list of star systems to you. Another set is going to call you and tell you the League's combined fleet is going to be headquartered right here. Or at least, in this star system, with Base HQ right here on Columbia. They're going to pull in every ship they can. This raid scared the pants off the Brits, and they'll be able to sign up every government who gets a look at that tape. We're both here to warn you that company's coming."

Randall Metcalf stared at Pete. "You do good guessing," he said.

"But why here?" Driscoll demanded.

"Columbia is a natural for an HQ. The reasons for putting the search team here are obvious—you guys run the Survey Service already, and that's a lot like what the search team here will be doing. And there are good reasons to put the fleet here as well. It's near enough Kennedy so you've got a easy job supplying the place with foodstuffs and so on, there's an intact crew and base here and in orbit that knows how to handle ships. Your people are used to spacers from every planet and language wandering through—and here on the surface of Columbia is an atmosphere that's not only poisonous, it's unique. Unless the Guards breed something specifically intended for this moon's air, Columbia's own weird half-way terraformed air, the atmosphere would kill it."

"And if they breed something that *can* survive here, the air anywhere else would kill it, and the rest of the League is safe. It makes a grim kind of sense," Driscoll conceded. "Is this an official message to the effect that the combined League fleet will be here?"

"More sort of semi non-official. All the delegates back at Earth's Moon will bicker and scream for a while, but the fix is in. The U.S., the Japanese, the British and the Brit Commonwealth nations are going to say Columbia—and Kennedy will agree, and all the other planets will be glad to stick someone else with it. Especially Earth. Who the hell would want to tempt the Guards into a raid on good old Mother Earth? You'll probably get the official orders cut for you in about 200 hours."

"But why does Kennedy's government want the fleet right next door? The same dangers of drawing fire apply here as Earth," Randall asked.

"I think they figure we must be next on the list anyway, after Britannica," Pete said. "The Guards would probably hesitate about hitting Earth. The Yanks, the Brits, and the Japanese finally managed to cut a deal with the Brazilians and the Czar. They've linked all the space defense and detection systems—and that means coordinated listening posts on moons of all the outer planets, *and* in deep space. Their spotting is probably ten times as good as Britannica's, and you can bet there's lots of firepower to back it up. So if Earth is too scary for the Guards, Kennedy's the next-juiciest military target. Couldn't hurt to have a great big combined fleet in the system."

"Uh huh. What about a commander?" Randall asked.

"You're going to love it," Pete said. "Politics again. The Brits insisted on naming one of their own as commander. They've been hit the hardest, except for the Finns, and the Finns don't have the pull—or the amount of hardware—the Brits do. The Brits are very concerned that the show be run the right way—their way. So they said you want to play with our ships—and our battle data—fine, but we get to be team captain or we take our ball and go home."

"Wait a minute, Pete," Mac said, "you just got through telling us all their senior line officers were killed—"

"Except Captain and soon to be Admiral Sir George Wilfred Thomas. Right."

Randall's mouth fell open, he closed it, opened it, spluttered a bit and finally said "*Thomas*? The man's a world class drunk. You can't take a Brit into a U.S. Navy officer's club without someone telling a Thomas joke. And the man's nine thousand years old."

"He's only 67, Earthside," Pete said. "I'll grant you, the

poop is they were going to put him out to pasture before all hell broke loose. But now he's all they got left. And he did damn well against the Guards in that raid."

"I notice he lost three major combatant ships."

Pete pulled out the recording he had shown and waved it in the air. "To the crawlies. He beat the Guard fleet. The *worms* took out the ships. So you tell me how he should have defended against *them*."

"Well, I don't have to like it," Randall said.

"No, you don't," Pete said agreeably. "You just have to get used to it."

Three hours later, late night had turned into early morning. Mac, unable to get back to sleep, had decided he might as well head to his office, put a pot of coffee on, and get some paperwork done.

He wasn't too surprised when a knock came at the door and Driscoll came in. "Figured I might find you here," she said. "Everyone else managed to sack out?"

"Yeah," Mac said, pushing back his chair as Driscoll sat down in the visitor's chair. "A long, hard day for everyone."

"So it was," Driscoll said. "And so it will be." Driscoll shifted uncomfortably in her seat, as if she could not quite bring herself to speak.

"Was there something you wanted to see me about?" Mac asked.

"Yeah," she said. "Yeah, there was." Another pause, and then at least she seemed ready to plunge in. "Mac," Captain Driscoll said. "When your captain's bars come through, would you mind terribly hanging them up for a while? Very temporary, a brevet demotion?"

"What?" Mac demanded. "*Now* what have I done?"

Driscoll smiled and shook her head. "Nothing like that. It's *my* problem. If we're going to have half the ships in space descending on us, this base has gone to be run right. And my executive officer got killed on the *Imp*. I want you in that job as a brevet commander, my XO, until we can get things a bit sorted out. It's no time to bring in an officer who doesn't know the layout. You know the base, the way things run, who the right people are. You're known, you have a name. People will listen to you, respect you. I need you, at least until the Fleet sails. Then you'll be wanted there, with the Fleet. But I need you flying a desk until then. Will you do it?"

Mac sighed, and stared down at his desk, at his empty hands, at the cold stale coffee in the cup on his desk. He had just been starting to get used to the idea of being a captain. In the midst of all the disastrous news, the reversal of his conviction and the promotion had been the one happy note. He had already started looking forward to the respect, the privileges, of the rank. And, be it confessed, there wasn't a naval officer anywhere who could hear the word "captain" without thinking "admiral." The idea wasn't impossible. Well, yes, it nearly was, after the court-martial. Conviction overturned or no, it wasn't the sort of thing that impressed a promotion board.

Still, being a captain would have been no bad thing in its own right. He was being paid as a lieutenant commander at the moment. A captaincy would practically double his current salary, for starters. The system owed him a little something, and the captaincy would have been a way to pay him back. And he was entitled, after all he had been through. Why should he say yes and settle for a commander's pay?

No, wait, Driscoll had thought of that. She wanted him to take the permanent grade *before* the brevet move to commander—so Mac could draw pay at his new permanent rank, captain. But how would yet another brevet move look on his record? It seemed to Mac he never retained one rank long enough for the ink to be dry on the paperwork. Not that it mattered. His military career was a crazy hodge-podge already. One more cobbled-together assignment wasn't going to hurt.

And besides, if the Navy owed him one, then he owed one to Driscoll. He knew damn well she had pulled strings to get him assigned back to the Survey base after he was convicted and demoted. Being in a place he knew, where he was a familiar face and not a face in the news—that had helped him a lot.

"Sure Captain," he said at last, very slowly. "I'd be glad to do it."

"Thanks, Mac. I appreciate it."

Mac lifted his mug and swallowed the last of his coffee, more for the sake of having some way of covering the awkward silence than because he wanted to drink it.

The dregs of the cup were bitter, and that seemed about right. Mac had never asked for reward or recognition for his part in the war. That was for others to offer, not his to demand.

But he had always trusted people when they *had* offered reward—and somehow it was always snatched away. He was always asked to do one more thing he couldn't say no to, always asked to understand why he was being shunted to one side for the very best of reasons. He was slowly starting to realize that the arrears would never be paid to him in full.

But if the damnable war had killed Joslyn, they could never even begin to pay them.

Chapter Sixteen

Survey Service HQ
The Moon Columbia

If he had time, Mac might have found ways to worry himself to death over Joslyn, but there was work to do, a great deal of it. Suddenly everything had to be done at once, and there wasn't time to think of anything but the job at hand. Mac knew he wasn't the first—or last—man to hide from his fears in the exhaustion of overwork, but he was grateful for that exhaustion anyway.

There was the fleet's arrival to prepare for, the search for Capital to plan. Driscoll, concerned with the task of providing facilities for hundreds of ships, put Mac in charge of the search for Capital while she worried about everything else. There should have been a dozen officers, all kinds of specialists on call to plan the search, but there simply weren't enough warm bodies, or enough time, to allow such luxury. And Driscoll liked it that way—she was a great believer in lean, mean organizations. She wanted the search operations underway before the League brass could wander in and strangle it in months of studies of how to do it quickly.

Mac was, therefore, left with a bit of a challenge.

George and Randall had arrived with a list of thirty-one star systems that met their criteria. The system had to be a binary with rotation periods of at least seventy years, with the stars sufficiently distant from each other for planets to exist in stable orbits. The system had to be unexplored and had to have at least one star of a brightness, age, and mass that could support life.

At first glance, the job was simple. All they had to do was send a ship to each system until one of them found Capital. In practice, things were a lot trickier. Any attack on Capital would benefit greatly from the element of surprise, which meant the search ships could not risk being detected themselves. If the Guards didn't know they had been found, they might be less on the alert. It made an optimistic sort of sense. Besides, the Guards would be sure to go nuts trying to blow any search ship they spotted.

Of course, if a ship didn't come back, that would tell them something right there, but not as much as they'd like to know. Besides, other things besides the Guards could keep a ship from coming back, and searching for lost ships could mean the loss of time and effort on wild goose chases. Mac made it clear he wanted every ship to play it safe and come back in one piece—a sentiment the ships' crews agreed with.

But the Guards' anti-ship missile system in New Finland had shown just how good they were at ship detection.

Therefore, the search ships were going to have to look for signs of civilization from extreme distances. Obviously, they would use only passive systems. They would monitor radio frequencies, make telescopic observation, do infrared checks, use neutrino detectors. No active radar. Fortunately, a world-sized civilization was easier to detect than a ship, or even a fleet of ships. But, surprisingly enough, it was not that much easier to spot. The planet *itself* would be spotted easily enough, but it could be tricky to spot a civilization that wanted to hide.

It all depended on how hard the Guards worked at camouflage. No search ship could possibly risk getting close enough to observe a planet optically and, for example, detect the lights of cities. But there were other things that could be spotted from fairly extreme range. Heat, radio, neutrinos, fusion flames would all be giveaways. The trouble was, the Guards could shield themselves pretty effectively if they were willing to expend the effort. Power sources could be disguised, all-but-impossible-to-detect laser communication and transmission over cable could be substituted for radio broadcasts.

If the Guards wanted to avoid neutrino emissions, they

could forego fusion power plants, and use chemical instead of fusion rockets. That would be inconvenient and expensive as all hell, but they could do it.

There were lots of concealment techniques they could use, if they were willing to go to extremes that would cripple their technology. But none of them could hide the planet itself, or long fool anyone observing with sensitive equipment, unless the Guards were willing to forego anything that went past nineteenth-century technology.

On the plus side, they had George Prigot and the information from the POWs taken on New Finland. They had a lot of evidence that the Guards *didn't* make extreme efforts at hiding, and instead trusted to their isolation—and, until recently, to the fact that no one knew they existed.

There was something else that helped narrow the odds. The odds were against a given star system having a planet in its biosphere, that range of distances from the star where a planet would get the right amount of light and heat from the star to support Earth-like life. On average, about one "G" class star in twenty had a planet in the right place. That was the figure for single stars, and the odds were somewhat worse for binary star systems. Therefore if *any* of the target stars had a properly located planet, the odds were good that it was *the* planet, Capital.

Mac, after considerable thought, and a hard look at all the facts, concluded that the Guards would be best served if they hid themselves well enough to hide from a ship just happening by and taking a cursory look, but not well enough to hide from a ship deliberately arrived in the system and intent on a thorough-going search. Concealment of a whole civilization from someone who knew what they were looking for, someone who was determined to find the civilization—that would be impossible, or at least impossibly expensive. It meant the search for Capital was do-able, and could be done with off-the-shelf gear.

All they had to do was search thirty-one star systems,

scattered far and wide, the closest of them ninety light-years out from Earth.

Not that it had taken much forethought, but Driscoll had figured out months before that the Survey ships would be needed in the search for Capital. She had grounded the ships as they came in. Now she turned the Survey's small fleet over to Mac to deploy as he saw fit. Not that it gave him a lot to work with. Only six of the Survey Service's ten fast frigates were in home port orbit around Columbia. The *Joslyn Marie* was still undergoing repairs in the New Finland system. She wouldn't be available for service anytime soon. *Spotter* was expected to return from a Survey mission any time now—though you couldn't exactly set your watch by an exploration ship's arrival. The *Ismene Schell* had been launched just before Driscoll had shut down the Survey project for the duration, and *Vasco da Gama* was overdue and feared lost. Mac had the other six ships to count on, and possibly two more drifting in, someday. Maybe three, if *Vasco* showed up. He needed more. Unfortunately, the moment when the whole League was finally scared into mobilizing wasn't exactly the moment when there were a lot of ships available for duty, though he fully intended to scrounge for some.

In the meantime, the six ships he had needed to be cranked up for detection duty. Spotting habitable worlds was the original prime task of the Survey, and the ships had been outfitted accordingly. Spotting an industrial civilization was a similar task, but it required somewhat different instrumentation. Optical and spectroscopic devices would still be handy, but Mac managed to come with neutrino spotters from New Harvard University, infrared sensors that could be patched into the fast frigate's telescopes from a mining company working the Kennedy system's outer planets, and other bits and pieces from all over.

Mac wanted to get his frigates out toward their first targets *fast*. He spent days studying the star-charts, playing with a dozen variables in his head, trying to figure which were the most likely stars to harbor Capital. He juggled the distance from Earth, the distance to suspected ship hijack points and the limits of space technology at the time the Guards had left Earth. He even dug up the specs on their colony ship, the *Oswald Mosley*.

And the *Mosley* specs told him something, told him that distance was a phony issue. With the C^2 drive, it wasn't the *distance* between stars that mattered so much, but their *velocity*, relative to each other, as they moved through space. A century before, with far less powerful and efficient ship's engines, and less sophisticated ships that tended to be much massier than modern designs, it had mattered a great deal more than it did now. Crudely put, the *Mosley* couldn't go very fast, and so couldn't catch up with a star system that was moving more than about one hundred twenty kilometers a second, relative to Earth.

Mac did the velocity calculations, and they led him to throw out four of the target systems altogether—the *Mosley* couldn't possibly have matched velocity with them. However, the same numbers also pulled five new systems out of Randall and George's "lower-probability" list and into the prime running. Now he had thirty-*two* target systems.

At long last he had sifted the data and made as many hunches and badly-educated guesses as he could. He had equipped the ships and briefed the crews as best he could. There was nothing more that could be done to prepare.

Three hundred fifty hours after Pete had brought news of the *Imp*, the first frigates headed out across the sky.

Chapter Seventeen

Guardian Contact Camp
The Planet Outpost

The forklift rolled another crate of rifles out of the cargo hold. Romero, watching from the viewport of his private office, smiled at the sight. Contact Camp was growing by leaps and bounds now. It was no longer a mere research station—it was a trading center, with warehouses and shipping clerks and inventory control. The Nihilists and the Guards were making lots of deals.

Romero had a letter in his tunic, tucked inside a pocket next to his heart, from Jules Jacquet himself, crediting Romero with the idea that had led to the destruction of three of the enemy's largest ships at Britannica. The foamworms had done their work. Romero smiled at the thought of the letter, and resisted the temptation to pull it out and read it again.

Promotion. Promotion was in the air for one Captain Lewis Romero. Things were breaking his way. That suicidal escape attempt by that half-breed Calder was the turning point. That had given Romero the excuse to yank that damned Gustav out of the Contact Camp and put *him* in charge of that dreary orbital station. Captain Lewis Romero had been forced to take charge of the now all-important Contact Camp himself.

Across the camp were the labs that made it important, where the Nihilists brought their horrors to explain and demonstrate to the men of the Guardian Navy's new BioWeapons Command.

The Nihilists were smart—all of the bios they brought in were "ecologic engulfers," as the BioWeapons men called them—once the first generation hatched, that was it, the things would breed and breed and breed to the limits of the ecology's carrying capacity—and beyond, until the only things left were the bios, and the bios would starve, eat each other's dead bodies, and finally die in their own waste products. Nothing but death could halt the cycle.

The Nihilists showed the Guards how to trigger breeding, how to bring the horrors out of dormancy so they would hatch from their eggs or pods or whatever—but not how to stop it again. Once the things had started breeding, the only way the Guards could stop them was to kill them, wipe them out to the last. There was no way for the Guardians to set up controlled hatches or breeding groups independent of the Nihilists. They would always have to go back to their hosts for more.

The Guards, in their own way, played the same game. They practically gave away their rifles, their lasers, their heavy weapons—and then traded hard for ammo and power packs, once the 'Posters had seen the value of their new toys.

Romero had been worried a bit when he learned that the Nihilists already had projectile weapons—slugthrowing guns, cannon, and so on. But the native-built guns weren't as sophisticated or accurate as the Guards' stuff—and the native weapons barely had any range at all. From the largest to the smallest, they were made for stopping power, the ability to throw a round hard at short range, elephant guns in all calibers. All were intended for defense against animals, not warfare.

And it seemed the source of supply for native-built weapons was limited for a very good reason. The Outposters who made the guns would certainly stop trading with the Nihilists when the Nihilists started their attacks.

The Guards had more to sell than weapons. The 'Posters had fought among themselves in the past, but their tactics had never gotten much past the two sides slamming into each other for an all-out brawl. The Guardians taught them strategy, and military formations, and the concept of specialized troops.

Romero felt pleased with himself. Things couldn't be going any better. Except—

Except now there was a new element. Jacquet, in his letter, had instructed Romero to show the Guardians' gratitude to the Nihilists for their aid against the League. Romero was to modify the controls of a small passenger lander so Outposters could fly her. Romero was then to train a crew of 'Posters—and present the ship to the Nihilists. Jacquet made it very clear that the Outposters' ship was to be capable of no more than the roundtrip to Capital. No C^2 unit. No navigation system capable of plotting interstellar journeys. It was to be an embassy ship, a dramatic way to convey an invitation to the Outposters to visit their friends on Capital.

Romero had hesitated as long as he could before obeying the order. It worried him a bit to give the Nihilists the power of spaceflight. It might be wiser to keep them safely on Outpost without giving them ideas. It would *definitely* be smarter. And safer. But Jacquet had ordered it, and Jacquet was backing Romero at the moment. It was no time to rock the boat.

He picked up his phone and asked the Camp's chief engineer to his office. He could find no good reason to delay any longer. The Nihilists would have their ship. What harm could one little inter-system lander do?

Chapter Eighteen

Survey Service HQ,
The Moon Columbia

The ballistic shuttle settled down on its landing legs, the pilot throttled back thrust to zero and quickly set about securing the ship. Outside, the ground crew was already operating the remote equipment, rolling out an access tunnel, the autofueler wheeling itself into position.

Mac Larson stared out the port at the grounded ship, beside himself with excitement and anxiety. Why couldn't they hurry with that damn access tunnel? No, finally they were pressurizing it. At last it was linked and sealed. *Now* they'd open it.

But there was some unexplained delay, and the airlocks on the lander and the terminal building remained stubbornly shut. A small crowd shuffled around inside the terminal, held back by the rope barrier, patient for the moment but annoyed by the wait. Nothing happening. Mac rushed back to the viewport. The ship just sat there.

Was she even aboard? All the communique had said was that Admiral Thomas was arriving with staff. Mac had still gotten no certain word that she had survived the attack. Was this even Thomas' lander? This was supposed to be her, but schedules had been hashed up before. The *clunk, clunk thud* of a hatch opening came from behind him. He rushed back to the airlock, peered along the access tunnel as far as he could, until it curved away to hide the rest of its length.

There she—no, his imagination was playing tricks on his eyes. How could so many people fit on such a small lander—

And he was over the silly rope barrier and halfway down

the access tunnel before his conscious mind registered that his eye had spotted her.

"Mac!" Joslyn dropped her bags and leaped up into his arms.

"Joslyn, you really are alive!"

"Mac, how did you know I was—"

"I didn't. I just hoped. Oh, thank God. Lord, you look good."

"Mac, I would have sent word, but they've gone absolutely potty with paranoia back home, not that I can blame them— " She looked up into his eyes, heedless of all the people coming past them from the lander, and the two of them were in a passionate embrace. Finally, almost reluctantly, they ended the kiss. She reached out and touched his face. "Oh, Mac. Let's get out of this tunnel and get home. With all these personnel coming in, it must be crowded here—"

"Swinging from the rafters."

"—But if we can't get nice, private married-couple quarters I think I'll scream."

"Cancel the scream. I managed to wangle us our old stateroom, and even the adjoining compartment. Just like before. Being XO has its advantages."

"You're Base XO?"

"Flying the second-biggest desk in the place. Privacy I had covered, but I wish I'd had some notice so I could have gotten some kind of meal—"

"Oh, Mac, I've got you. Who needs food? But I wanted to send word. I'm sorry, I tried like mad to write and say that I was all right, that I was coming, but Uncle George ordered *everything* shut down. No mail, no nothing."

"Well, you can tell your dear old Admiral Uncle Sir George Wilfred Thomas that he's taken five years off my life worrying."

"No need," came a deep and cheery voice behind him. "He's heard already."

Mac let go of Joslyn, turned, and found the admiral grinning at him. He saluted and took the admiral's proffered hand. "I beg your pardon, sir, I—"

"Never mind. To offer a scandalous suggestion, if I was married to my great-niece here and some old duffer kept her away from for this great length of time, I'd box his ears instead of saluting. Glad to meet you, Lieutenant Commander."

"Ah, actually, it's Captain, sir, but currently serving as a Commander. Full Commander."

"Mac! Not again! You never could have just one rank!" Joslyn said happily.

"Congratulations, then. But let's get out of this mob. The regs say all these people have to salute me and this tunnel's not wide enough for all these flying elbows. Come along."

Mac was worried that his reunion with his wife would be interrupted by a nice visit with the admiral, but fortunately, Thomas had his own reception committee decorously waiting at the roped barrier. Thomas was led away from the terminal and into the base proper, and Joslyn and Mac were left to their own devices for the first time in far too long.

For their sake—and his—Thomas was glad to be steered clear of the reunited couple. If ever a pair of young people needed some private time together—and deserved it—they did. In any event, he had his own concerns. "Ensign—I think I'd prefer to go straight to the situation room. I'd like to get right down to business."

"Certainly, sir."

The Survey Service base was a maze of corridors that looked like any base built on a tight budget. The situation room was behind an unmarked, double-locked door, guarded by a beefy marine who demanded Thomas' credentials before she let him through.

Inside, in holo tanks and displays and printouts, the story was told: The Combined League Fleet was slowly, quietly, with as much secrecy and misdirection as possible, drifting into Kennedy's star system. No large concentrations of ships this time—they were dispersed throughout the system, with small formations orbiting every planet in the system, and some ships in free orbit of Kennedy's sun. This time the neatly labeled spots of light moving in their displays hid no chaos. The calm of the situation room was reflected in the real world. No raiding fleet would be able to hit them all at once, worms or no worms.

The worms. The damned, horrible, nightmare worms. Thomas shivered, felt a twinge in the pit of his stomach. The worms would visit his dreams for the rest of his life. Even now, in the order of the situation room, the very thought of them raised his hackles. Worse than the worst delirium tremens he had ever had.

Wide dispersal in space was vital in protecting against the vermin. They were killed by vacuum. Praise be to God, for the eggs were killed by vacuum as well. They could survive no more than thirty seconds in zero-pressure. A raider, a saboteur, might get a few ships with the damn things, but the Combined Fleet itself would be safe.

Which was not to say there were no headaches. Even so simple a thing as rigging *Eagle* for flag ops had been a challenge. No one really liked the idea of using a carrier for a flag, not after Britannica, but the plain fact was that there was no other combatant ship that could carry all the specialized gear and equipment, to say nothing of billeting the specialists who would use that gear.

Combined League Fleet. In a more romantic age, it would have been called the Grand Fleet, perhaps, and would have been named by a sailor awestruck by its mighty size, and not by a bureaucratic technician who saw the numbers and not the ships.

Never had so many spacecraft, under so many flags, been joined together in one task. A procedure for coordinating their movements should have taken years to invent, but this was wartime, and those same soulless technicians had come up with the computer programming and the comm system in weeks. Practice at simply *talking* ship to ship, working through the Babylon of languages and the dozen "standard" radio frequencies, was the most important thing for these craft at the moment, and would be until the Search teams finally located the enemy.

You could hear the capital "S" in Search when people talked about it. Nothing was more important, and yet it had to be done by the tiny number of ships that could be equipped with the proper sensing devices.

Far Shore was still out there, and so were the *Jodrell Bank* and newly reappeared *Vasco Da Gama*. The *Vasco* had arrived in-system, and found herself turned around and sent back out within three hundred hours. One of the Survey ships might have succeeded. But for Sir George, it was time to do little more than wait.

Except for one project, and Sir George was following it closely. It was based on what some of the scientific johnnies had said about what was to be found at the barycenter of a binary star system.

It was a frightening idea, and a daring one. But try as he might, Admiral Thomas could think of no reason why it would not work. The research team had already come up with operational recommendations.

They gave it the code name Bannister. It seemed to Thomas that the deadliest schemes always had innocuous codenames.

Joslyn tried to let herself fall into the blissful mood of a happy, romantic reunion in the days that followed, and even succeeded to a certain extent. But there were too many things on her mind for her to manage it completely. At least Mac didn't seem to notice her worries, and she was very glad of that.

She fretted about their new admiral, dear old Sir George. Their lives were in his hands now. She loved her great-uncle, but she worried. She knew him better than anyone else in the fleet, knew his strengths and weaknesses, and even *she* had no answer to the central question: *Was* he the man for such a command? If not for the foamworms, he would have had a major victory in his pocket at Britannica. Was that just luck, chance, or had old Sir George simply been given his first decent chance after a lifetime of being shunted aside?

And she worried about the drinking. She could just about keep his boozing under some control when she was around, but she couldn't nursemaid her uncle constantly.

But a drinking uncle and a unreliable commander were not the worst of it. The death of the *Impervious* preyed on her mind more than anything else. She resolved never to talk about it with her husband. Joslyn was glad Mac hadn't seen that nightmare with his own eyes, glad that he couldn't know it was even worse than he imagined it being.

She herself had no desire to remember, but she had no choice but to do so. The disaster came into her dreams, and her waking thought, unbidden, time and time again. The nightmare trip from aux control to the emergency airlock, after the worms had done their worst and the *Imp* was dead, that was burned into her mind for all time. She could still hear the horrible shriek of the air roaring out the lock when they blew the outer door while the lock was full of air, because the pumps were dead. She could still see Ensign McCrae dying, strangling, screaming in silence before their eyes because the worms had eaten a hole in his suit somewhere. She could see the waiting cutter, framed by the worms that had gotten into the lock's vent system and so been sucked out with the air. The worms' ghastly, flaccid bodies bursting in the vacuum, and the cutter's lasers burning anything that even looked the size of a worm before it would allow them aboard.

And, the worst of it, somehow, the look on Sir George's face when they had half-dragged him out of the *Imp*'s lock and into the cutter. The *Imp* had been more than his ship for ten long years—she had been his life, his hope, his plan for salvaging something out of his life's work. Now she was scrap metal, the grisly grave for hundreds.

Had she, Joslyn done the right thing then? Aboard the cutter, she had *handed* him the bottle of gin, and let him drink as much as he would. What the worms had done to Sir George's world was more than any man should be expected to face, and Joslyn could not begrudge him his means of escape. But should she have given him one more lesson in hiding from failure? Should she have fed the weakness of the man who now commanded them?

Uncle George in command. He was the man with the job.

But was he the man *for* the job?

Chapter Nineteen

Comm Center
Survey Service HQ
The Moon Columbia

The comm center had standing orders, but they were the sort of orders an ensign stuck with the lobster trick was hesitant to obey. Even so, 0330 hours local or not, the admiral had said he wanted to be notified. Ensign Timility swallowed hard and picked up the phone. It rang twice, and then he heard the noise of curses as the admiral slapped at the answer button.

"What?"

"Ah, Admiral Thomas?"

"No, laddie, it's the bloody Queen of Sheba. Who is this, and why the hell are you calling at this time of night?"

"Well, ah, sir, this is Timility in comm. We're—we're picking up something from a returning Search ship. *Far Shore.*"

"And?"

"It looks like they found it. They are transmitting a long text message now. I'll have a hard copy in five minutes."

"The devil you say. Jolly good! You did right to wake me, Tumulty. Let me jump into my pants and I'll be there straight away."

Sir George showed up in his pants, but not much else. He had thrown on a disreputable dressing gown, a long, threadbare thing of indeterminate color that might have looked smart twenty years before. Sir George was barechested, and a sparse thatch of grey peeped through when the gown slipped a bit. Ensign Timility could smell the port on the admiral's breath, but Sir George seemed nothing if not sober and in control.

The admiral grabbed at the hard copy as it plopped out of the printer and riffled through the pages, growling to himself. "By damn, they've got it," he said. "They bloody damn well have it." He flipped through the pages, and then looked up at Timility. "Dimity, I want everyone in tactics and planning roused out of bed and to work on this *now*. I want enough copies of this report to paper every wall in the base."

"Ah, yes sir," Timility said.

But the admiral did not seem to hear him. "My God, they actually found it," he said, speaking to himself more than the ensign. "This calls for a bit of celebrating."

Sir George stuck the report under one arm, dug an enormous black cigar out of his dressing gown pocket, and bit the end off it. "I've been saving this for the right moment," he said. "A chum of mine got me a box straight from old Cuba. Last one left." He fussed about, trying to light it for a minute before it began drawing properly, and then stood, puffing smoke like a dragon, reading the *Far Shore*'s report. At last he looked up and noticed that Timility hadn't moved a muscle. "Well, get on it, Dimity. Rouse 'em! We've finally got some work to do."

Timility started working the intercom system, bringing the experts in. It was going to be a long night.

Second Lieutenant George Prigot, Royal Britannic Navy (Naval Intelligence) got one of the first calls. George had never been much good after a sudden awakening, and it took him a while to get his bearings. The call, a rather peremptory call to the comm center without explanation, didn't help. For that matter, his bearing had been a little off ever since Admiral Thomas had breezed into the Survey base.

As usual, no one had figured out what to *do* with George at Survey base, and he was apologetically packed into some broom closet they called guest quarters. Then Admiral Thomas had noticed George Prigot's card going past, somehow—and that was that. The Admiral didn't like anomalies, and Mr. Prigot was one. *Lieutenant* Prigot would *not* be one. The Royal Navy permitted non-British persons to enlist, and Intelligence was an odd barrel of fish that wouldn't mind one more. George had gone along with it. It would be nice to belong to something.

Intelligence. Why was it that every bureaucrat and brass hat in the League thought George Prigot belonged in Intelligence? He was an engineer, not a spy. Okay, so he was a native of Capital, and he knew which end of a Guardian screwdriver to hold. What good did that do them in intelligence?

George had used his brand-new clearance to peek at his own file, and the words there explained a lot about the cold shoulder he got from the rest of the Britannic Intel staff. All of them, right up and down, had urged that he was a bad security risk and should not be allowed to take up a commission. But Thomas had overruled them all. "There are times," the Admiral's comment read, "when you have to have a little faith in people. Clearance approved."

George pulled on his brand new uniform and staggered his way down the corridor to the head. He automatically went through the motions of trying to make himself look presentable and made his way to the comm center. Comm was crowded and confused, and getting more so by the minute. There must have been a couple of dozen people jammed into the tiny room and more coming all the time. A harried rating handed George a copy of the printout from *Far Shore*, and he found a quiet corner to sit down and start reading it.

Before he could get a fair start, the section chief of the Comm center ordered everyone to get the hell out of her radio room and move into the auditorium on the next level down.

George followed the rest of the herd down to the auditorium and took a seat in the back row. There were about fifty pages to get through. Like any good engineer, he wanted to read all the specs and have all the data before he reached any conclusions.

Others around him were of a different opinion. By now, there were thirty or forty standing around in the aisle or perched in chairs, arguing over what it all meant and what should be done about it.

Finally, Driscoll jumped up on the small stage, grabbed a mike and shouted into it. "PIPE DOWN OUT THERE."

The hubbub slowly died out.

"All right," Driscoll went on in a quieter voice. "Everyone take a seat and we'll go over this together."

The murmur of voices rose up again for a moment as people sat down. George spotted Mac and Joslyn sitting near the front of the house. He waved, and Joslyn waved back. Mac was too busy reading to notice anything else.

"TEN-SHUN!" Everybody got to their feet as Admiral Thomas came in a side door and took the three steps up to the stage. He looked trim and alert. He had put on his uniform and had a shave, and he was smoking a huge and malodorous cigar. He looked more cheerful and alert than anyone had a right to be at this hour.

"At ease, all of you. Take your seats and let's get on with it. As you have all seen, *Far Shore* has found the little spot our Guardian friends call home. The big surprise is that planets of *both* star systems seem to be inhabited. At least *Far Shore* picked up radio traffic from both sources. One of the two planets was definitely identified as Capital, and the other planet seemed to be called Outpost. *Far Shore* picked up numerous radio calls in clear referring to the planet names. Captain Toshiro and his crew did an excellent job—not only did they find our quarry, but they also managed to sift through the radio traffic and come up with some rough figures on numbers of ships and how and where they are based. Most of their Navy seems to be stationed in orbit about Outpost.

"Another bit of information. The anti-ship missile systems the Guards are so good at. There are no less than *three* of them in the system. One deployed around Nova Sol A, and so protecting Capital. A second deployed about Nova Sol B, shielding Outpost.

"And a third is being built around the barycenter. Toshiro's crew listened in on the chatter of the construction tugs, and Toshiro's best estimate is that the barycenter system is less than a third complete. Which sounds like an engraved invitation—though we haven't much time to exploit it.

"All this begs the question—what are we going to do? What is our plan? What are our war aims? Now we're all military here, and war aims are more properly a question for the politicians."

"So we drop the question of what to do in their laps. And when they come back with the answer, we will be ready, because you lot here are going to break off into separate planning groups, each to plan for a different contingency. You will have your specific assignments within the hour, and some of you will stick with the jobs you have now, and simply be expected to keep informed and assist.

"But we are going to plan for:

"A peaceful and open arrival, a show of strength that will scare the pants off the Central Guards and convince them to give up. Then I suppose we go around and hand out flowers to the people who attacked us without the barest hint of a provocation and then murdered our allies and friends using the most barbaric weapons imaginable, invaded our star systems and came bloody close to wiping out my fleet, and who have probably been kidnapping our kith and kin and enslaving them since before any of us were born. As you might have gathered, I rate the sweetness-and-light approach as not likely to work, and not bloody likely to be tried.

"Second, choosing among the various military options to find the one most likely to gain us a military victory with the greatest cost to the Guards and the least hurt to ourselves. In parallel with this, we will want to look at ways and means of rescuing any and all League-member citizens kidnapped by the Guards. I am certain that we *can* defeat the Guards, even in their home system, even against their loathsome bioweapons."

Admiral Thomas paused for a moment, and something

in his ice-cold tone of voice horrified George Prigot before the new intelligence officer understood what the Admiral was saying. "The third option is simple. And since the Battle of Britannica, I must admit that it is more likely than it once was. Personally, I would oppose it strenuously. However: That third option is extermination. We wipe them out, down to the last. Bomb every city, every satellite, every ship, sterilize the planets of Nova Sol, and ensure that the damned worms and whatever other monstrosities they have created are wiped out along with their masters.

"This, too, I am certain we could do."

Chapter Twenty

G.O.S. Ariadne
In Orbit of the Planet Outpost

Have they forgotten us?

No one asked that question anymore, at least not out loud. But all the CIs asked it of themselves, every time they saw the stars or thought of home. "Home" was gradually becoming a mythic place for each of them, an ideal that would never be seen again.

It had been a year and a half and more that they had been here, cooped up on Ariadne. The former members of the Survey Service's first class didn't think of themselves as being with the Survey, or the League, or as citizens of their own nations anymore. It was a feat of selective memory, defense against pain. To forget what they had been helped resign them to what they were. But that made it easier for them to think of themselves as CIs—and Conscripted Immigrant was a polite term for slave.

Yet that defense of forgetfulness, acceptance, surrender to the situation, was only skin deep. Every now and again, a certain look would pass across someone's face. The look of sorrow, the look of loss—the look of *being* lost. The outside universe thought they were dead, had given up on them. The CIs had lost hope.

Hope had sprung up for a time after the Main Strike Fleet and *Leviathan* had failed to return. Rumors had swept the station, whispers that said the Guards had suffered a grave defeat. That had helped morale for a while, and the CIs watched the screens and monitors, waiting for the great League fleet that would come chase the Guards back to their home system.

But Sam Schiller, the CIs' best astronomer, had been

pessimistic then, and he had been right. The League had to *find* the Guards first, and whatever else had happened with the Main Strike Fleet, the Guardians at least had kept their home system hidden. No great League fleet ever appeared, and morale slumped lower than ever.

The CIs had no solid information about the outside world at all, beyond what they could see and hear for themselves, and what they picked up from the more talkative Guards as rumor. The CIs joked the time of day was a state secret, and Security was trying to track down who kept leaking the information.

At least there were the Outposters. Officially, they too were a secret. In reality, of course, everyone knew about them. Hiding their existence from the CIs was an obvious impossibility when it was the CIs themselves who manned the communications and traffic control consoles. Starting with Lucy's first trip to the surface, pictures and words had been bootlegged onto every screen and speaker in the station. Tremendous amounts of cargo and any number of personnel had moved through Ariadne en route to the Contact camp. Everyone knew about the 'Posters, and everyone was fascinated by them.

And there was Lucy herself, and the strange truce that had developed between Gustav and the CIs. Only Cynthia Wu and Sam Schiller knew for certain that Lucy had escaped to the surface of Outpost—and even they had no idea why. Rumors swept the station, and it was hard to miss the connection between Lucy vanishing, a lander vanishing, a drugged doctor, one dead Guard and one badly wounded.

But only Cynthia knew for certain that Lucy was still alive, or at least that the beacon still moved. . . . On the time-honored principle that you can't tell what you don't know, Cynthia chose not to risk either the knowledge or her friends' safety by telling them what was going on, not even Sam. The two of them never discussed what had happened that night.

And Cynthia had yet to figure out Gustav's motives. Cynthia was ready to bet that Lucy and Gustav were up to something.

What, why, and how she had no idea. Neither Gustav or Lucy had told *Cynthia* anything, either. All she knew was that Lucy had to be made to disappear, and that she had a hunch that Gustav knew why. His arrival back at Ariadne just after her escape was too interesting a coincidence.

And so now the XO was running the show on Ariadne. He seemed to have his own ideas about what sort of game he wanted to play. Twenty hours after he got back aboard, Gremloid vanished from the computers without a trace. In fact, *every* supposedly covert computer operation went missing, without explanation, without reprimand or arrest. Gustav, the former intelligence officer, must have known about the underground files long ago. For a time, it scared the CIs. They waited for the other shoe to drop. It never did. Gustav didn't touch them.

But diddling the computer was what the CIs did best, and a few of the bolder—and more bored—hackers couldn't resist the temptation. They went back to work, invading the computers again, this time hiding everything better, using more sophisticated locks and encryptions. They waited for detection, arrest, punishment—but nothing happened. It was as if Gustav had merely been telling them to cover their tracks better.

Disciplinary actions against the CIs all but came to a halt. Minor infractions went unpunished, and serious violations were met with proportionate responses, not Draconian punishment. Gustav stopped Romero's policy of unannounced searches and seizures, and instead posted a schedule of regular inspections of quarters and working spaces—almost as if he wanted the CIs to have time to hide what needed hiding. The inspections themselves took on an entirely new complexion. Instead of the old, crude, and rough searches for contraband goods and printouts, caches of food and information, the inspections came to resemble boot-camp checks for cleanliness and order—two things that had, Cynthia admitted to herself, come to be in short supply. The XO treated the CIs like a station crew, not a gang of imprisoned criminals.

Somehow, the CIs remembered at least a part of what they had been. After long months of using bare surnames, they came back to calling each other by their old ranks. Gradually, their captors picked up the habit. The Guardians troopers found themselves calling their prisoners "sir," "ma'am," "Lieutenant," and even started treating the CIs with the respect due officers.

Ensign Cynthia Wu thought she knew whom to credit. By firm proddings and decent treatment, Gustav had brought the CIs back to pride and self respect in themselves, and self respect breeds the respect of others. Slowly, grudgingly, morale, health, and efficiency all began to climb out of the murky bogs they had been in.

Gustav seemed to be working toward some purpose—and he seemed to be *waiting* for something. The mood spread to the CIs. There was only one thing worth waiting for in their minds, of course, and if Gustav was expecting it, then so would they.

And so, very slowly, the question changed. It was no longer *Have they forgotten us*, but *when will they get here?*.

Sam Schiller finally knew where the Nova Sol system was—and where old Sol, the *real* Sol, Earth's sun, was. It had been a slow, maddeningly piecemeal job, but he had managed to get his bearings.

Strangely enough, it was the Outposters who had led the way. The Guardian scientists working with the locals had wanted to find out just how much astronomy the 'Posters had, and requested several reference tapes on the subject—a trickier thing than it seemed, as all of astronomy was classified material to the Guards. The request had to go all the way up to Romero's office. Wu was working the comm board that relayed the order to Capital. She had copied the message traffic and passed it to Schiller. He read it over, and found what looked like a series of library catalog numbers with no titles. He ran a search through the data files—and by God if they weren't astronomy texts that had been tucked deep inside Ariadne's computer all that time. Schiller printed out copies of the textbooks, and found what he was after—precise spectra of several well-known bright stars. Spectra were to stars what fingerprints or retina scans were to humans—infallible means of identification. Armed with them, he could scan the starfield, find some familiar stars, and triangulate back into Earth's position.

Even with the spectra in front of him, it took months of sneaking telescope time to find any of the stars in question—the chart hadn't given sky positions as seen from the Nova Sol system. But then he nailed Aldebaran, and that was the turning point. A week later he had Vega, and Deneb. With those three bright signposts in the sky precisely located, far more than half the battle was done. His doctorate was in astrocartography—he knew the relative positions of those three giants to Earth's Sun as well as he knew the family farmyard back home. An hour or two of computer time and he had what should have been the sky position of Sol as seen from Ariadne.

And so, deep into a night shift, a tiny yellow dot of light, too dim to be seen by the naked eye, lay centered in the crosshairs of Ariadne's largest 'scope. The sentries seemed to blunder past every ten minutes, and Schiller had to hide what he was doing, abort the job and start over a half dozen times. It took most of the shift to gather enough light to produce a spectrum.

But when the charge-coupled particle imager had finally accumulated enough photons, and a hard copy rolled out of the printer, Sam Schiller took that paper in his hands, looked over the slightly blurry pattern of dark lines, and wept. There was that dear old strong calcium line. He would know it anywhere. His professors had pointed that line out to him on the first spectrum he had ever made, a reading taken on the warm, friendly sunlight of a clear Cambridge spring day—but the light that formed *this* spectrum had left Sol decades before his professors were born. Those blurry lines were an indisputable portrait of the Sun. Home. Earth. The smell of honest dirt and the corn plants waving in the breeze and his mother sitting on the porch swing and the song of the barn swallows and the chirrup of the bats swooping through twilight, the harvest moon hanging low in the sky.

He should have burned that spectrum. It was evidence. It could get him shot. But he tucked it inside his pillow, and no one would ever know.

For what could they do? Radio for help? Even if the transmission was strong enough to be detected across the distance, Earth was one hundred fifty light-years away—and none of the other populated worlds were much closer. A radio message would take a century and a half to get through. They couldn't wait on rescue that long.

There wasn't much better hope, in short term, of stealing a ship. Lucy had managed to swipe a lander, but the lander couldn't get them home. And security had been tightened up after Lucy's escapade. Even before her little adventure, nothing with a C^2 capability had been allowed to dock with the station. Besides, there was still the question of navigation. Sam knew just how rough his fix on Sol was. They'd be lucky to get within ten light-years of the place, using the numbers Sam could get using the Guard hardware.

Maybe, someday, at just the right moment, knowledge of where home was would do them good, but until then, what point in raising false hopes? Why let frustration wreck morale? Why risk endangering the knowledge itself if someone let slip the wrong chance remark? Why tempt someone besides Lucy into a fool stunt?

So Schiller slept with a portrait of Sol in his pillow, and dreamt of the cornfields.

But his search for home had been the thing that held him together, gave some semblance of meaning to his life. With the hunt successfully concluded, both his time and his mind were far less occupied. He was left with little more to do than watch the radar screens, track the meaningless points of light on the screen—and think.

There seemed to be fewer of those points of light every day. Ariadne, with the job of supporting the Contact Camp, was a bustling and busy enterprise, but the other installations around Outpost were turning into ghost towns—or vanishing altogether, as the stations were towed up out of orbit to some other duty in space. Schiller watched, day by day, as the Guards pulled back from Outpost. A second attack fleet, this time made up of fifty small fast corvettes, was formed and launched. The fleet as such was never seen again. Long weeks later, fewer than ten of the corvettes straggled back into orbit of Outpost.

There were other things to be seen. The shield of anti-ship missiles around Outpost's sun had been completed, and the ships that had been involved with emplacing the missiles left. Then, there was suddenly a lot of radio traffic in the vicinity of the Nova Sol system's barycenter, encrypted in a way that seemed familiar. When Schiller trained his telescopes on the barycenter, he could detect the light of dozens of fusion engines.

So the Guards were building another anti-ship missile web around the barycenter. Not good news. It would further seal the Nova Sol system off from the outside universe, make it that much harder for the League to attack.

That was why Schiller kept his eye on the barycenter, tried to watch it through the scopes and the radio detectors.

And that was why he spotted the strange, far-off flickering lights in the 'center when they came.

Chapter Twenty-One

Eight Hundred Kilometers north of Guardian Contact Camp
The Planet Outpost

The Road had been long, and hard. Lucy's wagon rolled on, endlessly, it seemed. The Z'ensam kept to the Road, and the trade routes, forever going on. Lucy peered through the wagon's single small window and watched the landscape roll past. She estimated that the column was doing about forty kilometers an hour, a pretty good speed, all things considered. Some of the Z'ensam would get out of their carriers and gallop alongside the column for a while, easily keeping pace, just stretching their legs before climbing back aboard. Lucy knew damn well that was far beyond the abilities of a halfwalking monster from beyond the stars such as herself.

She had to settle for being cooped up in her own specially built truck, or mobile home, or lorry, or wagon, whatever you wanted to call it. Wagon was close enough. It was airlocked and the Z'ensam had not only managed to keep the carbon dioxide down to a level she could stand, they had gotten the worst of the stench of Outpost out of the air. They provided food for her that hadn't poisoned or starved her yet, and she had a chance at a sponge bath every day or so. She was being as well cared for as she could expect to be, under the circumstances. And her wagon rolled along with the rest of them. It seemed to be powered by some sort of liquid fuel that powered a smoothly purring engine beneath the floorboards. At least some sort of fluid was poured into a hole in the wagon every night. For all Lucy knew, that could be the feed for animals running on treadmills. She was never quite sure if machines were machines or some bizarre biological *thing* bred and grown for a tool. Her wagon didn't seem to have a driver. She assumed that some specially bred species of driving-beast sat in some tiny cab at the front of the thing, controlling it—but she couldn't be sure. They didn't tell her a lot. Aside from C'astille, the Z'ensam kept their distance.

Much of the transport was animal-powered, pulled by six-legged beasts, larger than elephants, that had speed and endurance far surpassing any draft horse on Earth. The Z'ensam were awesomely skilled in bio-engineering, and took their miracles for granted as easily as humans accepted light bulbs, or refrigeration, or star travel. The road itself was a living thing, or at least the product of a living thing. C'astille had tried to explain, and had quickly run into language trouble. The best analog Lucy had come up with was to think of the Road as a variety of dry-land coral trained or bred or forced to grow in long, precise strips a half-dozen meters wide and hundreds of kilometers long.

Apparently, the Z'ensam road engineers did little more than sow road-seed like a farmer planting a crop. The roadplant would grow, take root, dig down into the soil to form its own roadbed, and then produce a hard, porous carapace that formed the surface of the road and provided excellent traction. The Z'ensam were able to control the road-plant's growth exactly; Lucy paced out the width of the roads again and again as it crossed forests and fields, mountains and plains, and never did its measure vary by more than half the length of her foot.

The column seemed to be stopping again. There came booming and thumping and roars. Lucy sighed and slumped back against the wall of the wagon. The Hungry Ones were at it again. Sometimes Lucy had thought the Outposters, the Z'ensam as they called themselves, *couldn't* wipe them out, other times she thought they simply chose not to.

The hungries had certainly lived up to their name in the long days before C'astille had found her lander and taken her to safety with her Group, which C'astille called the Refiners. What they refined—sugar, ideas, oil, behavior in polite society, Lucy wasn't quite clear, though most of the Groups did tend to be bound by philosophical grounds. In any event several huge beasts had tried to *eat* the lander—and one had nearly succeeded. The Hungry Ones weren't any one species—any wild animal qualified as hungry—very, very hungry, and without the qualms of the Hungry Tiger in Oz. As far as Lucy could see, nature apparently didn't make much of a distinction between carnivore and herbivore on Outpost—anything would pretty much try to eat anything else. It was, however, the bigger species that gave the Z'ensam the worst time of it. On the other hand, Lucy had seen one species of pack-hunting animals, no bigger than mice, that didn't hesitate to attack the Z'ensam.

The sound of her landing must have scared off the animal life for a day or two, but when the great beasts returned they were terrifying. Lucy had at first thought that she had chanced into an area full of particularly voracious carnivores for some reason, but when the Z'ensam came to rescue her, C'astille assured her that, if anything, things were a bit on the quiet side around her lander.

Riding in her specially built wagon, traveling with the Z'ensam, she had seen enough to convince her that was true. Compared to the violence, the liveliness, the voraciousness of life in the temperate zones of Outpost, the lushest tropics of the Amazon were barren deserts. This world was far fuller of life than Earth. And, therefore, far fuller of death.

Now, as best Lucy could see through her window, the caravan was stopped by some pack of three-meter high, six-legged, befanged, warty, moss-colored, slavering horrors. The Z'ensam brought up their guns and weapons and calmly wiped the monsters out. There was a further delay while the massive corpses were shoved off the roadway, and then the caravan moved on.

Lucy had come to realize that the Nihilists must have been constantly patrolling the perimeter of the Guardian Contact Camp, killing or shooing away any and all animal life. Otherwise, the hungries would have wiped out the humans long ago. No doubt the need to cordon off the area around the landing zone had caused the delay between landing and First Contact. The idea that they stayed away because they didn't like the rain had never made much sense. Not for beings who evolved in this climate. At least that was one little mystery cleared up.

There were certainly enough others to take its place. What drove the Z'ensam to venture out on the road, to move from where they were to a town that might have been abandoned a week ago or a hundred years ago, to live there for a time, and then move on? They certainly had a high enough technology to settle down and build real cities and stay in one place. They didn't *have* to be nomads. But when Lucy asked why they didn't settle down, C'astille couldn't understand why anyone would want to do that in the first place. Trade had something to do with the constant travel, but that seemed as much a holdover from pre-technical times than out of any real need. The towns had started as trading posts, but the Z'ensam didn't need trading bazaars anymore. Their machine-powered and animal-powered transports could carry as much and as fast as, say, nineteenth century European rail or road cargo handlers on Earth. Why move the entire population to the goods when it should have been easier to move the goods to the population?

Lucy gradually discovered that there *were* a small number of settled folk, who lived pretty much permanently in a few larger cities. They seemed to be there to operate the manufacturing concerns too large to be made portable, to serve as brokers and to operate the communications centers, to use and operate the research libraries. All the permanently populated towns were such "company" towns or "college" towns. What slight central government there was emanated, more or less by default, from the cities, though no one much bothered with claiming territory or jurisdiction.

The settled Z'ensam had stepped off the Road and stayed in one place for much the same incentives that would tempt humans to accept hardship posts—wealth, power, the desire to escape from old ways, perhaps research into some subject. Some actually grew to like the settled life, but that was rare. Few accepted it for a lifetime.

It would have been easy for Lucy to form a comforting parallel with the settlement of Sumer, the birth of cities, primitive nomads inventing agriculture and settling down. It would make the Z'ensam seem comfortably primitive, and provide a nice, tidy, condescendingly anthropomorphic framework to explain their culture. Simple nomads just beginning the transition to the city-state.

But these simple nomads had radio, electricity and explosives far more powerful than gunpowder. They were skilled in chemistry, knowledgeable of astronomy and masters of bio-engineering. Theirs was a mature, sophisticated civilization.

Except that it wasn't. Lucy couldn't escape the notion that the Z'ensam should have gotten further than they had. They had the tools, the intelligence, the drive to do so much, and there seemed no doubt they had been around for a while. So what was holding them back?

Lucy's wagon started up again with a slight jerk. She glared at its interior, tired of trading one prison for another. The Guards might have locked her up on the *Venera*, on Ariadne, kept her confined to base on Outpost, but at least they had never locked her in a small, utterly blank room on wheels with nothing to read, nothing to do, no one to talk to. After some wheedling, and a lot of drawing and explaining, she had managed to get a table and chair built. Neither quite fit her proportions, but it was a big improvement over squatting in a corner to eat, and made keeping her journal easier too.

If only something worth reporting would happen. C'astille came sometimes, but not often enough to ease her boredom. The rest of the Z'ensam kept their distance. The higher-ups, the Guidance and the First Advice of this crowd didn't entirely trust her, didn't quite believe she had told C'astille the truth. Why believe there was to be a terrible war among humans, and the Nihilists were in an unholy alliance with M'Calder's enemies? There was no proof of that, yet. Until there was, the Refiners would harbor her, but they would keep their distance, and keep her existence a secret from outsiders. Potentially, she was of great value to the Refiners. But that potential had yet to be proved, and no one really liked looking at the weird little two-legged monster.

It seemed strange to be bored to tears while in the midst of a wholly alien culture traveling in an alien land—but Lucy was a prisoner again, able to do little more than stare out the window, and that got old mighty fast.

Her few possessions—a rather worn and dirty-looking pressure suit, a sleeping bag, a toilet kit, a few pair of work overalls that served as changes of clothes, her laser pistols, some emergency rations, a first-aid kit—were neatly stacked up by the rear wall. There hadn't been much else in the lander worth the carrying—and lugging even that lot around while wearing a pressure suit hadn't been a picnic.

She worried about keeping sane. That was what the journal was about. Every day she carefully noted down everything that had happened, forcing her mind to focus on present reality, to keep track of the passage of time. She knew she'd be in real trouble if she ever lost track of how many days and hours it had been. So far it had been just over 3000 hours. About four months, Earthside.

It seemed like a lot longer than that. And she was just about out of pages in her journal.

Worst of all was the open-endedness of the situation. She had to wait it out here until the League arrived. The League would need her, because she could speak to the Z'ensam and supposedly knew their ways.

But what she came to realize was that *she* needed the League. The League *ought* to come, logically. But Lucy could dream up a half-dozen reasons why they never would. In which case she would live here, among the Z'ensam, and die among them. Suppose the League never came? How long could she hang on, stay sane and healthy? A year? A decade? Fifty years? Three more days? She didn't know.

There was one bright spot—the Refiners were planning to move into a small, crossroads village tonight. They expected to arrive at it toward evening, and settle in to live there for perhaps ten or twenty days while they repaired the wagons and waited for another Group that was headed toward the town from the opposite direction. The two Groups had struck a trade deal over the radio, and planned to carry out its provisions in the village.

For Lucy, it meant she would get a break from the endless days cooped up in her rolling cage. And perhaps these new Z'ensam would take more of an interest in her—if she were even allowed to see them.

The kilometers rolled past, and Lucy returned to her window to watch the scenery. A huge bird zipped across her field of view. At least Lucy called them birds, because they flew. She had noted dozens of flying species. Like most of the life on this world, they were six-limbed, but with the middle pair of legs modified into wings. The flyers of Outpost didn't look quite as graceful as Earth's birds, but they were strong and agile on the wing. Air pressure here was about twenty percent higher than Earth sea-level, which must have been a help.

There was one particular breed of flyer that Lucy especially liked. Things about the size of a big house cat, with gaudy, brightly colored wings that reminded her of giant butterflies. They were not the most graceful of flyers, and Lucy named them stumblebugs.

The Z'ensam seemed to keep them as pets, or at least the Z'ensam tolerated the stumblebugs and let them follow the Group from camp to camp.

The stumblebugs' front paws could serve for hands about as well as a squirrel's could, and Lucy enjoyed feeding them bits of food, getting them to swoop down and grab a morsel from her hand, or even land and waddle up to get a treat. They seemed to have the vocal skills of the comical parrots Lucy had kept when she was a kid, and she even managed to teach one or two of them to say a few words in English in exchange for a bite of food.

She named them, and played with them, and, like many other lonely people, found pleasure and solace in the company of her pets. None of the Z'ensam seemed to approve of her spending time with the stumblebugs, but Lucy didn't let that bother her. There was very little she did that they *did* approve of, and she needed some pleasure to keep from going mad.

The line of wagons and lorries turned off the road into a small village. Good. They had arrived on schedule. Lucy was eager to get out and stretch her legs.

She heard a triple thump three times on the outer wall of the wagon. That was C'astille's signal that the hungries had been shooed off and it was safe to come out. Eagerly, Lucy climbed into her pressure suit and cycled through the lock. It was good to be out of her rolling prison, if only for a few hours, and if only in a shabby pressure suit.

It was a lovely evening, clear and still. As she hopped down from the airlock, Lucy was almost glad to be behind the glass of her suit's helmet—it kept out the overwhelming smell of mold and rotting plant life. Shielded from the stench, she could almost imagine it as a perfect night for a stroll back in Sydney, the air cool and clean, the stars shining brightly down, God up in heaven and everything in its place. A huge shape, hard to see in the twilight, shifted its stance and turned toward her.

"Hello, Lucy."

"Hello, C'astille. English tonight?"

"It is that you need less of the practice than I have need of."

"I don't know about that—but I certainly have more need of your language than you have of mine."

C'astille paused for a moment before answering, no doubt trying to sort out the difficult statements about knowledge and relative needs that Lucy had crammed into one sentence. C'astille could make herself understood in English, but she could not yet manage the compression, the conciseness, with which Lucy spoke.

"I have less need *now*. There will be a time when my

skills in Human talk will be of great value. So let me practice it tonight."

"Of course, my friend. I was only teasing you."

C'astille only grunted at that. Teasing didn't seem to be a part of Z'ensam humor, or even a Z'ensam concept.

Lucille Calder stepped away from her wagon and walked toward the center of the clearing. Around her, the bustle of unpacking and setting the village to rights went on. Light began to glow in the low one-storey structures, and there were snatches of conversation—and of song.

A pack of Z'ensam children rushed past, chasing each other around the clearing in a game of tag that any human child would have recognized at once. The kids here had long ago gotten used to the halfwalker monster in the Group, and some would even gather round once in a while to hear stories about Earth and Space. For the most part, though, they paid her no more mind than the adults did. Lucy barely realized how little she knew about Z'ensam family life.

All she really knew was that a child's name began with the prefix "O." C'astille was very proud of the fact that she had stopped being O'astille at a very early age.

Lucy looked through the scuffed plastic of her bubble helmet at the sky, the stars, Nova Sol A outshining all the rest, beaming down far more brightly than a full moon, casting crisp shadows. The night sky was lovely and clean, dark, studded with the glory of the stars.

She knew she belonged up there. But she was only gradually coming to accept that she might be trapped where she was for the rest of her life. Strange to think that all humans, less than two centuries ago, were so trapped, and never realized that there were any other worlds, that they were in any sort of trap at all.

And strange to think that this was the first generation of Z'ensam which knew for certain that there was more than one world. But the Z'ensam didn't seem to have invented flying machines. Perhaps they weren't interested in getting off the ground.

"Would you travel there, C'astille? Would you be willing to go through the sky?"

Her friend moved closer to her, bumped her long, rough flank against the pressure suit, and placed a long, four-fingered arm on Lucy's shoulder. C'astille looked up at the darkness. "Willing? That is a weak word. The mightiest traveler of the Z'ensam, the heroes who have crossed every overland route, the seafarers who have spanned the globe—none of them has ever found a Road, a way, as long as your shortest journeys. I *yearn* to go that way, and see everything, everywhere, all the worlds the Humans have found and all the ones they have not."

"You'll get there."

"Yes. As passengers on your ships. But one day we will have our own ships, and grow our own star roads. But come. I must eat, and see to it that our chemists have grown enough of that dull stuff we force you to live on."

The two of them headed toward the mess wagons, the stars in their hearts.

Of all the Refiners, only L'awdasi, the lifemaker, was a stargazer. L'awdasi was in charge of caring for all the workbeasts of the Group, and she had campaigned hard before the Guidance allowed her to care for M'Calder as well. It gave her access to the halfwalker, and gave her the chance to talk with Lucy for hours about the sky. L'awdasi had a fine telescope, a rugged reflector of about 30 centimeters aperture, built by the craftworkers of a distant city. It had been well worth the journey there, and even worth enduring the company of the eccentric citydwellers, to obtain such a fine instrument. Recently, L'awdasi had a new goal to seek for among the stars. This halfwalker had spoken of a "barycenter," a place between the twin suns where matter would accrete. It was even possible that there was a small planet at the barycenter. The idea fired her imagination. A new world! L'awdasi searched each night, joyously engaged in the hopeless task of detecting a hypothetical dim and tiny dot of light.

And so only L'awdasi saw the faint, flickering lights, all but lost in the glare from Nova Sol A, that sparked and shone for a time about the barycenter. A strange phenomenon. Tomorrow she would ask the halfwalker about it. After all, the halfwalker knew about barycenters.

Chapter Twenty-Two

Barycenter
Nova Sol System

The skies flamed and flickered in the view screen, and the Republic of Kennedy Starship *Eagle's* external radiation meters quivered, crawled a bit closer to the high end of the scale. All hell was breaking loose out there, exactly on schedule.

The *Eagle* and the rest of the League fleet stood well off from the barycenter of the Guardian/Outpost star system, and let the Snipe do their work.

All that wooing of the Bandwidthers had paid off. Admiral Thomas had sent them little more than a sketch on the back of a envelope, and they had responded a month later with five thousand custom-designed decoy drones. No other planet could have responded that quickly or effectively. Sir George was just glad the Bandwidthers were on the same side he was on.

The drones had gotten christened Snipe somewhere along the line (someone claimed the name stood for Special Nonexplosive Intrusive Probe Experiment, but obviously they had backed that acronym into the name). By any name, they were out there doing their job right now.

A Snipe was the size and shape of a standard torpedo, the smallest thing ever to get a C^2 generator crammed inside—and the Bandwidthers managed that mainly because the generators didn't have to be very precise, and because there was very little *else* that needed to go inside a Snipe. The big advantage to torpedo-size was that Snipe could be fired by practically any ship in the League fleet. At the moment, practically every ship in the fleet *was* firing them.

The League fleet stood off from the barycenter by about

a twentieth of a light-year, surrounding it in a vast ring, facing the 'center from every point of the compass. The ships themselves stayed well out of range of the defensive missiles, and the Snipe went in. Once fired from a torpedo tube, a Snipe would burst in and out of C^2 space in a millisecond or so, jumping from the fleet's encircling position to the vicinity of the barycenter, making as much radio noise and calling as much attention to itself as possible.

The Guards' automatic anti-ship missiles, designed to sense and home in on ships arriving from C^2, were drawn to the Snipe like lambs to the slaughter. A Guard missile would home on a Snipe and blow itself up—taking out the cheap, mass-produced drone instead of a warship, and there was suddenly one less Guard anti-ship missile to worry about. The real warships, the fleet, would wait until the anti-ship missiles stopped coming, until the skies about the barycenter were no longer lit by the fire of nuclear explosions.

Salvo after salvo of Snipe blipped into the barycenter and died, saturating the Guardian defenses before the main attack even began. The Snipe were a rich man's weapon, a brute force solution to the problem of getting through the Guards' missiles.

But Admiral Sir George Thomas, watching from the battle information center of his flagship, the *Eagle*, had never much cared about subtlety for subtlety's sake. He would settle for the irony of bombing the hell out of the enemy's defenses with their own bombs.

Computer-controlled sensors, quite unconcerned by such things, counted and mapped the explosions, and monitored the "I'm still-here" telemetry from the thousands of Snipe.

After long hours, the number of flashes in the darkness began to decline, and more and more Snipe survived longer and longer. Admiral Thomas, a guest on *Eagle*'s Bridge, turned to *Eagle*'s master, Captain Josiah Robinson. "Well, Captain, either our friends have run out of missiles or they're shutting down the missile system until we run out of drones."

"Either way, Sir George, that leaves a nice hole in their defenses."

"My thoughts exactly. What say we keep sending in the Snipe and start slipping in some fighters among them? It's time that trigger-happy younger generation of ours had a chance."

Captain Robinson nodded to the comm officer, and the order was relayed to the appropriate units. This moment was planned for. Robinson, a short, middle-age, dark-skinned black man with a peppery temper, rubbed his bald spot with the palm of his hand, noticed what he was doing, and stopped. Occasionally he wondered what he had done for a nervous gesture when he still had a full head of hair.

And there was plenty to be nervous about. *Eagle* was half the size of the *Imp*, but she still made a nice juicy target, not just for the worms or whatever other horrors the Guards had cooked up, but for a plain old-fashioned nuke. One of those pretty flashes of light would be enough to knock *Eagle* out of the game for good.

In the event, that didn't happen. The fighters went in, and some of them died. The Guardian ships that deployed the anti-ship missiles were blown. Sir George sent in frigates and corvettes and resupply ships, gradually establishing coherent force around the tiny worldlet that sat right where the astrophysicists said it would, exactly at the barycenter. A few minor Guard warships fought hard, killed and were killed. Slowly, methodically, Sir George peeled back the barycenter's defenses. Finally the League fleet moved in, and found itself astride the centerpoint of the whole star system. No Guard ship could move between Outpost and Capital in normal space without battling its way through the League fleet. The League forces could also intercept and/or jam most radio and laser communications between the two worlds. Most important, they were in under the range of the anti-ship missile systems around Capital and Outpost. As long as the League ships stayed in normal space, they could move against the two worlds without fear of the robot missiles. Of course, the Guards would see them coming, and the anti-ship missiles could probably be fired by remote control to go for ships in normal space. The fight wasn't over.

The planning for this attack had been hideously complex, the timing and communications problems mind-boggling. But it all paid off, with a clean, careful, methodical, smoothly run—and almost dull—operation. Captain Robinson liked it that way. So far, *Eagle* hadn't even had her paint job scratched.

Sir George was equally pleased, at the end of it. He had been in the Task Force Control Center seemingly every minute, always fresh and calm looking. It was time to put Bannister into operation. The specialists went down to the baryworld, and Thomas kept himself carefully appraised of their progress.

Thomas didn't want to hack through the defenses of the two worlds. He wanted the Guards to come to him, force them to fight on his turf.

He intended to keep building up his power at the barycenter, bringing in an endless stream of supplies and ships. Sooner or later, the Guards would have to try and put a stop to it, or face the prospect of a huge and impregnable enemy fleet in their own back yard. He had to wait. But waiting was slow torture to Sir George—and he had spent a lifetime in that torture already.

One evening, Sir George invited Robinson to dinner in the admiral's cabin. It wasn't until the mess steward had cleared the last of the dishes and left them to their port and cigars that Thomas really spoke. "We've managed to outflank ourselves, Captain Robinson," he said cheerfully. "We've hopped smack into the middle of it, and now the enemy has us surrounded without moving at all." He paused for a moment. "Things look good. We outgun them, we have more ships, we have the resources of every world in space to draw on. There are only two things to be afraid of. The unknown is the first. *Something* could happen, God knows what. And the second is the more dangerous, the more likely. If they have a genius for a commander. A genius, a truly great admiral and not a tired-out old man like me, he could wipe us out more certainly than a planet-load of worms and ten thousand nuclear weapons." He was silent for a long moment, and then slapped his hands together and spoke again, in a louder, more cheerful voice. "So—we prepare to defend ourselves once the Guards arrive, plan our next attack, and give praise for the rarity of genius."

Sir George reached for the port decanter again, a bit too eagerly, and filled his glass to the brim for the third time, while Robinson stared hard past him at nothing at all. How the hell did you keep an admiral dried out?

Aboard G.O.S. Ariadne
Orbiting the Planet Outpost

Schiller had waited twelve long hours before he had a chance to talk with Wu in private. Work schedules and sleep shifts had conspired to slow him down. Finally, he caught her as she was heading back on shift. He cornered her in a bend of the corridor and set her heart racing with two words.

"They're here."

Wu looked up at him sharply, her eyes opened wide. There was no point in asking who "they" were. That was in his tone of voice, the gleam in his eye. "Oh, Sam! Thank God." She grabbed his arm and looked up at him. "When? How long ago? What are they doing? How do you know?"

"Quiet, calm. Take it easy. We're talking about how bad the coffee is here. Okay? Good. Now, I've been tracking the construction of the anti-ship missile system at the barycenter—and all of a sudden the center is full of flashes of light, fusion engine lights, the x-ray and gamma detectors start doing a dance—don't ask me who's winning, but there's a pitched battle going on out there. No other possible explanation."

"Who else knows?"

"I haven't told anyone, and I haven't made any records. We've got to let this out slowly, carefully, or else this crowd is going to mutiny and get itself killed to no purpose. You and I need to talk, figure out a plan of action. Once we decide what to do, then, when we spread the word, we're doing more than starting a riot."

"So why pick me to tell?"

"I need help with this from somebody. You've kept your lip zipped over that Lucy-and-the-Lander bit, never mentioned it again. And besides this dull-witted Iowa farmboy, the lady from the inscrutable East seemed the most level-headed type left in the crowd."

Wu gave him the ghost of a smile, started to speak, but then he shushed her. "Meet me for a nice cup of bad coffee at your lunch break. Think on it all between now and then. So will I. Then we make a plan."

Cynthia Wu wasn't capable of much thought for a while. After so long, the League, their rescuers, had arrived. After a hundred years of kidnapping CIs, the League was here to smash the Guards and set them free! She could dare to think of home again—family, friends . . .

She went through the motions of powering up her console on automatic, not really thinking about the dull housekeeping chores that went with running the system. Check the power source, check the comm links, test antennae control, test beacon—

Beacon! It had almost ceased to have meaning for her, the hidden beacon she bade the computer check every morning. At first, the signal had sat tight in one spot for a long time, and Cynthia had assumed that Lucy was in the lander, staying safe. At least Cynthia had been able to mark the lander's location. But then the beacon had started moving, and Cynthia couldn't make sense of what the beacon signal told her. Lucy was supposed to be on the other end of that link, and if she was, she was moving endlessly about the surface of Outpost, why and toward what Cynthia didn't know. It was perfectly possible that Lucy was dead, and the beacon was transmitting its signal from inside the belly of the beast that had eaten her. There was no way to know.

But if the League was here—then Lucy would be damned

important. She knew more about the 'Posters than anyone. Cynthia would have to get a message to her somehow.

Cynthia called up the computer's tracking report of the beacon's movements, and got the second biggest shock of the day.

Lucy, or at least whoever had the beacon, had been moving at high speed straight for the lander for the last twelve hours.

North of Guardian Contact Camp
The Planet Outpost

A thing like a six-legged elephant with saber-toothed fangs blew up in a bloody pink fog, and the three wagons kept rolling down the Road at top speed, not even slowing as they ran over pulped carcass. The gunner on the lead wagon reloaded his cannon and got ready for the next one.

"Your lander is close now, Lucille M'Calder," C'astille said in her own tongue. "We will be with her in a few more hours." C'astille had grown more formal in her speech with Lucy, more careful to say the right thing. They were too close to what might be a last goodbye to risk hurting her friend with the wrong words. The two friends rode atop the second wagon, Lucy in her pressure suit, both of them too keyed up and excited to sit inside the wagon. The lead and rearward wagon were the Refiner versions of battle tanks, capable of killing anything that moved.

They might actually be used as battle tanks, soon. There were frightening reports that the Nihilists had begun their attack on other Groups.

C'astille hesitated for a moment, then spoke. "Still it is possible for me to be with you on this skyroad."

Lucy sighed deeply. "C'astille, it would make my job easier if you could come—they'd be forced to believe me. But you *can't* come along. There's no crash couch to fit you, and when I take off, I'll be doing six gees. You'd be crushed. And no offense, but you're just too damn big and heavy! I must travel as fast, as hard, as I can. I will throw everything I can off the lander, make her as light as possible, to let me go fast and save on fuel. I may not have the fuel for such a trip as it is—and with two along—besides, I have no food for you, no device to make our air breathable to you."

"All this can be solved—"

"*No!* Much as I want you to come, I can't risk failure, or everything has been for nothing. I'm sorry." She patted C'astille's muscular shoulder and stared down the road, straining for a view of the lander she knew perfectly well was far out of sight of the road. What sort of shape would it be in? Had some local hungry managed to take a bite out of it? Had some bug-eyed monster torn the hatch off and turned it into a nest?

If she managed a launch, would her luck go the wrong way? Would the Guards nail her and return her to Outpost in the form of a cloud of radioactive isotopes? She prayed for Gustav. If *he* had survived, she might.

Aboard G.O.S. Ariadne
Orbiting the Planet Outpost

Lieutenant Johnson Gustav was alive, and he knew things. He was ex-Intelligence. It was his job, his professional skill, to know things. Wu was unaware of it, but Gustav also watched Lucy's beacon. Schiller didn't know it, but Gustav watched Schiller, and monitored his use of the astronomical instruments. He knew when Schiller found Earth, and now, when Schiller found the League battle fleet as they cut the Guards' barycenter garrison into pieces, Gustav knew that too.

And he knew that this was the day he had dreaded all along. It was time to pay the piper. It would be so easy to turn back. Push a few buttons, call in a few of the troopers, have Schiller and Wu and the rest of the schemers arrested. Call Nike Station and Lucy's lander would be dust settling into a crater an hour later. A soldier's job. None who lived would reproach him for fighting on his own side.

Easier still to do nothing, to let Lucy take her chances when she boosted and ran through the Guard ships around

Outpost, heading for the barycenter and the League, to let the CIs on Ariadne stage some hopeless and bloody revolt to liberate the station once they knew their friends were here.

But then how many would die? How long could Jacquet and his thugs bleed the people of Capital white before they inevitably lost? How many dead? How many ships, factories, families smashed? What nightmare bioweapons were the Nihilists cooking up, and what horrible vengeance would the League exact for their use? The Guardians could not win. And the longer the Guardians fought, the more likely Capital was to be but a smoking ruin.

He had to act. But he had to act carefully. And privately.

It was toward the end of the morning. Cynthia hadn't had a chance to talk with Schiller yet, when she felt a tap on her shoulder.

She had almost gotten used to the sudden, bottomless fear at the pit of her stomach that came with any sudden, unwanted attention from the Guards. It had happened so many times before. When it did, you acted calmly, didn't turn around immediately, and innocently hit a few keys, so that whatever the hell you had been working on vanished off the screen. Then you turned around calmly and asked the sentry what was up. Usually it was nothing at all, the sentry wanted to borrow a book or a cigarette or wanted you to cover for him while he ducked down to the head. So this time, she casually cleared her screen, turned around—

—And there was Gustav himself. "Ensign Wu. Good day. I was just passing, and it occurred to me there were one or two questions about the comm schedule I wanted to talk with you about. Why don't you step down to my office with me?"

"Yes, of course, sir." Already her coverall was damp with sweat. She followed him through the corridors and into his office. He was very casual, calm; all was routine. It scared hell out of Wu.

He went behind his desk and took his chair. "Sit down, Ensign. I need to tell you a few things. First, in case he hasn't told you, Schiller found Earth some time ago. *Did* he tell you? Or anyone, to your knowledge?"

Wu was too shocked to think up a lie. "No . . . he—he didn't."

"Good. I suspected he had good sense. That confirms it. Let me tell some other things. I know you assisted in Lucille Calder's escape some time ago. But you should know that *I* helped too—in fact she and I plotted that escape together. At a guess, Schiller has told you that the League has taken the barycenter. Don't bother to answer, your face just did. Luc—Lieutenant Calder seems to have already discovered that fact for herself. She would have no other reason for heading for the lander. This saves us the trouble of trying to contact her. She too has a good deal of sense, so she won't try to make a run for it until both Ariadne and Nike are below her local horizon. The two stations are in fixed orbits, her lander's computers will know where they are. It's Guardian ships that are the danger. But you know how to check the orbits and figure out which will be where when. Can you hit the lander with a tight radio beam on a frequency she'd be likely to listen on?"

Cynthia caught her breath and said, "Yes."

"Good. Note that I have given you no instructions as to what to do. You should know that you must assume normal surveillance of your activities, whatever they should be. If you are caught, you might be able to avoid implicating me under mild interrogation. If you are caught, I cannot try to defend you, or else I will be caught and shot as well. And if you fail, I can still try to help. But you are in a better position for covert acts. So be careful. I will say one more thing. Ariadne will be of much greater value in saving lives if it holds together. A revolt here, and more people—League and Guardian—die. You might think of ways to keep the lid on. Now take a moment to calm yourself, then go."

✧ ✧ ✧

Cynthia wasn't much use until the lunch break. When she carried her tray over and sat by Schiller in the mess hall, he immediately noticed something was wrong.

"Cynthia, have you got some kind of flu? This is one hell of a bad moment to get sick."

"No, no. Sam. Is there a word for—I don't quite know how to put it—for when the officers or the *captain* mutinies?"

"Yeah, it's called barratry. Any court of inquiry treats it as about twice as slimy and rotten as mutiny or treason. You won't even find it listed in the *Bluejacket's Manual*. The Navy leaves it out of the glossary with the other dirty words. Why?"

"It came up in a crossword puzzle."

"Oh. But let's get to the serious stuff then. What do we do about welcoming the new neighbors?"

"I think," she said, "that it might be wisest if we didn't do anything at all."

Chapter Twenty-Three

The Planet Outpost

The dear old lander was still there, God bless her, squatting in the middle of the field she had come down in. Tarnished and entangled in undergrowth, half-hidden by vines and her once-gleaming hull begrimed and dull, but there—and whole. The Z'ensam from the lead and follower wagons started firing blank rounds to scare any squatters away from the lander. There was a brief stampede out from under the belly of the small ship, and the Z'ensam from the lead wagon got down and cautiously poked around the strange machine from the skies. Finally, they signaled all clear and Lucy climbed down from her own wagon.

"We'll need long knives or something to hack all this plant life back," Lucy said.

"That job is ours," C'astille replied. "You must be in that thing and see if it is ready to go."

Lucy walked up to the side of the stubby little ship, and patted its hull affectionately. A ship, a ticket out, a way back to the clean skies and her proper life. "Aboard," she said to C'astille in English. "You don't say 'in,' you say 'aboard.' And never 'it'—this is a 'she.' "

"Someday I'll actually understand your pronouns," C'astille said. "That will be a great day."

Lucy grinned at her. "*This* is a great day. I'm getting back into space." The ladder to the personnel hatch was still extruded from the hull, and Lucy scrambled up it. *There* was a reason right there that C'astille couldn't come along. Maybe the descendants of apes and monkeys could climb that ladder, but the descendants of what must have been like six-legged horses certainly couldn't.

Even ten meters off the ground, thick creepers had grown

up to ensnare the little ship, and one of them had grown straight over the personnel hatch. Lucy wrapped her arm around the top rung of the ladder and pulled her knife out of its belt sheath.

It was a copy of the classic Bowie knife, forged of a steel that would never lose its edge. She was careful with its sharp point around her nearly-decrepit pressure suit. She wouldn't need that suit much longer, but that would be no comfort if she ripped it and died of carbon dioxide poisoning three meters from breathable air.

The upper rung of the ladder was just to the left of the hatch itself, and the manual controls for the airlock were placed so they were right in front of Lucy's face as she stood at the top of the ladder. But vines blocked the hatch itself. Leaving her left foot on the ladder and hanging on to the top rung with her left hand, Lucy calmly swung over and hooked her right foot through a loop of vine that hung free of the ship, unaware of the fact that she was scaring the hell out of the distinctly non-arboreal Z'ensam below. Lucy got her leg around the vine and gave it a good yank. Enough of it came free so that she could get her knife underneath and saw through it. She resheathed the knife and peeled back the lower end of the vine from the lower lip of the hatch, then pulled the upper half off the hatch itself with one good tug.

Lucy got herself back onto the ladder, pulled the cover plate off the manual crank, unfolded the handle, and started cranking. Probably there was plenty of power aboard, but if some fluke had drained the batteries, she didn't want to find out she had wasted three ergs too many and so had three ergs less than she needed to start the generators.

Hanging onto the ladder, cranking the awkwardly placed handle, starting to work up more of a sweat than the worn-out suit could handle; peering at the world through the scuffed and dirty glass of her bubble helmet, breathing air that smelled of a mixture of unwashed Lucy and the moldy-bog aroma of Outpost, First Lieutenant Lucille Calder was happier than she had been since the *Venera* was peacefully cruising through space, two or three lifetimes ago. She was going home. The League was out there, past an obstacle or two.

And better still, there was an honest-to-God shower aboard the lander. And a fresh pair of coveralls, and *coffee*. Even the Guardian's emergency field rations would taste better than the nutritious glup the Refiners gave her. You'd think an advanced culture might have invented cooking instead of eating raw what they foraged and hunted. But there was no accounting for taste.

The hatch, hinged at its base, slowly swung down from the vertical to form a platform she could step onto easily from the ladder. She hopped across, stepped into the airlock, and used the inner manual to crank the outer door shut.

From the base of the lander, the watching Z'ensam realized the acrobatics were over and got back to clearing the vines and undergrowth away from the lander.

C'astille, standing on guard against any Hungry Ones that might come for a visit, snorted, lashed her tail, and gripped her long-gun harder. She had forgotten the way humans climbed and jumped and scrambled to reach a height. They thought nothing of it all, seemed to have no fear of falling. It was a little thing, but it reminded her that Lucy M'Calder wasn't just a mutated Z'ensam with the back half missing. She was alien—a mystery so complete that she could never be solved.

And C'astille called her *friend*, and aided her cause against her own kind.

Something big growled at the edge of the clearing. C'astille fired a few rounds at it on general principle, and as the roaring boom of her gun faded she heard a heavy body slump over and collapse into the brush.

There was electric power. Plenty of it. The cryo-stable tanks had lived up to their name and held the liquid oxygen and hydrogen at temperature all this time. The air, which was probably a little musty in reality, was totally, blissfully odorless to Lucy's Outpost-acclimated nose. Lights came on at the flick of a switch, and Lucy had forgotten how *friendly* a warm yellow light could be, after so many days of Outpost's gloomy clouds and rare days of too-white sun.

So the lander had held together. The next jobs she could do better if she was clean. The shower. Clean clothes. Food.

It wasn't until she had sat down in a real chair—well, a crash couch—but it was designed by and for a human and had a cup of properly hot, fresh coffee that she remembered her escort. It took her a minute to find the external mikes and speakers on the unfamiliar comm control panel. She switched on the mike and spoke in English. "Can you hear me?"

"Very well, far too well," C'astille's voice replied a bit testily. "We all just bolted and ran half across the field out of reflex."

"Sorry. Let me turn it down. Is that quiet enough?"

"Much better. Now perhaps we won't attract every Hungry for a day's gallop around. What have you been doing? Night is coming on."

"Sorry, C'astille. I was just cleaning myself and getting some human food and drink. Things I even forgot I missed. I lost track of the time. But if it's night, perhaps I'd better just sit tight here for the night. It would take a while to get into a suit and get out to the wagons."

"Very well, though you could have mentioned it sooner. We were getting nervous, and I had no way of contacting you. I thought the air might have gone bad in there and killed you."

"Thank you for being concerned, C'astille, and I apologize for worrying you."

"No more will be said. Is your lander well?"

"She seems to be in very good shape, though it will take some hours more of work to get her powered up and operational. Tomorrow will be time enough. Rest well, and I'll see you in the morning. I'll leave the hearing and speaking devices on so you can call me."

Lucy watched through the display screens as C'astille,

no doubt a bit miffed by being made to wait so long for no good reason, summed up the English exchange to her companions, and the Z'ensam retreated to the protection of the wagons.

If the truth be known, it wasn't the difficulty and delay of suiting up that kept Lucy inside the lander, but the comfort of being in human air, human light, with human food in her gut. The thought of sleeping in a proper bed, even a collapsible mattress, was an overwhelming temptation.

She left the comm station on standby, and besides the external pickups, she set the radio on scanner/receive without even thinking, unfamiliar board or not. That was standard operating procedure, one of a thousand things they bashed into a pilot's skull. It was one of the thousand things that kept pilots alive.

Left to itself, the cabin air was lovely in its scentlessness. With the air-conditioning on, bringing the temperature down from the usual high thirties of Outpost to a sinfully cool eighteen degrees centigrade, it was paradise. Lucy dragged the fold-up mattress out into the center of the cabin deck and flopped it down. Sheets, top and bottom! A pillow! She felt that she truly appreciated civilization for the first time.

She dropped off to sleep the moment she had cuddled herself into a comfy position, the now-familiar growls and screams of an Outpost night coming through the external mikes to serve for a lullaby.

Half an hour after Lucy dozed off, the emergency alarm blared into life, and she was in front of the comm board before she was fully awake. Where was the bloody alarm cut-off? There. The yowling of the siren cut off in mid scream.

What the bloody hell was going on—a *text* message on channel 30? She shunted the message over to the computer screen.

URGENT YOU DEPART FOR BARYCENTER DURING TIME PERIOD STARTING IN ONE HOUR TWO MINUTES AND ENDING IN ONE HOUR

NINETEEN MINUTES. MANY SHIPS IN ORBIT AND THIS WILL BE ONLY CLEAR WINDOW FOR SOME DAYS DEPENDING ON SHIP MOVEMENTS. GOOD LUCK FRIEND WU MAINTAIN RADIO SILENCE DO NOT REPLY WE'LL KNOW IF YOU GO. MESSAGE REPEATS: URGENT YOU—

Jesus! Lucy cleared the screen and rubbed her eyes. How the hell did Cynthia—of course, the beacon. Thank God for that.

A loud thumping noise came from the external pickups. Lucy kicked in the cameras. It was C'astille, pounding on the hull. Damn! That reminded Lucy that she had wanted to record some images of the Z'ensam, get some sort of proof they existed. She had planned to do it in the morning, but it was too late now. She twisted a few knobs and set the external cameras to record. "Yes, C'astille. What is it?"

"We heard a loud scream come from the talking device that comes from your ship. Are you all right?"

"Yes, thank you. It was an emergency message, from, from one of my Group who guessed I would be here. She tells me I must leave this place very soon, or not at all, because later the enemy will be where it can find me as I launch."

"You must leave now?"

"Yes." Lucy hesitated and shifted to Z'ensam. "You will sense me again. I will be here again, and we shall journey more. But there is a thing you must do. The device I called a beacon, the radio-direction finder. It is in the wagon. Keep it with you. It will show me the Road that leads to you, no matter where you are."

"It will be with me. Good luck." The last C'astille spoke in English. There was no way to say it in her own speech.

"Thank you. Now, bright lights will come on for a few minutes. My camera will get pictures of you for my Group to see, so they will have knowledge that you truly exist. My people still have never sensed you. The lights will stop before too many large night animals are attracted."

"Very well. There is no time for your descent from the machine for a true goodbye?"

"No." There wasn't much else she could say. "I wish there were time." she said, switching back to English. "But let me get your picture, and then you must all get quite far away, for the lander is dangerous to those outside."

"I have seen many landers fly. We will get well out of the way. When will you launch?"

"In about an hour. I'm sorry, I can't think well enough to convert that to your measures."

"I know what an hour is. We will be out of the way in time."

The floodlight blossomed on, blanketing the area around the lander in a harsh white light. C'astille shielded her eyes with her hand and waited for her eyes to adjust. She told herself to act intelligent, to convince this mysterious halfwalker Group of Lucy's that she wasn't just an animal. She wondered what, exactly, would constitute intelligent behavior.

Unsure of what to do, she did what billions in the same situation had done before. She waved at the camera.

Lucy would have smiled at that if she had been watching the monitors, but she was already over her head in calculations. How the hell to get off the planet without being converted into radioactive gases? If the Guards were in line of sight of her, they would spot the plume of her lander's fusion engines instantly. It would be impossible to miss. Having spotted her, they would know who it had to be, and where she had to be going. They would blow her out of the sky, and probably bomb her launch point just to be on the safe side.

She had to stay out of line of sight while firing her engine. Okay, fine. That meant a short boost at high thrust so she could get up to escape velocity and shut down the engine *fast*. She had to dive toward the barycenter, and that would help. She knew from running the radar on Ariadne that there was very little surveillance of that direction—and what there was was run from Ariadne—and if the Guards didn't breathe down their necks too hard, there were fair odds that the CIs could manage to look the other way. Cynthia Wu would make sure of that.

Then, a long run powered-down, to get far, far away before she relit her fusion engines for an extended burn that would get her to the barycenter, seven plus billion kilometers away. The further from Outpost she was when she lit up, the better a head start she would have on any pursuit. And if they couldn't backtrack her launchpoint, they couldn't identify her—and that meant that, with their hands full with an invading fleet, they wouldn't be likely to bother with her.

But she had to get this tub ticking along, bring her to life carefully after her months-long slumber. God only knew what systems had gummed themselves up without maintenance. Lucy had hoped to take at least a day or two to check things out, but it looked like it was time to have faith in the backups. Engine test cycle go. Fuel system at go. Fuel tanks at 90 percent, and she was going to need every drop of it. Food, water—there should be enough aboard for this trip, and if not she could stay alive on not much for a few days. No time to take an inventory now. Guidance. The computers seemed sane, and seemed to know where the sky was. She would have to trust it. No benchmark to test it against, and with 45 minutes until her launch window opened, no time to calibrate against the sextant.

Damn! No time to toss the deadweight mass out of the lander. Well, she'd have to deadhead it to escape velocity, then toss it through the airlock when she was running doggo, all engines powered down.

What about the hull? Did it still have integrity, or had some damned Outpost plant secreted some weird acid that had weakened it so it'd split a seam and start losing air under the stress of acceleration and vacuum? No time and no way to check. But she could take precautions. The second pressure suit. Lucy dug it out of the storage locker, and didn't realize she was buck naked until she started to put the suit on over bare skin. It had felt good to sleep in the nude, but time to get back into a damned monkey suit again. At least it was a clean one.

There was a rather awkward series of mechanisms on the suit that would take care of wastes, a sipping straw that would stave off death by dehydration, and even a little airlock gizmo that would let her pass food in toward the general direction of her mouth. If the hull leaked, she could stay alive in the suit long enough to get to the barycenter. But it wouldn't be fun.

She was on the clock and the minutes were dying. Back to the pilot's station. Fusion chamber pressure okay. Atmosphere engines cranked up and ready. She was tempted to skip them and boost on fusion, but C'astille and company might be too close. If the plume of fusion rocket exhaust brushed past them as she was on the way up, they'd never feel it before they died. Even if they were out of range, the actinic light of fusion could blind them.

No, she'd have to go up on the old liquid oxygen/liquid hydrogen engines. Half a tick. Why not ride the lox/l.h. as far as she could? It'd be the most efficient way to dump the mass of the liquid oxygen, and burning conventional propellant produced a much less noticeable flame—oh, they could spot it if they knew to look—but more than likely they wouldn't be rigged to spot such an inefficient fuel combination.

Lucy knew that she might begrudge every gram of hydrogen wasted in the lox/l.h. burn later on, but she knew damn well there might not be a later on if she didn't take the gamble.

She wasn't the sort to look back once she made a decision. She'd use the lox/l.h. system. Eighteen minutes until the window—and when it opened, she'd jump through it, with any sort of luck.

Luck. And there she was on a nameless lander. It wouldn't do. She did nothing but *think* of the name. That was enough to ward off bad luck. *Halfwalker*. C'astille was possibly the only person of any species who would appreciate the humor in that. Lucy resolved to stay alive long enough to tell her about it.

Working quickly and carefully, Lucy brought *Halfwalker* to life. The minutes vanished, all too fast. Too many systems were taken on faith, too much she just had to cross her fingers on.

Three minutes. She had a course, of sorts, laid in.

Two minutes, one, none. Show time. Power to take-off engines—

And a red light came on. Lucy's fingers rattled over the keyboard, demanding details on the malfunction, and her heart hammered in her chest. She had only seventeen minutes to solve it, fix it, or else—oh bloody hell, it was only the damn manual crank on the outer airlock. She had forgotten to fold the thing and close the cover on it. More than likely it would be sheared off by air resistance as she headed out of the atmosphere.

So be it. Lucy hit one last button, and *Halfwalker* grabbed for sky.

C'astille watched with a full heart as the pillar of flame clawed its way toward the stars, and the roar of the engines made the very ground shake. She had tried to describe this thing, *launch* the humans called it, to her companions. But words failed. To ride that pillar of flame, to race through a skyful of enemies to some sparkles of light in the night sky that you hoped was a mighty fleet—C'astille marveled at her friend's courage and wondered if she herself had the nerve, the spirit, to do such a thing, to ride flame toward the risk of death.

But the stars. The stars lay at the end of that Road of fire.

C'astille watched the lander climb out of sight, leaving a ropy vapor trail behind that quickly dispersed into the wind. And she realized that she might be the first of all her kind to dream of flying without revulsion, for none of her kind had ever flown and kept a whole name.

Chapter Twenty-Four

Outpost, Nihilist Encampment

D'etallis was a veteran of endless political infighting; she knew the value of good intelligence. From a half-dozen sources—Z'ensam who had befriended Guardians, from taps and listen-ins on radio traffic that the halfwalkers thought the Z'ensam didn't know about, through any number of little tricks—D'etallis knew the League had arrived at the barycenter.

She didn't know exactly what the League was, besides the fact that they were human and the enemies of the Guards. That was all she really needed to know. And the timing was just about perfect for her purposes.

D'etallis had made grand progress in her projects, but she discovered that her motives, her plans, her desires changed even as she went from victory to victory.

She had seen Eltipa divide. That was the turning point. Even after all the scheming, all the lies, all the manipulations, D'etallis had discovered that she still loved her old Guidance at that last, horrible moment. Too late to deny her the indignity of madness, idiocy, the loss of her name, D'etallis had killed her Guidance, and sworn that this would be the last generation that would suffer Division. She would kill every Z'ensam who showed the slightest symptoms.

Her Guardian friends had helped bring that dream closer. The Nihilists were on the march, attacking and slaughtering whoever got in their way. With their Guardian weapons and tactics, D'etallis's followers, still half-herd-mob and half army, would soon conquer or absorb every Group for an eight-day gallop in every direction. The Refiners still stayed ahead of her, stayed out of it, and a few others, but the day was not far off when she would have taken the entire heart of the continent.

And, under her direction, there would be no Divisions. That was the main thing, or at least it should have been. D'etallis had found herself up against a paradox. An end to Division was merely a first step. The only absolutely certain way to ensure an end to Division was to ensure the end of the race. Which meant having a large enough base of power to support an army that could do the actual killing. Which, clearly enough, meant having a lot of live Z'ensam around. If there *weren't* enough Nihilist Z'ensam around, Nihilism would collapse. If it had gotten big enough first, it might manage to take some or all of the rest of Z'ensam civilization with it. But inevitably, some small number would have to survive, and Divide, and the species would continue, and repopulate the world.

Worse, there were some sub-Groups of Nihilists not at all interested in the great work of genocide. They had found the power in a rifle barrel, were living well, and weren't too keen to wipe out the Z'ensam that served them at gunpoint. They had lost the purity of their ideals to luxury. D'etallis was forced by her successes to realize that she was doomed to failure, if she went on the way she was.

But all good politicians knew how to twist failure into victory, how to exploit advantages and chance opportunities while sidestepping problems.

D'etallis had worked it all out very clearly. First was the principle that *all* intelligent life was an abomination. There was equal merit in killing halfwalkers as in killing Z'ensam. More importantly, it should be easier to talk Z'ensam into killing ugly aliens—especially when the aliens had such interesting toys to serve as booty. The Guardians obviously had weapons far more powerful than what they gave to the Nihilists. Get her hands on those, and the job of wiping out the Z'ensam could be done. *Starsight* was another piece of the puzzle. The Guardians had made the formal presentation of the spacecraft a few days ago. D'etallis herself had christened the craft. The name was calculated to please and reassure the humans, and apparently it had.

Best of all was the news from the Nihilists' biological

labs. They had carefully collected bits of human skin scraped from inside pressure suits; saliva from used drinking containers, even blood drawn from Captain Romero himself. The good captain had been strolling the grounds of the camp without a pressure suit, wearing a neck-sealed bubble helmet instead. C'ischin had "accidentally" bumped into him and driven a tiny collection syringe into him and pulled it out before the fool halfwalker even had time to feel pain. It was perilously close to medicine, of course, but crimes had been committed in the service of a greater good before this. The biologists had burrowed in the human garbage dumps and latrines for samples. Discarded toenail clippings, mucus on a tissue, bacteria from human feces—all of it went into the labs for examination.

And now the biologists knew enough to build their plagues.

The Guards would be distracted by their war with the League. Presumably, they would try to keep it secret from the Nihilists. D'etallis knew how to take advantage of that, too.

The Guards had taught her a lot about strategy. It was time to strike.

Chapter Twenty-Five

Barycenter
Nova Sol System

The whole fleet was on alert, thanks to one tiny ship. *Eagle's* tracking had spotted her two days ago, coming toward the 'center from Outpost. It was the only response the Guards had made so far to the League's invasion.

It was easy to imagine a superweapon aboard, a bomb that could vaporize the entire barycenter, or a bioweapon that would make the foam-worms seem benign by comparison.

But there were some strange things about that ship. She had started her boost from millions of kilometers this side of Outpost. And if she kept to the course and thrust she was using, about forty hours from now she would come to a halt, a hundred thousand kilometers away from the 'center. It was tempting to think that she wanted to stand off so as to not get too close and appear threatening. Or was she just trying to stay out of range of whatever she was going to lob at the fleet? Captain Robinson wanted to blast her out of space, but Admiral Thomas had some faint hope that she was a peace ship, negotiators aboard. If there was the slightest chance to limit the killing, he would take it. Besides, the League needed time to build up its supply and expand its beachhead in the barycenter. They had pretty much shot their bolt, coming in with all guns blazing.

Robinson found himself wishing more than once for the use of the matter-transmitter they had used to get the troops to New Finland. It would have come in handy, but apparently the damn thing was hideously expensive to run. More seriously, no one knew exactly why the one existing transmitter had spontaneously melted down a month after it was used to transmit the troops to New Finland.

So supply ships shuttled in and out of the barycenter, bearing fuel and ammunition and food. The League fleet built up its strength, and waited. And with every day of waiting, Robinson noticed, Sir George was just a trifle later getting out of bed, and his cheeks were just a trifle rosier when he turned in.

Under the League's careful watch, the Guards likewise made no dramatic moves, but carefully reordered their forces. There were two large flotillas, each about a third the size of the League fleet, one orbiting Capital and the other about Outpost. Every day a ship or two launched away from Outpost and disappeared into C^2, only to reappear some time later on approach to Capital. Slowly, carefully, the Guards were shifting their strength to a direct defense of the home world. Presumably, in some computer simulator on Capital, they were planning the best way to dislodge the League. But an attack by hundreds of ships was not something to organize in an hour or two. It took time.

It could be weeks before either side was prepared for a major fleet movement.

In the meantime, there was that one tiny mystery ship, growing closer all the time. Robinson didn't like mysteries, especially this one. The *Eagle* stood ready to vaporize the visitor at a moment's notice. The comm crews tried to reach her over a hundred different frequencies, in a dozen languages. Since the Guards spoke English, it was hard to see the point of broadcasting to the visitor in Russian, but it kept the comm crews busy and happy, and that counted for something.

That was its only benefit; the visitor did not transmit a syllable in response.

Robinson deployed a half-dozen unmanned probes into the vicinity of space toward which the visitor seemed to be headed. One of these was the first to get a good visual on her when her engines finally cut off and the ship itself was no longer hidden in their glare. Robinson and Thomas were both on the bridge for the arrival, watching everything comm could pipe up to them. It was a lander, a rather weathered one, with Guard markings all right. No real shocker there, Robinson thought. Who else's ship would it be?

It was the first transmission from the lander that surprised him. It was a general broadcast in a woman's voice. "I have no directional radio gear. This is a wide broadcast transmission. Please jam this frequency for reception at Outpost and Capital. Do not respond until this is done."

Robinson hesitated a moment, then shrugged. He could play that sort of game. What harm could come from jamming the enemy's radio? He punched the intercom key and talked to the comm chief. "Comply with that, and give us a good overlap. Jam well above and below that frequency. Reply to our new friend when you've done it. And keep us patched in up here."

There was a few moments' pause as the comm section set up directionalized antennae and aimed them at the two planets. There was an increase in the background hiss as some of the signal leaked over, and then *Eagle*'s radio operator spoke again.

"*Eagle* to unidentified ship. Jamming commenced. Please identify yourself now."

There was another short pause. "This is Lieutenant Lucille Calder, Royal Australian Navy, on detached duty with the League of Planets Survey Service. I was last known by you to be aboard the *Venera*, and I suppose I'm listed as missing and presumed dead. I have a lot to tell you. I don't want the Guards to know I'm still alive. That's why the jamming. But I don't think I should broadcast my report, even so. Request permission to come aboard."

That started a hubbub. The *Venera*! She was more than a lost ship to spacers, she was a quick-born legend, a *Mary Celeste* or a Flying Dutchman, a mysterious story that had never had a proper end. The usual murmur of voices around the bridge rose to a dull roar until Robinson called out. "Put a lid on it! Admiral, your opinion?"

"Well, if it's some kind of trick, it's a damn clever one, and I can't quite see the point of it. If this Calder truly was with the Survey, Captain Larson and my niece can both identify her. I say let her aboard—with extreme precautions."

"I agree."

The decontamination boat launched from *Eagle* forty-five minutes later, Mac and Joslyn aboard. Mac could still not believe it. Calder, alive! Pete had been right all along, the *Venera* had been hijacked. Oh, it had all but been taken for granted after a while as a great theory, but here was *proof*. Joslyn and he had never known Calder all that well—she had been a smile in the mess hall, not a close friend. But if *she* lived. . . .

The decon boat was little more than a control panel, vacuum, engines, and fuel, cobbled together out of spare parts months ago in case the task force had to rescue anyone from a worm-ridden ship. Mac and Joslyn rode in crash couches welded to the midsection of the I-beam that made up the fuselage. At one end of the thirty-meter long beam were the engines, and at the other was a specially built personnel decon station. Midway between the bow and the pilot's station was a lethal-looking weapons pod, plus a disinfectant sprayer and other things to kill worms. Mac and Joslyn wore armored pressure suits. No exposed part of the ship or their suits was edible to the worms, so far as anyone knew. They had learned how to kill worms, and hoped they knew how to kill whatever else the Guards had dreamed up.

But how the hell did Calder get here?

Joslyn moved the decon boat at a stately one gee toward Calder's lander, a careful, deliberate pace. It was easy to remember that any weapon not trained on Calder's ship was now trained on their decon boat. It was just over a four hour run, accelerating for two hours, then turning the decon boat bow-to-stern and decelerating for another two hours.

"Mac, what can this mean?" Joslyn asked. "How the hell did she manage to steal a Guard lander? What's been going on out here?"

"Your imagination is as good as mine. Make up your own answers."

"I suppose. But the *Venera* alive! It makes a chill run down my spine."

"You're not alone. Just think of how Pete must feel. He was the only one who ever really thought that they weren't just a shipwreck."

"I'll bet he's glad he came along with the fleet."

"Watch your radar. We're coming up on her."

"Who's the pilot in this marriage?"

"Okay, so watch where we're goin—"

The engines stopped suddenly, and the decon ship was dead in space to Calder, not ten kilometers away from her. Calder had switched on the lander's navigation lights, and they could see them blinking across the darkness of the brilliant starfield.

Mac grinned and reached across to squeeze Joslyn's armored shoulder. "Very sweet, pilot. Very sweet."

"Shut up and open the secure channel, Cap'n."

"Aye, aye, ma'am." Mac told the computer to train a laser link back on the *Eagle*. "*Eagle*, this is Captain Larson speaking over a secure line. We are in position."

Mac switched on the radio, and took a deep breath as he prepared to talk with a woman who had been a ghost to him. "Lucille, this is Mac Larson. Do you know me?"

The answer came back instantly, and there was delight and pleasure in the voice. "Mac! Dear lord, what are you doing here?"

"I could ask you the same question. But, look, Lucille, the big shots want proof that you're you. . . ."

"As well they should."

Joslyn plugged her suit into the radio. "Lucille! Who am I and who married me to Mac?"

"Joslyn! Hello! That dreadful Reverend Farnsworth Buxley. He put half the congregation to sleep."

Joslyn turned and grinned at Mac. "If you're not you, you do a great imitation. Now, we've got a whole decontamination rigamarole to get through. Did *Eagle* explain to you?"

"Yes they did. I'm in my suit and the ship is in vacuum. I have my personal stuff in a vacuum-sealed carrybag. Switching to suit radio. You might have to boost your gain, it's not a very powerful set."

"Yes, your signal just got a lot weaker."

"Okay, coming out the lock. Jumping free, toward you, and lordy it's a big first step."

"Don't worry, we'll get you."

"Oh, I'm glad to be here. I've been cooped up so long. The stars look so *lovely* and I don't care if I'm babbling—I'm free!"

The telephoto cameras showed a tiny human figure sliding away from the shabby-looking lander.

"Okay, Luce. Now listen. We're going to move in on you. If I come in too fast, let me know."

"Oh, don't treat me like a groundhog, Joslyn! This is more fun than I've had in ages!"

Joslyn played with the low-powered trim jets, and nudged the decon ship toward the suited figure. In spite of Lucille's urging, she moved the ship slowly, carefully, closing the distance from kilometers to meters to centimeters, until the suited figure reached out a hand and gently pulled herself onto the I-beam fuselage.

"Welcome aboard. And welcome to League territory." Mac watched with anxious eyes as Lucille swung herself around and waved.

"Thank you, thank you, thank you! Which way to the showers?"

"Straight toward the bow. Strip to skin in the airlock there. Once you're in the decon tank use the inside controls to open the outer lock and jettison the suit and everything else."

Lucy felt herself bubbling with delight. She had escaped! It didn't matter what happened next, didn't matter that the League would have to come down on her like a ton of bricks to get every bit of information on the Guards and the Outposters and Ariadne—well, that was the way it had to be. She owed that to Wu and Schiller and everyone else back on the station. And she owed Johnson Gustav.

She pulled herself along the I-beam toward the decon chamber. The outer hatch was open. She clambered into it, and shut the hatch behind her. The lock itself was a standard issue aluminum and plastic box, little bigger than a closet. It didn't take long to pressurize. She wriggled out of the suit and her clothes and shoved them into a corner. She opened the inner hatch and tossed her carrybag into the decontamination tank. She followed the bag in and, working in the dark, dogged the inner hatch shut. She found a light switch and turned it on. Then she used the remotes to open the outer hatch with the lock still pressurized. There was a shower there, and several bottles of very strong, nasty-smelling soap. The paranoia about decontamination told her they had met with bioweapons already.

She didn't have to ask what the outcome had been.

Mac saw the outer lock open and the pressure suit and other clothes zip out into space, pulled along by the escaping air. He powered up the infra-red laser in the weapons pod, aimed and fired as Joslyn played with the attitude jets to match velocity with the debris. The suit melted and then vaporized in the intense heat. Mac zapped the rest of the clothes, and then Joslyn moved the boat alongside the lander. Mac pulled a pair of heatflash grenades out of a satchel and tossed them through the open airlock into the lander's cabin.

"Pull her back, Joz."

The control jets flared, the boat pulled back, Mac hit the radio trigger, and the lander's interior flared with a sullen, killing heat. They headed for home.

Decontamination. Bioweapons. First Contact. The League still had no idea that they were mixed up in a First Contact. Sobering thoughts. There was so much to tell them, but how to start? Scrubbing herself, carefully drying herself and getting into fresh coveralls, Lucy pondered the question. In all her time of waiting, she had never considered *how* to tell them. Now she did, and resolved to say nothing until she was sure of her words, until the right people were there to listen. Lucy kept her silence on the journey back to *Eagle*, except to reassure Mac and Joslyn she was all right. She smiled and waved and said nothing of consequence to the small crowd that cheered her arrival in the hangar deck, smiled her way up into the conference room where the Intelligence staff was waiting.

She looked out across the faces, and thought of the Nihilists and lost her smile. And she knew how to begin. "You're fighting the wrong war," she said.

Chapter Twenty-Six

Aboard RKS *Eagle*
The Barycenter
Nova Sol System

Lieutenant George Prigot sat there, silent and glad to be forgotten in the hubbub. The command staff and the Intelligence units had been in joint session for endless hours now, and the voices of argument swirled around him.

"We can't make First Contact in the middle of a war!"

"The bloody Guards made *First* Contact. We'll have to settle for second—and we don't have much choice about making Contact. How can we avoid it?"

"But in the middle of a war? How? Who? How can we get through the Guard ships around Outpost?"

Captain Robinson listened to it all for a while before banging his gavel and attempting to bring the talk back to the point. "Lieutenant Calder, I have seen the results of the attack on the *Impervious*, and I am willing to grant that bioweapons are dangerous. I can't quite credit your claim that these Nihilists could or would wipe out the human race. For starters, how could they get to us? They have no starships, no spacecraft of any kind—"

"But they *will* get them, Captain," Lucy said, with the weary voice of someone who has said the same thing many times before. "By trade or theft or by building their own, sooner or later they will have ships, now that they know such things exist. The Nihilists regard intelligent life as an abomination. Before anyone can ask me why, I'm not quite sure. The Nihilists want to keep growing in power—and they lose lots of friends if they start genocide against their own kind. Mostly, as I understand it, the Nihilists limit themselves to killing Outposters as they enter old age, which doesn't really seem to bother anyone. Again, don't ask me why, I don't know.

"But out of all this come some key points: They *can* kill us, and kill us by the millions. You have seen the results of weapons that can breed more weapons. They are, I assure you, actively seeking to get ships so they can get to us. That's opinion on my part, but every Refiner Z'ensam I've talked to agrees with that assumption.

"And *killing us has got to be politically healthier for them than killing other Z'ensam*—other Outposters. We are very ugly to the Z'ensam. Worse than ugly—mortifying to look on. The Guards are the only humans any Outposter has met, and they aren't the best ambassadors of good will. A lot of Z'ensam would stand back and let the Nihilists go after us—and if the Nihilists, say, take Capital, wipe out the population there, the weapons and the ships and the technology there would let them take over all of Outpost. And if they got starships, and they came hunting the rest of us—imagine, just for starters, a breed of those worms that *was* designed to attack a planet."

There was a long silence. Finally one of the New Finnish officers broke it. "Just once, right there at the end, did you mention Capital, the Guardians. *They* are our reason for being here. Your aliens are all very interesting, but we are here to fight the Guards! You know what those monsters did to my world. Why should we defend them against these Nihilists of yours? Let it happen. We would be well rid of the Guards. *Let* the Nihilists wipe them out. We of the League can handle the Nihilists afterwards. I would consent to that course of action, but even it would not satisfy me altogether. *I* say we must ignore these creatures who don't even have spacecraft. *We* must flatten Capital. We have waited in this dreary barycenter of yours long enough, Admiral. Enough of caution. We New Finns at least, came here to kill Guardians!"

George's blood turned cold. This crazy Finn was talking genocide—and no one was disagreeing! They were concerned with the tactics of battle. No one raised the moral issues against allowing the Nihilists to exterminate the people of his planet. He wished Mac or Joslyn were in on this meeting. They would have spoken up. George knew damn well no one would listen to *him* on this subject. Anything he could say would only make things worse.

Captain Robinson turned to Admiral Thomas, but the admiral didn't seem to want to say anything. Robinson looked to the Finnish contingent. "Gentlemen, we understand your feelings. But I don't think the situation is simple enough for a simple answer. We are not properly prepared to do a First Contact, we do not have the experts in xenosociology and so on available, but nonetheless I think we must establish some sort of relations with at least this group of Outposters that Lieutenant Calder traveled with."

The Finns did not reply, but a murmur of agreement came from the rest of the table. "So how do we do it?" Robinson asked.

"Ah, Captain?" A nervous-looking young black woman, an Intelligence lieutenant, spoke up timidly. "We *can* get a team down there, with a minimum of risk. We just can't get them back—at least not for a while. We have those covert landers."

"Right! I'd clean forgotten about them. Thank you, Lieutenant Krebs."

"Wait a minute," came a voice from the rear. "What's a covert lander—and what was that about not getting back?"

Krebs leaned in toward the center of the table so she could be heard. "The coverts are one-shot landers designed to be transparent to radar and other detection systems. We have a number along so we could drop spies and saboteurs on Capital. Each can carry six and some cargo. You can't get back in one because they don't carry much fuel—and they land a little rough, too. A covert lander could follow that beacon down, we could get some people in there, and they'd have to sit tight until we could get them out. They'd have radios and so on, of course."

"Lovely," said the same voice from the rear.

Pete Gesseti sighed and stood up. "Ah, Captain Robinson.

I really hate to admit this, but it seems to me that I'm the logical one to send on this trip."

Robinson had given up looking to Thomas. The admiral was willing to just sit there and listen. "I'm afraid I had just come to the same conclusion. Talk with me afterwards and we'll put together a team. Obviously, Lieutenant Calder should be on it, if you feel up to it, Lieutenant."

"I've been assuming that I'd go back. You'll need an interpreter, Mr. Gesseti."

"I need my head examined for volunteering," Pete said.

"Very well. Krebs, you get them organized after we're done here. But now we must move on to your other news about this Guardian officer, Johnson Gustav. Can he be trusted?"

Lucy opened her mouth to speak, shut it again, played with a pencil for a moment. "Johnson is a good and honorable man, but you must understand his viewpoint," she said finally. "He is a citizen of Capital, and his planet is at war with us. He makes a very clear distinction between the planet Capital and the political association called the Guardians. He hinted to me once or twice about an illegal opposition group called Settlers, but I don't know much about them. He doesn't want the League here. I don't think he actually *wants* the League to win. But he has concluded that those persons in power, the Central Guardians, have gotten Capital into a hopeless situation. Capital *will* lose. He sees that as inevitable. He wants to make that defeat as painless as possible. He believes that the use of bioweapons can only make the League more eager for revenge.

"I should emphasize that Johns—that Gustav is in a very delicate situation. I have had no contact with him for months. He may be dead. He may have been drugged and tortured into revealing every plan he and I made. The CIs on Ariadne might be dead by now, or simply transferred to another posting. So the *situation* cannot be trusted. But, if he lives, Johnson Gustav *can* be trusted. If we receive any transmissions from Ariadne, you must judge for yourself who is sending them."

"And at this range, we can't possibly be certain that a laser link would be secure," Robinson said thoughtfully. "We can't risk talking back to them. Somehow, this seems like a very new kind of war, and a very old kind, both at once.

"Meeting adjourned. We all have a lot to think about."

Chapter Twenty-Seven

Hangar Deck
RKS *Eagle*
The Barycenter
Nova Sol System

"Lucy has a point," Joslyn said. "A ship needs a name."

Mac grunted and stared up at the thing. The covert lander was an ungainly arrowhead, a dingy grey aerodynamic lump. It looked like a blob of clay some giant had half-formed into an airplane shape before he got bored and went away. She had been pulled in from her usual outside-of-hull docking to be checked out. Mac slapped his hand on the hull and it felt like crumbly concrete mixed with styrofoam. "How about the *Sick Moose*?"

"A real romantic, that's you, Mac," Lucy said. "A true sense of history. How's *Sick Moose* going in the books side-by-side with your name going to look to the unborn generations?"

Joslyn laughed and twined her arm through her husband's. "I was on your side until you said that, Luce. Think of all the schoolkids that are going to have to write dull reports about the First Contact for history class. Let's make it *Sick Moose* and give them some comic relief."

Lucy shrugged, grinned, and kicked the lander's hull. "*Sick Moose* it is, then. I must say that I expected a little more sense of awe and wonder and fewer dumb jokes from you two on the subject of meeting aliens."

"I don't think either of us really quite believe it all yet," Mac said, his voice turning serious. "You've had a long, long time to get used to it. We found out an hour ago when Pete said he had volunteered us to pilot this thing down to Outpost. I wanted to laugh and cry at the same time and then hurry there to meet C'astille."

"I'll second that," Joslyn said.

"Of course," Mac said, "I'm also scared to death. Not just for me personally, but with the idea that *I'll* be the one to make the dreadful mistake that wrecks our relations with them for all time. Maybe dumb jokes are the best cover we have for all that."

"And maybe we'd best change the subject before we bog down for hours discussing the Wonder of It All," Joslyn said. "George, you're the only real engineer here. Is this thing really going to work? Can we get through without being spotted?"

George Prigot shrugged. "I'm not going along, so I don't have the same stake in the answer you do. But it *should* work. Their radar isn't going to be geared to watch for an all-ceramic ship, and even if it was, it'd be hard to get a decent echo off this thing."

Joslyn snorted. "They won't be looking for it because no one has ever been enough of a damn fool to make a spaceship out of glass before."

"It's not glass," George objected. "It's more like a clay pot, though it should be a lot tougher."

" 'Should be' are the very words I'm worried about," Joslyn said. "And I say she's a glass ship because radar will see right through—and she'll shatter if you drop her hard. I'd love to know more about the propulsion system, though. Supposed to be some sort of cross between magneto-hydrodynamics and a linear accelerator. Extremely secret. She uses straight liquid oxygen for boost-mass. Not as efficient as fusion, but just try spotting the thrust plume."

George walked to the stern of the *Moose* and looked up into the engine bells. "Neat. It must jet the oxy at only a couple hundred degrees. Very hard to detect if you're watching for fusion plasmas."

"Neat it is. But I'd trade it for a hull you couldn't smash with a hammer."

Pete came through a hatch into the hangar bay and wandered into earshot as Joslyn was speaking. "Say, you're just the sort of pilot that inspires confidence in a passenger."

"Hello, Peter," Joslyn said with a smile. "What's the situation?"

"Well, this is a top secret operation, so I only had to clear it with ten departments instead of twenty. They dug up a biologist, a South African kid by the name of Charles Sisulu. Civilian kid who knows a lot about bioengineering. They brought him along to work on the bioweapons, so he might as well go straight to the source. So with Mac, Joz, Lucy, this Sisulu character and me, we have five and this crate can carry six. Any suggestions for the empty slot?"

"I've got one," Joslyn said. "Madeline Madsen. She's a Royal Britannic Navy second lieutenant, a pilot. I know she's checked out on the covert lander, and she's a big outdoorswoman."

Lucy sounded unconvinced. "She have any ground combat training?"

"Standard RBN basic training, I guess. Why do we need combat for this trip?"

"Because Outpost is a very nasty place. Any animal that sees us is likely to try eating us. And Mr. Gesseti, with all due respect, we're going to be in armored pressure suits for that same reason, for long hours at a stretch. Are you up to that?"

"I dunno, but I'm sure as hell in better shape than the other diplomatic types along for the ride. I'm fifteen years younger than any of 'em. One reason I volunteered."

Lucy grunted non-commitally. It was a motley crew, a hurry-up job, but maybe that was the best she dare hope for. "All right, Mr. Gesseti. That'll have to do. Any word about when we launch?"

"As soon as possible, they said, so I guess it's in your hands. Mac, how soon can we be ready?"

Mac hesitated for a moment, figuring loading and checkouts and a little extra for glitches. "We'll go in eighteen hours."

Lucy was ready long before that. Aside from getting fitted for a pressure suit, there really wasn't much for her to do.

The *Eagle*'s purser put her up in a VIP cabin for her one night aboard. It was a kindly gesture, a welcome-back to the ex-prisoner who had to depart at once for a harsh and dangerous field assignment. A huge bed, plush carpeting on the deck, books she'd have no time to read, recorded music and films she'd have no chance to run—but still, it was good to at least be near such things again.

Lucy thought of C'astille and decided that she had to bring a gift back for her friend. Even as she had the idea of bringing a present, her eyes fell upon the perfect thing. A book, a great big, old-fashioned picture book lying on the coffee table of her stateroom. It was called *Works of Our Hands: Humans Shape the Solar System*. It was full of pictures of grand buildings and structures, old and new, and each was set against a glorious background. C'astille would love it.

Lucy felt only mildly guilty about swiping it as she tucked it into her carry sack.

Chapter Twenty-Eight

Aboard the *Sick Moose*
Approaching the Planet Outpost

The long-range cameras tracked the great shape, brought it more frighteningly close than it truly was. "That's Nike," Lucy whispered. "She's big."

"That much we already knew," Mac replied in a whisper of his own. Logically, they could all be shouting at the top of their lungs and it wouldn't make any difference. But under the very nose of the huge military orbital command station, sneaking in past their radar, the desire to keep quiet went past the logical.

"Maddy, what can you see on passive detection?" Joslyn asked.

"Plenty enough," Madeline said, "and I've got everything cranked down to minimum power. But it looks to me that we should have Nike and Ariadne below our horizon when we hit the atmosphere."

"A bit of luck running our way," Joslyn said. "Even if this flying teapot is supposed to be invisible, I don't see any reason to experiment."

"Well, for what it's worth," Mac said, "we have now sailed through at least six different radars, apparently without being spotted."

"Mac, how are we, as far as the beacon signal?"

Mac was riding the comm station, which left him without much to do *besides* watch the beacon. He had gotten caught up on his reading this trip. "Right on the money. No change in its position since we picked it up. So do your bit and land us right on top of it."

The *Sick Moose*'s one small cabin was crowded with six people who had been forced to sleep and eat in each other's pockets for several rather long and uneventful days, but the two civilians had managed to carve out a small corner for their own. Charlie Sisulu had taken advantage of the long trip and methodically skinned Pete Gesseti's hide in four kinds of card game. Now Pete was grimly trying to win it all back in chess, fifty Kennedy dollars a game. Even with chess, his strong suit, Pete was just about holding his own. If he was even managing that, he thought, as he sadly watched his second bishop join its ancestors. "Charlie, isn't there any game you're not good at?"

Charlie grinned as he collected the bishop. He was a short, pudgy young man, perfect white teeth set off against his dark-skinned face. His hair was trimmed very short, and his rounded features and alert eyes suggested a quick and clever mind working behind the laughter and smiles. "If there was, why should I tell you? I figure you've paid for a month's vacation on Bandwidth already."

"And on what a diplomat makes. You should be ashamed of yourself. Seriously though, how'd you get so good?"

"Easy. It's how I worked my way through college. My part of South Africa used to be one of those phony homelands. Technically not under South African law, which banned gambling, among other things.

"The Afrikaners'd come in to make a killing at roulette and we'd skin 'em alive. After we got pulled back into the nation, we had the smarts and the luck to hang on to our special exemption to the gambling laws.

"These days marks might come in more than one color, but they still come, and we still clean 'em out and send 'em home. During the southern winter, that is the northern summer, I lived at home with my folks and played poker for a living. When September rolled around I'd fly to America and live off my earnings while I studied at the University of California. If I got short of money, I'd spend a weekend at Las Vegas. Later on, when I started research at Wood's Hole, I'd go to Atlantic City."

"That's the last time I play with anyone before I check their resume," Pete said, pulling his queen back into what looked like a safer position. "So how do you like our odds here?"

Charlie shrugged. "No way to calculate them. But I'm a *biologist!* When they waved the foam-worms at me, I signed every security agreement in sight—I *had* to work on that, top secret or no. And now I'll get to talk to someone who *designs* living things, from scratch! For a biologist, that's like a chat with God." Charlie moved in his own queen, took Pete's, and grinned. "Check. Mate in two moves. I'll take an IOU."

When they were about two hours from atmosphere, Mac called a meeting of all hands, which simply meant that everyone turned around and faced the center of the tiny cabin in their chairs.

"All right," Mac said, "let me go over the situation one more time. So far the Guard radars haven't picked us up, but that could change at any time. This ship might be invisible to radar, but she's slow, she's hard to maneuver, and she's unarmed. And I don't care if she's made out of special-purpose ceramics or prune danish, when she hits the atmosphere, the light and heat of atmospheric entry are going to be detectable. We're going in on the daylight side, at a time when the bigger stations can't see our entry window. But we still might get spotted.

"Obviously, if we use our own radar, the Guards will spot us immediately, so that's out. But that means we're relying on inertial tracking and on visual. Those aren't really good enough for precise navigation in this situation. We don't have this system very well charted yet, we don't have maps of Outpost's surface, and we don't really know enough about the performance of this ship. There's some degree of uncertainty about where and when we'll hit air. We've exhausted our fuel already, as you know. That was planned. In theory there's nothing to worry about. Once we do hit air, this thing is a glider, and it should be a good enough one to get us where we're going.

"The main point is that we're literally going in on a wing

and a prayer. But while this will be a somewhat hairier landing than most, all of this was taken into account when we planned this flight. We *should* be all right. Mostly I want to tell this last to Pete and Mr. Sisulu, but it can't hurt for us rough-and-ready pilot types to be reminded too—when we go in, things might look worse than they really are. Relax and hang on, and the hottest pilot I know will pull this one off. Right, Joz?"

"No worries," she said. "Mac's just trying to make it sound hard so when we come in you won't think it was too easy."

Mac played it very conservatively. He had them all in pressure suits, strapped into crash couches and secured half an hour before they expected to hit air. He felt justified when the first faint quivering and thrumming sounded against the hull, fifteen minutes ahead of schedule. Now they were in Joslyn's hands. Mac had already watched Madeline enough to wish he were in the back-up pilot's station. Maddy was good, but she wasn't seasoned, she didn't have that air of being calmly ready for disaster that combat pilots gained if they lived long enough. But it was too late for second guessing, and Mac couldn't think of anything that could take Joslyn out without killing the rest of them anyway.

Joslyn was trying to get the feel of the *Moose*. She seemed to be a pretty clumsy thing so far, and Joslyn was already worried about cross-ranges. Every second in atmosphere slowed them down, stole kilometers from the distance they could travel. There was enough fat in the landing program to cover the current situation, but just barely. She fought an impulse to tighten her grasp on the stick. This was her show, she had to keep calm and loose, ready for whatever the gods threw at her. She threw switches and let the computer handle the initial entry while she got a look around and tried to track that beacon. The planet's rotation had swung it out of their line of sight, but—hah! There she was, happily blinking away, and still within range of what the on-board computers were figuring was their likely glide-radius.

Then the *Moose* hit thicker air, and re-entry, and rode long minutes cut off from the outside world by a sheath of ionized air molecules and heat-shield ablation. This was the dangerous moment, when the *Moose* could not see, but was most easily seen. If there were any ships orbiting above them, and anyone aboard happened to look planetward, the *Moose* would be a blazing fire streaking across the dawn sky. No one aboard the *Moose* spoke as the computer dully went through its paces, maintaining ship's attitude at the right heading, keeping the shielding between the hull and disaster.

They went in, surrounded by a ball of flame that thundered through the skies of sunrise. The *Moose* shuddered and groaned, and the hull pinged and clicked as it absorbed the heat.

Slowly, the ball of fire guttered down, and the *Moose*, her hull still faintly glowing, coursed through the skies of Outpost. Joslyn pulled control back from the computer and took a look around. They were still nearly a hundred thousand meters up, still had line of sight on the beacon, though they might lose it as they glided lower. But they were in, and safe—

"Joslyn," Mac called. "I'm not up on reading Outpost weather, but it looks to me as if that beacon is right in the middle of one hell of a storm."

Joslyn's eye jumped from the beacon display to the pilot's window and back, mentally combining the two into one. "Damn! Mac, you're right. I wish to hell there had been time to put some decent viewing gear on this bird. I can't really get a good fix on where the beacon is compared to the cloud cover."

"We've got the gear," Mac said, "it's just that we can't use it without giving our position away."

"Then I wish they had yanked it out so this thing'd be light enough to glide. We've got to go straight through that muck to get where we're going."

In the rear seats, Pete and Charlie Sisulu exchanged nervous glances. This might get to be too exciting a trip.

The *Moose* glided onward and down, Joslyn stretching every horizontal meter she could out of the clumsy craft. The storm clouds came up around them, engulfed them, the dark cobalt blue of the upper atmosphere vanished into a witch's cauldron of angry, writhing grey clouds that grabbed at the *Moose* and flung her to and fro. Lightning flashed about them, thunder exploded at deafeningly short range, and Joslyn wrapped both hands around the stick, braced her arms as best she could to retain control of the bucking, rearing ship. The interior lights flickered once, twice, and then came back on, and the hull rattled and clattered as hailstones and wind-driven rain slammed into it.

Joslyn knew the hull simply wasn't built to take this kind of abuse. Her every pilot's instinct was to get them down fast, now, anywhere, to wait out the storm. But the crew of the *Moose* was going to be stranded on Outpost, and their chances for survival rested with the Refiners. They had to hang on, travel as far as they could in the *Moose*. Joslyn held onto the stick and swore through clenched teeth as a hailstone smashed into the pilot's window, starring the glass, making it that much harder to see.

"Maddy! Kick in the look-down radar and get me some hard numbers! If the Guards can spot our radar emissions through this bloody great storm, they *deserve* to win."

"Yes ma'am." Maddy started flicking switches. "Give it a second to get some returns back—now! Airspeed, altitude, range and bearing to beacon and descent rate on your panel."

Damn! Those numbers weren't good. They were going to land a good fifty kilometers short of the beacon. Joslyn dragged back desperately on the stick, pulling the wallowing *Moose*'s nose up as far as she could, risking a stall to try and drag some more range out of her.

With no consciousness of what she was doing, Joslyn felt an updraft in the thrumming of the wings and the tricks of the wind. She grabbed at it, rode it as far as she could, felt the ship wallow back down into stiller air. The updraft might have bought them a kilometer, maybe two. Joslyn prayed for a tailwind, and got it, and then wished she didn't have it, a roaring, wailing banshee of a gust that almost knocked the *Moose* off her tail and into a fatal spin.

In the crash and the roar of the storm, Joslyn wrestled with the elements of air and wind and water, battling to keep her craft on course and in one piece.

They were getting lower now. They broke through the base of the cloud deck and looked upon the rain-soaked, wind-torn face of Outpost.

They were too low and too damn slow now, almost out of airspeed, headed for a stall. Joslyn swore and pushed the *Moose*'s nose down, trading altitude she could ill afford for the airspeed she needed to keep her bird in the air. The ship seemed to wallow in the air, felt clumsier than ever, if that was possible. The damn porous ceramic hull must have soaked up the rainwater. And water was heavy. The added weight was dragging them down.

At least here, below the cloud deck, the winds had steadied down. No gusts or air pockets, just a hard, steady crosswind that did her no good but no great harm, either. Joslyn turned into the wind and held her nose as close to where it should be as she could.

Now they were really coming down. *Don't try anything fancy*, Joslyn told herself. *Just keep this thing in the air as long as it'll stay there*. There was nothing but unbroken forest land below, no cozy meadow to set down in. It was time to hope the local equivalent of trees had soft branches. How far from the beacon? Seventy kilometers. Sixty five. Sixty. Still slowing. Come on! Fifty five. Fifty! And they were still a few klicks up in the air. Forty five. Every klick was a gift from the gods of the air, now. Forty. There came the ground straight up for them. Thirty five. What was that in miles? Never mind, figure it on the ground. They were only a thousand meters up now.

The wind came about to their nose, blowing them back against their course. Joslyn pulled the *Moose*'s nose down and to port, trying to avoid a stall and maybe still make some headway. She kept it level, trying to pancake it down, spread the shock evenly—

—and the *Moose* ran out of sky.

She plowed into the treetops with terrible force, a roaring, screaming, keening crash of branches breaking and wings snapping off and shouts of frightened people and the horrible whistle of air screaming out of a broken hull. The *Moose* slammed on and on through the trees, far longer than seemed possible, treelimbs whipping past the cockpit windows, until finally a tree trunk stood its ground and the *Moose* shattered her nose square on against it. The ruined ship tilted over to port and fell the last ten meters to the ground on its side.

Suddenly, the world, which had been so full of noise, was silent, or nearly so, with nothing but the creak of treelimbs, the muted roar of the rain, and the moans of people to be heard.

"Everyone still with us?" Mac called out, and got a ragged chorus of *yes*'s. "Good. That was some kind of flying, Joz."

Joslyn shook herself and forced her hands to peel themselves away from the stick. "Thanks, Mac. Though that has to be the least covert landing I've ever made." She felt herself trembling. Perhaps no one else would ever realize it, but *she* would always know just how close it had been.

Mac took a few minutes to check again that everyone was all right. They had all taken some bumps and bruises, but no one seemed much the worse for wear. All the pressure suits were behaving themselves, and that was a blessing. There was one spare aboard, but getting anyone into it with the *Moose*'s hull cracked and breached would have been a challenge, to say the least.

It was tempting to sit tight and wait for the rain to end, but Lucy warned them just how long the rains could last—there was nothing for it but to get moving. Within a half hour of landing, they had their carrypacks strapped on, rifles and other weapons at the ready, and the direction finder pointing twenty nine kilometers *that* way to the beacon.

The six of them stepped from the wreckage of the *Sick Moose*, their hearts and spirits as gloomy as the dismal rainswept forest that surrounded them. Lucy's helmet started to blur over with rain, and she switched on the wiper arm. The others followed her lead, turned to her. She was the only one who could guide them on this trek. She looked to Mac, and he nodded.

"You're our native guide, Lucy. We follow your commands on this leg."

"Right, then. Everyone make sure your external mikes are up, so you can hear them coming. You've seen what a Z'ensam—an Outposter looks like. If you see *anything* else move, kill it. I don't care if it looks like a sweet little baby fawn that only wants to nibble the grass. *Kill* it! There *are* no harmless wild animals on this planet. Any creature that spots us will try to eat us. So kill them, without hesitation. And make sure it stays dead. Don't worry about offending the locals either—it's the same way they deal with the wildlife. Is all that grimly clear?"

No one said anything.

"Mac, you take the rear. I'll lead. Lieutenant Madsen, you get behind me with the direction finder. Joslyn, you watch her back while she's watching our route. Mr. Sisulu, Mr. Gesseti, if you would follow Joslyn. Let's go."

Chapter Twenty-Nine

The Planet Outpost

Charlie Sisulu didn't like the odds. He was sweating, not from exertion, but from fear. The forest was a grim, gloomy, wet and dismal place, claustrophobic, the vegetation shaded in livid greens that seemed horrid parodies of Earth's lovely plant life. His suit's external mikes picked up no birdsong, no musical calls of one beast to another, but instead an endless screaming, roaring challenge of defiance and death, set to the refrain of staccato, bone-rattling bursts of thunder. The rain came on and on, pouring down off his pressure suit, the wiper blade on his helmet barely able to keep his helmet halfway clear. And Charlie Sisulu had never been in a pressure suit before in his life. He felt trapped, sealed up, entombed in the clumsy suit.

This Lieutenant Lucy Calder led them on at a reckless speed, crashing through the thick underbrush, using a laser pistol or machete to hack down anything she couldn't get through. Twice she had dropped the laser, unholstered a heavy machine pistol and fired at *something* before Charlie had even seen whatever it was. Twice she had reholstered the heavy gun, scooped up the laser, and pressed on before whatever she had killed had finished falling to the ground. Twice he had stepped over shattered corpses that seemed nothing but teeth and claws.

And they had only gone about one kilometer.

He was scared, scared of drowning in the endless rain; scared of getting his foot mired in the ankle-deep mud they seemed to stumble into constantly; scared of some pocket-sized monster leaping out of the lurid greed fronds and weeds that hung down to brush against his suit with every step; scared of encountering some wild-living relative of the foam worm that might already be gnawing its way through some part of his suit where no one would notice it until it was too late; scared of his faceplate shattering; scared he might die of a carbon dioxide reaction, his lungs hyperventilating, panic setting in—he forced himself not to think of such things. His breath was growing short, his heart was pounding, he felt himself close to vomiting, and *that* was a real nightmare in a pressure suit. Claustrophobia. Xenophobia. Did giving it names make it easier? He forced himself to look up, forced himself to watch more than the slogging feet and lumbering backpack of the figure ahead of him, forced himself to look around, told himself that this was a whole new world of life to explore, that his tutors in a new universe of biology, themselves a wondrous find, were just a few kilometers ahead.

It seemed to help. A little. It felt like his heart rate was down.

A rifle slug screamed past his helmet and splattered the muzzle of a brightly colored, fox-sized flying beast that was diving straight for him, keening for his blood in a high-pitched shriek. It fell out of the air and landed at his feet. That Captain Larson was a good man to have at your back.

Charlie had never seen a flying animal that size. It was a whole new taxonomy, a discovery of the first importance. Time for that when they were safe. He stepped on the ruined, lovely little body rather than break stride, and kept on.

At the rear of the little column, Mac wasn't in much better shape. He devoutly wished for someone to be at *his* back. That fox-bat thing had gotten too damn close. He decided to shift to heavier firepower, unloaded the slugs from the rifle and slapped in a long clip of mini-rocket rounds with explosive warheads. Those should stop damn near anything.

He got the chance to find out almost immediately. A low-slung lizard with two cruel, grasping arms that reached up for Joslyn burst out from the shadows and Mac blasted it into bloody confetti. Lucy didn't even look back, she just shouted "Come on!" over the suit radio and upped the pace to a dog-trot. Even for Mac, that wasn't easy in the armored suit, carrying equipment. It must be real hell on Pete, but the middle-age diplomat made no protest.

They slogged on and on, not going a kilometer that some nightmare beast didn't burst out at them to die under their guns. It was a grueling, mind-numbing nightmare, Lucy setting an arrow-straight course toward the beacon, Maddy just behind her, dividing her attention between the direction finder and putting one foot after another. The relentless pace ground them down into automata, capable of nothing but marching on, and gunning down anything that moved. The rain never ended, the morbid forest never ended, the cacophony of animal cries never let up. All there was left to life was the simple act of marching on.

None of them knew it had happened until it was over, and of course Madeline Madsen never knew it happened at all. Or perhaps she did, because she threw the direction finder clear, unless the herd of whatever they were simply knocked it from her grasp as they plummeted past.

One moment they were alone in the forest, just stepping out onto an empty game trail, and the next, they were watching the backs of some tawny-colored, fleet-footed herd flashing back down the pathway, carrying Madeline's new-made corpse away.

They had moved so fast! Mac had seen just the slightest flicker of movement, and then a single moment frozen in his memory—a long, lanky body, its claws already raking open the armor of the pressure suit as if it weren't there, life's blood already gushing from her chest, her death scream cut short, and then hunter and prey alike were gone, followed by a small herd of the fleet killers, and Pete was down, the arm of his suit torn up, and he was bleeding.

Before Mac could bring his rifle up to fire, they were vanished into the forest. Too fast! The five remaining humans stood frozen to the ground in shock, and the fear grew in all of them. Mac shook his head, came to himself, and suddenly knew that, Pete injured or no, it was death to stay near that trail. He scooped up the older man over one shoulder, and shouted "Joslyn! The finder! Lucy! Go! Go! Maddy's dead, for God's sake. Go before they come back! Sisulu—get your gun out and stop playing tourist. Move it!"

Lucy took off again, full tilt, and they didn't stop again until they had another five klicks between themselves and Maddy's killers. Mac called the halt, and carefully set Pete down. The three military people surrounded Pete and Charlie and stood a frightened watch as the biologist tended the wound.

Charlie did the best he could for his patient. Pete was semi-conscious, and the injury itself was pretty ugly. The claws of one of those fiends had ripped clear through the armor of the suit and torn up Pete's arm pretty badly. He was bleeding, had already lost a lot of blood. Worse, Pete was already in carbon-dioxide shock, his face grey, his breath fast and shallow. Charlie used the chest panel on Pete's suit to up the oxygen flow and set up a positive pressure flow, flushing the CO_2 out of the suit through the torn-up sleeve. Charlie pulled the first-aid kit off his backpack, cut away as little of the suit arm as possible, slathered an antiseptic/local anesthetic on the wound, and bandaged it up as best he could.

He hesitated, then used the kit's jet hypodermic to give Pete heady doses of anti-shock drugs and a stimulant. With the loss of blood the drugs were risky, a temptation to a heart attack. But if the group was to keep any sort of pace through this nightmare world, Pete would have to be on his feet. Mac was the only person big enough to carry Pete more than a few meters, and if Mac was crippled by exhaustion, that would put everyone else at greater risk.

The first-aid kit included pressure suit patches, and Charlie slapped the largest one on the hole. Charlie worked the suit's chest panel again, backing off the pressure setting but keeping the oxy count high. Pete's color already looked better, and his breathing seemed easier. "That's all I can do," Charlie said carefully. "He should be all right if the blood loss wasn't too bad. Let him rest easy for just a few minutes before we go on. The patch on the suit needs to set."

Joslyn, watching the forest for whatever else was out there, felt a streak of moisture run down her cheek, and hoped it was a tear and not perspiration. She wanted to mourn Maddy Madsen, a bright young kid who had come a very long way to get killed, a fine young woman entrusted to Joslyn's care, who *died* in Joslyn's care. Joslyn wanted to feel guilt, wanted to feel sorrow, wanted to cherish Madeline's memory. But danger surrounded them still, and adrenalin coursed through her veins, and fear left no room for other emotion.

Groggy, shaky, Pete came back to himself and insisted he was strong enough to walk. He barely seemed aware of what had happened. Charlie helped him to his feet, grateful for the drugs that were holding the older man together.

They marched on.

Chapter Thirty

Refiner Camp
The Planet Outpost

The far-sentries to the south of the camp had reported the sound of a faint far-off crash in the midst of the storm, and then an occasional ripple of rapid explosions, like many guns going off at once, and animals came charging out of the south as if pursued by something terrifying. It all brought the damnable Nihilists quite rapidly to mind. Who else would crash through the underbrush, unannounced, traveling through the hazards of the woodland instead of the relative safety of the Road?

C'astille was the only one who thought of an alternate explanation, but she did not suggest it, for she hardly dared hope it was true. She volunteered to lead the team that would venture cross-country to investigate the disturbance. Ten of them set out, on foot, heavily armed, not only against the hypothetical enemy, but against the forest beasts.

C'astille led them at a good pace, and soon heard the noise of rapid-fire guns for herself. Moving cautiously, the Z'ensam let their ears guide them toward the sound. It soon became clear that not only were they moving toward the sound, but the sound was moving toward them. C'astille, for no logical reason, became more and more convinced that they were tracking something far more exciting than a band of marauding Nihilists, and urged her companions onward.

It was a miracle that humans and Z'ensam didn't open fire on each other when the two groups nearly tripped over each other toward midafternoon. But C'astille was the first to spot the humans, and fortunately had the good sense to call out "Lucy! Lucy!" instead of galloping blindly forward to greet her friend. If she had taken the latter course, unquestionably she would have gotten her head blown off.

As it was, the worst she had happen to her was near-strangulation when Lucy ran to her and flung her arms around C'astille's long neck. "Oh, C'astille! Thank God! I don't know how much further we could have gone."

C'astille returned her friend's embrace. "Lucy!" she said in English. "You did come back. Welcome!" C'astille stepped back from her friend and turned to the other humans, who looked just a trifle alarmed at being suddenly surrounded by natives bearing what were quite obviously weapons. And it occurred to C'astille that the Z'ensam must look rather large and threatening to a human. She holstered her weapon.

She carefully addressed the other humans in English. "My name is C'astille. In the name of D'chimchaw, Guidance of the Refiners, I bid you welcome and offer our hospitality." She had rehearsed that speech a long time, waiting for the day Lucy would bring her friends back.

The largest of the humans—in fact the largest human C'astille had yet seen—came forward and bowed. The big human, indeed all the humans, seemed exhausted to the point of collapse.

"My name is Terrance MacKenzie Larson. This is Joslyn Marie Cooper Larson, Charles Sisulu, and Peter William Gesseti. In the name of the League of Planets, we thank you for your welcome."

C'astille hesitated a moment, and then recalled a thing the Guards had done. She stepped forward and reached out her four-thumbed hand to Terranz Mac whatever-the-name-was. She could practice saying it later.

Mac seemed surprised by the gesture, but then he looked C'astille straight in her jet-black eyes and shook her hand in the pouring rain of Outpost's woodlands.

The weary humans were relieved beyond measure to find themselves with an armed escort through the deadly forest. There was something almost anticlimactic about their meeting with the natives. C'astille and Lucy walked side by side, chattering like two long-separated schoolgirl chums in a mixture of O-1 and English that no one else could follow. The other Outposters seemed curious about these new and strange halfwalkers, but they were used to seeing Lucy about and some of the novelty had worn off. Besides, none of them could speak English.

Mac, Pete, Joslyn and Charlie could do little but try not to stare at their hosts. But safety, and a pressurized wagon where they could peel off their suits, lay ahead, and that added a spring to their step. Even so, it was near nightfall when they finally reached the Refiners' camp, and the humans were just barely able to do more than stagger into the wagon and collapse that night. By then, Pete was being half carried by Mac and Charlie. C'astille and Lucy agreed it would be wise to wait until morning to meet with the Guidance.

Lucy re-entered her old pressurized wagon with mixed feelings. She was glad to see C'astille, glad to be out of that suit, but—all that effort, simply to return to her mobile prison! Nothing had changed in the time she had been gone. One table, one oddly-shaped chair, the possessions she had left behind neatly stacked in a corner, the beacon whose signal they had followed so far carefully hung on the wall. At least she wasn't alone anymore.

Pete was weakening, rapidly, his last burst of energy barely enough to get him to the wagon. The humans rushed him inside as quickly as possible. Pete fainted dead away in the airlock. They got him into the main room and stripped the pressure suit off.

Inside it, Pete was a bloody mess, and the stink of blood and sweat filled the wagon the moment they got his helmet off. The bandages must have worked themselves loose, and Pete had bled for a long time before the wound finally clotted up. He was pale and weak. They got his clothes off. Lucy grabbed some washing sponges and soaked them at the wagon's water spigot. They washed him down as best they could and wrapped him in blankets to keep him warm, to try and ward off shock. Charlie peeled the old dressing off and took a look at the wound. Nasty, but not dangerous. "I think he'll be all right," Charlie said. "The wound seems to have just about closed, just oozing a little bit. His real problem now is loss of blood."

Charlie was just about to put a new dressing on when the airlock thunked and an Outposter came in. He stood up. With five humans and one Outposter the size of a house in it, the wagon's interior suddenly seemed quite crowded. And Charlie was just a bit nervous about their hosts.

Lucy recognized the newcomer. "You are sensed, L'awdasi," she said in O-1.

"As are you, M'Calder. Welcome."

"Who is this, Luce?" Joslyn asked.

"This is L'awdasi. She helped to care for me, growing food, controlling the air, when I was here. I'm going to introduce you all. When I gesture toward you, bow." Lucy shifted to O-1. "L'awdasi, here are Terrance MacKenzie Larson, Joslyn Marie Cooper Larson, and Charles Sisulu. The one lying down is Peter Gesseti. He is unconscious. He was hurt by a beast in the forest, and we fear that he might not live. Another of our party was killed at the same time."

"Yes, C'astille told me of this, and I came to see for myself." L'awdasi stepped forward to get a look at Pete, and Lucy noticed the Outposter had a satchel slung over her neck. L'awdasi pointed at Pete's arm. "This is the wound? This is the danger?"

"Yes, though the wound itself should heal. But he has lost much—a word I do not know. You see the red fluid oozing from the cut? It is called *blood*. It carries oxygen through our bodies and does other important things."

Lucy was unaware of it, but perhaps the best description of L'awdasi's occupation might be veterinarian. L'awdasi was keenly interested in the halfwalkers' biology, and had even secured a few samples of Lucy's skin, hair, and waste products. She had gotten the samples without telling anyone or asking permission, as she had the feeling someone was bound to disapprove.

But circulatory fluid was one thing she hadn't gotten. She had never seen a wound, never seen any part of the *insides* of a human. When she had heard of what had happened, she had scooped up her work satchel and come, not quite sure what she intended. She craned her neck down to get a better look at Pete's arm. The wound was still oozing . . . L'awdasi *had* to have a sample of that fluid—perhaps she could even do the halfwalkers some good. Hardly believing her own daring, she pulled a glass sample tube from her satchel, knelt, and filled the tube from the slow stream of red dribbling out of the wound.

Lucy looked on, astonished. None of the other humans dared to move. L'awdasi stoppered the sample tube, slipped it back in her work satchel. She looked around at the alien faces, staring at her with great intensity. She decided it would be wisest to retreat, offer them no chance to demand an explanation. "Departure is now," she said to Lucy, careful formality in her voice and bearing. Without another word, she left.

Charlie was dumbfounded. "What in the devil was *that* all about?"

Lucy shook her head, as baffled as the rest. "I don't know. I wish I did." It took moments like that to remind her just how little she knew about the Z'ensam. "Come on, let's get Mr. Gesseti as comfortable as we can and then get some rest. We all need it."

L'awdasi couldn't sleep that night. She was too excited. For the first time, she had *living* samples, functioning cells, from a human being, from an entirely new and novel field of biology. She lumbered around her laboratory, examining the blood under microscopes, through filters, in a gaseous emissions tester, in a dozen devices. Human biochemists wouldn't recognize most of the machinery. If Charlie Sisulu knew what L'awdasi could do in her lab, he would have gladly traded off his soul for the chance to do a day's work there.

L'awdasi worked tirelessly. The clues she had gathered

from Lucy's dead cells and waste-product bacteria were a great help. She understood everything she saw, almost *before* she saw it. She examined the various forms of white blood cells, and instantly realized these were the descendants of some free-living form that had married itself to the bloodstream long, long ago, earning its keep by warding off less benign invaders. She admired the economy of the red blood cells. No nucleus, just the bare bones of hemoglobin transfer. But without a nucleus, the red cells could not reproduce themselves. Could they? She searched the red cells, and found no means by which they could breed themselves. But clearly the whites could and did reproduce themselves. She caught one in the very act of becoming two, and learned much. The gene structure was fantastic, clearly far more resistant to mutation than the Outposter equivalent of chromosomes. Then why was there such a great variation within the human population? L'awdasi had seen five humans with her own eyes, and pictures of many more—and *none* of them looked much alike. If the genes resisted mutation, everyone should look and be the same. Stranger still, there seemed to be no mechanism for transfer of acquired characteristics. The life of the human world must evolve with glacial slowness! But that same mutation resistance meant the human cell-stuff could be safely manipulated. And if the red cells were manufactured by some means external to themselves . . . L'awdasi got what was a wild idea, even for her. The plasma would be trivial. But how to spawn the cells?

She dove into the problem with manic enthusiasm.

It was a long night, but perhaps the most exciting one of L'awdasi's life. The rain had stopped, and the sun was creeping up the eastern sky when she cantered back to the humans' wagon. She cycled through the airlock as quietly as she could, restraining a sneeze when the chill-smelling, lifeless air the humans breathed tickled her blowhole. The air mix would sicken her if she stayed too long, but L'awdasi thought she could work fast. The four healthy ones slept, wrapped up in blankets on the floor. They must have been exhausted, for she managed to move her bulky self without waking them, carrying her gear carefully to keep it from clattering and clacking.

The injured one, M'Gegetty Lucy had called him, lay still and pale on the floor, his skin cool, almost transparent. There was some sort of covering on the wound, no doubt to shield its ugliness from view for the humans.

There was one last challenge, the most trivial, and yet one that almost stymied her. But she understood circulatory systems. Working by guess, luck, logic, intuition and analogy, she found a vein and gently inserted the needle. But then she was stuck holding the bottle aloft by hand.

Thirteen hours after seeing human blood for the first time, L'awdasi had invented transfusion.

Charlie awoke with a start to see L'awdasi's rather ample hindquarters taking up his entire field of vision. Cautiously, he got up to see what she was doing—and let out a shout that woke everyone else and almost spooked L'awdasi into stampeding through the wall.

The damn fool 'Poster was doing sympathetic magic! Something red had come out, so it was putting something red in. Pete jerked his arm as he woke, his color better and his mind clear the moment he woke. He looked up into the face of a leather-skinned monster who was holding what looked like a three-liter bottle of blood in midair, and decided he was still hallucinating.

Joslyn, Mac, and Lucy jumped to their feet and saw an alarmed L'awdasi backing away from a spluttering, horrified Charlie. The biologist wanted to rip out the needle, but God knows what damage that could do. He reached in and pinched the feedline, cutting off the flow of blood, careful to stay as far from the Outposter as possible.

"Lieutenant Calder! Tell it to stop! Tell it to get that needle out of his arm!" The poor son of a bitch was probably as good as dead already, with red paint coursing through his veins, but there might still be hope if they stopped it in time.

"L'awdasi!" Lucy shouted in O-1. "What action is this? Do you seek M'Gesetti's death? That needle must come out at once!"

L'awdasi looked from one human to another, shocked, terrified. Her mad enthusiasm for the experiment vanished in a moment. These were not animals, these were thinking beings! And she had dared to practice *medicine* on them. The enormity of the insult to them was beyond exaggeration.

Without a word, she pulled the needle, handed the transfusion bottle to Charlie, and left, leaving all her equipment behind.

There would a terrible reckoning for this. She had to speak with the Guidance, confess what she had done, before the damage was made worse.

If it *could* be made worse.

Charlie wasted not a moment. If he could identify the stuff L'awdasi had been pumping into Pete, maybe there was something in his portable field lab or the first aid kit to counteract it. There was a sophisticated miniature automated analyzer in the lab. He got it out, gave it a sample from the 'Poster's bottle full of fluid, and set it running. He pulled his rugged field microscope from the lab kit, got a sample of the stuff onto a slide, and took a look at it.

And took another look. He squirted a little of the red liquid onto his fingertip and sniffed it. He hesitated a moment, then tasted it. That same salty flavor he got from a cut lip. The analyzer pinged and ejected a hard copy of its report. It had matched the sample with some substance stored in its memory. Charlie didn't really have to look at the read-out, but he examined it with great care anyway. It eased the shock, somehow, to see it in print like that.

"It's blood," he said, dumbfounded. "Perfectly normal whole human blood. Red cells, all the white cells, plasma, clotting factors, everything. Type A positive. The Outposter matched it from the sample she took last night."

Pete fainted dead away.

Lucy was the first of them to regain her wits. She ate a quick breakfast and hurried out in search of C'astille. She was gone a few hours, during which time the rest of the humans were left completely alone, and elected not to venture outside the wagon. When Pete awakened, looking much recovered and alert, all of them had a field-ration breakfast.

When Lucy returned, she seemed more baffled than when she left. "I had to wait on C'astille until after a meeting of the Guidance and all the other grand poohbahs," she said. "C'astille suggested that both sides agree that nothing ever happened," she said. "It sounded like the best idea to me. Apparently, L'awdasi went straight to the Guidance and confessed her terrible crime, and the whole controlling group nearly went bouncing off the wall that she would dare perform medicine on a thinking species. The way she put it, trying to save Pete's life was a deadly insult, a breach of a strong taboo like incest or cannibalism. They think *that's* why we got upset, not because L'awdasi blundered in here and treated him without explaining what she was doing. They were quite relieved that we weren't insulted enough to call in an air strike. I seriously think they were expecting us to react that harshly."

Lucy took a cup of tea and went on. "C'astille was always a little cool toward L'awdasi when I was here before, and I think I've found out why. She's the camp veterinarian, more or less, and she was in charge of taking care of me. Veterinary medicine, I guess, is just barely socially acceptable. Don't ask me why being fed and cared for by the vet isn't an insult."

Charlie stared at her. "Wait a minute. Medicine is *taboo*? But these guys are the greatest bio-engineers anyone has ever seen!"

"Only with animals and plants. Not on themselves. Now that I come to think of it, I've never seen any Outposter treated for any illness, but on the other hand I never really noticed anyone who was taken sick, and their hides are tough enough to protect them against most natural enemies."

"But it doesn't make sense," Charlie insisted. "A really good strong taboo like incest or cannibalism always has some good strong practical reason behind it, even if people aren't aware of it. Commit incest and you get inbred, sickly babies. Commit cannibalism and you're liable to catch whatever killed the other guy—besides getting the dinner's family very mad at you. What could drive a medicine taboo?"

Lucy shook her head. "I don't know."

Mac looked worried, and he had every good reason to be. "Lucy, I think we've got to think about the bug-out option."

"Already?" Lucy said. She thought for a moment, and sighed. "I suppose you're right. If we're into this much of a mess before breakfast, what could happen by dinner?"

Pete spoke. "Hold it. What's the bug-out option?"

Mac started gathering up the litter of breakfast. "Lucy and I worked it out before we left the *Eagle*. We thought it might be possible that we would have to get the hell out of here before the League was in a position to come get us." He hesitated. "And if the League loses, God forbid, we still want a way out of here. We've got the beacon. The Guards, so far as we know, don't monitor that frequency—which is why Lucy and Gustav picked it. But Cynthia Wu aboard Ariadne is watching it. It's just sending a steady tone now—but we can hook a mike into it, tell Wu to send to us on another frequency we've got the gear to listen on, and talk."

"And we tell Ariadne to send us a pick-up ship, something we can run like hell in if we have to. Some ship that can reach the barycenter or the League, and tell them what we have learned about the Outposters."

Pete was astonished. "Mac, we came down here knowing we were risking our lives. If we're going to cut and run the moment we're in danger, we shouldn't have bothered coming. And this Gustav character sounds like a valuable asset. Our side can't risk him just for our sakes."

Joslyn knew her husband, understood what he was thinking. "It's not us dying, it's the *knowledge* dying, or the knowledge going straight to the Guards and not to our people," she said. "With what we've found out today, already, we are the best-informed League personnel. It happens that the knowledge we've gained makes our hosts think they've insulted us. Suppose that runs the other way? Suppose some innocent bit of knowledge about us is a deadly insult to them? Suppose they kill us, and sign up with the Nihilists? We have to be ready to warn our side."

Lucy wanted to protest Joslyn's hypothetical case, but there was too much truth in it. She had lived among these people for months, and still was shocked by what she learned. "A little knowledge," she said, "is a dangerous thing."

Chapter Thirty-One

Aboard G.O.S. Ariadne
In Orbit of the Planet Outpost

"You're certain the signals were authentic?" Gustav asked.

"Absolutely," Cynthia Wu replied. "It was Lucille Calder, and she handed the mike to both Mac and Joslyn Larson. I recognized all three voices."

Gustav allowed himself to close his eyes and breathe a sigh of relief. So far, she was still alive. But there were other considerations. He thought carefully, and stared up at the ceiling. He looked tired, drawn. "Okay. Two reports. One, Cynthia Wu shot trying to escape. Tonight. You vanish now. Two, loss of a ballistic lander two days from now. That's still putting the incidents too close together, but I don't know what else to do. I'll tell them a fusion system malfunction on the lander forced us to cut it loose and dump it into the planet's oceans by remote control before it blew. You stow away in the lander tonight, and don't touch the controls until the remote system is cut off. In the report, I try and distract them from my incompetence by complaining that this is the third fusion malf in two months, and that we were just lucky to get the first two under control. I ignore the fact that the previous complaints were phonies I sent in myself for verisimilitude in case I needed a lander to vanish. I assume your people found the unaccounted-for C^2 generator that wound up in the quartermaster's shop last week? It wasn't easy to arrange."

"Spotted it the day it arrived. The crate's already filled with scrap instead, and we have the C^2 unit hidden. Schiller will smuggle it aboard the lander tonight, and I can wait to do the actual installation once I'm on the planet."

"Good. Any questions?" Still, Gustav stared at the

featureless ceiling. His fingers fussed anxiously with the buttons of his tunic.

"Two. First off, how sure can you be that they won't catch on?"

"They'll be too busy. In a few days time the Guardians launch their counter-offensive. I don't know exactly when. No one in the fleet will have time to investigate a penny-ante engineering malf, and who ever cares about a CI to start with? I hope. And once that battle is over, no matter who wins, this little scheme won't really affect me one way or the other. If the Guards win, and have the leisure to investigate what's been going on around here—they can only shoot me once. If the League wins, I don't know and never have known what happens to me. What was the other question?"

"You want the war ended so it won't expand any more than it has. You want the killing to stop. I understand that. But this—it's not directly related. Why are you doing it? Why are you risking so much for this?"

For the first time, Gustav looked down, and stared straight at Cynthia. "Because," he said, "*she's* down there."

Chapter Thirty-Two

Refiner Camp
The Planet Outpost

Everything was a bit stuck until Pete got stronger. He was the only one of the League group empowered to discuss much of anything with any real authority. He was prepared to discuss technology trades, exchanges of ambassadors (or whatever the local equivalent was), and most importantly, a mutual assistance pact against the Guards and the Nihilists. But it would have to wait—and the flap over the transfusion made the situation that much more delicate.

All the humans were dumbfounded by the way L'awdasi, by all accounts a mere hobbyist in such things, had duplicated human blood overnight, but Charlie Sisulu was hit much harder by it than the rest. He knew better than the others just how complicated blood was. And if one amateur Outposter could do that overnight, what could a team of crack professionals do in a week, given the raw materials of a few human cells to work with? Clone a man? Clone an army of men? If they could make blood, surely they could make diseases, nightmare plagues. And none of them had even *seen* a human before last year. And with such biological power, what could they do to each *other*? With a biological science that powerful, Charlie could almost understand the medical taboo. Better the thousand natural shocks than the unnatural horrors a thousand L'awdasis might accidentally whip up any weekend.

And yet, it didn't quite play. Any element of human medicine could be abused, used to kill, from a scalpel used to slash a throat to an overdose of aspirin. Humankind had had the knowledge to unleash plagues at will for 150 years—but that didn't make anyone want to ban doctors.

Well, no percentage in playing until he understood the game. And Charlie did not yet know enough.

Lucy had mentioned to C'astille that Charlie was a biologist, and C'astille had instantly wanted to talk with him. There were a hundred questions she wanted to ask. Charlie, needless to say, was delighted with the chance himself. So, an hour or two after getting the message safely off to Ariadne, C'astille met the two humans by the entrance of their wagon and the three of them went for a walk. C'astille led them to a quiet corner of the clearing. The two humans sat down on the ground, a bit awkward in their pressure suits. C'astille folded her legs up beneath herself and curled her long tail around her body. Lucy thought the moment proper to offer her gift, the big picture book of Earth and the Solar System. She pulled it out of her carrypack. "Here you go, C'astille," she said. "Take a look at this, and you'll be all set to play tourist when you get there."

C'astille took the book eagerly, and spent a delighted half-hour with the humans, pointing to the pictures and asking Lucy endless questions.

But Charlie could not relax enough to join in. He found it very strange and incongruous to sit back in the grasslands, here on this world, with the sun shining, the sky blue, the area cleared of rapacious animals. To Charlie, Outpost would always be that deadly trek through the forest, and all the planet's other moods mere trickery and misdirection.

It was stranger still to sit with a six-limbed thinking creature nearly the size of a small horse, with a long reptilian tail, and big doll's eyes set in the front of that strange, egg-on-its-side shaped skull, a creature who thought nothing of creating whole human blood from scratch overnight.

He found himself watching her hands most of all. Four long, slender fingers, all opposable to each other. Those were graceful, toolmaker's hands. It was strange to watch their fluid motions that did what human hands did, though Outposter hands did it in a radically different way.

Finally, he got a bit tired of Lucy and the 'Poster oohing and aahing over pictures of Paris and the Outback and the space colonies. "C'astille," he said at last, in as cheerful a tone as he could manage. "We need to get started. I am curious about you and *your* world. You said you wished to ask me questions, and I promise you, I can match you, bafflement for bafflement. Time is short, so perhaps we might begin?"

C'astille nodded and regretfully closed the picture book. "You are right. The lovely pictures must wait until later. You have traveled far, at great risk, and the time might come quickly when we will need knowledge of each other."

"Good!" Charlie replied. "But let me say one more thing. Our peoples are quite strange to each other, and there is much we would know. Some questions might be delicate, but we have no way of knowing which ones. So if I speak rudely, I do not mean to, and I ask that you excuse me. Lucy and I will likewise not take offense, for we know none is meant."

"Thank you!" C'astille said. "I have been hunting the words to say that to you. I am glad you found them for me. And I'll test your promise about taking offense at once," she said with a cheerful tone. "L'awdasi, in the non-incident of this morning, noted something about your genes. Due to their structure, they are far less liable to mutation than our own. That would suggest that your species should look much more like one another than ours does—and yet just the opposite is true."

Charlie smiled thinly. He thought of a lot of people back home on Earth who would say otherwise—"they all look the same to me." Black, yellow, white, whatever, he had heard people of every color say that about people of every other color. "Let me save you some time, C'astille. You're leading up to asking why I in particular look so much more different than the other humans you have seen. Why is my skin so dark, why is my hair curly, why are my nose and lips wider?"

"Yes, I suppose that you're one example. But this Mac

M'Larson must be twice the size of Lucy here, and she and Joslyn have quite different proportions than the rest of you."

Charlie found himself vaguely embarrassed. What could this extra-terrestrial know of racial tension, of guilt and anger for deeds done a hundred, a thousand years before? She asked about variation in a population and he got his back up on the old prejudices. "Hmmm. Well, let me explain my case. Maybe that would help illustrate the others. Forgive me if I simplify a bit, but here is the basic explanation.

"All our people probably started out looking pretty much alike, when they all lived in one place, one climate. But our race, *homo sapiens*, human kind, had settled over pretty much all of our home world, Earth, by about 40,000 years ago, maybe a bit earlier. Some people lived in cold parts that didn't get much sun. Mac's ancestors came from such a place. Light-skinned people can absorb a lot of something in sunlight that humans need to stay healthy, because their skin is transparent enough to let in a large fraction of the light. My ancestors grew up in a warm place with very strong sunlight. Their skin needed to be dark to protect them from getting *too much* light.

"In Mac's part of the world, if your skin was too dark, you were likely to get sick and die from a lack of this special thing in sunlight. So mostly light-skinned people, with genes for light skin, survived to pass on their genes. In my part of the world if you were too light-skinned the sun was so strong it could kill you. So only darker people, with genes for dark skin, survived. People in temperate climates survived best with a skin color somewhere in the middle. Once people had invented civilization, and could control their environments more, it didn't really matter what color you were, so there were no selection pressures for one shade over another and people moved about as they wished. The other differences between us have similar explanations. The people who survived in various spots on the globe and lived to have children were the ones who, by chance, had traits and genes for those traits that gave them a little edge over everyone else. Obviously, they passed their genes on to their children. But in terms of evolution, these differences are trivial. We are all one species, but with each individual still carrying around adaptations to whatever climate his or her ancestors lived in."

The explanation didn't seem to satisfy C'astille altogether. "I see. But while she was with us, Lucy's skin grew darker, and she explained this was a reaction to the sunlight. Suppose that she bore children while she was here and her skin was dark. Wouldn't those children start out darker, inheriting the tendency for darker skin?"

"No, no, of course not. That would be inheritance of acquired traits. Let's see. What would be a clearer example? Okay. There's an animal on Earth called a giraffe. It has a very long neck, perhaps two meters long, and the long neck helps it eat leaves at the tops of trees no other animal can reach.

"Long ago, it used to be thought that some short-necked proto-giraffe managed to stretch its neck through exercise, and passed that slightly longer neck along to its offspring, and the offspring did the same, and so on. The theory had the physical shape of the body affecting the genes, and not the other way around. That's the classic example of inheritance of acquired characteristics, or Lamarckism, after the man who thought of it. But it doesn't work."

C'astille looked straight at Charlie, and pulled her head in toward her body in surprise. "On Outpost, it *does* work," she said, in a strange, querulous voice. "If I cut off my finger, within a month the regulator cells of my body will record the change and implant it in my ovaries. My children, and their children, and theirs, will have a finger missing. Or perhaps they will carry the gene for a missing finger from one generation to the next, until it shows up again, after skipping many generations."

Charlie stared back at her, astonished. Real, honest-to-God Lamarckian biology? It was incredible, but it explained so much. He was tempted to contradict her, to say that it must be a superstition, that she had to be wrong. But these people were *master* biologists. They would *know*. The implications went reeling through his head. It was a revelation of the greatest importance. Lamarckism! It must have shaped their skill in modifying and creating life-forms, been the very core and basis of it. It must have been easy to create a new and different animal with simply surgery. They would have been past masters at bio-engineering before they even invented the microscope and learned to manipulate genes directly.

All of that shot through his mind in a moment. "That's *fantastic*, C'astille," he said. "It's so unexpected, so astonishing I don't know what to say. The implications— My God, they're endless!"

Lucy looked from her human companion to the Outposter and back. There was a strange sense in the air, a feeling of being on the edge of a terrible truth. "Charlie—C'astille. What's the big deal? You both look so shocked. So Outposters and humans evolve in different ways. So what?"

"Lucy," C'astille said, speaking with a cautious precision. "Charlie and I have just stumbled across a fact that explains many of the differences between our peoples. It makes you more different from us than I had ever imagined. We Z'ensam wondered at your lack of skill in shaping life. Now I understand. It must take a dozen generations to shape even the slightest modification of Earth-life. Given the restraint you have worked under, I am amazed that you have learned as much as you have."

Charlie wasn't listening. A thousand new ideas were racing through his head. "Medicine!" he cried out, so wrapped up in his own amazement that he didn't consider the results of what he was saying. "Given Lamarckian biology, the taboo against medicine makes sense! A clumsy doctor's mistake could cripple not just one person, but all the generations unborn. An early experiment, say equivalent to boring a hole in the skull to let evil spirits out, could literally leave scars that would last forever. If the genes were recessive, old artificial genetic flaws, inherited injuries like that, would lie dormant. They could pop up anywhere, anytime, dozens of generations later!"

"They do 'pop up,'" C'astille said grimly. "Down to the present generation, we pay the price for the mischief the body-carvers made thousands of years ago. There are endless folktales of the too-proud fool who promised to 'solve' an illness and left a hideous wreck of a creature behind, one who would pass her deformities down through the genes of all her descendants."

C'astille's powerful tail lashed angrily back and forth through the grass. She seemed suddenly much larger, much fiercer, more alien, more unknowable, than she had a moment before. "Lucy, you must answer a most distasteful question. This Charlie has implied that medicine is *not* taboo among humans. Is this true? Does your kind willingly and shamelessly allow the body-carvers, the animal-healers, to play God with your bodies?"

Lucy was tempted to lie. There was nothing but trouble in an honest answer. But she thought of Pete Gesseti. They had made no effort to hide the bandage Charlie had put on his arm. And short of not treating Pete, of pulling the bandages off, how could they avoid exposing the human use of medicine?

Worse, C'astille counted Lucy as trustworthy, and being *worthy* of trust required that Lucy speak truly when the truth could but hurt her. She spoke at last, and spoke slowly, choosing each word. "There is no taboo against medicine. We call our body-carvers 'doctors' and hold their profession in the highest esteem. In its own way, the skill of our healers is as great as the skill of your bio-engineers. They have eliminated many diseases and causes of death altogether. Our race has benefited greatly from medicine, and for creatures made as we are, there is no cause to ban the practice of healing."

Clearly, to C'astille, it was as if Lucy had claimed there was no harm in being a child molester, or a murderer. "Revulsion is within me," the native said in her own tongue.

"C'astille! Judge not," Lucy said, replying in English.

"My ways are not yours. Your culture and mine were shaped by our biology. I have heard time and time again about frequent, even routine, death by suicide and *murder* among your elderly. No words of this have been spoken between us, for one must not judge what one does not understand. *I* still have no understanding. Yet, among humans, such things would be grave crimes, sins of the darkest kind. Your complaints against the Nihilists are subdued, as if you mildly objected to some of their techniques. To me, they are merciless, amoral killers.

"The early would-be healers among the Z'ensam killed and maimed, and so you banned healing. So be it. Very well. It must be that your clinging to that taboo means your people die of infection and injury and illness, though with your current skill you could save them. But I will not judge.

"*Our* healers save our lives, and our childrens' lives, and do great good. I do not apologize for them, or for us."

C'astille grunted, a deep, guttural, non-committal noise, before she replied. "You say that you do not condone suicide and mercy-killing for those humans near Division, 'elderly' as you say. You call it amoral. What honor, what morality, in letting them go their way to foolishness and idiocy?"

"You make my point for me. Foolishness and idiocy rarely come to an elder human. Some small number, yes. But the risk is small."

"Then humans remain sane after Division, after becoming implanters?" There was shocked surprise in C'astille's voice.

And that was the moment. Lucy opened her mouth to reply, but before she could speak, suddenly she understood. She stared at C'astille. It all fell into place. The cryptic remarks, the Outposter's confusion over pronouns, the obsession with "Division" suddenly made sense. Terrible, nightmare sense. She wished desperately for time to think, but there was none. *This* was the moment. "Charlie, C'astille," she said. "I've just figured it out! C'astille, there is a horrible, ghastly misunderstanding here, and it's all my fault, because all the human understanding of your culture is based on *my* work, my initial translation of your language. And I made a terrible mistake. From the first time I heard the term 'Division' I assumed it was a euphemism, a prettied-up, polite word for 'death.' But that's wrong. It means something else, doesn't it?"

"Death!" C'astille said in amazement. "No! Division is—Division is the revenge Life takes on us for our intelligence. That is what the Nihilists, and all the other similar Groups of the past, have had as a starting point. To them, death is a welcome means of escape from Division. Our studiers of society say that our population has never been large enough to support a city-based culture *because* so many escape into death."

Lucy nodded emphatically. "This is all suddenly making sense in my mind. Let me ask you another question. The English terms 'male' and 'female,' 'man' and 'woman'—what do they mean to you?"

C'astille clenched and unclenched her fingers, the Outposter equivalent of a shrug. "They refer to the two basic body-shapes for humans. You are female, and Charlie is male. That much I understand. But you have always attached great importance to the concepts, and to using the proper pronoun for male and female. I've never quite understood why. Why do your pronouns focus on that minor a difference? Why not a pronoun-set based on height, or eye color? Such would make as much sense."

"Did you ever get the idea that the reason might have something to do with—Jesus, Charlie, me and my bloody Baptist upbringing! I don't think I ever got around to explaining the words 'sex' or 'reproduction.' C'astille, did you ever get the idea 'male' and 'female' might refer to the way humans make more humans?"

"No, not really. Perhaps in the vaguest little way, some slight hint, but I did not wish to ask about such a distasteful thing."

"Ah."

Charlie couldn't contain himself anymore. "Excuse us a

minute, C'astille. I think I just need to have Lucy bring me up to date." He pulled the phono jack from his suit and plugged it into the comm panel on Lucy's suit. Both of them cut their external mikes and radio. "Lucy, what's going on here?" he demanded. "How could they *not* have the concepts of male and female? I got a good look at C'astille and that L'awdasi. They were both obviously female. And I saw some little ones around the camp."

"Charlie. Take a look around at all the Z'ensam when we're back at camp. *All* of them look to be 'obviously female.' Until now I took it to mean that appearances were deceiving, or else they had some sort of divided society. I never figured it out.

"Until now. Shut up and listen. And for God's sake, if you have to talk, be careful what you say." Lucy pulled the connection, and switched her radio back on.

Lucy felt her heart pounding. She knew, somehow she *knew*, that she was at the crux of everything, at the threshold of the central fact of being an Outposter, a Z'ensam. And she also *knew* that there was danger, terrible danger, in the knowledge. "Our apologies, C'astille. Charlie wasn't clear on why I was asking such things," she said in a gentle, quiet voice. "Tell me something. Tell me the life cycle of the Z'ensam. Tell me it as if I knew nothing. Tell me the way you'd explain it to a child."

C'astille stared at Lucy for a long moment. "There is a rhyme for young ones," she said at last. "Well, let me try and recite the sense of it in English for Charlie's benefit.

> First there are babies, to play and learn.
> Then the adults, to bear young, reason, and teach.
> Then the adult is taken by Division in the cocoon's fast womb.
> At last, the implanter, more foolish than any child, is flown from its cocoon, reason having flown long ago.
> Bewitched by the implanter, the adult makes a child, and so the middle link joins end with beginning.

Lucy said "C'astille, I think I understand. But there must

be no mistakes. The time has come when we must risk knowing each other, even if we don't like what we find. Tell me."

"You are right. That poem is so cryptic that I must say more. Especially to aliens. But, please, this is very difficult for me, for any Z'ensam, to speak of. Your medicine is polite conversation by comparison! So—each individual goes through the phases. There is first the child, born to adult. Adult, such as myself. There is no clear line between child and adult. One day it is recognized that a child has learned enough. It was a proud day when I was called C'astille and not O'astille, 'O' being the name-prefix of a child.

"The name prefixes are based on social status, by the way, not biological state. Someday, I will be M'astille, and then perhaps D'astille. I am still young, and there are perhaps thirty of your years before I must face the process of Division, the next biological phase. When Division comes, it takes only a few days. The first sign is a long red welt that forms down the length of the body.

"That is the sign for a Z'ensam to find a safe place. The body—collapses. The skin turns rock-hard to protect against predators. Internally, the body—I do not know a better English word—the body *digests* itself, reforms itself. Only a very small fraction of the body weight emerges from the body-cocoon, as an implanter.

"These implanters, then—when they find an adult who is ready to bear young, they—they *come* to that adult, join with the adult. The implanter places within the adult their seed, which combine with the adult's seed, and grow into children, born some months later. When the implanter comes for you—it is a terrible and debasing experience. It has only happened a few times to me, and as yet I have no children. But, when the implanter comes you are *compelled*, by feelings and sensations strong beyond imagining, to submit and cooperate. Nature would have it so, or else the Z'ensam would be no more. But be it unavoidable, be it beyond our control, be it necessary, we find it shameful to be taken so by the mindless implanters, and mortifying to know we will one day be like them. So we do not fault the Nihilists overmuch for offering escape.

"That is our way. I have gradually realized your way is different. Now you must explain it."

A thousand thoughts flashed through Lucy's mind, and she wished desperately for a chance to talk with Charlie privately. But C'astille was already suspicious; another humans-only chat would make it seem as if they were lying, trying to make up a story.

But no wonder the 'Posters didn't understand the male/female dichotomy. Each 'Poster was first sentient female—"adult"—and later non-sentient male—"implanter"—in turn.

Obviously whether or not you had a mind was more important in defining yourself than what shape your genitals were. The concept of female/male was subsumed completely into the concept of thinking/nonthinking. Lucy knew how careful she would have to be in her answer. "It is quite different. One is born either an immature adult or immature implanter. In either case, one grows up, lives and dies as one or the other. The two kinds come together, as your two kinds do, and the adults bear the children, usually only one at a time."

There was a strange, half envious, half-astonished tone to C'astille's voice when she responded. "You—you adults. You never lose the power of thought? You remain sane and wise all your lives?"

"The vast majority do. But as the body ages and wears out, occasionally the brain, the seat of the mind, wears out as well, and in such cases the mind weakens with the brain. But this is much rarer than it once was." The moment Lucy had finished the last sentence, she wished she had withheld it.

" 'Less often' thanks to your wonderful medicine, no doubt," C'astille said bitterly. She shook her head, a human mannerism she had picked up. "Whatever god formed your kind was kindlier than our creators. My life, my culture, my people, are formed, warped, distorted by the certainty that madness and idiocy will overtake any who do not choose to flee the world by suicide. To have the foreknowledge that I would stay sane . . ."

"C'astille." Charlie spoke, for the first time in a long time. "I would like to ask for something, a favor. It might not be possible for you to do it, or it might be painful or distasteful for you. If so, I will withdraw the request. But I would like to see one of your kind in the implanter phase."

The skin on the Outposter's head wrinkled up in humorless amusement. "Then you have seen them and not known it. Did you not know what they were, Lucy? Did you not wonder why we kept them around? Come, I will show you." Abruptly, she got to her feet and trotted off into the underbrush, forcing the humans to scramble after to keep up. "Let me ask you another two words I never quite learned, Lucy." C'astille stared straight ahead, not looking back at her companions, and there was a brittle sharpness to her voice. "The adult who gave birth to me, what is the English for that? And what would you call the responsible implanter."

Lucy ran to catch up, drew up alongside C'astille's head. In a low, hushed, voice, Lucy said, "Mother. The English is mother. And the implanter who joined with her to form you—that would be your father."

"Ah. I see. Thank you." C'astille slowed her pace slightly. "We'll be there in a few minutes."

Lucy trudged along in her armored pressure-suit cocoon, shielded from the stench and the dangers of Outpost, only the visual beauty of the day able to penetrate to her. She felt tired, ashamed, guilty, appalled. Madness! Madness, idiocy, and the *foreknowledge* of coming madness and idiocy the common lot of *every person*. Nature, Earth's kindly Mother Nature, had shielded her children far better. Could humans have built a culture if their biological heritage had been as cruel as the Z'ensams'? The caravans, the fledgling cities, the tiny population that wouldn't—no, she realized, *couldn't* control the rapacious Hungry Ones. Those were accomplishments to rival anything humans had done, in the face of such a mocking, demeaning life cycle.

C'astille led them into a tiny glade. "They like this place, when we camp here. It is near us, and yet they can play undisturbed. They will be nearby." C'astille raised her head and let out a strange, high-pitched keening.

It took Lucy a second or two to recognize that call. That was the sound they used to call the—

And there they were. Stumblebugs. Wings flapping, coming from all around them, fluttering down to landings in the grass. The laughing, giggling comedians, the silly pets the Z'ensam kept, the pretty, multi-colored, cat-sized flying beasts that Lucy had loved to play with, the cute little things that knew a word or two of O-1. Lucy had even taught a few of them a word or two of English.

She recognized one of them. The most foolish of them all, the one she had named Zipper for the way he flew so fast.

Zipper spotted Lucy, and let out a cheerful squeak. He hopped over to her, swished his tail back and forth, and chirped "Cookie? Cookie?"

In a voice near to breaking, C'astille said, "Lucy M'Calder. Charlie M'Sisulu. Allow me to present Ameser, whom you call Zipper. Allow me to present my father."

"Cookie?"

Lucy tried to speak, but the tears welled up in her eyes, ran down her cheek. Her voice choked up, and she let out a strangled sob. She raised her hands to her face, tried to wipe away the tears, but the helmet stopped her hands. She sobbed uncontrollably.

Charlie felt his bile rising, felt the urge to run home to Earth, to claw his way up the sky to a place where the rules of life were not so brutish. These were civilized people, but their Creator was a barbarian.

"Cookie?"

Slowly, all too slowly, Lucy forced herself to be calm. She tried to think coldly, to analyze. The irony of it! For she could see at once that culture-making, intelligence itself, were lethal mutations here. From the point of view of a reproductive strategy, from the viewpoint of evolution, the transition of each individual from female to male made good sense. The ancestors of the Z'ensam, who had not yet evolved intelligence, must have been served well by the pattern of their lives. It was the females, the mothers, that needed the smarts, the big brains, the brawn, to shelter and protect the children. And child-rearing would be a shared duty in a herd species. The herds, ancestors of the Groups, would have co-operated in raising young. And the males, the flying males, would have been capable of traveling great distances, keeping the gene pool well-mixed in the small, widely dispersed population. They could spread any advantageous mutation rapidly, and also ensure that the species stayed genetically cohesive. And each individual had a double chance to spread her/his genes around.

Only when the females developed true sentience, only when they developed the ability to reason and remember and communicate, would the strategy backfire. A thinking creature would *know* she was the offspring of a mindless animal, fated to mate with an animal, fated to *become* an animal.

How many humans, suffering brain damage or disease, confronted with the prospect of madness, had killed themselves rather than degenerate? And that happened to *all* the Z'ensam!

No wonder it was impossible for them to maintain a stable population. No wonder it was easy to find empty camps, the buildings left by some group of Z'ensam that had just given up . . .

Lucy thought of her own mother, still strong and sturdy, warm-hearted and sharp-witted, if a bit greyed and tired. Senility at worst a faint and far-off danger, was nowadays largely preventable. And her father. Her strong, happy, laughing, clever, kindly father, full of wisdom and understanding when his children needed him.

What would she, Lucy, be like, what bitterness would every human child carry inside, if they knew their fathers were mindless brutes?

"Well, then," C'astille said. She looked down at the pathetic, bewildered Zipper, the little fool wondering why his friends were all so sad. "You have seen my future. A gibbering fool who can be trained, with great effort, to ask for a cookie.

"And this will not happen to you, and that will scar the relations of our species for the rest of time. That saddens me.

"But, I must confess some curiosity. Something I have wondered about, and never dared to ask. But you have seen ours, and turnabout is fair play. You didn't bring them along, of course. But tell me about them. Describe your implanters to me."

Charlie looked sharply at Lucy.

My God, Lucy thought. *My little description of our life-cycle. I left out that males had* minds! *C'astille still thinks Charlie is a female!* Charlie. He caught Lucy's eye, and she nodded. He knew, he understood, he agreed. The truth was going to be bad news, probably disastrous. But they owed C'astille the truth, and lying would only make the inevitable discovery of the truth even worse later on. "We did bring them along," she said. "Our name for an adult is 'female.' Our name for an implanter is 'male.'

"You're talking to one of each."

Chapter Thirty-Three

Aboard *Reunion*,
En Route from Outpost Orbit to Refiner Camp

The ocean waters exploded into a raging cloud of superheated steam and molecules disassociated into component atoms, heated by the lander *Reunion*'s roaring fusion engine. The very air flamed as superheated oxygen and hydrogen cooled enough to recombine, setting a halo of faint-blue fire around the lander. The lander actually *submerged* below sea level before rising again and settling to a steady hover. But the heat of fusion and the pulse of expanding air and steam forced the water back, and the lander stayed dry.

Cynthia Wu was glad for small favors. It had been a hell of a ride. Gustav was trying to convince anyone who watched on radar that *Reunion* was being ditched, crashed into the ocean before she blew. It had been a hard entry. The autopilot had run an unpowered punch through the atmosphere, relying on air drag for braking, not lighting the fusion engines until *Reunion* was a bare five kilometers up—wavetop level for a spacecraft. The flare of the fusion engines and the roaring cloud of steam should look plenty enough like an explosion and impact for anyone watching from orbit.

More importantly, the ion sheath formed by the burning should foul up their radar. Cynthia took the control, checked her location against the last ground-track of the beacon, had the computer spit out a minimum-burn ballistic jump to the beacon, and throttled up the engines.

Reunion pogoed back up into the air, and instantly cut her engines. Nike and Ariadne would both be below the horizon by now, but there was no sense taking chances.

Reunion skittered up through the sky, headed north, then

turned tail, and fell back toward the planet. The beacon signal came back over the horizon, Cynthia tweaked up her course to head for, and rode on it.

It would be good to see Lucy and Mac and Joslyn again. Cynthia had named *Reunion* with this meeting in mind. She could hardly wait. She kicked in the chemical landing rockets and looked for a place to put her down.

Reunion landed without incident about five kilometers from the Refiner site. Cynthia was still buttoning up the craft when the line of pressure-suited figures came into sight of the external cameras. There was Mac, all right, gigantic in his pressure suit. And Joslyn! After God knows how long without seeing them, they still looked the same. Cynthia smiled and laughed out loud with the sheer joy of seeing people from home.

But something was wrong out there. She could see it in their tense, nervous movements. She hurried through the airlock and down the ladder to the ground. Mac crossed the ground scorched by the lander engines and hurried over to her.

"Cynthia. Damn, are we glad you're here," he said.

"Oh, Mac. It's good to see you." She looked at him, his face half-hidden behind the faceplate. And she inhaled sharply. She saw something she had never seen before. Mac was *scared*.

"Cynthia, let's get aboard and make sure that lander is cranked up and ready to go when we need her. We're going to camp aboard her instead of with the Refiners. Things have gone very wrong. Not just for us here. The Refiners might not help us against the Guards and Nihilists. Lucy is scared they might *help* the Nihilists get rid of us. We might have to get out of here fast, carrying a warning."

G.O.S. Ariadne
In Orbit of the Planet Outpost

Commander Richard Sprunt, commander of Nike Station's radar room, opened the door to Gustav's office and walked in without knocking or announcement. "You have some explaining to do, Gustav. And you'd better do it now."

Gustav calmly signed his name, put down his pen, tossed the paperwork into his out box, and leaned back in his chair. "Have a seat, Commander."

Sprunt pulled off his hat and sat down heavily. He was a pale-faced, sandy-haired man, medium height, with angry pale grey eyes and sharp, abrupt mannerisms. "Twice now, Lieutenant Gustav, CIs have vanished from this station, and twice landers have been lost. The official reports from this station say the CIs are dead and the landers crashed. Once I could buy, but not twice. Escapes, Gustav. Those were escapes. I saw both of them go down personally on Nike's radar, and the visual evidence could go either way—*if* it had happened once. Not twice. I'm here to do you a favor. I'm using a perfectly good three-day pass to come over from Nike to tell you, man-to-man, quietly, that you can't go covering up escapes. I knew your father, and he was a good officer. You owe it to him to straighten up, fly right, investigate these incidents properly, and take your lumps like a man."

"I've been expecting you, Commander Sprunt, though I admit it's a bonus that you came on liberty. Obviously, you haven't filed a report, and no one will have to know where you were for three days."

"WHAT? Just what the hell are you saying?" Sprunt roared, his eyes almost popping out of his head.

"Your crew must be pretty good, I admit that," Gustav said. "But not great. They missed the first lander launching toward the barycenter a week or two ago. And they missed the covert glider/lander that went in a few days ago. And they never had wit enough to do a frequency sweep-check and spot the Refiner's beacon. Of course, the Outposters use radio all the time. Maybe they thought that was just one of the Refiner's normal signals, so I can't really fault them there. But my CIs didn't miss anything, not even the covert. Schiller nailed that, just barely. A very tough target. I can't blame you for missing that one either."

"Gustav, you bloody traitor—" Sprunt rose half out of his chair at Gustav, and froze. A laser pistol had appeared in Gustav's hand, pointed right at Sprunt's chest.

"Sit down again, Commander. Let me tell you a version of the truth. You know I'm ex-Intelligence. Suppose I told you that I was working desperately, taking enormous risks, playing the most daring games with the enemy, to prevent what I believe is a possible attack on Capital that could wipe out our nation?"

"I'd say that you were a bloody traitor with paranoid delusions of grandeur," Sprunt said.

Gustav realized his visitor was angry, not scared. Give Sprunt that credit. "In a few days' time, Commander, I doubt it will matter very much what you think. But right now it might matter, and in blindly doing what I grant is your duty, you could doom millions. So I will put you under extremely quiet arrest. I think I might lie to the computer and put you on a flight down to the Contact Camp, a tourist going to see the aliens. There are already one or two cases of men wandering off into the woodlands and vanishing. Sometimes the searchers find the torn-up remains of pressure suits. The native life is vicious. I grant you that would be a dangerous game, too. But know that I am prepared to kill you and cover it up as best I can if you force me to it.

"But I'll make you a promise. If I fail in what I'm trying to do, I'll hand you this gun and surrender to you. Let you take me to justice, arrange a court-martial.

"But if I fail, I doubt you or I or any other human in this star system will survive long enough for a court-martial to convene in the first place."

Chapter Thirty-Four

Guardian Contact Camp
The Planet Outpost

Captain Lewis Romero was scared to death. With the distinct and uncomfortable feeling of entering a trap, Romero walked up the broad gangplank to board *Starsight*, the intersystem ship the Guards had given to the Nihilists.

D'etallis clumped solidly up the ramp behind him, followed by the Outposter pilot and co-pilot, L'anijmeb and L'etmlich.

Starsight had been up and down into orbit a few times, shakedown cruises. The last two flights had been made solo by the Outposter pilots. But this was the first trip that would actually take the ship anywhere. D'etallis had requested a chance to visit Capital, and the response had been a warm and eager invitation from Jules Jacquet himself. For the sake of wartime security, the flight itself would be a closely held secret, but once on Capital, the Outposters were sure to be a grand center of attention. The Central Guardians were understandably curious to get a look at their new allies—and Romero had been ordered to accompany them. Career-wise, it was a splendid moment for Romero, but this was one honor he would have been willing to forego. He had no faith in the Outposter pilots, no faith that the *Starsight* could stay out of trouble in the midst of interstellar war.

Romero had wit enough about him to read the reports and figure out what was up. Odds were a major battle would shape up while the Nihilists were away from home. Supposedly, the *Starsight* and those aboard would never know. The ship's course was laid in by Guard astrogators under orders to keep their guests the hell away from the war zone. *Starsight*'s detection and communications equipment were deliberately not very powerful, and the odds against accidentally blundering into some patrol ship in the vastness of space were nil. Especially since the course laid in for *Starsight* arced far out of the plane of mutual orbit for the two stars. She would never get within five hundred million kilometers of the barycenter. There was enough natural debris and sky junk in the vicinity of the baryworld that such precautions would have been prudent even if the enemy fleet hadn't been anywhere near the place.

But flying through a war wasn't smart. Lewis Romero could understand putting the best face on things for the Nihilists, but he knew there was trouble in the future.

What he didn't know was that the *Starsight* was carrying it.

D'etallis genuinely enjoyed the bustle and fuss of getting strapped in and ready for a voyage into space. And she was genuinely looking forward to the great adventure of travel on the longest Road any Z'ensam had ever traveled. It would be a leisurely journey of some days, and there would be great delight in seeing the stars, in seeing Outpost from space. But this was no pleasure trip.

Romero would have fainted dead away if he had realized just how much the Nihilists knew about the military situation. The Nihilists' radio gear was good, as was their skill at opening burn bags, examining the contents, and resealing the bags before anyone noticed. D'etallis knew what was going on in space, and knew that a time of turmoil, with the Guards occupied elsewhere, was the time to strike.

Starsight might have been headed for Capital at the Guards' bidding, but the Nihilists had their own plans upon arrival. Once she was there, once she had landed, D'etallis would take a Guardian-provided mortar from the hold, set it up on the landing field, and fire the specially modified rounds. The rounds were set to fire straight up and explode in midair, releasing an air-borne plague. Within days, every human on Capital would be dead. The Nihilists' plague was deadly to humans, and not to Z'ensam—several of the Guards thought to have wandered off from Contact Base had actually been kidnapped by the Nihilists and exposed to the plague virus. They had died quickly and nastily—and the corpses proved to be highly contagious. With the humans of Capital dead, *Starsight* would begin shuttling back and forth between Capital and Outpost, bringing in more Nihilists, the heirs of the Guardians' industrial base. There would be much to learn there.

In a stroke, the Nihilists would have shipyards, the plans for the human stardrive, star charts that could lead them to the other human worlds.

Within the year there would be many other emptied worlds, full of gleaming machines and vast stores of knowledge, waiting for their Nihilist inheritors.

The Z'ensam radio did not offer anything like a news service; the closest thing to reporting of events was what amounted to the neighbors gossiping over the back fence—one radio operator chatting with unseen friends in other Groups. But that sufficed; word traveled.

The launch of *Starsight* was a secret among humans but to the Z'ensam it was a most public event, and the Nihilists made no secret of it—though they made no mention of the real purpose of the mission, either. They announced it and described it as an embassy mission.

That didn't fool C'astille. She heard the news as she came out of the Guidance's house. The Guidance and all the leadership had, of course, been appalled by the news that humans had committed so grave an insult as to send implanters, "males," to negotiate. The adult, "female" humans were the ones to blame, of course. That was too repellent to think about. No one was to have any further contact with the humans. Shun them, ignore them, allow them to leave, be done with them.

But *Starsight*. C'astille knew the Nihilists well, knew their plans and schemes, and how what they did compared to what they said. She *knew*, instantly, that the *Starsight* was intent on a bio-attack. And she knew how hopelessly unprepared the humans, Guards or League, would be to defend against that.

The humans. Lucy had seemed a *friend*, and C'astille felt dirtied by the thoughtless, unmeant betrayal. Medicine. Supposedly "intelligent" implanters. Treating implanters as equals, and tricking all the Z'ensam into doing the same.

Disgusting, half-formed creatures, with their shameless ways, their perversities unpunished. C'astille knew, somehow, that it was no trick of hormones, no sublimation of conscious will, that forced the human females to mate with the males. They would go to it willingly, perhaps even eagerly, rutting like filthy, mindless beasts.

To hear the humans say it, their kind was never dragged down to the level of animals. But C'astille knew better. The humans never, once in their life-cycle, rose *above* the animals.

She wished the Nihilists and *Starsight* well.

Let the humans die. All of them.

Chapter Thirty-Five

RKS *Eagle*
The Barycenter
Nova Sol System

The first thing Chief Petty Officer Nguyen Chi Prihn noticed was the slight wear on the status panel's hold-down screws; the Phillips-heads were slightly chewed up. Someone had overtightened the screws, or perhaps used the wrong sized screwdriver. In any event, the screws were damaged, and *that* was something to bear down on the maintenance techs about. It was just the sort of minor sloppiness that could lead to disaster. If those screwheads got much more chewed up, it might suddenly get very difficult to unscrew the screws to lift that panel and repair the innards in a hurry, in the midst of battle. And that panel reported on flight status of some very important birds. If the status panel went out, it could incapacitate the whole port side launch ops bay.

Who had done the last work on this panel? He or she needed a good bawling out. Prihn signed on to a computer terminal and pulled up the maintenance log for the status panel. He studied it for a moment, then let out a string of curses that could be traced right back to old Saigon. He, Prihn, was listed as the last person to work on that panel, over a thousand hours ago. And Prihn would bet his life that those screws hadn't been damaged two days ago.

Someone was going to be lucky to be alive after Prihn got through with him. Doing repairs without logging them! But wait a second. Prihn knew his spacers well. All of them knew, and believed, that lives, the fortunes of battle, the tide of history itself, could easily depend on how well they did their work. Overtightening a screw was one thing, that might happen accidentally, but none of his kids would play around with logging procedure. Writing up a careful description of what they had done was second nature to all of them. They knew that not to was one of the quickest shortcuts to catastrophic failure. Prihn chewed on his finger for a moment, then ran a beefy hand over his perfectly combed, well-brilliantined head of hair. Something was seriously wrong here.

He pulled a toolkit out of the cabinet, grabbed a screwdriver, and opened up the panel. And there was no string of curses suitable for what he saw.

Someone had rewired the panel-lights to give phony readings. Sabotage. Clear cut, unmistakable sabotage. It took him a moment to trace the reworked wiring. The telltale lights on the number three Rapid-Deployment Docking Port had been shorted out so as to show green on all counts no matter what the real situation was. *Covert Lander Two* was supposed to be hanging there.

The external cameras. One after another, he punched up the cams that should have shown RDDP-3. All of them were dead. He switched in the intercom. "Comm room, this is CPO Prihn at port side launch control. Emergency Priority. Request any ships at close station-keeping distance with *Eagle* to feed us a visual of our hull in the area of the port side Rapid Deployment Docking Ports. Pipe the feed to me."

"Stand by, Port Side Launch. One moment. We have a feed from *Bismarck*."

The video screen came to life, showing nothing but space. Then the camera panned over and locked in on the huge cylinder that was *Eagle*, dimly lit by the distant suns. Then *Bismarck* powered up her searchlights, and the big ship seemed to shine against the darkness of space, proud and stately in her rotation about her long axis. *Bismarck*'s camera zoomed in toward the RDDP ports, but they slipped out of view with *Eagle*'s spin before Prihn could get a good look. The camera pitched up slightly to catch the docking ports as they came about again. There should have been four Covert landers docked to the external hull.

There were only three.

Prihn swore again, and felt a cold knot of fear and anxiety twisting together in his stomach. "Comm. Prihn again. Emergency Priority. Get me the Captain. We've got trouble."

Zeus Orbital Command Station,
Orbiting the planet Capital

The radio signal came out of nowhere. Long-range interferometry placed the source very close, only thirty thousand kilometers away, but radar hadn't and still couldn't detect anything. The radio source, whatever it was, was requesting permission to rendezvous and dock with *Zeus* Station, but the commodore would have none of that. He didn't want any ship that radar couldn't see getting too near his command. It could be a sneak-attack, a trick bomb. He deployed a squad of fighters and ordered them to home in on the radio signal, pick up any crew or passengers, and then leave the ship, or whatever it was, in a stable orbit far from any Guardian installation.

Not only *Zeus*, but the entire ring of bases and ships around Capital went on alert. There might be more of these invisible ships out there.

The fighters made the personnel pick-up without incident, reporting that there was only one person aboard the strange ship. The fighters hurried home, and their passenger was taken aboard *Zeus* and hustled straight into the Intelligence section. Captain Phillips himself decided to interrogate this one. There was only one place that ship could have come from. And to get a voluntary defection, flying such an advanced ship—it could be the sort of intelligence bonanza that changed the course of a war. Captain Phillips took a look at his visitor—tired, frightened, worried. He decided this one required gentle handling.

"All right, son," he said. "You gave us a quite a start there for a moment, but now here you are. Who are you, and why did you come here?"

"I came to warn you of the Nihilists' plans," the visitor said. "They'll betray you. They're going to launch a plague attack that could wipe out every person on Capital. My name is George Prigot, and I'm a native of Capital."

After a four-hour interrogation, Phillips was forced to conclude that he had a credible witness. A check with Central Military Records matched this fellow's fingerprints and retinal patterns with one George Prigot, listed as Missing and Presumed Dead on New Finland. And this Prigot knew too many things, his story fit together too well.

"You realize, Mr. Prigot, that by coming here you place yourself in grave danger. Whatever your reasons for coming here, by your own admission you are a deserter from the Guardian Army, and by your own admission, you have repeatedly committed acts of high treason against Capital. When your case is brought before the proper authorities, the only question left open to debate would be whether to shoot you as a spy or hang you as a traitor."

"I realize all that, sir," George said, his voice steady, only his eyes betraying his agitation. "But whatever my feelings about the government of Capital, I couldn't just sit back and allow the Nihilists to wipe out every human being on the planet. I decided I couldn't live with myself if I didn't try to stop them."

"And you are convinced that the Nihilists mean to turn on us?"

"Yes sir."

"But your only reason for so thinking is the report of this Calder woman, who in turned based her conclusions on what one single Outposter, a member of a Group that opposes the Nihilists, had to say."

"Sir. I don't have to tell you that the truth isn't determined by majority rule. The truth is just as true if *no one* believes it. And that's *not* my only reason for distrusting the Nihilists. I saw the tapes of what their foam worms did to the *Impervious*. Whoever invented *those* had no love for humanity. And why should they care about us? Their philosophy says intelligent life is an abomination. Alien intelligent life must be a double abomination. They kill their own kind. Why not us, too? And if they wipe us out, they get Capital. A whole world, and all our technology. Think of all the power that would represent, and tell me that wouldn't tempt them.

"Hang me as a traitor if you like, but listen to me first. *Stop the Nihilists*, before it's too late."

It was not until this George Prigot character had been led off to a fairly comfortable cell, not until Captain Phillips had befouled the station's air conditioning system with two pipefuls of the most hideously expensive and malodorous out-system tobacco, not until Phillips had sat there in thought for a solid hour, that the intelligence chief came to the conclusion that he believed Prigot. Not only that Prigot was telling a story and voicing a warning that he, Prigot, thought was honest. Phillips decided that the story and the warning themselves were legitimate. The Nihilists *were* going to attack Capital. He had never really trusted them in the first place. The bioweapons deal had been too rushed, too rashly and hurriedly considered.

But Mr. George Prigot, late of both the Britannic and the Guardian armed forces, had sent other messages by coming here, though such had not been his intention.

With Prigot flown the coop, the League forces would be forced to assume that all their plans had been exposed, all their schemes revealed, all their traps turned around. That meant they would be forced to change their plans. And that meant the enemy would lose time, would be somewhat more vulnerable for a while.

Even though he had not brought a scrap of tactical planning material with him, Prigot, by his very presence, had wrecked all the League's schemes and forced them to start over. Captain Phillips could see the advantages in that—great but fleeting advantages. He powered up his terminal, and rattled off a priority preliminary assessment to flag HQ.

But there was another point, a more private one. Prigot had never mentioned the name, never mentioned any Guardian Navy officer involved in the plans that had gotten Calder to the League fleet. But there had to have been one. Phillips *knew* that. Johnson Gustav, Phillips' former aide in Naval Intelligence, was assigned to Ariadne station. Gustav had dealt with Calder; Phillips had seen action summaries written by Gustav that mentioned her by name.

The connections were tenuous enough, but Phillips knew Gustav, knew what he would do in a given situation. And Phillips had read the report that Gustav had written so long ago. The one that had flatly stated that Capital would lose the war, suffering greater and greater loss of life and political freedom the longer the war was allowed to drag on. The report that had cost Gustav a step in rank, gotten him thrown out of the Intelligence service, and nearly gotten him shot.

Yes, Gustav's fingerprints were all over the place. He was mixed up in this scheme.

There was only one last important fact that Phillips had kept secret from everyone until now. But now, at last, it was time to act. For the fact was, Phillips had agreed with every word of that report.

It was time to contact Gustav, privately, over a secure channel. Phillips had a lot to talk about with him.

Chapter Thirty-Six

Captain's Cabin,
RKS *Eagle*
The Barycenter
Nova Sol System

Captain Robinson poured himself another cup of coffee and shoved his untouched and now-cold breakfast away. Hot, black, strong coffee—his morning repast was down to that. He was losing weight, he knew that without getting on a scale. He always stopped eating properly when he was nervous, on edge. Tension made his appetite vanish. Robinson had never been more tense and on edge than he was now.

He thought of his wife, Mildred, back home on Kennedy, and knew how she would worry if she saw him now. She knew the danger signs, the tiny twitches and microscopically small nervous gestures that warned things were not good.

And they weren't. For the first time, Robinson was seriously entertaining the thought that he might not get home to Mildred. He raised the cup to his mouth, sipped at the coffee, and burned his tongue. Too hot.

Prigot. Prigot was the last damn straw. They had mustered the ship's complement the moment *Covert Lander Two* turned up missing, of course. Prigot was the only person unaccounted for. The bloody twice-told traitor. He was competent enough to crack into any data file aboard and make a copy. It had to be assumed the Guards knew exactly where every ship had been—and so all of them had to be moved, or else be sitting ducks. Every plan, every disposition of forces had to be thrown out and reworked, and that was a crippling blow; the League forces were forced into their second-best plans. Time, energy, and fuel chewed up.

Well, maybe not *time* lost due to Prigot. They had been wasting that right along without any help from traitors. The League forces had simply been sitting astride the barycenter for weeks now, not attacking, not being attacked. Admiral Thomas seemed quite content to wait the Guards out. He did nothing all day, every day, but putter around the Bridge, watching this report, talking to that ship's captain. The only thing Thomas really seemed interested in was the exploratory team going over the lump of rock called the baryworld. Robinson couldn't see any great value to a roughly spherical lump of skyrock barely 100 kilometers across. Certainly nothing to merit such close attention from the Commander-in-Chief. He vanished into his stateroom each night, and early each morning the mess steward brought out an empty bottle of port. Hours later the admiral himself would emerge, looking very bright and chipper, his skin flushed, a twinkle in his eye. He *had* to be constantly drunk, putting away that much booze day after day. But it never showed. He was always sharp, always alert, always in control. But Robinson knew about drinkers and false fronts. Sooner or later the facade would crack, unless something was done.

His great-niece, Joslyn Larson, she seemed to have some effect on him, some ability to keep him from drinking. But she was on Outpost, chatting with the natives. There wasn't even any real way to know that the League's tiny, improvised First Contact crew was still alive. With Guard stations and spacecraft orbiting Outpost, reporting via radio would have been suicide. No, dealing with the company of the *Sick Moose* would have to wait upon the outcome of battle.

There might be some way to contact Ariadne station and Johnson Gustav, but to what point? What could they say to each other that would be worth the risk of communicating?

Robinson's coffee had gotten cold as he sat there, worrying. He drank it down anyway, throwing his head back and downing it in one swallow. He winced at the taste and his stomach kicked up a fuss, but it was time to go to work.

Guardian Orbital Command Station *Zeus*
Orbiting the Planet Capital

George Prigot wasn't sure about why he had been brought into the Intelligence section again, but he didn't like being there. He was brought from his cell straight to Phillips' office.

"Prigot," Captain Phillips said. "I thought you'd like to know. Thanks to your arrival, our attack on the barycenter was brought forward by fifty hours. The first craft are already launching. If we move quickly, we should catch the League while it's still repositioning its forces, while their ships are at their most vulnerable. The change in plans should allow us to do a great deal of damage."

"But why are they repositioning their forces? What's that got to do with me?"

"Didn't you work that out when you risked this trip of yours? The League will be forced to assume you betrayed every bit of information you had access to. Every battle plan. Any other assumption on their part would be risking suicide."

"But I didn't betray any League battle plans. I never *knew* them!"

"But they are forced to assume otherwise. Didn't you realize that? Tell me, Prigot, having betrayed both of them, which side *do* you want to win?"

But George Prigot was too stunned to answer.

RKS *Eagle*
The Barycenter

"Jesus H. Christ! Bridge, this is Detection! Bogie contacts all of a sudden, all over the place! Repeat, many contacts, presumed bandits and closing fast! Bridge, do you copy?"

"Captain here, on the bridge," Robinson said. "We've got 'em on the repeater here, too, son. Don't go shouting and bouncing off walls. Get us numbers and vectors."

"Ah, yessir. Still more blips coming in—tactical plot shows they're all popping out of C^2 on trajectories that track back to Capital—

"Oh, my God. A whole new family of 'em—at least fifty *more* targets, with track-back at Outpost."

"Damn good break-out pattern," Robinson said. His voice was calm, but his stomach was suddenly twisted into a monstrous knot. "Comm, call battle stations and relay all our information to the fleet. Then call the admiral and inform him that we are under attack."

Klaxons hooted, the usual murmur of background noise on the Bridge grew louder as relief crews and specialists rushed in from their quarters. Normally, only a third of the consoles were occupied. Within four minutes, they all were. Within five minutes, every combat station had reported in.

Except one. Robinson shouted out without turning his head. "Comm! Where the hell is Admiral Thomas?"

"No answer in his cabin, sir. It might be a intercom malfunction. I've dispatched a runner already."

"Thank you, Ensign." They both knew damn well it wasn't the intercom. Robinson was ready to bet that the admiral was passed-out dead drunk.

Comm Technician Third Class Carl Lieber was already pounding at the admiral's door by that time. He cursed as the spin-down alert was called, and the *Eagle* abruptly cut her rotation with her attitude jets. Lieber could do nothing but hold on to a stanchion for 45 long seconds—during which time the admiral still hadn't responded. Lieber hesitated only a moment longer before he pulled out the passkey he had been carrying for a week now. Commander Whitehead, the head of the Comm section, had given it to him after the rumors of the Old Man's drinking had gotten as far as the Comm department. Whitehead wanted to make sure that no drunk could lock a door and keep his men from their duties. Lieber used the key and entered the cabin.

Admiral Sir George Wilfred Thomas was peacefully asleep, drifting in mid-air over the bed.

Lieber tried shouting, but Thomas slept on. Lieber shoved himself off the deck and grabbed Thomas by the shoulder.

He gave the older man a good shaking, but nothing came of it. Lieber could smell the port on the admiral's breath. The spacer knew the next thing to try in waking a drunk, and decided this was enough of an emergency to risk it. Mentally kissing his rating and career goodbye, he towed Thomas into the head, shoved him into the shower, and twisted the nozzle over to *cold*.

Thomas awoke, spluttering, infuriated, and woozy. "What—what the devil is the meaning of this? Who the hell are you?"

"Sir. Spacer Lieber. The Guards have launched their attack on us, and you're wanted at the Task Force Command Center."

Thomas stopped his spluttering on the instant and reached to shut off the shower. Suddenly he looked more alert than he had for a long time. "The devil you say! Finally decided that they'd kept me waiting long enough, I suppose. Well, get out of my way and let an old man get dressed."

Thomas launched himself from the shower and made his way into his stateroom, leaving a trail of water blobs quivering in the air behind him. He peeled off his soaking-wet pajamas, and Spacer Lieber found himself in the presence of a naked—and rather scrawny looking—admiral. Thomas tossed his pajamas aside and they splattered flat against the overhead. He quickly ran a towel over his body, then pulled undershorts and socks out of a bureau, an undress uniform out of the closet, and was dressed in seconds. He bounced back into the head for a moment, shaved quickly, returned, jammed his hat down on his head to keep it on securely in zero-gee, and left Lieber behind in the stateroom completely forgotten, as he headed for the Task Force Command Center.

The combat staff was already in place, pulling in data from the *Eagle*'s sensors and from other ships. None of the TFCC crew so much as looked up as he arrived. Good enough. Pomp and circumstance could wait until they had all lived through this.

"This is TFCC Comm to Bridge. Admiral Thomas has arrived."

Thomas caught his comm officer's eye and gestured for a direct patch through to the *Eagle*'s bridge. "Good morning, Captain. This is where you and I earn our pay. What can you say about their disposition of forces?"

"Well sir, it's a pretty classic enfolding maneuver, in fact so far it's a lot—"

"A lot like the one we performed against them," Thomas agreed cheerfully. "You are quite right. I have been hoping against hope that they'd come after us. The half-built barycenter defenses were tough enough. I wouldn't want to try cracking through their completed missile screens around Outpost and Capital. Now they've saved us the trouble."

"An optimistic viewpoint, Admiral."

"True, Captain. But I believe you will see it borne out. Task Force Command Center out." Thomas turned and studied his screens, feeling good, feeling useful. Yes, an enfolding attack, from both sides. And that after the slow, cautious shifting of forces that was supposed to look like preparations for an assault from Capital alone.

Either the whole force-shifting had been a feint all along, or else this Prigot person's defection had led the Guards to shift their plans. It didn't matter. None of it mattered. Thomas' plan, the real plan, had been kept too close a secret to be endangered by anything Prigot could have known.

Thomas smiled to himself and busily worked through all the reports and data coming at him. There was a fear underlying his chipper enthusiasm, and he knew it. Now was not the time to analyze it, or acknowledge it, but there it was, the same old fear that had dogged him—and overwhelmed him—so often throughout his life. Not fear of death. He was an old man, quite pleased that he was still alive, but having long since accepted his own mortality.

No, he feared failure, disaster. Fear of finding out that the bottle had stolen his soul, his ability to think and feel, even as it deadened his capacity for fear, his loneliness and frustration at the endless waiting. He had told himself that work, and battle, and necessity would conquer the bottle when the time came. Now he would find out.

"Comm, order the fleet to prepare a phased fighting withdrawal away from the Capital fleet bringing us toward the Outpost fleet. All personnel off the baryworld *now*, and I want all League ships at least one million kilometers away from the baryworld, headed toward the Outpost fleet. Only once pull-back has *commenced*, drop anti-radar chaff and begin radar jamming. I want them to know we're moving, but not to where."

Aboard GSS *Adversary*, the Guardian Fleet Flagship
The Barycenter

Admiral Bernard Strickland, Guardian Navy, was pleased by the performance of his ships and men. The breakout into the space around the barycenter had been performed with impressive skill and precision. It had taken endless maneuvering, constant stops and starts of the engines for every ship in the fleet, in order to jockey everyone into position.

But they had come in on the League at exceedingly close range. The baryworld was a rather small lump of rock and there was no other large mass in the area to speak of—the two Guardian fleets had been able to drop back into normal space almost right on top of the League forces. The lead ships of the Capital fleet would be within range of the enemy in minutes. The Outpost fleet, which was flying practically as an autonomous unit, was smaller and moving not quite as crisply, but they'd pass muster. So far all was going well. No cat-and-mouse sneak attack as at Britannica this time—the Guard forces were staging an all-out frontal attack from two directions at once.

The League ships were maneuvering, pulling back away from the baryworld. Suddenly his tactical display scrambled, blanked out, and restarted, showing only empty space. For a wild half-second, Strickland thought the entire League force had entered C^2 space *en masse*. But no, that was ridiculous. The tactical display started to show a few League ships again, very faintly. Obviously they were using some sort of jamming equipment to cover their pullback. "Tactics officer! Clear the real-time display and give me projections based on tracks up until jamming commenced. Detection. Punch through that jamming somehow! Weapons! How long until we are in effective range?"

"Allowing for our best guess at enemy maneuvers, they'll be within engagement range of the Outpost fleet in twenty minutes, sir."

"So they take their first crack at the smaller fleet. Very well. Let's see how they do," Strickland said.

TFCC, RKS *Eagle*

Admiral Thomas watched his screens intently. In the vastness of space, even the high-speed maneuvers of the two fleets seemed to move in slow motion. But slowly, gradually, the League fleet was pulling away from the baryworld. Left behind on its surface was a collection of sophisticated sensing equipment, even now relaying information to the Task Force Command Center. The baryworld sensors would be destroyed in hours, but by then they would have done their job. But now it was time to look forward instead of back. Their retreat from the Capital fleet was moving them straight for the smaller Outpost fleet. "Comm, give me all-ships relay."

"You have the relay, Admiral."

"This is Admiral Sir George Wilfred Thomas to all ships. All ships without specialized assignments are to attack the smaller enemy fleet coming from Outpost." There *was* only one ship with a "specialized" assignment—*Sapper*—but never mind that now. "Their ships and ours should be in range of each other's weapons in a few minutes. Should your ship be hit by any sort of missile, I need hardly emphasize the need for the strictest decontamination procedures. We must assume that any and all Guard weapons include a biological component. I want a moving attack, not a stationary defense. I want to pass *through* their fleet. Good luck."

The two fleets moved toward each other at a pace that was almost leisurely by the standards of modern spaceflight. Thomas watched his screens intently. This was it, the make-or-break moment.

"Admiral, Captain Robinson wishes to speak with you," the comm officer said.

"Thank you, I'll take it on the private channel." It was just about time for Robinson to get a little nervous. Thomas couldn't blame him for that—if he was as much in the dark as the master of the *Eagle* was, he'd be a little on edge, too. Especially since he was dealing with an alcoholic Commander-in-Chief. . . .

Thomas slipped on a headset and punched up the private channel. "Yes, Captain."

"Admiral, with all due respect, you're aware that by passing *through* the Outpost fleet, you're leaving nothing between them and the Capital fleet. The two of them can form up into a larger combined force."

"I am aware of that, Captain. That is in fact my intention in ordering the maneuver."

"Sir? Could you elaborate?"

"Captain, I *am* sorry, but no. We have had a very serious breach of security already. That Prigot might have put some sort of tap on our internal communications. I may have said too much already. But I assure you that the situation is under control. Thomas out." *At least I bloody well hope the situation is under control,* Sir George thought. If Bannister worked as advertised, all would be well. A quick drink would have gone down very well just then, but Sir George shook his head to clear his mind of *that* idea, and concentrated on the evolution of the battle.

The League and Outpost fleets drifted into each other, pretty colors on the screen. A dot of League-green light labeled *Bismarck* took the first hit, flared into incandescence and nothingness. But a pair of fast frigates revenged *Bismarck*, their lasers tearing open her killer's hull from stem to stern. Thomas gripped the armrests of his crash couch hard, and tried to think of dots of light and not ruined young bodies.

Elsewhere aboard the *Eagle*, Captain Robinson sweated the battle far more personally as the flagship went into harm's way. This was his ship, the lives aboard were in his care, and he was following the orders of a man he no longer had faith in. At least his fighters were staying close to home, assigned to protecting the flag rather than forward attack. After what one torpedo full of foamworm eggs had done to *Britannica*, no one wanted to risk a capital ship in the fore of the action. If the *Eagle* hadn't been the only operational combatant large enough to carry a planning staff, a full tactical system, bio specialists, a clutch of diplomats and so on, she would have stayed behind in orbit of Kennedy. At the moment, that sounded just fine to Josiah Robinson.

A Guard destroyer got entirely too close to the *Eagle*, barely a thousand kilometers away, and let off a salvo of torps. The fighters got all the torps, but the enemy ship got away. Robinson considered dispatching a flight of fighters after her, but instead he let her go. *Eagle* was to defend herself, nothing more. No grand attacks. The most powerful ship in either fleet, and they didn't dare risk her.

Score one for Mac Larson.

Chapter Thirty-Seven

Barycenter Battle Zone

Both the Guards and the Nihilists had improved their deployment techniques for the bioweapons since Britannica. The Nihilists had developed ways to deliver adult animals instead of eggs, and techniques to hold the beasts in a species of suspended animation using a special gas mixture. The Guards had abandoned torpedoes that crashed through hulls and opened compartments to vacuum. Now they used limpet mines that attached themselves to the hull and carefully bored a hole through it. A torpedo could carry a stack of six limpets, and release them when it got close enough to the target ship. The limpets would slap themselves onto the ship, the hull-borers would do their jobs, the bioweapons would be awakened by the fresh air aboard the ship, climb, slither, or crawl aboard, and go to their deadly work.

And there were new types of bios, each of which could wreck a ship in its own way.

The USS *Benjamin Franklin* was killed by a swarm of beetle-like things the size of a man's thumb. Each beetle, as it crawled, excreted a chain-molecule monofilament thread too thin to be seen by the unaided eye, a thread capable of slicing through virtually anything without resistance. The beetle dragged the thread behind itself. The tail end of the thread was adhesive, and stuck firmly to the first spot of hull the beetle landed on. Two limpets successfully attached to *Franklin*, one amidships and one near the engine compartment. The limpets cut their holes through the hull and the slice-beetles wandered off. Almost immediately, one of them sliced through a hydrogen feed line, and the explosive gas was injected into the cabin air mixture. Fifteen minutes later, another beetle caused a spark as its thread cut a high-voltage cable. The ship blew up.

Europa, pride of that planet's fleet, was wrecked by a cloud of air-borne micro-organisms that metabolized atmospheric nitrogen and oxygen with most sorts of plastic, and left hydrochloric acid and poison gases behind as waste products.

Maxwell, a super-sophisticated heavy cruiser from Bandwidth, was attacked not only by the foam worms, but by a species of spider-things bred to eat human flesh. The latter murdered the crew before the former could wreck the ship.

Conventional armament spread its more familiar sort of horror as well; lasers, torpedoes, exploding limpets—all did their work and League ships died.

Thomas tried to ignore the death, the destruction, and concentrate on the battle itself, the progress of the opposing forces.

It was working, as well it should be. The Guard's Outpost fleet was passing through the League's fleet to link up with the Capital fleet around the baryworld. The combined Guard fleet was eagerly taking the chance to form into one fighting force. And the Guard fleet seemed to be significantly larger than anyone expected, with any number of smaller and slower ships deployed. After their losses at New Finland and Britannica, it was incredible that they could field that many ships. But then, this battle was for all the chips. If they lost here, they lost altogether. No point in holding reserves. They must have stripped their docking ports clean, must have taken along every space tug and broken-down old rustbucket.

The elderly admiral watched the screens. Yes, the Guards were forming up nicely about the baryworld. It was almost time. "Comm. Raise HMS *Sapper* if you please."

"*Sapper* is standing by, laser link ready."

"Very good." Suddenly, the admiral's voice shifted and he spoke in a stern, abrupt tone of voice. "*Sapper*, this is Admiral Sir George Wilfred Thomas. I hereby instruct you to proceed with Procedure A1A in exactly ten minutes from my mark—3, 2, 1, mark."

"Order received and acknowledged, Admiral," said an efficient-sounding voice from *Sapper*. "Activation codes to be transmitted in 9 minutes, 55 seconds. Allowing for speed-of-light delays, you should detect first results in 10 minutes, 38 seconds."

"Thank you, *Sapper*. Good luck." Thomas swung around to face the comm officer, and spoke with the same crisp severity in his voice. "Send to all ships. Emergency Priority. Break off any and all engagements with the enemy and proceed at full thrust away from the baryworld. You must be underway within nine minutes. That is an Emergency Priority order. Send it *now*. Clear the tactical view off the main screen and get me the highest magnification you can on the baryworld. Those of you here in this room are about to find out about the closest-held secret of the war. Officially, it's called Bannister."

The moment he had given the Bannister orders, Thomas wanted to countermand them. There *had* to be another way. But it was already too late for that by the time *Eagle*'s own engines lit, for *Sapper* had sent the start codes, and nothing could bring them back.

The main screen shifted to the view from a long-range camera that was already zooming in on the dark, barren, cold lump of rock. Here and there, tiny sparkles of white flame could be seen as Guard ships maneuvered and lit their engines.

"It will start in a moment," Thomas said quietly. "Unofficially, everyone called it WorldBomb."

The viewscreen was filled by the rough, worn old face of the unnamed baryworld, formed by the slowest and most tedious process of gradual accretion over billions of years. It was a very old, very tired-looking sort of world. Suddenly, there was a bright lance of fire, and then another, and another, across its scarred and cratered face, and then it seemed as if the entire surface of the tiny world was afire.

"Implosion phase," Thomas said. "Hundreds of small

explosions, from shaped nuclear explosives placed all over the surface of the planetoid. The bombs shatter the rock, and force shockwaves in toward its core to concentrate the explosion—smashing the structure of the world."

From equally spaced points around its surface, a dozen huge and terrible tongues of blood-red fire shot out from the baryworld, reaching out far into space, casting a horrible ocher tint across the universe.

"There go the larger nukes, the deep bombs. The flame is jetting back up the tunnels we dug to place them."

And then, in a blast of pure white radiance, the baryworld itself swelled up, expanded, exploded, the little planet shattering into a billion bits of shrapnel that were flung out into space at terrible velocity.

Ninety percent of the Guard fleet was within 50,000 kilometers of the baryworld when the WorldBomb was detonated. None of them had a chance. A huge pulse of electromagnetic energy, born of the nuclear explosions, flashed through the Guard fleet, scrambling computer banks, throwing circuit-breakers, forcing arcs and shorts in electronic equipment. The Guards ships were instantly blinded and crippled. Hard on the heels of the electromagnetic pulse came a virtually solid wall of rock fragments, from mountain-sized boulders down to grains of dust and molecules, all moving at terrible speed. All of it rushed out from the world that was no more, slamming into ships, ripping through their hulls, tumbling ships end for end, crashing one ship into another. A large fraction of the baryworld's mass had been vaporized altogether, and expanded out into vacuum as a shock wave of terrible force, popping hulls and ports and hatches that were meant to hold pressure *in*, not keep it out.

The problem with explosive weapons in space was the lack of an atmosphere to carry the shockwave, the absence of debris to be thrown. In short, in a vacuum, an explosion has no mass to throw around. By destroying a small world, the League had solved these problems.

✧ ✧ ✧

The command center crew watched the screen in stunned silence. Then the comm officer let out a low-pitched wail, and Thomas could hear the sound of quiet sobbing. "That's horrible, that's horrible," a voice whispered over and over, so quietly that at first Thomas thought the chanting was inside his own head. But no, it was the detection officer, his face ashen-white, unable to tear his eyes from the screen as the cloud of dust and debris that was once a tiny world and a proud fleet of ship expanded out into space.

"Even though that is a terrible, terrible end," Thomas said, "at least it *is* an end. And I shall ask myself if I truly had to do this for the rest of my days. But the war is over."

But Admiral Sir George Wilfred Thomas didn't know about *Starsight*.

Chapter Thirty-Eight

Starsight
Deep Space
The Nova Sol System

Captain Romero happened to be watching the monitors when the flaring light that was the baryworld's death blossomed across the dark of space. It took him a moment to realize where and what that terrible light had to be, and he was suddenly afraid. Who had done that, Guard or League? The great battle had begun, and he was here, still days out from Capital, cooped up with aliens he had grown to distrust.

D'etallis was irritated by the human's bothersome nervousness, and once again toyed with the idea of killing Romero immediately. But no, they might need a human face to parade in front of the cameras later on. She could endure Romero's company a while longer. He could die with lots of company, on Capital.

G.O.S. Ariadne
Orbiting the Planet Outpost

Perhaps there was no practical, rational need for caution anymore. Any fool who could count the number of ships left knew the days of the Guardians were over. After the barycenter disaster, there was nothing much left to oppose the League forces *with*. But Gustav knew warriors were not always practical or rational in defeat. Even *he* burned with a white-hot anger, a new hatred of the League that had smashed so many ships, killed so many young men, humiliated his planet and his nation. Johnson Gustav, who knew the Guards had started this war, who had known all along that the Guards must lose, even Johnson Gustav, who still might be executed as a traitor—even *he* thirsted for mindless revenge against the League for what they had done.

And Nike Station was still there in orbit, bristling with weapons that could leave a smoking crater where *Reunion* was. No, there were still plenty of reasons to be careful when talking to the League Contact party and *Reunion*. He waited until Nike was below the horizon, and then Gustav went to the comm room and set up the link himself.

He didn't know that Nike had deployed snooper buoys in orbit.

Reunion
On the Planet Outpost

Reunion's radio crackled and came to life. "Gustav to *Reunion*. Come in please."

Mac looked up from his work at the computer. He hit the right buttons and said "This is *Reunion*. Captain Larson speaking. Stand by a moment." He shut off the mike for a second and shouted down to the lower deck. "Message coming through from Gustav!" As the others scrambled up the ladder, he kicked the mike back on. "Go ahead, Gustav."

"There's some news you ought to know—the League has just plain destroyed the Guard fleet. We pulled every ship we *had* into the fight, and they were all virtually wiped out. It's all over but tidying up the details. The war is over, and—and your side won, in spite of the data that Prigot fellow seems to have given us." Gustav couldn't resist that dig into League sensibilities.

"Prigot?" Mac cried out. "What the hell are you talking about?"

"According to a report I've gotten, a man claiming to be a citizen of Capital, calling himself George Prigot, slipped through both the League and Guard detection systems, and got to a station orbiting Capital. I just got a very brief description of what he had to say, but apparently his information had a lot to do with the timing of the Guard attack on the League—for whatever good it did us."

There was a pause, and then Gustav's voice went on. "In any event, I'm not clear if Prigot claimed to have been a prisoner of the League or if he was pretending to cooperate with you. But he crossed the line to the Guardians the first moment he could, so obviously he was a double agent. I don't know all of what he told us. One thing he *did* say was that the Nihilists would betray us. No one seems to be taking him seriously on that. I take it you've heard of this Prigot?"

Mac felt suddenly sick inside. George a turncoat? A double agent? No, it was impossible. It couldn't be. The two of them had risked their lives for each other a dozen times on New Finland, and George had again and again provided information vital to the League war effort. Gustav had to be lying. There was no other explanation. But how the hell could he have known who George was, or that he was with the League fleet? What motive would Gustav have for lying?

And George *had* changed sides once before . . .

Joslyn took her husband by the arm, tried to comfort him with a quiet touch. She knew how much George meant to Mac, how responsible her husband felt for his friend.

Mac shook his head and tried to collect his thoughts. "Yes, I've heard of Prigot," he said angrily. "But that's to one side. Lucy has told me time and time again that you want to cut this war short, end it before too many die. It seems to me that this is the time for you to move."

"I quite agree," Gustav's voice replied over *Reunion*'s speakers. "I called asking for your advice in how best to proceed. The same person who told me about Prigot was primarily interested in getting contact with your side to start some very quiet talks. I believe you have a League diplomat along with you. Is he available?"

"Right here, Lieutenant," Pete called out. "My name is Gesseti, Peter Gesseti. Exactly what would the topic of those quiet talks be?"

"Very simply, Mr. Gesseti, we want to kno—"

The speaker went dead.

Nike Station,
Orbiting the Planet Outpost

Nike's comm center had been jumpy ever since Sprunt had vanished. They were the ones who finally picked up the chatter Ariadne was broadcasting, though they weren't able to locate the receiving station or locate the answering frequency. They only heard Gustav's side of it, but that was enough.

Laser Gunner's Mate Henderson didn't get told what was behind his orders, but he could guess. The damned CIs. They must have taken over Ariadne altogether. For Henderson's money, he wished they had ordered him to blow the place up, except there were probably still loyal Guards alive on her, prisoners. If there had been any ships at all left docked to the station, or orbiting the planet for that matter, they could have sent someone to arrest them all, but there weren't any ships. Which left things to Henderson. He powered up his laser cannon, tweaked up its long-range aiming unit, waited for the next close pass, and sliced every aerial and antennae clear off Ariadne. That would shut them up. And if a comm station was silenced, it couldn't do any harm.

Reunion
On the Planet Outpost

Cynthia worked the comm controls frantically. "They're gone! Nothing, no carrier. Not just our signal, but everything that should be coming off Ariadne is gone. Oh my God. Nike must have blown the station."

"No!" Lucy cried out, grabbing at the microphone. "Johnson! Damn it, come in!" Suddenly tears welled up in Lucy's eyes, the first tears she had allowed herself in a long, long time.

"Cyn, shut the radio off," Mac ordered. "Before they can trace us, too. I'm sorry, Luce."

Thousands of kilometers away, Johnson Gustav closed his eyes, sighed, and felt defeat. The game was up. They had caught him. He thought of all the things he had never been able to tell Lucy, and cursed the universe that had brought them together only to tear them away from each other.

Task Force Command Center, *Eagle*
The Barycenter

Thomas felt drained, used up. He knew the reasons all those ships had had to die, but he didn't have to like it, or feel good about killing them. No man or woman goes into space without falling in love with spacecraft—with all spacecraft—with the very *idea* of those splendid miracles of metal and glass and plastic that spanned the dark between the planets.

And the WorldBomb had smashed hundreds of those wondrous machines, killed thousands of people who had no greater flaw than being born on the wrong side of the line.

But he had a job to do now, still. He ordered prize crews to pick up survivors, and then turned his attention to the next task.

Unless the Guards saw sense and surrendered, he was going to have to bleed his fleet white trying to break through Capital's defense screen.

Chapter Thirty-Nine

Aboard *Starsight*

L'anijmeb performed the navigation check slowly, carefully, and then ran the whole test over again. All was well. They were on course, and no human group, League or Guardian, seemed to have spotted them yet. No human but the Guard's first Guidance, Jacquet, and a very few Guard officers, knew they were coming—and now that the Nihilists had changed the ship's course, the humans would have no idea where or when *Starsight* would arrive. There was some danger that the humans would realize what was happening and attempt to stop *Starsight*, but that was of no matter. If L'anijmeb could even get *Starsight* into the atmosphere for a few moments, that would suffice. Like most Nihilists, L'anijmeb didn't much care about dying. She glanced across the cabin at the pathetic little halfwalker.

"You'll want knowledge, M'Romero," L'anijmeb said in her slow English. "We should be landed in just over twenty-six of your hours." *And you, little halfwalker, will be dead in twenty-seven,* she thought.

Reunion
On the Planet Outpost

Mac stuck his head up through the opening in the deck plates and shouted through the overhead hatch. "Okay, Cynthia, run the phase three calibration." Mac ducked back into the underdeck and watched the test meters hooked up to the C^2 generator. The displays flickered briefly and settled down to satisfactory settings. Joslyn nodded at the figures. "That's it. It ought to work. Only way to be surer than we are now is to try it." She starting unplugging the test gear.

A strange sense of calm had come over the *Reunion*. It was all over now. All they had to do was sit tight and wait for some word from the League. Suddenly, there was time on their hands.

Charlie watched as Mac and Joslyn climbed out of the underdeck. "I still don't see why you're bothering to hook that thing up anyway," he said. "Or even why Cynthia swiped it off Ariadne in the first place."

"In case we needed to get the hell out of this star system on our own," Cynthia said, climbing down from the control room.

"Yeah, but the League *won*," Charlie objected. "We won't need it. The League can come get us or we can fly out to the barycenter and meet them. Why hook it up now?"

"*Could* be we won't need it," Mac said. "If so, we've kept ourselves busy instead of just sitting around doing nothing. And let me put it this way: If we *do* need a C^2 generator for some reason, we'll *really* need it. They just blew up their own comm station to silence Gustav. If they track *us* down, and come for us, we've going to want to be able to run and run fast."

Pete Gesseti applauded, and winced slightly as he did. He arm was still pretty sore. "Spoken like a true paranoid pioneer. Take a lesson or two from Mac, Charlie. He's gotten out of *plenty* of nasty situations. And you do that by being sure you can use any advantage you've got, and thinking of all the unpleasant possibilities. If we keep that in mind, we might up the odds on getting out of here alive. But I sure as hell wish I knew what Gustav was going to say. Poor guy."

"Poor Lucy," Joslyn said. "It didn't take much imagination to see there was something there. Where did she go, anyway?"

Charlie shrugged. "Out. Just put on her suit and left without a word while you guys were in the underdeck hooking that thing up."

"What's she up to?" Joslyn asked. "Do you think she was going to try and patch things up with the Outposters?"

"Joslyn, you weren't there when C'astille and Lucy and I dropped our little bombshells on each other," Charlie said. "I doubt very much that *any* Outposters will even *talk* to her."

Joslyn shook her head sadly. "I still can't get over it all. The poor, poor Outposters. To have your sex drives force you into sex with mindless animals, the bloody *stumblebugs*—it amounts to bestiality. And to *know* your whole life long that you're *sure* to turn into a dribbling idiot."

"You know, they can't possibly have any notion of an afterlife or a soul," Pete said thoughtfully. "They know for *sure* there is no life after death—they see death *in* life every time a stumblebug flutters past. They see the death of mind *during* life. They see life as *detached* from mind. Our life cycle allows us what are probably comfortable illusions about the soul and the afterlife."

"The poor Outposters," Joslyn said again. "Their whole lives warped by their reproductive cycle."

Charlie snorted. "And ours *aren't*? Then what's marriage? Where did divorce come from? Why the very, very large importance we place on the male/female dichotomy? Think about child custody. Pornography. Incest taboos. Monogamy. Polygamy, polyandry. Rules and traditions that encourage marriage with someone from outside the tribe. Homosexuality. Age of legal consent, and statutory rape. Family reunions. Teen-age dances that are rehearsals for courtship. Royal lineages. Inheritance laws. Dowries. Adoption. Illegitimacy. Keeping women at home, the way the Guards and a lot of other cultures do. Prostitution. Birth control. Population pressures and immigration. Hell, any shrink will tell you *gambling* is related to sexual impulses, and a lot of them will tell you starships are the ultimate phallic symbol. You could make a pretty good argument for just about every human activity being affected by our reproductive urges.

"Practically all of the things I just mentioned, and a thousand more that are basic to human society, must not only be unheard of for the Z'ensam, they must be impossible.

And all of them are tied up, directly or indirectly, in the way we make babies, or avoid making babies, or decide who should make a baby when, and who stands in what relation to the child. We define so much of ourselves, and our culture sexually. And all of that is right out the window with the Z'ensam.

"*Every* human culture invents marriage and marriage rituals. It's so ingrained into us, we don't notice it. But can you imagine a human culture where there were no marriages, for anyone, anytime, throughout all of history? Can you imagine there being a dichotomy more important than male/female for humans? Our lives are every bit as warped by biology and reproductive strategy. But human and Z'ensam are used to being the way they are."

Cynthia squatted down on the decking and stared at the gun-metal grey of the cabin bulkhead. Her mind's eye saw the murky, dismal green fields and forests beyond. "I don't envy them their way one little bit," she whispered.

For the hundredth time, C'astille resisted the urge to fling her picture book into the pond and be done with it. But she *couldn't*. She was so angry with the humans, so infuriated with all they did and built. They were *blessed* by their perversities. Without foreknowledge of doom, with intelligence lasting to the end of life, they had apparently invented the bizarre idea of the mind actually *outliving* the body—if she was inferring from the captions of the pictures properly. Their self-confidence, their incurable optimism, their huge monuments to themselves, all stemming from the crazy idea that they would live forever. And that live-forever idea stemmed directly from their weird, disgusting sexual practices! Practices that they probably saw as natural and right.

C'astille flipped through the pictures. Paris. The Moon colonies. The great bridges. The space stations and the huge starships. The observatory in the rings of Saturn, the lab nestled in among the craters of Mercury, the towers of New York, the Kremlin, Ulan Bator, the Taj Mahal, Machu

Picchu, the Great Wall, the Washington Monument, the Pyramids, the Parthenon, Kennedy Space Center. All of them so *big*, so *grand*. And the Roads! Grand highways that made the widest Road on Outpost look like a rough-and-tumble game path. How had these puny halfwalkers done it all?

Their self-confidence, their life-long intelligence, and their foul, foul medicine that extended lives, were the difference between humans building futures glories, and Z'ensam at best barely holding onto their modest present; between huge cities suffering from *overpopulation*, of all things, and a tiny Z'ensam populace that wasn't big or organized enough to build proper cities.

Their perversions had not been punished, they had been rewarded. Their vile ways had been their Road to the stars!

She wanted so much to hate them. Her jealousy was so strong, her anger at being accidentally deceived so great, her pride so wounded by talking to *implanters* all these months. She tried to hate them, tried to keep her anger alive. All she had to do was keep silent, offer no warning of the *Starsight*, and the humans would soon be no more.

But the picture book, and the grand works of the human hand—she wanted to *see* those things. Could she really let the Nihilists inherit them through murder? And Lucy was her friend. Lucy could not help being what she was.

With a sudden burst of understanding, C'astille realized something more—the worst, the absolute worst. The *humans* would feel *sorry* for the *Z'ensam*, would pity them. But she remembered their shock and fear at L'awdasi's simple trick of making their blood, and their fear of the Nihilist bioweapons. The humans would have some fear and respect, as well. Perhaps that would be enough. But perhaps not. She turned the pages of the book and stared hard at a picture of Earth as seen from orbit. She wanted to see that! Her very soul was knotted in anger and confusion.

Lucy had been walking in the clearing for hours, at first with no clearer aim in mind than getting away from people, being out by herself, but after a while, she found herself looking for C'astille. The other Z'ensam gave her a wide berth. They didn't want to interfere with her, and meet with the revenge of her people in return—but they certainly wanted nothing to do with her. Lucy knew she couldn't rely on non-interference for long; she had the very definite sense of being surrounded by a stiff-necked, angry tolerance that was near its end.

When she spotted C'astille lying on folded-up legs by the pond, looking at her book, Lucy was almost afraid to approach. So much accidental damage had been done—but she suddenly wanted someone to talk to, a friend to be with. She walked slowly toward the pond. And C'astille was looking at the book. That was a good sign. Perhaps there was still a chance some of the damage could be undone. For the moment, at least, Lucy managed to forget her own troubles and worry about someone else's.

C'astille saw Lucy approaching but did not acknowledge her in any way. Instead, she pretended to be fascinated by her book. Lucy hesitated a few meters off, and then came to sit alongside her friend. Neither of them spoke for a long time.

It was Lucy who broke the silence. "I'm sorry, C'astille."

No response. Lucy tried again. "C'astille, I wish there was some way to make it all right, some way that your people and mine could see each other, know the way each other lived, and not be horrified." Still no response, but at least she was listening. "Because you are good people. I like you, I like most of the Z'ensam. And the Z'ensam who can stand the way we humans look seem to like us. Even if it means I die here and now, I wouldn't regret having known you and your people. I would never give up that experience. But you must accept the way we are, perversions and all. We must accept you, and not be afraid of your great bio-skills, and try not to blame all Z'ensam for what the Nihilists do."

"Mmmmph," C'astille grunted. "I *know*. I *know* all that. But it will take time for my anger and my disgust to die."

C'astille said nothing for a long moment, and closed her book, her prize possession that cataloged the great works of humanity.

"There is at least one piece of good news," Lucy said. "My Group has defeated the Guardians in a great battle. That will put an end to the Guards and their Nihilist bioweapons. I suppose the League will try to ban such things. A treaty like the ones banning germ warfare," Lucy said absently.

"What is germ warfare?" C'astille asked.

"Mmmm. I suppose you might call it war-medicine. Medicine deliberately used to kill instead of cure."

C'astille sat bolt upright. War-medicine! The term translated well into her language, as one of the worst obscenities, one of the gravest sins possible. The Nihilists had stooped that low, and C'astille *knew* about it, knew what *Starsight* had to be intending, and had *done nothing*, as if the humans were pests that needed elimination. C'astille looked down again at the picture book, at the gift Lucy had impulsively filched from the VIP stateroom of the *Eagle*, and thought again of the fine and mighty things these humans could do. Weird star-mutants or not, these halfwalkers were thinking, talking *people*, not animals, not Hungry Ones to be killed off if they became inconvenient.

And this was war-medicine to be committed against *Lucy*! Sooner or later her people would die—her family, her Group. Wiping out the faceless Guardians was too huge and impersonal an assault to engage C'astille's imagination. But the Nihilists wanted to kill *Lucy* along with the rest of humanity. Lucy, the human sitting next to her now, the adult—no, the *female* who had risked so much for the sake of others. A strange creature, but as brave and civilized as any Z'ensam. It had taken Lucy, an alien pervert, to remind C'astille of the horrible wrongness in what the *Starsight* was up to. "Lucy, there is something you must know. . . ."

Lucy broke all records getting across the clearing to *Reunion*. She tried using the suit radio to get word back that much quicker, but she was breathing too hard and the radio's range was too short for that.

She rushed through the airlock and collapsed in a corner, panting hard. She wrenched off her helmet, and the others gathered round.

She took a big gulp of air. "C'astille said that the damn Guards were fool enough to give the Nihilists a spacecraft. The Nihilists named her *Starsight* and launched her on a course that should have her on Capital later *today*—and C'astille is pretty damn sure *Starsight* is carrying a shipload of plague virus, and anything they'd develop would make the Black Death look like a bad cold. It'll wipe out every human on Capital—and let the Nihilists take over there."

All of them stood in shock for a moment. Mac was the first to respond. "How sure of this is she? How does she know?"

"The only hard fact she has is that *Starsight* launched. But she knows the way the Nihilists think, what their plans are. And why the hell else would they risk a flight in the middle of a war?"

Mac thought hard for a minute. "Cynthia, can you raise the League fleet at the barycenter, warn them, so maybe they can shoot her down?"

Cynthia shook her head. "Not with this ship's gear. This is a Guard ship with a very dumbed-down comm system. Not in a million years. All the frequencies are preset, and there's a scrambler built into the system. I could get a signal to the barycenter, but not at any frequency they use, and not with the scramble disabled. The only reason we could talk to Gustav was that we had the beacon modified for voice. And the portable radio we used to talk back to him just doesn't have the range."

"Can you get a beam strong enough and tight enough to hit Capital? Can we call one of their stations and warn them, let their ships do the job?"

"I think so."

"Mac! Hold it a second," Pete said. "Gustav told us the had thrown every ship into the barycenter battle. And th way he talked, I think he meant *every* ship. Certainly every combatant went. There may be nothing besides a few unarmed tugs left around Capital."

"Hold it," Mac said. He held up his hand for quiet and sat leaned back against the bulkhead. "Hold it. Let me get this all clear in my head: We can't contact Ariadne because it isn't there any more. We don't dare contact Nike station. They just blew Ariadne, and if we radio to them, they'll drop a bomb on us the moment they track the signal. And you can bet they won't listen to what we have to say. We can't contact the League. We *can* contact the Guard orbital stations, but they won't have any ships.

"Which boils down to the fact that this is the only ship in the whole double star system with any sort of chance of stopping *Starsight*."

Chapter Forty

Reunion, surface of Outpost

"Mac, yes, *Reunion* can make it," Joslyn said. "With the C^2 generator installed, we could be in the Capital system four hours after launch—but we don't have the codes or the signaling equipment that will let us through the anti-ship missile system *around* Capital. That system is still intact, don't forget."

"Won't it stop the Nihilist ship as well?" Charlie asked hopefully.

"No, the anti-ship missiles use a sensor that detects a ship's arrival from C^2 space," Mac said. "There's a very specific burst of radiation given off. They can probably control the missiles manually to attack a target moving through normal space, but *Starsight* is an invited guest. She had clearance, and she's probably inside the defense shell already, where the missiles can't get to her. And once she's inside the defense shell, they probably will have trouble tracking her. She could change course and vanish from their screens."

"Can we radio them, tell them to shut off the system, and then go in?" Pete asked.

"Who'd listen to us? Who'd believe us?" Cynthia asked. " 'Hey guys, let down your last line of defenses just after we've smashed your fleet so we can rescue you. Honest, it's not a trick.' "

"I can think of one guy who'd believe us," Mac said quietly. "Or at least believe me."

"Mac!" Joslyn said. "Not George. He's somewhere around Capital, yes, but he's there because he *betrayed* us!"

"I don't believe that," Mac said firmly. "No offense, Joslyn but I know George. Gustav must have gotten it wrong

And even if it's true, that means he betrayed the *League*, not me. He's my friend, he'll know I wouldn't lie."

"But how could we know he'd hear it? How do we know he could convince anyone else?" Joslyn asked.

"We don't. But do you have any better ideas? And if the Nihilists get Capital, they'll have ships and material and technology and starmaps—they'll be able to drop plagues onto League worlds two weeks from now. Unless someone else has an idea, we've got no choice but to try it."

No one said anything for a while.

"I guess we have to chance it, Mac," Charlie said quietly.

Ten minutes later, Cynthia, Mac, Joslyn, and Lucy were at work in the control room.

"There's a big problem," Mac said. "We have to give the radio signal time to cross from here to Capital. We're twelve billion kilometers away—it'll be nearly twelve hours until they get the message. If we wait for a reply, confirming that the way is open, that's at least *another* twelve hours—and we can't afford to wait. The damn Nihilists will be there by then."

"So we send the signal," Joslyn said, "then wait twelve hours—plus say two to give them time to think about it and shut down the system, and then launch. No, wait half a tick—we'll have to boost well away from Outpost before we're far off enough to use C^2. We can subtract about four hours. So we launch ten hours after we send the signal."

"That's a hell of a big risk," Cynthia said.

Lucy shrugged. "We're taking a lot of risks already. And by rights all of us should be dead twenty ways each by now. I don't see we have any choice. Do it. We send the message, figure our course, and *go*."

"Okay, I guess I'm the one to do the talking," Mac said. "I want to send an audio message rather than text, so George can recognize my voice."

"Let me set up the recorder," Cynthia said. "Okay, everyone else keep quiet. Mac—go."

He took a deep breath and thought before he began.

What to say? What words were strong enough to convince George, strong enough to convince anyone else who happened to hear it if he didn't?

"This is Terrance MacKenzie Larson, calling George Prigot or anyone else in the Capital star system. George: I trust you. I don't know why you are where you are, but I have faith in you. I know you would never deliberately do anything to harm me, or any other person. I ask you to trust me, as you have many times in the past.

"There is a Nihilist ship coming toward you. She intends to land on Capital and release a deadly plague into the ecosystem. The plague will kill everyone on the planet. You should know by now the Nihilists are willing and able to do such things. If you have ships that can find her and stop her, use them, do it, stop her whatever it costs. Do not let that ship into the atmosphere.

"But I know your fleet has been wrecked in the war, and probably left you without combat pilots or ships. I cannot contact the League fleet and get them to stop the Nihilists. The ship I am in, *Reunion*, might just be able to do the job. But it can't get through your anti-ship defenses. I ask you to shut down those defenses two hours after this message arrives. We will have no way of knowing if you have shut down the defenses. *Reunion* will launch toward you in any event, and those of us aboard will simply have to trust that you have opened the way. If you haven't, the missiles will get us, a quick and painless death.

"But if *Starsight* isn't stopped, everyone on Capital will die. And they will not die pleasantly."

"I trust you. I beg you to trust me. The war between us is over. Please let us help you. For God's sake, shut down the missile screen and let us in!"

Some hours later, C'astille watched the pillar of flame that was *Reunion* roar into the sky. They were gone. They might die. But her world, she herself, would never be the same. Change was like the Nihilist plague—infectious.

"Good luck, my odd little halfwalkers," she whispered.

Chapter Forty-One

Zeus Station,
Orbiting the Planet Capital

Phillips shut off the recorder and stared across his desk at George. "That came in fifteen minutes ago. We have about another fifteen minutes left until we have to send the shut-down signal, since the actual anti-ship missiles are about ninety light minutes away. So. Ignoring the question of how he knows you're here, ignoring the fact that Larson somehow knew the top-secret fact that *Starsight* was en route, and has been since before the battle began, ignoring the fact that *Starsight* is overdue, ignoring a hundred other things my suspicious Intelligence officer's mind thinks of, *do you trust and believe this Larson*?"

George squirmed in the visitor's chair and felt the cold sweat of fear pouring out of his body. He was just a dumb engineer who liked playing with gadgets and didn't like to see people get hurt. Now he was mixed up in the fate of worlds. And intentionally or not, he *had* betrayed Mac and the League. George *knew*, deep down in his gut, that League people had died because of his run for Capital. Who could blame Mac if he did scheme for revenge, if this was all an elaborate plot to get the Capital defenses down so the League fleet could pour through and bomb the planet down to radioactive cinders? The League had just demonstrated they could and would blow up a planet. If George wrongly trusted Mac, Capital was a corpse of a world.

But this was *Mac*. And if George wrongly *dis*trusted Mac, Capital was just as doomed by the Nihilist plague. George was plenty ready to believe they could invent a disease that could wipe everyone out. The risks were equally balanced.

And then, suddenly, in the middle of his knot of fear

and turmoil, George found his answer. George could kill millions if he answered either way and was wrong. He had no control over that. But he, and only he, had control over whether he had faith in people. And if Mac was telling the truth, then Mac was deliberately putting his life in George's hands.

George decided he could live with himself, somehow, if millions died because he made an honest mistake. But he couldn't live with himself if he let a friend down. *You had to have a little faith in people.* Admiral Thomas had scrawled that across the bottom of George's Britannic Navy commission papers. Well, if he had betrayed the admiral's trust, then here was the time to make amends.

"I trust Mac Larson," George said in a strong, firm voice that was nonetheless near tears. "I would, and do, trust Terrance MacKenzie Larson with my life and the life of every human being on this planet."

"And leaves it on me," Phillips said. "You've just put the 50-50 odds, the head-or-tails gamble with the fate of the planet Capital in *my* hands now."

"So what will you do?" George asked.

"I will sit here remembering I trust George Prigot. My father always taught me trust was trust. No middle ground to it, no way to water it down and have it be any use to anyone."

The room was silent and still for a long moment before Phillips reached out and picked up the intercom phone. "Get me the defense control room," he said.

Both men felt a great burden rise off their shoulders. It was up to others now.

Aboard *Reunion*,
En Route from Outpost to Capital

Lucy had *seen* it, seen it with her own eyes through the computer-aimed long-range camera as *Reunion* headed for deep space. Ariadne was still there in orbit, not blown at all. Nothing but the bloody comm antennae gone! Johnson Gustav was alive.

Joslyn snuck another quick peek at Lucy, and smiled. Joz was pretty good at reading expressions, and true love was an easy one to spot. And it did tend to crop up in the oddest times and places.

But there was other work now. They were well clear of Outpost, far enough from her gravity well to make the jump. When Joslyn hit one last button, the computer would take over and fling them across C^2, to whatever awaited them. "Mac," she said. "It's now or never. We go?"

Mac's face was stern and solemn, and he was an honest enough man to let a little fear show through as well. But he looked at his lovely wife and grinned—a brave, open smile, because living with love and courage and faith was the only worthwhile way *to* live. "We go. I love you, Joz."

"And I love you, Mac. Always." She had to blink away the tears as she hit the button.

The bootleg C^2 box beneath the lower deck grabbed at space around *Reunion*, carried the ship for an incredibly brief moment, and dropped them down deep inside the Capital system.

Mac shushed the cheer that came from Charlie and Pete in the lower cabin. "Hold the applause down there!" he shouted. "We've got at least ten minutes before we're sure the missiles aren't coming."

Joslyn powered up the radar. The Guards knew right where they were anyway, and trying to hide wouldn't exactly inspire confidence. "Space is clear as best I can tell."

"Cynthia," Mac called, "use the radio and tell the Guards to kick in the defense screen again, just to prove we're sincere."

"Will do, Mac."

Mac turned to the two hot pilots, Joslyn and Lucy, trying to be cool, calm, rational. There was far too much at stake for him to get excited and make a wrong move. "Okay, here we are. And since we're not a radioactive cloud, we must be doing something right. So how do we find *Starsight*?"

"And short of ramming, how do we stop them?" Joslyn

asked. "We have lasers if we get within range for them, but no torps or any other sort of weapons."

"I was afraid you'd bring that up," Mac said in what he hoped was a cheerful-sounding voice. "But one thing at a time. We've got to find them first. Lucy. Try and think like a Nihilist. Never been in space before, probably getting your plots from a Guard astrogator who knows the straight-line route to take you right though the barycenter and the battle zone. Where do you go? What's your flight path?"

Lucy shut her eyes and concentrated. "I'd say they'd tend to a very simple and conservative route, and also assume they'd change course from their pre-plotted course somewhere along the line. That way, if the Guards got wind of them, they'd still have a chance to avoid interception. But they can't have any very sophisticated ideas about how to hide in space. Which makes waiting until the Guards are busy elsewhere very smart. If the Guards were in any shape to fly, the Nihilists wouldn't have a chance." Lucy powered up the tactical display and fiddled with a joystick to sketch things in as Mac and Joslyn watched on their repeaters. "I'd say put us *here*, over the leading limb of the planet. If they had an existing course that took them well clear of the barycenter, standard operating procedure would be to lead the target. Easier to run a transfer orbit from there. But it means there are a limited number of ways for the ship to change course. I figure they'd head in *this* way, looping back to come in straight over the Southern hemisphere. It brings them in right over the populated areas to give the plague a chance, and they don't approach the planet straight from Outpost. But that's a long-odds guess, Mac. No guarantees."

"But it makes sense, and we've been on the long end of the odds for quite a piece now. Do it. Put us there, and we watch and wait."

Starsight

The long journey down the space Road was nearly at an end. The lovely globe of Capital grew in the viewscreen.

It was time to slow the ship. L'etmlich swung the ship around and fired the fusion engine.

Reunion

"Fusion light!" Cynthia cried, after hours of watching a screen that showed nothing. It had been a long and wearing wait. "Lucy, go in for xeno-psychology—they're headed almost right down the path you figured."

"Range and rate!" Joslyn demanded.

"Stand by, still tracking. But they lit awfully close. Hang on, getting a Doppler. Okay, here come the numbers to your screen, Joslyn. Call it about 70,000 kilometers from the planet and closing at 500 klicks a second. If they hold course, they'll pass about 20,000 klicks in front of us. Heavy gee-load, but I'll need a better track to give any good figures."

"Are our movements shielded by their fusion plume?"

"No way. We're in plain sight. But I don't get any active radar from them. I doubt they'll spot us unless we advertise. They're nearly in decent laser range."

Mac thought fast. If the lasers didn't work, the Nihilists would still be out there—and they'd know someone was gunning for them. But if they could take *Starsight* out here and now—"Lasers," he said, with more confidence than he felt. There were times he hated being a commanding officer.

Starsight

L'anijmeb shouted in surprise. The image of Capital in the viewscreen turned a bright, horrid red, and then the screen died altogether.

Romero would have jumped straight out of his crash couch, but for the safety harness. "Laser attack!" he cried. That terrible flash in the barycenter—that was the *League*. They had won, and now they had taken over the skies of Capital itself. "Put the ship in a slow roll, spread the heat evenly! And pitch us around, run for the planet! Drop and get out of here!"

D'etallis almost told the human to shut up, but then she

remembered who aboard knew the most about space, fool or not. "L'anijmeb. Do what it says. And kindly use the radar to find our attacker."

Reunion

"Damn it!" Cynthia cried. "Real even heat pattern. I think they're rolling the ship. Fusion light gone, radar on, they'll have spotted us for sure now. Whoa! Fusion light, right down our nose! Now they're running. Diving for the planet—accelerating instead of braking."

"Chase 'em, Joslyn!" Mac yelled. "Lucy! Crank up the damn lasers right into their fusion flame. Try to overheat them!"

Joslyn powered up *Reunion*'s own engines and quickly brought them up to full thrust. Slowly, they started to gain on the Nihilist ship. She watched the fusion light ahead of her on the scopes. She pitched up and back—hard, suddenly. *Starsight* had come about, tried to fry *Reunion* in her exhaust.

"Skin temps high and going up!" Cynthia shouted.

An alarm sounded, and Lucy slapped the cutoff. "Mac, we've lost the laser. I think we caught the edge of their fusion plume and that toasted it."

"How the hell do we play this one?" Joslyn yelled over the roar of the engines.

Sweet Jesus. Mac stared hard at the screen, and felt his heart hammering in his chest. Damn it, there was only one chance, no time to fiddle with this tactic or that. He had to call it right the first time. A stern chase was no good, not with these short ranges. All the advantages were with the pursued. But how to outguess an alien pilot? And they had to get that ship in space. If they chased her into the atmosphere, blowing *Starsight* up would probably serve to throw the plague germs into the atmosphere.

The planet was coming up fast now. Okay. Cool, calm, collected thought. Those were inexperienced pilots up ahead. Someone with lots of entry practice could take a ship down with all ship stresses shoved right up to the limit, but could a green jockey do it? "Run a hot-box on them,

Joslyn. Put their backs to the wall on entry. Back off, then jump down their god-damned throats when they get close."

Starsight

L'anijmeb was scared. The planet was getting close, very close. They had to start braking *now* if they were to survive. L'anijmeb swung the ship around and started into the braking pattern. *Starsight* slowed her headlong rush. Gradually, all too gradually, she decreased her madcap speed to a sane level. Behind her, her pursuer matched her maneuver for maneuver, but hanging far back.

Now *Starsight* was a bare 1000 kilometers above the cloud tops, and her pursuer was far above, no longer interfering. L'anijmeb didn't even know exactly how long a kilometer was, but that almost didn't matter. She just had to follow the meters, keep within the tolerance the Guards had taught her. Now 900 klicks. Eight hundred, She snorted nervously through her blowhole, and wished endlessly that someone else could do this job. 700, 600 klicks. 500, 450, 400. Very close now, and maybe they had slowed enough.

Reunion

Mac watched the meters, the screens, the planet rising up around them. They were headed straight in. The Nihilists would have to keep braking if they were to survive.

But the same was true of *Reunion*.

"Do it, Joz," he said. "Rush 'em. Give it everything you have."

Starsight

D'etallis' face crinkled in pleasure. They had outrun them. They were nearly there. No point in even bothering to land. Three hundred kilometers. They could fire the plague shells out the airlock while they were hovering. More effective, and probably safer all around—

That loathsome Romero screamed again, and pointed at the radar screen.

D'etallis' jaw dropped in horror.

The chase ship had reversed thrust again, and was diving, accelerating, straight for *Starsight*.

Reunion

Eight gees. For a brief moment, nine. Watching her spacetrack and *Starsight* and her attitude and her skin temps all at once, Joslyn dove nose first for her enemy. The two ships closed at a terrifying rate, dead for each other. Split seconds from a crash, Joslyn spun ship one last time. There was no radar to guide her; she aimed her fusion flame by luck and feel.

And *Starsight*'s hull was clawed open by the heat of a sun's core. The tongues of starflame sliced through to the hydrogen tanks, bursting their pressure seals, the escaping hydrogen flaring into fusion itself. A tenth of a second later, what was left of the Nihilist ship exploded.

Reunion shook from stem to stern as she dove through the cloud of debris. Tiny fragments of the enemy ship bounced off her hull with terrifying reports, and suddenly *Reunion* was in the midst of atmospheric entry, pointed in the wrong attitude, moving at far too high a speed.

Joslyn held the engines to eight gees, and felt their speed begin to die. Slowly, painfully, *Reunion* clawed its way back up into the dark of space, and scrabbled into a stable orbit. Joslyn cut the engines and started breathing again, staring at a status board with more red lights than green on it.

That was as close to ramming another ship as she ever wanted to get.

Chapter Forty-Two

RKS *Eagle*
The Barycenter

It was a week later when Pete Gesseti set off down the corridors of *Eagle*'s officer's country, intent on barging into Admiral Thomas's stateroom. And it had been a *hell* of a week. Peace so far had been anything but peaceful. At least *Reunion*'s flight back from Capital had been less nervewracking than the trip out. The impromptu ceasefire that Thomas had ordered was holding, but negotiations were just about under way. Another three days and they'd settle on the shape of the table.

The Guards still had their defense screens around Outpost and Capital, but the League had the only intact fleet around and a decisive victory in its pocket. Conditions were right for cutting a deal. Pete had a hunch the Settlers, whoever exactly they were, were delaying things until this Jules Jacquet could be neatly deposed with the rest of the Central Guardians and they could move in.

Lucy Calder was champing at the bit to fly the rescue ship that would pick up the Survey Service CIs from Ariadne, and just incidentally reunite her with Johnson Gustav, once the anti-ship defense screens were down.

Pete was hoping and betting and expecting that Mac and Joslyn would call it quits from the military and settle back to have some kids and name one of them Peter. But knowing the two of them, they'd probably outfit their own ship and have their kids out in space on the flip side of nowhere.

George Prigot was probably going to end up as hero and villain to boot, for history books written by both sides. No one ever *had* known what to do with him. Another loose end. At the moment, it seemed that he was drawing pay from the Britannic navy and the Guard army at the same time. It would get worked out. That was what diplomats were used for after a war—to come in and tidy up the mess, somehow.

The Guards still held stocks of bioweapons. Pete had a feeling that they wouldn't last long. Pete had made it very clear to the officials on *Zeus* that the League would have two absolutely unnegotiable demands: repatriation of all Conscripted Immigrants (and any of their descendants who chose to leave), and the verified destruction of the bios. After what the *Starsight* had nearly done, the Guards didn't seem likely to argue.

When Thomas allowed an unarmed Guard lander (with a New Finn officer aboard to keep everyone honest) to make the transit from Capital to Outpost, they found every human soul at the Guardian Contact Camp was dead and rotting, massacred. The Nihilists themselves were nowhere to be found. They were out there on the planet somewhere, with their Guard-provided combat weapons. *They* would have to be dealt with.

And no one knew exactly what to do with the Outposters—no, the *Z'ensam*—in general. Pete was doing his best to learn the one known Outposter language quickly. Someone would have to negotiate with them. He hadn't made much progress there on his first trip to the planet, but the second time round he expected a more dignified journey than a crash-landing, a forced march, plus getting a chunk of his arm taken off and artificial blood put in. Pete, however, didn't want to be in *charge* of deals with the natives. Too much paperwork. No, he'd need a boss to take the flak and do all the dull ceremonial work.

And Pete knew himself well enough to know he'd need a boss of wisdom and experience, someone who might be able to understand the Z'ensam.

Which brought him to the point of his present visit. He arrived at Thomas' cabin. Pete had gotten a key from somewhere, and somehow it just happened the admiral's door was unguarded at the moment. He used his key and walked, in uninvited and unannounced.

Sir George was at his desk, in the act of quietly pouring a good strong spine-stiffener. At that exact moment, that dreadful Gesseti person barged in, calmly walked up and knocked both bottle and glass out of the admiral's hands and onto the deck.

"You not only just went on the wagon, you just decided to retire," Pete announced cheerfully.

"Mr. Gesseti! How dare you barge in li—"

"How do I dare? Easy." Pete took the visitor's chair and settled back comfortably. "Work it out, Admiral. It's time you hung up your gold braid. Oh, if you harrumph loud and long enough, they'd let you stay on. But to do what?"

"I hadn't quite had time to think about—"

"But I have. I'll tell you what I think. *I* think you're going to be the first League Diplomatic Representative to the Z'ensam. No one knows what the legal ramifications of diplomacy with aliens are. No one has had any time to make any up. But you and I are on the scene, so *we* get to make them up."

"Diplomatic Representative?"

"Sort of an over-ambassador is how I see the post. It'd be damn sloppy to have God knows how many League signatories each with their own ambassador, each following an uncoordinated policy. And on the other side, Lucy Calder estimates there are at least 120 major Groups to deal with. We'll need some centralized organization. And I like you for top man."

Thomas was trying hard to be angry at this cheeky upstart who had barged in, but it was hard. "I see. And why should I fill this post?"

For the first time, Pete hesitated a moment. "I could say because your grand victory here puts you in the public eye, would give you the prestige to do what has to be done. I could say you deserve it for the way you've fought this war. But though that would be true, it's only part of the reason. With all due respect, Admiral, you should have this job because this job *demands* a tired, cynical, embittered old man."

Sir George almost lunged across the desk to bash Pete's face in, but Pete raised his hand, very gently, very slightly, and gestured for Sir George to sit down. There was something in Pete's tone and manner that forced the admiral to listen. Pete started to speak again, in a far more gentle voice. "By virtue of your unhappy life, you're the best qualified to understand the Z'ensam, Admiral. Your until-recently undistinguished career, your rather advanced age, your fear of failure, your obvious search after oblivion in your heavy drinking.

"And think of what you've seen—the bioweapons, ships wrecked, an entire small world literally destroyed. You know what power, their kind and ours, can do when it goes rogue. You know we can avoid destroying ourselves and each other only if we make a conscious decision *not* to destroy. Both humans and Z'ensam must control *themselves*, for so much that we both *do* can escape our control.

"You've seen all that. And you see grand victories through eyes that have seen a lifetime of defeat and humiliation.

"And you've seen death. You understand how final death is, far better than any sleek young career diplomat could.

"Perhaps most importantly, Admiral, only someone who has chased oblivion so hard and so long through the bottle could understand the Z'ensam's fear of losing themselves in Division.

"All that tempers your great successes here, gives you a sense of proportion. But here's a frightening fact: Failure is impossible now, Admiral, because you've already won. I'd bet my life you've dreamed for generations about what you could do, given half the chance. Now you have the chance. Grab at it with both hands.

"Admiral, it's time to climb out of the bottle full time and take hold of the long hard work that your victories have won for you."

Thomas spluttered and felt himself ready to explode ir

anger, when the smell of the spilled liquor wafted its way to his nose. Suddenly he wanted, no, he *needed*, a little something. A soother, just a drop that would calm him and help him avoid this argument—

And at that moment, in that instant, for the first time, he really caught himself. For the first time, he didn't wave off his problem, or ignore it. Everything this snide young fellow was saying was true. Damn him. He ought to chase the little sod out, slam the door and get some peace and quiet, so he could—

—So he could what? Sir George looked at the broken bottle on the floor and knew how he had intended to complete that thought.

Damn the fellow for being right! The truth hurt. But—if Gesseti actually thought he could maneuver Thomas into that super-ambassadorship . . . A post like that, with real work, a hundred lifetimes' work to keep him busy, keep him occupied, a job with endless challenges . . . Thomas decided he didn't want that drink after all. Oh, of course Gesseti's schemes were all pie in the sky, one-in-a-thousand shots of coming off, but Sir George knew he'd gain more in trying and failing than he ever would in not trying at all.

"Mr. Gesseti," he said at last. "You are a very rude person, and I look forward to working with you. I am forced to admit I see your point. I must further admit that the job sounds a lot better than collecting dust in a corner office until I keel over stone-dead from boredom. You will have my most energetic—and sober—cooperation.

"But you are taking a grave chance, Mr. Gesseti. You and I both know that. You just got through saying I'm a drunken old fool, who might just have finished his streak of luck. Granted, you might have read me right, there might just still be enough marbles clattering around upstairs for me to do the job. But you can't *know* that. No matter how much my background qualifies me, it also damns me as a likely flop. Why are you taking that risk with such important work?"

Pete grinned. "You know what?" he asked. "Things are in six kinds of a mess around here, but that's the normal human condition. It's all going to be all right." Pete shook his head and let out a deep, contented sigh before he said anything more. He was the very portrait of a man who had just finished the last bit of a long tough job, a man pleased with the results of his handiwork. " 'Why,' Admiral? Because I have a real gut feeling you're the man for it. I really believe that. And there's another thing.

"When *Reunion* docked with *Zeus* Station and we were getting the first cease-fire worked out, I asked George Prigot why the *hell* he had trusted Mac with the fate of George's whole planet."

Pete stood up and got ready to go. The admiral rose from behind his desk. Pete offered his hand. Admiral Thomas took it, and asked, "But what *did* Mr. Prigot say?"

Pete laughed out loud, shook the admiral's hand, and opened the door to the corridor. "He said, if I might quote him exactly—'You've got to have a little faith in people.' I wonder where he heard that?"

THE WORLDS OF CHARLES SHEFFIELD

Reigning Master of Hard Science Fiction

"He has the scientific grounding of a Clarke, the story-telling skills of a Heinlein, the dry wit of a Pohl or a Kornbluth, and the universe-building prowess of a Niven."

—Spider Robinson

A scientist of internationally recognized stature, Charles Sheffield is equally renowned as an award-winning author and a master of hard SF. Explore his dazzling future worlds in these exciting volumes from Baen.

Proteus Combined 87603-1 • $5.99 ☐

Proteus in the Underworld 87659-7 • $5.99 ☐

In the 22nd century, technology gives man the power to alter his shape at will. Behrooz Wolf invented the form change process—now he will have to tame it.... "Earmarked with intriguing technology, intricately plotted, full of suspense..." —*Publishers Weekly*

The Mind Pool 72165-8 • $5.99 ☐

A revised and expanded version of the author's 1986 novel *The Nimrod Hunt*. "A considerable feat of both imagination and storytelling." —*Chicago Sun-Times*